DAN BROWN

is one of the world's bestselling authors. He first
introduced the world to Harvard symbologist Robert
Langdon in *Angels & Demons*. Since then Langdon
has gone on to conquer the globe in four further
bestselling adventures: *The Da Vinci Code*, *The Lost
Symbol*, *Inferno* and, most recently, *Origin*. Director
Ron Howard adapted three of Brown's Langdon
novels into films starring Tom Hanks. Dan Brown
is also the author of the international bestsellers
Digital Fortress and *Deception Point*. He lives
in New England with his wife.

www.danbrown.com
www.danbrownofficial.co.uk

www.**penguin**.co.uk

BY DAN BROWN

FORTRESS

An impossibly complex code threatens to obliterate the balance
of world power forever . . .

'Fascinating'
Washington Post

Deception
POINT

An apparently miraculous scientific discovery might change the
future of the planet if its truth is revealed . . .

'Thundering'
Chicago Tribune

THE ROBERT LANGDON
NOVELS

DEMONS

ROME: An ancient secret brotherhood arises once more to launch a
devastating new weapon against an unthinkable target . . .

'Heart-racing'
San Francisco Chronicle

The Da Vinci
CODE

PARIS: A quest almost as old as time itself for an object thought lost
forever becomes a deadly race against the clock . . .

'Blockbuster perfection'
New York Times

SYMBOL

The kidnapping of a friend will lead Langdon into the shadowy
world of freemasonry and a hell-for-leather chase across Washington DC.

'So compelling that several times I came close
to cardiac arrest . . . As perfectly constructed as the
Washington architecture it escorts us around'
Sunday Express

Inferno

Robert Langdon races against time to try to save the world from a terrifying
threat, armed only with a few lines from Dante's *Inferno* to help him.

'Jam-packed with tricks . . . A book-length scavenger
hunt that Mr Brown creates so energetically'
New York Times

RIGIN

Langdon must follow a trail marked only by enigmatic symbols and elusive
modern art to discover the truth about an astonishing scientific breakthrough, and
come face-to-face with a breathtaking truth that has remained buried – until now.

'Fans will not be disappointed'
The Times

DAN BROWN

The Lost SYMBOL

CORGI BOOKS

TRANSWORLD PUBLISHERS
61–63 Uxbridge Road, London W5 5SA
A Random House Group Company
www.rbooks.co.uk

THE LOST SYMBOL
A CORGI BOOK: 9780552161237

First published in Great Britain
in 2009 by Bantam Press
an imprint of Transworld Publishers
Corgi edition published 2010

Addresses for Random House Group Ltd companies outside the UK
can be found at: www.randomhouse.co.uk
The Random House Group Ltd Reg. No. 954009

The Random House Group Limited supports The Forest Stewardship
Council (FSC), the leading international forest certification organisation. All
our titles that are printed on Greenpeace approved FSC certified paper carry
the FSC logo. Our paper procurement policy can be found at
www.rbooks.co.uk/environment

Typeset in 11.5/13.5pt Palatino by Falcon Oast Graphic Art Ltd.
Printed in the UK by Clays Ltd, Elcograf S.p.A.

25

FOR BLYTHE

Acknowledgments

My profound thanks to three dear friends with whom I have the great luxury of working: my editor, Jason Kaufman; my agent, Heide Lange; and my counselor, Michael Rudell. In addition, I would like to express my immense gratitude to Doubleday, to my publishers around the world, and, of course, to my readers.

This novel could not have been written without the generous assistance of countless individuals who shared their knowledge and expertise. To all of you, I extend my deep appreciation.

The Lost
SYMBOL

To live in the world without becoming
aware of the meaning of the world is
like wandering about in a great library
without touching the books.

**The Secret Teachings
of All Ages**

FACT:

In 1991, a document was locked in
the safe of the director of the CIA. The
document is still there today. Its cryptic
text includes references to an ancient
portal and an unknown location
underground. The document also contains
the phrase *'It's buried out there somewhere.'*

All organizations in this novel exist,
including the Freemasons, the Invisible
College, the Office of Security, the SMSC,
and the Institute of Noetic Sciences.

All rituals, science, artwork,
and monuments in this novel are real.

Prologue

The secret is how to die.

Since the beginning of time, the secret had always been how to die.

The thirty-four-year-old initiate gazed down at the human skull cradled in his palms. The skull was hollow, like a bowl, filled with bloodred wine.

Drink it, he told himself. *You have nothing to fear.*

As was tradition, he had begun this journey adorned in the ritualistic garb of a medieval heretic being led to the gallows, his loose-fitting shirt gaping open to reveal his pale chest, his left pant leg rolled up to the knee, and his right sleeve rolled up to the elbow. Around his neck hung a heavy rope noose – a 'cable-tow' as the brethren called it. Tonight, however, like the brethren bearing witness, he was dressed as a master.

The assembly of brothers encircling him all were adorned in their full regalia of lambskin aprons, sashes, and white gloves. Around their necks hung ceremonial jewels that glistened like ghostly eyes in the muted light. Many of these men held powerful stations in life, and yet the initiate knew their worldly

17

ranks meant nothing within these walls. Here all men were equals, sworn brothers sharing a mystical bond.

As he surveyed the daunting assembly, the initiate wondered who on the outside would ever believe that this collection of men would assemble in one place . . . much less *this* place. The room looked like a holy sanctuary from the ancient world.

The truth, however, was stranger still.

I am just blocks away from the White House.

This colossal edifice, located at 1733 Sixteenth Street NW in Washington, D.C., was a replica of a pre-Christian temple – the temple of King Mausolus, the original *mausoleum* . . . a place to be taken after death. Outside the main entrance, two seventeen-ton sphinxes guarded the bronze doors. The interior was an ornate labyrinth of ritualistic chambers, halls, sealed vaults, libraries, and even a hollow wall that held the remains of two human bodies. The initiate had been told every room in this building held a secret, and yet he knew no room held deeper secrets than the gigantic chamber in which he was currently kneeling with a skull cradled in his palms.

The Temple Room.

This room was a perfect square. And cavernous. The ceiling soared an astonishing one hundred feet over-head, supported by monolithic columns of green granite. A tiered gallery of dark Russian walnut seats with hand-tooled pigskin encircled the room. A thirty-three-foot-tall throne dominated the western wall, with a concealed pipe organ opposite it. The walls were a kaleidoscope of ancient symbols . . . Egyptian, Hebraic, astronomical, alchemical, and others yet unknown.

Tonight, the Temple Room was lit by a series of

precisely arranged candles. Their dim glow was aided only by a pale shaft of moonlight that filtered down through the expansive oculus in the ceiling and illuminated the room's most startling feature – an enormous altar hewn from a solid block of polished Belgian black marble, situated dead center of the square chamber.

The secret is how to die, the initiate reminded himself.

'It is time,' a voice whispered.

The initiate let his gaze climb the distinguished white-robed figure standing before him. *The Supreme Worshipful Master.* The man, in his late fifties, was an American icon, well loved, robust, and incalculably wealthy. His once-dark hair was turning silver, and his famous visage reflected a lifetime of power and a vigorous intellect.

'Take the oath,' the Worshipful Master said, his voice soft like falling snow. 'Complete your journey.'

The initiate's journey, like all such journeys, had begun at the first degree. On that night, in a ritual similar to this one, the Worshipful Master had blindfolded him with a velvet hoodwink and pressed a ceremonial dagger to his bare chest, demanding: 'Do you seriously declare on your honor, uninfluenced by mercenary or any other unworthy motive, that you freely and voluntarily offer yourself as a candidate for the mysteries and privileges of this brotherhood?'

'I do,' the initiate had lied.

'Then let this be a sting to your consciousness,' the master had warned him, 'as well as instant death should you ever betray the secrets to be imparted to you.'

At the time, the initiate had felt no fear. *They will never know my true purpose here.*

Tonight, however, he sensed a foreboding solemnity

in the Temple Room, and his mind began replaying all the dire warnings he had been given on his journey, threats of terrible consequences if he ever shared the ancient secrets he was about to learn: *Throat cut from ear to ear . . . tongue torn out by its roots . . . bowels taken out and burned . . . scattered to the four winds of heaven . . . heart plucked out and given to the beasts of the field—*

'Brother,' the gray-eyed master said, placing his left hand on the initiate's shoulder. 'Take the final oath.'

Steeling himself for the last step of his journey, the initiate shifted his muscular frame and turned his attention back to the skull cradled in his palms. The crimson wine looked almost black in the dim candle-light. The chamber had fallen deathly silent, and he could feel all of the witnesses watching him, waiting for him to take his final oath and join their elite ranks.

Tonight, he thought, *something is taking place within these walls that has never before occurred in the history of this brotherhood. Not once, in centuries.*

He knew it would be the spark . . . and it would give him unfathomable power. Energized, he drew a breath and spoke aloud the same words that countless men had spoken before him in countries all over the world.

'*May this wine I now drink become a deadly poison to me . . . should I ever knowingly or willfully violate my oath.*'

His words echoed in the hollow space.

Then all was quiet.

Steadying his hands, the initiate raised the skull to his mouth and felt his lips touch the dry bone. He closed his eyes and tipped the skull toward his mouth, drinking the wine in long, deep swallows. When the last drop was gone, he lowered the skull.

For an instant, he thought he felt his lungs growing tight, and his heart began to pound wildly. *My God, they know!* Then, as quickly as it came, the feeling passed.

A pleasant warmth began to stream through his body. The initiate exhaled, smiling inwardly as he gazed up at the unsuspecting gray-eyed man who had foolishly admitted him into this brotherhood's most secretive ranks.

Soon you will lose everything you hold most dear.

1

The Otis elevator climbing the south pillar of the Eiffel Tower was overflowing with tourists. Inside the cramped lift, an austere businessman in a pressed suit gazed down at the boy beside him. 'You look pale, son. You should have stayed on the ground.'

'I'm okay . . .' the boy answered, struggling to control his anxiety. 'I'll get out on the next level.' *I can't breathe.*

The man leaned closer. 'I thought by now you would have gotten over this.' He brushed the child's cheek affectionately.

The boy felt ashamed to disappoint his father, but he could barely hear through the ringing in his ears. *I can't breathe. I've got to get out of this box!*

The elevator operator was saying something reassuring about the lift's articulated pistons and puddled-iron construction. Far beneath them, the streets of Paris stretched out in all directions.

Almost there, the boy told himself, craning his neck and looking up at the unloading platform. *Just hold on.*

As the lift angled steeply toward the upper viewing deck, the shaft began to narrow, its massive struts contracting into a tight, vertical tunnel.

'Dad, I don't think—'

23

Suddenly a staccato crack echoed overhead. The carriage jerked, swaying awkwardly to one side. Frayed cables began whipping around the carriage, thrashing like snakes. The boy reached out for his father.

'Dad!'

Their eyes locked for one terrifying second.

Then the bottom dropped out.

Robert Langdon jolted upright in his soft leather seat, startling out of the semiconscious daydream. He was sitting all alone in the enormous cabin of a Falcon 2000EX corporate jet as it bounced its way through turbulence. In the background, the dual Pratt & Whitney engines hummed evenly.

'Mr. Langdon?' The intercom crackled overhead. 'We're on final approach.'

Langdon sat up straight and slid his lecture notes back into his leather daybag. He'd been halfway through reviewing Masonic symbology when his mind had drifted. The daydream about his late father, Langdon suspected, had been stirred by this morning's unexpected invitation from Langdon's longtime mentor, Peter Solomon.

The other man I never want to disappoint.

The fifty-eight-year-old philanthropist, historian, and scientist had taken Langdon under his wing nearly thirty years ago, in many ways filling the void left by Langdon's father's death. Despite the man's influential family dynasty and massive wealth, Langdon had found humility and warmth in Solomon's soft gray eyes.

Outside the window the sun had set, but Langdon could still make out the slender silhouette of the world's largest obelisk, rising on the horizon like the spire of an ancient gnomon. The 555-foot marble-faced obelisk marked this nation's heart. All around the spire, the meticulous geometry of streets and monuments radiated outward.

Even from the air, Washington, D.C., exuded an almost mystical power.

Langdon loved this city, and as the jet touched down, he felt a rising excitement about what lay ahead. The jet taxied to a private terminal somewhere in the vast expanse of Dulles International Airport and came to a stop.

Langdon gathered his things, thanked the pilots, and stepped out of the jet's luxurious interior onto the foldout staircase. The cold January air felt liberating.

Breathe, Robert, he thought, appreciating the wide-open spaces.

A blanket of white fog crept across the runway, and Langdon had the sensation he was stepping into a marsh as he descended onto the misty tarmac.

'Hello! Hello!' a singsong British voice shouted from across the tarmac. 'Professor Langdon?'

Langdon looked up to see a middle-aged woman with a badge and clipboard hurrying toward him, waving happily as he approached. Curly blond hair protruded from under a stylish knit wool hat.

'Welcome to Washington, sir!'

Langdon smiled. 'Thank you.'

'My name is Pam, from passenger services.' The woman spoke with an exuberance that was almost unsettling. 'If you'll come with me, sir, your car is waiting.'

Langdon followed her across the runway toward the Signature terminal, which was surrounded by glistening private jets. *A taxi stand for the rich and famous.*

'I hate to embarrass you, Professor,' the woman said, sounding sheepish, 'but you *are* the Robert Langdon who writes books about symbols and religion, aren't you?'

Langdon hesitated and then nodded.

'I thought so!' she said, beaming. 'My book group read your book about the sacred feminine and the church! What a delicious scandal that one caused! You do enjoy putting the fox in the henhouse!'

Langdon smiled. 'Scandal wasn't really my intention.'

The woman seemed to sense Langdon was not in the mood to discuss his work. 'I'm sorry. Listen to me rattling on. I know you probably get tired of being recognized . . . but it's your own fault.' She playfully motioned to his clothing. 'Your uniform gave you away.'

My uniform? Langdon glanced down at his attire. He was wearing his usual charcoal turtleneck, Harris Tweed jacket, khakis, and collegiate cordovan loafers . . . his standard attire for the classroom, lecture circuit, author photos, and social events.

The woman laughed. 'Those turtlenecks you wear are so dated. You'd look much sharper in a tie!'

No chance, Langdon thought. *Little nooses.*

Neckties had been required six days a week when Langdon attended Phillips Exeter Academy, and despite the headmaster's romantic claims that the origin of the cravat went back to the silk *fascalia* worn by Roman orators to warm their vocal cords, Langdon knew that, etymologically, *cravat* actually derived from a ruthless band of 'Croat' mercenaries who donned knotted neckerchiefs before they stormed into battle. To this day, this ancient battle garb was donned by modern office warriors hoping to intimidate their enemies in daily boardroom battles.

'Thanks for the advice,' Langdon said with a chuckle. 'I'll consider a tie in the future.'

Mercifully, a professional-looking man in a dark suit got out of a sleek Lincoln Town Car parked near the terminal and held up his finger. 'Mr. Langdon? I'm Charles with Beltway Limousine.' He opened the passenger door. 'Good evening, sir. Welcome to Washington.'

Langdon tipped Pam for her hospitality and then climbed into the plush interior of the Town Car. The driver showed him the temperature controls, the bottled water, and the basket of hot muffins. Seconds later, Langdon was speeding away on a private access road. *So this is how the other half lives.*

As the driver gunned the car up Windsock Drive, he consulted his passenger manifest and placed a quick call. 'This is Beltway Limousine,' the driver said with professional efficiency. 'I was asked to confirm once my passenger had landed.' He paused. 'Yes, sir. Your guest, Mr. Langdon, has arrived, and I will deliver him to the Capitol Building by seven P.M. You're welcome, sir.' He hung up.

Langdon had to smile. *No stone left unturned.* Peter Solomon's attention to detail was one of his most potent assets, allowing him to manage his substantial power with apparent ease. *A few billion dollars in the bank doesn't hurt either.*

Langdon settled into the plush leather seat and closed his eyes as the noise of the airport faded behind him. The U.S. Capitol was a half hour away, and he appreciated the time alone to gather his thoughts. Everything had happened so quickly today that Langdon only now had begun to think in earnest about the incredible evening that lay ahead.

Arriving under a veil of secrecy, Langdon thought, amused by the prospect.

Ten miles from the Capitol Building, a lone figure was eagerly preparing for Robert Langdon's arrival.

2

The one who called himself Mal'akh pressed the tip of the needle against his shaved head, sighing with pleasure as the sharp tool plunged in and out of his flesh. The soft hum of the electric device was addictive . . . as was the bite of the needle sliding deep into his dermis and depositing its dye.

I am a masterpiece.

The goal of tattooing was never beauty. The goal was *change.* From the scarified Nubian priests of 2000 B.C., to the tattooed acolytes of the Cybele cult of ancient Rome, to the *moko* scars of the modern Maori, humans have tattooed themselves as a way of offering up their bodies in partial sacrifice, enduring the physical pain of embellishment and emerging changed beings.

Despite the ominous admonitions of Leviticus 19:28, which forbade the marking of one's flesh, tattoos had become a rite of passage shared by millions of people in the modern age – everyone from clean-cut teenagers to hard-core drug users to suburban housewives.

The act of tattooing one's skin was a transformative

declaration of power, an announcement to the world: *I am in control of my own flesh.* The intoxicating feeling of control derived from physical transformation had addicted millions to flesh-altering practices ... cosmetic surgery, body piercing, bodybuilding, and steroids ... even bulimia and transgendering. *The human spirit craves mastery over its carnal shell.*

A single bell chimed on Mal'akh's grandfather clock, and he looked up. Six thirty P.M. Leaving his tools, he wrapped the Kiryu silk robe around his naked, six-foot-three body and strode down the hall. The air inside this sprawling mansion was heavy with the pungent fragrance of his skin dyes and smoke from the beeswax candles he used to sterilize his needles. The towering young man moved down the corridor past priceless Italian antiques – a Piranesi etching, a Savonarola chair, a silver Bugarini oil lamp.

He glanced through a floor-to-ceiling window as he passed, admiring the classical skyline in the distance. The luminous dome of the U.S. Capitol glowed with solemn power against the dark winter sky.

This is where it is hidden, he thought. *It is buried out there somewhere.*

Few men knew it existed ... and even fewer knew its awesome power or the ingenious way in which it had been hidden. To this day, it remained this country's greatest untold secret. Those few who *did* know the truth kept it hidden behind a veil of symbols, legends, and allegory.

Now they have opened their doors to me, Mal'akh thought.

Three weeks ago, in a dark ritual witnessed by America's most influential men, Mal'akh had ascended to the thirty-third degree, the highest echelon of the world's oldest surviving brotherhood. Despite Mal'akh's new rank, the brethren had told him nothing. *Nor will they,* he knew. That was not how it worked. There were circles within circles . . . brotherhoods within brotherhoods. Even if Mal'akh waited years, he might never earn their ultimate trust.

Fortunately, he did not need their trust to obtain their deepest secret.

My initiation served its purpose.

Now, energized by what lay ahead, he strode toward his bedroom. Throughout his entire home, audio speakers broadcast the eerie strains of a rare recording of a castrato singing the 'Lux Aeterna' from the Verdi Requiem – a reminder of a previous life. Mal'akh touched a remote control to bring on the thundering 'Dies Irae.' Then, against a backdrop of crashing timpani and parallel fifths, he bounded up the marble staircase, his robe billowing as he ascended on sinewy legs.

As he ran, his empty stomach growled in protest. For two days now, Mal'akh had fasted, consuming only water, preparing his body in accordance with the ancient ways. *Your hunger will be satisfied by dawn,* he reminded himself. *Along with your pain.*

Mal'akh entered his bedroom sanctuary with reverence, locking the door behind him. As he moved toward his dressing area, he paused, feeling himself drawn to the enormous gilded mirror. Unable to resist, he turned and faced his own reflection. Slowly, as if unwrapping a priceless gift, Mal'akh opened his robe to unveil his naked form. The vision awed him.

I am a masterpiece.

His massive body was shaved and smooth. He lowered his gaze first to his feet, which were tattooed with the scales and talons of a hawk. Above that, his muscular legs were tattooed as carved pillars – his left leg spiraled and his right vertically striated. *Boaz and Jachin.* His groin and abdomen formed a decorated archway, above which his powerful chest was emblazoned with the double-headed phoenix . . . each head in profile with its visible eye formed by one of Mal'akh's nipples. His shoulders, neck, face, and shaved head were completely covered with an intricate tapestry of ancient symbols and sigils.

I am an artifact . . . an evolving icon.

One mortal man had seen Mal'akh naked, eighteen hours earlier. The man had shouted in fear. 'Good God, you're a demon!'

'If you perceive me as such,' Mal'akh had replied, understanding as had the ancients that angels and demons were identical – interchangeable archetypes – all a matter of polarity: the guardian angel who conquered your enemy in battle was perceived by your enemy as a demon destroyer.

Mal'akh tipped his face down now and got an oblique view of the top of his head. There, within the crownlike halo, shone a small circle of pale, untattooed flesh. This carefully guarded canvas was Mal'akh's only remaining piece of virgin skin. The sacred space had waited patiently . . . and tonight, it would be filled. Although Mal'akh did not yet possess what he required to complete his masterpiece, he knew the moment was fast approaching.

Exhilarated by his reflection, he could already feel his power growing. He closed his robe and walked to

31

the window, again gazing out at the mystical city before him. *It is buried out there somewhere.*

Refocusing on the task at hand, Mal'akh went to his dressing table and carefully applied a base of concealer makeup to his face, scalp, and neck until his tattoos had disappeared. Then he donned the special set of clothing and other items he had meticulously prepared for this evening. When he finished, he checked himself in the mirror. Satisfied, he ran a soft palm across his smooth scalp and smiled.

It is out there, he thought. *And tonight, one man will help me find it.*

As Mal'akh exited his home, he prepared himself for the event that would soon shake the U.S. Capitol Building. He had gone to enormous lengths to arrange all the pieces for tonight.

And now, at last, his final pawn had entered the game.

3

Robert Langdon was busy reviewing his note cards when the hum of the Town Car's tires changed pitch on the road beneath him. Langdon glanced up, surprised to see where they were.

Memorial Bridge already?

He put down his notes and gazed out at the calm waters of the Potomac passing beneath him. A heavy mist hovered on the surface. Aptly named, Foggy Bottom had always seemed a peculiar site on which to build the nation's capital. Of all the places in the New

World, the forefathers had chosen a soggy riverside marsh on which to lay the cornerstone of their utopian society.

Langdon gazed left, across the Tidal Basin, toward the gracefully rounded silhouette of the Jefferson Memorial – America's Pantheon, as many called it. Directly in front of the car, the Lincoln Memorial rose with rigid austerity, its orthogonal lines reminiscent of Athens's ancient Parthenon. But it was farther away that Langdon saw the city's centerpiece – the same spire he had seen from the air. Its architectural inspiration was far, far older than the Romans or the Greeks.

America's Egyptian obelisk.

The monolithic spire of the Washington Monument loomed dead ahead, illuminated against the sky like the majestic mast of a ship. From Langdon's oblique angle, the obelisk appeared ungrounded tonight . . . swaying against the dreary sky as if on an unsteady sea. Langdon felt similarly ungrounded. His visit to Washington had been utterly unexpected. *I woke up this morning anticipating a quiet Sunday at home . . . and now I'm a few minutes away from the U.S. Capitol.*

This morning at four forty-five, Langdon had plunged into dead-calm water, beginning his day as he always did, swimming fifty laps in the deserted Harvard Pool. His physique was not quite what it had been in his college days as a water-polo all-American, but he was still lean and toned, respectable for a man in his forties. The only difference now was the amount of effort it took Langdon to keep it that way.

When Langdon arrived home around six, he began his morning ritual of hand-grinding Sumatra coffee beans and savoring the exotic scent that filled his kitchen. This morning, however, he was surprised to see the blinking red light on his voice-mail display. *Who calls at six A.M. on a Sunday?* He pressed the button and listened to the message.

'Good morning, Professor Langdon, I'm terribly sorry for this early-morning call.' The polite voice was noticeably hesitant, with a hint of a southern accent. 'My name is Anthony Jelbart, and I'm Peter Solomon's executive assistant. Mr. Solomon told me you're an early riser . . . he has been trying to reach you this morning on short notice. As soon as you receive this message, would you be so kind as to call Peter directly? You probably have his new private line, but if not, it's 202-329-5746.'

Langdon felt a sudden concern for his old friend. Peter Solomon was impeccably well-bred and courteous, and certainly not the kind of man to call at daybreak on a Sunday unless something was very wrong.

Langdon left his coffee half made and hurried toward his study to return the call.

I hope he's okay.

Peter Solomon had been a friend, mentor, and, although only twelve years Langdon's senior, a father figure to him ever since their first meeting at Princeton University. As a sophomore, Langdon had been required to attend an evening guest lecture by the well-known young historian and philanthropist. Solomon had spoken with a contagious passion, presenting a dazzling vision of semiotics and archetypal history that had sparked in Langdon what would later become his lifelong passion for symbols. It was not Peter Solomon's brilliance, however, but the humility in his gentle gray eyes that had given Langdon the courage to write him a thank-you letter.

The young sophomore had never dreamed that Peter Solomon, one of America's wealthiest and most intriguing young intellectuals, would ever write back. But Solomon did. And it had been the beginning of a truly gratifying friendship.

A prominent academic whose quiet manner belied his powerful heritage, Peter Solomon came from the ultrawealthy Solomon family, whose names appeared on buildings and universities all over the nation. Like the Rothschilds in Europe, the surname Solomon had always carried the mystique of American royalty and success. Peter had inherited the mantle at a young age after the death of his father, and now, at fifty-eight, he had held numerous positions of power in his life. He currently served as the head of the Smithsonian Institution. Langdon occasionally ribbed Peter that the lone tarnish on his sterling pedigree was his diploma from a second-rate university – Yale.

Now, as Langdon entered his study, he was surprised to see that he had received a fax from Peter as well.

Peter Solomon

OFFICE OF THE SECRETARY

THE SMITHSONIAN INSTITUTION

Good morning, Robert,

I need to speak with you at once.
Please call me this morning as soon
as you can at 202-329-5746.

Peter

Langdon immediately dialed the number, sitting down at his hand-carved oak desk to wait as the call went through.

'Office of Peter Solomon,' the familiar voice of the assistant answered. 'This is Anthony. May I help you?'

'Hello, this is Robert Langdon. You left me a message earlier—'

'Yes, Professor Langdon!' The young man sounded relieved. 'Thank you for calling back so quickly. Mr. Solomon is eager to speak to you. Let me tell him you're on the line. May I put you on hold?'

'Of course.'

As Langdon waited for Solomon to get on the line, he gazed down at Peter's name atop the Smithsonian letterhead and had to smile. *Not many slackers in the Solomon clan.* Peter's ancestral tree burgeoned with the names of wealthy business magnates, influential politicians, and a number of distinguished scientists, some even fellows of London's Royal Society. Solomon's only living family member, his younger sister, Katherine, had apparently inherited the science gene, because she was now a leading figure in a new cutting-edge discipline called Noetic Science.

All Greek to me, Langdon thought, amused to recall Katherine's unsuccessful attempt to explain Noetic Science to him at a party at her brother's home last year. Langdon had listened carefully and then replied, 'Sounds more like magic than science.'

Katherine winked playfully. 'They're closer than you think, Robert.'

Now Solomon's assistant returned to the phone. 'I'm sorry, Mr. Solomon is trying to get off a conference call. Things are a little chaotic here this morning.'

'That's not a problem. I can easily call back.'

'Actually, he asked me to fill you in on his reason for contacting you, if you don't mind?'

'Of course not.'

The assistant inhaled deeply. 'As you probably know, Professor, every year here in Washington, the board of the Smithsonian hosts a private gala to thank our most generous supporters. Many of the country's cultural elite attend.'

Langdon knew his own bank account had too few zeros to qualify him as culturally elite, but he wondered if maybe Solomon was going to invite him to attend nonetheless.

'This year, as is customary,' the assistant continued, 'the dinner will be preceded by a keynote address. We've been lucky enough to secure the National Statuary Hall for that speech.'

The best room in all of D.C., Langdon thought, recalling a political lecture he had once attended in the dramatic semicircular hall. It was hard to forget five hundred folding chairs splayed in a perfect arc, surrounded by thirty-eight life-size statues, in a room that had once served as the nation's original House of Representatives chamber.

'The problem is this,' the man said. 'Our speaker has fallen ill and has just informed us she will be unable to give the address.' He paused awkwardly. 'This means we are desperate for a replacement speaker. And Mr. Solomon is hoping you would consider filling in.'

Langdon did a double take. 'Me?' This was not at all what he had expected. 'I'm sure Peter could find a far better substitute.'

'You're Mr. Solomon's first choice, Professor, and

you're being much too modest. The institution's guests would be thrilled to hear from you, and Mr. Solomon thought you could give the same lecture you gave on Bookspan TV a few years back? That way, you wouldn't have to prepare a thing. He said your talk involved symbolism in the architecture of our nation's capital – it sounds absolutely perfect for the venue.'

Langdon was not so sure. 'If I recall, that lecture had more to do with the Masonic history of the building than—'

'Exactly! As you know, Mr. Solomon is a Mason, as are many of his professional friends who will be in attendance. I'm sure they would love to hear you speak on the topic.'

I admit it would be easy. Langdon had kept the lecture notes from every talk he'd ever given. 'I suppose I could consider it. What date is the event?'

The assistant cleared his throat, sounding suddenly uncomfortable. 'Well, actually, sir, it's tonight.'

Langdon laughed out loud. 'Tonight?!'

'That's why it's so hectic here this morning. The Smithsonian is in a deeply embarrassing predicament . . .' The assistant spoke more hurriedly now. 'Mr. Solomon is ready to send a private jet to Boston for you. The flight is only an hour, and you would be back home before midnight. You're familiar with the private air terminal at Boston's Logan Airport?'

'I am,' Langdon admitted reluctantly. *No wonder Peter always gets his way.*

'Wonderful! Would you be willing to meet the jet there at say . . . five o'clock?'

'You haven't left me much choice, have you?' Langdon chuckled.

'I just want to make Mr. Solomon happy, sir.'

Peter has that effect on people. Langdon considered it a long moment, seeing no way out. 'All right. Tell him I can do it.'

'Outstanding!' the assistant exclaimed, sounding deeply relieved. He gave Langdon the jet's tail number and various other information.

When Langdon finally hung up, he wondered if Peter Solomon had ever been told no.

Returning to his coffee preparation, Langdon scooped some additional beans into the grinder. *A little extra caffeine this morning,* he thought. *It's going to be a long day.*

4

The U.S. Capitol Building stands regally at the eastern end of the National Mall, on a raised plateau that city designer Pierre L'Enfant described as 'a pedestal waiting for a monument.' The Capitol's massive footprint measures more than 750 feet in length and 350 feet deep. Housing more than sixteen acres of floor space, it contains an astonishing 541 rooms. The neoclassical architecture is meticulously designed to echo the grandeur of ancient Rome, whose ideals were the inspiration for America's founders in establishing the laws and culture of the new republic.

The new security checkpoint for tourists entering the Capitol Building is located deep within the recently completed subterranean visitor center, beneath a magnificent glass skylight that frames the Capitol Dome.

Newly hired security guard Alfonso Nuñez carefully studied the male visitor now approaching his checkpoint. The man had a shaved head and had been lingering in the lobby, completing a phone call before entering the building. His right arm was in a sling, and he moved with a slight limp. He was wearing a tattered army-navy surplus coat, which, combined with his shaved head, made Nuñez guess military. Those who had served in the U.S. armed forces were among the most common visitors to Washington.

'Good evening, sir,' Nuñez said, following the security protocol of verbally engaging any male visitor who entered alone.

'Hello,' the visitor said, glancing around at the nearly deserted entry. 'Quiet night.'

'NFC play-offs,' Nuñez replied. 'Everyone's watching the Redskins tonight.' Nuñez wished he were, too, but this was his first month on the job, and he'd drawn the short straw. 'Metal objects in the dish, please.'

As the visitor fumbled to empty the pockets of his long coat with his one working hand, Nuñez watched him carefully. Human instinct made special allowances for the injured and handicapped, but it was an instinct Nuñez had been trained to override.

Nuñez waited while the visitor removed from his pockets the usual assortment of loose change, keys, and a couple of cell phones. 'Sprain?' Nuñez asked, eyeing the man's injured hand, which appeared to be wrapped in a series of thick Ace bandages.

The bald man nodded. 'Slipped on the ice. A week ago. Still hurts like hell.'

'Sorry to hear that. Walk through, please.'

The visitor limped through the detector, and the machine buzzed in protest.

The visitor frowned. 'I was afraid of that. I'm wearing a ring under these bandages. My finger was too swollen to get it off, so the doctors wrapped right over it.'

'No problem,' Nuñez said. 'I'll use the wand.'

Nuñez ran the metal-detection wand over the visitor's wrapped hand. As expected, the only metal he detected was a large lump on the man's injured ring finger. Nuñez took his time rubbing the metal detector over every inch of the man's sling and finger. He knew his supervisor was probably monitoring him on the closed circuit in the building's security center, and Nuñez needed this job. *Always better to be cautious.* He carefully slid the wand up inside the man's sling.

The visitor winced in pain.

'Sorry.'

'It's okay,' the man said. 'You can't be too careful these days.'

'Ain't that the truth.' Nuñez liked this guy. Strangely, that counted for a lot around here. Human instinct was America's first line of defense against terrorism. It was a proven fact that human intuition was a more accurate detector of danger than all the electronic gear in the world – the *gift of fear,* as one of their security reference books termed it.

In this case, Nuñez's instincts sensed nothing that caused him any fear. The only oddity that he noticed, now that they were standing so close, was that this tough-looking guy appeared to have used some kind of self-tanner or concealer makeup on his face. *Whatever. Everyone hates to be pale in the winter.*

41

'You're fine,' Nuñez said, completing his sweep and stowing the wand.

'Thanks.' The man started collecting his belongings from the tray.

As he did, Nuñez noticed that the two fingers protruding from his bandage each bore a tattoo; the tip of his index finger bore the image of a crown, and the tip of his thumb bore that of a star. *Seems everyone has tattoos these days,* Nuñez thought, although the pads of his fingertips seemed like painful spots to get them. 'Those tats hurt?'

The man glanced down at his fingertips and chuckled. 'Less than you might think.'

'Lucky,' Nuñez said. 'Mine hurt a lot. I got a mermaid on my back when I was in boot camp.'

'A mermaid?' The bald man chuckled.

'Yeah,' he said, feeling sheepish. 'The mistakes we make in our youth.'

'I hear you,' the bald man said. 'I made a big mistake in my youth, too. Now I wake up with her every morning.'

They both laughed as the man headed off.

Child's play, Mal'akh thought as he moved past Nuñez and up the escalator toward the Capitol Building. The entry had been easier than anticipated. Mal'akh's slouching posture and padded belly had hidden his true physique, while the makeup on his face and hands had hidden the tattoos that covered his body. The true genius, however, was the sling, which disguised the potent object Mal'akh was transporting into the building.

A gift for the one man on earth who can help me obtain what I seek.

5

The world's largest and most technologically advanced museum is also one of the world's best-kept secrets. It houses more pieces than the Hermitage, the Vatican Museum, and the New York Metropolitan . . . combined. Yet despite its magnificent collection, few members of the public are ever invited inside its heavily guarded walls.

Located at 4210 Silver Hill Road just outside of Washington, D.C., the museum is a massive zigzag-shaped edifice constructed of five interconnected pods – each pod larger than a football field. The building's bluish metal exterior barely hints at the strangeness within – a six-hundred-thousand-square-foot alien world that contains a 'dead zone,' a 'wet pod,' and more than twelve miles of storage cabinets.

Tonight, scientist Katherine Solomon was feeling unsettled as she drove her white Volvo up to the building's main security gate.

The guard smiled. 'Not a football fan, Ms. Solomon?' He lowered the volume on the Redskins play-off pregame show.

Katherine forced a tense smile. 'It's Sunday night.'

'Oh, that's right. Your meeting.'

'Is he here yet?' she asked anxiously.

He glanced down at his paperwork. 'I don't see him on the log.'

'I'm early.' Katherine gave a friendly wave and continued up the winding access road to her usual parking spot at the bottom of the small, two-tiered lot. She began collecting her things and gave herself a quick check in the rearview mirror – more out of force of habit than actual vanity.

Katherine Solomon had been blessed with the resilient Mediterranean skin of her ancestry, and even at fifty years old she had a smooth olive complexion. She used almost no makeup and wore her thick black hair unstyled and down. Like her older brother, Peter, she had gray eyes and a slender, patrician elegance.

You two might as well be twins, people often told them.

Their father had succumbed to cancer when Katherine was only seven, and she had little memory of him. Her brother, eight years Katherine's senior and only fifteen when their father died, had begun his journey toward becoming the Solomon patriarch much sooner than anyone had ever dreamed. As expected, though, Peter had grown into the role with the dignity and strength befitting their family name. To this day, he still watched over Katherine as though they were just kids.

Despite her brother's occasional prodding, and no shortage of suitors, Katherine had never married. Science had become her life partner, and her work had proven more fulfilling and exciting than any man could ever hope to be. Katherine had no regrets.

Her field of choice – Noetic Science – had been virtually unknown when she first heard of it, but in recent years it had started opening new doors of understanding into the power of the human mind.

Our untapped potential is truly shocking.

Katherine's two books on Noetics had established her as a leader in this obscure field, but her most recent discoveries, when published, promised to make

Noetic Science a topic of mainstream conversation around the world.

Tonight, however, science was the last thing on her mind. Earlier in the day, she had received some truly upsetting information relating to her brother. *I still can't believe it's true.* She'd thought of nothing else all afternoon.

A pattering of light rain drummed on her windshield, and Katherine quickly gathered her things to get inside. She was about to step out of her car when her cell phone rang.

She checked the caller ID and inhaled deeply.

Then she tucked her hair behind her ears and settled in to take the call.

Six miles away, Mal'akh was moving through the corridors of the U.S. Capitol Building with a cell phone pressed to his ear. He waited patiently as the line rang.

Finally, a woman's voice answered. 'Yes?'

'We need to meet again,' Mal'akh said.

There was a long pause. 'Is everything all right?'

'I have new information,' Mal'akh said.

'Tell me.'

Mal'akh took a deep breath. 'That which your brother believes is hidden in D.C. . . . ?'

'Yes?'

'It can be found.'

Katherine Solomon sounded stunned. 'You're telling me – it is *real*?'

Mal'akh smiled to himself. 'Sometimes a legend that endures for centuries . . . endures for a reason.'

6

'Is this as close as you can get?' Robert Langdon felt a sudden wave of anxiety as his driver parked on First Street, a good quarter mile from the Capitol Building.

'Afraid so,' the driver said. 'Homeland Security. No vehicles near landmark buildings anymore. I'm sorry, sir.'

Langdon checked his watch, startled to see it was already 6:50. A construction zone around the National Mall had slowed them down, and his lecture was to begin in ten minutes.

'Weather's turning,' the driver said, hopping out and opening Langdon's door for him. 'You'll want to hurry.' Langdon reached for his wallet to tip the driver, but the man waved him off. 'Your host already added a very generous tip to the charge.'

Typical Peter, Langdon thought, gathering his things. 'Okay, thanks for the ride.'

The first few raindrops began to fall as Langdon reached the top of the gracefully arched concourse that descended to the new 'underground' visitors' entrance.

The Capitol Visitor Center had been a costly and controversial project. Described as an underground city to rival parts of Disney World, this subterranean space reportedly provided over a half-million square feet of space for exhibits, restaurants, and meeting halls.

Langdon had been looking forward to seeing it, although he hadn't anticipated quite this long a walk. The skies were threatening to open at any moment, and he broke into a jog, his loafers offering almost no

46

traction on the wet cement. *I dressed for a lecture, not a four-hundred-yard downhill dash through the rain!*

When he arrived at the bottom, he was breathless and panting. Langdon pushed through the revolving door, taking a moment in the foyer to catch his breath and brush off the rain. As he did, he raised his eyes to the newly completed space before him.

Okay, I'm impressed.

The Capitol Visitor Center was not at all what he had expected. Because the space was underground, Langdon had been apprehensive about passing through it. A childhood accident had left him stranded at the bottom of a deep well overnight, and Langdon now lived with an almost crippling aversion to enclosed spaces. But this underground space was . . . airy somehow. *Light. Spacious.*

The ceiling was a vast expanse of glass with a series of dramatic light fixtures that threw a muted glow across the pearl-colored interior finishes.

Normally, Langdon would have taken a full hour in here to admire the architecture, but with five minutes until showtime, he put his head down and dashed through the main hall toward the security checkpoint and escalators. *Relax,* he told himself. *Peter knows you're on your way. The event won't start without you.*

At the security point, a young Hispanic guard chatted with him while Langdon emptied his pockets and removed his vintage watch.

'Mickey Mouse?' the guard said, sounding mildly amused.

Langdon nodded, accustomed to the comments. The collector's edition Mickey Mouse watch had been a gift from his parents on his ninth birthday. 'I wear it to remind me to slow down and take life less seriously.'

'I don't think it's working,' the guard said with a smile. 'You look like you're in a serious hurry.'

Langdon smiled and put his daybag through the X-ray machine. 'Which way to the Statuary Hall?'

The guard motioned toward the escalators. 'You'll see the signs.'

'Thanks.' Langdon grabbed his bag off the conveyor and hurried on.

As the escalator ascended, Langdon took a deep breath and tried to gather his thoughts. He gazed up through the rain-speckled glass ceiling at the mountainous form of the illuminated Capitol Dome overhead. It was an astonishing building. High atop her roof, almost three hundred feet in the air, the Statue of Freedom peered out into the misty darkness like a ghostly sentinel. Langdon always found it ironic that the workers who hoisted each piece of the nineteen-and-a-half-foot bronze statue to her perch were slaves – a Capitol secret that seldom made the syllabi of high school history classes.

This entire building, in fact, was a treasure trove of bizarre arcana that included a 'killer bathtub' responsible for the pneumonic murder of Vice President Henry Wilson, a staircase with a permanent bloodstain over which an inordinate number of guests seemed to trip, and a sealed basement chamber in which workers in 1930 discovered General John Alexander Logan's long-deceased stuffed horse.

No legends were as enduring, however, as the claims of thirteen different ghosts that haunted this building. The spirit of city designer Pierre L'Enfant frequently was reported wandering the halls, seeking payment of his bill, now two hundred years overdue. The ghost of a worker who fell from the Capitol Dome during construction was seen wandering the corridors with a tray of tools. And, of course, the most famous apparition of all, reported numerous times in the Capitol basement – an ephemeral black cat that prowled the substructure's eerie maze of narrow passageways and cubicles.

Langdon stepped off the escalator and again checked his watch. *Three minutes.* He hurried down the wide corridor, following the signs toward the Statuary Hall and rehearsing his opening remarks in his head. Langdon had to admit that Peter's assistant had been correct; this lecture topic would be a perfect match for an event hosted in Washington, D.C., by a prominent Mason.

It was no secret that D.C. had a rich Masonic history. The cornerstone of this very building had been laid in a full Masonic ritual by George Washington himself. This city had been conceived and designed by Master Masons – George Washington, Ben Franklin, and Pierre L'Enfant – powerful minds who adorned their new capital with Masonic symbolism, architecture, and art.

Of course, people see in those symbols all kinds of crazy ideas.

Many conspiracy theorists claimed the Masonic forefathers had concealed powerful secrets throughout Washington along with symbolic messages hidden in the city's layout of streets. Langdon never paid any attention. Misinformation about the Masons was so commonplace that even educated Harvard students seemed to have surprisingly warped conceptions about the brotherhood.

Last year, a freshman had rushed wild-eyed into

Langdon's classroom with a printout from the Web. It was a street map of D.C. on which certain streets had been highlighted to form various shapes – satanic pentacles, a Masonic compass and square, the head of Baphomet – proof apparently that the Masons who designed Washington, D.C., were involved in some kind of dark, mystical conspiracy.

'Fun,' Langdon said, 'but hardly convincing. If you draw enough intersecting lines on a map, you're bound to find all kinds of shapes.'

'But this can't be coincidence!' the kid exclaimed.

Langdon patiently showed the student that the same exact shapes could be formed on a street map of Detroit.

The kid seemed sorely disappointed.

'Don't be disheartened,' Langdon said. 'Washington *does* have some incredible secrets . . . just none on this street map.'

The young man perked up. 'Secrets? Like what?'

'Every spring I teach a course called Occult Symbols. I talk a lot about D.C. You should take the course.'

'*Occult* symbols!' The freshman looked excited again. 'So there *are* devil symbols in D.C.!'

Langdon smiled. 'Sorry, but the word *occult*, despite conjuring images of devil worship, actually means "hidden" or "obscured." In times of religious oppression, knowledge that was counterdoctrinal had to be kept hidden or "occult," and because the church felt threatened by this, they redefined anything "occult" as evil, and the prejudice survived.'

'Oh.' The kid slumped.

Nonetheless, that spring, Langdon spotted the freshman seated in the front row as five hundred students bustled into Harvard's Sanders Theatre, a hollow old lecture hall with creaking wooden benches.

'Good morning, everybody,' Langdon shouted from the expansive stage. He turned on a slide projector, and an image materialized behind him. 'As you're getting settled, how many of you recognize the building in this picture?'

'U.S. Capitol!' dozens of voices called out in unison. 'Washington, D.C.!'

'Yes. There are nine million pounds of ironwork in that dome. An unparalleled feat of architectural ingenuity for the 1850s.'

'Awesome!' somebody shouted.

Langdon rolled his eyes, wishing somebody would ban that word. 'Okay, and how many of you have ever been to Washington?'

A scattering of hands went up.

'So few?' Langdon feigned surprise. 'And how many of you have been to Rome, Paris, Madrid, or London?'

Almost all the hands in the room went up.

As usual. One of the rites of passage for American college kids was a summer with a Eurorail ticket before the harsh reality of real life set in. 'It appears many more of you have visited Europe than have visited your own capital. Why do you think that is?'

'No drinking age in Europe!' someone in back shouted.

Langdon smiled. 'As if the drinking age *here* stops any of you?'

Everyone laughed.

It was the first day of school, and the students were taking longer than usual to get settled, shifting and creaking in their wooden pews. Langdon loved teaching in this hall because he always knew how engaged the students were simply by listening to how much they fidgeted in their pews.

'Seriously,' Langdon said, 'Washington, D.C., has some of the world's finest architecture, art, and symbolism. Why would you go overseas before visiting your own capital?'

'Ancient stuff is cooler,' someone said.

'And by ancient stuff,' Langdon clarified, 'I assume you mean castles, crypts, temples, that sort of thing?'

Their heads nodded in unison.

'Okay. Now, what if I told you that Washington, D.C., has *every* one of those things? Castles, crypts, pyramids, temples . . . it's all there.'

The creaking diminished.

'My friends,' Langdon said, lowering his voice and moving to the front of the stage, 'in the next hour, you will discover that our nation is overflowing with secrets and hidden history. And exactly as in Europe, all of the best secrets are hidden in plain view.'

The wooden pews fell dead silent.

Gotcha.

Langdon dimmed the lights and called up his second slide. 'Who can tell me what George Washington is doing here?'

The slide was a famous mural depicting George Washington dressed in full Masonic regalia standing before an odd-looking contraption – a giant wooden tripod that supported a rope-and-pulley system from which was suspended a massive block of stone. A group of well-dressed onlookers stood around him.

'Lifting that big block of stone?' someone ventured.

Langdon said nothing, preferring that a student make the correction if possible.

'Actually,' another student offered, 'I think Washington is *lowering* the rock. He's wearing a Masonic costume. I've seen pictures of Masons laying cornerstones before. The ceremony always uses that tripod thing to lower the first stone.'

'Excellent,' Langdon said. 'The mural portrays the Father of Our Country using a tripod and pulley to lay the cornerstone of our Capitol Building on September 18, 1793, between the hours of eleven fifteen and twelve thirty.' Langdon paused, scanning the class. 'Can anyone tell me the significance of that date and time?'

Silence.

'What if I told you that precise moment was chosen by three famous Masons – George Washington, Benjamin Franklin, and Pierre L'Enfant, the primary architect for D.C.?'

More silence.

'Quite simply, the cornerstone was set at that date and time because, among other things, the auspicious Caput Draconis was in Virgo.'

Everyone exchanged odd looks.

'Hold on,' someone said. 'You mean . . . like *astrology*?'

'Exactly. Although a different astrology than we know today.'

A hand went up. 'You mean our Founding Fathers believed in astrology?'

Langdon grinned. 'Big-time. What would you say if I told you the city of Washington, D.C., has more astrological signs in its architecture than *any* other city in the world – zodiacs, star charts, cornerstones laid at precise astrological dates and times? More than half of the framers of our Constitution were Masons, men who strongly believed that the stars and fate were intertwined, men who paid close attention to the layout of the heavens as they structured their new world.'

'But that whole thing about the Capitol cornerstone being laid while Caput Draconis was in Virgo – who cares? Can't that just be coincidence?'

'An impressive coincidence considering that the cornerstones of the three structures that make up Federal Triangle – the Capitol, the White House, the Washington Monument – were all laid in different years but were carefully timed to occur under this *exact* same astrological condition.'

Langdon's gaze was met by a room full of wide eyes. A number of heads dipped down as students began taking notes.

A hand in back went up. 'Why did they do that?'

Langdon chuckled. 'The answer to that is an entire semester's worth of material. If you're curious, you should take my mysticism course. Frankly, I don't think you guys are emotionally prepared to hear the answer.'

'What?' the person shouted. 'Try us!'

Langdon made a show of considering it and then shook his head, toying with them. 'Sorry, I can't do that. Some of you are only freshmen. I'm afraid it might blow your minds.'

'Tell us!' everyone shouted.

Langdon shrugged. 'Perhaps you should join the Masons or Eastern Star and learn about it from the source.'

'We can't get in,' a young man argued. 'The Masons are like a supersecret society!'

'Supersecret? Really?' Langdon remembered the large Masonic ring that his friend Peter Solomon wore proudly on his right hand. 'Then why do Masons wear obvious Masonic rings, tie clips, or pins? Why are Masonic buildings clearly marked? Why are their meeting times in the newspaper?' Langdon smiled at all the puzzled faces. 'My friends, the Masons are not a secret society . . . they are a society with secrets.'

'Same thing,' someone muttered.

'Is it?' Langdon challenged. 'Would you consider Coca-Cola a secret society?'

'Of course not,' the student said.

'Well, what if you knocked on the door of corporate headquarters and asked for the recipe for Classic Coke?'

'They'd never tell you.'

'Exactly. In order to learn Coca-Cola's deepest secret, you would need to join the company, work for many years, prove you were trustworthy, and eventually rise to the upper echelons of the company, where that information might be shared with you. Then you would be sworn to secrecy.'

'So you're saying Freemasonry is like a corporation?'

'Only insofar as they have a strict hierarchy and they take secrecy very seriously.'

'My uncle is a Mason,' a young woman piped up. 'And my aunt hates it because he won't talk about it with her. She says Masonry is some kind of strange religion.'

'A common misperception.'

'It's not a religion?'

'Give it the litmus test,' Langdon said. 'Who here has taken Professor Witherspoon's comparative religion course?'

Several hands went up.

'Good. So tell me, what are the three prerequisites for an ideology to be considered a religion?'

'ABC,' one woman offered. 'Assure, Believe, Convert.'

'Correct,' Langdon said. 'Religions *assure* salvation; religions *believe* in a precise theology; and religions *convert* nonbelievers.' He paused. 'Masonry, however, is batting zero for three. Masons make no promises of salvation; they have no specific theology; and they do not seek to convert you. In fact, within Masonic lodges, discussions of religion are prohibited.'

'So . . . Masonry is *anti*religious?'

'On the contrary. One of the prerequisites for becoming a Mason is that you *must* believe in a higher power. The difference between Masonic spirituality and organized religion is that the Masons do not impose a specific definition or name on a higher power. Rather than definitive theological identities like God, Allah, Buddha, or Jesus, the Masons use more general terms like Supreme Being or Great Architect of the Universe. This enables Masons of different faiths to gather together.'

'Sounds a little far-out,' someone said.

'Or, perhaps, refreshingly open-minded?' Langdon offered. 'In this age when different cultures are killing each other over whose definition of God is better, one could say the Masonic tradition of tolerance and open-mindedness is commendable.' Langdon paced the stage. 'Moreover, Masonry is open to men of all races, colors, and creeds, and provides a spiritual fraternity that does not discriminate in any way.'

'Doesn't discriminate?' A member of the university's Women's Center stood up. 'How many *women* are permitted to be Masons, Professor Langdon?'

Langdon showed his palms in surrender. 'A fair point. Freemasonry had its roots, traditionally, in the stone masons' guilds of Europe and was therefore a man's organization. Several hundred years ago, some say as early as 1703, a women's branch called Eastern Star was founded. They have more than a million members.'

'Nonetheless,' the woman said, 'Masonry is a powerful organization from which women are excluded.'

Langdon was not sure how *powerful* the Masons really were anymore, and he was not going to go down that road; perceptions of the modern Masons ranged from their being a group of harmless old men who liked to play dress up . . . all the way to an underground cabal of power brokers who ran the world. The truth, no doubt, was somewhere in the middle.

'Professor Langdon,' called a young man with curly hair in the back row, 'if Masonry is not a secret society, not a corporation, and not a religion, then what is it?'

'Well, if you were to ask a Mason, he would offer the following definition: Masonry is a system of morality, veiled in allegory and illustrated by symbols.'

'Sounds to me like a euphemism for "freaky cult." '

'*Freaky*, you say?'

'Hell yes!' the kid said, standing up. 'I heard what they do inside those secret buildings! Weird candlelight rituals with coffins, and nooses, and drinking wine out of skulls. Now *that's* freaky!'

Langdon scanned the class. 'Does that sound freaky to anyone else?'

'Yes!' they all chimed in.

Langdon feigned a sad sigh. 'Too bad. If that's too freaky for you, then I know you'll never want to join *my* cult.'

Silence settled over the room. The student from the Women's Center looked uneasy. '*You're* in a cult?'

Langdon nodded and lowered his voice to a conspiratorial whisper. 'Don't tell anyone, but on the pagan day of the sun god Ra, I kneel at the foot of an ancient instrument of torture and consume ritualistic symbols of blood and flesh.'

The class looked horrified.

Langdon shrugged. 'And if any of you care to join me, come to the Harvard chapel on Sunday, kneel beneath the crucifix, and take Holy Communion.'

The classroom remained silent.

Langdon winked. 'Open your minds, my friends. We all fear what we do not understand.'

The tolling of a clock began echoing through the Capitol corridors.

Seven o'clock.

Robert Langdon was now running. *Talk about a dramatic entrance.* Passing through the House Connecting Corridor, he spotted the entrance to the National Statuary Hall and headed straight for it.

As he neared the door, he slowed to a nonchalant stroll and took several deep breaths. Buttoning his jacket, he lifted his chin ever so slightly and turned the corner just as the final chime sounded.

Showtime.

As Professor Robert Langdon strode into the National Statuary Hall, he raised his eyes and smiled warmly. An instant later, his smile evaporated. He stopped dead in his tracks.

Something was very, very wrong.

7

Katherine Solomon hurried across the parking lot through the cold rain, wishing she had worn more than jeans and a cashmere sweater. As she neared the building's main entrance, the roar of the giant air purifiers got louder. She barely heard them, her ears still ringing from the phone call she'd just received.

That which your brother believes is hidden in D.C. . . . it can be found.

Katherine found the notion almost impossible to believe. She and the caller still had much to discuss and had agreed to do so later that evening.

Reaching the main doors, she felt the same sense of excitement she always felt upon entering the gargantuan building. *Nobody knows this place is here.*

The sign on the door announced:

SMITHSONIAN MUSEUM SUPPORT CENTER (SMSC)

The Smithsonian Institution, despite having more than a dozen massive museums on the National Mall, had a collection so huge that only 2 percent of it could be on display at any one time. The other 98 percent of the collection had to be stored somewhere. And that somewhere . . . was *here*.

Not surprisingly, this building was home to an astonishingly diverse array of artifacts – giant Buddhas, handwritten codices, poisoned darts from New Guinea, jewel-encrusted knives, a kayak made of baleen. Equally mind-boggling were the building's *natural* treasures – plesiosaur skeletons, a priceless meteorite collection, a giant squid, even a collection of elephant skulls brought back from an African safari by Teddy Roosevelt.

But none of this was why the Smithsonian secretary, Peter Solomon, had introduced his sister to the SMSC three years ago. He had brought her to this place not to *behold* scientific marvels, but rather to *create* them. And that was exactly what Katherine had been doing.

Deep within this building, in the darkness of the most remote recesses, was a small scientific laboratory unlike any other in the world. The recent break-throughs Katherine had made here in the field of Noetic Science had ramifications across every discipline – from physics, to history, to philosophy, to religion. *Soon everything will change,* she thought.

As Katherine entered the lobby, the front desk guard quickly stashed his radio and yanked the earplugs from his ears. 'Ms. Solomon!' He smiled broadly.

'Redskins?'

He blushed, looking guilty. 'Pregame.'

She smiled. 'I won't tell.' She walked to the metal detector and emptied her pockets. When she slid the gold Cartier watch from her wrist, she felt the usual pang of sadness. The timepiece had been a gift from her mother for Katherine's eighteenth birthday. Almost ten years had now passed since her mother had died violently . . . passing away in Katherine's arms.

'So, Ms. Solomon?' the guard whispered jokingly. 'Are you ever gonna tell anybody what you're doing back there?'

She glanced up. 'Someday, Kyle. Not tonight.'

'Come on,' he pressed. 'A secret lab . . . in a

secret museum? You must be doing something cool.'

Miles beyond cool, Katherine thought as she collected her things. The truth was that Katherine was doing science so advanced that it no longer even resembled science.

8

Robert Langdon stood frozen in the doorway of the National Statuary Hall and studied the startling scene before him. The room was precisely as he remembered it – a balanced semicircle built in the style of a Greek amphitheater. The graceful arched walls of sandstone and Italian plaster were punctuated by columns of variegated breccia, interspersed with the nation's statuary collection – life-size statues of thirty-eight great Americans standing in a semicircle on a stark expanse of black-and-white marble tile.

It was exactly as Langdon had recalled from the lecture he had once attended here.

Except for one thing.

Tonight, the room was empty.

No chairs. No audience. No Peter Solomon. Just a handful of tourists milling around aimlessly, oblivious to Langdon's grand entrance. *Did Peter mean the Rotunda?* He peered down the south corridor toward the Rotunda and could see tourists milling around in there, too.

The echoes of the clock chime had faded. Langdon was now officially late.

He hurried back into the hallway and found a

docent. 'Excuse me, the lecture for the Smithsonian event tonight? Where is that being held?'

The docent hesitated. 'I'm not sure, sir. When does it start?'

'Now!'

The man shook his head. 'I don't know about any Smithsonian event this evening – not here, at least.'

Bewildered, Langdon hurried back toward the center of the room, scanning the entire space. *Is Solomon playing some kind of joke?* Langdon couldn't imagine it. He pulled out his cell phone and the fax page from this morning and dialed Peter's number.

His phone took a moment to locate a signal inside the enormous building. Finally, it began to ring.

The familiar southern accent answered. 'Peter Solomon's office, this is Anthony. May I help you?'

'Anthony!' Langdon said with relief. 'I'm glad you're still there. This is Robert Langdon. There seems to be some confusion about the lecture. I'm standing in the Statuary Hall, but there's nobody here. Has the lecture been moved to a different room?'

'I don't believe so, sir. Let me check.' His assistant paused a moment. 'Did you confirm with Mr. Solomon directly?'

Langdon was confused. 'No, I confirmed with *you*, Anthony. This morning!'

'Yes, I recall that.' There was a silence on the line. 'That was a bit careless of you, don't you think, Professor?'

Langdon was now fully alert. 'I beg your pardon?'

'Consider this . . .' the man said. 'You received a fax asking you to call a number, which you did. You spoke to a total stranger who said he was Peter Solomon's assistant. Then you willingly boarded a private plane to Washington and climbed into a waiting car. Is that right?'

Langdon felt a chill race through his body. 'Who the hell is this? Where is Peter?'

'I'm afraid Peter Solomon has no idea you're in Washington today.' The man's southern accent disappeared, and his voice morphed into a deeper, mellifluous whisper. 'You are here, Mr. Langdon, because *I* want you here.'

9

Inside the Statuary Hall, Robert Langdon clutched his cell phone to his ear and paced in a tight circle. 'Who the hell are you?'

The man's reply was a silky calm whisper. 'Do not be alarmed, Professor. You have been summoned here for a reason.'

'Summoned?' Langdon felt like a caged animal. 'Try kidnapped!'

'Hardly.' The man's voice was eerily serene. 'If I wanted to harm you, you would be dead in your Town Car right now.' He let the words hang for a moment. 'My intentions are purely noble, I assure you. I would simply like to offer you an invitation.'

No thanks. Ever since his experiences in Europe over the last several years, Langdon's unwanted celebrity had made him a magnet for nutcases, and this one had just crossed a very serious line. 'Look, I don't know what the hell is going on here, but I'm hanging up—'

'Unwise,' said the man. 'Your window of

opportunity is very small if you want to save Peter Solomon's soul.'

Langdon drew a sharp breath. 'What did you say?'

'I'm sure you heard me.'

The way this man had uttered Peter's name had stopped Langdon cold. 'What do you know about Peter?'

'At this point, I know his deepest secrets. Mr. Solomon is my guest, and I can be a persuasive host.'

This can't be happening. 'You don't have Peter.'

'I answered his private cell phone. That should give you pause.'

'I'm calling the police.'

'No need,' the man said. 'The authorities will join you momentarily.'

What is this lunatic talking about? Langdon's tone hardened. 'If you have Peter, put him on the phone right now.'

'That's impossible. Mr. Solomon is trapped in an unfortunate place.' The man paused. 'He is in the Araf.'

'Where?' Langdon realized he was clutching his phone so tightly his fingers were going numb.

'The Araf? Hamistagan? That place to which Dante devoted the canticle immediately following his legendary *Inferno*?'

The man's religious and literary references solidified Langdon's suspicion that he was dealing with a madman. *The second canticle.* Langdon knew it well; nobody escaped Phillips Exeter Academy without reading Dante. 'You're saying you think Peter Solomon is . . . in *purgatory*?'

'A crude word you Christians use, but yes, Mr. Solomon is in the *in-between*.'

The man's words hung in Langdon's ear. 'Are you saying Peter is . . . *dead*?'

'Not exactly, no.'

'Not exactly?!' Langdon yelled, his voice echoing sharply in the hall. A family of tourists looked over at him. He turned away and lowered his voice. '*Death* is usually an all-or-nothing thing!'

'You surprise me, Professor. I expected you to have a better understanding of the mysteries of life and death. There *is* a world in between – a world in which Peter Solomon is hovering at the moment. He can either return to your world, or he can move on to the next . . . depending on your actions right now.'

Langdon tried to process this. 'What do you want from me?'

'It's simple. You have been given access to something quite ancient. And tonight, you will share it with me.'

'I have no idea what you're talking about.'

'No? You pretend not to understand the ancient secrets that have been entrusted to you?'

Langdon felt a sudden sinking sensation, now guessing what this was probably about. *Ancient secrets.* He had not uttered a word to anyone about his experiences in Paris several years earlier, but Grail fanatics had followed the media coverage closely, some connecting the dots and believing Langdon was now privy to secret information regarding the Holy Grail – perhaps even its location.

'Look,' Langdon said, 'if this is about the Holy Grail, I can assure you I know nothing more than—'

'Don't insult my intelligence, Mr. Langdon,' the man snapped. 'I have no interest in anything so frivolous as the Holy Grail or mankind's pathetic debate over whose version of history is correct. Circular arguments over the semantics of faith hold no interest for me. Those are questions answered only through death.'

The stark words left Langdon confused. 'Then what the hell is this about?'

The man paused for several seconds. 'As you may know, there exists within this city an ancient portal.'

An ancient portal?

'And tonight, Professor, you will unlock it for me. You should be honored I contacted you – this is the invitation of your lifetime. You alone have been chosen.'

And you have lost your mind. 'I'm sorry, but you've chosen poorly,' Langdon said. 'I don't know anything about any ancient portal.'

'You don't understand, Professor. It was not *I* who chose you . . . it was *Peter Solomon.*'

'What?' Langdon replied, his voice barely a whisper.

'Mr. Solomon told me how to find the portal, and he confessed to me that only one man on earth could unlock it. And he said that man is *you.*'

'If Peter said that, he was mistaken . . . or lying.'

'I think not. He was in a fragile state when he confessed that fact, and I am inclined to believe him.'

Langdon felt a stab of anger. 'I'm warning you, if you hurt Peter in any—'

'It's far too late for *that,*' the man said in an amused tone. 'I've already taken what I need from Peter Solomon. But for his sake, I suggest you provide what I need from *you.* Time is of the essence . . . for *both* of you. I suggest you find the portal and unlock it. Peter will point the way.'

Peter? 'I thought you said Peter was in "purgatory." '

'As above, so below,' the man said.

Langdon felt a deepening chill. This strange

response was an ancient Hermetic adage that proclaimed a belief in the physical connection between heaven and earth. *As above, so below.* Langdon eyed the vast room and wondered how everything had veered so suddenly out of control tonight. 'Look, I don't know how to find any ancient portal. I'm calling the police.'

'It really hasn't dawned on you yet, has it? Why you were chosen?'

'No,' Langdon said.

'It *will*,' he replied, chuckling. 'Any moment now.'

Then the line went dead.

Langdon stood rigid for several terrifying moments, trying to process what had just happened.

Suddenly, in the distance, he heard an unexpected sound.

It was coming from the Rotunda.

Someone was screaming.

10

Robert Langdon had entered the Capitol Rotunda many times in his life, but never at a full sprint. As he ran through the north entrance, he spotted a group of tourists clustered in the center of the room. A small boy was screaming, and his parents were trying to console him. Others were crowding around, and several security guards were doing their best to restore order.

'He pulled it out of his sling,' someone said frantically, 'and just *left* it there!'

As Langdon drew nearer, he got his first glimpse of

what was causing all the commotion. Admittedly, the object on the Capitol floor was odd, but its presence hardly warranted screaming.

The device on the floor was one Langdon had seen many times. The Harvard art department had dozens of these – life-size plastic models used by sculptors and painters to help them render the human body's most complex feature, which, surprisingly, was not the human face but rather the human hand. *Someone left a mannequin hand in the Rotunda?*

Mannequin hands, or *handequins* as some called them, had articulated fingers enabling an artist to pose the hand in whatever position he wanted, which for sophomoric college students was often with the middle finger extended straight up in the air. This handequin, however, had been positioned with its index finger and thumb pointing up toward the ceiling.

As Langdon drew nearer, though, he realized this handequin was unusual. Its plastic surface was not smooth like most. Instead, the surface was mottled and slightly wrinkled, and appeared almost . . .

Like real skin.

Langdon stopped abruptly.

Now he saw the blood. *My God!*

The severed wrist appeared to have been skewered onto a spiked wooden base so that it would stand up. A wave of nausea rushed over him. Langdon inched closer, unable to breathe, seeing now that the tips of the index finger and thumb had been decorated with tiny tattoos. The tattoos, however, were not what held Langdon's attention. His gaze moved instantly to the familiar golden ring on the fourth finger.

No.

Langdon recoiled. His world began to spin as he realized he was looking at the severed right hand of Peter Solomon.

11

Why isn't Peter answering? Katherine Solomon wondered as she hung up her cell phone. Where is he?

For three years, Peter Solomon had always been the first to arrive for their weekly seven P.M. Sunday-night meetings. It was their private family ritual, a way to remain connected before the start of a new week, and for Peter to stay up-to-date on Katherine's work at the lab.

He's never late, she thought, *and he always answers his phone.* To make matters worse, Katherine was still not sure what she was going to say to him when he *did* finally arrive. *How do I even begin to ask him about what I found out today?*

Her footsteps clicked rhythmically down the cement corridor that ran like a spine through the SMSC. Known as 'The Street,' the corridor connected the building's five massive storage pods. Forty feet overhead, a circulatory system of orange ductwork throbbed with the heartbeat of the building – the pulsing sounds of thousands of cubic feet of filtered air being circulated.

Normally, during her nearly quarter-mile walk to her lab, Katherine felt calmed by the breathing sounds of the building. Tonight, however, the pulsing had her on edge. What she had learned about her brother

69

today would have troubled anyone, and yet because Peter was the only family she had in the world, Katherine felt especially disturbed to think he might be keeping secrets from her.

As far as she knew, he had kept a secret from her only *once* . . . a wonderful secret that was hidden at the end of this very hallway. Three years ago, her brother had walked Katherine down this corridor, introducing her to the SMSC by proudly showing off some of the building's more unusual items – the Mars meteorite ALH-84001, the handwritten pictographic diary of Sitting Bull, a collection of wax-sealed Ball jars containing original specimens collected by Charles Darwin.

At one point, they walked past a heavy door with a small window. Katherine caught a glimpse of what lay beyond and gasped. 'What in the world is *that*?!'

Her brother chuckled and kept walking. 'Pod Three. It's called Wet Pod. Pretty unusual sight, isn't it?'

Terrifying is more like it. Katherine hurried after him. This building was like another planet.

'What I really want to show you is in Pod Five,' her brother said, guiding her down the seemingly endless corridor. 'It's our newest addition. It was built to house artifacts from the basement of the National Museum of Natural History. That collection is scheduled for relocation here in about five years, which means Pod Five is sitting empty at the moment.'

Katherine glanced over. 'Empty? So why are we looking at it?'

Her brother's gray eyes flashed a familiar mischief. 'It occurred to me that because nobody is using the space, maybe *you* could use it.'

'Me?'

'Sure. I thought maybe you could use a dedicated lab space – a facility where you can actually *perform* some of the theoretical experiments you've been developing for all these years.'

Katherine stared at her brother in shock. 'But, Peter, those experiments *are* theoretical! To actually *perform* them would be almost impossible.'

'Nothing is impossible, Katherine, and this building is perfect for you. The SMSC is not just a warehouse of treasures; it's one of the world's most advanced scientific research facilities. We're constantly taking pieces from the collection and examining them with the best quantitative technologies money can buy All the equipment you could possibly need would be here at your disposal.'

'Peter, the technologies required to run these experiments are—'

'Already in place.' He smiled broadly. 'The lab is done.'

Katherine stopped short.

Her brother pointed down the long corridor. 'We're going to see it now.'

Katherine could barely speak. 'You . . . you built me a lab?'

'It's my job. The Smithsonian was established to advance scientific knowledge. As secretary, I must take that charge seriously. I believe the experiments you've proposed have the potential to push the boundaries of science into uncharted territory.' Peter stopped and looked her squarely in the eyes. 'Whether or not you were my sister, I would feel obliged to support this research. Your ideas are brilliant. The world deserves to see where they lead.'

'Peter, I can't possibly—'

'Okay, relax . . . it was my own money, and nobody's using Pod Five right now. When you're done with your experiments, you'll move out. Besides, Pod Five has some unique properties that will be perfect for your work.'

Katherine could not imagine what a massive, empty pod might offer that would serve her research, but she sensed she was about to find out. They had just reached a steel door with boldly stenciled letters:

Pod 5

Her brother inserted his key card into a slot and an electronic keypad lit up. He raised his finger to type his access code, but paused, arching his eyebrows in the same mischievous way he always had as a boy. 'You sure you're ready?'

She nodded. *My brother, always the showman.*

'Stand back.' Peter hit the keys.

The steel door hissed loudly open.

Beyond the threshold was only inky blackness . . . a yawning void. A hollow moan seemed to echo out of the depths. Katherine felt a cold blast of air emanating from within. It was like staring into the Grand Canyon at night.

'Picture an empty airline hangar waiting for a fleet of Airbuses,' her brother said, 'and you get the basic idea.'

Katherine felt herself take a step backward.

'The pod itself is far too voluminous to be heated, but your lab is a thermally insulated cinder-block room, roughly a cube, located in the farthest corner of the pod for maximum separation.'

Katherine tried to picture it. *A box inside a box.* She strained to see into the darkness, but it was absolute. 'How far back?'

'Pretty far . . . a football field would fit easily in here. I should warn you, though, the walk is a little un-nerving. It's exceptionally dark.'

Katherine peered tentatively around the corner. 'No light switch?'

'Pod Five is not yet wired for electricity.'

'But . . . then how can a lab function?'

He winked. 'Hydrogen fuel cell.'

Katherine's jaw dropped. 'You're kidding, right?'

'Enough clean power to run a small town. Your lab enjoys full radio-frequency separation from the rest of the building. What's more, all pod exteriors are sealed with photo-resistant membranes to protect the artifacts inside from solar radiation. Essentially, this pod is a sealed, energy-neutral environment.'

Katherine was starting to comprehend the appeal of Pod 5. Because much of her work centered on quanti-fying previously unknown energy fields, her experiments needed to be performed in a location isolated from any extraneous radiation or 'white noise.' This included interference as subtle as 'brain radiation' or 'thought emissions' generated by people nearby. For this reason, a university campus or hospital lab wouldn't work, but a deserted pod at the SMSC could not have been more perfect.

'Let's go back and have a look.' Her brother was grinning as he stepped into the vast darkness. 'Just follow me.'

Katherine stalled at the threshold. *Over a hundred*

yards in total darkness? She wanted to suggest a flash-light, but her brother had already disappeared into the abyss.

'Peter?' she called.

'Leap of faith,' he called back, his voice already fading away. 'You'll find your way. Trust me.'

He's kidding, right? Katherine's heart was pounding as she stepped a few feet over the threshold, trying to peer into the darkness. *I can't see a thing!* Suddenly the steel door hissed and slammed shut behind her, plunging her into total blackness. Not a speck of light anywhere. 'Peter?!'

Silence.

You'll find your way. Trust me.

Tentative, she inched forward blindly. *Leap of faith?* Katherine could not even see her hand directly in front of her face. She kept moving forward, but within a matter of seconds, she was entirely lost. *Where am I going?*

That was three years ago.

Now, as Katherine arrived at the same heavy metal door, she realized how far she had come since that first night. Her lab – nicknamed the Cube – had become her home, a sanctuary within the depths of Pod 5. Exactly as her brother had predicted, she had found her way through the darkness that night, and every day since – thanks to an ingeniously simple guidance system that her brother had let her discover for herself.

Far more important, her brother's other prediction had come true as well: Katherine's experiments had produced astonishing results, particularly in the last six months, breakthroughs that would alter entire paradigms of thinking. Katherine and her brother had agreed to keep her results absolutely secret until the implications were more fully understood. One day soon, however, Katherine knew she would publish some of the most transformative scientific revelations in human history.

A secret lab in a secret museum, she thought, inserting her key card into the Pod 5 door. The keypad lit up, and Katherine typed her PIN.

The steel door hissed open.

The familiar hollow moan was accompanied by the same blast of cold air. As always, Katherine felt her pulse rate start to climb.

Strangest commute on earth.

Steeling herself for the journey, Katherine Solomon glanced at her watch as she stepped into the void. Tonight, however, a troubled thought followed her inside. *Where is Peter?*

12

Capitol police chief Trent Anderson had overseen security in the U.S. Capitol Complex for over a decade. A burly, square-chested man with a chiseled face and red hair, he kept his hair cropped in a buzz cut, giving him an air of military authority. He wore a visible sidearm as a warning to anyone foolish enough to question the extent of his authority.

Anderson spent the majority of his time co-ordinating his small army of police officers from a high-tech surveillance center in the basement of the Capitol. Here he oversaw a staff of technicians who watched visual monitors, computer readouts, and a telephone switchboard that kept him in contact with the many security personnel he commanded.

This evening had been unusually quiet, and Anderson was pleased. He had been hoping to catch a bit of the Redskins game on the flat-panel television in his office. The game had just kicked off when his intercom buzzed.

'Chief?'

Anderson groaned and kept his eyes on the television as he pressed the button. 'Yeah.'

'We've got some kind of disturbance in the Rotunda. I've got officers arriving now, but I think you'll want to have a look.'

'Right.' Anderson walked into the security nerve center – a compact, neomodern facility packed with computer monitors. 'What have you got?'

The technician was cueing a digital video clip on his monitor. 'Rotunda east balcony camera. Twenty seconds ago.' He played the clip.

Anderson watched over the technician's shoulder.

The Rotunda was almost deserted today, dotted with just a few tourists. Anderson's trained eye went immediately to the one person who was alone and moving faster than all the others. Shaved head. Green army-surplus jacket. Injured arm in a sling. Slight limp. Slouched posture. Talking on a cell phone.

The bald man's footfalls echoed crisply on the audio feed until, suddenly, arriving at the exact center of the Rotunda, he stopped short, ended his phone call, and then knelt down as if to tie his shoe. But instead of tying a shoe, he pulled something out of his sling and set it on the floor. Then he stood up and limped briskly toward the east exit.

Anderson eyed the oddly shaped object the man had left behind. *What in the world?* It was about eight inches tall and standing vertically. Anderson crouched closer to the screen and squinted. *That can't be what it looks like!*

As the bald man hurried off, disappearing through the east portico, a little boy nearby could be heard saying, 'Mommy, that man dropped something.' The boy drifted toward the object but suddenly stopped short. After a long, motionless beat, he pointed and let out a deafening scream.

Instantly, the police chief spun and ran for the door, barking orders as he went. 'Radio all points! Find the bald guy with the sling and detain him! NOW!'

Dashing out of the security center, he bounded up the treads of the well-worn staircase three at a time. The security feed had shown the bald man with the sling leave the Rotunda via the east portico. The shortest route out of the building would therefore take him through the east-west corridor, which was just ahead.

I can head him off.

As he reached the top of the stairs and rounded the corner, Anderson surveyed the quiet hallway before him. An elderly couple strolled at the far end, hand in hand. Nearby, a blond tourist wearing a blue blazer was reading a guidebook and studying the mosaic ceiling outside the House chamber.

'Excuse me, sir!' Anderson barked, running toward him. 'Have you seen a bald man with a sling on his arm?'

The man looked up from his book with a confused expression.

'A bald man with a sling!' Anderson repeated more firmly. 'Have you seen him?'

The tourist hesitated and glanced nervously toward the far eastern end of the hallway. 'Uh . . . yes,' he said. 'I think he just ran past me . . . to that staircase over there.' He pointed down the hall.

Anderson pulled out his radio and yelled into it. 'All points! The suspect is headed for the southeast exit. Converge!' He stowed the radio and yanked his sidearm from its holster, running toward the exit.

Thirty seconds later, at a quiet exit on the east side of the Capitol, the powerfully built blond man in the blue blazer stepped into the damp night air. He smiled, savoring the coolness of the evening.

Transformation.

It had been so easy.

Only a minute ago he had limped quickly out of the Rotunda in an army-surplus coat. Stepping into a darkened alcove, he shed his coat, revealing the blue blazer he wore underneath. Before abandoning his surplus jacket, he pulled a blond wig from the pocket and fit it snugly on his head. Then he stood up straight, pulled a slim Washington guidebook from his blazer, and stepped calmly from the niche with an elegant gait.

Transformation. This is my gift.

As Mal'akh's mortal legs carried him toward his waiting limousine, he arched his back, standing to his full six-foot-three height and throwing back his shoulders. He inhaled deeply, letting the air fill his lungs. He could feel the wings of the tattooed phoenix on his chest opening wide.

If they only knew my power, he thought, gazing out at the city. *Tonight my transformation will be complete.*

Mal'akh had played his cards artfully within the Capitol Building, showing obeisance to all the ancient etiquettes. *The ancient invitation has been delivered.* If Langdon had not yet grasped his role here tonight, soon he would.

13

For Robert Langdon, the Capitol Rotunda – like St. Peter's Basilica – always had a way of taking him by surprise. Intellectually, he knew the room was so large that the Statue of Liberty could stand comfortably inside it, but somehow the Rotunda always felt larger and more hallowed than he anticipated, as if there were spirits in the air. Tonight, however, there was only chaos.

Capitol police officers were sealing the Rotunda while attempting to herd distraught tourists away from the hand. The little boy was still crying. A bright light flashed – a tourist taking a photo of the hand – and several guards immediately detained the man, taking his camera and escorting him off. In the confusion, Langdon felt himself moving forward in a trance, slipping through the crowd, inching closer to the hand.

Peter Solomon's severed right hand was standing upright, the flat plane of the detached wrist skewered down onto the spike of a small wooden stand. Three of the fingers were closed in a fist, while the thumb and index finger were fully extended, pointing up toward the soaring dome.

'Everyone back!' an officer called.

Langdon was close enough now that he could see dried blood, which had run down from the wrist and coagulated on the wooden base. *Postmortem wounds don't bleed . . . which means Peter is alive.* Langdon didn't know whether to be relieved or nauseated. *Peter's hand was removed while he was alive?* Bile rose in his throat. He thought of all the times his dear friend had extended this same hand to shake Langdon's or offer a warm embrace.

For several seconds, Langdon felt his mind go blank, like an untuned television set broadcasting only static. The first clear image that broke through was utterly unexpected.

A crown . . . and a star.

Langdon crouched down, eyeing the tips of Peter's thumb and index finger. *Tattoos?* Incredibly, the monster who had done this appeared to have tattooed tiny symbols on Peter's fingertips.

On the thumb – a crown. On the index finger – a star.

This can't be. The two symbols registered instantly in Langdon's mind, amplifying this already horrific scene into something almost otherworldly. These symbols had appeared together many times in history, and always in the same place – on the fingertips of a hand. It was one of the ancient world's most coveted and secretive icons.

The Hand of the Mysteries.

The icon was rarely seen anymore, but throughout history it had symbolized a powerful call to action. Langdon strained to comprehend the grotesque artifact now before him. *Someone crafted the Hand of the Mysteries out of Peter's hand?* It was unthinkable. Traditionally, the icon was sculpted in stone or wood or rendered as a drawing. Langdon had never heard of the Hand of the Mysteries being fashioned from actual flesh. The concept was abhorrent.

'Sir?' a guard said behind Langdon. 'Please step back.'

Langdon barely heard him. *There are other tattoos.* Although he could not see the fingertips of the three clenched fingers, Langdon knew these fingertips would bear their own unique markings. That was the tradition. Five symbols in total. Through the millennia, the symbols on the fingertips of the Hand of the Mysteries had never changed . . . nor had the hand's iconic purpose.

The hand represents . . . an invitation.

Langdon felt a sudden chill as he recalled the words of the man who had brought him here. *Professor, tonight you are receiving the invitation of your lifetime.* In ancient times, the Hand of the Mysteries actually served as the most coveted invitation on earth. To receive this icon was a sacred summons to join an elite group – those who were said to guard the secret wisdom of all the ages. The invitation not only was a great honor, but it signified that a master believed you were worthy to receive this hidden wisdom. *The hand of the master extended to the initiate.*

'Sir,' the guard said, putting a firm hand on Langdon's shoulder. 'I need you to back up right now.'

'I know what this means,' Langdon managed. 'I can help you.'

'Now!' the guard said.

'My friend is in trouble. We have to—'

Langdon felt powerful arms pulling him up and leading him away from the hand. He simply let it happen . . . feeling too off balance to protest. A formal invitation had just been delivered. Someone was summoning Langdon to unlock a mystical portal that would unveil a world of ancient mysteries and hidden knowledge.

But it was all madness.

Delusions of a lunatic.

14

Mal'akh's stretch limousine eased away from the U.S. Capitol, moving eastward down Independence Avenue. A young couple on the sidewalk strained to see through the tinted rear windows, hoping to glimpse a VIP.

I'm in front, Mal'akh thought, smiling to himself.

Mal'akh loved the feeling of power he got from driving this massive car all alone. None of his other five cars offered him what he needed tonight – the *guarantee* of privacy. Total privacy. Limousines in this city enjoyed a kind of unspoken immunity. *Embassies on wheels.* Police officers who worked near Capitol Hill were never certain what power broker they might mistakenly pull over in a limousine, and so most simply chose not to take the chance.

As Mal'akh crossed the Anacostia River into Maryland, he could feel himself moving closer to Katherine, pulled onward by destiny's gravity. *I am being called to a second task tonight . . . one I had not imagined.* Last night, when Peter Solomon told the last of his secrets, Mal'akh had learned of the existence of a secret lab in which Katherine Solomon had performed miracles – staggering breakthroughs that Mal'akh realized would change the world if they were ever made known.

Her work will unveil the true nature of all things.

For centuries the 'brightest minds' on earth had ignored the ancient sciences, mocking them as ignorant superstitions, arming themselves instead with smug skepticism and dazzling new technologies – tools that led them only further from the truth. *Every generation's breakthroughs are proven false by the next generation's technology.* And so it had gone through the ages. The more man learned, the more he realized he did not know.

For millennia, mankind had wandered in the darkness . . . but now, as had been prophesied, there was a change coming. After hurtling blindly through history, mankind had reached a crossroads. This moment had been predicted long ago, prophesied by the ancient texts, by the primeval calendars, and even by the stars themselves. The date was specific, its arrival imminent. It would be preceded by a brilliant explosion of knowledge . . . a flash of clarity to illuminate the darkness and give mankind a final chance to veer away from the abyss and take the path of wisdom.

I have come to obscure the light, Mal'akh thought. *This is my role.*

Fate had linked him to Peter and Katherine Solomon. The breakthroughs Katherine Solomon had made within the SMSC would risk opening floodgates of new thinking, starting a new Renaissance. Katherine's revelations, if made public, would become a catalyst that would inspire mankind to rediscover the knowledge he had lost, empowering him beyond all imagination.

Katherine's destiny is to light this torch.
Mine is to extinguish it.

15

In total darkness, Katherine Solomon groped for the outer door of her lab. Finding it, she heaved open the lead-lined door and hurried into the small entry room. The journey across the void had taken only ninety seconds, and yet her heart was pounding wildly. *After three years, you'd think I'd be used to that.* Katherine always felt relieved to escape the blackness of Pod 5 and step into this clean, well-lit space.

The 'Cube' was a massive windowless box. Every inch of the interior walls and ceiling was covered with a stiff mesh of titanium-coated lead fiber, giving the impression of a giant cage built inside a cement enclosure. Dividers of frosted Plexiglas separated the space into different compartments – a laboratory, a control room, a mechanical room, a bathroom, and a small research library.

Katherine strode briskly into the main lab. The bright and sterile work space glistened with advanced quantitative equipment: paired electroencephalographs, a femtosecond comb, a magneto-optical trap, and quantum-indeterminate electronic noise REGs, more simply known as Random Event Generators.

Despite Noetic Science's use of cutting-edge technologies, the discoveries themselves were far more mystical than the cold, high-tech machines that were producing them. The stuff of magic and myth was fast becoming reality as the shocking new data poured in, all of it supporting the basic ideology of Noetic Science – the untapped potential of the human mind.

The overall thesis was simple: *We have barely scratched the surface of our mental and spiritual capabilities.*

Experiments at facilities like the Institute of Noetic Sciences (IONS) in California and the Princeton Engineering Anomalies Research Lab (PEAR) had categorically proven that human thought, if properly focused, had the ability to affect and change *physical* mass. Their experiments were no 'spoon-bending' parlor tricks, but rather highly controlled inquiries that all produced the same extraordinary result: our *thoughts* actually interacted with the physical world, whether or not we knew it, effecting change all the way down to the subatomic realm.

Mind over matter.

In 2001, in the hours following the horrifying events of September 11, the field of Noetic Science made a quantum leap forward. Four scientists discovered that as the frightened world came together and focused in shared grief on this single tragedy, the outputs of thirty-seven different Random Event Generators around the world suddenly became significantly *less* random. Somehow, the oneness of this shared experience, the coalescing of millions of minds, had affected the randomizing function of these machines, organizing their outputs and bringing order from chaos.

The shocking discovery, it seemed, paralleled the ancient spiritual belief in a 'cosmic consciousness' – a vast coalescing of human intention that was actually capable of interacting with physical matter. Recently, studies in mass meditation and prayer had produced similar results in Random Event Generators, fueling the claim that *human consciousness*, as Noetic author Lynne McTaggart described it, was a substance *outside* the confines of the body . . . a highly ordered energy capable of changing the physical world.

Katherine had been fascinated by McTaggart's book *The Intention Experiment*, and her global, Web-based study – theintentionexperiment.com – aimed at discovering how human intention could affect the world. A handful of other progressive texts had also piqued Katherine's interest.

From this foundation, Katherine Solomon's research had vaulted forward, proving that 'focused thought' could affect literally *anything* – the growth rate of plants, the direction that fish swam in a bowl, the manner in which cells divided in a petri dish, the synchronization of separately automated systems, and the chemical reactions in one's own body. Even the crystalline structure of a newly forming solid was rendered mutable by one's mind; Katherine had created beautifully symmetrical ice crystals by sending loving thoughts to a glass of water as it froze. Incredibly, the *converse* was also true: when she sent negative, polluting thoughts to the water, the ice crystals froze in chaotic, fractured forms.

Human thought can literally transform the physical world.

As Katherine's experiments grew bolder, her results became more astounding. Her work in this lab had proven beyond the shadow of a doubt that 'mind over matter' was not just some New Age self-help mantra. The mind had the ability to alter the state of matter itself, and, more important, the mind had the power to encourage the physical world to move in a specific direction.

We are the masters of our own universe.

At the subatomic level, Katherine had shown that particles themselves came in and out of existence based solely on her *intention* to observe them. In a sense, her desire to see a particle . . . manifested that particle. Heisenberg had hinted at this reality decades ago, and now it had become a fundamental principle of Noetic Science. In the words of Lynne McTaggart: 'Living consciousness somehow is the influence that turns the *possibility* of something into something *real*. The most essential ingredient in creating our universe is the consciousness that observes it.'

The most astonishing aspect of Katherine's work, however, had been the realization that the mind's ability to affect the physical world could be *augmented* through practice. Intention was a *learned* skill. Like meditation, harnessing the true power of 'thought' required practice. More important . . . some people were born more skilled at it than others. And throughout history, there had been those few who had become true masters.

This is the missing link between modern science and ancient mysticism.

Katherine had learned this from her brother, Peter, and now, as her thoughts turned back to him, she felt a deepening concern. She walked to the lab's research library and peered in. Empty.

The library was a small reading room – two Morris chairs, a wooden table, two floor lamps, and a wall of mahogany bookshelves that held some five hundred books. Katherine and Peter had pooled their favorite texts here, writings on everything from particle physics to ancient mysticism. Their collection had grown into an eclectic fusion of new and old . . . of cutting-edge and historical. Most of Katherine's books bore titles like *Quantum Consciousness*, *The New Physics*, and *Principles of Neural Science*. Her brother's bore older, more esoteric titles like the *Kybalion*, the *Zohar*, *The*

Dancing Wu Li Masters, and a translation of the Sumerian tablets from the British Museum.

'The key to our scientific future,' her brother often said, 'is hidden in our past.' A lifelong scholar of history, science, and mysticism, Peter had been the first to encourage Katherine to boost her university science education with an understanding of early Hermetic philosophy. She had been only nineteen years old when Peter sparked her interest in the link between modern science and ancient mysticism.

'So tell me, Kate,' her brother had asked while she was home on vacation during her sophomore year at Yale. 'What are Elis reading these days in theoretical physics?'

Katherine had stood in her family's book-filled library and recited her demanding reading list.

'Impressive,' her brother replied. 'Einstein, Bohr, and Hawking are modern geniuses. But are you reading anything older?'

Katherine scratched her head. 'You mean like . . . Newton?'

He smiled. 'Keep going.' At twenty-seven, Peter had already made a name for himself in the academic world, and he and Katherine had grown to savor this kind of playful intellectual sparring.

Older than Newton? Katherine's head now filled with distant names like Ptolemy, Pythagoras, and Hermes Trismegistus. *Nobody reads that stuff anymore.*

Her brother ran a finger down the long shelf of cracked leather bindings and old dusty tomes. 'The scientific wisdom of the ancients was staggering . . . modern physics is only *now* beginning to comprehend it all.'

'Peter,' she said, 'you already told me that the

Egyptians understood levers and pulleys long before Newton, and that the early alchemists did work on a par with modern chemistry, but so what? *Today's* physics deals with concepts that would have been unimaginable to the ancients.'

'Like what?'

'Well . . . like *entanglement theory*, for one!' Subatomic research had now proven categorically that all matter was interconnected . . . entangled in a single unified mesh . . . a kind of universal oneness. 'You're telling me the ancients sat around discussing *entanglement* theory?'

'Absolutely!' Peter said, pushing his long, dark bangs out of his eyes. 'Entanglement was at the core of primeval beliefs. Its names are as old as history itself . . . Dharmakaya, Tao, Brahman. In fact, man's oldest spiritual quest was to perceive his own entanglement, to sense his own interconnection with all things. He has always wanted to become "one" with the universe . . . to achieve the state of "at-one-ment." '

Her brother raised his eyebrows. 'To this day, Jews and Christians still strive for "atonement" . . . although most of us have forgotten it is actually "at-one-ment" we're seeking.'

Katherine sighed, having forgotten how hard it was to argue with a man so well versed in history. 'Okay, but you're talking in generalities. I'm talking *specific* physics.'

'Then *be* specific.' His keen eyes challenged her now.

'Okay, how about something as simple as *polarity* – the positive/negative balance of the subatomic realm. Obviously, the ancients didn't underst—'

'Hold on!' Her brother pulled down a large dusty text, which he dropped loudly on the library table.

'Modern polarity is nothing but the "dual world" described by Krishna here in the Bhagavad Gita over two thousand years ago. A dozen other books in here, including the *Kybalion*, talk about binary systems and the opposing forces in nature.'

Katherine was skeptical. 'Okay, but if we talk about modern discoveries in *subatomics* – the Heisenberg uncertainty principle, for example—'

'Then we must look *here*,' Peter said, striding down his long bookshelf and pulling out another text. 'The sacred Hindu Vendantic scriptures known as the Upanishads.' He dropped the tome heavily on the first. 'Heisenberg and Schrödinger *studied* this text and credited it with helping them formulate some of their theories.'

The showdown continued for several minutes, and the stack of dusty books on the desk grew taller and taller. Finally Katherine threw up her hands in frustration. 'Okay! You made your point, but I want to study cutting-edge *theoretical* physics. The future of science! I really doubt Krishna or Vyasa had much to say about superstring theory and multidimensional cosmological models.'

'You're right. They didn't.' Her brother paused, a smile crossing his lips. 'If you're talking superstring theory . . .' He wandered over to the bookshelf yet again. 'Then you're talking *this* book here.' He heaved out a colossal leather-bound book and dropped it with a crash onto the desk. 'Thirteenth-century translation of the original medieval Aramaic.'

'Superstring theory in the thirteenth century?!' Katherine wasn't buying it. 'Come on!'

Superstring theory was a brand-new cosmological model. Based on the most recent scientific observations, it suggested the multidimensional universe was made up not of *three* ... but rather of *ten* dimensions, which all interacted like vibrating strings, similar to resonating violin strings.

Katherine waited as her brother heaved open the book, ran through the ornately printed table of contents, and then flipped to a spot near the beginning of the book. 'Read this.' He pointed to a faded page of text and diagrams.

Dutifully, Katherine studied the page. The translation was old-fashioned and very hard to read, but to her utter amazement, the text and drawings clearly outlined the *exact* same universe heralded by modern superstring theory – a ten-dimensional universe of resonating strings. As she continued reading, she suddenly gasped and recoiled. 'My God, it even describes how six of the dimensions are entangled and act as one?!' She took a frightened step backward. 'What *is* this book?!'

Her brother grinned. 'Something I'm hoping you'll read one day.' He flipped back to the title page, where an ornately printed plate bore three words.

The Complete Zohar.

Although Katherine had never read the *Zohar,* she knew it was the fundamental text of early Jewish mysticism, once believed so potent that it was reserved only for the most erudite rabbis.

Katherine eyed the book. 'You're saying the early mystics *knew* their universe had ten dimensions?'

'Absolutely.' He motioned to the page's illustration of ten intertwined circles called Sephiroth. 'Obviously, the nomenclature is esoteric, but the physics is very advanced.'

Katherine didn't know how to respond. 'But ... then why don't more people study this?'

Her brother smiled. 'They *will*.'

'I don't understand.'

'Katherine, we have been born into wonderful times. A change is coming. Human beings are poised on the threshold of a new age when they will begin turning their eyes back to nature and to the old ways . . . back to the ideas in books like the *Zohar* and other ancient texts from around the world. Powerful truth has its own gravity and eventually pulls people back to it. There will come a day when modern science begins in earnest to study the wisdom of the ancients . . . that will be the day that mankind begins to find answers to the big questions that still elude him.'

That night, Katherine eagerly began reading her brother's ancient texts and quickly came to understand that he was right. *The ancients possessed profound scientific wisdom.* Today's science was not so much making 'discoveries' as it was making 'rediscoveries.' Mankind, it seemed, had once grasped the true nature of the universe . . . but had let go . . . and forgotten.

Modern physics can help us remember! This quest had become Katherine's mission in life – to use advanced science to rediscover the lost wisdom of the ancients. It was more than academic thrill that kept her motivated. Beneath it all was her conviction that the world *needed* this understanding . . . now more than ever.

At the rear of the lab, Katherine saw her brother's white lab coat hanging on its hook along with her own. Reflexively, she pulled out her phone to check for messages. Nothing. A voice echoed again in her memory. *That which your brother believes is hidden in D.C. . . . it can be found. Sometimes a legend*

that endures for centuries . . . endures for a reason.
'No,' Katherine said aloud. 'It can't possibly be real.'
Sometimes a legend was just that – a legend.

16

Security chief Trent Anderson stormed back toward the Capitol Rotunda, fuming at the failure of his security team. One of his men had just found a sling and an army-surplus jacket in an alcove near the east portico.

The goddamn guy walked right out of here!

Anderson had already assigned teams to start scanning exterior video, but by the time they found anything, this guy would be long gone.

Now, as Anderson entered the Rotunda to survey the damage, he saw that the situation had been contained as well as could be expected. All four entrances to the Rotunda were closed with as inconspicuous a method of crowd control as Security had at its disposal – a velvet swag, an apologetic guard, and a sign that read THIS ROOM TEMPORARILY CLOSED FOR CLEANING. The dozen or so witnesses were all being herded into a group on the eastern perimeter of the room, where the guards were collecting cell phones and cameras; the last thing Anderson needed was for one of these people to send a cell-phone snapshot to CNN.

One of the detained witnesses, a tall, dark-haired man in a tweed sport coat, was trying to break away from the group to speak to the chief. The man was currently in a heated discussion with the guards.

'I'll speak to him in a moment,' Anderson called over to the guards. 'For now, please hold everyone in the main lobby until we sort this out.'

Anderson turned his eyes now to the hand, which stood at attention in the middle of the room. *For the love of God.* In fifteen years on security detail for the Capitol Building, he had seen some strange things. But nothing like this.

Forensics had better get here fast and get this thing out of my building.

Anderson moved closer, seeing that the bloody wrist had been skewered on a spiked wooden base to make the hand stand up. *Wood and flesh,* he thought. *Invisible to metal detectors.* The only metal was a large gold ring, which Anderson assumed had either been wanded or casually pulled off the dead finger by the suspect as if it were his own.

Anderson crouched down to examine the hand. It looked as if it had belonged to a man of about sixty. The ring bore some kind of ornate seal with a two-headed bird and the number 33. Anderson didn't recognize it. What really caught his eye were the tiny tattoos on the tips of the thumb and index finger.

A goddamn freak show.

'Chief?' One of the guards hurried over, holding out a phone. 'Personal call for you. Security switchboard just patched it through.'

Anderson looked at him like he was insane. 'I'm in the middle of something here,' he growled.

The guard's face was pale. He covered the mouth-piece and whispered. 'It's CIA.'

Anderson did a double take. *CIA heard about this already?!*

'It's their Office of Security.'

Anderson stiffened. *Holy shit.* He glanced uneasily at the phone in the guard's hand.

In Washington's vast ocean of intelligence agencies, the CIA's Office of Security was something of a Bermuda Triangle – a mysterious and treacherous region from which all who knew of it steered clear whenever possible. With a seemingly self-destructive mandate, the OS had been created by the CIA for one strange purpose – to spy on the CIA itself. Like a powerful internal-affairs office, the OS monitored all CIA employees for illicit behavior: misappropriation of funds, selling of secrets, stealing classified technologies, and use of illegal torture tactics, to name a few.

They spy on America's spies.

With investigative carte blanche in all matters of national security, the OS had a long and potent reach. Anderson could not fathom why they would be interested in this incident at the Capitol, or how they had found out so fast. Then again, the OS was rumored to have eyes everywhere. For all Anderson knew, they had a direct feed of U.S. Capitol security cameras. This incident did not match OS directives in any way, although the timing of the call seemed too coincidental to Anderson to be about anything other than this severed hand.

'Chief?' The guard was holding the phone out to him like a hot potato. 'You need to take this call right now. It's . . .' He paused and silently mouthed two syllables. 'SA-TO.'

Anderson squinted hard at the man. *You've got to be kidding.* He felt his palms begin to sweat. *Sato is handling this personally?*

The overlord of the Office of Security – Director

Inoue Sato – was a legend in the intelligence community. Born inside the fences of a Japanese internment camp in Manzanar, California, in the aftermath of Pearl Harbor, Sato was a toughened survivor who had never forgotten the horrors of war, or the perils of insufficient military intelligence. Now, having risen to one of the most secretive and potent posts in U.S. intelligence work, Sato had proven an uncompromising patriot as well as a terrifying enemy to any who stood in opposition. Seldom seen but universally feared, the OS director cruised the deep waters of the CIA like a leviathan who surfaced only to devour its prey.

Anderson had met Sato face-to-face only once, and the memory of looking into those cold black eyes was enough to make him count his blessings that he would be having this conversation by telephone.

Anderson took the phone and brought it to his lips. 'Director Sato,' he said in as friendly a voice as possible. 'This is Chief Anderson. How may I—'

'There is a man in your building to whom I need to speak immediately.' The OS director's voice was unmistakable – like gravel grating on a chalkboard. Throat cancer surgery had left Sato with a profoundly unnerving intonation and a repulsive neck scar to match. 'I want you to find him for me immediately.'

That's all? You want me to page someone? Anderson felt suddenly hopeful that maybe the timing of this call was pure coincidence. 'Who are you looking for?'

'His name is Robert Langdon. I believe he is inside your building right now.'

Langdon? The name sounded vaguely familiar, but Anderson couldn't quite place it. He was now wondering if Sato knew about the hand. 'I'm in the

Rotunda at the moment,' Anderson said, 'but we've got some tourists here . . . hold on.' He lowered his phone and called out to the group, 'Folks, is there anyone here by the name of Langdon?'

After a short silence, a deep voice replied from the crowd of tourists. 'Yes. I'm Robert Langdon.'

Sato knows all. Anderson craned his neck, trying to see who had spoken up.

The same man who had been trying to get to him earlier stepped away from the others. He looked distraught . . . but familiar somehow.

Anderson raised the phone to his lips. 'Yes, Mr. Langdon is here.'

'Put him on,' Sato said coarsely.

Anderson exhaled. *Better him than me.* 'Hold on.' He waved Langdon over.

As Langdon approached, Anderson suddenly realized why the name sounded familiar. *I just read an article about this guy. What the hell is* he *doing here?*

Despite Langdon's six-foot frame and athletic build, Anderson saw none of the cold, hardened edge he expected from a man famous for surviving an explosion at the Vatican and a manhunt in Paris. *This guy eluded the French police . . . in loafers?* He looked more like someone Anderson would expect to find hearthside in some Ivy League library reading Dostoyevsky.

'Mr. Langdon?' Anderson said, walking halfway to meet him. 'I'm Chief Anderson. I handle security here. You have a phone call.'

'For *me*?' Langdon's blue eyes looked anxious and uncertain.

Anderson held out the phone. 'It's the CIA's Office of Security.'

'I've never heard of it.'

Anderson smiled ominously. 'Well, sir, *it's* heard of *you.*'

Langdon put the phone to his ear. 'Yes?'

'Robert Langdon?' Director Sato's harsh voice blared in the tiny speaker, loud enough that Anderson could hear.

'Yes?' Langdon replied.

Anderson stepped closer to hear what Sato was saying.

'This is Director Inoue Sato, Mr. Langdon. I am handling a crisis at the moment, and I believe you have information that can help me.'

Langdon looked hopeful. 'Is this about Peter Solomon? Do you know where he is?!'

Peter Solomon? Anderson felt entirely out of the loop.

'Professor,' Sato replied. 'I am asking the questions at the moment.'

'Peter Solomon is in very serious trouble,' Langdon exclaimed. 'Some madman just—'

'Excuse me,' Sato said, cutting him off.

Anderson cringed. *Bad move.* Interrupting a top CIA official's line of questioning was a mistake only a civilian would make. *I thought Langdon was supposed to be smart.*

'Listen carefully,' Sato said. 'As we speak, this nation is facing a crisis. I have been advised that you have information that can help me avert it. Now, I am going to ask you again. What information do you possess?'

Langdon looked lost. 'Director, I have no idea what you're talking about. All I'm concerned with is finding Peter and—'

'No idea?' Sato challenged.

Anderson saw Langdon bristle. The professor now took a more aggressive tone. 'No, sir. No damned idea at all.'

Anderson winced. *Wrong. Wrong. Wrong.* Robert Langdon had just made a very costly mistake in dealing with Director Sato.

Incredibly, Anderson now realized it was too late. To his astonishment, Director Sato had just appeared on the far side of the Rotunda, and was approaching fast behind Langdon. *Sato is in the building!* Anderson held his breath and braced for impact. *Langdon has no idea.*

The director's dark form drew closer, phone held to ear, black eyes locked like two lasers on Langdon's back.

Langdon clutched the police chief's phone and felt a rising frustration as the OS director pressed him. 'I'm sorry, sir,' Langdon said tersely, 'but I can't read your mind. What do you want from me?'

'What do I want from you?' The OS director's grating voice crackled through Langdon's phone, scraping and hollow, like that of a dying man with strep throat.

As the man spoke, Langdon felt a tap on his shoulder. He turned and his eyes were drawn down . . . directly into the face of a tiny Japanese woman. She had a fierce expression, a mottled complexion, thinning hair, tobacco-stained teeth, and an unsettling white scar that sliced horizontally across her neck. The woman's gnarled hand held a cell phone to her ear, and when her lips moved, Langdon heard the familiar raspy voice through his cell phone.

'What do I want from you, Professor?' She calmly closed her phone and glared at him. 'For starters, you can stop calling me "sir." '

Langdon stared, mortified. 'Ma'am, I . . . apologize. Our connection was poor and—'.

'Our connection was fine, Professor,' she said. 'And I have an extremely low tolerance for bullshit.'

17

Director Inoue Sato was a fearsome specimen – a bristly tempest of a woman who stood a mere four feet ten inches. She was bone thin, with jagged features and a dermatological condition known as vitiligo, which gave her complexion the mottled look of coarse granite blotched with lichen. Her rumpled blue pantsuit hung on her emaciated frame like a loose sack, the open-necked blouse doing nothing to hide the scar across her neck. It had been noted by her coworkers that Sato's only acquiescence to physical vanity appeared to be that of plucking her substantial mustache.

For over a decade, Inoue Sato had overseen the CIA's Office of Security. She possessed an off-the-chart IQ and chillingly accurate instincts, a combination which girded her with a self-confidence that made her terrifying to anyone who could not perform the impossible. Not even a terminal diagnosis of aggressive throat cancer had knocked her from her perch. The battle had cost her one month of work, half her voice box, and a third of her body weight, but she returned to the office as if nothing had happened. Inoue Sato appeared to be indestructible.

Robert Langdon suspected he was probably not the first to mistake Sato for a man on the phone, but the director was still glaring at him with simmering black eyes.

'Again, my apologies, ma'am,' Langdon said. 'I'm still trying to get my bearings here – the person who claims to have Peter Solomon tricked me into coming to D.C. this evening.' He pulled the fax from his jacket. 'This is what he sent me earlier. I wrote down the tail number of the plane he sent, so maybe if you call the FAA and track the—'

Sato's tiny hand shot out and snatched the sheet of paper. She stuck it in her pocket without even opening it. 'Professor, I am running this investigation, and until you start telling me what I want to know, I suggest you not speak unless spoken to.'

Sato now spun to the police chief.

'Chief Anderson,' she said, stepping entirely too close and staring up at him through tiny black eyes, 'would you care to tell me what the hell is going on here? The guard at the east gate told me you found a human hand on the floor. Is that true?'

Anderson stepped to the side and revealed the object in the center of the floor. 'Yes, ma'am, only a few minutes ago.'

She glanced at the hand as if it were nothing more than a misplaced piece of clothing. 'And yet you didn't mention it to me when I called?'

'I . . . I thought you knew.'

'Do *not* lie to me.'

Anderson wilted under her gaze, but his voice

remained confident. 'Ma'am, this situation is under control.'

'I really doubt that,' Sato said, with equal confidence.

'A forensics team is on the way. Whoever did this may have left fingerprints.'

Sato looked skeptical. 'I think someone clever enough to walk through your security checkpoint with a human hand is probably clever enough not to leave fingerprints.'

'That may be true, but I have a responsibility to investigate.'

'Actually, I am relieving you of your responsibility as of this moment. I'm taking over.'

Anderson stiffened. 'This is not exactly OS domain, is it?'

'Absolutely. This is an issue of national security.'

Peter's hand? Langdon wondered, watching their exchange in a daze. *National security?* Langdon was sensing that his own urgent goal of finding Peter was not Sato's. The OS director seemed to be on another page entirely.

Anderson looked puzzled as well. 'National security? With all due respect, ma'am—'

'The last I checked,' she interrupted, 'I outrank you. I suggest you do exactly as I say, and that you do it without question.'

Anderson nodded and swallowed hard. 'But shouldn't we at least print the fingers to confirm the hand belongs to Peter Solomon?'

'I'll confirm it,' Langdon said, feeling a sickening certainty. 'I recognize his ring . . . and his hand.' He paused. 'The tattoos are new, though. Someone did that to him recently.'

'I'm sorry?' Sato looked unnerved for the first time since arriving. 'The hand is *tattooed*?'

Langdon nodded. 'The thumb has a crown. And the index finger a star.'

Sato pulled out a pair of glasses and walked toward the hand, circling like a shark.

'Also,' Langdon said, 'although you can't see the other three fingers, I'm certain they will have tattoos on the fingertips as well.'

Sato looked intrigued by the comment and motioned to Anderson. 'Chief, can you look at the other fingertips for us, please?'

Anderson crouched down beside the hand, being careful not to touch it. He put his cheek near the floor and looked up under the clenched fingertips. 'He's right, ma'am. All of the fingertips have tattoos, although I can't quite see what the other—'

'A sun, a lantern, and a key,' Langdon said flatly.

Sato turned fully to Langdon now, her small eyes appraising him. 'And how exactly would you know that?'

Langdon stared back. 'The image of a human hand, marked in this way on the fingertips, is a very old icon. It's known as "the Hand of the Mysteries." '

Anderson stood up abruptly. 'This thing has a *name*?'

Langdon nodded. 'It's one of the most secretive icons of the ancient world.'

Sato cocked her head. 'Then might I ask what the hell it's doing in the middle of the U.S. Capitol?'

Langdon wished he would wake up from this nightmare. 'Traditionally, ma'am, it was used as an invitation.'

'An invitation . . . to what?' she demanded.

Langdon looked down at the symbols on his friend's severed hand. 'For centuries, the Hand of the Mysteries served as a mystical summons. Basically, it's an invitation to receive secret knowledge – protected wisdom known only to an elite few.'

Sato folded her thin arms and stared up at him with jet-black eyes. 'Well, Professor, for someone who claims to have no clue why he's here . . . you're doing quite well so far.'

18

Katherine Solomon donned her white lab coat and began her usual arrival routine – her 'rounds' as her brother called them.

Like a nervous parent checking on a sleeping baby, Katherine poked her head into the mechanical room. The hydrogen fuel cell was running smoothly, its backup tanks all safely nestled in their racks.

Katherine continued down the hall to the data-storage room. As always, the two redundant holographic backup units hummed safely within their temperature-controlled vault. *All of my research*, she thought, gazing in through the three-inch-thick shatter-proof glass. Holographic data-storage devices, unlike their refrigerator-size ancestors, looked more like sleek stereo components, each perched atop a columnar pedestal.

Both of her lab's holographic drives were synchro-nized and identical – serving as redundant backups to safeguard identical copies of her work. Most backup protocols advocated a secondary backup system *off-site* in case of earthquake, fire, or theft, but Katherine and her brother agreed that secrecy was paramount; once this data left the building to an off-site server, they could no longer be certain it would stay private.

Content that everything was running smoothly here, she headed back down the hallway. As she rounded the corner, however, she spotted something unexpected across the lab. *What in the world?* A muted glow was glinting off all the equipment. She hurried in to have a look, surprised to see light emanating from behind the Plexiglas wall of the control room.

He's here. Katherine flew across the lab, arriving at the control-room door and heaving it open. 'Peter!' she said, running in.

The plump woman seated at the control room's terminal jumped up. 'Oh my God! Katherine! You scared me!'

Trish Dunne – the only other person on earth allowed back here – was Katherine's metasystems analyst and seldom worked weekends. The twenty-six-year-old redhead was a genius data modeler and had signed a nondisclosure document worthy of the KGB. Tonight, she was apparently analyzing data on the control room's plasma wall – a huge flat-screen display that looked like something out of NASA mission control.

'Sorry,' Trish said. 'I didn't know you were here yet. I was trying to finish up before you and your brother arrived.'

'Have you spoken to him? He's late and he's not answering his phone.'

Trish shook her head. 'I bet he's still trying to figure

out how to use that new iPhone you gave him.'

Katherine appreciated Trish's good humor, and Trish's presence here had just given her an idea. 'Actually, I'm glad you're in tonight. You might be able to help me with something, if you don't mind?'

'Whatever it is, I'm sure it beats football.'

Katherine took a deep breath, calming her mind. 'I'm not sure how to explain this, but earlier today, I heard an unusual story . . .'

Trish Dunne didn't know what story Katherine Solomon had heard, but clearly it had her on edge. Her boss's usually calm gray eyes looked anxious, and she had tucked her hair behind her ears three times since entering the room – a nervous 'tell,' as Trish called it. *Brilliant scientist. Lousy poker player.*

'To me,' Katherine said, 'this story sounds like fiction . . . an old legend. And yet . . .' She paused, tucking a wisp of hair behind her ears once again.

'And yet?'

Katherine sighed. 'And yet I was told today by a trusted source that the legend is true.'

'Okay . . .' *Where is she going with this?*

'I'm going to talk to my brother about it, but it occurs to me that maybe you can help me shed some light on it before I do. I'd love to know if this legend has ever been corroborated anywhere else in history.'

'In all of history?'

Katherine nodded. 'Anywhere in the world, in any language, at any point in history.'

Strange request, Trish thought, *but certainly feasible.* Ten years ago, the task would have been impossible. Today, however, with the Internet, the World Wide

106

Web, and the ongoing digitization of the great libraries and museums in the world, Katherine's goal could be achieved by using a relatively simple search engine equipped with an army of translation modules and some well-chosen keywords.

'No problem,' Trish said. Many of the lab's research books contained passages in ancient languages, and so Trish was often asked to write specialized Optical Character Recognition translation modules to generate English text from obscure languages. She had to be the only metasystems specialist on earth who had built OCR translation modules in Old Frisian, Maek, and Akkadian.

The modules would help, but the trick to building an effective search spider was all in choosing the right key words. *Unique but not overly restrictive.*

Katherine looked to be a step ahead of Trish and was already jotting down possible keywords on a slip of paper. Katherine had written down several when she paused, thought a moment, and then wrote several more. 'Okay,' she finally said, handing Trish the slip of paper.

Trish perused the list of search strings, and her eyes grew wide. *What kind of crazy legend is Katherine investigating?* 'You want me to search for *all* of these key phrases?' One of the words Trish didn't even recognize. *Is that even English?* 'Do you really think we'll find all of these in one place? Verbatim?'

'I'd like to try.'

Trish would have said *impossible,* but the I-word was banned here. Katherine considered it a dangerous mind-set in a field that often transformed pre-conceived falsehoods into confirmed truths. Trish

Dunne seriously doubted this key-phrase search would fall into that category.

'How long for results?' Katherine asked.

'A few minutes to write the spider and launch it. After that, maybe fifteen for the spider to exhaust itself.'

'So fast?' Katherine looked encouraged.

Trish nodded. Traditional search engines often required a full day to crawl across the entire online universe, find new documents, digest their content, and add it to their searchable database. But this was not the kind of search spider Trish would write.

'I'll write a program called a *delegator*,' Trish explained. 'It's not entirely kosher, but it's fast. Essentially, it's a program that orders other people's search engines to do our work. Most databases have a search function built in – libraries, museums, universities, governments. So I write a spider that finds *their* search engines, inputs your keywords, and asks them to search. This way, we harness the power of thousands of engines, working in unison.'

Katherine looked impressed. 'Parallel processing.'

A kind of metasystem. 'I'll call you if I get anything.'

'I appreciate it, Trish.' Katherine patted her on the back and headed for the door. 'I'll be in the library.'

Trish settled in to write the program. Coding a search spider was a menial task far below her skill level, but Trish Dunne didn't care. She would do anything for Katherine Solomon. Sometimes Trish still couldn't believe the good fortune that had brought her here.

You've come a long way, baby.

Just over a year ago, Trish had quit her job as a meta-systems analyst in one of the high-tech industry's many cubicle farms. In her off-hours, she did some freelance programming and started an industry blog – 'Future Applications in Computational Metasystem Analysis' – although she doubted anyone read it. Then one evening her phone rang.

'Trish Dunne?' a woman's voice asked politely.

'Yes, who's calling, please?'

'My name is Katherine Solomon.'

Trish almost fainted on the spot. *Katherine Solomon?* 'I just read your book – *Noetic Science: Modern Gateway to Ancient Wisdom – and* I wrote about it on my blog!'

'Yes, I know,' the woman replied graciously. 'That's why I'm calling.'

Of course it is, Trish realized, feeling dumb. *Even brilliant scientists Google themselves.*

'Your blog intrigues me,' Katherine told her. 'I wasn't aware metasystems modeling had come so far.'

'Yes, ma'am,' Trish managed, starstruck. 'Data models are an exploding technology with far-reaching applications.'

For several minutes, the two women chatted about Trish's work in metasystems, discussing her experience analyzing, modeling, and predicting the flow of massive data fields.

'Obviously, your book is way over my head,' Trish said, 'but I understood enough to see an intersection with my metasystems work.'

'Your blog said you believe metasystems modeling can *transform* the study of Noetics?'

'Absolutely. I believe metasystems could turn Noetics into real science.'

'*Real* science?' Katherine's tone hardened slightly. 'As opposed to . . . ?'

Oh shit, that came out wrong. 'Um, what I meant is that Noetics is more . . . esoteric.'

Katherine laughed. 'Relax, I'm kidding. I get that all the time.'

I'm not surprised, Trish thought. Even the Institute of Noetic Sciences in California described the field in arcane and abstruse language, defining it as the study of mankind's 'direct and immediate access to knowledge beyond what is available to our normal senses and the power of reason.'

The word *noetic,* Trish had learned, derived from the ancient Greek *nous* – translating roughly to 'inner knowledge' or 'intuitive consciousness.'

'I'm interested in your metasystems work,' Katherine said, 'and how it might relate to a project I'm working on. Any chance you'd be willing to meet? I'd love to pick your brain.'

Katherine Solomon wants to pick my *brain?* It felt like Maria Sharapova had called for tennis tips.

The next day a white Volvo pulled into Trish's driveway and an attractive, willowy woman in blue jeans got out. Trish immediately felt two feet tall. *Great,* she groaned. *Smart, rich, and thin – and I'm supposed to believe God is good?* But Katherine's unassuming air set Trish instantly at ease.

The two of them settled in on Trish's huge back porch overlooking an impressive piece of property.

'Your house is amazing,' Katherine said.

'Thanks. I got lucky in college and licensed some software I'd written.'

'Metasystems stuff?'

'A precursor to metasystems. Following 9/11, the government was intercepting and crunching enormous data fields – civilian e-mail, cell phone, fax, text, Web sites – sniffing for keywords associated with terrorist communications. So I wrote a piece of software that let them process their data field in a second way . . . pulling from it an additional intelligence product.' She smiled. 'Essentially, my software let them take America's temperature.'

'I'm sorry?'

Trish laughed. 'Yeah, sounds crazy, I know. What I mean is that it quantified the nation's *emotional* state. It offered a kind of cosmic consciousness barometer, if you will.' Trish explained how, using a data field of the nation's communications, one could assess the nation's *mood* based on the 'occurrence density' of certain keywords and emotional indicators in the data field. Happier times had happier language, and stressful times vice versa. In the event, for example, of a terrorist attack, the government could use data fields to measure the shift in America's psyche and better advise the president on the emotional impact of the event.

'Fascinating,' Katherine said, stroking her chin. 'So essentially you're examining a population of individuals . . . as if it were a *single* organism.'

'Exactly. A *metasystem*. A single entity defined by the sum of its parts. The human body, for example, consists of millions of individual cells, each with different attributes and different purposes, but it functions as a single entity.'

Katherine nodded enthusiastically. 'Like a flock of birds or a school of fish moving as one. We call it convergence or entanglement.'

Trish sensed her famous guest was starting to see the potential of metasystem programming in her own field of Noetics. 'My software,' Trish explained, 'was designed to help government agencies better evaluate and respond appropriately to wide-scale crises – pandemic diseases, national tragedies, terrorism, that sort of thing.' She paused. 'Of course, there's always the potential that it could be used in other directions ... perhaps to take a snapshot of the national mind-set and predict the outcome of a national election or the direction the stock market will move at the opening bell.'

'Sounds powerful.'

Trish motioned to her big house. 'The *government* thought so.'

Katherine's gray eyes focused in on her now. 'Trish, might I ask about the *ethical* dilemma posed by your work?'

'What do you mean?'

'I mean you created a piece of software that can easily be abused. Those who possess it have access to powerful information not available to everyone. You didn't feel any hesitation creating it?'

Trish didn't blink. 'Absolutely not. My software is no different than say ... a flight simulator program. Some users will practice flying first-aid missions into under-developed countries. Some users will practice flying passenger jets into skyscrapers. Knowledge is a tool, and like all tools, its impact is in the hands of the user.'

Katherine sat back, looking impressed. 'So let me ask you a hypothetical question.'

Trish suddenly sensed their conversation had just turned into a job interview.

Katherine reached down and picked up a tiny speck of sand off the deck, holding it up for Trish to see. 'It occurs to me,' she said, 'that your metasystems work essentially lets you calculate the weight of an entire sandy beach ... by weighing one grain at a time.'

'Yes, basically that's right.'

'As you know, this little grain of sand has *mass*. A very small mass, but mass nonetheless.'

Trish nodded.

'And *because* this grain of sand has mass, it therefore exerts *gravity*. Again, too small to feel, but there.'

'Right.'

'Now,' Katherine said, 'if we take trillions of these sand grains and let them attract one another to form . . . say, the *moon*, then their combined gravity is enough to move entire oceans and drag the tides back and forth across our planet.'

Trish had no idea where this was headed, but she liked what she was hearing.

'So let's take a hypothetical,' Katherine said, discarding the sand grain. 'What if I told you that a *thought* . . . any tiny idea that forms in your mind . . . actually has *mass*? What if I told you that a thought is an actual *thing*, a measurable entity, with a measurable mass? A minuscule mass, of course, but *mass* nonetheless. What are the implications?'

'Hypothetically speaking? Well, the obvious implications are . . . if a thought has mass, then a thought exerts gravity and can pull things toward it.'

Katherine smiled. 'You're good. Now take it a step further. What happens if many people start focusing on the *same* thought? All the occurrences of that same thought begin to merge into one, and the cumulative mass of this thought begins to grow. And therefore, its gravity grows.'

'Okay.'

'Meaning . . . if enough people begin thinking the same thing, then the gravitational force of that thought becomes tangible . . . and it exerts actual force.' Katherine winked. 'And it can have a measurable effect in our physical world.'

19

Director Inoue Sato stood with her arms folded, her eyes locked skeptically on Langdon as she processed what he had just told her. 'He said he wants you to unlock an ancient portal? What am I supposed to do with that, Professor?'

Langdon shrugged weakly. He was feeling ill again and tried not to look down at his friend's severed hand. 'That's exactly what he told me. An ancient portal . . . hidden somewhere in this building. I told him I knew of no portal.'

'Then why does he think *you* can find it?'

'Obviously, he's insane.' *He said Peter would point the way.* Langdon looked down at Peter's upstretched finger, again feeling repulsed by his captor's sadistic play on words. *Peter will point the way.* Langdon had already permitted his eyes to follow the pointing finger up to the dome overhead. *A portal? Up there? Insane.*

'This man who called me,' Langdon told Sato, 'was the *only* one who knew I was coming to the Capitol tonight, so whoever informed *you* I was here tonight, that's your man. I recommend—'

'Where I got my information is not your concern,' Sato interrupted, voice sharpening. 'My top priority at the moment is to cooperate with this man, and I have information suggesting *you* are the only one who can give him what he wants.'

'And *my* top priority is to find my friend,' Langdon replied, frustrated.

Sato inhaled deeply, her patience clearly being tested. 'If we want to find Mr. Solomon, we have one course of action, Professor – to start cooperating with the one person who seems to know where he is.' Sato checked her watch. 'Our time is limited. I can assure you it is imperative we comply with this man's demands quickly.'

'How?' Langdon asked, incredulous. 'By locating and unlocking an ancient portal? There *is* no portal, Director Sato. This guy's a lunatic.'

Sato stepped close, less than a foot from Langdon. 'If I may point this out . . . your *lunatic* deftly manipulated two fairly smart individuals already this morning.' She stared directly at Langdon and then glanced at Anderson. 'In my business, one learns there is a fine line between insanity and genius. We would be wise to give this man a little respect.'

'He *cut off* a man's hand!'

'My point exactly. That is hardly the act of an uncommitted or uncertain individual. More important, Professor, this man obviously believes you can help him. He brought you all the way to Washington – and he must have done it for a reason.'

'He said the only reason he thinks I can unlock this "portal" is that *Peter* told him I can unlock it,' Langdon countered.

'And why would Peter Solomon say that if it weren't true?'

'I'm sure Peter said no such thing. And if he did, then he did so under duress. He was confused . . . or frightened.'

'Yes. It's called interrogational torture, and it's quite

115

effective. All the more reason Mr. Solomon would tell the truth.' Sato spoke as if she'd had personal experience with this technique. 'Did he explain *why* Peter thinks you alone can unlock the portal?'

Langdon shook his head.

'Professor, if your reputations are correct, then you and Peter Solomon both share an interest in this sort of thing – secrets, historical esoterica, mysticism, and so on. In all of your discussions with Peter, he never once mentioned to you anything about a secret portal in Washington, D.C.?'

Langdon could scarcely believe he was being asked this question by a high-ranking officer of the CIA. 'I'm certain of it. Peter and I talk about some pretty arcane things, but believe me, I'd tell him to get his head examined if he ever told me there was an ancient portal hidden anywhere at all. Particularly one that leads to the Ancient Mysteries.'

She glanced up. 'I'm sorry? The man told you *specifically* what this portal leads to?'

'Yes, but he didn't have to.' Langdon motioned to the hand. 'The Hand of the Mysteries is a formal invitation to pass through a mystical gateway and acquire ancient secret knowledge – powerful wisdom known as the Ancient Mysteries . . . or the lost wisdom of all the ages.'

'So you've *heard* of the secret he believes is hidden here.'

'A lot of historians have heard of it.'

'Then how can you say the portal does not exist?'

'With respect, ma'am, we've all heard of the Fountain of Youth and Shangri-la, but that does not mean they exist.'

The loud squawk of Anderson's radio interrupted them.

'Chief?' the voice on the radio said.

Anderson snatched his radio from his belt. 'Anderson here.'

'Sir, we've completed a search of the grounds. There's no one here that fits the description. Any further orders, sir?'

Anderson shot a quick glance at Sato, clearly expecting a reprimand, but Director Sato seemed uninterested. Anderson moved away from Langdon and Sato, speaking quietly into his radio.

Sato's unwavering focus remained on Langdon. 'You're saying the secret he believes is hidden in Washington . . . is a *fantasy*?'

Langdon nodded. 'A very old myth. The secret of the Ancient Mysteries is pre-Christian, actually. Thousands of years old.'

'And yet it's *still* around?'

'As are many equally improbable beliefs.' Langdon often reminded his students that most modern religions included stories that did not hold up to scientific scrutiny: everything from Moses parting the Red Sea . . . to Joseph Smith using magic eyeglasses to translate the Book of Mormon from a series of gold plates he found buried in upstate New York. *Wide acceptance of an idea is not proof of its validity.*

'I see. So what exactly *are* these . . . Ancient Mysteries?'

Langdon exhaled. *Have you got a few weeks?* 'In short, the Ancient Mysteries refer to a body of secret knowledge that was amassed long ago. One intriguing aspect of this knowledge is that it allegedly enables its practitioners to access powerful abilities that lie dormant in the human mind. The enlightened Adepts who possessed this knowledge vowed to keep it veiled from the masses because it was considered far too potent and dangerous for the uninitiated.'

'Dangerous in what way?'

'The information was kept hidden for the same reason we keep matches from children. In the correct hands, fire can provide illumination ... but in the wrong hands, fire can be highly destructive.'

Sato took off her glasses and studied him. 'Tell me, Professor, do you believe such powerful information could truly exist?'

Langdon was not sure how to respond. The Ancient Mysteries had always been the greatest paradox of his academic career. Virtually every mystical tradition on earth revolved around the idea that there existed arcane knowledge capable of imbuing humans with mystical, almost godlike, powers: tarot and *I Ching* gave men the ability to see the future; alchemy gave men immortality through the fabled Philosopher's Stone; Wicca permitted advanced practitioners to cast powerful spells. The list went on and on.

As an academic, Langdon could not deny the historical record of these traditions – troves of documents, artifacts, and artwork that, indeed, clearly suggested the ancients had a powerful wisdom that they shared only through allegory, myths, and symbols, ensuring that only those properly initiated could access its power. Nonetheless, as a realist and a skeptic, Langdon remained unconvinced.

'Let's just say I'm a skeptic,' he told Sato. 'I have never seen anything in the real world to suggest the Ancient Mysteries are anything other than legend – a recurring mythological archetype. It seems to me that if it were *possible* for humans to acquire miraculous powers, there would be evidence. And yet, so far, history has given us no men with superhuman powers.'

Sato arched her eyebrows. 'That's not entirely true.'

Langdon hesitated, realizing that for many religious people, there was indeed a precedent for human gods, Jesus being the most obvious. 'Admittedly,' he said, 'there are plenty of educated people who believe this empowering wisdom truly exists, but I'm not yet convinced.'

'Is Peter Solomon one of those people?' Sato asked, glancing toward the hand on the floor.

Langdon could not bring himself to look at the hand. 'Peter comes from a family lineage that has always had a passion for all things ancient and mystical.'

'Was that a yes?' Sato asked.

'I can assure you that even if Peter believes the Ancient Mysteries are real, he does *not* believe they are accessible through some kind of portal hidden in Washington, D.C. He understands metaphorical symbolism, which is something his captor apparently does not.'

Sato nodded. 'So you believe this portal is a *metaphor*.'

'Of course,' Langdon said. 'In theory, anyway. It's a very common metaphor – a mystical portal through which one must travel to become enlightened. Portals and doorways are common symbolic constructs that represent transformative rites of passage. To look for a *literal* portal would be like trying to locate the actual Gates of Heaven.'

Sato seemed to consider this momentarily. 'But it

sounds like Mr. Solomon's captor believes you can unlock an *actual* portal.'

Langdon exhaled. 'He's made the same error many zealots make – confusing metaphor with a literal reality.' Similarly, early alchemists had toiled in vain to transform lead into gold, never realizing that lead-to-gold was nothing but a metaphor for tapping into true human potential – that of taking a dull, ignorant mind and transforming it into a bright, enlightened one.

Sato motioned to the hand. 'If this man wants you to locate some kind of portal for him, why wouldn't he simply *tell* you how to find it? Why all the dramatics? Why give you a tattooed hand?'

Langdon had asked himself the same question and the answer was unsettling. 'Well, it seems the man we are dealing with, in addition to being mentally unstable, is also highly educated. This hand is proof that he is well versed in the Mysteries as well as their codes of secrecy. Not to mention with the history of this room.'

'I don't understand.'

'Everything he has done tonight was done in perfect accordance with ancient protocols. Traditionally, the Hand of the Mysteries is a sacred invitation, and therefore it must be presented in a sacred place.'

Sato's eyes narrowed. 'This is the Rotunda of the U.S. Capitol Building, Professor, not some sacred shrine to ancient mystical secrets.'

'Actually, ma'am,' Langdon said, 'I know a great number of historians who would disagree with you.'

At that moment, across town, Trish Dunne was seated in the glow of the plasma wall inside the Cube. She finished preparing her search spider and typed in the five key phrases Katherine had given her.

Here goes nothing.

Feeling little optimism, she launched the spider, effectively commencing a worldwide game of Go Fish. At blinding speed, the phrases were now being compared to texts all over the world . . . looking for a perfect match.

Trish couldn't help but wonder what this was all about, but she had come to accept that working with the Solomons meant never quite knowing the entire story.

20

Robert Langdon stole an anxious glance at his wristwatch: 7:58 P.M. The smiling face of Mickey Mouse did little to cheer him up. *I've got to find Peter. We're wasting time.*

Sato had stepped aside for a moment to take a phone call, but now she returned to Langdon. 'Professor, am I keeping you from something?'

'No, ma'am,' Langdon said, pulling his sleeve down over his watch. 'I'm just extremely concerned about Peter.'

'I can understand, but I assure you the best thing you can do to help Peter is to help me understand the mind-set of his captor.'

Langdon was not so sure, but he sensed he was not going anywhere until the OS director got the information she desired.

'A moment ago,' Sato said, 'you suggested this Rotunda is somehow *sacred* to the idea of these Ancient Mysteries?'

'Yes, ma'am.'

'Explain that to me.'

Langdon knew he would have to choose his words sparingly. He had taught for entire semesters on the mystical symbolism of Washington, D.C., and there was an almost inexhaustible list of mystical references in this building alone.

America has a hidden past.

Every time Langdon lectured on the symbology of America, his students were confounded to learn that the *true* intentions of our nation's forefathers had absolutely nothing to do with what so many politicians now claimed.

America's intended destiny has been lost to history.

The forefathers who founded this capital city first named her 'Rome.' They had named her river the Tiber and erected a classical capital of pantheons and temples, all adorned with images of history's great gods and goddesses – Apollo, Minerva, Venus, Helios, Vulcan, Jupiter. In her center, as in many of the great classical cities, the founders had erected an enduring tribute to the ancients – the Egyptian obelisk. This obelisk, larger even than Cairo's or Alexandria's, rose 555 feet into the sky, more than thirty stories, proclaiming thanks and honor to the demigod forefather for whom this capital city took its newer name.

Washington.

Now, centuries later, despite America's separation of church and state, this state-sponsored Rotunda glistened with ancient religious symbolism. There were over a dozen different gods in the Rotunda – more than the original Pantheon in Rome. Of course, the Roman Pantheon had been converted to Christianity in 609 . . . but *this* pantheon was never converted; vestiges of its true history still remained in plain view.

'As you may know,' Langdon said, 'this Rotunda was designed as a tribute to one of Rome's most venerated mystical shrines. The Temple of Vesta.'

'As in the vestal virgins?' Sato looked doubtful that Rome's virginal guardians of the flame had anything to do with the U.S. Capitol Building.

'The Temple of Vesta in Rome,' Langdon said, 'was circular, with a gaping hole in the floor, through which the sacred fire of enlightenment could be tended by a sisterhood of virgins whose job it was to ensure the flame never went out.'

Sato shrugged. 'This Rotunda is a circle, but I see no gaping hole in this floor.'

'No, not anymore, but for years the center of this room had a large opening precisely where Peter's hand is now.' Langdon motioned to the floor. 'In fact, you can still see the marks in the floor from the railing that kept people from falling in.'

'What?' Sato demanded, scrutinizing the floor. 'I've never heard that.'

'Looks like he's right.' Anderson pointed out the circle of iron nubs where the posts had once been. 'I've seen these before, but I never had any idea why they were there.'

You're not alone, Langdon thought, imagining the thousands of people every day, including famous lawmakers, who strode across the center of the Rotunda having no idea there was once a day when they would have plunged down into the Capitol Crypt – the level beneath the Rotunda floor.

'The hole in the floor,' Langdon told them, 'was eventually covered, but for a good while, those who visited the Rotunda could see straight down to the fire that burned below.'

Sato turned. 'Fire? In the U.S. Capitol?'

'More of a large torch, actually – an eternal flame that burned in the crypt directly beneath us. It was supposed to be visible through the hole in the floor, making this room a modern Temple of Vesta. This building even had its own vestal virgin – a federal employee called the Keeper of the Crypt – who successfully kept the flame burning for fifty years, until politics, religion, and smoke damage snuffed out the idea.'

Both Anderson and Sato looked surprised.

Nowadays, the only reminder that a flame once burned here was the four-pointed star compass embedded in the crypt floor one story below them – a symbol of America's eternal flame, which once shed illumination toward the four corners of the New World.

'So, Professor,' Sato said, 'your contention is that the man who left Peter's hand here *knew* all this?'

'Clearly. And much, much more. There are symbols all over this room that reflect a belief in the Ancient Mysteries.'

'Secret wisdom,' Sato said with more than a hint of sarcasm in her voice. 'Knowledge that lets men acquire godlike powers?'

'Yes, ma'am.'

'That hardly fits with the Christian underpinnings of this country.'

'So it would seem, but it's true. This transformation of man into God is called *apotheosis*. Whether or not you're aware of it, this theme – transforming man into god – is the core element in this Rotunda's symbolism.'

'Apotheosis?' Anderson spun with a startled look of recognition.

'Yes.' *Anderson works here. He knows.* 'The word *apotheosis* literally means "divine transformation" – that of man becoming God. It's from the ancient Greek: *apo* – "to become," *theos* – "god." '

Anderson looked amazed. '*Apotheosis* means 'to become God'? I had no idea.'

'What am I missing?' Sato demanded.

'Ma'am,' Langdon said, 'the largest painting in this building is called *The Apotheosis of Washington*. And it clearly depicts George Washington being *transformed* into a god.'

Sato looked doubtful. 'I've never seen anything of the sort.'

'Actually, I'm sure you *have*.' Langdon raised his index finger, pointing straight up. 'It's directly over your head.'

21

The Apotheosis of Washington – a 4,664-square-foot fresco that covers the canopy of the Capitol Rotunda – was completed in 1865 by Constantino Brumidi.

Known as 'The Michelangelo of the Capitol,' Brumidi had laid claim to the Capitol Rotunda in the same way Michelangelo had laid claim to the Sistine Chapel, by painting a fresco on the room's most lofty canvas – the ceiling. Like Michelangelo, Brumidi had done some of his finest work inside the Vatican. Brumidi, however, emigrated to America in 1852, abandoning God's largest shrine in favor of a new shrine, the U.S. Capitol, which now glistened with examples of his mastery – from the trompe l'oeil of the Brumidi Corridors to the frieze ceiling of the Vice President's Room. And yet it was the enormous image hovering above the Capitol Rotunda that most historians considered to be Brumidi's masterwork.

Robert Langdon gazed up at the massive fresco that covered the ceiling. He usually enjoyed his students' startled reactions to this fresco's bizarre imagery, but at the moment he simply felt trapped in a nightmare he had yet to understand.

Director Sato was standing next to him with her hands on her hips, frowning up at the distant ceiling. Langdon sensed she was having the same reaction many had when they first stopped to examine the painting at the core of their nation.

Utter confusion.

You're not alone, Langdon thought. For most people, *The Apotheosis of Washington* got stranger and stranger the longer they looked at it. 'That's George Washington on the central panel,' Langdon said, pointing 180 feet upward into the middle of the dome. 'As you can see, he's dressed in white robes, attended by thirteen maidens, and ascending on a cloud above mortal man. This is the moment of his apotheosis . . . his transformation into a god.'

Sato and Anderson said nothing.

'Nearby,' Langdon continued, 'you can see a strange, anachronistic series of figures: ancient gods presenting our forefathers with advanced knowledge. There's Minerva giving technological inspiration to our

126

nation's great inventors – Ben Franklin, Robert Fulton, Samuel Morse.' Langdon pointed them out one by one. 'And over there is Vulcan helping us build a steam engine. Beside them is Neptune demonstrating how to lay the transatlantic cable. Beside that is Ceres, goddess of grain and root of our word *cereal;* she's sitting on the McCormick reaper, the farming break-through that enabled this country to become a world leader in food production. The painting quite overtly portrays our forefathers receiving great wisdom from the gods.' He lowered his head, looking at Sato now. 'Knowledge is power, and the *right* knowledge lets man perform miraculous, almost godlike tasks.'

Sato dropped her gaze back down to Langdon and rubbed her neck. 'Laying a phone cable is a far cry from being a god.'

'Perhaps to a *modern* man,' Langdon replied. 'But if George Washington knew that we had become a race that possessed the power to speak to one another across oceans, fly at the speed of sound, and set foot on our moon, he would assume that we had become gods, capable of miraculous tasks.' He paused. 'In the words of futurist Arthur C. Clarke, "Any sufficiently advanced technology is indistinguishable from magic."'

Sato pursed her lips, apparently deep in thought. She glanced down at the hand, and then followed the direction of the outstretched index finger up into the dome. 'Professor, you were told, "Peter will point the way." Is that correct?'

'Yes, ma'am, but—'

'Chief,' Sato said, turning away from Langdon, 'can you get us a closer look at the painting?'

Anderson nodded. 'There's a catwalk around the interior of the dome.'

Langdon looked way, way up to the tiny railing visible just beneath the painting and felt his body go rigid. 'There's no need to go up there.' He had experienced that seldom-visited catwalk once before, as the guest of a U.S. senator and his wife, and he had almost fainted from the dizzying height and perilous walkway.

'No need?' Sato demanded. 'Professor, we have a man who believes this room contains a portal that has the potential to make him a god; we have a ceiling fresco that symbolizes the transformation of a man into a god; and we have a hand pointing straight at that painting. It seems everything is urging us *upward*.'

'Actually,' Anderson interjected, glancing up, 'not many people know this, but there is *one* hexagonal coffer in the dome that actually swings open like a portal, and you can peer down through it and—'

'Wait a second,' Langdon said, 'you're missing the point. The portal this man is looking for is a *figurative* portal – a gateway that doesn't exist. When he said, "Peter will point the way," he was talking in meta-phorical terms. This pointing-hand gesture – with its index finger *and* thumb extended upward – is a well-known symbol of the Ancient Mysteries, and it appears all over the world in ancient art. This same gesture appears in three of Leonardo da Vinci's most famous encoded masterpieces – *The Last Supper*, *Adoration of the Magi*, and *Saint John the Baptist*. It's a symbol of man's mystical connection to God.' *As above, so below.* The madman's bizarre choice of words was starting to feel more relevant now.

'I've never seen it before,' Sato said.

Then watch ESPN, Langdon thought, always amused to see professional athletes point skyward in gratitude to God after a touchdown or home run. He wondered how many knew they were continuing a pre-Christian mystical tradition of acknowledging the mystical power above, which, for one brief moment, had transformed them into a god capable of miraculous feats.

'If it's of any help,' Langdon said, 'Peter's hand is not the first such hand to make an appearance in this Rotunda.'

Sato eyed him like he was insane. 'I beg your pardon?'

Langdon motioned to her BlackBerry. 'Google "George Washington Zeus." '

Sato looked uncertain but started typing. Anderson inched toward her, looking over her shoulder intently.

Langdon said, 'This Rotunda was once dominated by a massive sculpture of a bare-chested George Washington . . . depicted as a god. He sat in the same exact pose as Zeus in the Pantheon, bare chest exposed, left hand holding a sword, right hand raised with thumb and finger extended.'

Sato had apparently found an online image, because Anderson was staring at her BlackBerry in shock. 'Hold on, *that's* George Washington?'

'Yes,' Langdon said. 'Depicted as Zeus.'

'Look at his hand,' Anderson said, still peering over Sato's shoulder. 'His right hand is in the same exact position as Mr. Solomon's.'

As I said, Langdon thought, *Peter's hand is not the first to make an appearance in this room.* When Horatio Greenough's statue of a naked George Washington was first unveiled in the Rotunda, many joked that Washington must be reaching skyward in a desperate attempt to find some clothes. As American religious ideals changed, however, the joking criticism turned to controversy, and the statue was removed, banished to a shed in the east garden. Currently, it made its home at the Smithsonian's National Museum of American History, where those who saw it had no reason to suspect that it was one of the last vestigial links to a time when the father of the country had watched over the U.S. Capitol as a god . . . like Zeus watching over the Pantheon.

Sato began dialing a number on her BlackBerry, apparently seeing this as an opportune moment to check in with her staff. 'What have you got?' She listened patiently. 'I see . . .' She glanced directly at Langdon, then at Peter's hand. 'You're certain?' She listened a moment longer. 'Okay, thanks.' She hung up and turned back toward Langdon. 'My support staff did some research and confirms the existence of your so-called Hand of the Mysteries, corroborating everything you said: five fingertip markings – the star, the sun, the key, the crown, and the lantern – as well as the fact that this hand served as an ancient invitation to learn secret wisdom.'

'I'm glad,' Langdon said.

'Don't be,' she replied curtly. 'It appears we're now at a dead end until you share whatever it is you're still not telling me.'

'Ma'am?'

Sato stepped toward him. 'We've come full circle, Professor. You've told me nothing I could not have learned from my own staff. And so I will ask you once more. Why were you brought here tonight? What makes you so special? What is it that *you* alone know?'

'We've been through this,' Langdon fired back. 'I don't know why this guy thinks I know anything at all!'

Langdon was half tempted to demand how the hell *Sato* knew that he was in the Capitol tonight, but they'd been through that, too. *Sato isn't talking.* 'If I knew the next step,' he told her, 'I'd tell you. But I don't. Traditionally, the Hand of the Mysteries is extended by a teacher to a student. And then, shortly afterward, the hand is followed up with a set of instructions . . . directions to a temple, the name of the master who will teach you – *something*! But all this guy left for us is five tattoos! Hardly—' Langdon stopped short.

Sato eyed him. 'What is it?'

Langdon's eyes shot back to the hand. *Five tattoos.* He now realized that what he was saying might not be entirely true.

'Professor?' Sato pressed.

Langdon inched toward the gruesome object. *Peter will point the way.* 'Earlier, it crossed my mind that maybe this guy had left an object clenched in Peter's palm – a map, or a letter, or a set of directions.'

'He didn't,' Anderson said. 'As you can see, those three fingers are not clenched tightly.'

'You're right,' Langdon said. 'But it occurs to me . . .' He crouched down now, trying to see up under the fingers to the hidden part of Peter's palm. 'Maybe it's not written on paper.'

'Tattooed?' Anderson said.

Langdon nodded.

'Do you see anything on the palm?' Sato asked.

Langdon crouched lower, trying to peer up under the loosely clenched fingers. 'The angle is impossible. I can't—'

'Oh, for heaven's sake,' Sato said, moving toward him. 'Just open the damned thing!'

Anderson stepped in front of her. 'Ma'am! We

should really wait for forensics before we touch—'

'I want some answers,' Sato said, pushing past him. She crouched down, edging Langdon away from the hand.

Langdon stood up and watched in disbelief as Sato pulled a pen from her pocket, sliding it carefully under the three clenched fingers. Then, one by one, she pried each finger upward until the hand stood fully open, with its palm visible.

She glanced up at Langdon, and a thin smile spread across her face. 'Right again, Professor.'

22

Pacing the library, Katherine Solomon pulled back the sleeve of her lab coat and checked her watch. She was not a woman accustomed to waiting, but at the moment, she felt as if her whole world were on hold. She was waiting for Trish's search-spider results, she was waiting for word from her brother, and also, she was waiting for a callback from the man who was responsible for this entire troubling situation.

I wish he hadn't told me, she thought. Normally, Katherine was extremely careful about making new acquaintances, and although she had met this man for the first time only this afternoon, he had earned her trust in a matter of minutes. *Completely.*

His call had come this afternoon while Katherine was at home enjoying her usual Sunday-afternoon pleasure of catching up on the week's scientific journals.

'Ms. Solomon?' an unusually airy voice had said. 'My name is Dr. Christopher Abaddon. I was hoping I might speak to you for a moment about your brother?'

'I'm sorry, *who* is this?' she had demanded. *And how did you get my private cell-phone number?*

'Dr. Christopher Abaddon?'

Katherine did not recognize the name.

The man cleared his throat, as if the situation had just become awkward. 'I apologize, Ms. Solomon. I was under the impression your brother had told you about me. I'm his doctor. Your cell number was listed as his emergency contact.'

Katherine's heart skipped. *Emergency contact?* 'Is something wrong?'

'No . . . I don't think so,' the man said. 'Your brother missed an appointment this morning, and I can't reach him on any of his numbers. He never misses appointments without calling, and I'm just a little worried. I hesitated to phone you, but—'

'No, no, not at all, I appreciate the concern.' Katherine was still trying to place the doctor's name. 'I haven't spoken to my brother since yesterday morning, but he probably just forgot to turn on his cell.' Katherine had recently given him a new iPhone, and he still hadn't taken the time to figure out how to use it.

'You say you're his *doctor*?' she asked. *Does Peter have an illness he's keeping from me?*

There was a weighty pause on the line. 'I'm terribly sorry, but I've obviously just made a rather serious professional error by calling you. Your brother told me you were aware of his visits to me, but now I see that's not the case.'

My brother lied to his doctor? Katherine's concern was now growing steadily. 'Is he sick?'

133

'I'm sorry, Ms. Solomon, doctor-patient con-fidentiality precludes me from discussing your brother's condition, and I've already said too much by admitting he is my patient. I'm going to hang up now, but if you hear from him today, please ask him to call me so I know he's okay.'

'Wait!' Katherine said. 'Please tell me what's wrong with Peter!'

Dr. Abaddon exhaled, sounding displeased with his mistake. 'Ms. Solomon, I can hear you're upset, and I don't blame you. I'm sure your brother is fine. He was in my office just yesterday.'

'Yesterday? And he's scheduled again *today*? This sounds urgent.'

The man heaved a sigh. 'I suggest we give him a little more time before we—'

'I'm coming by your office right now,' Katherine said, heading for the door. 'Where are you located?'

Silence.

'Dr. Christopher Abaddon?' Katherine said. 'I can look up your address myself, or you can simply give it to me. Either way, I'm coming over.'

The doctor paused. 'If I meet with you, Ms. Solomon, would you please do me the courtesy of saying nothing to your brother until I've had a chance to explain my misstep?'

'That's fine.'

'Thank you. My office is in Kalorama Heights.' He gave her an address.

Twenty minutes later, Katherine Solomon was navigating the stately streets of Kalorama Heights. She had phoned all of her brother's numbers with no reply. She did not feel overly concerned about her brother's whereabouts, and yet, the news that he was secretly seeing a doctor . . . was troubling.

When Katherine finally located the address, she stared up at the building in confusion. *This is a doctor's office?*

The opulent mansion before her had a wrought-iron security fence, electronic cameras, and lush grounds. As she slowed to double-check the address, one of the security cameras rotated toward her, and the gate swung open. Tentatively, Katherine drove up the driveway and parked next to a six-car garage and a stretch limo.

What kind of doctor is *this guy?*

As she got out of her car, the front door of the mansion opened, and an elegant figure drifted out onto the landing. He was handsome, exceptionally tall, and younger than she had imagined. Even so, he projected the sophistication and polish of an older man. He was impeccably dressed in a dark suit and tie, and his thick blond hair was immaculately coiffed.

'Ms. Solomon, I'm Dr. Christopher Abaddon,' he said, his voice a breathy whisper. When they shook hands, his skin felt smooth and well tended.

'Katherine Solomon,' she said, trying not to stare at his skin, which was unusually smooth and bronzed. *Is he wearing makeup?*

Katherine felt a growing disquiet as she stepped into the home's beautifully appointed foyer. Classical music played softly in the background, and it smelled as if someone had burned incense. 'This is lovely,' she said, 'although I expected more of . . . an office.'

'I'm fortunate to work out of my home.' The man led her into a living room, where there was a crackling fire. 'Please make yourself comfortable. I'm just steeping some tea. I'll bring it out, and we can talk.'

He strode toward the kitchen and disappeared.

Katherine Solomon did not sit. Female intuition was a potent instinct that she had learned to trust, and something about this place was making her skin crawl. She saw nothing that looked anything like any doctor's office she had ever seen. The walls of this antique-adorned living room were covered with classical art, primarily paintings with strange mythical themes. She paused before a large canvas depicting the Three Graces, whose nude bodies were spectacularly rendered in vivid colors.

'That's the original Michael Parkes oil.' Dr. Abaddon appeared without warning beside her, holding a tray of steaming tea. 'I thought we'd sit by the fire?' He led her over to the living room and offered her a seat. 'There's no reason to be nervous.'

'I'm not nervous,' Katherine said entirely too quickly.

He gave her a reassuring smile. 'Actually, it is my business to know when people are nervous.'

'I beg your pardon?'

'I'm a practicing psychiatrist, Ms. Solomon. That is my profession. I've been seeing your brother for almost a year now. I'm his therapist.'

Katherine could only stare. *My brother is in therapy?*

'Patients often choose to keep their therapy to themselves,' the man said. 'I made a mistake by calling you, although in my defense, your brother did mislead me.'

'I . . . I had no idea.'

'I apologize if I made you nervous,' he said, sounding embarrassed. 'I noticed you studying my face when we met, and yes, I do wear makeup.' He touched his own cheek, looking self-conscious. 'I have a dermatological condition, which I prefer to hide. My wife usually puts the makeup on for me, but when she's not here, I have to rely on my own heavy touch.'

Katherine nodded, too embarrassed to speak.

'And this lovely hair . . .' He touched his lush blond mane. 'A wig. My skin condition affected my scalp follicles as well, and all my hair jumped ship.' He shrugged. 'I'm afraid my one sin is vanity.'

'Apparently *mine* is rudeness,' Katherine said.

'Not at all.' Dr. Abaddon's smile was disarming. 'Shall we start over? Perhaps with some tea?'

They sat in front of the fire and Abaddon poured tea. 'Your brother got me in the habit of serving tea during our sessions. He said the Solomons are tea drinkers.'

'Family tradition,' Katherine said. 'Black, please.'

They sipped their tea and made small talk for a few minutes, but Katherine was eager for information about her brother. 'Why was my brother coming to you?' she asked. *And why didn't he tell me?* Admittedly, Peter had endured more than his fair share of tragedy in his life – losing his father at a young age, and then, within a span of five years, burying his only son and then his mother. Even so, Peter had always found a way to cope.

Dr. Abaddon took a sip of tea. 'Your brother came to me because he trusts me. We have a bond beyond that of normal patient and doctor.' He motioned to a framed document near the fireplace. It looked like a diploma, until Katherine spied the double-headed phoenix.

'You're a Mason?' *The highest degree, no less.*

'Peter and I are brothers of sorts.'

'You must have done something important to be invited into the thirty-third degree.'

'Not really,' he said. 'I have family money, and I give a lot of money to Masonic charities.'

Katherine now realized why her brother trusted this young doctor. *A Mason with family money, interested in philanthropy and ancient mythology?* Dr. Abaddon had more in common with her brother than she had initially imagined.

'When I asked why my brother came to you,' she said, 'I didn't mean why did he *choose* you. I meant, why is he seeking the services of a psychiatrist?'

Dr. Abaddon smiled. 'Yes, I know. I was trying to sidestep the question politely. It's really not something I should be discussing.' He paused. 'Although I must say I'm puzzled that your brother would keep our discussions from you, considering that they relate so directly to your research.'

'My research?' Katherine said, taken totally off guard. *My brother talks about my research?*

'Recently, your brother came to me looking for a professional opinion about the psychological impact of the breakthroughs you are making in your lab.'

Katherine almost choked on the tea. 'Really? I'm . . . surprised,' she managed. *What is Peter thinking? He told his shrink about my work?!* Their security protocol involved not discussing with *anyone* what Katherine was working on. Moreover, the confidentiality had been her brother's idea.

'Certainly you are aware, Ms. Solomon, that your brother is deeply concerned about what will happen when your research goes public. He sees the potential for a significant philosophical shift in the world . . . and he came here to discuss the possible ramifications . . . from a *psychological* perspective.'

'I see,' Katherine said, her teacup now shaking slightly.

'The questions we discuss are challenging ones: What happens to the human condition if the great mysteries of life are finally revealed? What happens when those beliefs that we accept on *faith* ... are suddenly categorically proven as *fact*? Or disproved as *myth*? One could argue that there exist certain questions that are best left unanswered.'

Katherine could not believe what she was hearing, and yet she kept her emotions in check. 'I hope you don't mind, Dr. Abaddon, but I'd prefer not to discuss the details of my work. I have no immediate plans to make anything public. For the time being, my discoveries will remain safely locked in my lab.'

'Interesting.' Abaddon leaned back in his chair, lost in thought for a moment. 'In any event, I asked your brother to come back today because yesterday he suffered a bit of a *break*. When that happens, I like to have clients—'

'Break?' Katherine's heart was pounding. 'As in breakdown?' She couldn't imagine her brother breaking down over anything.

Abaddon reached out kindly. 'Please, I can see I've upset you. I'm sorry. Considering these awkward circumstances, I can understand how you might feel entitled to answers.'

'Whether I'm entitled or not,' Katherine said, 'my brother is all I have left of my family. Nobody knows him better than I do, so if you tell me what the hell happened, maybe I can help you. We all want the same thing – what's best for Peter.'

Dr. Abaddon fell silent for several long moments and then began slowly nodding as if Katherine might

139

have a point. Finally, he spoke. 'For the record, Ms. Solomon, if I decide to share this information with you, I would do so only because I think your insights might help me assist your brother.'

'Of course.'

Abaddon leaned forward, putting his elbows on his knees. 'Ms. Solomon, as long as I've been seeing your brother, I've sensed in him a deep struggle with feelings of guilt. I've never pressed him on it because that's not why he comes to me. And yet yesterday, for a number of reasons, I finally asked him about it.' Abaddon locked eyes with her. 'Your brother opened up, rather dramatically and unexpectedly. He told me things I had not expected to hear . . . including everything that happened the night your mother died.'

Christmas Eve – almost exactly ten years ago. She died in my arms.

'He told me your mother was murdered during a robbery attempt at your home? A man broke in looking for something he believed your brother was hiding?'

'That's correct.'

Abaddon's eyes were appraising her. 'Your brother said he shot the man dead?'

'Yes.'

Abaddon stroked his chin. 'Do you recall what the intruder was looking for when he broke into your home?'

Katherine had tried in vain for ten years to block out the memory. 'Yes, his demand was very specific. Unfortunately, none of us knew what he was talking about. His demand never made sense to any of us.'

'Well, it made sense to your brother.'

'What?' Katherine sat up.

'At least according to the story he told me yesterday, Peter knew exactly what the intruder was looking for. And yet your brother did not want to hand it over, so he pretended not to understand.'

'That's absurd. Peter couldn't possibly have known what the man wanted. His demands made no sense!'

'Interesting.' Dr. Abaddon paused and took a few notes. 'As I mentioned, however, Peter told me he *did* know. Your brother believes if he had only cooperated with the intruder, maybe your mother would be alive today. This decision is the source of all his guilt.'

Katherine shook her head. 'That's crazy . . .'

Abaddon slumped, looking troubled. 'Ms. Solomon, this has been useful feedback. As I feared, your brother seems to have had a little break with reality. I must admit, I was afraid this might be the case. That's why I asked him to come back today. These delusional episodes are not uncommon when they relate to traumatic memories.'

Katherine shook her head again. 'Peter is far from delusional, Dr. Abaddon.'

'I would agree, except . . .'

'Except *what*?'

'Except that his recounting of the attack was just the beginning . . . a tiny fraction of the long and far-fetched tale he told me.'

Katherine leaned forward in her seat. 'What did Peter tell you?'

Abaddon gave a sad smile. 'Ms. Solomon, let me ask you this. Has your brother ever discussed with you what he believes is hidden here in Washington,

D.C. . . . or the role he believes he plays in protecting a great treasure . . . of lost ancient wisdom?'

Katherine's jaw fell open. 'What in the world are you talking about?'

Dr. Abaddon heaved a long sigh. 'What I am about to tell you will be a bit shocking, Katherine.' He paused and locked eyes with her. 'But it will be immeasurably helpful if you can tell me *anything* you may know about it.' He reached for her cup. 'More tea?'

23

Another tattoo.

Langdon crouched anxiously beside Peter's open palm and examined the seven tiny symbols that had been hidden beneath the lifeless clenched fingers.

'They appear to be numbers,' Langdon said, surprised. 'Although I don't recognize them.'

'The first is a Roman numeral,' Anderson said.

'Actually, I don't think so,' Langdon corrected. 'The Roman numeral I-I-I-X doesn't exist. It would be written V-I-I.'

'How about the rest of it?' Sato asked.

'I'm not sure. It looks like eight-eight-five in Arabic numbers.'

'Arabic?' Anderson asked. 'They look like normal numbers.'

'Our normal numbers *are* Arabic.' Langdon had become so accustomed to clarifying this point for his students that he'd actually prepared a lecture about the scientific advances made by early Middle Eastern cultures, one of them being our modern numbering system, whose advantages over Roman numerals included 'positional notation' and the invention of the number zero. Of course, Langdon always ended this lecture with a reminder that Arab culture had also given mankind the word *al-kuhl* – the favorite beverage of Harvard freshmen – known as *alcohol*.

Langdon scrutinized the tattoo, feeling puzzled. 'And I'm not even sure about the eight-eight-five. The rectilinear writing looks unusual. Those may not be numbers.'

'Then what are they? Sato asked.

'I'm not sure. The whole tattoo looks almost . . . runic.'

'Meaning?' Sato asked.

'Runic alphabets are composed solely of straight lines. Their letters are called runes and were often used for carving in stone because curves were too difficult to chisel.'

'If these are runes,' Sato said, 'what is their meaning?'

Langdon shook his head. His expertise extended only to the most rudimentary runic alphabet – Futhark – a third-century Teutonic system, and this was not Futhark. 'To be honest, I'm not even sure these are runes. You'd need to ask a specialist. There are dozens of different forms – Hälsinge, Manx, the "dotted" Stungnar—'

'Peter Solomon is a Mason, is he not?'

Langdon did a double take. 'Yes, but what does that have to do with this?' He stood up now, towering over the tiny woman.

'*You* tell me. You just said that runic alphabets are used for stone carvings, and it is my understanding that the original Freemasons were stone craftsmen. I mention this only because when I asked my office to search for a connection between the Hand of the Mysteries and Peter Solomon, their search returned one link in particular.' She paused, as if to emphasize the importance of her finding. 'The Masons.'

Langdon exhaled, fighting the impulse to tell Sato the same thing he constantly told his students: '*Google*' *is not a synonym for* '*research.*' In these days of massive, worldwide keyword searches, it seemed everything was linked to everything. The world was becoming one big entangled web of information that was getting denser every day.

Langdon maintained a patient tone. 'I'm not surprised the Masons appeared in your staff's search. Masons are a very obvious link between Peter Solomon and any number of esoteric topics.'

'Yes,' Sato said, 'which is another reason I have been surprised this evening that you have not yet mentioned the Masons. After all, you've been talking about secret wisdom protected by an enlightened few. That sounds very Masonic, does it not?'

'It does . . . and it also sounds very Rosicrucian, Kabbalistic, Alumbradian, and any number of other esoteric groups.'

'But Peter Solomon is a Mason – a very powerful Mason, at that. It seems the Masons would come to mind if we were talking about secrets. Heaven knows the Masons love their secrets.'

Langdon could hear the distrust in her voice, and he wanted no part of it. 'If you want to know anything about the Masons, you would be far better served to ask a Mason.'

'Actually,' Sato said, 'I'd prefer to ask someone I can trust.'

Langdon found the comment both ignorant and offensive. 'For the record, ma'am, the entire Masonic philosophy is built on honesty and integrity. Masons are among the most trustworthy men you could ever hope to meet.'

'I have seen persuasive evidence to the contrary.'

Langdon was liking Director Sato less and less with each passing moment. He had spent years writing about the Masons' rich tradition of metaphorical iconography and symbols, and knew that Masons had always been one of the most unfairly maligned and misunderstood organizations in the world. Regularly accused of everything from devil worship to plotting a one-world government, the Masons also had a policy of never responding to their critics, which made them an easy target.

'Regardless,' Sato said, her tone biting, 'we are again at an impasse, Mr. Langdon. It seems to me there is either something you are missing . . . or something you are not telling me. The man we're dealing with said that Peter Solomon chose you specifically.' She leveled a cold stare at Langdon. 'I think it's time we move this conversation to CIA headquarters. Maybe we'll have more luck there.'

Sato's threat barely registered with Langdon. She had just said something that had lodged in his mind. *Peter Solomon chose you.* The comment, combined with the mention of Masons, had hit Langdon strangely. He looked down at the Masonic ring on Peter's finger. The ring was one of Peter's most prized possessions – a Solomon family heirloom that bore the symbol of the double-headed phoenix – the ultimate mystical icon of Masonic wisdom. The gold glinted in the light, sparking an unexpected memory.

Langdon gasped, recalling the eerie whisper of Peter's captor: *It really hasn't dawned on you yet, has it? Why you were chosen?*

Now, in one terrifying moment, Langdon's thoughts snapped into focus and the fog lifted.

All at once, Langdon's purpose here was crystal clear.

Ten miles away, driving south on Suitland Parkway, Mal'akh heard a distinctive vibration on the seat beside him. It was Peter Solomon's iPhone, which had proven a powerful tool today. The visual caller ID now displayed the image of an attractive middle-aged woman with long black hair.

INCOMING CALL – KATHERINE SOLOMON

Mal'akh smiled, ignoring the call. *Destiny pulls me closer.*

He had lured Katherine Solomon to his home this afternoon for one reason only – to determine if she had information that could assist him . . . perhaps a family secret that might help Mal'akh locate what he sought. Clearly, however, Katherine's brother had told her nothing of what he had been guarding all these years.

Even so, Mal'akh had learned something else from Katherine. *Something that has earned her a few extra hours of life today.* Katherine had confirmed for him that all of her research was in *one* location, safely locked inside her lab.

I must destroy it.

Katherine's research was poised to open a new door of understanding, and once the door was opened even a crack, others would follow. It would just be a matter of time before everything changed. *I cannot let that happen. The world must stay as it is . . . adrift in ignorant darkness.*

The iPhone beeped, indicating Katherine had left a voice mail. Mal'akh retrieved it.

'Peter, it's me again.' Katherine's voice sounded concerned. 'Where are you? I'm still thinking about my conversation with Dr. Abaddon . . . and I'm worried. Is everything okay? Please call me. I'm at the lab.'

The voice mail ended.

Mal'akh smiled. *Katherine should worry less about her brother, and more about herself.* He turned off Suitland Parkway onto Silver Hill Road. Less than a mile later, in the darkness, he spotted the faint outline of the SMSC nestled in the trees off the highway to his right. The entire complex was surrounded by a high razor-wire fence.

A secure building? Mal'akh chuckled to himself. *I know someone who will open the door for me.*

24

The revelation crashed over Langdon like a wave.

I know why I am here.

Standing in the center of the Rotunda, Langdon felt a powerful urge to turn and run away . . . from Peter's hand, from the shining gold ring, from the suspicious eyes of Sato and Anderson. Instead, he stood dead still, clinging more tightly to the leather daybag that hung on his shoulder. *I've got to get out of here.*

His jaw clenched as his memory began replaying the scene from that cold morning, years ago in Cambridge. It was six A.M. and Langdon was entering his classroom as he always did following his ritual morning laps in the Harvard Pool. The familiar smells of chalk dust and steam heat greeted him as he crossed the threshold. He took two steps toward his desk but stopped short.

A figure was waiting there for him – an elegant gentleman with an aquiline face and regal gray eyes.

'Peter?' Langdon stared in shock.

Peter Solomon's smile flashed white in the dimly lit room. 'Good morning, Robert. Surprised to see me?' His voice was soft, and yet there was power there.

Langdon hurried over and warmly shook his friend's hand. 'What in the world is a Yale blue blood doing on the Crimson campus before dawn?'

'Covert mission behind enemy lines,' Solomon said, laughing. He motioned to Langdon's trim waistline. 'Laps are paying off. You're in good shape.'

'Just trying to make you feel old,' Langdon said, toying with him. 'It's great to see you, Peter. What's up?'

'Short business trip,' the man replied, glancing around the deserted classroom. 'I'm sorry to drop in on you like this, Robert, but I have only a few minutes. There's something I needed to ask you . . . in person. A favor.'

That's a first. Langdon wondered what a simple college professor could possibly do for the man who had everything. 'Anything at all,' he replied, pleased for any opportunity to do something for someone who had given him so much, especially when Peter's life of good fortune had also been marred by so much tragedy.

Solomon lowered his voice. 'I was hoping you would consider looking after something for me.'

Langdon rolled his eyes. 'Not Hercules, I hope.' Langdon had once agreed to take care of Solomon's hundred-fifty-pound mastiff, Hercules, during Solomon's travels. While at Langdon's home, the dog apparently had become homesick for his favorite leather chew toy and had located a worthy substitute in Langdon's study – an original vellum, hand-calligraphed, illuminated Bible from the 1600s. Somehow 'bad dog' didn't quite seem adequate.

'You know, I'm still searching for a replacement,' Solomon said, smiling sheepishly.

'Forget it. I'm glad Hercules got a taste of religion.'

Solomon chuckled but seemed distracted. 'Robert, the reason I came to see you is I'd like you to keep an eye on something that is quite valuable to me. I inherited it a while back, but I'm no longer comfortable leaving it in my home or in my office.'

Langdon immediately felt uncomfortable. Anything 'quite valuable' in Peter Solomon's world had to be worth an absolute fortune. 'How about a safe-deposit box?' *Doesn't your family have stock in half the banks in America?*

'That would involve paperwork and bank employees; I'd prefer a trusted friend. And I know you can keep secrets.' Solomon reached in his pocket and pulled out a small package, handing it to Langdon.

Considering the dramatic preamble, Langdon had expected something more impressive. The package was a small cube-shaped box, about three inches square, wrapped in faded brown packing paper and tied with twine. From the package's heavy weight and size, it felt like its contents must be rock or metal. *This is it?* Langdon turned the box in his hands, now noticing the twine had been carefully secured on one side with an embossed wax seal, like an ancient edict. The seal bore a double-headed phoenix with the number 33 emblazoned on its chest – the traditional symbol of the highest degree of Freemasonry.

'Really, Peter,' Langdon said, a lopsided grin creeping across his face. 'You're the Worshipful Master of a Masonic lodge, not the pope. Sealing packages with your ring?'

Solomon glanced down at his gold ring and gave a chuckle. 'I didn't seal this package, Robert. My great-grandfather did. Almost a century ago.'

Langdon's head snapped up. 'What?!'

Solomon held up his ring finger. 'This Masonic ring was his. After that, it was my grandfather's, then my father's . . . and eventually mine.'

Langdon held up the package. 'Your great-grandfather wrapped this a *century* ago and nobody has opened it?'

'That's right.'

'But . . . why not?'

Solomon smiled. 'Because it's not time.'

Langdon stared. 'Time for *what*?'

'Robert, I know this will sound odd, but the less you know, the better. Just put this package somewhere safe, and please tell no one I gave it to you.'

Langdon searched his mentor's eyes for a glint of playfulness. Solomon had a propensity for dramatics, and Langdon wondered if he wasn't being played a bit here. 'Peter, are you sure this isn't just a clever ploy to make me think I've been entrusted with some kind of ancient Masonic secret so I'll be curious and decide to join?'

'The Masons do not recruit, Robert, you know that. Besides, you've already told me you'd prefer not to join.'

This was true. Langdon had great respect for Masonic philosophy and symbolism, and yet he had decided never to be initiated; the order's vows of secrecy would prevent him from discussing Freemasonry with his students. It had been for this same reason that Socrates had refused to formally participate in the Eleusinian Mysteries.

As Langdon now regarded the mysterious little box and its Masonic seal, he could not help but ask the obvious question. 'Why not entrust this to one of your Masonic brothers?'

'Let's just say I have an instinct it would be safer stored *outside* the brotherhood. And please don't let the size of this package fool you. If what my father told me is correct, then it contains something of substantial power.' He paused. 'A talisman, of sorts.'

Did he say a talisman? By definition, a talisman was an object with magical powers. Traditionally, talismans were used for bringing luck, warding off evil spirits, or aiding in ancient rituals. 'Peter, you *do* realize that talismans went out of vogue in the Middle Ages, right?'

Peter laid a patient hand on Langdon's shoulder. 'I know how this sounds, Robert. I've known you a long time, and your skepticism is one of your greatest strengths as an academic. It is also your greatest weakness. I know you well enough to know you're not a man I can ask to *believe* . . . only to *trust*. So now I am asking you to trust me when I tell you this talisman is powerful. I was told it can imbue its possessor with the ability to bring order from chaos.'

Langdon could only stare. The idea of 'order from chaos' was one of the great Masonic axioms. *Ordo ab chao*. Even so, the claim that a talisman could impart *any* power at all was absurd, much less the power to bring order from chaos.

'This talisman,' Solomon continued, 'would be dangerous in the wrong hands, and unfortunately, I have reason to believe powerful people want to steal it from me.' His eyes were as serious as Langdon could ever recall. 'I would like you to keep it safe for me for a while. Can you do that?'

That night, Langdon sat alone at his kitchen table with the package and tried to imagine what could possibly be inside. In the end, he simply chalked it up to Peter's eccentricity and locked the package in his library's wall safe, eventually forgetting all about it.

That was . . . until this morning.

The phone call from the man with the southern accent.

'Oh, Professor, I almost forgot!' the assistant had said after giving Langdon the specifics of his travel arrangements to D.C. 'There is one more thing Mr. Solomon requested.'

'Yes?' Langdon replied, his mind already moving to the lecture he had just agreed to give.

'Mr. Solomon left a note here for you.' The man began reading awkwardly, as if trying to decipher Peter's penmanship. ' "Please ask Robert ... to bring ... the small, sealed package I gave him many years ago." ' The man paused. 'Does this make any sense to you?'

Langdon felt surprised as he recalled the small box that had been sitting in his wall safe all this time. 'Actually, yes. I know what Peter means.'

'And you can bring it?'

'Of course. Tell Peter I'll bring it.'

'Wonderful.' The assistant sounded relieved. 'Enjoy your speech tonight. Safe travels.'

Before leaving home, Langdon had dutifully retrieved the wrapped package from the back of his safe and placed it in his shoulder bag.

Now he was standing in the U.S. Capitol, feeling certain of only one thing. Peter Solomon would be horrified to know how badly Langdon had failed him.

25

My God, Katherine was right. As usual.

Trish Dunne stared in amazement at the search-spider results that were materializing on the plasma wall before her. She had doubted the search would turn up *any* results at all, but in fact, she now had over a dozen hits. And they were still coming in.

One entry in particular looked quite promising.

Trish turned and shouted in the direction of the library. 'Katherine? I think you'll want to see this!'

It had been a couple of years since Trish had run a

search spider like this, and tonight's results astounded her. *A few years ago, this search would have been a dead end.* Now, however, it seemed that the quantity of searchable digital material in the world had exploded to the point where someone could find literally anything. Incredibly, one of the keywords was a word Trish had never even heard before . . . and the search even found *that*.

Katherine rushed through the control-room door. 'What have you got?'

'A *bunch* of candidates.' Trish motioned to the plasma wall. 'Every one of these documents contains all of your key phrases verbatim.'

Katherine tucked her hair behind her ear and scanned the list.

'Before you get too excited,' Trish added, 'I can assure you that most of these documents are *not* what you're looking for. They're what we call black holes. Look at the file sizes. Absolutely enormous. They're things like compressed archives of millions of e-mails, giant unabridged encyclopedia sets, global message boards that have been running for years, and so forth. By virtue of their size and diverse content, these files contain so many potential keywords that they suck in any search engine that comes anywhere near them.'

Katherine pointed to one of the entries near the top of the list. 'How about *that* one?'

Trish smiled. Katherine was a step ahead, having found the sole file on the list that had a small file size. 'Good eyes. Yeah, that's really our only candidate so far. In fact, *that* file's so small it can't be more than a page or so.'

'Open it.' Katherine's tone was intense.

Trish could not imagine a one-page document containing *all* the strange search strings Katherine had provided. Nonetheless, when she clicked and opened the document, the key phrases were there . . . crystal clear and easy to spot in the text.

Katherine strode over, eyes riveted to the plasma wall. 'This document is . . . *redacted*?'

Trish nodded. 'Welcome to the world of digitized text.'

Automatic redaction had become standard practice when offering digitized documents. Redaction was a process wherein a server allowed a user to search the entire text, but then revealed only a small portion of it – a teaser of sorts – only that text immediately flanking the requested keywords. By omitting the vast majority of the text, the server avoided copyright infringement and also sent the user an intriguing message: *I have the information you're searching for, but if you want the rest of it, you'll have to buy it from me.*

'As you can see,' Trish said, scrolling through the heavily abridged page, 'the document contains all of your key phrases.'

Katherine stared up at the redaction in silence.

Trish gave her a minute and then scrolled back to the top of the page. Each of Katherine's key phrases was underlined in capital letters and accompanied by a small sample of teaser text – the two words that appeared on either side of the requested phrase.

secret location <u>UNDERGROUND</u> where the ■■

████████████████████████ . . . ██

████████████████████████████

████████████████████████████

somewhere in <u>WASHINGTON, D.C.,</u> the coordinates ████████████████████

█████████████████████████ . . .

████████████████████████████

████████████████████████████

████████████████████████████

██████████████████ uncovered an <u>ANCIENT PORTAL</u> that led ████████

████████████████████████████

████████████████████████████

███████ . . . ████████████████

████████████████████████████

████████████████████████████

████████ warning the <u>PYRAMID</u> holds dangerous ████████████████ . . . ██

████████████████████████████

████████ decipher this <u>ENGRAVED</u> <u>SYMBOLON</u> to unveil ████████████

████████████████████████████

████████████████████████████

████████████████████████████

Trish could not imagine what this document was referring to. *And what the heck is a 'symbolon'?*

Katherine stepped eagerly toward the screen. 'Where did this document come from? Who wrote it?'

Trish was already working on it. 'Give me a second. I'm trying to chase down the source.'

'I need to know who wrote this,' Katherine repeated, her voice intense. 'I need to see the *rest* of it.'

'I'm trying,' Trish said, startled by the edge in Katherine's tone.

Strangely, the file's location was not displaying as a traditional Web address but rather as a numeric Internet Protocol address. 'I can't unmask the IP,' Trish said. 'The domain name's not coming up. Hold on.' She pulled up her terminal window. 'I'll run a traceroute.'

Trish typed the sequence of commands to ping all the 'hops' between her control room's machine and whatever machine was storing this document.

'Tracing now,' she said, executing the command.

Traceroutes were extremely fast, and a long list of network devices appeared almost instantly on the plasma wall. Trish scanned down ... down ... through the path of routers and switches that connected her machine to ...

What the hell? Her trace had stopped before reaching the document's server. Her ping, for some reason, had hit a network device that swallowed it rather than bouncing it back. 'It looks like my traceroute got blocked,' Trish said. *Is that even possible?*

'Run it again.'

Trish launched another traceroute and got the same result. 'Nope. Dead end. It's like this document is on a server that is untraceable.' She looked at the last few hops before the dead end. 'I *can* tell you, though, it's located somewhere in the D.C. area.'

'You're kidding.'

'Not surprising,' Trish said. 'These spider programs spiral out geographically, meaning the first results are always local. Besides, one of your search strings was "Washington, D.C." '

'How about a "who is" search?' Katherine prompted. 'Wouldn't that tell you who owns the domain?'

A bit lowbrow, but not a bad idea. Trish navigated to the 'who is' database and ran a search for the IP, hoping to match the cryptic numbers to an actual domain name. Her frustration was now tempered by rising curiosity. *Who has this document?* The 'who is' results appeared quickly, showing no match, and Trish held up her hands in defeat. 'It's like this IP address doesn't exist. I can't get any information about it at all.'

'Obviously the IP *exists*. We've just searched a document that's stored there!'

True. And yet whoever had this document apparently preferred not to share his or her identity. 'I'm not sure what to tell you. Systems traces aren't really my thing, and unless you want to call in someone with hacking skills, I'm at a loss.'

'Do you know someone?'

Trish turned and stared at her boss. 'Katherine, I was kidding. It's not exactly a great idea.'

'But it *is* done?' She checked her watch.

'Um, yeah . . . all the time. Technically it's pretty easy.'

'Who do you know?'

'Hackers?' Trish laughed nervously. 'Like half the guys at my old job.'

'Anyone you trust?'

Is she serious? Trish could see Katherine was dead serious. 'Well, yeah,' she said hurriedly. 'I know this one guy we could call. He was our systems security specialist – serious computer geek. He wanted to date me, which kind of sucked, but he's a good guy, and I'd trust him. Also, he does freelance.'

'Can he be discreet?'

'He's a hacker. Of course he can be discreet. That's what he does. But I'm sure he'd want at least a thousand bucks to even look—'

'Call him. Offer him double for fast results.'

Trish was not sure what made her more uncomfortable – helping Katherine Solomon hire a hacker . . . or calling a guy who probably still found it impossible to believe a pudgy, redheaded meta-systems analyst would rebuff his romantic advances. 'You're sure about this?'

'Use the phone in the library,' Katherine said. 'It's got a blocked number. And obviously don't use my name.'

'Right.' Trish headed for the door but paused when she heard Katherine's iPhone chirp. With luck, the incoming text message might be information that would grant Trish a reprieve from this distasteful task. She waited as Katherine fished the iPhone from her lab coat's pocket and eyed the screen.

Katherine Solomon felt a wave of relief to see the name on her iPhone.

At last.

PETER SOLOMON

'It's a text message from my brother,' she said, glancing over at Trish.

Trish looked hopeful. 'So maybe we should ask him about all this . . . before we call a hacker?'

Katherine eyed the redacted document on the plasma wall and heard Dr. Abaddon's voice. *That which your brother believes is hidden in D.C. . . . it can be found.* Katherine had no idea what to believe anymore, and this document represented information about the far-fetched ideas with which Peter had apparently become obsessed.

Katherine shook her head. 'I want to know who wrote this and where it's located. Make the call.'

Trish frowned and headed for the door.

Whether or not this document would be able to explain the mystery of what her brother had told Dr. Abaddon, there was at least *one* mystery that had been solved today. Her brother had finally learned how to use the text-messaging feature on the iPhone Katherine had given him.

'And alert the media,' Katherine called after Trish. 'The great Peter Solomon just sent his first text message.'

In a strip-mall parking lot across the street from the SMSC, Mal'akh stood beside his limo, stretching his legs and waiting for the phone call he knew would be coming. The rain had stopped, and a winter moon had started to break through the clouds. It was the same moon that had shone down on Mal'akh through the oculus of the House of the Temple three months ago during his initiation.

The world looks different tonight.

As he waited, his stomach growled again. His two-day fast, although uncomfortable, was critical to his preparation. Such were the ancient ways. Soon all physical discomforts would be inconsequential.

As Mal'akh stood in the cold night air, he chuckled to see that *fate* had deposited him, rather ironically, directly in front of a tiny church. Here, nestled between Sterling Dental and a minimart, was a tiny sanctuary.

LORD'S HOUSE OF GLORY.

Mal'akh gazed at the window, which displayed part of the church's doctrinal statement: WE BELIEVE THAT JESUS CHRIST WAS BEGOTTEN BY THE HOLY SPIRIT, AND BORN OF THE VIRGIN MARY, AND IS BOTH TRUE MAN AND GOD.

Mal'akh smiled. *Yes, Jesus is indeed both – man and God – but a virgin birth is not the prerequisite for divinity. That is not how it happens.*

The ring of a cell phone cut the night air, quickening his pulse. The phone that was now ringing was Mal'akh's *own* – a cheap disposable phone he had purchased yesterday. The caller ID indicated it was the call he had been anticipating.

A local call, Mal'akh mused, gazing out across Silver Hill Road toward the faint moonlit outline of a zigzag roofline over the treetops. Mal'akh flipped open his phone.

'This is Dr. Abaddon,' he said, tuning his voice deeper.

'It's Katherine,' the woman's voice said. 'I finally heard from my brother.'

'Oh, I'm relieved. How is he?'

'He's on his way to my lab right now,' Katherine said. 'In fact, he suggested you join us.'

'I'm sorry?' Mal'akh feigned hesitation. 'In your . . . lab?'

'He must trust you deeply. He never invites *anyone* back there.'

'I suppose maybe he thinks a visit might help

our discussions, but I feel like it's an intrusion.'

'If my *brother* says you're welcome, then you're welcome. Besides, he said he has a lot to tell us both, and I'd love to get to the bottom of what's going on.'

'Very well, then. *Where* exactly is your lab?'

'At the Smithsonian Museum Support Center. Do you know where that is?'

'No,' Mal'akh said, staring across the parking lot at the complex. 'I'm actually in my car right now, and I have a guidance system. What's the address?'

'Forty-two-ten Silver Hill Road.'

'Okay, hold on. I'll type it in.' Mal'akh waited for ten seconds and then said, 'Ah, good news, it looks like I'm closer than I thought. The GPS says I'm only about ten minutes away.'

'Great. I'll phone the security gate and tell them you're coming through.'

'Thank you.'

'I'll see you shortly.'

Mal'akh pocketed the disposable phone and looked out toward the SMSC. *Was I rude to invite myself?* Smiling, he now pulled out Peter Solomon's iPhone and admired the text message he had sent Katherine several minutes earlier.

> Got your messages. All's fine. Busy day.
> Forgot appointment with Dr. Abaddon. Sorry
> not to mention him sooner. Long story. Am
> headed to lab now. If available, have Dr.
> Abaddon join us inside. I trust him fully, and I
> have much to tell you both. – Peter

Not surprisingly, Peter's iPhone now pinged with an incoming reply from Katherine.

peter, congrats on learning to text! relieved
you're okay. spoke to dr. A., and he is coming
to lab. see you shortly! – k

Clutching Solomon's iPhone, Mal'akh crouched
down under his limousine and wedged the phone
between the front tire and the pavement. This phone
had served Mal'akh well . . . but now it was time it
became untraceable. He climbed behind the wheel,
put the car in gear, and crept forward until he heard
the sharp crack of the iPhone imploding.

Mal'akh put the car back in park and stared out at
the distant silhouette of the SMSC. *Ten minutes.* Peter
Solomon's sprawling warehouse housed over thirty
million treasures, but Mal'akh had come here tonight
to obliterate only the two most valuable.

All of Katherine Solomon's research.

And Katherine Solomon herself.

26

'Professor Langdon?' Sato said. 'You look like you've
seen a ghost. Are you okay?'

Langdon hoisted his daybag higher onto his
shoulder and laid his hand on top of it, as if somehow
this might better hide the cube-shaped package he was
carrying. He could feel his face had gone ashen.
'I'm . . . just worried about Peter.'

Sato cocked her head, eyeing him askew.

Langdon felt a sudden wariness that Sato's involvement tonight might relate to this small package that

Solomon had entrusted to him. Peter had warned Langdon: *Powerful people want to steal this. It would be dangerous in the wrong hands.* Langdon couldn't imagine why the CIA would want a little box containing a talisman . . . or even what the talisman could be. *Ordo ab chao?*

Sato stepped closer, her black eyes probing. 'I sense you've had a revelation?'

Langdon felt himself sweating now. 'No, not exactly.'

'What's on your mind?'

'I just . . .' Langdon hesitated, having no idea what to say. He had no intention of revealing the existence of the package in his bag, and yet if Sato took him to the CIA, his bag most certainly would be searched on the way in. 'Actually . . .' he fibbed, 'I have another idea about the numbers on Peter's hand.'

Sato's expression revealed nothing. 'Yes?' She glanced over at Anderson now, who was just arriving from greeting the forensics team that had finally arrived.

Langdon swallowed hard and crouched down beside the hand, wondering what he could possibly come up with to tell them. *You're a teacher, Robert – improvise!* He took one last look at the seven tiny symbols, hoping for some sort of inspiration.

$$\text{III} \text{X} \square\square \text{5}$$

Nothing. Blank.

As Langdon's eidetic memory skimmed through his mental encyclopedia of symbols, he could find only one possible point to make. It was something that had occurred to him initially, but had seemed unlikely. At the moment, however, he had to buy time to think.

'Well,' he began, 'a symbologist's first clue that he's on the wrong track when deciphering symbols and codes is when he starts interpreting symbols using multiple symbolic languages. For example, when I told you this text was Roman and Arabic, that was a poor analysis because I used multiple symbolic systems. The same is true for Roman and runic.'

Sato crossed her arms and arched her eyebrows as if to say, 'Go on.'

'In general, communications are made in *one* language, not multiple languages, and so a symbologist's first job with any text is to find a *single* consistent symbolic system that applies to the entire text.'

'And you see a single system now?'

'Well, yes . . . and no.' Langdon's experience with the rotational symmetry of ambigrams had taught him that symbols sometimes had meanings from multiple angles. In this case, he realized there was indeed a way to view all seven symbols in a single language. 'If we manipulated the hand slightly, the language will become consistent.' Eerily, the manipulation Langdon was about to perform was one that seemed to have been suggested by Peter's captor already when he spoke the ancient Hermetic adage. *As above, so below.*

Langdon felt a chill as he reached out and grasped the wooden base on which Peter's hand was secured. Gently, he turned the base upside down so that Peter's extended fingers were now pointing straight down. The symbols on the palm instantly transformed themselves.

5BB XIII

'From this angle,' Langdon said, 'X-I-I-I becomes a valid Roman numeral – thirteen. Moreover, the rest of the characters can be interpreted using the Roman alphabet – SBB.' Langdon assumed the analysis would elicit blank shrugs, but Anderson's expression immediately changed.

'SBB?' the chief demanded.

Sato turned to Anderson. 'If I'm not mistaken, that sounds like a familiar numbering system here in the Capitol Building.'

Anderson looked pale. 'It is.'

Sato gave a grim smile and nodded to Anderson. 'Chief, follow me, please. I'd like a word in private.'

As Director Sato led Chief Anderson out of earshot, Langdon stood alone in bewilderment. *What the hell is going on here? And what is SBB XIII?*

Chief Anderson wondered how this night could possibly get any stranger. *The hand says SBB13?* He was amazed any outsider had even heard of SBB . . . much less SBB13. Peter Solomon's index finger, it seemed, was not directing them upward as it had appeared . . . but rather was pointing in quite the opposite direction.

Director Sato led Anderson over to a quiet area near the bronze statue of Thomas Jefferson. 'Chief,' she said, 'I trust you know exactly where SBB Thirteen is located?'

'Of course.'

'Do you know what's inside?'

'No, not without looking. I don't think it's been used in decades.'

'Well, you're going to open it up.'

Anderson did not appreciate being told what he would do in his own building. 'Ma'am, that may be problematic. I'll have to check the assignment roster first. As you know, most of the lower levels are private offices or storage, and security protocol regarding private—'

'You will unlock SBB Thirteen for me,' Sato said, 'or I will call OS and send in a team with a battering ram.'

Anderson stared at her a long moment and then pulled out his radio, raising it to his lips. 'This is Anderson. I need someone to unlock the SBB. Have someone meet me there in five minutes.'

The voice that replied sounded confused. 'Chief, confirming you said SBB?'

'Correct. SBB. Send someone immediately. And I'll need a flashlight.' He stowed his radio. Anderson's heart was pounding as Sato stepped closer, lowering her voice even further.

'Chief, time is short,' she whispered, 'and I want you to get us down to SBB Thirteen as quickly as possible.'

'Yes, ma'am.'

'I also need something else from you.'

In addition to breaking and entering? Anderson was in no position to protest, and yet it had not gone unnoticed by him that Sato had arrived within minutes of Peter's hand appearing in the Rotunda, and that she now was using the situation to demand access to private sections of the U.S. Capitol. She seemed so far ahead of the curve tonight that she was practically defining it.

167

Sato motioned across the room toward the professor. 'The duffel bag on Langdon's shoulder.'

Anderson glanced over. 'What about it?'

'I assume your staff X-rayed that bag when Langdon entered the building?'

'Of course. All bags are scanned.'

'I want to see that X-ray. I want to know what's in his bag.'

Anderson looked over at the bag Langdon had been carrying all evening. 'But . . . wouldn't it be easier just to ask him?'

'What part of my request was unclear?'

Anderson pulled out his radio again and called in her request. Sato gave Anderson her BlackBerry address and requested that his team e-mail her a digital copy of the X-ray as soon as they had located it. Reluctantly Anderson complied.

Forensics was now collecting the severed hand for the Capitol Police, but Sato ordered them to deliver it directly to her team at Langley. Anderson was too tired to protest. He had just been run over by a tiny Japanese steamroller.

'And I want that ring,' Sato called over to Forensics.

The chief technician seemed ready to question her but thought better of it. He removed the gold ring from Peter's hand, placed it in a clear specimen bag, and gave it to Sato. She slipped it into her jacket pocket, and then turned to Langdon.

'We're leaving, Professor. Bring your things.'

'Where are we going?' Langdon replied.

'Just follow Mr. Anderson.'

Yes, Anderson thought, *and follow me closely.* The SBB was a section of the Capitol that few ever visited. To reach it, they would pass through a sprawling labyrinth of tiny chambers and tight passages buried beneath the crypt. Abraham Lincoln's youngest son, Tad, had once gotten lost down there and almost perished. Anderson was starting to suspect that if Sato had her way, Robert Langdon might suffer a similar fate.

27

Systems security specialist Mark Zoubianis had always prided himself on his ability to multitask. At the moment, he was seated on his futon along with a TV remote, a cordless phone, a laptop, a PDA, and a large bowl of Pirate's Booty. With one eye on the muted Redskins game and one eye on his laptop, Zoubianis was speaking on his Bluetooth headset with a woman he had not heard from in over a year.

Leave it to Trish Dunne to call on the night of a play-off game.

Confirming her social ineptitude yet again, his former colleague had chosen the Redskins game as a perfect moment to chat him up and request a favor. After some brief small talk about the old days and how she missed his great jokes, Trish had gotten to her point: she was trying to unmask a hidden IP address, probably that of a secure server in the D.C. area. The server contained a small text document, and she wanted access to it . . . or at the very least, some information about whose document it was.

Right guy, wrong timing, he had told her. Trish then showered him with her finest geek flattery, most of which was true, and before Zoubianis knew it, he was typing a strange-looking IP address into his laptop.

Zoubianis took one look at the number and immediately felt uneasy. 'Trish, this IP has a funky format. It's written in a protocol that isn't even publicly available yet. It's probably gov intel or military.'

'Military?' Trish laughed. 'Believe me, I just pulled a redacted document off this server, and it was *not* military.'

Zoubianis pulled up his terminal window and tried a traceroute. 'You said your traceroute died?'

'Yeah. Twice. Same hop.'

'Mine, too.' He pulled up a diagnostic probe and launched it. 'And what's so interesting about this IP?'

'I ran a delegator that tapped a search engine at this IP and pulled a redacted document. I need to see the rest of the document. I'm happy to pay them for it, but I can't figure out who owns the IP or how to access it.'

Zoubianis frowned at his screen. 'Are you sure about this? I'm running a diagnostic, and this firewall coding looks . . . pretty serious.'

'That's why you get the big bucks.'

Zoubianis considered it. They'd offered him a fortune for a job this easy. 'One question, Trish. Why are you so hot on this?'

Trish paused. 'I'm doing a favor for a friend.'

'Must be a special friend.'

'She is.'

Zoubianis chuckled and held his tongue. *I knew it.*

'Look,' Trish said, sounding impatient. 'Are you good enough to unmask this IP? Yes or no?'

'Yes, I'm good enough. And yes, I know you're playing me like a fiddle.'

'How long will it take you?'

'Not long,' he said, typing as he spoke. 'I should be able to get into a machine on their network within ten minutes or so. Once I'm in and know what I'm looking at, I'll call you back.'

'I appreciate it. So, are you doing well?'

Now she asks? 'Trish, for God's sake, you called me on the night of a play-off game and now you want to chat? Do you want me to hack this IP or not?'

'Thanks, Mark. I appreciate it. I'll be waiting for your call.'

'Fifteen minutes.' Zoubianis hung up, grabbed his bowl of Pirate's Booty, and unmuted the game.

Women.

28

Where are they taking me?

As Langdon hurried with Anderson and Sato into the depths of the Capitol, he felt his heart rate increasing with each downward step. They had begun their journey through the west portico of the Rotunda, descending a marble staircase and then doubling back through a wide doorway into the famous chamber directly beneath the Rotunda floor.

The Capitol Crypt.

The air was heavier here, and Langdon was already feeling claustrophobic. The crypt's low ceiling and soft uplighting accentuated the robust girth of the forty Doric columns required to support the vast stone floor directly overhead. *Relax, Robert.*

'This way,' Anderson said, moving quickly as he

angled to the left across the wide circular space.

Thankfully, this particular crypt contained no bodies. Instead it contained several statues, a model of the Capitol, and a low storage area for the wooden catafalque on which coffins were laid for state funerals. The entourage hurried through, without even a glance at the four-pointed marble compass in the center of the floor where the Eternal Flame had once burned.

Anderson seemed to be in a hurry, and Sato once again had her head buried in her BlackBerry. Cellular service, Langdon had heard, was boosted and broadcast to all corners of the Capitol Building to support the hundreds of government phone calls that took place here every day.

After diagonally crossing the crypt, the group entered a dimly lit foyer and began winding through a convoluted series of hallways and dead ends. The warren of passages contained numbered doorways, each of which bore an identification number. Langdon read the doors as they snaked their way around.

S154 . . . S153 . . . S152 . . .

He had no idea what lay behind these doors, but at least one thing now seemed clear – the meaning of the tattoo on Peter Solomon's palm. SBB13 appeared to be a numbered doorway somewhere in the bowels of the U.S. Capitol Building.

'What are all these doorways?' Langdon asked, clutching his daybag tightly to his ribs and wondering what Solomon's tiny package could possibly have to do with a door marked SBB13.

'Offices and storage,' Anderson said. '*Private* offices and storage,' he added, glancing back at Sato.

Sato did not even glance up from her BlackBerry.

'They look tiny,' Langdon said.

'Glorified closets, most of them, but they're still some of the most sought-after real estate in D.C. This is the heart of the original Capitol, and the old Senate chamber is two stories above us.'

'And SBB. Thirteen?' Langdon asked. 'Whose office is that?'

'Nobody's. The SBB is a private storage area, and I must say, I'm puzzled how—'

'Chief Anderson,' Sato interrupted without looking up from her BlackBerry. 'Just take us there, please.'

Anderson clenched his jaw and guided them on in silence through what was now feeling like a hybrid self-storage facility and epic labyrinth. On almost every wall, directional signs pointed back and forth, apparently attempting to locate specific office blocks in this network of hallways.

S142 to S152 . . .

ST1 to ST70 . . .

H1 to H166 & HT1 to HT67 . . .

Langdon doubted he could ever find his way out of here alone. *This place is a maze.* From all he could gather, office numbers began with either an *S* or an *H* depending on whether they were on the Senate side of the building or the House side. Areas designated ST and HT were apparently on a level that Anderson called Terrace Level.

Still no signs for SBB.

Finally they arrived at a heavy steel security door with a key-card entry box.

SB Level

Langdon sensed they were getting closer.

Anderson reached for his key card but hesitated, looking uncomfortable with Sato's demands.

'Chief,' Sato prompted. 'We don't have all night.'

Anderson reluctantly inserted his key card. The steel door released. He pushed it open, and they stepped through into the foyer beyond. The heavy door clicked shut behind them.

Langdon wasn't sure what he had hoped to see in this foyer, but the sight in front of him was definitely not it. He was staring at a descending stairway. 'Down again?' he said, stopping short. 'There's a level *under* the crypt?'

'Yes,' Anderson said. '*SB* stands for "Senate Basement." '

Langdon groaned. *Terrific*.

29

The headlights winding up the SMSC's wooded access road were the first the guard had seen in the last hour. Dutifully, he turned down the volume on his portable TV set and stashed his snacks beneath the counter. Lousy timing. The Redskins were completing their opening drive, and he didn't want to miss it.

As the car drew closer, the guard checked the name on the notepad in front of him.

Dr. Christopher Abaddon.

Katherine Solomon had just called to alert Security of this guest's imminent arrival. The guard had no idea who this doctor might be, but he was apparently very good at doctoring; he was arriving in a black stretch limousine. The long, sleek vehicle rolled to a stop beside the guardhouse, and the driver's tinted window lowered silently.

'Good evening,' the chauffeur said, doffing his cap. He was a powerfully built man with a shaved head. He was listening to the football game on his radio. 'I have Dr. Christopher Abaddon for Ms. Katherine Solomon?'

The guard nodded. 'Identification, please.'

The chauffeur looked surprised. 'I'm sorry, didn't Ms. Solomon call ahead?'

The guard nodded, stealing a glance at the television. 'I'm still required to scan and log visitor identification. Sorry, regulations. I'll need to see the doctor's ID.'

'Not a problem.' The chauffeur turned backward in his seat and spoke in hushed tones through the privacy screen. As he did, the guard stole another peek at the game. The Redskins were breaking from the huddle now, and he hoped to get this limo through before the next play.

The chauffeur turned forward again and held out the ID that he'd apparently just received through the privacy screen.

The guard took the card and quickly scanned it into his system. The D.C. driver's license showed one Christopher Abaddon from Kalorama Heights. The photo depicted a handsome blond gentleman wearing a blue blazer, a necktie, and a satin pocket square. *Who the hell wears a pocket square to the DMV?*

A muffled cheer went up from the television set, and the guard wheeled just in time to see a Redskins player dancing in the end zone, his finger pointed skyward. 'I missed it,' the guard grumbled, returning to the window.

'Okay,' he said, returning the license to the chauffeur. 'You're all set.'

As the limo pulled through, the guard returned to his TV, hoping for a replay.

As Mal'akh drove his limo up the winding access road, he couldn't help but smile. Peter Solomon's secret museum had been simple to breach. Sweeter still, tonight was the second time in twenty-four hours that Mal'akh had broken into one of Solomon's private spaces. Last night, a similar visit had been made to Solomon's home.

Although Peter Solomon had a magnificent country estate in Potomac, he spent much of his time in the city at his penthouse apartment at the exclusive Dorchester Arms. His building, like most that catered to the super-rich, was a veritable fortress. High walls. Guard gates. Guest lists. Secured underground parking.

Mal'akh had driven this very limousine up to the building's guardhouse, doffed his chauffeur's cap from his shaved head, and proclaimed, 'I have Dr. Christopher Abaddon. He is an invited guest of Mr. Peter Solomon.' Mal'akh spoke the words as if he were announcing the Duke of York.

The guard checked a log and then Abaddon's ID. 'Yes, I see Mr. Solomon is expecting Dr. Abaddon.' He pressed a button and the gate opened. 'Mr. Solomon is in the penthouse apartment. Have your guest use the *last* elevator on the right. It goes all the way up.'

'Thank you.' Mal'akh tipped his hat and drove through.

As he wound deep into the garage, he scanned for

security cameras. Nothing. Apparently, those who lived here were neither the kind of people who broke into cars nor the kind of people who appreciated being watched.

Mal'akh parked in a dark corner near the elevators, lowered the divider between the driver's compartment and the passenger compartment, and slithered through the opening into the back of the limo. Once in back, he got rid of his chauffeur's cap and donned his blond wig. Straightening his jacket and tie, he checked the mirror to make sure he had not smeared his makeup. Mal'akh was not about to take any chances. Not tonight.

I have waited too long for this.

Seconds later, Mal'akh was stepping into the private elevator. The ride to the top was silent and smooth. When the door opened, he found himself in an elegant, private foyer. His host was already waiting.

'Dr. Abaddon, welcome.'

Mal'akh looked into the man's famous gray eyes and felt his heart begin to race. 'Mr. Solomon, I appreciate your seeing me.'

'Please, call me Peter.' The two men shook hands. As Mal'akh gripped the older man's palm, he saw the gold Masonic ring on Solomon's hand . . . the same hand that had once aimed a gun at Mal'akh. A voice whispered from Mal'akh's distant past. *If you pull that trigger, I will haunt you forever.*

'Please come in,' Solomon said, ushering Mal'akh into an elegant living room whose expansive windows offered an astonishing view of the Washington skyline.

'Do I smell tea steeping?' Mal'akh asked as he entered.

Solomon looked impressed. 'My parents always

greeted guests with tea. I've carried on that tradition.' He led Mal'akh into the living room, where a tea service was waiting in front of the fire. 'Cream and sugar?'

'Black, thank you.'

Again Solomon looked impressed. 'A purist.' He poured them both a cup of black tea. 'You said you needed to discuss something with me that was sensitive in nature and could be discussed only in private.'

'Thank you. I appreciate your time.'

'You and I are Masonic brothers now. We have a bond. Tell me how I can help you.'

'First, I would like to thank you for the honor of the thirty-third degree a few months ago. This is deeply meaningful to me.'

'I'm glad, but please know that those decisions are not mine alone. They are by vote of the Supreme Council.'

'Of course.' Mal'akh suspected Peter Solomon had probably voted against him, but within the Masons, as with all things, money was power. Mal'akh, after achieving the thirty-second degree in his own lodge, had waited only a month before making a multimillion-dollar donation to charity in the name of the Masonic Grand Lodge. The unsolicited act of self-lessness, as Mal'akh anticipated, was enough to earn him a quick invitation into the elite thirty-third degree. *And yet I have learned no secrets.*

Despite the age-old whispers – 'All is revealed at the thirty-third degree' – Mal'akh had been told nothing new, nothing of relevance to his quest. But he had never expected to be told. The inner circle of Freemasonry contained smaller circles still . . . circles

Mal'akh would not see for years, if ever. He didn't care. His initiation had served its purpose. Something unique had happened within that Temple Room, and it had given Mal'akh power over all of them. *I no longer play by your rules.*

'You do realize,' Mal'akh said, sipping his tea, 'that you and I met many years ago.'

Solomon looked surprised. 'Really? I don't recall.'

'It was quite a long time ago.' *And Christopher Abaddon is not my real name.*

'I'm so sorry. My mind must be getting old. Remind me how I know you?'

Mal'akh smiled one last time at the man he hated more than any other man on earth. 'It's unfortunate that you don't recall.'

In one fluid motion, Mal'akh pulled a small device from his pocket and extended it outward, driving it hard into the man's chest. There was a flash of blue light, the sharp sizzle of the stun-gun discharge, and a gasp of pain as one million volts of electricity coursed through Peter Solomon's body. His eyes went wide, and he slumped motionless in his chair. Mal'akh stood up now, towering over the man, salivating like a lion about to consume his injured prey.

Solomon was gasping, straining to breathe.

Mal'akh saw fear in his victim's eyes and wondered how many people had ever seen the great Peter Solomon cower. Mal'akh savored the scene for several long seconds. He took a sip of tea, waiting for the man to catch his breath.

Solomon was twitching, attempting to speak. 'Wh-why?' he finally managed.

'Why do you think?' Mal'akh demanded.

Solomon looked truly bewildered. 'You want . . . money?'

Money? Mal'akh laughed and took another sip of tea. 'I gave the Masons millions of dollars; I have no need of wealth.' *I come for wisdom, and he offers me wealth.*

'Then what . . . do you want?'

'You possess a secret. You will share it with me tonight.'

Solomon struggled to lift his chin so he could look Mal'akh in the eye. 'I don't . . . understand.'

'No more lies!' Mal'akh shouted, advancing to within inches of the paralyzed man. 'I know what is hidden here in Washington.'

Solomon's gray eyes were defiant. 'I have no idea what you're talking about!'

Mal'akh took another sip of tea and set the cup on a coaster. 'You spoke those same words to me ten years ago, on the night of your mother's death.'

Solomon's eyes shot wide open. 'You . . . ?'

'She didn't have to die. If you had given me what I demanded . . .'

The older man's face contorted in a mask of horrified recognition . . . and disbelief.

'I warned you,' Mal'akh said, 'if you pulled the trigger, I would haunt you forever.'

'But you're—'

Mal'akh lunged, driving the Taser hard into Solomon's chest again. There was another flash of blue light, and Solomon went completely limp.

Mal'akh put the Taser back in his pocket and calmly finished his tea. When he was done, he dabbed his lips with a monogrammed linen napkin and peered down at his victim. 'Shall we go?'

Solomon's body was motionless, but his eyes were wide and engaged.

Mal'akh got down close and whispered in the man's ear. 'I'm taking you to a place where only truth remains.'

Without another word, Mal'akh wadded up the monogrammed napkin and stuffed it into Solomon's mouth. Then he hoisted the limp man onto his broad shoulders and headed for the private elevator. On his way out, he picked up Solomon's iPhone and keys from the hall table.

Tonight you will tell me all your secrets, Mal'akh thought. *Including why you left me for dead all those years ago.*

30

SB level.
   Senate basement.
   Robert Langdon's claustrophobia gripped him more tightly with every hastening step of their descent. As they moved deeper into the building's original foundation, the air became heavy, and the ventilation seemed nonexistent. The walls down here were an uneven blend of stone and yellow brick.

Director Sato typed on her BlackBerry as they walked. Langdon sensed a suspicion in her guarded manner, but the feeling was quickly becoming reciprocal. Sato still hadn't told him how she knew Langdon was here tonight. *An issue of national security?* He had a hard time understanding any relation between ancient mysticism and national security. Then again, he had a hard time understanding much of anything about this situation.

Peter Solomon entrusted me with a talisman . . . a deluded lunatic tricked me into bringing it to the Capitol and wants me to use it to unlock a mystical portal . . . possibly in a room called SBB13.

Not exactly a clear picture.

As they pressed on, Langdon tried to shake from his mind the horrible image of Peter's tattooed hand, transformed into the Hand of the Mysteries. The gruesome picture was accompanied by Peter's voice: *The Ancient Mysteries, Robert, have spawned many myths . . . but that does not mean they themselves are fiction.*

Despite a career studying mystical symbols and history, Langdon had always struggled intellectually with the idea of the Ancient Mysteries and their potent promise of apotheosis.

Admittedly, the historical record contained indisputable evidence that secret wisdom had been passed down through the ages, apparently having come out of the Mystery Schools in early Egypt. This knowledge moved underground, resurfacing in Renaissance Europe, where, according to most accounts, it was entrusted to an elite group of scientists within the walls of Europe's premier scientific think tank – the Royal Society of London – enigmatically nicknamed the Invisible College.

This concealed 'college' quickly became a brain trust of the world's most enlightened minds – those of Isaac Newton, Francis Bacon, Robert Boyle, and even Benjamin Franklin. Today, the list of modern 'fellows' was no less impressive – Einstein, Hawking, Bohr, and Celsius. These great minds had all made quantum leaps in human understanding, advances that, according to some, were the result of their exposure to ancient wisdom hidden within the Invisible College. Langdon doubted this was true, although certainly there had been an unusual amount of 'mystical work' taking place within those walls.

The discovery of Isaac Newton's secret papers in 1936 had stunned the world by revealing Newton's all-consuming passion for the study of ancient alchemy and mystical wisdom. Newton's private papers included a handwritten letter to Robert Boyle in which he exhorted Boyle to keep 'high silence' regarding the mystical knowledge they had learned. 'It cannot be communicated,' Newton wrote, 'without immense damage to the world.'

The meaning of this strange warning was still being debated today.

'Professor,' Sato said suddenly, glancing up from her BlackBerry, 'despite your insistence that you have no idea why you're here tonight, perhaps you could shed light on the meaning of Peter Solomon's ring.'

'I can try,' Langdon said, refocusing.

She produced the specimen bag and handed it to Langdon. 'Tell me about the symbols on his ring.'

Langdon examined the familiar ring as they moved through the deserted passageway. Its face bore the image of a double-headed phoenix holding a banner proclaiming ORDO AB CHAO, and its chest was emblazoned with the number 33. 'The double-headed phoenix with the number thirty-three is the emblem of the highest Masonic degree.' Technically, this prestigious degree existed solely within the Scottish Rite. Nonetheless, the rites and degrees of Masonry were a complex hierarchy that Langdon had no desire to detail for Sato tonight. 'Essentially, the thirty-third degree is an elite honor reserved for a small group of highly accomplished Masons. All the other degrees can be attained by successful completion of the previous degree, but ascension to the thirty-third degree is controlled. It's by invitation only.'

'So you were aware that Peter Solomon was a member of this elite inner circle?'

'Of course. Membership is hardly a secret.'

'And he is their highest-ranking official?'

'Currently, yes. Peter heads the Supreme Council Thirty-third Degree, which is the governing body of the Scottish Rite in America.' Langdon always loved visiting their headquarters – the House of the Temple – a classical masterpiece whose symbolic orna-mentation rivaled that of Scotland's Rosslyn Chapel.

'Professor, did you notice the engraving on the ring's band? It bears the words "All is revealed at the thirty-third degree." '

Langdon nodded. 'It's a common theme in Masonic lore.'

'Meaning, I assume, that if a Mason is admitted to this highest thirty-third degree, then something special is *revealed* to him?'

'Yes, that's the lore, but probably not the reality. There's always been conspiratorial conjecture that a select few within this highest echelon of Masonry are made privy to some great mystical secret. The truth, I suspect, is probably far less dramatic.'

Peter Solomon often made playful allusions to the existence of a precious Masonic secret, but Langdon always assumed it was just a mischievous attempt to coax him into joining the brotherhood. Unfortunately, tonight's events had been anything but playful, and there had been nothing mischievous about the seriousness with which Peter had urged Langdon to protect the sealed package in his daybag.

Langdon glanced forlornly at the plastic bag containing Peter's gold ring. 'Director,' he asked, 'would you mind if I held on to this?'

She looked over. 'Why?'

'It's very valuable to Peter, and I'd like to return it to him tonight.'

She looked skeptical. 'Let's hope you get that chance.'

'Thanks.' Langdon pocketed the ring.

'Another question,' Sato said as they hastened deeper into the labyrinth. 'My staff said that while cross-checking the concepts of the "thirty-third degree" and "portal" with Masonry, they turned up literally hundreds of references to a "*pyramid*"?'

'That's not surprising, either,' Langdon said. 'The pyramid builders of Egypt are the forerunners of the modern stonemasons, and the pyramid, along with Egyptian themes, is very common in Masonic symbolism.'

'Symbolizing what?'

'The pyramid essentially represents enlightenment. It's an architectural symbol emblematic of ancient man's ability to break free from his earthly plane and ascend upward toward heaven, toward the golden sun, and ultimately, toward the supreme source of illumination.'

She waited a moment. 'Nothing else?'

Nothing else?! Langdon had just described one of history's most elegant symbols. *The structure through which man elevated himself into the realm of the gods.*

'According to my staff,' she said, 'it sounds like there is a much more relevant connection tonight.

They tell me there exists a popular legend about a *specific* pyramid here in Washington – a pyramid that relates specifically to the Masons and the Ancient Mysteries?'

Langdon now realized what she was referring to, and he tried to dispel the notion before they wasted any more time. 'I *am* familiar with the legend, Director, but it's pure fantasy. The Masonic Pyramid is one of D.C.'s most enduring myths, probably stemming from the pyramid on the Great Seal of the United States.'

'Why didn't you mention it earlier?'

Langdon shrugged. 'Because it has no basis in fact. Like I said, it's a myth. One of many associated with the Masons.'

'And yet *this* particular myth relates directly to the Ancient Mysteries?'

'Sure, as do plenty of others. The Ancient Mysteries are the foundation for countless legends that have survived in history – stories about powerful wisdom protected by secret guardians like the Templars, the Rosicrucians, the Illuminati, the Alumbrados – the list goes on and on. They are *all* based on the Ancient Mysteries . . . and the Masonic Pyramid is just one example.'

'I see,' Sato said. 'And what does this legend actually say?'

Langdon considered it for a few steps and then replied, 'Well, I'm no specialist in conspiracy theory, but I am educated in mythology, and most accounts go something like this: The Ancient Mysteries – the lost wisdom of the ages – have long been considered mankind's most sacred treasure, and like all great treasures, they have been carefully protected. The enlightened sages who understood the true power of this wisdom learned to fear its awesome potential. They knew that if this secret knowledge were to fall into uninitiated hands, the results could be devastating; as we said earlier, powerful tools can be used either for good or for evil. So, in order to protect the Ancient Mysteries, and mankind in the process, the early practitioners formed secret fraternities. Inside these brotherhoods, they shared their wisdom only with the properly initiated, passing the wisdom from sage to sage. Many believe we can look back and see the historical remnants of those who mastered the Mysteries . . . in the stories of sorcerers, magicians, and healers.'

'And the Masonic Pyramid?' Sato asked. 'How does that fit in?'

'Well,' Langdon said, striding faster now to keep pace, 'this is where history and myth begin to merge. According to some accounts, by the sixteenth century in Europe, almost all of these secret fraternities had become extinct, most of them exterminated by a growing tide of religious persecution. The Freemasons, it is said, became the last surviving custodians of the Ancient Mysteries. Understandably, they feared that if their own brotherhood one day died off like its predecessors, the Ancient Mysteries would be lost for all time.'

'And the *pyramid*?' Sato again pressed.

Langdon was getting to it. 'The legend of the Masonic Pyramid is quite simple. It states that the Masons, in order to fulfill their responsibility of protecting this great wisdom for future generations, decided to hide it in a great fortress.' Langdon tried to gather his recollections of the story. 'Again, I stress this is all myth, but allegedly, the Masons transported their secret wisdom from the Old World to the New

World – here, to America – a land they hoped would remain free from religious tyranny. And here they built an impenetrable fortress – a hidden *pyramid* – designed to protect the Ancient Mysteries until the time that *all* of mankind was ready to handle the awesome power that this wisdom could communicate. According to the myth, the Masons crowned their great pyramid with a shining, solid-gold capstone as symbol of the precious treasure within – the ancient wisdom capable of empowering mankind to his full human potential. Apotheosis.'

'Quite a story,' Sato said.

'Yes. The Masons fall victim to all kinds of crazy legends.'

'Obviously you don't believe such a pyramid exists.'

'Of course not,' Langdon replied. 'There's no evidence whatsoever to suggest that our Masonic fore-fathers built any kind of pyramid in America, much less in D.C. It's pretty difficult to hide a pyramid, especially one large enough to hold all the lost wisdom of the ages.'

The legend, as Langdon recalled, never explained exactly *what* was supposed to be inside the Masonic Pyramid – whether it was ancient texts, occult writings, scientific revelations, or something far more mysterious – but the legend *did* say that the precious information inside was ingeniously encoded . . . and understandable only to the most enlightened souls.

'Anyway,' Langdon said, 'this story falls into a category we symbologists call an "archetypal hybrid" – a blend of other classic legends, borrowing so many elements from popular mythology that it could only be a fictional *construct* . . . not historical fact.'

When Langdon taught his students about archetypal

hybrids, he used the example of fairy tales, which were recounted across generations and exaggerated over time, borrowing so heavily from one another that they evolved into homogenized morality tales with the same iconic elements – virginal damsels, handsome princes, impenetrable fortresses, and powerful wizards. By way of fairy tales, this primeval battle of 'good vs. evil' is ingrained into us as children through our stories: Merlin vs. Morgan le Fay, Saint George vs. the Dragon, David vs. Goliath, Snow White vs. the Witch, and even Luke Skywalker battling Darth Vader.

Sato scratched her head as they turned a corner and followed Anderson down a short flight of stairs. 'Tell me this. If I'm not mistaken, pyramids were once considered mystical *portals* through which the deceased pharaohs could ascend to the gods, were they not?'

'True.'

Sato stopped short and caught Langdon's arm, glaring up at him with an expression somewhere between surprise and disbelief. 'You're saying Peter Solomon's captor told you to find a hidden *portal,* and it didn't occur to you that he was talking about the Masonic Pyramid from this legend?'

'By *any* name, the Masonic Pyramid is a fairy tale. It's purely fantasy.'

Sato stepped closer to him now, and Langdon could smell her cigarette breath. 'I understand your position on that, Professor, but for the sake of my investigation, the parallel is hard to ignore. A portal leading to secret knowledge? To my ear, this sounds a lot like what Peter Solomon's captor claims you, alone, can unlock.'

'Well, I can hardly believe—'

'What *you* believe is not the point. No matter what

189

you believe, you must concede that this man might *himself* believe that the Masonic Pyramid is real.'

'The man's a lunatic! He may well believe that SBB Thirteen is the entrance to a giant underground pyramid that contains all the lost wisdom of the ancients!'

Sato stood perfectly still, her eyes seething. 'The crisis I am facing tonight is *not* a fairy tale, Professor. It is quite real, I assure you.'

A cold silence hung between them.

'Ma'am?' Anderson finally said, gesturing to another secure door ten feet away. 'We're almost there, if you'd like to continue.'

Sato finally broke eye contact with Langdon, motioning for Anderson to move on.

They followed the security chief through the secure doorway, which deposited them in a narrow passage. Langdon looked left and then right. *You've got to be kidding.*

He was standing in the longest hallway he had ever seen.

31

Trish Dunne felt the familiar surge of adrenaline as she exited the bright lights of the Cube and moved into the raw darkness of the void. The SMSC's front gate had just called to say that Katherine's guest, Dr. Abaddon, had arrived and required an escort back to Pod 5. Trish had offered to bring him back, mostly out of curiosity. Katherine had said very little about the man who would be visiting them, and Trish was intrigued. The man was apparently someone Peter Solomon trusted deeply; the Solomons never invited anyone back to the Cube. This was a first.

I hope he handles the crossing okay, Trish thought as she moved through the frigid darkness. The last thing she needed was Katherine's VIP panicking when he realized what he had to do to get to the lab. *The first time is always the worst.*

Trish's first time had been about a year ago. She had accepted Katherine's job offer, signed a nondisclosure, and then come to the SMSC with Katherine to see the lab. The two women had walked the length of 'The Street,' arriving at a metal door marked POD 5. Even though Katherine had tried to prepare her by describing the lab's remote location, Trish was not ready for what she saw when the pod door hissed open.

The void.

Katherine stepped over the threshold, walked a few feet into the perfect blackness, and then motioned for Trish to follow. 'Trust me. You won't get lost.'

Trish pictured herself wandering in a pitch-black, stadium-size room and broke a sweat at the mere thought.

'We have a guidance system to keep you on track.' Katherine pointed to the floor. 'Very low-tech.'

Trish squinted through the darkness at the rough cement floor. It took a moment to see it in the darkness, but there was a narrow carpet runner that had been laid down in a straight line. The carpet ran like a roadway, disappearing into the darkness.

'See with your feet,' Katherine said, turning and walking off. 'Just follow right behind me.'

As Katherine disappeared into the blackness, Trish

swallowed her fear and followed. *This is insane!* She had taken only a few steps down the carpet when the Pod 5 door swung shut behind her, snuffing out the last faint hint of light. Pulse racing, Trish turned all of her attention to the feeling of the carpet beneath her feet. She had ventured only a handful of steps down the soft runner when she felt the side of her right foot hit hard cement. Startled, she instinctively corrected to the left, getting both feet back on soft carpet.

Katherine's voice materialized up ahead in the blackness, her words almost entirely swallowed by the lifeless acoustics of this abyss. 'The human body is amazing,' she said. 'If you deprive it of one sensory input, the other senses take over, almost instantly. Right now, the nerves in your feet are literally "tuning" themselves to become more sensitive.'

Good thing, Trish thought, correcting course again.

They walked in silence for what seemed entirely too long. 'How much farther?' Trish finally asked.

'We're about halfway.' Katherine's voice sounded more distant now.

Trish sped up, doing her best to stay composed, but the breadth of the darkness felt like it would engulf her. *I can't see one millimeter in front of my face!* 'Katherine? How do you know when to stop walking?'

'You'll know in a moment,' Katherine said.

That was a year ago, and now, tonight, Trish was once again in the void, heading in the opposite direction, out to the lobby to retrieve her boss's guest. A sudden change in carpet texture beneath her feet alerted her that she was three yards from the exit. *The warning track,* as it was called by Peter Solomon, an avid baseball fan. Trish stopped short, pulled out her key card, and groped in the darkness along the wall until she found the raised slot and inserted her card.

The door hissed open.

Trish squinted into the welcoming light of the SMSC hallway.

Made it . . . again.

Moving through the deserted corridors, Trish found herself thinking about the bizarre redacted file they had found on a secure network. *Ancient portal? Secret location underground?* She wondered if Mark Zoubianis was having any luck figuring out where the mysterious document was located.

Inside the control room, Katherine stood in the soft glow of the plasma wall and gazed up at the enigmatic document they had uncovered. She had isolated her key phrases now and felt increasingly certain that the document was talking about the same far-flung legend that her brother had apparently shared with Dr. Abaddon.

> . . . secret location <u>UNDERGROUND</u> where the . . .
> . . . somewhere in <u>WASHINGTON, D.C.,</u> the coordinates . . .
> . . . uncovered an <u>ANCIENT PORTAL</u> that led . . .
> . . . warning the <u>PYRAMID</u> holds dangerous . . .
> . . . decipher this <u>ENGRAVED SYMBOLON</u> to unveil . . .

I need to see the rest of the file, Katherine thought.

She stared a moment longer and then flipped the plasma wall's power switch. Katherine always turned off this energy-intensive display so as not to waste the fuel cell's liquid hydrogen reserves.

She watched as her keywords slowly faded, collapsing down into a tiny white dot, which hovered in the middle of the wall and then finally twinkled out.

She turned and walked back toward her office. Dr. Abaddon would be arriving momentarily, and she wanted to make him feel welcome.

32

'Almost there,' Anderson said, guiding Langdon and Sato down the seemingly endless corridor that ran the entire length of the Capitol's eastern foundation. 'In Lincoln's day, this passage had a dirt floor and was filled with rats.'

Langdon felt grateful the floor had been tiled; he was not a big fan of rats. The group continued on, their footfalls drumming up an eerie, uneven echo in the long passageway. Doorways lined the long hallway, some closed but many ajar. Many of the rooms down on this level looked abandoned. Langdon noticed the numbers on the doors were now descending and, after a while, seemed to be running out.

SB4 . . . SB3 . . . SB2 . . . SB1 . . .

They continued past an unmarked door, but Anderson stopped short when the numbers began ascending again.

HB1 . . . HB2 . . .

'Sorry,' Anderson said. 'Missed it. I almost never come down this deep.'

The group backed up a few yards to an old metal door, which Langdon now realized was located at the hallway's central point – the meridian that divided the Senate Basement (SB) and the House Basement (HB).

As it turned out, the door was indeed marked, but its engraving was so faded, it was almost imperceptible.

SBB

'Here we are,' Anderson said. 'Keys will be arriving any moment.'

Sato frowned and checked her watch.

Langdon eyed the SBB marking and asked Anderson, 'Why is this space associated with the *Senate* side even though it's in the middle?'

Anderson looked puzzled. 'What do you mean?'

'It says SBB, which begins with an *S*, not an *H*.'

Anderson shook his head. 'The *S* in SBB doesn't stand for Senate. It—'

'Chief?' a guard called out in the distance. He came jogging up the hallway toward them, holding out a key. 'Sorry, sir, it took a few minutes. We couldn't locate the main SBB key. This is a spare from an auxiliary box.'

'The original is missing?' Anderson said, sounding surprised.

'Probably lost,' the guard replied, arriving out of breath. 'Nobody has requested access down here for ages.'

Anderson took the key. 'No secondary key for SBB Thirteen?'

'Sorry, so far we're not finding keys for *any* of the rooms in the SBB. MacDonald's on it now.' The guard pulled out his radio and spoke into it. 'Bob? I'm with the chief. Any additional info yet on the key for SBB Thirteen?'

The guard's radio crackled, and a voice replied, 'Actually, yeah. It's strange. I'm seeing no entries since we computerized, but the hard logs indicate all the storage rooms in the SBB were cleaned out and abandoned more than twenty years ago. They're now listed as unused space.' He paused. 'All except for SBB Thirteen.'

Anderson grabbed the radio. 'This is the chief. What do you mean, all *except* SBB Thirteen?'

'Well, sir,' the voice replied, 'I've got a handwritten notation here that designates SBB Thirteen as "private." It was a long time ago, but it's written and initialed by the Architect himself.'

The term *Architect*, Langdon knew, was not a reference to the man who had designed the Capitol, but rather to the man who *ran* it. Similar to a building manager, the man appointed as Architect of the Capitol was in charge of everything including maintenance, restoration, security, hiring personnel, and assigning offices.

'The strange thing . . .' the voice on the radio said, 'is that the Architect's notation indicates that this "private space" was set aside for the use of Peter Solomon.'

Langdon, Sato, and Anderson all exchanged startled looks.

'I'm guessing, sir,' the voice continued, 'that Mr. Solomon has our primary key to the SBB as well as any keys to SBB Thirteen.'

Langdon could not believe his ears. *Peter has a private room in the basement of the Capitol?* He had always known Peter Solomon had secrets, but this was surprising even to Langdon.

'Okay,' Anderson said, clearly unamused. 'We're hoping to get access to SBB Thirteen specifically, so keep looking for a secondary key.'

'Will do, sir. We're also working on the digital image that you requested—'

'Thank you,' Anderson interrupted, pressing the talk button and cutting him off. 'That will be all. Send that file to Director Sato's BlackBerry as soon as you have it.'

'Understood, sir.' The radio went silent.

Anderson handed the radio back to the guard in front of them.

The guard pulled out a photocopy of a blueprint and handed it to his chief. 'Sir, the SBB is in gray, and we've notated with an X which room is SBB Thirteen, so it shouldn't be hard to find. The area is quite small.'

Anderson thanked the guard and turned his focus to the blueprint as the young man hurried off. Langdon looked on, surprised to see the astonishing number of cubicles that made up the bizarre maze beneath the U.S. Capitol.

Anderson studied the blueprint for a moment, nodded, and then stuffed it into his pocket. Turning to the door marked SBB, he raised the key, but hesitated, looking uneasy about opening it. Langdon felt similar misgivings; he had no idea what was behind this door, but he was quite certain that whatever Solomon had hidden down here, he wanted to keep private. *Very private.*

Sato cleared her throat, and Anderson got the message. The chief took a deep breath, inserted the key, and tried to turn it. The key didn't move. For a split second, Langdon felt hopeful the key was wrong. On the second try, though, the lock turned, and Anderson heaved the door open.

As the heavy door creaked outward, damp air rushed out into the corridor.

Langdon peered into the darkness but could see nothing at all.

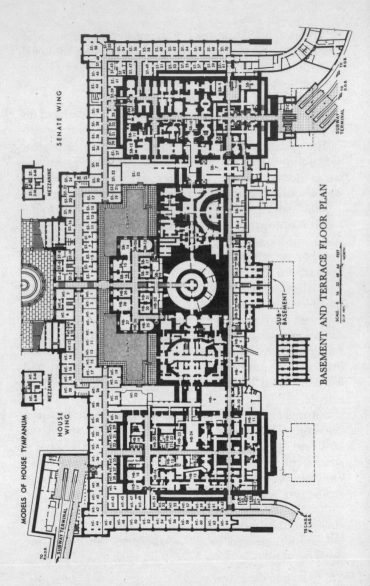

BASEMENT AND TERRACE FLOOR PLAN

SCALE: 0 16 32 48 64 FEET

C.I.F. 1971

NORTH

MODELS OF HOUSE TYMPANUM

HOUSE WING

SENATE WING

MEZZANINE

SUB-BASEMENT

SUBWAY TERMINAL

TO R.O.B.

TO R.O.B.

TO D.O.B.

TO C.H.O.B. & L.H.O.B.

'Professor,' Anderson said, glancing back at Langdon as he groped blindly for a light switch. 'To answer your question, the *S* in SBB doesn't stand for Senate. It stands for *sub*.'

'Sub?' Langdon asked, puzzled.

Anderson nodded and flicked the switch just inside the door. A single bulb illuminated an alarmingly steep staircase descending into inky blackness. 'SBB is the Capitol's subbasement.'

33

Systems security specialist Mark Zoubianis was sinking deeper into his futon and scowling at the information on his laptop screen.

What the hell kind of address is this?

His best hacking tools were entirely ineffective at breaking into the document or at unmasking Trish's mysterious IP address. Ten minutes had passed, and Zoubianis's program was still pounding away in vain at the network firewalls. They showed little hope of penetration. *No wonder they're overpaying me.* He was about to retool and try a different approach when his phone rang.

Trish, for Christ's sake, I said I'd call you. He muted the football game and answered. 'Yeah?'

'Is this Mark Zoubianis?' a man asked. 'At 357 Kingston Drive in Washington?'

Zoubianis could hear other muffled conversations in the background. *A telemarketer during the play-offs? Are they insane?* 'Let me guess, I won a week in Anguilla?'

'No,' the voice replied with no trace of humor. 'This is systems security for the Central Intelligence Agency. We would like to know why you are attempting to hack one of our classified databases?'

Three stories above the Capitol Building's sub-basement, in the wide-open spaces of the visitor center, security guard Nuñez locked the main entry doors as he did every night at this time. As he headed back across the expansive marble floors, he thought of the man in the army-surplus jacket with the tattoos.

I let him in. Nuñez wondered if he would have a job tomorrow.

As he headed toward the escalator, a sudden pounding on the outside doors caused him to turn. He squinted back toward the main entrance and saw an elderly African American man outside, rapping on the glass with his open palm and motioning to be let in.

Nuñez shook his head and pointed to his watch.

The man pounded again and stepped into the light. He was immaculately dressed in a blue suit and had close-cropped graying hair. Nuñez's pulse quickened. *Holy shit.* Even at a distance, Nuñez now recognized who this man was. He hurried back to the entrance and unlocked the door. 'I'm sorry, sir. Please, please come in.'

Warren Bellamy – Architect of the Capitol – stepped across the threshold and thanked Nuñez with a polite nod. Bellamy was lithe and slender, with an erect posture and piercing gaze that exuded the confidence of a man in full control of his surroundings. For the last twenty-five years, Bellamy had served as the supervisor of the U.S. Capitol.

'May I help you, sir?' Nuñez asked.

'Thank you, yes.' Bellamy enunciated his words with crisp precision. As a northeastern Ivy League graduate, his diction was so exacting he sounded almost British. 'I've just learned that you had an incident here this evening.' He looked deeply concerned.

'Yes, sir. It was—'

'Where's Chief Anderson?'

'Downstairs with Director Sato from the CIA's Office of Security.'

Bellamy's eyes widened with concern. 'The CIA is here?'

'Yes, sir. Director Sato arrived almost immediately after the incident.'

'Why?' Bellamy demanded.

Nuñez shrugged. *As if I was going to ask?*

Bellamy strode directly toward the escalators. 'Where are they?'

'They just went to the lower levels.' Nuñez hastened after him.

Bellamy glanced back with a look of concern. 'Downstairs? Why?'

'I don't really know – I just heard it on my radio.'

Bellamy was moving faster now. 'Take me to them right away.'

'Yes, sir.'

As the two men hurried across the open expanse, Nuñez caught a glimpse of a large golden ring on Bellamy's finger.

Nuñez pulled out his radio. 'I'll alert the chief that you're coming down.'

'No.' Bellamy's eyes flashed dangerously. 'I'd prefer to be unannounced.'

Nuñez had made some big mistakes tonight, but failing to alert Chief Anderson that the Architect was now in the building would be his last. 'Sir?' he said, uneasy. 'I think Chief Anderson would prefer—'

'You are aware that I *employ* Mr. Anderson?' Bellamy said.

Nuñez nodded.

'Then I think he would prefer you obey my wishes.'

34

Trish Dunne entered the SMSC lobby and looked up with surprise. The guest waiting here looked nothing like the usual bookish, flannel-clad doctors who entered this building – those of anthropology, oceanography, geology, and other scientific fields. Quite to the contrary, Dr. Abaddon looked almost aristocratic in his impeccably tailored suit. He was tall, with a broad torso, well-tanned face, and perfectly combed blond hair that gave Trish the impression he was more accustomed to luxuries than to laboratories. 'Dr. Abaddon, I presume?' Trish said, extending her hand.

The man looked uncertain, but he took Trish's plump hand in his broad palm. 'I'm sorry. And *you* are?'

'Trish Dunne,' she replied. 'I'm Katherine's assistant. She asked me to escort you back to her lab.'

'Oh, I see.' The man smiled now. 'Very nice to meet you, Trish. My apologies if I seemed confused. I was under the impression Katherine was here alone this evening.' He motioned down the hall. 'But I'm all yours. Lead the way.'

Despite the man's quick recovery, Trish had seen the flash of disappointment in his eyes. She now suspected the motive for Katherine's secrecy earlier about Dr. Abaddon. *A budding romance, maybe?* Katherine never discussed her social life, but her visitor was attractive and well-groomed, and although younger than Katherine, he clearly came from her world of wealth and privilege. Nonetheless, whatever Dr. Abaddon had imagined tonight's visit might entail, Trish's presence did not seem to be part of his plan.

At the lobby's security checkpoint, a lone guard quickly pulled off his headphones, and Trish could hear the Redskins game blaring. The guard put Dr. Abaddon through the usual visitor routine of metal detectors and temporary security badges.

'Who's winning?' Dr. Abaddon said affably as he emptied his pockets of a cell phone, some keys, and a cigarette lighter.

'Skins by three,' the guard said, sounding eager to get back. 'Helluva game.'

'Mr. Solomon will be arriving shortly,' Trish told the guard. 'Would you please send him back to the lab once he arrives?'

'Will do.' The guard gave an appreciative wink as they passed through. 'Thanks for the heads-up. I'll look busy.'

Trish's comment had been not only for the benefit of the guard but also to remind Dr. Abaddon that Trish was not the only one intruding on his private evening here with Katherine.

'So how do you know Katherine?' Trish asked, glancing up at the mysterious guest.

Dr. Abaddon chuckled. 'Oh, it's a long story. We've been working on something together.'

Understood, Trish thought. *None of my business.*

'This is an amazing facility,' Abaddon said, glancing around as they moved down the massive corridor. 'I've never actually been here.'

His airy tone was becoming more genial with every step, and Trish noticed he was actively taking it all in. In the bright lights of the hallway, she also noticed that his face looked like he had a fake tan. *Odd.* Nonetheless, as they navigated the deserted corridors, Trish gave him a general synopsis of the SMSC's purpose and function, including the various pods and their contents.

The visitor looked impressed. 'Sounds like this place has a treasure trove of priceless artifacts. I would have expected guards posted everywhere.'

'No need,' Trish said, motioning to the row of fish-eye lenses lining the ceiling high above. 'Security here is automated. Every inch of this corridor is recorded twenty-four/seven, and this corridor is the spine of the facility. It's impossible to access any of the rooms off this corridor without a key card and PIN number.'

'Efficient use of cameras.'

'Knock on wood, we've never had a theft. Then again, this is not the kind of museum anyone would rob – there's not much call on the black market for extinct flowers, Inuit kayaks, or giant squid carcasses.'

Dr. Abaddon chuckled. 'I suppose you're right.'

'Our biggest security threat is rodents and insects.' Trish explained how the building prevented insect infestations by freezing all SMSC refuse and also by an architectural feature called a 'dead zone' – an inhospitable compartment between double walls, which surrounded the entire building like a sheath.

'Incredible,' Abaddon said. 'So, where is Katherine and Peter's lab?'

'Pod Five,' Trish said. 'It's all the way at the end of this hallway.'

Abaddon halted suddenly, spinning to his right, toward a small window. 'My word! Will you look at *that*!'

Trish laughed. 'Yeah, that's Pod Three. They call it Wet Pod.'

'Wet?' Abaddon said, face pressed to the glass.

'There are over three thousand gallons of liquid ethanol in there. Remember the giant squid carcass I mentioned earlier?'

'That's the squid?!' Dr. Abaddon turned from the window momentarily, his eyes wide. 'It's huge!'

'A female Architeuthis,' Trish said. 'She's over forty feet.'

Dr. Abaddon, apparently enraptured by the sight of the squid, seemed unable to pull his eyes away from the glass. For a moment, the grown man reminded Trish of a little boy at a pet-store window, wishing he could go in and see a puppy. Five seconds later, he was still staring longingly through the window.

'Okay, okay,' Trish finally said, laughing as she inserted her key card and typed her PIN number. 'Come on. I'll show you the squid.'

As Mal'akh stepped into the dimly lit world of Pod 3, he scanned the walls for security cameras. Katherine's pudgy little assistant began rattling on about the specimens in this room. Mal'akh tuned her out. He had no interest whatsoever in giant squids. His only interest was in using this dark, private space to solve an unexpected problem.

35

The wooden stairs descending to the Capitol's sub-basement were as steep and shallow as any stairs Langdon had ever traversed. His breathing was faster now, and his lungs felt tight. The air down here was cold and damp, and Langdon couldn't help but flash on a similar set of stairs he had taken a few years back into the Vatican's Necropolis. *The City of the Dead.*

Ahead of him, Anderson led the way with his flashlight. Behind Langdon, Sato followed closely, her tiny hands occasionally pressing into Langdon's back. *I'm going as fast as I can.* Langdon inhaled deeply, trying to ignore the cramped walls on either side of him. There was barely room for his shoulders on this staircase, and his daybag now scraped down the sidewall.

'Maybe you should leave your bag above,' Sato offered behind him.

'I'm fine,' Langdon replied, having no intention of letting it out of his sight. He pictured Peter's little package and could not begin to imagine how it might relate to anything in the subbasement of the U.S. Capitol.

'Just a few more steps,' Anderson said. 'Almost there.'

The group had descended into darkness, moving beyond the reach of the staircase's lone lightbulb. When Langdon stepped off the final wooden tread, he could feel that the floor beneath his feet was dirt.

Journey to the center of the Earth. Sato stepped down behind him.

Anderson now raised his beam, examining their surroundings. The subbasement was less of a basement than it was an ultranarrow corridor that ran perpendicular to the stairs. Anderson shone his light left and then right, and Langdon could see the passage was only about fifty feet long and lined on both sides with small wooden doors. The doors abutted one another so closely that the rooms behind them could not have been more than ten feet wide.

ACME Storage meets the Catacombs of Domatilla, Langdon thought as Anderson consulted the blueprint. The tiny section depicting the subbasement was marked with an X to show the location of SBB13. Langdon couldn't help but notice that the layout was identical to a fourteen-tomb mausoleum – seven vaults facing seven vaults – with one removed to accommodate the stairs they had just descended. *Thirteen in all.*

He suspected America's 'thirteen' conspiracy theorists would have a field day if they knew there were exactly *thirteen* storage rooms buried beneath the U.S. Capitol. Some found it suspicious that the Great Seal of the United States had thirteen stars, thirteen arrows, thirteen pyramid steps, thirteen shield stripes, thirteen olive leaves, thirteen olives, thirteen letters in *annuit coeptis,* thirteen letters in *e pluribus unum,* and on and on.

'It *does* look abandoned,' Anderson said, shining the beam into the chamber directly in front of them. The heavy wooden door was wide open. The shaft of light illuminated a narrow stone chamber – about ten feet wide by some thirty feet deep – like a dead-end hallway to nowhere. The chamber contained nothing more than a couple of old collapsed wooden boxes and some crumpled packing paper.

Anderson shone his light on a copper plate mounted on the door. The plate was covered with verdigris, but the old marking was legible:

SBB IV

'SBB Four,' Anderson said.

'Which one is SBB Thirteen?' Sato asked, faint wisps of steam curling out of her mouth in the cold subterranean air.

Anderson turned the beam toward the south end of the corridor. 'Down there.'

Langdon peered down the narrow passage and shivered, feeling a light sweat despite the cold.

As they moved through the phalanx of doorways, all of the rooms looked the same, doors ajar, apparently abandoned long ago. When they reached the end of the line, Anderson turned to his right, raising the beam to peer into room SBB13. The flashlight beam, however, was impeded by a heavy wooden door.

Unlike the others, the door to SBB13 was closed.

This final door looked exactly like the others – heavy hinges, iron handle, and a copper number plate encrusted with green. The seven characters on the number plate were the same characters on Peter's palm upstairs.

Please tell me the door is locked, Langdon thought.

Sato spoke without hesitation. 'Try the door.'

The police chief looked uneasy, but he reached out, grasped the heavy iron handle, and pushed down on it. The handle didn't budge. He shone the light now, illuminating a heavy, old-fashioned lock plate and keyhole.

'Try the master key,' Sato said.

Anderson produced the main key from the entry door upstairs, but it was not even close to fitting.

'Am I mistaken,' Sato said, her tone sarcastic, 'or shouldn't Security have access to every corner of a building in case of emergency?'

Anderson exhaled and looked back at Sato. 'Ma'am, my men are checking for a secondary key, but—'

'Shoot the lock,' she said, nodding toward the key plate beneath the lever.

Langdon's pulse leaped.

Anderson cleared his throat, sounding uneasy. 'Ma'am, I'm waiting for news on a secondary key. I am not sure I'm comfortable blasting our way into—'

'Perhaps you'd be more comfortable in prison for obstructing a CIA investigation?'

Anderson looked incredulous. After a long beat, he reluctantly handed the light to Sato and unsnapped his holster.

'Wait!' Langdon said, no longer able to stand idly by. 'Think about it. Peter gave up his right hand rather than reveal whatever might be behind this door. Are you sure we want to do this? Unlocking this door is essentially complying with the demands of a terrorist.'

'Do you want to get Peter Solomon back?' Sato asked.

'Of course, but—'

'Then I suggest you do exactly what his captor is requesting.'

'Unlock an ancient portal? You think *this* is the portal?'

Sato shone the light in Langdon's face. 'Professor, I have no idea what the hell this is. Whether it's a storage unit or the secret entrance to an ancient pyramid, I intend to open it. Do I make myself clear?'

Langdon squinted into the light and finally nodded.

Sato lowered the beam and redirected it at the door's antique key plate. 'Chief? Go ahead.'

Still looking averse to the plan, Anderson extracted his sidearm very, very slowly, gazing down at it with uncertainty.

'Oh, for God's sake!' Sato's tiny hands shot out, and she grabbed the weapon from him. She stuffed the flashlight into his now empty palm. 'Shine the damned light.' She handled the gun with the confidence of someone who had trained with weapons, wasting no time turning off the pistol's safety, cocking the weapon, and aiming at the lock.

'*Wait!*' Langdon yelled, but he was too late.

The gun roared three times.

Langdon's eardrums felt like they had exploded. *Is she insane?!* The gunshots in the tiny space had been deafening.

Anderson also looked shaken, his hand wavering a bit as he shone the flashlight on the bullet-riddled door.

The lock mechanism was now in tatters, the wood surrounding it entirely pulverized. The lock had released, the door now having fallen ajar.

Sato extended the pistol and pressed the tip of the barrel against the door, giving it a push. The door swung fully into the blackness beyond.

Langdon peered in but could see nothing in the darkness. *What in the world is that smell?* An unusual, fetid odor wafted out of the darkness.

Anderson stepped into the doorway and shone the light on the floor, tracing carefully down the length of the barren dirt floor. This room was like the others – a long, narrow space. The sidewalls were rugged stone, giving the room the feel of an ancient prison cell. *But that smell . . .*

'There's nothing here,' Anderson said, moving the beam farther down the chamber floor. Finally, as the beam reached the end of the floor, he raised it up to illuminate the chamber's farthest wall.

'My God . . . !' Anderson shouted.

Everyone saw it and jumped back.

Langdon stared in disbelief at the deepest recess of the chamber.

To his horror, something was staring back.

36

'What in God's name . . . ?' At the threshold of SBB13, Anderson fumbled with his light and retreated a step.

Langdon also recoiled, as did Sato, who looked startled for the first time all night.

Sato aimed the gun at the back wall and motioned for Anderson to shine the light again. Anderson raised the light. The beam was dim by the time it reached the far wall, but the light was enough to illuminate the shape of a pallid and ghostly face, staring back at them through lifeless sockets.

A human skull.

The skull sat atop a rickety wooden desk positioned against the rear wall of the chamber. Two human leg bones sat beside the skull, along with a collection of other items that were meticulously arranged on the desk in shrinelike fashion – an antique hourglass, a crystal flask, a candle, two saucers of pale powder, and a sheet of paper. Propped against the wall beside the desk stood the fearsome shape of a long scythe, its curved blade as familiar as that of the grim reaper.

Sato stepped into the room. 'Well, now . . . it appears Peter Solomon keeps more secrets than I imagined.'

Anderson nodded, inching after her. 'Talk about skeletons in your closet.' He raised the light and surveyed the rest of the empty chamber. 'And that *smell*?' he added, crinkling his nose. 'What is it?'

'Sulfur,' Langdon replied evenly behind them. 'There should be two saucers on the desk. The saucer on the right will contain salt. And the other sulfur.'

Sato wheeled in disbelief. 'How the hell would you know *that*?!'

'Because, ma'am, there are rooms exactly like this all over the world.'

One story above the subbasement, Capitol security guard Nuñez escorted the Architect of the Capitol, Warren Bellamy, down the long hallway that ran the length of the eastern basement. Nuñez could have sworn that he had just heard three gunshots down here, muffled and underground. *There's no way.*

'Subbasement door is open,' Bellamy said, squinting down the hallway at a door that stood ajar in the distance.

Strange evening indeed, Nuñez thought. *Nobody goes down there.* 'I'll be glad to find out what's going on,' he said, reaching for his radio.

'Go back to your duties,' Bellamy said. 'I'm fine from here.'

Nuñez shifted uneasily. 'You sure?'

Warren Bellamy stopped, placing a firm hand on Nuñez's shoulder. 'Son, I've worked here for twenty-five years. I think I can find my way.'

37

Mal'akh had seen some eerie spaces in his life, but few rivaled the unearthly world of Pod 3. *Wet Pod.* The massive room looked as if a mad scientist had taken over a Walmart and packed every aisle and shelf with specimen jars of all shapes and sizes. Lit like a photographic darkroom, the space was bathed in a reddish haze of 'safelight' that emanated from beneath the shelves, filtering upward and illuminating the ethanol-filled containers. The clinical smell of preservative chemicals was nauseating.

'This pod houses over twenty thousand species,' the chubby girl was saying. 'Fish, rodents, mammals, reptiles.'

'All *dead*, I hope?' Mal'akh asked, making a show of sounding nervous.

The girl laughed. 'Yes, yes. All very much dead. I'll admit, I didn't dare come in for at least six months after I started work.'

Mal'akh could understand why. Everywhere he looked there were specimen jars of dead life-forms – salamanders, jellyfish, rats, bugs, birds, and other things he could not begin to identify. As if this collection were not unsettling enough on its own, the hazy red safelights that protected these photosensitive specimens from long-term light exposure gave the visitor the feeling he was standing inside a giant aquarium, where lifeless creatures were somehow congregating to watch from the shadows.

'That's a coelacanth,' the girl said, pointing to a big Plexiglas container that held the ugliest fish Mal'akh had ever seen. 'They were thought to be extinct with the dinosaurs, but this was caught off Africa a few years back and donated to the Smithsonian.'

Lucky you, Mal'akh thought, barely listening. He was busy scanning the walls for security cameras. He saw only one – trained on the entry door – not surprising, considering that entrance was probably the only way in.

'And here is what you wanted to see . . .' she said, leading him to the giant tank he had seen from the window. 'Our longest specimen.' She swept her arm out over the vile creature like a game-show host displaying a new car. 'Architeuthis.'

The squid tank looked like a series of glass phone booths had been laid on their sides and fused end to end. Within the long, clear Plexiglas coffin hovered a sickeningly pale and amorphous shape. Mal'akh gazed down at the bulbous, saclike head and its basketball-size eyes. 'Almost makes your coelacanth look handsome,' he said.

'Wait till you see her lit.'

Trish flipped back the long lid of the tank. Ethanol fumes wafted out as she reached down into the tank and flipped a switch just above the liquid line. A string of fluorescent lights flickered to life along the entire base of the tank. Architeuthis was now shining in all her glory – a colossal head attached to a slithery mass of decaying tentacles and razor-sharp suckers.

She began talking about how Architeuthis could beat a sperm whale in a fight.

Mal'akh heard only empty prattling.

The time had come.

Trish Dunne always felt a bit uneasy in Pod 3, but the chill that had just run through her felt different.

Visceral. Primal.

She tried to ignore it, but it grew quickly now, clawing deeply at her. Although Trish could not seem to place the source of her anxiety, her gut was clearly telling her it was time to leave.

'Anyhow, that's the squid,' she said, reaching into the tank and turning off the display light. 'We should probably get back to Katherine's—'

A broad palm clamped hard over her mouth, yanking her head back. Instantly, a powerful arm was wrapped around her torso, pinning her against a rock-hard chest. For a split second, Trish went numb with shock.

Then came the terror.

The man groped across her chest, grabbing her key

card and yanking down hard. The cord burned the back of her neck before snapping. The key card fell on the floor at their feet. She fought, trying to twist away, but she was no match for the man's size and strength. She tried to scream, but his hand remained tightly across her mouth. He leaned down and placed his mouth next to her ear, whispering, 'When I take my hand off your mouth, you will not scream, is that clear?'

She nodded vigorously, her lungs burning for air. *I can't breathe!*

The man removed his hand from her mouth, and Trish gasped, inhaling deeply.

'Let me go!' she demanded, breathless. 'What the hell are you doing?'

'Tell me your PIN number,' the man said.

Trish felt totally at a loss. *Katherine! Help! Who is this man?!* 'Security can see you!' she said, knowing full well·they were out of range of the cameras. *And nobody is watching anyway.*

'Your PIN number,' the man repeated. 'The one that matches your key card.'

An icy fear churned in her gut, and Trish spun violently, wriggling an arm free and twisting around, clawing at the man's eyes. Her fingers hit flesh and raked down one cheek. Four dark gashes opened on his flesh where she scratched him. Then she realized the dark stripes on his flesh were not blood. The man was wearing makeup, which she had just scratched off, revealing dark tattoos hidden underneath.

Who is this monster?!

With seemingly superhuman strength, the man spun her around and hoisted her up, pushing her out over the open squid tank, her face now over the ethanol. The fumes burned her nostrils.

'What is your PIN number?' he repeated.

Her eyes burned, and she could see the pale flesh of the squid submerged beneath her face.

'Tell me,' he said, pushing her face closer to the surface. 'What is it?'

Her throat was burning now. 'Zero-eight-zero-four!' she blurted, barely able to breathe. 'Let me go! Zero-eight-zero-four!'

'If you're lying,' he said, pushing down farther, her hair in the ethanol now.

'I'm not lying!' she said, coughing. 'August 4! It's my birthday!'

'Thank you, Trish.'

His powerful hands clasped her head tighter, and a crushing force rammed her downward, plunging her face into the tank. Searing pain burned her eyes. The man pressed down harder, driving her whole head under the ethanol. Trish felt her face pressing into the fleshy head of the squid.

Summoning all of her strength, she bucked violently, arching backward, trying to pull her head out of the tank. But the powerful hands did not budge.

I have to breathe!

She remained submerged, straining not to open her eyes or mouth. Her lungs burned as she fought the powerful urge to breathe in. *No! Don't!* But Trish's inhalation reflex finally took over.

Her mouth flew open, and her lungs expanded violently, attempting to suck in the oxygen that her body craved. In a searing rush, a wave of ethanol poured into her mouth. As the chemicals gushed down her throat into her lungs, Trish felt a pain like nothing she had ever imagined possible. Mercifully, it lasted only a few seconds before her world went black.

Mal'akh stood beside the tank, catching his breath and surveying the damage.

The lifeless woman lay slumped over the rim of the tank, her face still submerged in ethanol. Seeing her there, Mal'akh flashed on the only other woman he had ever killed.

Isabel Solomon.

Long ago. Another life.

Mal'akh gazed down now at the woman's flaccid corpse. He grabbed her ample hips and lifted with his legs, hoisting her up, pushing forward, until she began to slide over the rim of the squid tank. Trish Dunne slithered headfirst down into the ethanol. The rest of her body followed, sloshing down. Gradually, the ripples subsided, leaving the woman hovering limp over the huge sea creature. As her clothing got heavier, she began to sink, slipping into the darkness. Bit by bit, Trish Dunne's body settled on top of the great beast.

Mal'akh wiped his hands and replaced the Plexiglas lid, sealing the tank.

Wet Pod has a new specimen.

He retrieved Trish's key card from the floor and slipped it in his pocket: *0804.*

When Mal'akh had first seen Trish in the lobby, he'd seen a liability. Then he'd realized her key card and password were his insurance. If Katherine's data-storage room was as secure as Peter had implied, then Mal'akh was anticipating some challenges persuading Katherine to unlock it for him. *I now have my own set of keys.* He was pleased to know he would no longer have to waste time bending Katherine to his will.

As Mal'akh stood up straight, he saw his own reflection in the window and could tell his makeup was badly mangled. It didn't matter anymore. By the time Katherine put it all together, it would be too late.

38

'This room is Masonic?' Sato demanded, turning from the skull and staring at Langdon in the darkness.

Langdon nodded calmly. 'It's called a Chamber of Reflection. These rooms are designed as cold, austere places in which a Mason can reflect on his own mortality. By meditating on the inevitability of death, a Mason gains a valuable perspective on the fleeting nature of life.'

Sato looked around the eerie space, apparently not convinced. 'This is some kind of *meditation* room?'

'Essentially, yes. These chambers always incorporate the same symbols – skull and crossed bones, scythe, hourglass, sulfur, salt, blank paper, a candle, et cetera. The symbols of death inspire Masons to ponder how better to lead their lives while on this earth.'

'It looks like a death shrine,' Anderson said.

That's kind of the point. 'Most of my symbology students have the same reaction at first.' Langdon often assigned them *Symbols of Freemasonry* by Beresniak, which contained beautiful photos of Chambers of Reflection.

'And your students,' Sato demanded, 'don't find it unnerving that Masons meditate with skulls and scythes?'

'No more unnerving than Christians praying at the feet of a man nailed to a cross, or Hindus chanting in front of a four-armed elephant named Ganesh. Misunderstanding a culture's symbols is a common root of prejudice.'

Sato turned away, apparently in no mood for a lecture. She moved toward the table of artifacts. Anderson tried to light her way with the flashlight, but the beam was beginning to dim. He tapped the heel of the light and coaxed it to burn a little brighter.

As the threesome moved deeper into the narrow space, the pungent tang of sulfur filled Langdon's nostrils. The subbasement was damp, and the humidity in the air was activating the sulfur in the bowl. Sato arrived at the table and stared down at the skull and accompanying objects. Anderson joined her, doing his best to light the desk with the weakening beam of his flashlight.

Sato examined everything on the table and then placed her hands on her hips, sighing. 'What is all this junk?'

The artifacts in this room, Langdon knew, were carefully selected and arranged. 'Symbols of trans-formation,' he told her, feeling confined as he inched forward and joined them at the table. 'The skull, or *caput mortuum*, represents man's final transformation through decay; it's a reminder that we all shed our mortal flesh one day. The sulfur and salt are alchemical catalysts that facilitate transformation. The hourglass represents the transformational power of time.' He motioned to the unlit candle. 'And this candle represents the formative primordial fire and the awakening of man from his ignorant slumber – transformation through illumination.'

'And . . . *that*?' Sato asked, pointing into the corner.

Anderson swung his dimming flashlight beam to the giant scythe that leaned against the back wall.

'Not a death symbol, as most assume,' Langdon said. 'The scythe is actually a symbol of the transformative nourishment of nature – the reaping of nature's gifts.'

Sato and Anderson fell silent, apparently trying to process their bizarre surroundings.

Langdon wanted nothing more than to get out of the place. 'I realize this room may seem unusual,' he told them, 'but there's nothing to see here; it's really quite normal. A lot of Masonic lodges have chambers exactly like this one.'

'But this is not a Masonic lodge!' Anderson declared. 'It's the U.S. Capitol, and I'd like to know what the hell this room is doing in my building.'

'Sometimes Masons set aside rooms like this in their offices or private homes as meditation spaces. It is not uncommon.' Langdon knew a heart surgeon in Boston who had converted a closet in his office into a Masonic Chamber of Reflection so he could ponder mortality before going into surgery.

Sato looked troubled. 'You're saying Peter Solomon comes down here to reflect on death?'

'I really don't know,' Langdon said sincerely. 'Maybe he created it as a sanctuary for his Masonic brothers who work in the building, giving them a spiritual sanctuary away from the chaos of the material world . . . a place for a powerful lawmaker to reflect before making decisions that affect his fellow man.'

'Lovely sentiment,' Sato said, her tone sarcastic, 'but I have a feeling Americans might have a problem with

221

their leaders praying in closets with scythes and skulls.'

Well, they shouldn't, Langdon thought, imagining how different a world it might be if more leaders took time to ponder the finality of death before racing off to war.

Sato pursed her lips and carefully surveyed all four corners of the candlelit chamber. 'There must be *something* in here besides human bones and bowls of chemicals, Professor. Someone transported you all the way from your home in Cambridge to be in this precise room.'

Langdon clutched his daybag to his side, still unable to imagine how the package he carried might relate to this chamber. 'Ma'am, I'm sorry, but I don't see anything out of the ordinary here.' Langdon hoped that now at last they could get to the business of trying to find Peter.

Anderson's light flickered again, and Sato spun on him, her temper starting to show. 'For Christ's sake, is it too much to ask?' She plunged her hand into her pocket and yanked out a cigarette lighter. Striking her thumb on the flint, she held out the flame and lit the desk's lone candle. The wick sputtered and then caught, spreading a ghostly luminescence throughout the constricted space. Long shadows raked the stone walls. As the flame grew brighter, an unexpected sight materialized before them.

'Look!' Anderson said, pointing.

In the candlelight, they could now see a faded patch of graffiti – seven capital letters scrawled across the rear wall.

VITRIOL

'An odd choice of word,' Sato said as the candlelight cast a frightening skull-shaped silhouette across the letters.

'Actually, it's an acronym,' Langdon said. 'It's written on the rear wall of most chambers like this as a shorthand for the Masonic meditative mantra: *Visita interiora terrae, rectificando invenies occultum lapidem.*'

Sato eyed him, looking almost impressed. 'Meaning?'

'Visit the interior of the earth, and by rectifying, you will find the hidden stone.'

Sato's gaze sharpened. 'Does the hidden stone have any connection to a hidden pyramid?'

Langdon shrugged, not wanting to encourage the comparison. 'Those who enjoy fantasizing about hidden pyramids in Washington would tell you that *occultum lapidem* refers to the stone pyramid, yes. Others will tell you it's a reference to the Philosopher's Stone – a substance alchemists believed could bring them everlasting life or turn lead into gold. Others claim it's a reference to the Holy of Holies, a hidden stone chamber at the core of the Great Temple. Some say it's a Christian reference to the hidden teachings of Saint Peter – the Rock. Every esoteric tradition interprets "the stone" in its own way, but invariably the *occultum lapidem* is a source of power and enlightenment.'

Anderson cleared his throat. 'Is it possible Solomon lied to this guy? Maybe he told him there was something down here . . . and there really isn't.'

Langdon was having similar thoughts.

Without warning, the candle flame flickered, as if caught by a draft. It dimmed for a moment and then recovered, burning brightly again.

'That's odd,' Anderson said. 'I hope no one closed the door upstairs.' He strode out of the chamber into the darkness of the hallway. 'Hello?'

Langdon barely noticed him leave. His gaze had been drawn suddenly to the rear wall. *What just happened?*

'Did you see that?' Sato asked, also staring with alarm at the wall.

Langdon nodded, his pulse quickening. *What did I just see?*

A moment earlier, the rear wall seemed to have shimmered, as if a ripple of energy had passed through it.

Anderson now strode back into the room. 'No one's out there.' As he entered, the wall shimmered again. 'Holy shit!' he exclaimed, jumping back.

All three stood mute for a long moment, staring in unison at the back wall. Langdon felt another chill run through him as he realized what they were seeing. He reached out tentatively, until his fingertips touched the rear surface of the chamber. 'It's not a wall,' he said.

Anderson and Sato stepped closer, peering intently.

'It's a canvas,' Langdon said.

'But it billowed,' Sato said quickly.

Yes, in a very strange way. Langdon examined the surface more closely. The sheen on the canvas had refracted the candlelight in a startling manner because the canvas had just billowed *away* from the room . . . fluttering backward *through* the plane of the rear wall.

Langdon extended his outstretched fingers very gently, pressing the canvas backward. Startled, he yanked his hand back. *There's an opening!*

'Pull it aside,' Sato ordered.

Langdon's heart pounded wildly now. He reached

up and clutched the edge of the canvas banner, slowly pulling the fabric to one side. He stared in disbelief at what lay hidden behind it. *My God.*

Sato and Anderson stood in stunned silence as they looked through the opening in the rear wall.

Finally, Sato spoke. 'It appears we've just found our pyramid.'

39

Robert Langdon stared at the opening in the rear wall of the chamber. Hidden behind the canvas banner, a perfectly square hole had been hollowed out of the wall. The opening, about three feet across, appeared to have been created by removing a series of bricks. For a moment, in the darkness, Langdon thought the hole was a window to a room beyond.

Now he saw it was not.

The opening extended only a few feet into the wall before terminating. Like a rough-hewn cubbyhole, the recessed niche reminded Langdon of a museum alcove designed to hold a statuette. Fittingly, this niche displayed one small object.

About nine inches tall, it was a piece of carved, solid granite. The surface was elegant and smooth with four polished sides that shone in the candlelight.

Langdon could not fathom what it was doing here. *A stone pyramid?*

'From your look of surprise,' Sato said, sounding self-satisfied, 'I take it this object is not *typical* within a Chamber of Reflection?'

Langdon shook his head.

'Then perhaps you would like to reassess your previous claims regarding the legend of a Masonic Pyramid hidden in Washington?' Her tone now was almost smug.

'Director,' Langdon replied instantly, 'this little pyramid is *not* the Masonic Pyramid.'

'So it is merely coincidence that we found a pyramid hidden at the heart of the U.S. Capitol in a secret chamber belonging to a Masonic leader?'

Langdon rubbed his eyes and tried to think clearly. 'Ma'am, this pyramid doesn't resemble the myth in any way. The Masonic Pyramid is described as enormous, with a tip forged of solid gold.'

Moreover, Langdon knew, this little pyramid – with its flat top – was not even a *true* pyramid. Without its tip, this was another symbol entirely. Known as an Unfinished Pyramid, it was a symbolic reminder that man's ascent to his full human potential was always a work in progress. Though few realized it, this symbol was the most widely published symbol on earth. *Over twenty billion in print.* Adorning every one-dollar bill in circulation, the Unfinished Pyramid waited patiently for its shining capstone, which hovered above it as a reminder of America's yet-unfulfilled destiny and the work yet to be done, both as a country and as individuals.

'Lift it down,' Sato said to Anderson, motioning to the pyramid. 'I want a closer look.' She began making room on the desk by shoving the skull and crossed bones to one side with no reverence whatsoever.

Langdon was starting to feel like they were common grave robbers, desecrating a personal shrine.

Anderson maneuvered past Langdon, reached into

the niche, and clamped his large palms on either side of the pyramid. Then, barely able to lift at this awkward angle, he slid the pyramid toward him and lowered it with a hard thud onto the wooden desk. He stepped back to give Sato room.

The director repositioned the candle close to the pyramid and studied its polished surface. Slowly, she ran her tiny fingers over it, examining every inch of the flat top, and then the sides. She wrapped her hands around to feel the back, then frowned in apparent disappointment. 'Professor, earlier you said the Masonic Pyramid was constructed to protect secret information.'

'That's the legend, yes.'

'So, hypothetically speaking, if Peter's captor believed *this* was the Masonic Pyramid, he would believe it contained powerful information.'

Langdon nodded, exasperated. 'Yes, although even if he found this information, he probably would not be able to *read* it. According to legend, the contents of the pyramid are encoded, making them indecipherable . . . except to the most worthy.'

'I beg your pardon?'

Despite Langdon's growing impatience, he replied with an even tone. 'Mythological treasures are *always* protected by tests of worthiness. As you may recall, in the legend of the Sword in the Stone, the stone refuses to give up the sword except to Arthur, who was spiritually prepared to wield the sword's awesome power. The Masonic Pyramid is based on the same idea. In *this* case, the information is the treasure, and it is said to be written in an encoded language – a mystical tongue of lost words – legible only to the worthy.'

A faint smile crossed Sato's lips. 'That may explain why you were summoned here tonight.'

'I'm sorry?'

Calmly, Sato rotated the pyramid in place, turning it a full 180 degrees. The pyramid's fourth side now shone in the candlelight.

Robert Langdon stared at it with surprise.

'It appears,' Sato said, 'that someone believes you're worthy.'

40

What's taking Trish so long?

Katherine Solomon checked her watch again. She'd forgotten to warn Dr. Abaddon about the bizarre commute to her lab, but she couldn't imagine the darkness had slowed them down this much. *They should have arrived by now.*

Katherine walked over to the exit and heaved open the lead-lined door, staring out into the void. She listened for a moment, but heard nothing.

'Trish?' she called out, her voice swallowed by the darkness.

Silence.

Puzzled, she closed the door, took out her cell phone, and called the lobby. 'This is Katherine. Is Trish out there?'

'No, ma'am,' the lobby guard said. 'She and your guest headed back about ten minutes ago.'

'Really? I don't think they're even inside Pod Five yet.'

'Hold on. I'll check.' Katherine could hear the guard's fingers clicking on his computer keyboard. 'You're right. According to Ms. Dunne's key-card logs, she has not yet opened the Pod Five door. Her last access event was about eight minutes ago . . . at Pod Three. I guess she's giving your guest a little tour on his way in.'

Katherine frowned. *Apparently.* The news was a bit odd, but at least she knew Trish wouldn't be long in Pod 3. *The smell in there is terrible.* 'Thanks. Has my brother arrived yet?'

'No, ma'am, not yet.'

'Thank you.'

As Katherine hung up, she felt an unexpected twinge of trepidation. The uneasy feeling made her pause, but only for a moment. It was the same exact disquiet she'd felt earlier when she stepped into Dr. Abaddon's house. Embarrassingly, her feminine intuition had failed her there. Badly.

It's nothing, Katherine told herself.

41

Robert Langdon studied the stone pyramid. *This isn't possible.*

'An ancient encoded language,' Sato said without looking up. 'Tell me, does this qualify?'

On the newly exposed face of the pyramid, a series of sixteen characters was precisely engraved into the smooth stone.

Beside Langdon, Anderson's mouth now gaped open, mirroring Langdon's own shock. The security chief looked like he had just seen some kind of alien keypad.

'Professor?' Sato said. 'I assume you can read this?'

Langdon turned. 'Why would you assume that?'

'Because you were *brought* here, Professor. You were chosen. This inscription appears to be a code of some sort, and considering your reputation, it seems obvious to me that you were brought here to decipher it.'

Langdon had to admit that after his experiences in Rome and Paris, he'd received a steady flow of requests asking for his help deciphering some of history's great unsolved codes – the Phaistos Disk, the Dorabella Cipher, the mysterious Voynich Manuscript.

Sato ran her finger over the inscription. 'Can you tell me the meaning of these icons?'

They're not icons, Langdon thought. *They're symbols.* The language was one he had recognized immediately – an encrypted cipher language from the seventeenth century. Langdon knew very well how to break it. 'Ma'am,' he said, feeling hesitant, 'this pyramid is Peter's *private* property.'

'Private or not, if this code is indeed the reason you

were brought to Washington, I am not giving you a choice in the matter. I want to know what it says.'

Sato's BlackBerry pinged loudly, and she yanked the device from her pocket, studying the incoming message for several moments. Langdon was amazed that the Capitol Building's internal wireless network provided service this far down.

Sato grunted and raised her eyebrows, giving Langdon an odd look.

'Chief Anderson?' she said, turning to him. 'A word in private, if I may?' The director motioned for Anderson to join her, and they disappeared into the pitch-black hallway, leaving Langdon alone in the flickering candlelight of Peter's Chamber of Reflection.

Chief Anderson wondered when this night would end. *A severed hand in my Rotunda? A death shrine in my basement? Bizarre engravings on a stone pyramid?* Somehow, the Redskins game no longer felt significant.

As he followed Sato into the darkness of the hall, Anderson flicked on his flashlight. The beam was weak but better than nothing. Sato led him down the hall a few yards, out of sight of Langdon.

'Have a look at this,' she whispered, handing Anderson her BlackBerry.

Anderson took the device and squinted at the illuminated screen. It displayed a black-and-white image – the X-ray of Langdon's bag that Anderson had requested be sent to Sato. As in all X-rays, the objects of greatest density appeared in the brightest white. In Langdon's bag, a lone item outshone everything else. Obviously extremely dense, the object glowed like a dazzling jewel in a murky jumble of other items. Its shape was unmistakable.

He's been carrying that all night? Anderson looked over at Sato in surprise. 'Why didn't Langdon mention this?'

'Damned good question,' Sato whispered.

'The shape . . . it can't be coincidence.'

'No,' Sato said, her tone angry now. 'I would say not.'

A faint rustle in the corridor drew Anderson's attention. Startled, he pointed his flashlight down the black passageway. The dying beam revealed only a deserted corridor, lined with open doors.

'Hello?' Anderson said. 'Is somebody there?'

Silence.

Sato gave him an odd look, apparently having heard nothing.

Anderson listened a moment longer and then shook it off. *I've got to get out of here.*

Alone in the candlelit chamber, Langdon ran his fingers over the sharply carved edges of the pyramid's engraving. He was curious to know what the message said, and yet he was not about to intrude on Peter Solomon's privacy any more than they already had. *And why would this lunatic care about this small pyramid anyway?*

'We have a problem, Professor,' Sato's voice declared loudly behind him. 'I've just received a new piece of information, and I've had enough of your lies.'

Langdon turned to see the OS director marching in,

BlackBerry in hand and fire in her eyes. Taken aback, Langdon looked to Anderson for help, but the chief was now standing guard at the door, his expression unsympathetic. Sato arrived in front of Langdon and thrust her BlackBerry in his face.

Bewildered, Langdon looked at the screen, which displayed an inverted black-and-white photograph, like a ghostly film negative. The photo looked like a jumble of objects, and one of them shone very brightly. Though askew and off center, the brightest object was clearly a little, pointed pyramid.

A tiny pyramid? Langdon looked at Sato. 'What is this?'

The question seemed only to incense Sato further. 'You're pretending you don't know?'

Langdon's temper flared. 'I'm not *pretending* anything! I've never seen this before in my life!'

'Bullshit!' Sato snapped, her voice cutting through the musty air. 'You've been carrying it in your bag all night!'

'I—' Langdon stalled midsentence. His eyes moved slowly down to the daybag on his shoulder. Then he raised them again to the BlackBerry. *My God . . . the package.* He looked more closely at the image. Now he saw it. A ghostly cube, enclosing the pyramid. Stunned, Langdon realized he was looking at an X-ray of his bag . . . and also of Peter's mysterious cube-shaped package. The cube was, in fact, a hollow box . . . containing a small pyramid.

Langdon opened his mouth to speak, but his words failed him. He felt the breath go out of his lungs as a new revelation struck him.

Simple. Pure. Devastating.

My God. He looked back at the truncated stone

pyramid on the desk. Its apex was flat – a small square area – a blank space symbolically awaiting its final piece . . . that piece which would transform it from an Unfinished Pyramid into a True Pyramid.

Langdon now realized the tiny pyramid he was carrying was not a pyramid at all. *It's a capstone.* At that instant, he knew why he alone could unlock the mysteries of this pyramid.

I hold the final piece.

And it is indeed . . . a talisman.

When Peter had told Langdon the package contained a *talisman,* Langdon had laughed. Now he realized his friend was right. This tiny capstone *was* a talisman, but not the magic kind . . . the far older kind. Long before *talisman* had magical connotations, it had another meaning – 'completion.' From the Greek *telesma,* meaning 'complete,' a talisman was any object or idea that completed another and made it whole. *The finishing element.* A capstone, symbolically speaking, was the ultimate talisman, transforming the Unfinished Pyramid into a symbol of completed perfection.

Langdon now felt an eerie convergence that forced him to accept one very strange truth: with the exception of its size, the stone pyramid in Peter's Chamber of Reflection seemed to be transforming itself, bit by bit, into something vaguely resembling the Masonic Pyramid of legend.

From the brightness with which the capstone shone on the X-ray, Langdon suspected it was made of metal . . . a very *dense* metal. Whether or not it was solid gold, he had no way of knowing, and he was not about to let his mind start playing tricks on him. *This pyramid is too small. The code's too easy to read. And . . . it's a myth, for heaven's sake!*

Sato was watching him. 'For a bright man, Professor, you've made some dumb choices tonight. Lying to an intelligence director? Intentionally obstructing a CIA investigation?'

'I can explain, if you'll let me.'

'You will be explaining at CIA headquarters. As of this moment, I am detaining you.'

Langdon's body went rigid. 'You can't possibly be serious.'

'Deadly serious. I made it very clear to you that the stakes tonight were high, and you chose not to co-operate. I strongly suggest you start thinking about explaining the inscription on this pyramid, because when we arrive at the CIA . . .' She raised her BlackBerry and took a close-up snapshot of the engraving on the stone pyramid. 'My analysts will have had a head start.'

Langdon opened his mouth to protest, but Sato was already turning to Anderson at the door. 'Chief,' she said, 'put the stone pyramid in Langdon's bag and carry it. I'll handle taking Mr. Langdon into custody. Your weapon, if I may?'

Anderson was stone-faced as he advanced into the chamber, unsnapping his shoulder holster as he came. He gave his gun to Sato, who immediately aimed it at Langdon.

Langdon watched as if in a dream. *This cannot be happening.*

Anderson now came to Langdon and removed the daybag from his shoulder, carrying it over to the desk and setting it on the chair. He unzipped the bag, propped it open, and then hoisted the heavy stone pyramid off the desk and into the bag, along with Langdon's notes and the tiny package.

Suddenly there was a rustle of movement in the hallway. A dark outline of a man materialized in the doorway, rushing into the chamber and approaching fast behind Anderson. The chief never saw him coming. In an instant, the stranger had lowered his shoulder and crashed into Anderson's back. The chief launched forward, his head cracking into the edge of the stone niche. He fell hard, crumpling on the desk, sending bones and artifacts flying. The hourglass shattered on the floor. The candle toppled to the floor, still burning.

Sato reeled amid the chaos, raising the gun, but the intruder grabbed a femur and lashed out with it, striking her shoulder with the leg bone. Sato let out a cry of pain and fell back, dropping the weapon. The newcomer kicked the gun away and then wheeled toward Langdon. The man was tall and slender, an elegant African American whom Langdon had never seen before in his life.

'Grab the pyramid!' the man commanded. 'Follow me!'

42

The African American man leading Langdon through the Capitol's subterranean maze was clearly someone of power. Beyond knowing his way through all the side corridors and back rooms, the elegant stranger carried a key ring that seemed to unlock every door that blocked their way.

Langdon followed, quickly running up an

unfamiliar staircase. As they climbed, he felt the leather strap of his daybag cutting hard into his shoulder. The stone pyramid was so heavy that Langdon feared the bag's strap might break.

The past few minutes defied all logic, and now Langdon found himself moving on instinct alone. His gut told him to trust this stranger. Beyond saving Langdon from Sato's arrest, the man had taken dangerous action to protect Peter Solomon's mysterious pyramid. *Whatever the pyramid may be.* While his motivation remained a mystery, Langdon had glimpsed a telltale shimmer of gold on the man's hand – a Masonic ring – the double-headed phoenix and the number 33. This man and Peter Solomon were more than trusted friends. They were Masonic brothers of the highest degree.

Langdon followed him to the top of the stairs, into another corridor, and then through an unmarked door into a utilitarian hallway. They ran past supply boxes and bags of garbage, veering off suddenly through a service door that deposited them in an utterly unexpected world – a plush movie theater of some sort. The older man led the way up the side aisle and out the main doors into the light of a large atrium. Langdon now realized they were in the visitor center through which he had entered earlier tonight.

Unfortunately, so was a Capitol police officer.

As they came face-to-face with the officer, all three men stopped, staring at one another. Langdon recognized the young Hispanic officer from the X-ray machine earlier tonight.

'Officer Nuñez,' the African American man said. 'Not a word. Follow me.'

The guard looked uneasy but obeyed without question.

Who is this guy?

The three of them hurried toward the southeast corner of the visitor center, where they arrived at a small foyer and a set of heavy doors blocked with orange pylons. The doors were sealed with masking tape, apparently to keep the dust of whatever was happening beyond out of the visitor center. The man reached up and peeled off the tape on the door. Then he flipped through his key ring as he spoke to the guard. 'Our friend Chief Anderson is in the sub-basement. He may be injured. You'll want to check on him.'

'Yes, sir.' Nuñez looked as baffled as he did alarmed.

'Most important, you did *not* see us.' The man found a key, took it off the key ring, and used it to turn the heavy dead bolt. He pulled open the steel door and tossed the key to the guard. 'Lock this door behind us. Put the tape back on as best as you can. Pocket the key and say nothing. To *anyone*. Including the chief. Is that clear, Officer Nuñez?'

The guard eyed the key as if he'd just been entrusted with a precious gem. 'It is, sir.'

The man hurried through the door, and Langdon followed. The guard locked the heavy bolt behind them, and Langdon could hear him reapplying the masking tape.

'Professor Langdon,' the man said as they strode briskly down a modern-looking corridor that was obviously under construction. 'My name is Warren Bellamy. Peter Solomon is a dear friend of mine.'

Langdon shot a startled glance at the stately man. *You're Warren Bellamy?* Langdon had never met the

Architect of the Capitol, but he certainly knew the man's name.

'Peter speaks very highly of you,' Bellamy said, 'and I'm sorry we are meeting under these dreadful circumstances.'

'Peter is in terrible trouble. His hand . . .'

'I know.' Bellamy sounded grim. 'That's not the half of it, I'm afraid.'

They reached the end of the lit section of corridor, and the passageway took an abrupt left. The remaining length of corridor, wherever it went, was pitch-black.

'Hold on,' Bellamy said, disappearing into a nearby electrical room from which a tangle of heavy-duty orange extension cords snaked out, running away from them into the darkness of the corridor. Langdon waited while Bellamy rooted around inside. The Architect must have located the switch that sent power to the extension cords, because suddenly the route before them became illuminated.

Langdon could only stare.

Washington, D.C. – like Rome – was a city laced with secret passageways and underground tunnels. The passage before them now reminded Langdon of the *passetto* tunnel connecting the Vatican to Castel Sant'Angelo. *Long. Dark. Narrow.* Unlike the ancient *passetto,* however, this passage was modern and not yet complete. It was a slender construction zone that was so long it seemed to narrow to nothing at its distant end. The only lighting was a string of intermittent construction bulbs that did little more than accentuate the tunnel's impossible length.

Bellamy was already heading down the passage. 'Follow me. Watch your step.'

Langdon felt himself fall into step behind Bellamy, wondering where on earth this tunnel led.

At that moment, Mal'akh stepped out of Pod 3 and strode briskly down the deserted main corridor of the SMSC toward Pod 5. He clutched Trish's key card in his hand and quietly whispered, 'Zero-eight-zero-four.'

Something else was cycling through his mind as well. Mal'akh had just received an urgent message from the Capitol Building. *My contact has run into unforeseen difficulties.* Even so, the news remained encouraging: Robert Langdon now possessed *both* the pyramid and the capstone. Despite the unexpected way in which it had happened, the crucial pieces were falling into place. It was almost as if destiny itself were guiding tonight's events, ensuring Mal'akh's victory.

43

Langdon hurried to keep pace with Warren Bellamy's brisk footsteps as they moved without a word down the long tunnel. So far, the Architect of the Capitol appeared far more intent on putting distance between Sato and this stone pyramid than he did on explaining to Langdon what was going on. Langdon had a growing apprehension that there was far more going on than he could imagine.

The CIA? The Architect of the Capitol? Two Thirty-third-degree Masons?

The shrill sound of Langdon's cell phone cut the air.

He pulled his phone from his jacket. Uncertain, he answered. 'Hello?'

The voice that spoke was an eerie, familiar whisper. 'Professor, I hear you had unexpected company.'

Langdon felt an icy chill. 'Where the hell is Peter?!' he demanded, his words reverberating in the enclosed tunnel. Beside him, Warren Bellamy glanced over, looking concerned and motioning for Langdon to keep walking.

'Don't worry,' the voice said. 'As I told you, Peter is somewhere safe.'

'You cut off his hand, for God's sake! He needs a doctor!'

'He needs a priest,' the man replied. 'But you can save him. If you do as I command, Peter will live. I give you my word.'

'The word of a madman means nothing to me.'

'Madman? Professor, surely you appreciate the reverence with which I have adhered to the ancient protocols tonight. The Hand of the Mysteries guided you to a portal – the pyramid that promises to unveil ancient wisdom. I know you now possess it.'

'You think *this* is the Masonic Pyramid?' Langdon demanded. 'It's a chunk of rock.'

There was silence on the other end of the line. 'Mr. Langdon, you're too smart to play dumb. You know very well what you've uncovered tonight. A stone pyramid . . . hidden at the core of Washington, D.C. . . . by a powerful Mason?'

'You're chasing a *myth*! Whatever Peter told you, he told you in fear. The Legend of the Masonic Pyramid is *fiction*. The Masons never built any pyramid to protect secret wisdom. And even if they did, *this* pyramid is far too small to be what you think it is.'

The man chuckled. 'I see Peter has told you very little. Nonetheless, Mr. Langdon, whether or not you choose to accept what it is you now possess, you *will* do as I say. I am well aware that the pyramid you are carrying has an encrypted engraving. You *will* decipher that engraving for me. Then, and only then, will I return Peter Solomon to you.'

'Whatever you believe this engraving reveals,' Langdon said, 'it won't be the Ancient Mysteries.'

'Of course not,' he replied. 'The mysteries are far too vast to be written on the side of a little stone pyramid.'

The response caught Langdon off guard. 'But if this engraving is *not* the Ancient Mysteries, then this pyramid is *not* the Masonic Pyramid. Legend clearly states the Masonic Pyramid was constructed to protect the Ancient Mysteries.'

The man's tone was condescending now. 'Mr. Langdon, the Masonic Pyramid *was* constructed to preserve the Ancient Mysteries, but with a twist you've apparently not yet grasped. Did Peter never tell you? The power of the Masonic Pyramid is *not* that it reveals the mysteries themselves . . . but rather that it reveals the secret *location* where the mysteries are buried.'

Langdon did a double take.

'Decipher the engraving,' the voice continued, 'and it will tell you the hiding place of mankind's greatest treasure.' He laughed. 'Peter did not entrust you with the *treasure* itself, Professor.'

Langdon came to an abrupt halt in the tunnel. 'Hold on. You're saying this pyramid is . . . a *map*?'

Bellamy jolted to a stop now, too, his expression one of shock and alarm. Clearly, the caller had just hit a raw nerve. *The pyramid is a map.*

'This map,' the voice whispered, 'or pyramid, or

portal, or whatever you choose to call it . . . was created long ago to ensure the hiding place of the Ancient Mysteries would never be forgotten . . . that it would never be lost to history.'

'A grid of sixteen symbols doesn't look much like a map.'

'Appearances can be deceiving, Professor. But regardless, you alone have the power to read that inscription.'

'You're wrong,' Langdon fired back, picturing the simplistic cipher. '*Anyone* could decipher this engraving. It's not very sophisticated.'

'I suspect there is more to the pyramid than meets the eye. Regardless, you alone possess the capstone.'

Langdon pictured the little capstone in his bag. *Order from chaos?* He didn't know what to believe anymore, but the stone pyramid in his bag seemed to be getting heavier with every passing moment.

Mal'akh pressed the cell phone to his ear, enjoying the sound of Langdon's anxious breathing on the other end. 'Right now, I have business to attend to, Professor, and so do you. Call me as soon as you have deciphered the map. We will go together to the hiding place and make our trade. Peter's life . . . for all the wisdom of the ages.'

'I will do *nothing*,' Langdon declared. 'Especially not without proof Peter is alive.'

'I suggest you not test me. You are a very small cog in a vast machine. If you disobey me, or attempt to find me, Peter will die. This I swear.'

'For all I know, Peter is *already* dead.'

'He is very much alive, Professor, but he desperately needs your help.'

'What are you really looking for?' Langdon shouted into the phone.

Mal'akh paused before answering. 'Many people have pursued the Ancient Mysteries and debated their power. Tonight, I will prove the mysteries are real.'

Langdon was silent.

'I suggest you get to work on the map immediately,' Mal'akh said. 'I need this information *today*.'

'Today?! It's already after nine o'clock!'

'Exactly. *Tempus fugit*.'

44

New York editor Jonas Faukman was just turning off the lights in his Manhattan office when his phone rang. He had no intention of picking up at this hour – that is, until he glimpsed the caller-ID display. *This ought to be good*, he thought, reaching for the receiver.

'Do we still publish you?' Faukman asked, half serious.

'Jonas!' Robert Langdon's voice sounded anxious. 'Thank God you're there. I need your help.'

Faukman's spirits lifted. 'You've got pages for me to edit, Robert?' *Finally?*

'No, I need information. Last year, I connected you with a scientist named Katherine Solomon, the sister of Peter Solomon?'

Faukman frowned. *No pages.*

'She was looking for a publisher for a book on Noetic Science? Do you remember her?'

Faukman rolled his eyes. 'Sure. I remember. And

thanks a million for *that* introduction. Not only did she refuse to let me read the results of her research, she didn't want to publish anything until some magical date in the future.'

'Jonas, listen to me, I don't have time. I need Katherine's phone number. Right now. Do you have it?'

'I've got to warn you . . . you're acting a little desperate. She's great looking, but you're not going to impress her by—'

'This is no joke, Jonas, I need her number now.'

'All right . . . hold on.' Faukman and Langdon had been close friends for enough years that Faukman knew when Langdon was serious. Jonas typed the name Katherine Solomon into a search window and began scanning the company's e-mail server.

'I'm looking now,' Faukman said. 'And for what it's worth, when you call her, you may not want to call from the Harvard Pool. It sounds like you're in an asylum.'

'I'm not at the pool. I'm in a tunnel under the U.S. Capitol.'

Faukman sensed from Langdon's voice that he was not joking. *What is it with this guy?* 'Robert, why can't you just stay home and *write*?' His computer pinged. 'Okay, hold on . . . I got it.' He moused through the old e-mail thread. 'It looks like all I have is her cell.'

'I'll take it.'

Faukman gave him the number.

'Thanks, Jonas,' Langdon said, sounding grateful. 'I owe you one.'

'You *owe* me a manuscript, Robert. Do you have any idea how long—'

The line went dead.

Faukman stared at the receiver and shook his head.

Book publishing would be so much easier without the authors.

45

Katherine Solomon did a double take when she saw the name on her caller ID. She had imagined the incoming call was from Trish, checking in to explain why she and Christopher Abaddon were taking so long. But the caller was not Trish.

Far from it.

Katherine felt a blushing smile cross her lips. *Could tonight get any stranger?* She flipped open her phone.

'Don't tell me,' she said playfully. 'Bookish bachelor seeking single Noetic Scientist?'

'Katherine!' The deep voice belonged to Robert Langdon. 'Thank God you're okay.'

'Of course I'm okay,' she replied, puzzled. 'Other than the fact that you never called me after that party at Peter's house last summer.'

'Something has happened tonight. Please listen.' His normally smooth voice sounded ragged. 'I'm so sorry to have to tell you this . . . but Peter is in serious trouble.'

Katherine's smile disappeared. 'What are you talking about?'

'Peter . . .' Langdon hesitated as if searching for words. 'I don't know how to say it, but he's been . . . *taken*. I'm not sure how or by whom, but—'

'Taken?' Katherine demanded. 'Robert, you're scaring me. Taken . . . where?'

'Taken captive.' Langdon's voice cracked as if he were overwhelmed. 'It must have happened earlier today or maybe yesterday.'

'This isn't funny,' she said angrily. 'My brother is *fine*. I just spoke to him fifteen minutes ago!'

'You did?!' Langdon sounded stunned.

'Yes! He just texted me to say he was coming to the lab.'

'He *texted* you . . .' Langdon thought out loud. 'But you didn't actually hear his *voice*?'

'No, but—'

'Listen to me. The text you received was *not* from your brother. Someone has Peter's phone. He's dangerous. Whoever it is tricked me into coming to Washington tonight.'

'Tricked you? You're not making any sense!'

'I know, I'm so sorry.' Langdon seemed uncharacteristically disorientated. 'Katherine, I think you could be in danger.'

Katherine Solomon was sure that Langdon would never joke about something like this, and yet he sounded like he had lost his mind. 'I'm fine,' she said. 'I'm locked inside a secure building!'

'Read me the message you got from Peter's phone. *Please*.'

Bewildered, Katherine pulled up the text message and read it to Langdon, feeling a chill as she came to the final part referencing Dr. Abaddon. ' 'If available, have Dr. Abaddon join us inside. I trust him fully . . . '

'Oh God . . .' Langdon's voice was laced with fear. 'Did you invite this man inside?'

'Yes! My assistant just went out to the lobby to get him. I expect them back any—'

'Katherine, get out!' Langdon yelled. 'Now!'

* * *

At the other side of the SMSC, inside the security room, a phone began ringing, drowning out the Redskins game. The guard reluctantly pulled out his earbuds one more time.

'Lobby,' he answered. 'This is Kyle.'

'Kyle, it's Katherine Solomon!' Her voice sounded anxious, out of breath.

'Ma'am, your brother has not yet—'

'Where's Trish?!' she demanded. 'Can you see her on the monitors?'

The guard rolled his chair over to look at the screens. 'She hasn't gotten back to the Cube yet?'

'No!' Katherine shouted, sounding alarmed.

The guard now realized that Katherine Solomon was out of breath, as if she were running. *What's going on back there?*

The guard quickly worked the video joystick, skimming through frames of digital video at rapid speed. 'Okay, hold on, scrolling through playback . . . I've got Trish with your guest leaving the lobby . . . they move down the Street . . . fast-forwarding . . . okay, they're going into Wet Pod . . . Trish uses her key card to unlock the door . . . both of them step into Wet Pod . . . fast-forwarding . . . okay, here they are coming out of Wet Pod just a minute ago . . . heading down . . .' He cocked his head, slowing the playback. 'Wait a minute. That's odd.'

'What?'

'The gentleman came out of Wet Pod alone.'

'Trish stayed inside?'

'Yes, it looks that way. I'm watching your guest now . . . he's in the hall on his own.'

'*Where* is Trish?' Katherine asked more frantically.

'I don't see her on the video feed,' he replied, an edge of anxiety creeping into his voice. He looked back at the screen and noticed that the man's jacket sleeves appeared to be wet . . . all the way up to his elbows. *What in the world did he do in Wet Pod?* The guard watched as the man began to move purposefully down the main hallway toward Pod 5, clutching in his hand what looked like . . . a key card.

The guard felt the hair on the back of his neck stand on end. 'Ms. Solomon, we've got a serious problem.'

Tonight was a night of firsts for Katherine Solomon.

In two years, she had never used her cell phone inside the void. Nor had she ever crossed the void at a dead run. At the moment, however, Katherine had a cell phone pressed to her ear while she was dashing blindly along the endless length of carpet. Each time she felt a foot stray from the carpet, she corrected back to center, racing on through the sheer darkness.

'Where is he now?' Katherine asked the guard, breathless.

'Checking now,' the guard replied. 'Fast-forward-ing . . . okay, here he is walking down the hall . . . moving toward Pod Five . . .'

Katherine ran harder, hoping to reach the exit before she got trapped back here. 'How long until he gets to the Pod Five entrance?'

The guard paused. 'Ma'am, you don't understand. I'm still fast-forwarding. This is recorded playback. This *already* happened.' He paused. 'Hold on, let me check the entry event monitor.' He paused and then said, 'Ma'am, Ms. Dunne's key card shows a Pod Five entry event about a minute ago.'

Katherine slammed on the brakes, sliding to a halt in the middle of the abyss. 'He already unlocked Pod Five?' she whispered into the phone.

The guard was typing frantically. 'Yes, it looks like he entered . . . ninety seconds ago.'

Katherine's body went rigid. She stopped breathing. The darkness felt suddenly alive all around her.

He's in here with me.

In an instant, Katherine realized that the only light in the entire space was coming from her cell phone, illuminating the side of her face. 'Send help,' she whispered to the guard. 'And get to Wet Pod to help Trish.' Then she quietly closed her phone, extinguishing the light.

Absolute darkness settled around her.

She stood stock-still and breathed as quietly as possible. After a few seconds, the pungent scent of ethanol wafted out of the darkness in front of her. The smell got stronger. She could sense a presence, only a few feet in front of her on the carpet. In the silence, the pounding of Katherine's heart seemed loud enough to give her away. Silently, she stepped out of her shoes and inched to her left, sidestepping off the carpet. The cement felt cold under her feet. She took one more step to clear the carpet.

One of her toes cracked.

It sounded like a gunshot in the stillness.

Only a few yards away, a rustle of clothing suddenly came at her out of the darkness. Katherine bolted an instant too late and a powerful arm snagged her, groping in the darkness, hands violently attempting to gain purchase. She spun away as a viselike grip caught her lab coat, yanking her backward, reeling her in.

Katherine threw her arms backward, slithering out of her lab coat and slipping free. Suddenly, with no idea anymore which way was out, Katherine Solomon found herself dashing, dead blind, across an endless black abyss.

46

Despite containing what many have called 'the most beautiful room in the world,' the Library of Congress is known less for its breathtaking splendor than for its vast collections. With over five hundred miles of shelves – enough to stretch from Washington, D.C., to Boston – it easily claims the title of largest library on earth. And yet *still* it expands, at a rate of over ten thousand items per day.

As an early repository for Thomas Jefferson's personal collection of books on science and philosophy, the library stood as a symbol of America's commitment to the dissemination of knowledge. One of the first buildings in Washington to have electric lights, it literally shone like a beacon in the darkness of the New World.

As its name implies, the Library of Congress was established to serve Congress, whose venerated members worked across the street in the Capitol Building. This age-old bond between library and Capitol had been fortified recently by the construction of a physical connection – a long tunnel beneath Independence Avenue that linked the two buildings.

Tonight, inside this dimly lit tunnel, Robert

Langdon followed Warren Bellamy through a construction zone, trying to quell his own deepening concern for Katherine. *This lunatic is at her lab?!* Langdon didn't even want to imagine why. When he had called to warn her, Langdon had told Katherine exactly where to meet him before they hung up. *How much longer is this damned tunnel?* His head ached now, a roiling torrent of interconnected thoughts: Katherine, Peter, the Masons, Bellamy, pyramids, ancient prophecy . . . and a map.

Langdon shook it all off and pressed on. *Bellamy promised me answers.*

When the two men finally reached the end of the passage, Bellamy guided Langdon through a set of double doors that were still under construction. Finding no way to lock the unfinished doors behind them, Bellamy improvised, grabbing an aluminum ladder from the construction supplies and leaning it precariously against the outside of the door. Then he balanced a metal bucket on top. If anyone opened the door, the bucket would crash loudly to the floor.

That's our alarm system? Langdon eyed the perched bucket, hoping Bellamy had a more comprehensive plan for their safety tonight. Everything had happened so fast, and Langdon was only now starting to process the repercussions of his fleeing with Bellamy. *I'm a fugitive from the CIA.*

Bellamy led the way around a corner, where the two men began ascending a wide staircase that was cordoned off with orange pylons. Langdon's daybag weighed him down as he climbed. 'The stone pyramid,' he said, 'I still don't understand—'

'Not here,' Bellamy interrupted. 'We'll examine it in the light. I know a safe place.'

Langdon doubted such a place existed for anyone who had just physically assaulted the director of the CIA's Office of Security.

As the two men reached the top of the stairs, they entered a wide hallway of Italian marble, stucco, and gold leaf. The hall was lined with eight pairs of statues – all depicting the goddess Minerva. Bellamy pressed on, leading Langdon eastward, through a vaulted archway, into a far grander space.

Even in the dim, after-hours lighting, the library's great hall shone with the classical grandeur of an opulent European palace. Seventy-five feet overhead, stained-glass skylights glistened between paneled beams adorned with rare 'aluminum leaf' – a metal that was considered to be more precious than gold at one time. Beneath that, a stately course of paired pillars lined the second-floor balcony, accessible by two magnificent curling staircases whose newel posts supported giant bronze female figures raising torches of enlightenment.

In a bizarre attempt to reflect this theme of modern enlightenment and yet stay within the decorative register of Renaissance architecture, the stairway banisters had been carved with cupidlike putti portrayed as modern scientists. *An angelic electrician holding a telephone? A cherubic entomologist with a specimen box?* Langdon wondered what Bernini would have thought.

'We'll talk over here,' Bellamy said, leading Langdon past the bulletproof display cases that contained the library's two most valuable books – the Giant Bible of Mainz, handwritten in the 1450s, and America's copy of the Gutenberg Bible, one of only three perfect vellum copies in the world. Fittingly, the vaulted ceiling overhead bore John White Alexander's six-panel painting titled *The Evolution of the Book.*

Bellamy strode directly to a pair of elegant double doors at the center rear of the east-corridor wall. Langdon knew what room lay beyond those doors, but it seemed a strange choice for a conversation. Notwithstanding the irony of talking in a space filled with 'Silence Please' signs, this room hardly seemed like a 'safe place.' Located dead center of the library's cruciform-shaped floor plan, this chamber served as the heart of the building. Hiding in here was like breaking into a cathedral and hiding on the altar.

Nonetheless, Bellamy unlocked the doors, stepped into the darkness beyond, and groped for the lights. When he flipped the switch, one of America's great architectural masterpieces seemed to materialize out of thin air.

The famous reading room was a feast for the senses. A voluminous octagon rose 160 feet at its center, its eight sides finished in chocolate-brown Tennessee marble, cream-colored Siena marble, and apple-red Algerian marble. Because it was lit from eight angles, no shadows fell anywhere, creating the effect that the room itself was glowing.

'Some say it's the most striking room in Washington,' Bellamy said, ushering Langdon inside.

Maybe in the whole world, Langdon thought as he stepped across the threshold. As always, his gaze first ascended straight up to the towering central collar, where rays of arabesque coffers curled down the dome to an upper balcony. Encircling the room, sixteen bronze 'portrait' statues peered down from the balustrade. Beneath them, a stunning arcade of arch-ways formed a lower balcony. Down at floor level, three concentric circles of burnished wood desks radiated out from the massive octagonal circulation desk.

Langdon returned his focus to Bellamy, who was now propping the room's double doors wide open. 'I thought we were *hiding*,' Langdon said, confused.

'If anyone enters the building,' Bellamy said, 'I want to hear them coming.'

'But won't they find us instantly in here?'

'No matter *where* we hide, they'll find us. But if anyone corners us in this building, you'll be very glad I chose this room.'

Langdon had no idea why, but Bellamy apparently wasn't looking to discuss it. He was already on the move toward the center of the room, where he selected one of the available reading desks, pulled up two chairs, and flipped on the reading light. Then he motioned to Langdon's bag.

'Okay, Professor, let's have a closer look.'

Not wanting to risk scratching its polished surface with a rough piece of granite, Langdon hoisted his entire bag onto the desk and unzipped it, folding the sides all the way down to reveal the pyramid inside. Warren Bellamy adjusted the reading lamp and studied the pyramid carefully. He ran his fingers over the unusual engraving.

'I assume you recognize this language?' Bellamy asked.

'Of course,' Langdon replied, eyeing the sixteen symbols.

Known as the Freemason's Cipher, this encoded language had been used for private communication among early Masonic brothers. The encryption method had been abandoned long ago for one simple reason – it was much too easy to break. Most of the students in

Langdon's senior symbology seminar could break this code in about five minutes. Langdon, with a pencil and paper, could do it in under sixty seconds.

The notorious breakability of this centuries-old encryption scheme now presented a couple of paradoxes. First, the claim that Langdon was the only person on earth who could break it was absurd. Second, for Sato to suggest that a Masonic cipher was an issue of national security was like her suggesting our nuclear launch codes were encrypted with a Cracker Jack decoder ring. Langdon was still struggling to believe any of it. *This pyramid is a* map? *Pointing to the lost wisdom of the ages?*

'Robert,' Bellamy said, his tone grave. 'Did Director Sato tell you why she is so interested in this?'

Langdon shook his head. 'Not specifically. She just kept saying it was an issue of national security. I assume she's lying.'

'Perhaps,' Bellamy said, rubbing the back of his neck. He seemed to be struggling with something. 'But there is a far more troubling possibility.' He turned to look Langdon in the eye. 'It's possible that Director Sato has discovered this pyramid's true potential.'

47

The blackness engulfing Katherine Solomon felt absolute.

Having fled the familiar safety of the carpet, she was now groping blindly forward, her outstretched hands touching only empty space as she staggered deeper into the desolate void. Beneath her stockinged feet, the endless expanse of cold cement felt like a frozen lake . . . a hostile environment from which she now needed to escape.

No longer smelling ethanol, she stopped and waited in darkness. Standing dead still, she listened, willing her heart to stop pounding so loudly. The heavy footsteps behind her seemed to have stopped. *Did I lose him?* Katherine closed her eyes and tried to imagine where she was. *Which direction did I run? Where is the door?* It was no use. She was so turned around now that the exit could be anywhere.

Fear, Katherine had once heard, acted as a stimulant, sharpening the mind's ability to think. Right now, however, her fear had turned her mind into a tumbling torrent of panic and confusion. *Even if I find the exit, I can't get out.* Her key card had been lost when she'd shed her lab coat. Her only hope seemed to be that she was now a needle in a haystack – a single point on a thirty-thousand-square-foot grid. Despite the overwhelming urge to flee, Katherine's analytical mind told her instead to make the only logical move – no move at all. *Stay still. Don't make a sound.* The security guard was on his way, and for some unknown reason, her attacker smelled strongly of ethanol. *If he gets too close, I'll know it.*

257

As Katherine stood in silence, her mind raced over what Langdon had said. *Your brother . . . he's been taken.* She felt a bead of cold sweat materialize on her arm and trickle down, toward the cell phone still clenched in her right hand. It was a danger she had forgotten to consider. If the phone rang, it would give away her position, and she could not turn it off without opening it and illuminating the display.

Set down the phone . . . and move away from it.

But it was too late. The smell of ethanol approached on her right. And now it grew stronger. Katherine struggled to stay calm, forcing herself to override the instinct to run. Carefully, slowly, she took one step to her left. The faint rustle of her clothing was apparently all her attacker needed. She heard him lunge, and the smell of ethanol washed over her as a powerful hand grabbed at her shoulder. She twisted away, raw terror gripping her. Mathematical probability went out the window, and Katherine broke into a blind sprint. She veered hard to the left, changing course, dashing blindly now into the void.

The wall materialized out of nowhere.

Katherine hit it hard, knocking the wind from her lungs. Pain blossomed in her arm and shoulder, but she managed to stay on her feet. The oblique angle at which she had collided with the wall had spared her the full force of the blow, but it was little comfort now. The sound had echoed everywhere. *He knows where I am.* Doubled over in pain, she turned her head and stared out into the blackness of the pod and sensed him staring back at her.

Change your location. Now!

Still struggling to catch her breath, she began moving down the wall, touching her left hand quietly

258

to each exposed steel stud as she passed. *Stay along the wall. Slip past him before he corners you.* In her right hand, Katherine still clutched her cell phone, ready to hurl it as a projectile if need be.

Katherine was in no way prepared for the sound she heard next – the clear rustle of clothing directly in *front* of her . . . against the wall. She froze, stock-still, and stopped breathing. *How could he be on the wall already?* She felt a faint puff of air, laced with the stench of ethanol. *He's moving down the wall toward me!*

Katherine backed up several steps. Then, turning silently 180 degrees, she began moving quickly in the opposite direction down the wall. She moved twenty feet or so when the impossible happened. Once again, directly in front of her, along the wall, she heard the rustling sound of clothing. Then came the same puff of air and the smell of ethanol. Katherine Solomon froze in place.

My God, he's everywhere!

Bare-chested, Mal'akh stared into the darkness.

The smell of ethanol on his sleeves had proven a liability, and so he had transformed it into an asset, stripping off his shirt and jacket and using them to help corner his prey. Throwing his jacket against the wall to the right, he had heard Katherine stop short and change direction. Now, having thrown his shirt ahead to the left, Mal'akh had heard her stop again. He had effectively corralled Katherine against the wall by establishing points beyond which she dared not pass.

Now he waited, ears straining in the silence. *She has only one direction she can move – directly toward me.* Even so, Mal'akh heard nothing. Either Katherine was paralyzed with fear, or she had decided to stand still and wait for help to enter Pod 5. *Either way she loses.* Nobody would be entering Pod 5 anytime soon; Mal'akh had disabled the outer keypad with a very crude, yet very effective, technique. After using Trish's key card, he had rammed a single dime deep into the key-card slot to prevent any other key-card use without first dismantling the entire mechanism.

You and I are alone, Katherine . . . for as long as this takes.

Mal'akh inched silently forward, listening for any movement. Katherine Solomon would die tonight in the darkness of her brother's museum. A poetic end. Mal'akh looked forward to sharing the news of Katherine's death with her brother. The old man's anguish would be long-awaited revenge.

Suddenly in the darkness, to Mal'akh's great surprise, he saw a tiny glow in the distance and realized Katherine had just made a deadly error in judgment. *She's phoning for help?!* The electronic display that had just flickered to life was hovering waist high, about twenty yards ahead, like a shining beacon on a vast ocean of black. Mal'akh had been prepared to wait Katherine out, but now he wouldn't have to.

Mal'akh sprang into motion, racing toward the hovering light, knowing he had to reach her before she could complete her call for help. He was there in a matter of seconds, and he lunged, arms outstretched on either side of her glowing cell phone, preparing to engulf her.

Mal'akh's fingers jammed into a solid wall, bending backward and almost breaking. His head collided next, crashing into a steel beam. He cried out in pain as he crumpled beside the wall. Cursing, he clambered back to his feet, pulling himself up by the waist-high, horizontal strut on which Katherine Solomon had cleverly placed her open cell phone.

Katherine was running again, this time with no concern for the noise her hand was making as it bounced rhythmically off the evenly spaced metal studs of Pod 5. *Run!* If she followed the wall all the way around the pod, she knew that sooner or later she would feel the exit door.

Where the hell is the guard?

The even spacing of the studs continued as she ran with her left hand on the sidewall and her right out in front of her for protection. *When will I reach the corner?* The sidewall seemed to go on and on, but suddenly the rhythm of the studs was broken. Her left hand hit empty space for several long strides, and then the studs began again. Katherine slammed on the brakes and backed up, feeling her way across the smooth metal panel. *Why are there no studs here?*

She could hear her attacker lumbering loudly after her now, groping his way down the wall in her direction. Even so, it was a different sound that scared Katherine even more – the distant rhythmic banging of a security guard pounding his flashlight against the Pod 5 door.

The guard can't get in?

While the thought was terrifying, the *location* of his banging – diagonally to her right – instantly oriented Katherine. She could now picture where in Pod 5 she was located. The visual flash brought with it an unexpected realization. She now knew what this flat panel on the wall was.

Every pod was equipped with a specimen bay – a

giant movable wall that could be retracted for transporting oversize specimens in and out of the pods. Like those of an airplane hangar, this door was mammoth, and Katherine in her wildest dreams had never imagined needing to open it. At the moment, though, it seemed like her only hope.

Is it even operable?

Katherine fumbled blindly in the blackness, searching the bay door until she found the large metal handle. Grasping it, she threw her weight backward, trying to slide open the door. Nothing. She tried again. It didn't budge.

She could hear her attacker closing faster now, homing in on the sounds of her efforts. *The bay door is locked!* Wild with panic, she slid her hands all over the door, feeling the surface for any latch or lever. She suddenly hit what felt like a vertical pole. She followed it down to the floor, crouching, and could feel it was inserted into a hole in the cement. *A security rod!* She stood up, grabbed the pole, and, lifting with her legs, slid the rod up and out of the hole.

He's almost here!

Katherine groped now for the handle, found it again, and heaved back on it with all her might. The massive panel seemed barely to move, and yet a sliver of moonlight now sliced into Pod 5. Katherine pulled again. The shaft of light from outside the building grew wider. A *little more!* She pulled one last time, sensing her attacker was now only a few feet away.

Leaping toward the light, Katherine wriggled her slender body sideways into the opening. A hand materialized in the darkness, clawing at her, trying to pull her back inside. She heaved herself through the opening, pursued by a massive bare arm that was covered with tattooed scales. The terrifying arm writhed like an angry snake trying to seize her.

Katherine spun and fled down the long, pale outer wall of Pod 5. The bed of loose stones that surrounded the entire perimeter of the SMSC cut into her stockinged feet as she ran, but she pressed on, heading for the main entrance. The night was dark, but with her eyes fully dilated from the utter blackness of Pod 5, she could see perfectly – almost as if it were daylight. Behind her, the heavy bay door ground open, and she heard heavy footsteps accelerating in pursuit down the side of the building. The footsteps seemed impossibly fast.

I'll never outrun him to the main entrance. She knew her Volvo was closer, but even that would be too far. *I'm not going to make it.*

Then Katherine realized she had one final card to play.

As she neared the corner of Pod 5, she could hear his footsteps quickly overtaking her in the darkness. *Now or never.* Instead of rounding the corner, Katherine suddenly cut hard to her left, *away* from the building, out onto the grass. As she did so, she closed her eyes tightly, placed both hands over her face, and began running totally blind across the lawn.

The motion-activated security lighting that blazed to life around Pod 5 transformed night into day instantly. Katherine heard a scream of pain behind her as the brilliant floodlights seared into her assailant's hyperdilated pupils with over twenty-five-million candlepower of light. She could hear him stumbling on the loose stones.

Katherine kept her eyes tightly closed, trusting herself on the open lawn. When she sensed she was far enough away from the building and the lights, she opened her eyes, corrected her course, and ran like hell through the dark.

Her Volvo's keys were exactly where she always left them, in the center console. Breathless, she seized the keys in her trembling hands and found the ignition. The engine roared to life, and her headlights flipped on, illuminating a terrifying sight.

A hideous form raced toward her.

Katherine froze for an instant.

The creature caught in her headlights was a bald and bare-chested animal, its skin covered with tattooed scales, symbols, and text. He bellowed as he ran into the glare, raising his hands before his eyes like a cave-dwelling beast seeing sunlight for the first time. She reached for the gearshift but suddenly he was there, hurling his elbow through her side window, sending a shower of safety glass into her lap.

A massive scale-covered arm burst through her window, groping half blind, finding her neck. She threw the car in reverse, but her attacker had latched on to her throat, squeezing with unimaginable force. She turned her head in an attempt to escape his grasp, and suddenly she was staring at his face. Three dark stripes, like fingernail scratches, had torn through his face makeup to reveal the tattoos beneath. His eyes were wild and ruthless.

'I should have killed you ten years ago,' he growled. 'The night I killed your mother.'

As his words registered, Katherine was seized by a horrifying memory: that feral look in his eyes – she had seen it before. *It's him.* She would have screamed had it not been for the viselike grip around her neck.

She smashed her foot onto the accelerator, and the

car lurched backward, almost snapping her neck as he was dragged beside her car. The Volvo careened up an inclined median, and Katherine could feel her neck about to give way beneath his weight. Suddenly tree branches were scraping the side of her car, slapping through the side windows, and the weight was gone.

The car burst through the evergreens and out into the upper parking lot, where Katherine slammed on the brakes. Below her, the half-naked man clambered to his feet, staring into her headlights. With a terrifying calm, he raised a menacing scale-covered arm and pointed directly at her.

Katherine's blood coursed with raw fear and hatred as she spun the wheel and hit the gas. Seconds later, she was fishtailing out onto Silver Hill Road.

48

In the heat of the moment, Capitol police officer Nuñez had seen no option but to help the Capitol Architect and Robert Langdon escape. Now, however, back in the basement police headquarters, Nuñez could see the storm clouds gathering fast.

Chief Trent Anderson was holding an ice pack to his head while another officer was tending to Sato's bruises. Both of them were standing with the video surveillance team, reviewing digital playback files in an attempt to locate Langdon and Bellamy.

'Check the playback on every hallway and exit,' Sato demanded. 'I want to know where they went!'

Nuñez felt ill as he looked on. He knew it would be only a matter of minutes before they found the right video clip and learned the truth. *I helped them escape.* Making matters worse was the arrival of a four-man CIA field team that was now staging nearby, prepping to go after Langdon and Bellamy. These guys looked nothing like the Capitol Police. These guys were dead-serious soldiers . . . black camouflage, night vision, futuristic-looking handguns.

Nuñez felt like he would throw up. Making up his mind, he motioned discreetly to Chief Anderson. 'A word, Chief?'

'What is it?' Anderson followed Nuñez into the hall.

'Chief, I made a bad mistake,' Nuñez said, breaking a sweat. 'I'm sorry, and I'm resigning.' *You'll fire me in a few minutes anyway.*

'I beg your pardon?'

Nuñez swallowed hard. 'Earlier, I saw Langdon and Architect Bellamy in the visitor center on their way out of the building.'

'What?!' Anderson bellowed. 'Why didn't you say something?!'

'The Architect told me not to say a word.'

'You work for *me*, goddammit!' Anderson's voice echoed down the corridor. 'Bellamy smashed my head into a wall, for Christ's sake!'

Nuñez handed Anderson the key that the Architect had given him.

'What is this?' Anderson demanded.

'A key to the new tunnel under Independence Avenue. Architect Bellamy had it. That's how they escaped.'

Anderson stared down at the key, speechless.

Sato poked her head out into the hallway, eyes probing. 'What's going on out here?'

Nuñez felt himself go pale. Anderson was still holding the key, and Sato clearly had seen it. As the hideous little woman drew near, Nuñez improvised as best as he could, hoping to protect his chief. 'I found a key on the floor in the subbasement. I was just asking Chief Anderson if he knew what it might go to.'

Sato arrived, eyeing the key. 'And does the chief know?'

Nuñez glanced up at Anderson, who was clearly weighing all his options before speaking. Finally, the chief shook his head. 'Not offhand. I'd have to check the—'

'Don't bother,' Sato said. 'This key unlocks a tunnel off the visitor center.'

'Really?' Anderson said. 'How do you know that?'

'We just found the surveillance clip. Officer Nuñez here helped Langdon and Bellamy escape and then relocked that tunnel door behind them. Bellamy gave Nuñez that key.'

Anderson turned to Nuñez with a flare of anger. 'Is this true?!'

Nuñez nodded vigorously, doing his best to play along. 'I'm sorry, sir. The Architect told me not to tell a soul!'

'I don't give a damn *what* the Architect told you!' Anderson yelled. 'I expect—'

'Shut up, Trent,' Sato snapped. 'You're both lousy liars. Save it for your CIA inquisition.' She snatched the Architect's tunnel key from Anderson. 'You're done here.'

49

Robert Langdon hung up his cell phone, feeling increasingly worried. *Katherine's not answering her cell?* Katherine had promised to call him as soon as she was safely out of the lab and on her way to meet him here, but she had never done so.

Bellamy sat beside Langdon at the reading-room desk. He, too, had just made a call, his to an individual he claimed could offer them sanctuary – a safe place to hide. Unfortunately, this person was not answering either, and so Bellamy had left an urgent message, telling him to call Langdon's cell phone right away.

'I'll keep trying,' he said to Langdon, 'but for the moment, we're on our own. And we need to discuss a plan for this pyramid.'

The pyramid. For Langdon, the spectacular backdrop of the reading room had all but disappeared, his world constricting now to include only what was directly in front of him – a stone pyramid, a sealed package containing a capstone, and an elegant African American man who had materialized out of the darkness and rescued him from the certainty of a CIA interrogation.

Langdon had expected a modicum of sanity from the Architect of the Capitol, but now it seemed Warren Bellamy was no more rational than the madman claiming Peter was in purgatory. Bellamy was insisting this stone pyramid was, in fact, the Masonic Pyramid of legend. *An ancient map? That guides us to powerful wisdom?*

'Mr. Bellamy,' Langdon said politely, 'this idea that there exists some kind of ancient knowledge that can imbue men with great power . . . I simply can't take it seriously.'

Bellamy's eyes looked both disappointed and earnest, making Langdon's skepticism all the more awkward. 'Yes, Professor, I had imagined you might feel this way, but I suppose I should not be surprised. You are an outsider looking in. There exist certain Masonic realities that you will perceive as myth because you are not properly initiated and prepared to understand them.'

Now Langdon felt patronized. *I wasn't a member of Odysseus's crew, but I'm certain the Cyclops is a myth.* 'Mr. Bellamy, even if the legend is true . . . *this* pyramid cannot possibly be the Masonic Pyramid.'

'No?' Bellamy ran a finger across the Masonic cipher on the stone. 'It looks to me like it fits the description perfectly. A stone pyramid with a shining metal capstone, which, according to Sato's X-ray, is exactly what Peter entrusted to you.' Bellamy picked up the little cube-shaped package, weighing it in his hand.

'This stone pyramid is less than a foot tall,' Langdon countered. 'Every version of the story I've ever heard describes the Masonic Pyramid as enormous.'

Bellamy had clearly anticipated this point. 'As you know, the legend speaks of a pyramid rising so high that God Himself can reach out and touch it.'

'Exactly.'

'I can see your dilemma, Professor. However, both the Ancient Mysteries and Masonic philosophy celebrate the potentiality of God within each of us. Symbolically speaking, one could claim that anything within reach of an enlightened man . . . is within reach of God.'

Langdon felt unswayed by the wordplay.

'Even the Bible concurs,' Bellamy said. 'If we accept, as Genesis tells us, that "God created man in his own image," then we *also* must accept what this implies – that mankind was not created *inferior* to God. In Luke 17:20 we are told, "The kingdom of God is within you."'

'I'm sorry, but I don't know any Christians who consider themselves God's *equal*.'

'Of course not,' Bellamy said, his tone hardening. 'Because most Christians want it both ways. They want to be able to proudly declare they are believers in the Bible and yet simply ignore those parts they find too difficult or too inconvenient to believe.'

Langdon made no response.

'Anyhow,' Bellamy said, 'the Masonic Pyramid's age-old description as being tall enough to be touched by God . . . this has long led to misinterpretations about its size. Conveniently, it keeps academics like yourself insisting the pyramid is a legend, and nobody searches for it.'

Langdon looked down at the stone pyramid. 'I apologize that I'm frustrating you,' he said. 'I've simply always thought of the Masonic Pyramid as a myth.'

'Does it not seem perfectly fitting to you that a map created by stonemasons would be carved in stone? Throughout history, our most important guideposts have always been carved in stone – including the tablets God gave Moses – Ten Commandments to guide our human conduct.'

'I understand, and yet it is always referred to as the *Legend* of the Masonic Pyramid. *Legend* implies it is mythical.'

'Yes, *legend*.' Bellamy chuckled. 'I'm afraid you're suffering from the same problem Moses had.'

'I'm sorry?'

Bellamy looked almost amused as he turned in his seat, glancing up at the second-tier balcony, where sixteen bronze statues peered down at them. 'Do you see Moses?'

Langdon gazed up at the library's celebrated statue of Moses. 'Yes.'

'He has horns.'

'I'm aware of that.'

'But do you know *why* he has horns?'

Like most teachers, Langdon did not enjoy being lectured to. The Moses above them had horns for the same reason *thousands* of Christian images of Moses had horns – a mistranslation of the book of Exodus. The original Hebrew text described Moses as having '*karan 'ohr panav*' – 'facial skin that glowed with rays of light' – but when the Roman Catholic Church created the official Latin translation of the Bible, the translator bungled Moses's description, rendering it as '*cornuta esset facies sua,*' meaning 'his face was horned.' From that moment on, artists and sculptors, fearing reprisals if they were not true to the Gospels, began depicting Moses with horns.

'It was a simple mistake,' Langdon replied. 'A mistranslation by Saint Jerome around four hundred A.D.'

Bellamy looked impressed. 'Exactly. A mistranslation. And the result is . . . poor Moses is now misshapen for all history.'

'Misshapen' was a nice way to put it. Langdon, as a child, had been terrified when he saw Michelangelo's diabolical 'horned Moses' – the centerpiece of Rome's Basilica of St. Peter in Chains.

'I mention the horned Moses,' Bellamy now said, 'to illustrate how a single word, misunderstood, can rewrite history.'

You're preaching to the choir, Langdon thought, having learned the lesson firsthand in Paris a number of years back. *SanGreal: Holy Grail. SangReal: Royal Blood.*

'In the case of the Masonic Pyramid,' Bellamy continued, 'people heard whispers about a "legend." And the idea stuck. The *Legend* of the Masonic Pyramid sounded like a myth. But the word *legend* was referring to something else. It had been misconstrued. Much like the word *talisman*.' He smiled. 'Language can be very adept at hiding the truth.'

'That's true, but you're losing me here.'

'Robert, the Masonic Pyramid is a *map*. And like every map, it has a *legend* – a key that tells you how to read it.' Bellamy took the cube-shaped package and held it up. 'Don't you see? This capstone *is* the legend to the pyramid. It is the key that tells you how to read the most powerful artifact on earth . . . a map that unveils the hiding place of mankind's greatest treasure – the lost wisdom of the ages.'

Langdon fell silent.

'I humbly submit,' Bellamy said, 'that your towering Masonic Pyramid is only *this* . . . a modest stone whose golden capstone reaches high enough to be touched by God. High enough that an enlightened man can reach down and touch it.'

Silence hung between the two men for several seconds.

Langdon felt an unexpected pulse of excitement as he looked down at the pyramid, seeing it in a new light. His eyes moved again to the Masonic cipher. 'But this code . . . it seems so . . .'

'Simple?'

Langdon nodded. 'Almost *anyone* could decipher this.'

Bellamy smiled and retrieved a pencil and paper for Langdon. 'Then perhaps you should enlighten us?'

Langdon felt uneasy about reading the code, and yet considering the circumstances, it seemed a minor betrayal of Peter's trust. Moreover, whatever the engraving said, he could not imagine that it unveiled a secret hiding place of anything at all . . . much less that of one of history's greatest treasures.

Langdon accepted the pencil from Bellamy and tapped it on his chin as he studied the cipher. The code was so simple that he barely needed pencil and paper. Even so, he wanted to ensure he made no mistakes, and so he dutifully put pencil to paper and wrote down the most common decryption key for a Masonic cipher. The key consisted of four grids – two plain and two dotted – with the alphabet running through them in order. Each letter of the alphabet was now positioned inside a uniquely shaped 'enclosure' or 'pen.' The shape of each letter's *enclosure* became the *symbol* for that letter.

The scheme was so simple, it was almost infantile.

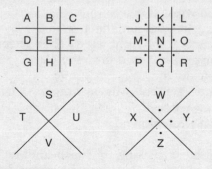

273

Langdon double-checked his handiwork. Feeling confident the decryption key was correct, he now turned his attention back to the code inscribed on the pyramid. To decipher it, all he had to do was to find the matching shape on his decryption key and write down the letter inside it.

∨⊡☐‹
⌐⟩✕⊙
∟∨⌐∨
⋏‹⊡⌐

The first character on the pyramid looked like a down arrow or a chalice. Langdon quickly found the chalice-shaped segment on the decryption key. It was located in the lower left-hand corner and enclosed the letter *S*.

Langdon wrote down *S*.

The next symbol on the pyramid was a dotted square missing its right side. That shape on the decryption grid enclosed the letter *O*.

He wrote down *O*.

The third symbol was a simple square, which enclosed the letter *E*.

Langdon wrote down *E*.

S O E . . .

He continued, picking up speed until he had completed the entire grid. Now, as he gazed down at his finished translation, Langdon let out a puzzled sigh. *Hardly what I'd call a eureka moment.*

Bellamy's face showed the hint of a smile. 'As you know, Professor, the Ancient Mysteries are reserved only for the truly enlightened.'

'Right,' Langdon said, frowning. *Apparently, I don't qualify.*

50

In a basement office deep inside CIA headquarters in Langley, Virginia, the same sixteen-character Masonic cipher glowed brightly on a high-definition computer monitor. Senior OS analyst Nola Kaye sat alone and studied the image that had been e-mailed to her ten minutes ago by her boss, Director Inoue Sato.

Is this some kind of joke? Nola knew it was not, of course; Director Sato had no sense of humor, and the events of tonight were anything but a joking matter. Nola's high-level clearance within the CIA's all-seeing Office of Security had opened her eyes to the shadow worlds of power. But what Nola had witnessed in the last twenty-four hours had changed her impressions forever of the secrets that powerful men kept.

'Yes, Director,' Nola now said, cradling the phone on her shoulder as she talked to Sato. 'The engraving is indeed the Masonic cipher. However, the cleartext is meaningless. It appears to be a grid of random letters.' She gazed down at her decryption.

```
S    O    E    U

A    T    U    N

C    S    A    S

V    U    N    J
```

'It must say *something*,' Sato insisted.

'Not unless it has a second layer of encryption that I'm not aware of.'

'Any guesses?' Sato asked.

'It's a grid-based matrix, so I could run the usual – Vigenère, grilles, trellises, and so forth – but no promises, especially if it's a onetime pad.'

'Do what you can. And do it fast. How about the X-ray?'

Nola swiveled her chair to a second system, which displayed a standard security X-ray of someone's bag. Sato had requested information on what appeared to be a small pyramid inside a cube-shaped box. Normally, a two-inch-tall object would not be an issue of national security unless it was made of enriched plutonium. This one was not. It was made of something almost equally startling.

'Image-density analysis was conclusive,' Nola said. 'Nineteen-point-three grams per cubic centimeter. It's pure gold. Very, very valuable.'

'Anything else?'

'Actually, yes. The density scan picked up minor irregularities on the surface of the gold pyramid. It turns out the gold is engraved with text.'

'Really?' Sato sounded hopeful. 'What does it say?'

'I can't tell yet. The inscription is extremely faint. I'm

trying to enhance with filters, but the resolution on the X-ray is not great.'

'Okay, keep trying. Call me when you have something.'

'Yes, ma'am.'

'And, Nola?' Sato's tone turned ominous. 'As with everything you have learned in the last twenty-four hours, the images of the stone pyramid and gold capstone are classified at the highest levels of security. You are to consult no one. You report to me directly. I want to make sure that is clear.'

'Of course, ma'am.'

'Good. Keep me posted.' Sato hung up.

Nola rubbed her eyes and looked blearily back at her computer screens. She had not slept in over thirty-six hours, and she knew damn well she would not sleep again until this crisis had reached its conclusion.

Whatever that may be.

Back at the Capitol Visitor Center, four black-clad CIA field-op specialists stood at the entrance to the tunnel, peering hungrily down the dimly lit shaft like a pack of dogs eager for the hunt.

Sato approached, having just hung up from a call. 'Gentlemen,' she said, still holding the Architect's key, 'are your mission parameters clear?'

'Affirmative,' the lead agent replied. 'We have *two* targets. The first is an engraved stone pyramid, approximately one foot tall. The second is a smaller, cube-shaped package, approximately two inches tall. Both were last seen in Robert Langdon's shoulder bag.'

'Correct,' Sato said. 'These two items must be

retrieved quickly and intact. Do you have any questions?'

'Parameters for use of force?'

Sato's shoulder was still throbbing from where Bellamy had struck her with a bone. 'As I said, it is of critical importance that these items be retrieved.'

'Understood.' The four men turned and headed into the darkness of the tunnel.

Sato lit a cigarette and watched them disappear.

51

Katherine Solomon had always been a prudent driver, but now she was pushing her Volvo at over ninety as she fled blindly up the Suitland Parkway. Her trembling foot had been lodged on the accelerator for a full mile before her panic began to lift. She now realized her uncontrollable shivering was no longer solely from fear.

I'm freezing.

The wintry night air was gushing through her shattered window, buffeting her body like an arctic wind. Her stockinged feet were numb, and she reached down for her spare pair of shoes, which she kept beneath the passenger seat. As she did, she felt a stab of pain from the bruise on her throat, where the powerful hand had latched on to her neck.

The man who had smashed through her window bore no resemblance to the blond-haired gentleman whom Katherine knew as Dr. Christopher Abaddon. His thick hair and smooth, tanned complexion had disappeared. His shaved head, bare chest, and makeup-smeared face had been unveiled as a terrifying tapestry of tattoos.

She heard his voice again, whispering to her in the howl of wind outside her broken window. *Katherine, I should have killed you years ago . . . the night I killed your mother.*

Katherine shivered, feeling no doubt. *That was him.* She had never forgotten the look of fiendish violence in his eyes. Nor had she ever forgotten the sound of her brother's single gunshot, which had killed this man, propelling him off a high ledge into the frozen river below, where he plummeted through the ice and never resurfaced. Investigators had searched for weeks, never finding his body, and finally decided it had been washed away by the current out to the Chesapeake Bay.

They were wrong, she now knew. *He is still alive. And he's back.*

Katherine felt angst-ridden as the memories flooded back. It was almost exactly ten years ago. Christmas Day. Katherine, Peter, and their mother – her entire family – were gathered at their sprawling stone mansion in Potomac, nestled on a two-hundred-acre wooded estate with its own river running through it.

As was tradition, their mother worked diligently in the kitchen, rejoicing in the holiday custom of cooking for her two children. Even at seventy-five years of age, Isabel Solomon was an exuberant cook, and tonight the mouthwatering smells of roast venison, parsnip gravy, and garlic mashed potatoes wafted through the house. While Mother prepared the feast, Katherine and her brother relaxed in the conservatory, discussing Katherine's latest fascination – a new field called

Noetic Science. An unlikely fusion of modern particle physics and ancient mysticism, Noetics had absolutely captivated Katherine's imagination.

Physics meets philosophy.

Katherine told Peter about some of the experiments she was dreaming up, and she could see in his eyes that he was intrigued. Katherine felt particularly pleased to give her brother something positive to think about this Christmas, since the holiday had also become a painful reminder of a terrible tragedy.

Peter's son, Zachary.

Katherine's nephew's twenty-first birthday had been his last. The family had been through a nightmare, and it seemed that her brother was only now finally learning how to laugh again.

Zachary had been a late bloomer, frail and awkward, a rebellious and angry teenager. Despite his deeply loving and privileged upbringing, the boy seemed determined to detach himself from the Solomon 'establishment.' He was kicked out of prep school, partied hard with the 'celebrati,' and shunned his parents' exhaustive attempts to provide him firm and loving guidance.

He broke Peter's heart.

Shortly before Zachary's eighteenth birthday, Katherine had sat down with her mother and brother and listened to them debating whether or not to withhold Zachary's inheritance until he was more mature. The Solomon inheritance – a centuries-old tradition in the family – bequeathed a staggeringly generous piece of the Solomon wealth to every Solomon child on his or her eighteenth birthday. The Solomons believed that an inheritance was more helpful at the *beginning* of someone's life than at the end. Moreover, placing large pieces of the Solomon fortune in the hands of eager young descendants had been the key to growing the family's dynastic wealth.

In this case, however, Katherine's mother argued that it was dangerous to give Peter's troubled son such a large sum of money. Peter disagreed. 'The Solomon inheritance,' her brother had said, 'is a family tradition that should not be broken. This money may well force Zachary to be more responsible.'

Sadly, her brother had been wrong.

The moment Zachary received the money, he broke from the family, disappearing from the house without taking any of his belongings. He surfaced a few months later in the tabloids. TRUST FUND PLAYBOY LIVING EUROPEAN HIGH LIFE.

The tabloids took joy in documenting Zachary's spoiled life of debauchery. The photos of wild parties on yachts and drunken disco stupors were hard for the Solomons to take, but the photos of their wayward teen turned from tragic to frightening when the papers reported Zachary had been caught carrying cocaine across a border in Eastern Europe: SOLOMON MILLIONAIRE IN TURKISH PRISON.

The prison, they learned, was called Soganlik – a brutal F-class detention center located in the Kartal district outside of Istanbul. Peter Solomon, fearing for his son's safety, flew to Turkey to retrieve him. Katherine's distraught brother returned empty-handed, having been forbidden even to visit with Zachary. The only promising news was that Solomon's influential contacts at the U.S. State Department were working on getting him extradited as quickly as possible.

Two days later, however, Peter received a horrifying

international phone call. The next morning, headlines blared: SOLOMON HEIR MURDERED IN PRISON.

The prison photos were horrific, and the media callously aired them all, even long after the Solomons' private burial ceremony. Peter's wife never forgave him for failing to free Zachary, and their marriage came to an end six months later. Peter had been alone ever since.

It was years later that Katherine, Peter, and their mother, Isabel, were gathered quietly for Christmas. The pain was still a presence in their family, but mercifully it was fading with each passing year. The pleasant rattle of pots and pans now echoed from the kitchen as their mother prepared the traditional feast. Out in the conservatory, Peter and Katherine were enjoying a baked Brie and relaxed holiday conversation.

Then came an utterly unexpected sound.

'Hello, Solomons,' an airy voice said behind them.

Startled, Katherine and her brother spun to see an enormous muscular figure stepping into the conservatory. He wore a black ski mask that covered all of his face except his eyes, which shone with feral ferocity.

Peter was on his feet in an instant. 'Who are you?! How did you get in here?!'

'I knew your little boy, Zachary, in prison. He told me where this key was hidden.' The stranger held up an old key and grinned like a beast. 'Right before I bludgeoned him to death.'

Peter's mouth fell open.

A pistol appeared, aimed directly at Peter's chest. 'Sit.'

Peter fell back into his chair.

As the man moved into the room, Katherine was frozen in place. Behind his mask, the man's eyes were wild like those of a rabid animal.

'Hey!' Peter yelled, as if trying to warn their mother in the kitchen. 'Whoever you are, take what you want, and get out!'

The man leveled his gun at Peter's chest. 'And what is it you think I want?'

'Just tell me how much,' Solomon said. 'We don't have money in the house, but I can—'

The monster laughed. 'Do not insult me. I have not come for money. I have come tonight for Zachary's other birthright.' He grinned. 'He told me about the pyramid.'

Pyramid? Katherine thought in bewildered terror. *What pyramid?*

Her brother was defiant. 'I don't know what you're talking about.'

'Don't play dumb with me! Zachary told me what you keep in your study vault. I want it. Now.'

'Whatever Zachary told you, he was confused,' Peter said. 'I don't know what you're talking about!'

'No?' The intruder turned and aimed the gun at Katherine's face. 'How about now?'

Peter's eyes filled with terror. 'You must believe me! I don't know what it is you want!'

'Lie to me one more time,' he said, still aiming at Katherine, 'and I swear I will take her from you.' He smiled. 'And from what Zachary said, your little sister is more precious to you than all your—'

'What's going on?!' Katherine's mother shouted, marching into the room with Peter's Browning Citori shotgun – which she aimed directly at the man's chest. The intruder spun toward her, and the feisty seventy-five-year-old woman wasted no time. She fired a deafening blast of pellets. The intruder staggered backward, firing his handgun wildly in all directions, shattering windows as he fell and crashed through the glass doorway, dropping the pistol as he fell.

Peter was instantly in motion, diving on the loose handgun. Katherine had fallen, and Mrs. Solomon hurried to her side, kneeling beside her. 'My God, are you hurt?!'

Katherine shook her head, mute with shock. Outside the shattered glass door, the masked man had clambered to his feet and was running into the woods, clutching his side as he ran. Peter Solomon glanced back to make sure his mother and sister were safe, and seeing they were fine, he held the pistol and raced out the door after the intruder.

Katherine's mother held her hand, trembling. 'Thank heavens you're okay.' Then suddenly her mother pulled away. 'Katherine? You're bleeding! There's blood! You're hurt!'

Katherine saw the blood. A lot of blood. It was all over her. But she felt no pain.

Her mother frantically searched Katherine's body for a wound. 'Where does it hurt!'

'Mom, I don't know, I don't feel anything!'

Then Katherine saw the source of the blood, and she went cold. 'Mom, it's not me . . .' She pointed to the side of her mother's white satin blouse, where blood was running freely, and a small tattered hole was visible. Her mother glanced down, looking more confused than anything else. She winced and shrank back, as if the pain had just hit her.

'Katherine?' Her voice was calm, but suddenly it carried the weight of her seventy-five years. 'I need you to call an ambulance.'

. Katherine ran to the hall phone and called for help. When she got back to the conservatory, she found her mother lying motionless in a pool of blood. She ran to her, crouching down, cradling her mother's body in her arms.

Katherine had no idea how much time had passed when she heard the distant gunshot in the woods. Finally, the conservatory door burst open, and her brother, Peter, rushed in, eyes wild, gun still in his hand. When he saw Katherine sobbing, holding their lifeless mother in her arms, his face contorted in anguish. The scream that echoed through the conservatory was a sound Katherine Solomon would never forget.

52

Mal'akh could feel the tattooed muscles on his back rippling as he sprinted back around the building toward the open bay door of Pod 5.

I must gain access to her lab.

Katherine's escape had been unanticipated . . . and problematic. Not only did she know where Mal'akh lived, she now knew his true identity . . . and that he was the one who had invaded their home a decade earlier.

Mal'akh had not forgotten that night either. He had come within inches of possessing the pyramid, but destiny had obstructed him. *I was not yet ready.* But he was ready now. More powerful. More influential. Having endured unthinkable hardship in preparation for his return, Mal'akh was poised tonight to fulfill his destiny at last. He felt certain that before the night was over, he would indeed be staring into the dying eyes of Katherine Solomon.

As Mal'akh reached the bay door, he reassured himself that Katherine had not truly escaped; she had only prolonged the inevitable. He slid through the opening and strode confidently across the darkness until his feet hit the carpet. Then he took a right turn and headed for the Cube. The banging on the door of Pod 5 had stopped, and Mal'akh suspected the guard was now trying to remove the dime Mal'akh had jammed into the key panel to render it useless.

When Mal'akh reached the door that led into the Cube, he located the outer keypad and inserted Trish's key card. The panel lit up. He entered Trish's PIN and went inside. The lights were all ablaze, and as he moved into the sterile space, he squinted in amazement at the dazzling array of equipment. Mal'akh was no stranger to the power of technology; he performed his own breed of science in the basement of his home, and last night some of that science had borne fruit.

The Truth.

Peter Solomon's unique confinement – trapped alone in the in-between – had laid bare all of the man's secrets. *I can see his soul.* Mal'akh had learned certain secrets he anticipated, and others he had not, including the news about Katherine's lab and her shocking discoveries. *Science is getting close,* Mal'akh had realized. *And I will not allow it to light the way for the unworthy.*

Katherine's work here had begun using modern science to answer ancient philosophical questions. *Does anyone hear our prayers? Is there life after death? Do humans have souls?* Incredibly, Katherine had answered all of these questions, and more. Scientifically. Conclusively. The methods she used were irrefutable. Even the most skeptical of people would be persuaded by the results of her experiments. If this information were published and made known, a fundamental shift would begin in the consciousness of man. *They will start to find their way.* Mal'akh's last task tonight, before his transformation, was to ensure that this did not happen.

As he moved through the lab, Mal'akh located the data room that Peter had told him about. He peered through the heavy glass walls at the two holographic data-storage units. *Exactly as he said they would be.* Mal'akh found it hard to imagine that the contents of these little boxes could change the course of human development, and yet Truth had always been the most potent of all the catalysts.

Eyeing the holographic storage units, Mal'akh produced Trish's key card and inserted it in the door's security panel. To his surprise, the panel did not light up. Apparently, access to this room was not a trust extended to Trish Dunne. He now reached for the key card he had found in Katherine's lab-coat pocket. When he inserted this one, the panel lit up.

Mal'akh had a problem. *I never got Katherine's PIN.* He tried Trish's PIN, but it didn't work. Stroking his chin, he stepped back and examined the three-inch-thick Plexiglas door. Even with an ax, he knew he would be unable to break through and obtain the drives he needed to destroy.

Mal'akh had planned for this contingency, however.

Inside the power-supply room, exactly as Peter had described, Mal'akh located the rack holding several metal cylinders resembling large scuba tanks. The cylinders bore the letters *LH,* the number 2, and the universal symbol for combustible. One of the canisters was connected to the lab's hydrogen fuel cell.

Mal'akh left one canister connected and carefully heaved one of the reserve cylinders down onto a dolly beside the rack. Then he rolled the cylinder out of the power-supply room, across the lab, to the Plexiglas door of the data-storage room. Although this location would certainly be plenty close enough, he had noticed one weakness in the heavy Plexiglas door – the small space between the bottom and the jamb.

At the threshold, he carefully laid the canister on its side and slid the flexible rubber tube beneath the door. It took him a moment to remove the safety seals and access the cylinder's valve, but once he did, ever so gently, he uncocked the valve. Through the Plexiglas, he could see the clear, bubbling liquid begin draining out of the tube onto the floor inside the storage room. Mal'akh watched the puddle expand, oozing across the floor, steaming and bubbling as it grew. Hydrogen remained in liquid form only when it was cold, and as it warmed up, it would start to boil off. The resulting gas, conveniently, was even more flammable than the liquid.

Remember the Hindenburg.

Mal'akh hurried now into the lab and retrieved the Pyrex jug of Bunsen-burner fuel – a viscous, highly flammable, yet noncombustible oil. He carried it to the Plexiglas door, pleased to see the liquid hydrogen canister was still draining, the puddle of boiling liquid inside the data-storage room now covering the entire floor, encircling the pedestals that supported the holographic storage units. A whitish mist now rose from the boiling puddle as the liquid hydrogen began turning to gas . . . filling the small space.

Mal'akh raised the jug of Bunsen-burner fuel and squirted a healthy amount on the hydrogen canister, the tubing, and into the small opening beneath the door. Then, very carefully, he began backing out of the lab, leaving an unbroken stream of oil on the floor as he went.

The dispatch operator handling 911 calls for Washington, D.C., had been unusually busy tonight. *Football, beer, and a full moon,* she thought as yet another emergency call appeared on her screen, this one from a gas station pay phone on the Suitland Parkway in Anacostia. *A car accident probably.*

'Nine-one-one,' she answered. 'What is your emergency?'

'I was just attacked at the Smithsonian Museum Support Center,' a panicked woman's voice said. 'Please send the police! Forty-two-ten Silver Hill Road!'

'Okay, slow down,' the operator said. 'You need to—'

'I need you to send officers also to a mansion in Kalorama Heights where I think my brother may be held captive!'

The operator sighed. *Full moon.*

53

'As I tried to tell you,' Bellamy was saying to Langdon, 'there is more to this pyramid than meets the eye.'

Apparently so. Langdon had to admit that the stone pyramid sitting in his unzipped daybag looked much more mysterious to him now. His decryption of the Masonic cipher had rendered a seemingly meaningless grid of letters.

Chaos.

S	O	E	U
A	T	U	N
C	S	A	S
V	U	N	J

For a long while, Langdon examined the grid, searching for any hint of meaning within the letters – hidden words, anagrams, clues of any sort – but he found nothing.

'The Masonic Pyramid,' Bellamy explained, 'is said to guard its secrets behind many veils. Each time you pull back a curtain, you face another. You have unveiled these letters, and yet they tell you nothing until you peel back another layer. Of course, the way to do that is known only to the one who holds the capstone. The *capstone*, I suspect, has an inscription as well, which tells you how to decipher the pyramid.'

Langdon glanced at the cube-shaped package on the desk. From what Bellamy had said, Langdon now understood that the capstone and pyramid were a 'segmented cipher' – a code broken into pieces. Modern cryptologists used segmented ciphers all the time, although the security scheme had been invented in ancient Greece. The Greeks, when they wanted to store secret information, inscribed it on a clay tablet and then shattered the tablet into pieces, storing each piece in a separate location. Only when all the pieces were gathered together could the secrets be read. This kind of inscribed clay tablet – called a symbolon – was in fact the origin of the modern word *symbol*.

'Robert,' Bellamy said, 'this pyramid and capstone have been kept apart for generations, ensuring the secret's safety.' His tone turned rueful. 'Tonight, however, the pieces have come dangerously close. I'm sure I don't have to say this . . . but it is our duty to ensure this pyramid is not assembled.'

Langdon found Bellamy's sense of drama to be somewhat overwrought. *Is he describing the capstone and pyramid . . . or a detonator and nuclear bomb?* He still couldn't quite accept Bellamy's claims, but it hardly seemed to matter. 'Even if this *is* the Masonic Pyramid, and even if this inscription does somehow reveal the location of ancient knowledge, how could that knowledge possibly impart the kind of power it is said to impart?'

'Peter always told me you were a hard man to convince – an academic who prefers proof to speculation.'

'You're saying you *do* believe that?' Langdon demanded, feeling impatient now. 'Respectfully . . . you are a modern, educated man. How could you believe such a thing?'

Bellamy gave a patient smile. 'The craft of Freemasonry has given me a deep respect for that which transcends human understanding. I've learned *never* to close my mind to an idea simply because it seems miraculous.'

54

Frantically, the SMSC perimeter patrolman dashed down the gravel pathway that ran along the outside of the building. He'd just received a call from an officer inside saying that the keypad to Pod 5 had been sabotaged, and that a security light indicated that Pod 5's specimen bay door was now open.

What the hell is going on?!

As he arrived at the specimen bay, sure enough he found the door open a couple of feet. *Bizarre,* he thought. *This can only be unlocked from the inside.* He took the flashlight off his belt and shone it into the inky blackness of the pod. Nothing. Having no desire to step into the unknown, he moved only as far as the threshold and then stuck the flashlight through the opening, swinging it to the left, and then to the—

Powerful hands seized his wrist and yanked him into the blackness. The guard felt himself being spun around by an invisible force. He smelled ethanol. The flashlight flew out of his hand, and before he could even process what was happening, a rock-hard fist collided with his sternum. The guard crumpled to the cement floor . . . groaning in pain as a large black form stepped away from him.

The guard lay on his side, gasping and wheezing for breath. His flashlight lay nearby, its beam spilling across the floor and illuminating what appeared to be a metal can of some sort. The can's label said it was fuel oil for a Bunsen burner.

A cigarette lighter sparked, and the orange flame illuminated a vision that hardly seemed human. *Jesus*

Christit! The guard barely had time to process what he was seeing before the bare-chested creature knelt down and touched the flame to the floor.

Instantly, a strip of fire materialized, leaping away from them, racing into the void. Bewildered, the guard looked back, but the creature was already slipping out the open bay door into the night.

The guard managed to sit up, wincing in pain as his eyes followed the thin ribbon of fire. *What the hell?!* The flame looked too small to be truly dangerous, and yet now he saw something utterly terrifying. The fire was no longer illuminating only the darkened void. It had traveled all the way to the back wall, where it was now illuminating a massive cinder-block structure. The guard had never been permitted inside Pod 5, but he knew very well what this structure must be.

The Cube.

Katherine Solomon's lab.

The flame raced in a straight line directly to the lab's outer door. The guard clambered to his feet, knowing full well that the ribbon of oil probably continued beneath the lab door . . . and would soon start a fire inside. But as he turned to run for help, he felt an unexpected puff of air sucking past him.

For a brief instant, all of Pod 5 was bathed in light.

The guard never saw the hydrogen fireball erupting skyward, ripping the roof off Pod 5 and billowing hundreds of feet into the air. Nor did he see the sky raining fragments of titanium mesh, electronic equipment, and droplets of melted silicon from the lab's holographic storage units.

* * *

Katherine Solomon was driving north when she saw the sudden flash of light in her rearview mirror. A deep rumble thundered through the night air, startling her.

Fireworks? she wondered. *Do the Redskins have a half-time show?*

She refocused on the road, her thoughts still on the 911 call she'd placed from the deserted gas station's pay phone.

Katherine had successfully convinced the 911 dispatcher to send the police to the SMSC to investigate a tattooed intruder and, Katherine prayed, to find her assistant, Trish. In addition, she urged the dispatcher to check Dr. Abaddon's address in Kalorama Heights, where she thought Peter was being held hostage.

Unfortunately, Katherine had been unable to obtain Robert Langdon's unlisted cell-phone number. So now, seeing no other option, she was speeding toward the Library of Congress, where Langdon had told her he was headed.

The terrifying revelation of Dr. Abaddon's true identity had changed everything. Katherine had no idea what to believe anymore. All she knew for certain was that the same man who had killed her mother and nephew all those years ago had now captured her brother and had come to kill her. *Who is this madman? What does he want?* The only answer she could come up with made no sense. *A pyramid?* Equally confusing was why this man had come to her lab tonight. If he wanted to hurt her, why hadn't he done so in the privacy of his own home earlier today? Why go to the trouble of sending a text message and risk breaking into her lab?

Unexpectedly, the fireworks in her rearview mirror

grew brighter, the initial flash followed by an un-expected sight – a blazing orange fireball that Katherine could see rising above the tree line. *What in the world?!* The fireball was accompanied by dark black smoke ... and it was nowhere near the Redskins' FedEx Field. Bewildered, she tried to determine what industry might be located on the other side of those trees ... just southeast of the parkway.

Then, like an oncoming truck, it hit her.

55

Warren Bellamy stabbed urgently at the buttons on his cell phone, trying again to make contact with someone who could help them, whoever that might be.

Langdon watched Bellamy, but his mind was with Peter, trying to figure out how best to find him. *Decipher the engraving,* Peter's captor had commanded, *and it will tell you the hiding place of mankind's greatest treasure ... We will go together ... and make our trade.*

Bellamy hung up, frowning. Still no answer.

'Here's what I don't understand,' Langdon said. 'Even if I could somehow accept that this hidden wisdom exists ... and that this pyramid somehow points to its underground location ... what am I looking for? A vault? A bunker?'

Bellamy sat quietly for a long moment. Then he gave a reluctant sigh and spoke guardedly. 'Robert, according to what I've heard through the years, the pyramid leads to the entrance of a spiral staircase.'

'A *staircase*?'

'That's right. A staircase that leads down into the earth . . . many hundreds of feet.'

Langdon could not believe what he was hearing. He leaned closer.

'I've heard it said that the ancient wisdom is buried at the bottom.'

Robert Langdon stood up and began pacing. *A spiral staircase descending hundreds of feet into the earth . . . in Washington, D.C.* 'And nobody has ever *seen* this staircase?'

'Allegedly the entrance has been covered with an enormous stone.'

Langdon sighed. The idea of a tomb covered with an enormous stone was right out of the biblical accounts of Jesus' tomb. This archetypal hybrid was the grandfather of them all. 'Warren, do *you* believe this secret mystical staircase into the earth exists?'

'I've never seen it personally, but a few of the older Masons swear it exists. I was trying to call one of them just now.'

Langdon continued pacing, uncertain what to say next.

'Robert, you leave me a difficult task with respect to this pyramid.' Warren Bellamy's gaze hardened in the soft glow of the reading lamp. 'I know of no way to *force* a man to believe what he does not want to believe. And yet I hope you understand your duty to Peter Solomon.'

Yes, I have a duty to help *him,* Langdon thought.

'I don't need you to believe in the power this pyramid can unveil. Nor do I need you to believe in the staircase it supposedly leads to. But I *do* need you to believe that you are morally obliged to protect this secret . . . whatever it may be.' Bellamy motioned to the little cube-shaped package. 'Peter entrusted the capstone to you because he had faith you would obey his wishes and keep it secret. And now you must do exactly that, even if it means sacrificing Peter's life.'

Langdon stopped short and wheeled around. 'What?!'

Bellamy remained seated, his expression pained but resolute. 'It's what he would want. You need to forget Peter. He's gone. Peter did his job, doing the best he could to protect the pyramid. Now it is *our* job to make sure his efforts were not in vain.'

'I can't believe you're saying this!' Langdon exclaimed, temper flaring. 'Even if this pyramid is everything you say it is, Peter is your Masonic brother. You're sworn to protect him above all else, even your country!'

'No, Robert. A Mason must protect a fellow Mason above all things . . . except one – the great secret our brotherhood protects for all mankind. Whether or not I believe this lost wisdom has the potential that history suggests, I have taken a vow to keep it out of the hands of the unworthy. And I would not give it over to anyone . . . even in exchange for Peter Solomon's life.'

'I know plenty of Masons,' Langdon said angrily, 'including the most advanced, and I'm damned sure these men are not sworn to sacrifice their lives for the sake of a stone pyramid. And I'm also damned sure none of them believes in a secret staircase that descends to a treasure buried deep in the earth.'

'There are circles *within* circles, Robert. Not every*one* knows every*thing*.'

Langdon exhaled, trying to control his emotions. He, like everyone, had heard the rumors of elite circles within the Masons. Whether or not it was true seemed irrelevant in the face of this situation. 'Warren, if this pyramid and capstone truly reveal the ultimate Masonic secret, then why would Peter involve *me*? I'm not even a brother . . . much less part of any inner circle.'

'I know, and I suspect that is precisely *why* Peter chose you to guard it. This pyramid has been targeted in the past, even by those who infiltrated our brotherhood with unworthy motives. Peter's choice to store it *outside* the brotherhood was a clever one.'

'Were you aware I had the capstone?' Langdon asked.

'No. And if Peter told anyone at all, it would have been only one man.' Bellamy pulled out his cell phone and hit redial. 'And so far, I've been unable to reach him.' He got a voice-mail greeting and hung up. 'Well, Robert, it looks like you and I are on our own for the moment. And we have a decision to make.'

Langdon looked at his Mickey Mouse watch. 9:42 P.M. 'You do realize that Peter's captor is waiting for me to decipher this pyramid *tonight* and tell him what it says.'

Bellamy frowned. 'Great men throughout history have made deep personal sacrifices to protect the Ancient Mysteries. You and I must do the same.' He stood up now. 'We should keep moving. Sooner or later Sato will figure out where we are.'

'What about Katherine?!' Langdon demanded, not wanting to leave. 'I can't reach her, and she never called.'

'Obviously, something happened.'

'But we can't just abandon her!'

'Forget Katherine!' Bellamy said, his voice

commanding now. 'Forget Peter! Forget everyone! Don't you understand, Robert, that you've been entrusted with a duty that is bigger than all of us – you, Peter, Katherine, myself?' He locked eyes with Langdon. 'We need to find a safe place to hide this pyramid and capstone far from— '

A loud metallic crash echoed in the direction of the great hall.

Bellamy wheeled, eyes filling with fear. 'That was fast.'

Langdon turned toward the door. The sound apparently had come from the metal bucket that Bellamy had placed on the ladder blocking the tunnel doors. *They're coming for us.*

Then, quite unexpectedly, the crash echoed again.

And again.

And again.

The homeless man on the bench in front of the Library of Congress rubbed his eyes and watched the strange scene unfolding before him.

A white Volvo had just jumped the curb, lurched across the deserted pedestrian walkway, and screeched to a halt at the foot of the library's main entrance. An attractive, dark-haired woman had leaped out, anxiously surveyed the area, and, spotting the homeless man, had shouted, 'Do you have a phone?'

Lady, I don't have a left shoe.

Apparently realizing as much, the woman dashed up the staircase toward the library's main doors. Arriving at the top of the stairs, she grabbed the handle and tried desperately to open each of the three giant doors.

The library's closed, lady.

But the woman didn't seem to care. She seized one of the heavy ring-shaped handles, heaved it backward, and let it fall with a loud crash against the door. Then she did it again. And again. And again.

Wow, the homeless man thought, *she must really need a book.*

56

When Katherine Solomon finally saw the massive bronze doors of the library swing open before her, she felt as if an emotional floodgate had burst. All the fear and confusion she had bottled up tonight came pouring through.

The figure in the library doorway was Warren Bellamy, a friend and confidant of her brother's. But it was the man behind Bellamy in the shadows whom Katherine felt happiest to see. The feeling was apparently mutual. Robert Langdon's eyes filled with relief as she rushed through the doorway . . . directly into his arms.

As Katherine lost herself in the comforting embrace of an old friend, Bellamy closed the front door. She heard the heavy lock click into place, and at last she felt safe. Tears came unexpectedly, but she fought them back.

Langdon held her. 'It's okay,' he whispered. 'You're okay.'

Because you saved me, Katherine wanted to tell him. *He destroyed my lab . . . all my work. Years of research*

. . . *up in smoke.* She wanted to tell him everything, but she could barely breathe.

'We'll find Peter.' Langdon's deep voice resonated against her chest, comforting her somehow. 'I promise.'

I know who did this! Katherine wanted to yell. *The same man who killed my mother and nephew!* Before she could explain herself, an unexpected sound broke the silence of the library.

The loud crash echoed up from beneath them in a vestibule stairwell – as if a large metal object had fallen on a tile floor. Katherine felt Langdon's muscles stiffen instantly.

Bellamy stepped forward, his expression dire. 'We're leaving. *Now.*'

Bewildered, Katherine followed as the Architect and Langdon hurried across the great hall toward the library's famed reading room, which was ablaze with light. Bellamy quickly locked the two sets of doors behind them, first the outer, then the inner.

Katherine followed in a daze as Bellamy hustled them both toward the center of the room. The threesome arrived at a reading desk where a leather bag sat beneath a light. Beside the bag, there was a tiny cube-shaped package, which Bellamy scooped up and placed inside the bag, alongside a—

Katherine stopped short. *A pyramid?*

Although she had never seen this engraved stone pyramid, she felt her entire body recoil in recognition. Somehow her gut knew the truth. Katherine Solomon had just come face-to-face with the object that had so deeply damaged her life. *The pyramid.*

Bellamy zipped up the bag and handed it to Langdon. 'Don't let this out of your sight.'

A sudden explosion rocked the room's outer doors. The tinkling of shattered glass followed.

'This way!' Bellamy spun, looking scared now as he rushed them over to the central circulation desk – eight counters around a massive octagonal cabinet. He guided them in behind the counters and then pointed to an opening in the cabinet. 'Get in there!'

'In *there*?' Langdon demanded. 'They'll find us for sure!'

'Trust me,' Bellamy said. 'It's not what you think.'

57

Mal'akh gunned his limousine north toward Kalorama Heights. The explosion in Katherine's lab had been bigger than he had anticipated, and he had been lucky to escape unscathed. Conveniently, the ensuing chaos had enabled him to slip out without opposition, powering his limousine past a distracted gate guard who was busy yelling into a telephone.

I've got to get off the road, he thought. If Katherine hadn't yet phoned the police, the explosion would certainly draw their attention. *And a shirtless man driving a limousine would be hard to miss.*

After years of preparation, Mal'akh could scarcely believe the night was now upon him. The journey to this moment had been a long, difficult one. *What began years ago in misery . . . will end tonight in glory.*

On the night it all began, he had not had the name Mal'akh. In fact, on the night it all began, he had not had any name at all. *Inmate 37.* Like most of the prisoners at the brutal Soganlik Prison outside of Istanbul, Inmate 37 was here because of drugs.

He had been lying on his bunk in a cement cell, hungry and cold in the darkness, wondering how long he would be incarcerated. His new cellmate, whom he'd met only twenty-four hours ago, was sleeping in the bunk above him. The prison administrator, an obese alcoholic who hated his job and took it out on the inmates, had just killed all the lights for the night.

It was almost ten o'clock when Inmate 37 heard the conversation filtering in through the ventilation shaft. The first voice was unmistakably clear – the piercing, belligerent accent of the prison administrator, who clearly did not appreciate being woken up by a late-night visitor.

'Yes, yes, you've come a long way,' he was saying, 'but there are no visitors for the first month. State regulations. No exceptions.'

The voice that replied was soft and refined, filled with pain. 'Is my son safe?'

'He is a drug addict.'

'Is he being treated well?'

'Well enough,' the administrator said. 'This is not a hotel.'

There was a pained pause. 'You do realize the U.S. State Department will request extradition.'

'Yes, yes, they always do. It will be granted, although the paperwork might take us a couple of weeks . . . or even a month . . . depending.'

'Depending on what?'

'Well,' the administrator said, 'we are understaffed.' He paused. 'Of course, sometimes concerned parties like yourself make donations to the prison staff to help us push things through more quickly.'

The visitor did not reply.

'Mr. Solomon,' the administrator continued, lowering his voice, 'for a man like yourself, for whom money is no object, there are always options. I know people in government. If you and I work together, we may be able to get your son out of here . . . *tomorrow*, with all the charges dropped. He would not even have to face prosecution at home.'

The response was immediate. 'Forgetting the legal ramifications of your suggestion, I refuse to teach my son that money solves all problems or that there is no accountability in life, especially in a serious matter like this.'

'You'd like to *leave* him here?'

'I'd like to speak to him. Right now.'

'As I said, we have rules. Your son is unavailable to you . . . unless you would like to negotiate his immediate release.'

A cold silence hung for several moments. 'The State Department will be contacting you. Keep Zachary safe. I expect him on a plane home within the week. Good night.'

The door slammed.

Inmate 37 could not believe his ears. *What kind of father leaves his son in this hellhole in order to teach him a lesson?* Peter Solomon had even rejected an offer to clear Zachary's record.

It was later that night, lying awake in his bunk, that Inmate 37 had realized how he would free himself. If money was the only thing separating a prisoner from freedom, then Inmate 37 was as good as free. Peter Solomon might not be willing to part with money, but as anyone who read the tabloids knew, his son, Zachary, had plenty of money, too. The next day,

Inmate 37 spoke privately to the administrator and suggested a plan – a bold, ingenious scheme that would give them both exactly what they wanted.

'Zachary Solomon would have to die for this to work,' explained Inmate 37. 'But we could both disappear immediately. You could retire to the Greek Islands. You would never see this place again.'

After some discussion, the two men shook hands.

Soon Zachary Solomon will be dead, Inmate 37 thought, smiling to think how easy it would be.

It was two days later that the State Department contacted the Solomon family with the horrific news. The prison snapshots showed their son's brutally bludgeoned body, lying curled and lifeless on the floor of his prison cell. His head had been bashed in by a steel bar, and the rest of him was battered and twisted beyond what was humanly imaginable. He appeared to have been tortured and finally killed. The prime suspect was the prison administrator himself, who had disappeared, probably with all of the murdered boy's money. Zachary had signed papers moving his vast fortune into a private numbered account, which had been emptied immediately following his death. There was no telling where the money was now.

Peter Solomon flew to Turkey on a private jet and returned with their son's casket, which they buried in the Solomon family cemetery. The prison administrator was never found. Nor *would* he be, Inmate 37 knew. The Turk's rotund body was now resting at the bottom of the Sea of Marmara, feeding the blue manna crabs that migrated in through the Bosporus Strait. The vast fortune belonging to Zachary Solomon had all been moved to an untraceable numbered account. Inmate 37 was a free man again – a free man with a massive fortune.

The Greek Islands were like heaven. The light. The water. The women.

There was nothing money couldn't buy – new identities, new passports, new hope. He chose a Greek name – Andros Dareios – *Andros* meaning 'warrior,' and *Dareios* meaning 'wealthy.' The dark nights in prison had frightened him, and Andros vowed never to go back. He shaved off his shaggy hair and shunned the drug world entirely. He began life anew – exploring never-before-imagined sensual pleasures. The serenity of sailing alone on the ink-blue Aegean Sea became his new heroin trance; the sensuality of sucking moist *arni souvlakia* right off the skewer became his new Ecstasy; and the rush of cliff diving into the foam-filled ravines of Mykonos became his new cocaine.

I am reborn.

Andros bought a sprawling villa on the island of Syros and settled in among the *bella gente* in the exclusive town of Possidonia. This new world was a community not only of wealth, but of culture and physical perfection. His neighbors took great pride in their bodies and minds, and it was contagious. The newcomer suddenly found himself jogging on the beach, tanning his pale body, and reading books. Andros read Homer's *Odyssey*, captivated by the images of powerful bronze men doing battle on these islands. The next day, he began lifting weights, and was amazed to see how quickly his chest and arms grew larger. Gradually, he began to feel women's eyes on him, and the admiration was intoxicating. He longed to grow stronger still. And he did. With the help of aggressive cycles of steroids intermixed with black-market growth hormones and endless hours of weight lifting, Andros transformed himself into something he had never imagined he could be – a perfect male specimen. He grew in both height and musculature, developing flawless pectorals and massive, sinewy legs, which he kept perfectly tanned.

Everyone was looking now.

As Andros had been warned, the heavy steroids and hormones changed not only his body, but also his voice box, giving him an eerie, breathy whisper, which made him feel more mysterious. The soft, enigmatic voice, combined with his new body, his wealth, and his refusal to speak about his mysterious past, served as catnip for the women who met him. They gave themselves willingly, and he satisfied them all – from fashion models visiting his island on photo shoots, to nubile American college girls on vacation, to the lonely wives of his neighbors, to the occasional young man. They could not get enough.

I am a masterpiece.

As the years passed, however, Andros's sexual adventures began to lose their thrill. As did everything. The island's sumptuous cuisine lost its taste, books no longer held his interest, and even the dazzling sunsets from his villa looked dull. *How could this be?* He was only in his midtwenties, and yet he felt old. *What more is there to life?* He had sculpted his body into a masterpiece; he had educated himself and nourished his mind with culture; he had made his home in paradise; and he had the love of anyone he desired.

And yet, incredibly, he felt as empty as he had in that Turkish prison.

What is it I am missing?

The answer had come to him several months later. Andros was sitting alone in his villa, absently surfing channels in the middle of the night, when he stumbled across a program about the secrets of Freemasonry. The show was poorly done, posing more questions than answers, and yet he found himself intrigued by the plethora of conspiracy theories surrounding the brotherhood. The narrator described legend after legend.

Freemasons and the New World Order . . .
The Great Masonic Seal of the United States . . .
The P2 Masonic Lodge . . .
The Lost Secret of Freemasonry . . .
The Masonic Pyramid . . .

Andros sat up, startled. *Pyramid.* The narrator began recounting the story of a mysterious stone pyramid whose encrypted engraving promised to lead to lost wisdom and unfathomable power. The story, though seemingly implausible, sparked in him a distant memory . . . a faint recollection from a much darker time. Andros remembered what Zachary Solomon had heard from his father about a mysterious pyramid.

Could it be? Andros strained to recall the details.

When the show ended, he stepped out onto the balcony, letting the cool air clear his mind. He remembered more now, and as it all came back, he began to sense there might be some truth to this legend after all. And if so, then Zachary Solomon – although long dead – still had something to offer.

What do I have to lose?

Three weeks later, his timing carefully planned, Andros stood in the frigid cold outside the conservatory of the Solomons' Potomac estate. Through the glass, he could see Peter Solomon chatting and laughing with his sister, Katherine. *It looks like they've had no trouble forgetting Zachary,* he thought.

Before he pulled the ski mask over his face, Andros took a hit of cocaine, his first in ages. He felt the familiar rush of fearlessness. He pulled out a handgun, used an old key to unlock the door, and stepped inside. 'Hello, Solomons.'

Unfortunately, the night had not gone as Andros had planned. Rather than obtaining the pyramid for which he had come, he found himself riddled with bird shot and fleeing across the snow-covered lawn toward the dense woods. To his surprise, behind him, Peter Solomon was giving chase, pistol glinting in his hand. Andros dashed into the woods, running down a trail along the edge of a deep ravine. Far below, the sounds of a waterfall echoed up through the crisp winter air. He passed a stand of oak trees and rounded a corner to his left. Seconds later, he was skidding to a stop on the icy path, narrowly escaping death.

My God!

Only feet in front of him, the path ended, plunging straight down into an icy river far below. The large boulder at the side of the path had been carved by the unskilled hand of a child:

Zach's bRiDge

On the far side of the ravine, the path continued on. *So where's the bridge?!* The cocaine was no longer working. *I'm trapped!* Panicking now, Andros turned to flee back up the path, but he found himself facing Peter Solomon, who stood breathless before him, pistol in hand.

Andros looked at the gun and took a step backward. The drop behind him was at least fifty feet to an ice-covered river. The mist from the waterfall upstream billowed around them, chilling him to the bone.

'Zach's bridge rotted out long ago,' Solomon said, panting. 'He was the only one who ever came down this far.' Solomon held the gun remarkably steady. 'Why did you kill my son?'

'He was nothing,' Andros replied. 'A drug addict. I did him a favor.'

Solomon moved closer, gun aimed directly at Andros's chest. 'Perhaps I should do *you* the same favor.' His tone was surprisingly fierce. 'You *bludgeoned* my son to death. How does a man do such a thing?'

'Men do the unthinkable when pushed to the brink.'

'You *killed* my son!'

'No,' Andros replied, hotly now. '*You* killed your son. What kind of man leaves his son in a prison when he has the option to get him out! *You* killed your son! Not me.'

'You know *nothing*!' Solomon yelled, his voice filled with pain.

You're wrong, Andros thought. *I know everything.*

Peter Solomon drew closer, only five yards away now, gun leveled. Andros's chest was burning, and he could tell he was bleeding badly. The warmth ran down over his stomach. He looked over his shoulder at the drop. Impossible. He turned back to Solomon. 'I know more about you than you think,' he whispered. 'I know you are not the kind of man who kills in cold blood.'

Solomon stepped closer, taking dead aim.

'I'm warning you,' Andros said, 'if you pull that trigger, I will haunt you forever.'

'You already will.' And with that, Solomon fired.

As he raced his black limousine back toward Kalorama Heights, the one who now called himself Mal'akh reflected on the miraculous events that had delivered him from certain death atop that icy ravine. He had been transformed forever. The gunshot had echoed only for an instant, and yet its effects had reverberated across decades. His body, once tanned and perfect, was now marred by scars from that night . . . scars he kept hidden beneath the tattooed symbols of his new identity.

I am Mal'akh.

This was my destiny all along.

He had walked through fire, been reduced to ashes, and then emerged again . . . transformed once more. Tonight would be the final step of his long and magnificent journey.

58

The coyly nicknamed explosive Key4 had been developed by Special Forces specifically for opening locked doors with minimal collateral damage. Consisting primarily of cyclotrimethylenetrinitramine with a diethylhexyl plasticizer, it was essentially a piece of C-4 rolled into paper-thin sheets for insertion into doorjambs. In the case of the library's reading room, the explosive had worked perfectly.

Operation leader Agent Turner Simkins stepped over the wreckage of the doors and scanned the massive octagonal room for any signs of movement. Nothing.

'Kill the lights,' Simkins said.

A second agent found the wall panel, threw the switches, and plunged the room into darkness. In unison, all four men reached up and yanked down their night-vision headgear, adjusting the goggles over their eyes. They stood motionless, surveying the reading room, which now materialized in shades of luminescent green inside their goggles.

The scene remained unchanged.

Nobody made a dash for it in the dark.

The fugitives were probably unarmed, and yet the field team entered the room with weapons raised. In the darkness, their firearms projected four menacing rods of laser light. The men washed the beams in all directions, across the floor, up the far walls, into the balconies, probing the darkness. Oftentimes, a mere glimpse of a laser-sighted weapon in a darkened room was enough to induce instant surrender.

Apparently not tonight.

Still no movement.

Agent Simkins raised his hand, motioning his team into the space. Silently, the men fanned out. Moving cautiously up the center aisle, Simkins reached up and flipped a switch on his goggles, activating the newest addition to the CIA's arsenal. Thermal imaging had been around for years, but recent advances in miniaturization, differential sensitivity, and dual-source integration had facilitated a new generation of vision-enhancing equipment that gave field agents eyesight that bordered on superhuman.

We see in the dark. We see through walls. And now . . . we see back in time.

Thermal-imaging equipment had become so sensitive to heat differentials that it could detect not only a person's location . . . but their *previous* locations. The ability to see into the past often proved the most valuable asset of all. And tonight, once again, it proved its worth. Agent Simkins now spied a thermal signature at one of the reading desks. The two wooden chairs luminesced in his goggles, registering a reddish-purple color, indicating those chairs were warmer than the other chairs in the room. The desk lamp's bulb glowed orange. Obviously the two men had been sitting at the desk, but the question now was in which direction they had gone.

He found his answer on the central counter that surrounded the large wooden console in the middle of the room. A ghostly handprint, glowing crimson.

Weapon raised, Simkins moved toward the octagonal cabinet, training his laser sight across the surface. He circled until he saw an opening in the side of the console. *Did they really corner themselves in a cabinet?* The agent scanned the trim around the opening and saw another glowing handprint on it. Clearly someone had grabbed the doorjamb as he ducked inside the console.

The time for silence was over.

'Thermal signature!' Simkins shouted, pointing at the opening. 'Flanks converge!'

His two flanks moved in from opposite sides, effectively surrounding the octagonal console.

Simkins moved toward the opening. Still ten feet away, he could see a light source within. 'Light inside the console!' he shouted, hoping the sound of his voice might convince Mr. Bellamy and Mr. Langdon to exit the cabinet with their hands up.

Nothing happened.

Fine, we'll do this the other way.

As Simkins drew closer to the opening, he could hear an unexpected hum rumbling from within. It sounded like machinery. He paused, trying to imagine what could be making such a noise in such a small space. He inched closer, now hearing voices over the sound of machinery. Then, just as he arrived at the opening, the lights inside went out.

Thank you, he thought, adjusting his night vision. *Advantage, us.*

Standing at the threshold, he peered through the opening. What lay beyond was unexpected. The console was less of a cabinet than a raised ceiling over a steep set of stairs that descended into a room below. The agent aimed his weapon down the stairs and began descending. The hum of machinery grew louder with every step.

What the hell is this place?

The room beneath the reading room was a small, industrial-looking space. The hum he heard was indeed machinery, although he was not sure whether it was running because Bellamy and Langdon had activated it, or because it ran around the clock. Either way, it clearly made no difference. The fugitives had left their telltale heat signatures on the room's lone exit – a heavy steel door whose keypad showed four clear fingerprints glowing on the numbers. Around the door, slivers of glowing orange shone beneath the doorjamb, indicating that lights were illuminated on the other side.

'Blow the door,' Simkins said. 'This was their escape route.'

It took eight seconds to insert and detonate a sheet

314

of Key4. When the smoke cleared, the field-team agents found themselves peering into a strange underground world known here as 'the stacks.'

The Library of Congress had miles and miles of bookshelves, most of them underground. The endless rows of shelves looked like some kind of 'infinity' optical illusion created with mirrors.

A sign announced

TEMPERATURE-CONTROLLED ENVIRONMENT
Keep this door closed at all times.

Simkins pushed through the mangled doors and felt cool air beyond. He couldn't help but smile. *Could this get any easier?* Heat signatures in controlled environments showed up like solar flares, and already his goggles revealed a glowing red smear on a banister up ahead, which Bellamy or Langdon had grabbed on to while running past.

'You can run,' he whispered to himself, 'but you can't hide.'

As Simkins and his team advanced into the maze of stacks, he realized the playing field was tipped so heavily in his favor that he would not even need his goggles to track his prey. Under normal circumstances, this maze of stacks would have been a respectable hiding place, but the Library of Congress used motion-activated lights to save energy, and the fugitives' escape route was now lit up like a runway. A narrow strip of illumination stretched into the distance, dodging and weaving as it went.

All the men ripped off their goggles. Surging ahead on well-trained legs, the field team followed the trail of lights, zigging and zagging through a seemingly endless labyrinth of books. Soon Simkins began seeing lights flickering on in the darkness up ahead. *We're gaining.* He pushed harder, faster, until he heard footsteps and labored breathing ahead. Then he saw a target.

'I've got visual!' he yelled.

The lanky form of Warren Bellamy was apparently bringing up the rear. The primly dressed African American staggered through the stacks, obviously out of breath. *It's no use, old man.*

'Stop right there, Mr. Bellamy!' Simkins yelled.

Bellamy kept running, turning sharp corners, weaving through the rows of books. At every turn, the lights kept coming on over his head.

As the team drew within twenty yards, they shouted again to stop, but Bellamy ran on.

'Take him down!' Simkins commanded.

The agent carrying the team's nonlethal rifle raised it and fired. The projectile that launched down the aisle and wrapped itself around Bellamy's legs was nicknamed Silly String, but there was nothing silly about it. A military technology invented at Sandia National Laboratories, this nonlethal 'incapacitant' was a thread of gooey polyurethane that turned rock hard on contact, creating a rigid web of plastic across the back of the fugitive's knees. The effect on a running target was that of jamming a stick into the spokes of a moving bike. The man's legs seized midstride, and he pitched forward, crashing to the floor. Bellamy slid another ten feet down a darkened aisle before coming to a stop, the lights above him flickering unceremoniously to life.

'I'll deal with Bellamy,' Simkins shouted. 'You keep going after Langdon! He must be up ahead some—' The team leader stopped, now seeing that the library stacks ahead of Bellamy were all pitch-black. Obviously, there was no one else running in front of Bellamy. *He's alone?*

Bellamy was still on his chest, breathing heavily, his legs and ankles all tangled with hardened plastic. The agent walked over and used his foot to roll the old man over onto his back.

'Where is he?!' the agent demanded.

Bellamy's lip was bleeding from the fall. 'Where is *who*?'

Agent Simkins lifted his foot and placed his boot squarely on Bellamy's pristine silk tie. Then he leaned in, applying some pressure. 'Believe me, Mr. Bellamy, you do not want to play this game with me.'

59

Robert Langdon felt like a corpse.

He lay supine, hands folded on his chest, in total darkness, trapped in the most confined of spaces. Although Katherine lay nearby in a similar position near his head, Langdon could not see her. He had his eyes closed to prevent himself from catching even a fleeting glimpse of his frightening predicament.

The space around him was small.

Very small.

Sixty seconds ago, with the double doors of the reading room crashing down, he and Katherine had followed Bellamy into the octagonal console, down a steep set of stairs, and into the unexpected space below.

Langdon had realized at once where they were. *The heart of the library's circulation system.* Resembling a small airport baggage distribution center, the circulation room had numerous conveyor belts that angled off in different directions. Because the Library of Congress was housed in three separate buildings, books requested in the reading room often had to be transported great distances by a system of conveyors through a web of underground tunnels.

Bellamy immediately crossed the room to a steel door, where he inserted his key card, typed a sequence of buttons, and pushed open the door. The space beyond was dark, but as the door opened, a span of motion-sensor lights flickered to life.

When Langdon saw what lay beyond, he realized he was looking at something few people ever saw. *The Library of Congress stacks.* He felt encouraged by Bellamy's plan. *What better place to hide than in a giant labyrinth?*

Bellamy did not guide them into the stacks, however. Instead, he propped the door open with a book and turned back to face them. 'I had hoped to be able to explain a lot more to you, but we have no time.' He gave Langdon his key card. 'You'll need this.'

'You're not coming with us?' Langdon asked.

Bellamy shook his head. 'You'll never make it unless we split up. The most important thing is to keep that pyramid and capstone in safe hands.'

Langdon saw no other way out except the stairs back up to the reading room. 'And where are *you* going?'

'I'll coax them into the stacks away from you,' Bellamy said. 'It's all I can do to help you escape.'

Before Langdon could ask where he and Katherine were supposed to go, Bellamy was heaving a large

318

crate of books off one of the conveyors. 'Lie on the belt,' Bellamy said. 'Keep your hands in.'

Langdon stared. *You cannot be serious!* The conveyor belt extended a short distance then disappeared into a dark hole in the wall. The opening looked large enough to permit passage of a crate of books, but not much more. Langdon glanced back longingly at the stacks.

'Forget it,' Bellamy said. 'The motion-sensor lights will make it impossible to hide.'

'Thermal signature!' a voice upstairs shouted. 'Flanks converge!'

Katherine apparently had heard all she needed to hear. She climbed onto the conveyor belt with her head only a few feet from the opening in the wall. She crossed her hands over her chest like a mummy in a sarcophagus.

Langdon stood frozen.

'Robert,' Bellamy urged, 'if you won't do this for me, do it for Peter.'

The voices upstairs sounded closer now.

As if in a dream, Langdon moved to the conveyor. He slung his daybag onto the belt and then climbed on, placing his head at Katherine's feet. The hard rubber conveyor felt cold against his back. He stared at the ceiling and felt like a hospital patient preparing for insertion headfirst into an MRI machine.

'Keep your phone on,' Bellamy said. 'Someone will call soon . . . and offer help. Trust him.'

Someone will call? Langdon knew that Bellamy had been trying to reach someone with no luck and had left a message earlier. And only moments ago, as they hurried down the spiral staircase, Bellamy had tried one last time and gotten through, speaking very briefly in hushed tones and then hanging up.

'Follow the conveyor to the end,' Bellamy said. 'And jump off quickly before you circle back. Use my key card to get out.'

'Get out of *where*?!' Langdon demanded.

But Bellamy was already pulling levers. All the different conveyors in the room hummed to life. Langdon felt himself jolt into motion, and the ceiling began moving overhead.

God save me.

As Langdon approached the opening in the wall, he looked back and saw Warren Bellamy race through the doorway into the stacks, closing the door behind him. An instant later, Langdon slid into the darkness, swallowed up by the library . . . just as a glowing red laser dot came dancing down the stairs.

60

The underpaid female security guard from Preferred Security double-checked the Kalorama Heights address on her call sheet. *This is it?* The gated driveway before her belonged to one of the neighborhood's largest and quietest estates, and so it seemed odd that 911 had just received an urgent call about it.

As usual with unconfirmed call-ins, 911 had contacted the local alarm company before bothering the police. The guard often thought the alarm company's motto – 'Your first line of defense' – could just as easily have been 'False alarms, pranks, lost pets, and complaints from wacky neighbors.'

Tonight, as usual, the guard had arrived with no details about the specific concern. *Above my pay grade.* Her job was simply to show up with her yellow bubble light spinning, assess the property, and report anything unusual. Normally, something innocuous had tripped the house alarm, and she would use her override keys to reset it. *This* house, however, was silent. No alarm. From the road, everything looked dark and peaceful.

The guard buzzed the intercom at the gate, but got no answer. She typed her override code to open the gate and pulled into the driveway. Leaving her engine running and her bubble light spinning, she walked up to the front door and rang the bell. No answer. She saw no lights and no movement.

Reluctantly following procedure, she flicked on her flashlight to begin her trek around the house to check the doors and windows for signs of break-in. As she rounded the corner, a black stretch limousine drove past the house, slowing for a moment before continuing on. *Rubbernecking neighbors.*

Bit by bit, she made her way around the house, but saw nothing out of place. The house was bigger than she had imagined, and by the time she reached the backyard, she was shivering from the cold. Obviously there was nobody home.

'Dispatch?' she called in on her radio. 'I'm on the Kalorama Heights call? Owners aren't home. No signs of trouble. Finished the perimeter check. No indication of an intruder. False alarm.'

'Roger that,' the dispatcher replied. 'Have a good night.'

The guard put her radio back on her belt and began retracing her steps, eager to get back to the warmth of her vehicle. As she did so, however, she spotted something she had missed earlier – a tiny speck of bluish light on the back of the house.

Puzzled, she walked over to it, now seeing the source – a low transom window, apparently to the home's basement. The glass of the window had been blacked out, coated on the inside with an opaque paint. *Some kind of darkroom maybe?* The bluish glow she had seen was emanating through a tiny spot on the window where the black paint had started to peel.

She crouched down, trying to peer through, but she couldn't see much through the tiny opening. She tapped on the glass, wondering if maybe someone was working down there.

'Hello?' she shouted.

There was no answer, but as she knocked on the window, the paint chip suddenly detached and fell off, affording her a more complete view. She leaned in, nearly pressing her face to the window as she scanned the basement. Instantly, she wished she hadn't.

What in the name of God?!

Transfixed, she remained crouched there for a moment, staring in abject horror at the scene before her. Finally, trembling, the guard groped for the radio on her belt.

She never found it.

A sizzling pair of Taser prongs slammed into the back of her neck, and a searing pain shot through her body. Her muscles seized, and she pitched forward, unable even to close her eyes before her face hit the cold ground.

61

Tonight was not the first time Warren Bellamy had been blindfolded. Like all of his Masonic brothers, he had worn the ritual 'hoodwink' during his ascent to the upper echelons of Masonry. That, however, had taken place among trusted friends. Tonight was different. These rough-handed men had bound him, placed a bag on his head, and were now marching him through the library stacks.

The agents had physically threatened Bellamy and demanded to know the whereabouts of Robert Langdon. Knowing his aging body couldn't take much punishment, Bellamy had told his lie quickly.

'Langdon never came down here with me!' he had said, gasping for air. 'I told him to go up to the balcony and hide behind the Moses statue, but I don't know where he is now!' The story apparently had been convincing, because two of the agents had run off in pursuit. Now the remaining two agents were marching him in silence through the stacks.

Bellamy's only solace was in knowing Langdon and Katherine were whisking the pyramid off to safety. Soon Langdon would be contacted by a man who could offer sanctuary. *Trust him.* The man Bellamy had called knew a great deal about the Masonic Pyramid and the secret it held – the location of a hidden spiral staircase that led down into the earth to the hiding place of potent ancient wisdom buried long ago. Bellamy had finally gotten through to the man as they were escaping the reading room, and he felt confident that his short message would be understood perfectly.

Now, as he moved in total darkness, Bellamy

pictured the stone pyramid and golden capstone in Langdon's bag. *It has been many years since those two pieces were in the same room.*

Bellamy would never forget that painful night. *The first of many for Peter.* Bellamy had been asked to come to the Solomon estate in Potomac for Zachary Solomon's eighteenth birthday. Zachary, despite being a rebellious child, was a Solomon, which meant tonight, following family tradition, he would receive his inheritance. Bellamy was one of Peter's dearest friends and a trusted Masonic brother, and therefore was asked to attend as a witness. But it was not only the transference of money that Bellamy had been asked to witness. There was far more than money at stake tonight.

Bellamy had arrived early and waited, as requested, in Peter's private study. The wonderful old room smelled of leather, wood fires, and loose-leaf tea. Warren was seated when Peter led his son, Zachary, into the room. When the scrawny eighteen-year-old saw Bellamy, he frowned. 'What are you doing here?'

'Bearing witness,' Bellamy offered. 'Happy birthday, Zachary.'

The boy mumbled and looked away.

'Sit down, Zach,' Peter said.

Zachary sat in the solitary chair facing his father's huge wooden desk. Solomon bolted the study door. Bellamy took a seat off to one side.

Solomon addressed Zachary in a serious tone. 'Do you know why you're here?'

'I think so,' Zachary said.

Solomon sighed deeply. 'I know you and I have not seen eye to eye for quite some time, Zach. I've done my best to be a good father and to prepare you for this moment.'

Zachary said nothing.

'As you know, every Solomon child, upon reaching adulthood, is presented with his or her birthright – a share of the Solomon fortune – which is intended to be a *seed* . . . a seed for you to nurture, make grow, and use to help nourish mankind.'

Solomon walked to a vault in the wall, unlocked it, and removed a large black folder. 'Son, this portfolio contains everything you need to legally transfer your financial inheritance into your own name.' He laid it on the desk. 'The aim is that you use this money to build a life of productivity, prosperity, and philanthropy.'

Zachary reached for the folder. 'Thanks.'

'Hold on,' his father said, putting his hand on the portfolio. 'There's something else I need to explain.'

Zachary shot his father a contemptuous look and slumped back down.

'There are aspects of the Solomon inheritance of which you are not yet aware.' His father was staring straight into Zachary's eyes now. 'You are my firstborn, Zachary, which means you are entitled to a choice.'

The teenager sat up, looking intrigued.

'It is a choice that may well determine the direction of your future, and so I urge you to ponder it carefully.'

'What choice?'

His father took a deep breath. 'It is the choice . . . between wealth or wisdom.'

Zachary gave him a blank stare. 'Wealth or wisdom? I don't get it.'

Solomon stood, walking again to the vault, where he pulled out a heavy stone pyramid with Masonic symbols carved into it. Peter heaved the stone onto the desk beside the portfolio. 'This pyramid was created long ago and has been entrusted to our family for generations.'

'A pyramid?' Zachary didn't look very excited.

'Son, this pyramid is a map . . . a map that reveals the location of one of humankind's greatest lost treasures. This map was created so that the treasure could one day be rediscovered.' Peter's voice swelled now with pride. 'And tonight, following tradition, I am able to offer it to you . . . under certain conditions.'

Zachary eyed the pyramid suspiciously. 'What's the treasure?'

Bellamy could tell that this coarse question was not what Peter had hoped for. Nonetheless, his demeanor remained steady.

'Zachary, it's hard to explain without a lot of background. But this treasure . . . in essence . . . is something we call the Ancient Mysteries.'

Zachary laughed, apparently thinking his father was joking.

Bellamy could see the melancholy growing now in Peter's eyes.

'This is very difficult for me to describe, Zach. Traditionally, by the time a Solomon is eighteen years of age, he is about to embark on his years of higher education in—'

'I told you!' Zachary fired back. 'I'm not interested in college!'

'I don't mean *college*,' his father said, his voice still calm and quiet. 'I'm talking about the brotherhood of Freemasonry. I'm talking about an education in the enduring mysteries of human science. If you had plans to join me within their ranks, you would be on the verge of receiving the education necessary to understand the importance of your decision tonight.'

Zachary rolled his eyes. 'Spare me the Masonic lecture again. I know I'm the first Solomon who doesn't want to join. But so what? Don't you get it? I have no interest in playing dress-up with a bunch of old men!'

His father was silent for a long time, and Bellamy noticed the fine age lines that had started to appear around Peter's still-youthful eyes.

'Yes, I get it,' Peter finally said. 'Times are different now. I understand that Masonry probably appears strange to you, or maybe even boring. But I want you to know, that doorway will *always* be open for you should you change your mind.'

'Don't hold your breath,' Zach grumbled.

'That's enough!' Peter snapped, standing up. 'I realize life has been a struggle for you, Zachary, but I am not your only guidepost. There are good men waiting for you, men who will welcome you within the Masonic fold and show you your true potential.'

Zachary chuckled and glanced over at Bellamy. 'Is that why *you're* here, Mr. Bellamy? So you Masons can gang up on me?'

Bellamy said nothing, instead directing a respectful gaze back at Peter Solomon – a reminder to Zachary of who held the power in this room.

Zachary turned back to his father.

'Zach,' Peter said, 'we're getting nowhere . . . so let me just tell you this. Whether or not you comprehend the responsibility being offered to you tonight, it is my family obligation to present it.' He motioned to the pyramid. 'It is a rare privilege to guard this pyramid. I urge you to consider this opportunity for a few days before making your decision.'

'Opportunity?' Zachary said. 'Babysitting a rock?'

'There are great mysteries in this world, Zach,' Peter said with a sigh. 'Secrets that transcend your wildest imagination. This pyramid protects those secrets. And even more important, there will come a time, probably within your lifetime, when this pyramid will at last be deciphered and its secrets unearthed. It will be a moment of great human transformation . . . and you have a chance to play a role in that moment. I want you to consider it very carefully. Wealth is common-place, but wisdom is rare.' He motioned to the portfolio and then to the pyramid. 'I beg you to remember that wealth without wisdom can often end in disaster.'

Zachary looked like he thought his father was insane. 'Whatever you say, Dad, but there's no way I'm giving up my inheritance for this.' He gestured to the pyramid.

Peter folded his hands before him. 'If you choose to accept the responsibility, I will hold your money and the pyramid for you until you have successfully completed your education within the Masons. This will take years, but you will emerge with the maturity to receive both your money *and* this pyramid. Wealth and wisdom. A potent combination.'

Zachary shot up. 'Jesus, Dad! You don't give up, do you? Can't you see that I don't give a damn about the Masons or stone pyramids and ancient mysteries?' He reached down and scooped up the black portfolio, waving it in front of his father's face. '*This* is my birthright! The same birthright of the Solomons who came before me! I can't believe you'd try to trick me out of my inheritance with lame stories about ancient treasure maps!' He tucked the portfolio under his arm and marched past Bellamy to the study's patio door.

'Zachary, wait!' His father rushed after him as Zachary stalked out into the night. 'Whatever you do, you can never speak of the pyramid you have seen!' Peter Solomon's voice cracked. 'Not to *anyone*! Ever!'

But Zachary ignored him, disappearing into the night.

Peter Solomon's gray eyes were filled with pain as he returned to his desk and sat heavily in his leather chair. After a long silence, he looked up at Bellamy and forced a sad smile. 'That went well.'

Bellamy sighed, sharing in Solomon's pain. 'Peter, I don't mean to sound insensitive . . . but . . . do you trust him?'

Solomon stared blankly into space.

'I mean . . .' Bellamy pressed, 'not to say anything about the pyramid?'

Solomon's face was blank. 'I really don't know what to say, Warren. I'm not sure I even know him anymore.'

Bellamy rose and walked slowly back and forth before the large desk. 'Peter, you have followed your family duty, but now, considering what just happened, I think we need to take precautions. I should return the capstone to you so you can find a new home for it. Someone else should watch over it.'

'Why?' Solomon asked.

'If Zachary tells anyone about the pyramid . . . and mentions my being present tonight . . .'

'He knows *nothing* of the capstone, and he's too immature to know the pyramid has any significance. We don't need a new home for it. I'll keep the pyramid in my vault. And you will keep the capstone wherever you keep it. As we always have.'

It was six years later, on Christmas Day, with the family still healing from Zachary's death, that the enormous man claiming to have killed him in prison broke into the Solomon estate. The intruder had come for the pyramid, but he had taken with him only Isabel Solomon's life.

Days later, Peter summoned Bellamy to his office. He locked the door and took the pyramid out of his vault, setting it on the desk between them. 'I should have listened to you.'

Bellamy knew Peter was racked with guilt over this. 'It wouldn't have mattered.'

Solomon drew a tired breath. 'Did you bring the capstone?'

Bellamy pulled a small cube-shaped package from his pocket. The faded brown paper was tied with twine and bore a wax seal of Solomon's ring. Bellamy laid the package on the desk, knowing the two halves of the Masonic Pyramid were closer together tonight than they should be. 'Find someone else to watch this. Don't tell me who it is.'

Solomon nodded.

'And I know where you can hide the pyramid,' Bellamy said. He told Solomon about the Capitol Building subbasement. 'There's no place in Washington more secure.'

Bellamy recalled Solomon liking the idea right away because it felt symbolically apt to hide the pyramid in the symbolic heart of our nation. *Typical Solomon*, Bellamy had thought. *The idealist even in a crisis*.

Now, ten years later, as Bellamy was being shoved blindly through the Library of Congress, he knew the crisis tonight was far from over. He also now knew whom Solomon had chosen to guard the capstone . . . and he prayed to God that Robert Langdon was up to the job.

330

62

I'm under Second Street.

Langdon's eyes remained tightly shut as the conveyor rumbled through the darkness toward the Adams Building. He did his best not to picture the tons of earth overhead and the narrow tube through which he was now traveling. He could hear Katherine breathing several yards ahead of him, but so far, she had not uttered a word.

She's in shock. Langdon was not looking forward to telling her about her brother's severed hand. *You have to, Robert. She needs to know.*

'Katherine?' Langdon finally said, without opening his eyes. 'Are you okay?'

A tremulous, disembodied voice replied somewhere up ahead. 'Robert, the pyramid you're carrying. It's Peter's, isn't it?'

'Yes,' Langdon replied.

A long silence followed. 'I think . . . that pyramid is why my mother was murdered.'

Langdon was well aware that Isabel Solomon had been murdered ten years ago, but he didn't know the details, and Peter had never mentioned anything about a pyramid. 'What are you talking about?'

Katherine's voice filled with emotion as she recounted the harrowing events of that night, how the tattooed man had broken into their estate. 'It was a long time ago, but I'll never forget that he demanded a pyramid. He said he heard about the pyramid in prison, from my nephew, Zachary . . . right before he killed him.'

Langdon listened in amazement. The tragedy

within the Solomon family was almost beyond belief. Katherine continued, telling Langdon that she had always believed the intruder was killed that night . . . that is, until this same man had resurfaced today, posing as Peter's psychiatrist and luring Katherine to his home. 'He knew private things about my brother, my mother's death, and even my *work*,' she said anxiously, 'things he could only have learned from my brother. And so I trusted him . . . and that's how he got inside the Smithsonian Museum Support Center.' Katherine took a deep breath and told Langdon she was nearly certain the man had destroyed her lab tonight.

Langdon listened in utter shock. For several moments, the two of them lay together in silence on the moving conveyor. Langdon knew he had an obligation to share with Katherine the rest of tonight's terrible news. He began slowly, and as gently as he possibly could he told her how her brother had entrusted him with a small package years earlier, how Langdon had been tricked into bringing this package to Washington tonight, and finally, about her brother's hand having been found in the Rotunda of the Capitol Building.

Katherine's reaction was deafening silence.

Langdon could tell she was reeling, and he wished he could reach out and comfort her, but lying end to end in the narrow blackness made it impossible. 'Peter's okay,' he whispered. 'He's alive, and we'll get him back.' Langdon tried to give her hope. 'Katherine, his captor *promised* me your brother would be returned alive . . . as long as I decipher the pyramid for him.'

Still Katherine said nothing.

Langdon kept talking. He told her about the stone

pyramid, its Masonic cipher, the sealed capstone, and, of course, about Bellamy's claims that this pyramid was in fact the Masonic Pyramid of legend . . . a map that revealed the hiding place of a long spiral staircase that led deep into the earth . . . down hundreds of feet to a mystical ancient treasure that had been buried in Washington long ago.

Katherine finally spoke, but her voice was flat and emotionless. 'Robert, open your eyes.'

Open my eyes? Langdon had no desire to have even the slightest glimpse of how cramped this space really was.

'Robert!' Katherine demanded, urgently now. 'Open your eyes! We're here!'

Langdon's eyes flew open as his body emerged through an opening similar to the one it had entered at the other end. Katherine was already climbing off the conveyor belt. She lifted his daybag off the belt as Langdon swung his legs over the edge and jumped down onto the tile floor just in time, before the conveyor turned the corner and headed back the way it came. The space around them was a circulation room much like the one they had come from in the other building. A small sign read ADAMS BUILDING: CIRCULATION ROOM 3.

Langdon felt like he had just emerged from some kind of subterranean birth canal. *Born again.* He turned immediately to Katherine. 'Are you okay?'

Her eyes were red, and she had obviously been crying, but she nodded with a resolute stoicism. She picked up Langdon's daybag and carried it across the room without a word, setting it on a cluttered desk. She lit the desk's halogen clamp lamp, unzipped the bag, folded down the sides, and peered inside.

The granite pyramid looked almost austere in the clean halogen light. Katherine ran her fingers over the engraved Masonic cipher, and Langdon sensed deep emotion churning within her. Slowly, she reached into the daybag and pulled out the cube-shaped package. She held it under the light, examining it closely.

'As you can see,' Langdon quietly said, 'the wax seal is embossed with Peter's Masonic ring. He said this ring was used to seal the package more than a century ago.'

Katherine said nothing.

'When your brother entrusted the package to me,' Langdon told her, 'he said it would give me the power to create order out of chaos. I'm not entirely sure what that means, but I've got to assume the capstone reveals something important, because Peter was insistent that it not fall into the wrong hands. Mr. Bellamy just told me the same thing, urging me to hide the pyramid and not let anyone open the package.'

Katherine turned now, looking angry. 'Bellamy told you *not* to open the package?'

'Yes. He was adamant.'

Katherine looked incredulous. 'But you said this capstone is the only way we can decipher the pyramid, right?'

'Probably, yes.'

Katherine's voice was rising now. 'And you said deciphering the pyramid is what you were told to do. It's the *only* way we can get Peter back, right?'

Langdon nodded.

'Then, Robert, why wouldn't we open the package and decipher this thing right now?!'

Langdon didn't know how to respond. 'Katherine, I had the same exact reaction, and yet Bellamy told me that keeping this pyramid's secret intact was more important than anything . . . including your brother's life.'

Katherine's pretty features hardened, and she tucked a wisp of hair behind her ears. When she spoke, her voice was resolved. 'This stone pyramid, whatever it is, has cost me my entire family. First my nephew, Zachary, then my mother, and now my brother. And let's face it, Robert, if you hadn't called tonight to warn me . . .'

Langdon could feel himself trapped between Katherine's logic and Bellamy's steadfast urging.

'I may be a scientist,' she said, 'but I also come from a family of well-known Masons. Believe me, I've heard all the stories about the Masonic Pyramid and its promise of some great treasure that will enlighten mankind. Honestly, I find it hard to imagine such a thing exists. However, if it _does_ exist . . . perhaps it's time to unveil it.' Katherine slid a finger beneath the old twine on the package.

Langdon jumped. 'Katherine, no! Wait!'

She paused, but her finger remained beneath the string. 'Robert, I'm not going to let my brother die for this. Whatever this capstone says . . . whatever lost treasures this engraving might reveal . . . those secrets end tonight.'

With that, Katherine yanked defiantly on the twine, and the brittle wax seal exploded.

63

In a quiet neighborhood just west of Embassy Row in Washington, there exists a medieval-style walled garden whose roses, it is said, spring from twelfth-century plants. The garden's Carderock gazebo – known as Shadow House – sits elegantly amid meandering pathways of stones dug from George Washington's private quarry.

Tonight the silence of the gardens was broken by a young man who rushed through the wooden gate, shouting as he came.

'Hello?' he called out, straining to see in the moonlight. 'Are you in here?'

The voice that replied was frail, barely audible. 'In the gazebo . . . just taking some air.'

The young man found his withered superior seated on the stone bench beneath a blanket. The hunched old man was tiny, with elfin features. The years had bent him in two and stolen his eyesight, but his soul remained a force to be reckoned with.

Catching his breath, the young man told him, 'I just . . . took a call . . . from your friend . . . Warren Bellamy.'

'Oh?' The old man perked up. 'About what?'

'He didn't say, but he sounded like he was in a big hurry. He told me he left you a message on your voice mail, which you need to listen to right away.'

'That's all he said?'

'Not quite.' The young man paused. 'He told me to ask you a question.' *A very strange question.* 'He said he needed your response right away.'

The old man leaned closer. 'What question?'

As the young man spoke Mr. Bellamy's question, the pall that crossed the old man's face was visible even in the moonlight. Immediately, he threw off his blanket and began struggling to his feet.

'Please help me inside. Right away.'

64

No more secrets, thought Katherine Solomon.

On the table in front of her, the wax seal that had been intact for generations now lay in pieces. She finished removing the faded brown paper from her brother's precious package. Beside her, Langdon looked decidedly uneasy.

From within the paper, Katherine extracted a small box made of gray stone. Resembling a polished granite cube, the box had no hinges, no latch, and no apparent way inside. It reminded Katherine of a Chinese puzzle box.

'It looks like a solid block,' she said, running her fingers over the edges. 'Are you sure the X-ray showed it was hollow? With a capstone inside?'

'It did,' Langdon said, moving next to Katherine and scrutinizing the mysterious box. He and Katherine peered at the box from different angles, attempting to find a way in.

'Got it,' Katherine said as her fingernail located the hidden slit along one of the box's top edges. She set the box down on the desk and then carefully pried open the lid, which rose smoothly, like the top of a fine jewelry box.

When the lid fell back, Langdon and Katherine both drew audible breaths. The interior of the box seemed to be glowing. The inside was shining with an almost supernatural effulgence. Katherine had never seen a piece of gold this large, and it took her an instant to realize that the precious metal was simply reflecting the radiance of the desk lamp.

'It's spectacular,' she whispered. Despite being sealed in a dark stone cube for over a century, the capstone had not faded or tarnished in any way. *Gold resists the entropic laws of decay; that's one of the reasons the ancients considered it magical.* Katherine felt her pulse quicken as she leaned forward, peering down over the small golden point. 'There's an inscription.'

Langdon moved closer, their shoulders now touching. His blue eyes flashed with curiosity. He had told Katherine about the ancient Greek practice of creating a symbolon – a code broken into parts – and how this capstone, long separated from the pyramid itself, would hold the key to deciphering the pyramid. Allegedly, this inscription, whatever it said, would bring order from this chaos.

Katherine held the little box up to the light and peered straight down over the capstone.

Though small, the inscription was perfectly visible – a small bit of elegantly engraved text on the face of one side. Katherine read the six simple words.

Then she read them again.

'*No!*' she declared. 'That *can't* be what it says!'

Across the street, Director Sato hurried up the long walkway outside the Capitol Building toward her rendezvous point on First Street. The update from her field team had been unacceptable. No Langdon. No pyramid. No capstone. Bellamy was in custody, but he was not telling them the truth. At least not yet.

I'll make him talk.

She glanced back over her shoulder at one of Washington's newest vistas – the Capitol Dome framed above the new visitor center. The illuminated dome only accentuated the significance of what was truly at stake tonight. *Dangerous times.*

Sato was relieved to hear her cell phone ring and see her analyst's ID on the screen.

'Nola,' Sato answered. 'What have you got?'

Nola Kaye gave her the bad news. The X-ray of the capstone's inscription was too faint to read, and the image-enhancing filters had not helped.

Shit. Sato chewed at her lip. 'How about the sixteen-letter grid?'

'I'm still trying,' Nola said, 'but so far I've found no secondary encryption scheme that's applicable. I've got a computer reshuffling the letters in the grid and looking for anything identifiable, but there are over twenty trillion possibilities.'

'Stay on it. Let me know.' Sato hung up, scowling. Her hopes of deciphering the pyramid using only a photograph and X-ray were fading fast. *I need that pyramid and capstone . . . and I'm running out of time.*

Sato arrived at First Street just as a black Escalade SUV with dark windows roared across the double yellow and skidded to a stop in front of her at their rendezvous point. A lone agent got out.

'Any word yet on Langdon?' Sato demanded.

'Confidence is high,' the man said, emotionless. 'Backup just arrived. All library exits are surrounded. We even have air support coming in. We'll flush him with tear gas, and he'll have nowhere to run.'

'And Bellamy?'

'Tied up in the backseat.'

Good. Her shoulder was still smarting.

The agent handed Sato a plastic Ziploc bag containing cell phone, keys, and wallet. 'Bellamy's effects.'

'Nothing else?'

'No, ma'am. The pyramid and package must still be with Langdon.'

'Okay,' Sato said. 'Bellamy knows plenty he's not telling. I'd like to question him personally.'

'Yes, ma'am. To Langley, then?'

Sato took a deep breath and paced a moment beside the SUV. Strict protocols governed the interrogation of U.S. civilians, and questioning Bellamy was highly illegal unless it was done at Langley on video with witnesses, attorneys, blah, blah, blah . . . 'Not Langley,' she said, trying to think of somewhere closer. *And more private.*

The agent said nothing, standing at attention beside the idling SUV, waiting for orders.

Sato lit a cigarette, took a long drag, and gazed down at the Ziploc bag of Bellamy's items. His key ring, she had noticed, included an electronic fob adorned with four letters – *USBG.* Sato knew, of course, which government building this fob accessed. The building was very close and, at this hour, very private.

She smiled and pocketed the fob. *Perfect.*

When she told the agent where she wanted to take Bellamy, she expected the man to look surprised, but he simply nodded and opened the passenger door for her, his cold stare revealing nothing.

Sato loved professionals.

* * *

Langdon stood in the basement of the Adams Building and stared in disbelief at the elegantly inscribed words on the face of the golden capstone.

That's all it says?

Beside him, Katherine held the capstone under the light and shook her head. 'There's got to be more,' she insisted, sounding cheated. '*This* is what my brother has been protecting all these years?'

Langdon had to admit he was mystified. According to Peter and Bellamy, this capstone was supposed to help them decipher the stone pyramid. In light of those claims, Langdon had expected something illuminating and helpful. *More like obvious and useless.* Once again, he read the six words delicately inscribed on the face of the capstone.

The
secret hides
within The Order

The secret hides within The Order?

At first glance, the inscription appeared to be stating the obvious – that the letters on the pyramid were out of 'order' and that their secret lay in finding their proper sequence. This reading, however, in addition to being self-evident, seemed unlikely for another reason. 'The words *the* and *order* are capitalized,' Langdon said.

Katherine nodded blankly. 'I saw that.'

The secret hides within The Order. Langdon could think of only one logical implication. ' "The Order" must be referencing *the Masonic Order.*'

'I agree,' Katherine said, 'but it's still no help. It tells us nothing.'

Langdon had to concur. After all, the entire story of the Masonic Pyramid revolved around a secret hidden within the Masonic Order.

'Robert, didn't my brother tell you this capstone would give you power to see *order* where others saw only *chaos*?'

He nodded in frustration. For the second time tonight, Robert Langdon was feeling unworthy.

65

Once Mal'akh had finished dealing with his un-expected visitor – a female security guard from Preferred Security – he fixed the paint on the window through which she had glimpsed his sacred work space.

Now, ascending out of the soft blue haze of the base-ment, he emerged through a hidden doorway into his living room. Inside, he paused, admiring his spectacular painting of the Three Graces and savoring the familiar smells and sounds of his home.

Soon I will be leaving forever. Mal'akh knew that after tonight he would be unable to return to this place. *After tonight,* he thought, smiling, *I will have no need for this place.*

He wondered if Robert Langdon yet understood the true power of the pyramid . . . or the importance of the role for which fate had chosen him. *Langdon has yet to call me,* Mal'akh thought, after double-checking for messages on his disposable phone. It was now 10:02 P.M. *He has less than two hours.*

Mal'akh went upstairs to his Italian-marble bathroom and turned on the steam shower to let it heat up. Methodically, he stripped off his clothes, eager to begin his cleansing ritual.

He drank two glasses of water to calm his starving stomach. Then he walked to the full-length mirror and studied his naked body. His two days of fasting had accentuated his musculature, and he could not help but admire that which he had become. *By dawn, I will be so much more.*

66

'We should get out of here,' Langdon said to Katherine. 'It's only a matter of time before they figure out where we are.' He hoped Bellamy had managed to escape.

Katherine still seemed fixated on the gold capstone, looking incredulous that the inscription was so unhelpful. She had taken the capstone out of the box, examined every side, and was now carefully putting it back in the box.

The secret hides within The Order, Langdon thought. *Big help.*

Langdon found himself wondering now if perhaps Peter had been misinformed about the contents of the box. This pyramid and capstone had been created long before Peter was born, and Peter was simply doing as his forefathers had told him, keeping a secret that was probably as much a mystery to him as it was to Langdon and Katherine.

What did I expect? Langdon wondered. The more he learned tonight about the Legend of the Masonic Pyramid, the less plausible it all seemed. *I'm searching for a hidden spiral staircase covered by a huge stone?* Something told Langdon he was chasing shadows. Nonetheless, deciphering this pyramid seemed his best chance at saving Peter.

'Robert, does the year 1514 mean anything to you?'

Fifteen-fourteen? The question seemed apropos of nothing. Langdon shrugged. 'No. Why?'

Katherine handed him the stone box. 'Look. The box is dated. Have a look under the light.'

Langdon took a seat at the desk and studied the cube-shaped box beneath the light. Katherine put a soft hand on his shoulder, leaning in to point out the tiny text she had found carved on the exterior of the box, near the bottom corner of one side.

'Fifteen-fourteen A.D.,' she said, pointing into the box.

Sure enough, the carving depicted the number 1514, followed by an unusual stylization of the letters *A* and *D*.

1514 🐓

'This date,' Katherine was saying, sounding suddenly hopeful, 'maybe it's the link we're missing? This dated cube looks a lot like a Masonic cornerstone, so maybe it's pointing to a real cornerstone? Maybe to a building built in 1514 A.D.?'

Langdon barely heard her.

Fifteen-fourteen A.D. is not a date.

The symbol 🔏, as any scholar of medieval art would recognize, was a well-known symbature – a symbol used in place of a signature. Many of the early philosophers, artists, and authors signed their work with their own unique symbol or monogram rather than their name. This practice added a mysterious allure to their work and also protected them from persecution should their writings or artwork be deemed counter establishment.

In the case of this symbature, the letters *A.D.* did not stand for *Anno Domini* . . . they were German for something else entirely.

Langdon instantly saw all the pieces fall into place. Within seconds, he was certain he knew exactly how to decipher the pyramid. 'Katherine, you did it,' he said, packing up. 'That's all we needed. Let's go. I'll explain on the way.'

Katherine looked amazed. 'The date 1514 A.D. actually *means* something to you?'

Langdon winked at her and headed for the door. 'A.D. isn't a date, Katherine. It's a *person*.'

67

West of Embassy Row, all was silent again inside the walled garden with its twelfth-century roses and Shadow House gazebo. On the other side of an entry road, the young man was helping his hunched superior walk across an expansive lawn.

He's letting me guide him?

Normally, the blind old man refused help, preferring to navigate by memory alone while on the grounds of his sanctuary. Tonight, however, he was apparently in a hurry to get inside and return Warren Bellamy's phone call.

'Thank you,' the old man said as they entered the building that held his private study. 'I can find my way from here.'

'Sir, I would be happy to stay and help—'

'That's all for tonight,' he said, letting go of his helper's arm and shuffling hurriedly off into the darkness. 'Good night.'

The young man exited the building and walked back across the great lawn to his modest dwelling on the grounds. By the time he entered his flat, he could feel his curiosity gnawing at him. The old man clearly had been upset by the question posed by Mr. Bellamy . . . and yet the question had seemed strange, almost meaningless.

Is there no help for the widow's son?

In his wildest imagination, he could not guess what this could mean. Puzzled, he went to his computer and typed in a search for this precise phrase.

To his great surprise, page after page of references appeared, all citing this exact question. He read the information in wonderment. It seemed Warren Bellamy was not the first person in history to ask this strange question. These same words had been uttered centuries ago . . . by King Solomon as he mourned a murdered friend. The question was allegedly still spoken today by Masons, who used it as a kind of encoded cry for help. Warren Bellamy, it seemed, was sending a distress call to a fellow Mason.

68

Albrecht Dürer?

Katherine was trying to put the pieces together as she hurried with Langdon through the basement of the Adams Building. *A.D. stands for Albrecht Dürer?* The famous sixteenth-century German engraver and painter was one of her brother's favorite artists, and Katherine was vaguely familiar with his work. Even so, she could not imagine how Dürer would be any help to them in this case. *For one thing, he's been dead more than four hundred years.*

'Dürer is symbolically perfect,' Langdon was saying as they followed the trail of illuminated EXIT signs. 'He was the ultimate Renaissance mind – artist, philosopher, alchemist, *and* a lifelong student of the Ancient Mysteries. To this day, nobody fully understands the messages hidden in Dürer's art.'

'That may be true,' she said. 'But how does "1514 Albrecht Dürer" explain how to decipher the pyramid?'

They reached a locked door, and Langdon used Bellamy's key card to get through.

'The number 1514,' Langdon said as they hurried up the stairs, 'is pointing us to a very specific piece of Dürer's work.' They came into a huge corridor. Langdon glanced around and then pointed left. 'This way.' They moved quickly again. 'Albrecht Dürer actually *hid* the number 1514 in his most mysterious piece of art – *Melencolia I* – which he completed in the year 1514. It's considered the seminal work of the Northern European Renaissance.'

Peter had once shown Katherine *Melencolia I* in an

old book on ancient mysticism, but she didn't recall any hidden number 1514.

'As you may know,' Langdon said, sounding excited, '*Melencolia I* depicts mankind's struggle to comprehend the Ancient Mysteries. The symbolism in *Melencolia I* is so complex it makes Leonardo da Vinci look overt.'

Katherine stopped abruptly and looked at Langdon. 'Robert, *Melencolia I* is here in Washington. It hangs in the National Gallery.'

'Yes,' he said with a smile, 'and something tells me *that's* not a coincidence. The gallery is closed at this hour, but I know the curator and—'

'Forget it, Robert, I know what happens when you go to museums.' Katherine headed off into a nearby alcove, where she saw a desk with a computer.

Langdon followed, looking unhappy.

'Let's do this the easier way.' It seemed Professor Langdon, the art connoisseur, was having an ethical dilemma about using the Internet when an original was so nearby. Katherine stepped behind the desk and powered up the computer. When the machine finally came to life, she realized she had another problem. 'There's no icon for a browser.'

'It's an internal library network.' Langdon pointed to an icon on the desktop. 'Try that.'

Katherine clicked on the icon marked DIGITAL COLLECTIONS. The computer accessed a new screen, and Langdon pointed again. Katherine clicked on his choice of icon: FINE PRINTS COLLECTION. The screen refreshed. FINE PRINTS: SEARCH.

'Type in "Albrecht Dürer." '

Katherine entered the name and then clicked the search key. Within seconds, the screen began displaying a series of thumbnail images. All of the images looked to be similar in style – intricate black-and-white engravings. Dürer had apparently done dozens of similar engravings.

Katherine scanned the alphabetical list of his artwork.

Adam and Eve
Betrayal of Christ
Four Horsemen of the Apocalypse
Great Passion
Last Supper

Seeing all the biblical titles, Katherine recalled that Dürer practiced something called Mystic Christianity – a fusion of early Christianity, alchemy, astrology, and science.

Science . . .

The image of her lab in flames rushed through her mind. She could barely process the long-term ramifications, but for the moment, her thoughts turned to her assistant, Trish. *I hope she made it out.*

Langdon was saying something about Dürer's version of the Last Supper, but Katherine was barely listening. She had just seen the link for *Melencolia I.*

She clicked the mouse, and the page refreshed with general information.

Melencolia I, 1514
Albrecht Dürer
(engraving on laid paper)
Rosenwald Collection
National Gallery of Art
Washington, D.C.

When she scrolled down, a high-res digital image of Dürer's masterpiece appeared in all its glory.

Katherine stared in bewilderment, having forgotten just how strange it was.

Langdon gave an understanding chuckle. 'As I said, it's cryptic.'

Melencolia I consisted of a brooding figure with giant wings, seated in front of a stone building, surrounded by the most disparate and bizarre collection of objects imaginable – measuring scales, an emaciated dog, carpenter's tools, an hourglass, various geometric solids, a hanging bell, a *putto*, a blade, a ladder.

Katherine vaguely recalled her brother telling her that the winged figure was a representation of 'human genius' – a great thinker with chin in hand, looking depressed, still unable to achieve enlightenment. The genius is surrounded with all of the symbols of his human intellect – objects of science, math, philosophy, nature, geometry, even carpentry – and yet is still unable to climb the ladder to true enlightenment. *Even the human genius has difficulty comprehending the Ancient Mysteries.*

'Symbolically,' Langdon said, 'this represents mankind's failed attempt to transform *human* intellect into *god*like power. In alchemical terms, it represents our inability to turn lead into gold.'

'Not a particularly encouraging message,' Katherine agreed. 'So how does it help us?' She did not see the hidden number 1514 that Langdon was talking about.

'Order from chaos,' Langdon said, flashing a lop-sided grin. 'Just as your brother promised.' He reached in his pocket and pulled out the grid of letters he had written earlier from the Masonic cipher. 'Right now, this grid is meaningless.' He spread the paper out on the desk.

S	O	E	U
A	T	U	N
C	S	A	S
V	U	N	J

Katherine eyed the grid. *Definitely meaningless.*

'But Dürer will transform it.'

'And how might he do that?'

'Linguistic alchemy.' Langdon motioned to the computer screen. 'Look carefully. Hidden in this masterpiece is something that will make sense of our sixteen letters.' He waited. 'Do you see it yet? Look for the number 1514.'

Katherine was in no mood to play classroom. 'Robert, I see nothing – an orb, a ladder, a knife, a polyhedron, a scale? I give up.'

'Look! There in the background. Carved into that building behind the angel? Beneath the bell? Dürer engraved a square that is full of numbers.'

Katherine now saw the square that contained numbers, among them 1514.

'Katherine, that square is the key to deciphering the pyramid!'

She shot him a surprised look.

'That's not just *any* square,' Langdon said, grinning. 'That, Ms. Solomon, is a *magic* square.'

69

Where the hell are they taking me?

Bellamy was still blindfolded in the back of an SUV. After a short stop somewhere close to the Library of Congress, the vehicle had continued on . . . but only for a minute. Now the SUV had stopped again, having again traveled only about a block.

Bellamy heard muffled voices talking.

'Sorry . . . impossible . . .' an authoritative voice was saying. ' . . . closed at this hour . . .'

The man driving the SUV replied with equal authority. 'CIA investigation . . . national security . . .' Apparently the exchange of words and IDs was persuasive, because the tone shifted immediately.

'Yes, of course . . . service entrance . . .' There was the loud grinding of what sounded like a garage door, and as it opened, the voice added, 'Shall I accompany you? Once you're inside, you won't be able to get through—'

'No. We have access already.'

If the guard was surprised, it was too late. The SUV was moving again. It advanced about fifty yards and then came to a stop. The heavy door rumbled closed again behind them.

Silence.

Bellamy realized he was trembling.

With a bang, the SUV's rear hatch flew open. Bellamy felt a sharp pain in his shoulders as someone dragged him out by his arms, then lifted him to his feet. Without a word, a powerful force led him across a wide expanse of pavement. There was a strange, earthy smell here that he could not place. There were footsteps of someone else walking with them, but whoever it was had yet to speak.

They stopped at a door, and Bellamy heard an electronic ping. The door clicked open. Bellamy was manhandled through several corridors and could not help but notice that the air was warmer and more humid. *An indoor pool, maybe? No.* The smell in the air was not chlorine . . . it was far more earthy and primal.

Where the hell are we?! Bellamy knew he could not be more than a block or two from the Capitol Building. Again they stopped, and again he heard the electronic beep of a security door. This one slid open with a hiss. As they pushed him through, the smell that hit him was unmistakable.

Bellamy now realized where they were. *My God!* He came here often, although never through the service entrance. This magnificent glass building was only three hundred yards from the Capitol Building and was technically part of the Capitol Complex. *I run this place!* Bellamy now realized it was his own key fob that was giving them access.

Powerful arms pushed him through the doorway, leading him down a familiar, winding walkway. The heavy, damp warmth of this place usually felt comforting to him. Tonight, he was sweating.

What are we doing here?!

Bellamy was halted suddenly and seated on a bench. The man with the muscles unhooked his handcuffs only long enough to reaffix them to the bench behind his back.

'What do you want from me?' Bellamy demanded, heart pounding wildly.

The only response he received was the sound of boots walking off and the glass door sliding shut.

Then silence.

Dead silence.

They're just going to leave me here? Bellamy was sweating more heavily now as he struggled to release his hands. *I can't even take off my blindfold?*

'Help!' he shouted. 'Anybody!'

Even as he called out in panic, Bellamy knew nobody was going to hear him. This massive glass room – known as the Jungle – was entirely airtight when the doors were closed.

They left me in the Jungle, he thought. *Nobody will find me until morning.*

Then he heard it.

The sound was barely audible, but it terrified Bellamy like no sound he had ever heard in his life. *Something breathing. Very close.*

He was not alone on the bench.

The sudden hiss of a sulfur match sizzled so close to his face that he could feel the heat. Bellamy recoiled, instinctively yanking hard at his chains.

Then, without warning, a hand was on his face, removing his blindfold.

The flame before him reflected in the black eyes of Inoue Sato as she pressed the match against the cigarette dangling from her lips, only inches away from Bellamy's face.

She glared at him in the moonlight that filtered down through the glass ceiling. She looked pleased to see his fear.

'So, Mr. Bellamy,' Sato said, shaking out the match. 'Where shall we begin?'

70

A magic square. Katherine nodded as she eyed the numbered square in Dürer's engraving. Most people would have thought Langdon had lost his mind, but Katherine had quickly realized he was right.

The term *magic square* referred not to something mystical but to something mathematical – it was the name given to a grid of consecutive numbers arranged in such a way that all the rows, columns, and diagonals added up to the same thing. Created some four thousand years ago by mathematicians in Egypt and India, magic squares were still believed by some to hold magical powers. Katherine had read that even nowadays devout Indians drew special three-by-three magic squares called the Kubera Kolam on their pooja altars. Primarily, though, modern man had relegated magic squares to the category of 'recreational mathematics,' some people still deriving pleasure from the quest to discover new 'magical' configurations. *Sudoku for geniuses.*

Katherine quickly analyzed Dürer's square, adding up the numbers in several rows and columns.

16	3	2	13
5	10	11	8
9	6	7	12
4	15	14	1

'Thirty-four,' she said. 'Every direction adds up to thirty-four.'

'Exactly,' Langdon said. 'But did you know that *this* magic square is famous because Dürer accomplished the seemingly impossible?' He quickly showed Katherine that in addition to making the rows, columns, and diagonals add up to thirty-four, Dürer had also found a way to make the four quadrants, the four center squares, and even the four corner squares add up to that number. 'Most amazing, though, was Dürer's ability to position the numbers 15 and 14 together in the bottom row as an indication of the year in which he accomplished this incredible feat!'

Katherine scanned the numbers, amazed by all the combinations.

Langdon's tone grew more excited now. 'Extraordinarily, *Melencolia I* represents the very first time in history that a magic square appeared in *European* art. Some historians believe this was Dürer's encoded way of indicating that the Ancient Mysteries had traveled outside the Egyptian Mystery Schools and were now held by the European secret societies.' Langdon paused. 'Which brings us back to . . . *this*.'

He motioned to the slip of paper bearing the grid of letters from the stone pyramid.

S	O	E	U
A	T	U	N
C	S	A	S
V	U	N	J

'I assume the layout looks familiar now?' Langdon asked.

'Four-by-four square.'

Langdon picked up the pencil and carefully transcribed Dürer's numbered magic square onto the slip of paper, directly beside the lettered square. Katherine was now seeing just how easy this was going to be. He stood poised, pencil in hand, and yet . . . strangely, after all this enthusiasm, he seemed to hesitate.

'Robert?'

He turned to her, his expression one of trepidation. 'Are you *sure* we want to do this? Peter expressly—'

'Robert, if *you* don't want to decipher this engraving, then *I* will.' She held out her hand for the pencil.

Langdon could tell there would be no deterring her and so he acquiesced, turning his attention back to the pyramid. Carefully, he superimposed the magic square over the pyramid's grid of letters and assigned each letter a number. Then he created a new grid, placing the Masonic cipher's letters in the new order as defined by the sequence in Dürer's magic square.

When Langdon was finished, they both examined the result.

J E O V

A S A N

C T U S

U N U S

Katherine immediately felt confused. 'It's still gibberish.'

Langdon remained silent a long moment. 'Actually,

Katherine, it's not gibberish.' His eyes brightened again with the thrill of discovery. 'It's . . . Latin.'

In a long, dark corridor, an old blind man shuffled as quickly as he could toward his office. When he finally arrived, he collapsed in his desk chair, his old bones grateful for the reprieve. His answering machine was beeping. He pressed the button and listened.

'It's Warren Bellamy,' said the hushed whisper of his friend and Masonic brother. 'I'm afraid I have alarming news . . .'

Katherine Solomon's eyes shot back to the grid of letters, reexamining the text. Sure enough, a Latin word now materialized before her eyes. *Jeova.*

J	E	O	V
A	S	A	N
C	T	U	S
U	N	U	S

Katherine had not studied Latin, but this word was familiar from her reading of ancient Hebrew texts. *Jeova. Jehovah.* As her eyes continued to trace downward, reading the grid like a book, she was surprised to realize she could read the *entire* text of the pyramid.

Jeova Sanctus Unus.

She knew its meaning at once. This phrase was ubiquitous in modern translations of Hebrew scripture. In the Torah, the God of the Hebrews was known by many names – *Jeova, Jehovah, Jeshua, Yahweh, the Source, the Elohim* – but many Roman translations had consolidated the confusing nomenclature into a single Latin phrase: *Jeova Sanctus Unus.*

'One true God?' she whispered to herself. The phrase certainly did not seem like something that would help them find her brother. 'That's this pyramid's secret message? One true God? I thought this was a map.'

Langdon looked equally perplexed, the excitement in his eyes evaporating. 'This decryption obviously is correct, but . . .'

'The man who has my brother wants to know a *location.*' She tucked her hair behind her ear. 'This is not going to make him very happy.'

'Katherine,' Langdon said, heaving a sigh. 'I've been afraid of this. All night, I've had a feeling we're treating as reality a collection of myths and allegories. Maybe this inscription is pointing to a *metaphorical* location – telling us that the true potential of man can be accessed only through the one true God.'

'But that makes no *sense!*' Katherine replied, her jaw now clenched in frustration. 'My family protected this pyramid for generations! One true God? *That's* the secret? And the CIA considers this an issue of national security? Either they're lying or we're missing something!'

Langdon shrugged in accord.

Just then, his phone began to ring.

In a cluttered office lined with old books, the old man hunched over his desk, clutching a phone receiver in his arthritic hand.

The line rang and rang.

At last, a tentative voice answered. 'Hello?' The voice was deep but uncertain.

The old man whispered, 'I was told you require sanctuary.'

The man on the line seemed startled. 'Who is this? Did Warren Bell—'

'No names, please,' the old man said. 'Tell me, have you successfully protected the map that was entrusted to you?'

A startled pause. 'Yes . . . but I don't think it matters. It doesn't say much. If it is a map, it seems to be more *metaphorical* than—'

'No, the map is quite real, I assure you. And it points to a very *real* location. You must keep it safe. I cannot impress upon you enough how important this is. You are being pursued, but if you can travel unseen to my location, I will provide sanctuary . . . and answers.'

The man hesitated, apparently uncertain.

'My friend,' the old man began, choosing his words carefully. 'There is a refuge in Rome, north of the Tiber, which contains ten stones from Mount Sinai, one from heaven itself, and one with the visage of Luke's dark father. Do you know my location?'

There was a long pause on the line, and then the man replied, 'Yes, I do.'

The old man smiled. *I thought you might, Professor.* 'Come at once. Make sure you're not followed.'

71

Mal'akh stood naked in the billowing warmth of his steam shower. He felt pure again, having washed off the last remaining scent of ethanol. As the eucalyptus-infused vapors permeated his skin, he could feel his pores opening to the heat. Then he began his ritual.

First, he rubbed depilatory chemicals across his tattooed body and scalp, removing any traces of body hair. *Hairless were the gods of the seven islands of Heliades.* Then he massaged Abramelin oil into his softened and receptive flesh. *Abramelin is the sacred oil of the great Magi.* Then he turned his shower lever hard to the left, and the water turned ice cold. He stood beneath the frigid water for a full minute to close his pores and trap the heat and energy within his core. The cold served as a reminder of the icy river in which this transformation had begun.

When he stepped from the shower, he was shivering, but within seconds, his core heat emanated up through his layers of flesh and warmed him. Mal'akh's insides felt like a furnace. He stood naked before the mirror and admired his form . . . perhaps the last time he would see himself as a mere mortal.

His feet were the talons of a hawk. His legs – Boaz and Jachin – were the ancient pillars of wisdom. His hips and abdomen were the archways of mystical power. Hanging beneath the archway, his massive sex organ bore the tattooed symbols of his destiny. In another life, this heavy shaft of flesh had been his source of carnal pleasure. But no longer.

I have been purified.

Like the mystical eunuch monks of Katharoi, Mal'akh had removed his testicles. He had sacrificed his physical potency for a more worthy one. *Gods have no gender.* Having shed the human imperfection of gender along with the earthly pull of sexual temptation, Mal'akh had become like Ouranos, Attis,

Sporus, and the great castrati magicians of Arthurian legend. *Every spiritual metamorphosis is preceded by a physical one.* Such was the lesson of all the great gods . . . from Osiris, to Tammuz, to Jesus, to Shiva, to the Buddha himself.

I must shed the man who clothes me.

Abruptly, Mal'akh drew his gaze upward, past the double-headed phoenix on his chest, past the collage of ancient sigils adorning his face, and directly to the top of his head. He tipped his head toward the mirror, barely able to see the circle of bare flesh that waited there. This location on the body was sacred. Known as the fontanel, it was the one area of the human skull that remained open at birth. *An oculus to the brain.* Although this physiological portal closes within a matter of months, it remains a symbolic vestige of the lost connection between the outer and inner worlds.

Mal'akh studied the sacred patch of virginal skin, which was enclosed by the crownlike circle of an *ouroboros* – a mystical snake devouring its own tail. The bare flesh seemed to stare back at him . . . bright with promise.

Robert Langdon soon would uncover the great treasure that Mal'akh required. Once Mal'akh possessed it, the void on top of his head would be filled, and he would at last be prepared for his final transformation.

Mal'akh padded across his bedroom and took from his bottom drawer a long strip of white silk. As he had done many times before, he wrapped it around his groin and buttocks. Then he went downstairs.

In his office, his computer had received an e-mail message.

It was from his contact:

Mal'akh smiled. It was time to make final preparations.

72

The CIA field agent was in a foul mood as he descended from the reading-room balcony. *Bellamy lied to us.* The agent had seen no heat signatures whatsoever upstairs near the Moses statue, nor anywhere else upstairs for that matter.

So where the hell did Langdon go?

The agent retraced his steps now to the only place they'd spotted any heat signatures at all – the library's distribution hub. He descended the stairs again, moving beneath the octagonal console. The noise of the rumbling conveyors was grating. Advancing into the space, he flipped down his thermal goggles and scanned the room. Nothing. He looked toward the stacks, where the mangled door still showed hot from the explosion. Other than that, he saw no—

Holy shit!

The agent jumped back as an unexpected luminescence drifted into his field of vision. Like a pair of ghosts, the dimly glowing imprints of two humanoids had just emerged from the wall on a conveyor belt. *Heat signatures.*

Stunned, the agent watched as the two apparitions circled the room on the conveyor loop and then disappeared headfirst into a narrow hole in the wall. *They rode the conveyor out? That's insanity.*

In addition to realizing they had just lost Robert Langdon through a hole in the wall, the field agent was now aware that he had another problem. *Langdon's not alone?*

He was just about to switch on his transceiver and call the team leader, but the team leader beat him to it.

'All points, we've got an abandoned Volvo on the plaza in front of the library. Registered to one Katherine Solomon. Eyewitness says she entered the library not long ago. We suspect she's with Robert Langdon. Director Sato has ordered that we find them both immediately.'

'I've got heat signatures for both of them!' shouted the field agent in the distribution room. He explained the situation.

'For Christ's sake!' the team leader replied. 'Where the hell does the conveyor go?'

The field agent was already consulting the employee reference schematic on the bulletin board. 'Adams Building,' he replied. 'One block from here.'

'All points. Redirect to the Adams Building! NOW!'

73

Sanctuary. Answers.

The words echoed in Langdon's mind as he and Katherine burst through a side door of the Adams Building and out into the cold winter night. The mysterious caller had conveyed his location cryptically, but Langdon had understood. Katherine's reaction to their destination had been surprisingly sanguine: *Where better to find One True God?*

Now the question was how to get there.

Langdon spun in place, trying to get his bearings. It was dark, but thankfully the weather had cleared. They were standing in a small courtyard. In the distance, the Capitol Dome looked startlingly far away, and Langdon realized this was the first moment he had stepped outside since arriving at the Capitol several hours ago.

So much for my lecture.

'Robert, look.' Katherine pointed toward the silhouette of the Jefferson Building.

Langdon's first reaction on seeing the building was astonishment that they had traveled so far underground on a conveyor belt. His second reaction, however, was alarm. The Jefferson Building was now abuzz with activity – trucks and cars pulling in, men shouting. *Is that a searchlight?*

Langdon grabbed Katherine's hand. 'Come on.'

They ran northeast across the courtyard, quickly disappearing from view behind an elegant U-shaped building, which Langdon realized was the Folger Shakespeare Library. This particular building seemed appropriate camouflage for them tonight, as it housed the original Latin manuscript of Francis Bacon's *New Atlantis*, the utopian vision on which the American forefathers had allegedly modeled a new world based on ancient knowledge. Even so, Langdon would not be stopping.

We need a cab.

They arrived at the corner of Third Street and East Capitol. The traffic was sparse, and Langdon felt fading hope as he scanned for taxis. He and Katherine hurried northward on Third Street, putting distance between themselves and the Library of Congress. It was not until they had gone an entire block that Langdon finally spotted a cab rounding the corner. He flagged it down, and the cab pulled over.

Middle Eastern music played on his radio, and the young Arab driver gave them a friendly smile. 'Where to?' the driver asked as they jumped into the car.

'We need to go to—'

'Northwest!' Katherine interjected, pointing up Third Street away from the Jefferson Building. 'Drive toward Union Station, then left on Massachusetts Avenue. We'll tell you when to stop.'

The driver shrugged, closed the Plexiglas divider, and turned his music back on.

Katherine shot Langdon an admonishing look as if to say: 'Leave no trail.' She pointed out the window, directing Langdon's attention to a black helicopter that was skimming in low, approaching the area. *Shit.* Sato was apparently dead serious about recovering Solomon's pyramid.

As they watched the helicopter land between the Jefferson and Adams buildings, Katherine turned to him, looking increasingly worried. 'Can I see your cell phone for a second?'

Langdon handed her his phone.

'Peter told me you have an eidetic memory?' she said, rolling down her window. 'And that you remember every phone number you've ever dialed?'

'That's true, but—'

Katherine hurled his phone out into the night. Langdon spun in his seat and watched as his cell phone cartwheeled and splintered into pieces on the pavement behind them. 'Why did you do that!'

'Off the grid,' Katherine said, her eyes grave. 'This pyramid is our only hope of finding my brother, and I have no intention of letting the CIA steal it from us.'

In the front seat, Omar Amirana bobbed his head and hummed along with his music. Tonight had been slow, and he felt blessed to finally have a fare. His cab was just passing Stanton Park, when the familiar voice of his company dispatcher crackled over the radio.

'This is Dispatch. All vehicles in the area of the National Mall. We have just received a bulletin from government authorities regarding two fugitives in the area of the Adams Building . . .'

Omar listened in amazement as Dispatch described the precise couple in his cab. He stole an uneasy glance in his rearview mirror. Omar had to admit, the tall guy *did* look familiar somehow. *Did I see him on* America's Most Wanted?

Gingerly, Omar reached for his radio handset. 'Dispatch?' he said, speaking quietly into the transceiver. 'This is cab one-three-four. The two people you asked about – they are in my cab . . . right now.'

Dispatch immediately advised Omar what to do. Omar's hands were trembling as he called the phone number Dispatch had given him. The voice that answered was tight and efficient, like that of a soldier.

'This is Agent Turner Simkins, CIA field ops. Who is this?'

'Um . . . I'm the taxi driver?' Omar said. 'I was told to call about the two—'

'Are the fugitives currently in your vehicle? Answer only yes or no.'

'Yes.'

'Can they hear this conversation? Yes or no?'

'No. The slider is—'

'Where are you taking them?'

'Northwest on Massachusetts.'

'Specific destination?'

'They didn't say.'

The agent hesitated. 'Is the male passenger carrying a leather bag?'

Omar glanced in the rearview mirror, and his eyes went wide. 'Yes! That bag doesn't have explosives or anything in—'

'Listen carefully,' the agent said. 'You are in no danger so long as you follow my directions exactly. Is that clear?'

'Yes, sir.'

'What is your name?'

'Omar,' he said, breaking a sweat.

'Listen, Omar,' the man said calmly. 'You're doing great. I want you to drive as slowly as possible while I get my team out in front of you. Do you understand?'

'Yes, sir.'

'Also, is your cab equipped with an intercom system so you can communicate with them in the backseat?'

'Yes, sir.'

'Good. Here's what I want you to do.'

74

The Jungle, as it is known, is the centerpiece of the U.S. Botanic Garden (USBG) – America's living museum –

located adjacent to the U.S. Capitol Building. Technically a rain forest, the Jungle is housed in a towering greenhouse, complete with soaring rubber trees, strangler figs, and a canopy catwalk for more daring tourists.

Normally, Warren Bellamy felt nurtured by the Jungle's earthy smells and the sunlight glinting through the mist that filtered down from the vapor nozzles in the glass ceiling. Tonight, however, lit only by moonlight, the Jungle terrified him. He was sweating profusely, writhing against the cramps that now stabbed at his arms, still pinned painfully behind him.

Director Sato paced before him, puffing calmly on her cigarette – the equivalent of ecoterrorism in this carefully calibrated environment. Her face looked almost demonic in the smoke-filled moonlight that streamed down through the glass ceiling overhead.

'So then,' Sato continued, 'when you arrived at the Capitol tonight, and you discovered that I was already there . . . you made a decision. Rather than making your presence known to me, you descended quietly into the SBB, where, at great risk to yourself, you attacked Chief Anderson and myself, and you helped Langdon escape with the pyramid and capstone.' She rubbed her shoulder. 'An interesting choice.'

A choice I would make again, Bellamy thought. 'Where is Peter?' he demanded angrily.

'How would *I* know?' Sato said.

'You seem to know everything else!' Bellamy fired back at her, making no attempt to hide his suspicion that she was somehow behind all this. 'You knew to go to the Capitol Building. You knew to find Robert Langdon. And you even knew to X-ray Langdon's bag to find the capstone. Obviously, someone is giving you a lot of inside information.'

Sato laughed coldly and stepped closer to him. 'Mr. Bellamy, is *that* why you attacked me? Do you think I'm the *enemy*? Do you think I'm trying to steal your little pyramid?' Sato took a drag on her cigarette and blew the smoke out of her nostrils. 'Listen carefully. No one understands better than I do the importance of keeping secrets. I believe, as you do, that there is certain information to which the masses should not be privy. Tonight, however, there are forces at work that I fear you have not yet grasped. The man who kidnapped Peter Solomon holds enormous power . . . a power that you apparently have yet to realize. Believe me, he is a walking time bomb . . . capable of initiating a series of events that will profoundly change the world as you know it.'

'I don't understand.' Bellamy shifted on the bench, his arms aching in his handcuffs.

'You don't *need* to understand. You need to obey. Right now, my only hope of averting a major disaster is to cooperate with this man . . . and to give him exactly what he wants. Which means, you are going to call Mr. Langdon and tell him to turn himself in, along with the pyramid and capstone. Once Langdon is in my custody, he will decrypt the pyramid's inscription, obtain whatever information this man is demanding, and provide him with exactly what he wants.'

The location of the spiral staircase that leads to the Ancient Mysteries? 'I can't do that. I've taken vows of secrecy.'

Sato erupted. 'I don't give a damn *what* you've vowed, I will throw you in prison so fast—'

'Threaten me all you like,' Bellamy said defiantly. 'I will not help you.'

Sato took a deep breath and spoke now in a fearsome whisper. 'Mr. Bellamy, you have no idea what's really going on tonight, do you?'

The tense silence hung for several seconds, finally broken by the sound of Sato's phone. She plunged her hand into her pocket and eagerly snatched it out. 'Talk to me,' she answered, listening carefully to the reply. 'Where is their taxi now? How long? Okay, good. Bring them to the U.S. Botanic Garden. Service entrance. And make sure you get me that goddamn pyramid and capstone.'

Sato hung up and turned back to Bellamy with a smug smile. 'Well then . . . it seems you're fast outliving your usefulness.'

75

Robert Langdon stared blankly into space, feeling too tired to urge the slow-moving taxi driver to pick up the pace. Beside him, Katherine had fallen silent, too, looking frustrated by their lack of understanding of what made the pyramid so special. They had again been through everything they knew about the pyramid, the capstone, and the evening's strange events; they still had no ideas as to how this pyramid could possibly be considered a map to anything at all.

Jeova Sanctus Unus? The secret hides within The Order?

Their mysterious contact had promised them answers if they could meet him at a specific place. *A refuge in Rome, north of the Tiber.* Langdon knew the forefathers' 'new Rome' had been renamed Washington early in her history, and yet vestiges of their original dream remained: the Tiber's waters still flowed into the Potomac; senators still convened beneath a replica of St. Peter's dome; and Vulcan and Minerva still watched over the Rotunda's long-extinguished flame.

The answers sought by Langdon and Katherine were apparently waiting for them just a few miles ahead. *Northwest on Massachusetts Avenue.* Their destination was indeed a refuge . . . north of Washington's Tiber Creek. Langdon wished the driver would speed up.

Abruptly, Katherine jolted upright in her seat, as if she had made a sudden realization. 'Oh my God, Robert!' She turned to him, her face going white. She hesitated a moment and then spoke emphatically. 'We're going the wrong way!'

'No, this is right,' Langdon countered. 'It's northwest on Massachu—'

'No! I mean we're going to the wrong *place*!'

Langdon was mystified. He had already told Katherine how he knew what location was being described by the mysterious caller. *It contains ten stones from Mount Sinai, one from heaven itself, and one with the visage of Luke's dark father.* Only one building on earth could make those claims. And that was exactly where this taxi was headed.

'Katherine, I'm certain the location is correct.'

'No!' she shouted. 'We don't need to go *there* anymore. I figured out the pyramid and capstone! I know what this is all about!'

Langdon was amazed. 'You understand it?'

'Yes! We have to go to Freedom Plaza instead!'

Now Langdon was lost. Freedom Plaza, although nearby, seemed totally irrelevant.

'*Jeova Sanctus Unus!*' Katherine said. 'The One True God of the Hebrews. The sacred symbol of the *Hebrews* is the Jewish star – the Seal of Solomon – an important symbol to the Masons!' She fished a dollar bill out of her pocket. 'Give me your pen.'

Bewildered, Langdon pulled a pen from his jacket.

'Look.' She spread the bill out on her thigh and took his pen, pointing to the Great Seal on the back. 'If you superimpose Solomon's seal on the Great Seal of the United States . . .' She drew the symbol of a Jewish star precisely over the pyramid. 'Look what you get!'

Langdon looked down at the bill and then back at Katherine as if she were mad.

'Robert, look more closely! Don't you see what I'm *pointing* at?'

He glanced back at the drawing.

What in the world is she getting at? Langdon had seen this image before. It was popular among conspiracy theorists as 'proof' that the Masons held secret influence over our early nation. When the six-pointed star was laid perfectly over the Great Seal of the United States, the star's top vertex fit perfectly over the Masonic all-seeing eye . . . and, quite eerily, the other five vertices clearly pointed to the letters *M-A-S-O-N*.

'Katherine, that's just a coincidence, and I still don't see how it has anything to do with Freedom Plaza.'

'Look again!' she said, sounding almost angry now. 'You're not looking where I am *pointing*! Right there. Don't you see it?'

An instant later, Langdon saw it.

CIA field-operations leader Turner Simkins stood outside the Adams Building and pressed his cell phone tightly to his ear, straining to hear the conversation now taking place in the back of the taxi. *Something just happened.* His team was about to board the modified Sikorsky UH-60 helicopter to head northwest and set up a roadblock, but now it seemed the situation had suddenly changed.

Seconds ago, Katherine Solomon had begun insisting they were going to the wrong destination. Her explanation – something about the dollar bill and Jewish stars – made no sense to the team leader, nor, apparently, to Robert Langdon. At least at first. Now, however, Langdon seemed to have grasped her meaning.

'My God, you're right!' Langdon blurted. 'I didn't see it earlier!'

Suddenly Simkins could hear someone banging on the driver's divider, and then it slid open. 'Change of plans,' Katherine shouted to the driver. 'Take us to Freedom Plaza!'

'Freedom Plaza?' the cabbie said, sounding nervous. 'Not northwest on Massachusetts?'

'Forget that!' Katherine shouted. 'Freedom Plaza! Go left here! Here! HERE!'

Agent Simkins heard the cab screeching around a corner. Katherine was talking excitedly again to Langdon, saying something about the famous bronze cast of the Great Seal embedded in the plaza.

'Ma'am, just to confirm,' the cabbie's voice interjected, sounding tense. 'We're going to Freedom Plaza – on the corner of Pennsylvania and Thirteenth?'

'Yes!' Katherine said. 'Hurry!'

'It's very close. Two minutes.'

Simkins smiled. *Nicely done, Omar.* As he dashed toward the idling helicopter, he shouted to his team. 'We've got them! Freedom Plaza! Move!'

76

Freedom Plaza is a map.

Located at the corner of Pennsylvania Avenue and Thirteenth Street, the plaza's vast surface of inlaid stone depicts the streets of Washington as they were originally envisioned by Pierre L'Enfant. The plaza is a popular tourist destination not only because the giant map is fun to walk on, but also because Martin Luther King Jr., for whom Freedom Plaza is named, wrote much of his 'I Have a Dream' speech in the nearby Willard Hotel.

D.C. cabdriver Omar Amirana brought tourists to Freedom Plaza all the time, but tonight, his two passengers were obviously no ordinary sightseers. *The CIA is chasing them?* Omar had barely come to a stop at the curb before the man and woman had jumped out.

'Stay right here!' the man in the tweed coat told Omar. 'We'll be right back!'

Omar watched the two people dash out onto the wide-open spaces of the enormous map, pointing and shouting as they scanned the geometry of intersecting streets. Omar grabbed his cell phone off the dashboard. 'Sir, are you still there?'

'Yes, Omar!' a voice shouted, barely audible over a thundering noise on his end of the line. 'Where are they now?'

'Out on the map. It seems like they're looking for something.'

'Do not let them out of your sight,' the agent shouted. 'I'm almost there!'

Omar watched as the two fugitives quickly found the plaza's famous Great Seal – one of the largest bronze medallions ever cast. They stood over it a moment and quickly began pointing to the southwest. Then the man in tweed came racing back toward the cab. Omar quickly set his phone down on the dashboard as the man arrived, breathless.

'Which direction is Alexandria, Virginia?' he demanded.

'Alexandria?' Omar pointed southwest, the exact same direction the man and woman had just pointed toward.

'I knew it!' the man whispered beneath his breath. He spun and shouted back to the woman. 'You're right! Alexandria!'

The woman now pointed across the plaza to an illuminated 'Metro' sign nearby. 'The Blue Line goes directly there. We want King Street Station!'

Omar felt a surge of panic. *Oh no.*

The man turned back to Omar and handed him entirely too many bills for the fare. 'Thanks. We're all set.' He hoisted his leather bag and ran off.

'Wait! I can drive you! I go there all the time!'

But it was too late. The man and woman were already dashing across the plaza. They disappeared down the stairs into the Metro Center subway station.

Omar grabbed his cell phone. 'Sir! They ran down into the subway! I couldn't stop them! They're taking the Blue Line to Alexandria!'

'Stay right there!' the agent shouted. 'I'll be there in fifteen seconds!'

Omar looked down at the wad of bills the man had given him. The bill on top was apparently the one they had been writing on. It had a Jewish star on top of the Great Seal of the United States. Sure enough, the star's points fell on letters that spelled *MASON*.

Without warning, Omar felt a deafening vibration all around him, as if a tractor trailer were about to collide with his cab. He looked up, but the street was deserted. The noise increased, and suddenly a sleek black helicopter dropped down out of the night and landed hard in the middle of the plaza map.

A group of black-clad men jumped out. Most ran toward the subway station, but one came dashing toward Omar's cab. He yanked open the passenger door. 'Omar? Is that you?'

Omar nodded, speechless.

'Did they say where they were headed?' the agent demanded.

'Alexandria! King Street Station,' Omar blurted. 'I offered to drive, but—'

377

'Did they say *where* in Alexandria they were going?'

'No! They looked at the medallion of the Great Seal on the plaza, then they asked about Alexandria, and they paid me with *this*.' He handed the agent the dollar bill with the bizarre diagram. As the agent studied the bill, Omar suddenly put it all together. *The Masons! Alexandria!* One of the most famous Masonic buildings in America was in Alexandria. 'That's it!' he blurted. 'The George Washington Masonic Memorial! It's directly across from King Street Station!'

'That it is,' the agent said, apparently having just come to the same realization as the rest of the agents came sprinting back from the station.

'We missed them!' one of the men yelled. 'Blue Line just left! They're not down there!'

Agent Simkins checked his watch and turned back to Omar. 'How long does the subway take to Alexandria?'

'Ten minutes at least. Probably more.'

'Omar, you've done an excellent job. Thank you.'

'Sure. What's this all about?!'

But Agent Simkins was already running back to the chopper, shouting as he went. 'King Street Station! We'll get there before they do!'

Bewildered, Omar watched the great black bird lift off. It banked hard to the south across Pennsylvania Avenue, and then thundered off into the night.

Underneath the cabbie's feet, a subway train was picking up speed as it headed away from Freedom Plaza. On board, Robert Langdon and Katherine Solomon sat breathless, neither one saying a word as the train whisked them toward their destination.

77

The memory always began the same way.

He was falling . . . plummeting backward toward an ice-covered river at the bottom of a deep ravine. Above him, the merciless gray eyes of Peter Solomon stared down over the barrel of Andros's handgun. As he fell, the world above him receded, everything disappearing as he was enveloped by the cloud of billowing mist from the waterfall upstream.

For an instant, everything was white, like heaven.

Then he hit the ice.

Cold. Black. Pain.

He was tumbling . . . being dragged by a powerful force that pounded him relentlessly across rocks in an impossibly cold void. His lungs ached for air, and yet his chest muscles had contracted so violently in the cold that he was unable even to inhale.

I'm under the ice.

The ice near the waterfall was apparently thin on account of the turbulent water, and Andros had broken directly through it. Now he was being washed downstream, trapped beneath a transparent ceiling. He clawed at the underside of the ice, trying to break out, but he had no leverage. The searing pain from the bullet hole in his shoulder was evaporating, as was the sting of the bird shot; both were blotted out now by the crippling throb of his body going numb.

The current was accelerating, slingshotting him around a bend in the river. His body screamed for oxygen. Suddenly he was tangled in branches, lodged against a tree that had fallen into the water. *Think!* He groped wildly at the branch, working his way toward the surface, finding the spot where the branch pierced up through the ice. His fingertips found the tiny space of open water surrounding the branch, and he pulled at the edges, trying to break the hole wider; once, twice, the opening was growing, now several inches across.

Propping himself against the branch, he tipped his head back and pressed his mouth against the small opening. The winter air that poured into his lungs felt warm. The sudden burst of oxygen fueled his hope. He planted his feet on the tree trunk and pressed his back and shoulders forcefully upward. The ice around the fallen tree, perforated by branches and debris, was weakened already, and as he drove his powerful legs into the trunk, his head and shoulders broke through the ice, crashing up into the winter night. Air poured into his lungs. Still mostly submerged, he wriggled desperately upward, pushing with his legs, pulling with his arms, until finally he was out of the water, lying breathless on the bare ice.

Andros tore off his soaked ski mask and pocketed it, glancing back upstream for Peter Solomon. The bend in the river obscured his view. His chest was burning again. Quietly, he dragged a small branch over the hole in the ice in order to hide it. The hole would be frozen again by morning.

As Andros staggered into the woods, it began to snow. He had no idea how far he had run when he stumbled out of the woods onto an embankment beside a small highway. He was delirious and hypothermic. The snow was falling harder now, and a single set of headlights approached in the distance. Andros waved wildly, and the lone pickup truck immediately pulled over. It had Vermont plates. An old man in a red plaid shirt jumped out.

Andros staggered toward him, holding his bleeding chest. 'A hunter . . . shot me! I need a . . . hospital!'

Without hesitation, the old man helped Andros up into the passenger seat of the truck and turned up the heater. 'Where's the nearest hospital?!'

Andros had no idea, but he pointed south. 'Next exit.' *We're not going to a hospital.*

The old man from Vermont was reported missing the next day, but nobody had any idea *where* on his journey from Vermont he might have disappeared in the blinding snowstorm. Nor did anyone link his disappearance to the other news story that dominated the headlines the next day – the shocking murder of Isabel Solomon.

When Andros awoke, he was lying in a desolate bedroom of a cheap motel that had been boarded up for the season. He recalled breaking in and binding his wounds with torn bedsheets, and then burrowing into a flimsy bed beneath a pile of musty blankets. He was famished.

He limped to the bathroom and saw the pile of bloody bird-shot pellets in the sink. He vaguely recalled prying them out of his chest. Raising his eyes to the dirty mirror, he reluctantly unwrapped his bloody bandages to survey the damage. The hard muscles of his chest and abdomen had stopped the bird shot from penetrating too deep, and yet his body, once perfect, was now ruined with wounds. The single bullet fired by Peter Solomon had apparently gone cleanly through his shoulder, leaving a bloody crater.

Making matters worse, Andros had failed to obtain that for which he had traveled all this distance. *The pyramid.* His stomach growled, and he limped outside to the man's truck, hoping maybe to find food. The pickup was now covered with heavy snow, and Andros wondered how long he had been sleeping in this old motel. *Thank God I woke up.* Andros found no food anywhere in the front seat, but he did find some arthritis painkillers in the glove compartment. He took a handful, washing them down with several mouthfuls of snow.

I need food.

A few hours later, the pickup that pulled out from behind the old motel looked nothing like the truck that had pulled in two days earlier. The cab cap was missing, as were the hubcaps, bumper stickers, and all of the trim. The Vermont plates were gone, replaced by those from an old maintenance truck Andros had found parked by the motel Dumpster, into which he had thrown all the bloody sheets, bird shot, and other evidence that he had ever been at the motel.

Andros had not given up on the pyramid, but for the moment it would have to wait. He needed to hide, heal, and above all, *eat*. He found a roadside diner where he gorged himself on eggs, bacon, hash browns, and three glasses of orange juice. When he was done, he ordered more food to go. Back on the road, Andros listened to the truck's old radio. He had not seen a television or newspaper since his ordeal, and when he finally heard a local news station, the report stunned him.

'FBI investigators,' a news announcer said, 'continue their search for the armed intruder who murdered Isabel Solomon in her Potomac home two days ago. The murderer is believed to have fallen through the ice and been washed out to sea.'

Andros froze. *Murdered Isabel Solomon?* He drove

on in bewildered silence, listening to the full report. It was time to get far, far away from this place.

The Upper West Side apartment offered breathtaking views of Central Park. Andros had chosen it because the sea of green outside his window reminded him of his lost view of the Adriatic. Although he knew he should be happy to be alive, he was not. The emptiness had never left him, and he found himself fixated on his failed attempt to steal Peter Solomon's pyramid.

Andros had spent long hours researching the Legend of the Masonic Pyramid, and although nobody seemed to agree on whether or not the pyramid was real, they all concurred on its famous promise of vast wisdom and power. *The Masonic Pyramid is real,* Andros told himself. *My inside information is irrefutable.*

Fate had placed the pyramid within Andros's reach, and he knew that ignoring it was like holding a winning lottery ticket and never cashing it in. *I am the only non-Mason alive who knows the pyramid is real . . . as well as the identity of the man who guards it.*

Months had passed, and although his body had healed, Andros was no longer the cocky specimen he had been in Greece. He had stopped working out, and he had stopped admiring himself naked in the mirror. He felt as if his body were beginning to show signs of age. His once-perfect skin was a patchwork of scars, and this only depressed him further. He still relied on the painkillers that had nursed him through his recovery, and he felt himself slipping back to the lifestyle that had put him in Soganlik Prison. He didn't care. *The body craves what the body craves.*

One night, he was in Greenwich Village buying

drugs from a man whose forearm had been tattooed with a long, jagged lightning bolt. Andros asked him about it, and the man told him the tattoo was covering a long scar he had gotten in a car accident. 'Seeing the scar every day reminded me of the accident,' the dealer said, 'and so I tattooed over it with a symbol of personal power. I took back control.'

That night, high on his new stash of drugs, Andros staggered into a local tattoo parlor and took off his shirt. 'I want to hide these scars,' he announced. *I want to take back control.*

'Hide them?' The tattoo artist eyed his chest. 'With *what*?'

'Tattoos.'

'Yes . . . I mean tattoos of *what*?'

Andros shrugged, wanting nothing more than to hide the ugly reminders of his past. 'I don't know. *You* choose.'

The artist shook his head and handed Andros a pamphlet on the ancient and sacred tradition of tattooing. 'Come back when you're ready.'

Andros discovered that the New York Public Library had in its collection fifty-three books on tattooing, and within a few weeks, he had read them all. Having rediscovered his passion for reading, he began carrying entire backpacks of books back and forth between the library and his apartment, where he voraciously devoured them while overlooking Central Park.

These books on tattoos had opened a door to a strange world Andros had never known existed – a world of symbols, mysticism, mythology, and the magical arts. The more he read, the more he realized how blind he had been. He began keeping notebooks of his ideas, his sketches, and his strange dreams. When he could no longer find what he wanted at the library, he paid rare-book dealers to purchase for him some of the most esoteric texts on earth.

De Praestigiis Daemonum ... *Lemegeton* ... *Ars Almadel* ... *Grimorium Verum* ... *Ars Notoria* ... and on and on. He read them all, becoming more and more certain that the world still had many treasures yet to offer him. *There are secrets out there that transcend human understanding.*

Then he discovered the writings of Aleister Crowley – a visionary mystic from the early 1900s – whom the church had deemed 'the most evil man who ever lived.' *Great minds are always feared by lesser minds.* Andros learned about the power of ritual and incantation. He learned that sacred *words*, if properly spoken, functioned like keys that opened gateways to other worlds. *There is a shadow universe beyond this one ... a world from which I can draw power.* And although Andros longed to harness that power, he knew there were rules and tasks to be completed beforehand.

Become something holy, Crowley wrote. *Make yourself sacred.*

The ancient rite of 'sacred making' had once been the law of the land. From the early Hebrews who made burnt offerings at the Temple, to the Mayans who beheaded humans atop the pyramids of Chichén Itzá, to Jesus Christ, who offered his body on the cross, the ancients understood God's requirement for *sacrifice*. Sacrifice was the original ritual by which humans drew favor from the gods and made themselves holy.

Sacra – sacred.
Face – make.
Even though the rite of sacrifice had been

abandoned eons ago, its power remained. There had been a handful of modern mystics, including Aleister Crowley, who practiced the Art, perfecting it over time, and transforming themselves gradually into something more. Andros craved to transform himself as they had. And yet he knew he would have to cross a dangerous bridge to do so.

Blood is all that separates the light from the dark.

One night, a crow flew through Andros's open bathroom window and got trapped in his apartment. Andros watched the bird flutter around for a while and then finally stop, apparently accepting its inability to escape. Andros had learned enough to recognize a sign. *I am being urged onward.*

Clutching the bird in one hand, he stood at the makeshift altar in his kitchen and raised a sharp knife, speaking aloud the incantation he had memorized.

'*Camiach, Eomiahe, Emial, Macbal, Emoii, Zazean . . . by the most holy names of the angels in the Book of Assamaian, I conjure thee that thou assist me in this operation by the power of the One True God.*'

Andros now lowered the knife and carefully pierced the large vein on the right wing of the panicked bird. The crow began to bleed. As he watched the stream of red liquid flowing down into the metal cup he had placed as a receptacle, he felt an unexpected chill in the air. Nonetheless, he continued.

'*Almighty Adonai, Arathron, Ashai, Elohim, Elohi, Elion, Asher Eheieh, Shaddai . . . be my aid, so that this blood may have power and efficacy in all wherein I shall wish, and in all that I shall demand.*'

That night, he dreamed of birds . . . of a giant phoenix rising from a billowing fire. The next morning, he awoke with an energy he had not felt since childhood. He went running in the park, faster and farther than he'd imagined possible. When he could run no longer, he stopped to do push-ups and sit-ups. Countless repetitions. Still he had energy.

That night, again, he dreamed of the phoenix.

Autumn had fallen again on Central Park, and the wildlife were scurrying about searching for food for winter. Andros despised the cold, and yet his carefully hidden traps were now overflowing with live rats and squirrels. He took them home in his backpack, performing rituals of increasing complexity.

Emanual, Massiach, Yod, He, Vaud . . . please find me worthy.

The blood rituals fueled his vitality. Andros felt younger every day. He continued to read day and night – ancient mystical texts, epic medieval poems, the early philosophers – and the more he learned about the true nature of things, the more he realized that all hope for mankind was lost. *They are blind . . . wandering aimlessly in a world they will never understand.*

Andros was still a man, but he sensed he was evolving into something else. Something greater. *Something sacred.* His massive physique had emerged from dormancy, more powerful now than ever before. He finally understood its true purpose. *My body is but a vessel for my most potent treasure . . . my mind.*

Andros knew his true potential had not yet been realized, and he delved deeper. *What is my destiny?* All the ancient texts spoke of good and evil . . . and of man's need to choose between them. *I made my choice long ago,* he knew, and yet he felt no remorse. *What is evil, if not a natural law?* Darkness followed light. Chaos followed order. Entropy was fundamental. Everything decayed. The perfectly ordered crystal eventually turned into random particles of dust.

There are those who create . . . and those who destroy.

It was not until Andros read John Milton's *Paradise Lost* that he saw his destiny materialize before him. He read of the great fallen angel . . . the warrior demon who fought against the light . . . the valiant one . . . the angel called Moloch.

Moloch walked the earth as a god. The angel's name, Andros later learned, when translated to the ancient tongue, became Mal'akh.

And so shall I.

Like all great transformations, this one had to begin with a sacrifice . . . but not of rats, nor birds. No, this transformation required a *true* sacrifice.

There is but one worthy sacrifice.

Suddenly he had a sense of clarity unlike anything he had ever experienced in his life. His entire destiny had materialized. For three straight days he sketched on an enormous sheet of paper. When he was done, he had created a blueprint of what he would become.

He hung the life-size sketch on his wall and gazed into it as if into a mirror.

I am a masterpiece.

The next day, he took his drawing to the tattoo parlor.

He was ready.

78

The George Washington Masonic Memorial stands atop Shuter's Hill in Alexandria, Virginia. Built in three distinct tiers of increasing architectural complexity from bottom to top – Doric, Ionic, and Corinthian – the structure stands as a physical symbol of man's intellectual ascent. Inspired by the ancient Pharos lighthouse of Alexandria, Egypt, this soaring tower is capped by an Egyptian pyramid with a flame-like finial.

Inside the spectacular marble foyer sits a massive bronze of George Washington in full Masonic regalia, along with the actual trowel he used to lay the cornerstone of the Capitol Building. Above the foyer, nine different levels bear names like the Grotto, the Crypt Room, and the Knights Templar Chapel. Among the treasures housed within these spaces are over twenty thousand volumes of Masonic writings, a dazzling replica of the Ark of the Covenant, and even a scale model of the throne room in King Solomon's Temple.

CIA agent Simkins checked his watch as the modified UH-60 chopper skimmed in low over the Potomac. *Six minutes until their train arrives.* He exhaled and gazed out the window at the shining Masonic Memorial on the horizon. He had to admit, the brilliantly shining tower was as impressive as any building on the National Mall. Simkins had never been inside the memorial, and tonight would be no different. If all went according to plan, Robert Langdon and Katherine Solomon would never make it out of the subway station.

'Over there!' Simkins shouted to the pilot, pointing

down at the King Street subway station across from the memorial. The pilot banked the helicopter and set it down on a grassy area at the foot of Shuter's Hill.

Pedestrians looked up in surprise as Simkins and his team piled out, dashed across the street, and ran down into King Street Station. In the stairwell, several departing passengers leaped out of the way, plastering themselves to the walls as the phalanx of armed men in black thundered past them.

The King Street Station was larger than Simkins had anticipated, apparently serving several different lines – Blue, Yellow, and Amtrak. He raced over to the Metro map on the wall, found Freedom Plaza and the direct line to this location.

'Blue Line, southbound platform!' Simkins shouted. 'Get down there and clear everyone out!' His team dashed off.

Simkins rushed over to the ticket booth, flashed his identification, and shouted to the woman inside. 'The next train from Metro Center – what time is it due?!'

The woman inside looked frightened. 'I'm not sure. Blue Line arrives every eleven minutes. There's no set schedule.'

'How long since the last train?'

'Five . . . six minutes, maybe? No more than that.'

Turner did the math. *Perfect.* The next train had to be Langdon's.

Inside a fast-moving subway car, Katherine Solomon shifted uncomfortably on the hard plastic seat. The bright fluorescent lights overhead hurt her eyes, and she fought the impulse to let her eyelids close, even for a second. Langdon sat beside her in the empty car, staring blankly down at the leather bag at his feet. His eyelids looked heavy, too, as if the rhythmic sway of the moving car were lulling him into a trance.

Katherine pictured the strange contents of Langdon's bag. *Why does the CIA want this pyramid?* Bellamy had said that Sato might be pursuing the pyramid because she knew its true potential. But even if this pyramid somehow *did* reveal the hiding place of ancient secrets, Katherine found it hard to believe that its promise of primeval mystical wisdom would interest the CIA.

Then again, she reminded herself, the CIA had been caught several times running parapsychological or psi programs that bordered on ancient magic and mysticism. In 1995, the 'Stargate/Scannate' scandal had exposed a classified CIA technology called remote viewing – a kind of telepathic mind travel that enabled a 'viewer' to transport his mind's eye to any location on earth and spy there, without being physically present. Of course, the technology was nothing new. Mystics called it astral projection, and yogis called it out-of-body experience. Unfortunately, horrified American taxpayers called it *absurd,* and the program had been scuttled. At least publicly.

Ironically, Katherine saw remarkable connections between the CIA's failed programs and her own break-throughs in Noetic Science.

Katherine felt eager to call the police and find out if they had discovered anything in Kalorama Heights, but she and Langdon were phoneless now, and making contact with the authorities would probably be a mistake anyway; there was no telling how far Sato's reach extended.

Patience, Katherine. Within minutes, they would be in a safe hiding place, guests of a man who had assured them he could provide answers. Katherine hoped his answers, whatever they might be, would help her save her brother.

'Robert?' she whispered, glancing up at the subway map. 'Next stop is ours.'

Langdon emerged slowly from his daydream. 'Right, thanks.' As the train rumbled toward the station, he collected his daybag and gave Katherine an uncertain glance. 'Let's just hope our arrival is uneventful.'

By the time Turner Simkins dashed down to join his men, the subway platform had been entirely cleared, and his team was fanning out, taking up positions behind the support pillars that ran the length of the platform. A distant rumble echoed in the tunnel at the other end of the platform, and as it grew louder, Simkins felt the push of stale warm air billowing around him.

No escape, Mr. Langdon.

Simkins turned to the two agents he had told to join him on the platform. 'Identification and weapons out. These trains are automated, but they all have a conductor who opens the doors. Find him.'

The train's headlamp now appeared down the tunnel, and the sound of squealing brakes pierced the air. As the train burst into the station and began slowing down, Simkins and his two agents leaned out over the track, waving CIA identification badges and straining to make eye contact with the conductor before he could open the doors.

The train was closing fast. In the third car, Simkins finally saw the startled face of the conductor, who was apparently trying to figure out why three men in black were all waving identification badges at him. Simkins jogged toward the train, which was now nearing a full stop.

'CIA!' Simkins shouted, holding up his ID. 'Do NOT open the doors!' As the train glided slowly past him, he went toward the conductor's car, shouting in at him. 'Do not open your doors! Do you understand?! Do NOT open your doors!'

The train came to a full stop, its wide-eyed conductor nodding repeatedly. 'What's wrong?!' the man demanded through his side window.

'Don't let this train move,' Simkins said. 'And don't open the doors.'

'Okay.'

'Can you let us into the first car?'

The conductor nodded. Looking fearful, he stepped out of the train, closing the door behind him. He escorted Simkins and his men to the first car, where he manually opened the door.

'Lock it behind us,' Simkins said, pulling his weapon. Simkins and his men stepped quickly into the stark light of the first car. The conductor locked the door behind them.

The first car contained only four passengers – three teenage boys and an old woman – all of whom looked understandably startled to see three armed men entering. Simkins held up his ID. 'Everything's fine. Just stay seated.'

Simkins and his men now began their sweep, pushing toward the back of the sealed train one car at a time – 'squeezing toothpaste,' as it was called during his training at the Farm. Very few passengers were on this train, and halfway to the back, the agents still had seen nobody even remotely resembling the description of Robert Langdon and Katherine Solomon. Nonetheless, Simkins remained confident. There was absolutely no place to hide on a subway car. No bathrooms, no storage, and no alternative exits. Even if the targets had seen them board the train and fled to the back, there was no way out. Prying open a door was almost impossible, and Simkins had men watching the platform and both sides of the train anyway.

Patience.

By the time Simkins reached the second-to-last car, however, he was feeling edgy. This penultimate car had only one passenger – a Chinese man. Simkins and his agents moved through, scanning for any place to hide. There was none.

'Last car,' Simkins said, raising his weapon as the threesome moved toward the threshold of the train's final section. As they stepped into the last car, all three of them immediately stopped and stared.

What the . . . ?! Simkins raced to the rear of the deserted cabin, searching behind all the seats. He spun back to his men, blood boiling. 'Where the hell did they go?!'

79

Eight miles due north of Alexandria, Virginia, Robert Langdon and Katherine Solomon strode calmly across a wide expanse of frost-covered lawn.

'You should be an actress,' Langdon said, still impressed by Katherine's quick thinking and improvisational skills.

'You weren't half bad yourself.' She gave him a smile.

At first, Langdon had been mystified by Katherine's abrupt antics in the taxi. Without warning, she had suddenly demanded they go to Freedom Plaza based on some revelation about a Jewish star and the Great Seal of the United States. She drew a well-known conspiracy-theory image on a dollar bill and then insisted Langdon look closely where she was *pointing*.

Finally, Langdon realized that Katherine was pointing *not* at the dollar bill but at a tiny indicator bulb on the back of the driver's seat. The bulb was so covered with grime that he had not even noticed it. As he leaned forward, however, he could see that the bulb was illuminated, emitting a dull red glow. He could also see the two faint words directly beneath the lit bulb.

– INTERCOM ON –

Startled, Langdon glanced back at Katherine, whose frantic eyes were urging him to look into the front seat. He obeyed, stealing a discreet glance through the divider. The cabby's cell phone was on the dash, wide open, illuminated, facing the intercom speaker. An instant later, Langdon understood Katherine's actions.

They know we're in this cab . . . they've been listening to us.

Langdon had no idea how much time he and Katherine had until their taxi was stopped and surrounded, but he knew they had to act fast. Instantly, he'd begun playing along, realizing that Katherine's desire to go to Freedom Plaza had nothing to do with the pyramid but rather with its being a large subway station – Metro Center – from which they could take the Red, Blue, or Orange lines in any of six different directions.

They jumped out of the taxi at Freedom Plaza, and Langdon took over, doing some improvising of his own, leaving a trail to the Masonic Memorial in Alexandria before he and Katherine ran down into the subway station, dashing past the Blue Line platforms and continuing on to the Red Line, where they caught a train in the opposite direction.

Traveling six stops northbound to Tenleytown, they emerged all alone into a quiet, upscale neighborhood. Their destination, the tallest structure for miles, was immediately visible on the horizon, just off Massachusetts Avenue on a vast expanse of manicured lawn.

Now 'off the grid,' as Katherine called it, the two of them walked across the damp grass. On their right was a medieval-style garden, famous for its ancient rose-bushes and Shadow House gazebo. They moved past the garden, directly toward the magnificent building to which they had been summoned. *A refuge containing ten stones from Mount Sinai, one from heaven itself, and one with the visage of Luke's dark father*.

'I've never been here at night,' Katherine said, gazing up at the brightly lit towers. 'It's spectacular.'

Langdon agreed, having forgotten how impressive this place truly was. This neo-Gothic masterpiece stood at the north end of Embassy Row. He hadn't been here for years, not since writing a piece about it for a kids' magazine in hopes of generating some excitement among young Americans to come see this amazing landmark. His article – 'Moses, Moon Rocks, and *Star Wars*' – had been part of the tourist literature for years.

Washington National Cathedral, Langdon thought, feeling an unexpected anticipation at being back after all these years. *Where better to ask about One True God?*

'This cathedral *really* has ten stones from Mount Sinai?' Katherine asked, gazing up at the twin bell towers.

Langdon nodded. 'Near the main altar. They symbolize the Ten Commandments given to Moses on Mount Sinai.'

'And there's a lunar rock?'

A rock from heaven itself. 'Yes. One of the stained-glass windows is called the Space Window and has a fragment of moon rock embedded in it.'

'Okay, but you can't be serious about the last thing.' Katherine glanced over, her pretty eyes flashing skepticism. 'A statue of . . . Darth Vader?'

Langdon chuckled. 'Luke Skywalker's dark father? Absolutely. Vader is one of the National Cathedral's most popular grotesques.' He pointed high into the west towers. 'Tough to see him at night, but he's there.'

'What in the world is Darth Vader doing on Washington National Cathedral?'

'A contest for kids to carve a gargoyle that depicted the face of evil. Darth won.'

They reached the grand staircase to the main entrance, which was set back in an eighty-foot archway beneath a breathtaking rose window. As they began climbing, Langdon's mind shifted to the mysterious stranger who had called him. *No names, please . . . Tell me, have you successfully protected the map that was entrusted to you?* Langdon's shoulder ached from carrying the heavy stone pyramid, and he was looking forward to setting it down. *Sanctuary and answers.*

As they approached the top of the stairs, they were met with an imposing pair of wooden doors. 'Do we just knock?' Katherine asked.

Langdon had been wondering the same thing, except that now one of the doors was creaking open.

'Who's there?' a frail voice said. The face of a withered old man appeared in the doorway. He wore priest's robes and a blank stare. His eyes were opaque and white, clouded with cataracts.

'My name is Robert Langdon,' he replied. 'Katherine Solomon and I are seeking sanctuary.'

The blind man exhaled in relief. 'Thank God. I've been expecting you.'

80

Warren Bellamy felt a sudden ray of hope.

Inside the Jungle, Director Sato had just received a phone call from a field agent and had immediately flown into a tirade. 'Well, you damn well *better* find them!' she shouted into her phone. 'We're running out of time!' She had hung up and was now stalking back and forth in front of Bellamy as if trying to decide what to do next.

Finally, she stopped directly in front of him and turned. 'Mr. Bellamy, I'm going to ask you this once, and only once.' She stared deep into his eyes. 'Yes or no – do you have any idea where Robert Langdon might have gone?'

Bellamy had more than a good idea, but he shook his head. 'No.'

Sato's piercing gaze had never left his eyes. 'Unfortunately, part of my job is to know when people are lying.'

Bellamy averted his eyes. 'Sorry, I can't help you.'

'Architect Bellamy,' Sato said, 'tonight just after seven P.M., you were having dinner in a restaurant outside the city when you received a phone call from a man who told you he had kidnapped Peter Solomon.'

Bellamy felt an instant chill and returned his eyes to hers. *How could you possibly know that?!*

'The man,' Sato continued, 'told you that he had sent Robert Langdon to the Capitol Building and given Langdon a task to complete . . . a task that required *your* help. He warned that if Langdon failed in this task, your friend Peter Solomon would die. Panicked, you called all of Peter's numbers but failed to reach him. Understandably, you then raced to the Capitol.'

Bellamy could not imagine how Sato knew about this phone call.

'As you fled the Capitol,' Sato said behind the smoldering tip of her cigarette, 'you sent a text message to Solomon's kidnapper, assuring him that you and Langdon had been successful in obtaining the Masonic Pyramid.'

Where is she getting her information? Bellamy wondered. *Not even Langdon knows I sent that text message.* Immediately after entering the tunnel to the Library of Congress, Bellamy had stepped into the electrical room to plug in the construction lighting. In the privacy of that moment, he had decided to send a quick text message to Solomon's captor, telling him about Sato's involvement, but reassuring him that he – Bellamy – and Langdon had obtained the Masonic Pyramid and would indeed cooperate with his demands. It was a lie, of course, but Bellamy hoped the reassurance might buy time, both for Peter Solomon and also to hide the pyramid.

'Who told you I sent a text?' Bellamy demanded.

Sato tossed Bellamy's cell phone on the bench next to him. 'Hardly rocket science.'

Bellamy now remembered his phone and keys had been taken from him by the agents who captured him.

'As for the rest of my inside information,' Sato said, 'the Patriot Act gives me the right to place a wiretap on the phone of anyone I consider a viable threat to national security. I consider Peter Solomon to be such a threat, and last night I took action.'

Bellamy could barely get his mind around what she was telling him. 'You're tapping Peter Solomon's phone?'

'Yes. This is how I knew the kidnapper called you at the restaurant. You called Peter's cell phone and left an anxious message explaining what had just happened.'

Bellamy realized she was right.

'We had also intercepted a call from Robert Langdon, who was in the Capitol Building, deeply confused to learn he had been tricked into coming there. I went to the Capitol at once, arriving before you because I was closer. As for how I knew to check the X-ray of Langdon's bag . . . in light of my realization that Langdon was involved in all of this, I had my staff reexamine a seemingly innocuous early-morning call between Langdon and Peter Solomon's cell phone, in which the kidnapper, posing as Solomon's assistant, persuaded Langdon to come for a lecture and also to bring a small package that Peter had entrusted to him. When Langdon was not forthcoming with me about the package he was carrying, I requested the X-ray of his bag.'

Bellamy could barely think. Admittedly, everything Sato was saying was feasible, and yet something was not adding up. 'But . . . how could you possibly think Peter Solomon is a threat to national security?'

'Believe me, Peter Solomon *is* a serious national-security threat,' she snapped. 'And frankly, Mr. Bellamy, so are *you*.'

Bellamy sat bolt upright, the handcuffs chafing against his wrists. 'I beg your pardon?!'

She forced a smile. 'You Masons play a risky game. You keep a very, *very* dangerous secret.'

Is she talking about the Ancient Mysteries?

'Thankfully, you've always done a good job of keeping your secrets hidden. Unfortunately, recently you've been careless, and tonight, your most dangerous secret is about to be unveiled to the world. And unless we can stop that from happening, I assure you the results will be catastrophic.'

Bellamy stared in bewilderment.

'If you had not attacked me,' Sato said, 'you would have realized that you and I are on the same team.'

The same team. The words sparked in Bellamy an idea that seemed almost impossible to fathom. *Is Sato a member of Eastern Star?* The Order of the Eastern Star – often considered a sister organization to the Masons – embraced a similar mystical philosophy of benevolence, secret wisdom, and spiritual open-mindedness. *The same team? I'm in handcuffs! She's tapping Peter's phone!*

'You will help me stop this man,' Sato said. 'He has the potential to bring about a cataclysm from which this country might not recover.' Her face was like stone.

'Then why aren't you *tracking* him?'

Sato looked incredulous. 'Do you think I'm not *trying*? My trace on Solomon's cell phone went dead before we got a location. His other number appears to be a disposable phone – which is almost impossible to track. The private-jet company told us that Langdon's flight was booked by Solomon's assistant, on Solomon's cell phone, with Solomon's Marquis Jet card. There is no trail. Not that it matters anyway. Even if we find out exactly where he is, I can't possibly risk moving in and trying to grab him.'

'Why not?!'

'I'd prefer not to share that, as the information is classified,' Sato said, patience clearly waning. 'I am asking you to trust me on this.'

'Well, I don't!'

Sato's eyes were like ice. She turned suddenly and shouted across the Jungle. 'Agent Hartmann! The briefcase, please.'

Bellamy heard the hiss of the electronic door, and an agent strode into the Jungle. He was carrying a sleek titanium briefcase, which he set on the ground beside the OS director.

'Leave us,' Sato said.

As the agent departed, the door hissed again, and then everything fell silent.

Sato picked up the metal case, laid it across her lap, and popped the clasps. Then she raised her eyes slowly to Bellamy. 'I did not want to do this, but our time is running out, and you've left me no choice.'

Bellamy eyed the strange briefcase and felt a swell of fear. *Is she going to torture me?* He strained at his cuffs again. 'What's in that case?!'

Sato smiled grimly. 'Something that will persuade you to see things *my* way. I guarantee it.'

81

The subterranean space in which Mal'akh performed the Art was ingeniously hidden. His home's basement, to those who entered, appeared quite normal – a typical cellar with boiler, fuse box, woodpile, and a hodgepodge of storage. This visible cellar, however, was only a portion of Mal'akh's underground space. A sizable area had been walled off for his clandestine practices.

Mal'akh's private work space was a suite of small rooms, each with a specialized purpose. The area's sole entrance was a steep ramp secretly accessible through his living room, making the area's discovery virtually impossible.

Tonight, as Mal'akh descended the ramp, the tattooed sigils and signs on his flesh seemed to come alive in the cerulean glow of his basement's special-ized lighting. Moving into the bluish haze, he walked past several closed doors and headed directly for the largest room at the end of the corridor.

The 'sanctum sanctorum,' as Mal'akh liked to call it, was a perfect twelve-foot square. *Twelve are the signs of the zodiac. Twelve are the hours of the day. Twelve are the gates of heaven.* In the center of the chamber was a stone table, a seven-by-seven square. *Seven are the seals of Revelation. Seven are the steps of the Temple.* Centered over the table hung a carefully calibrated light source that cycled through a spectrum of preordained colors, completing its cycle every six hours in accordance with the sacred Table of Planetary Hours. *The hour of Yanor is blue. The hour of Nasnia is red. The hour of Salam is white.*

Now was the hour of Caerra, meaning the light in the room had modulated to a soft purplish hue. Wearing only a silken loincloth wrapped around his buttocks and neutered sex organ, Mal'akh began his preparations.

He carefully combined the suffumigation chemicals that he would later ignite to sanctify the air. Then he folded the virgin silk robe that he would eventually don in place of his loincloth. And finally, he purified a flask of water for the anointing of his offering. When he was done, he placed all of these prepared ingredients on a side table.

Next he went to a shelf and retrieved a small ivory box, which he carried to the side table and placed with the other items. Although he was not yet ready to use it, he could not resist opening the lid and admiring this treasure.

The knife.

Inside the ivory box, nestled in a cradle of black velvet, shone the sacrificial knife that Mal'akh had been saving for tonight. He had purchased it for $1.6 million on the Middle Eastern antiquities black market last year.

The most famous knife in history.

Unimaginably old and believed lost, this precious blade was made of iron, attached to a bone handle. Over the ages, it had been in the possession of countless powerful individuals. In recent decades, however, it had disappeared, languishing in a secret private collection. Mal'akh had gone to enormous lengths to obtain it. The knife, he suspected, had not drawn blood for decades . . . possibly centuries. Tonight, this blade would again taste the power of the sacrifice for which it was honed.

Mal'akh gently lifted the knife from its cushioned compartment and reverently polished the blade with a silk cloth soaked in purified water. His skills had progressed greatly since his first rudimentary experiments in New York. The dark Art that Mal'akh practiced had been known by many names in many languages, but by any name, it was a precise science. This primeval technology had once held the key to the portals of power, but it had been banished long ago, relegated to the shadows of occultism and magic. Those few who still practiced this Art were considered madmen, but Mal'akh knew better. *This is not work for those with dull faculties.* The ancient dark Art, like modern science, was a discipline involving precise formulas, specific ingredients, and meticulous timing.

This Art was not the impotent black magic of today, often practiced halfheartedly by curious souls. This Art, like nuclear physics, had the potential to unleash enormous power. The warnings were dire: *The unskilled practitioner runs the risk of being struck by a reflux current and destroyed.*

Mal'akh finished admiring the sacred blade and turned his attention to a lone sheet of thick vellum lying on the table before him. He had made this vellum himself from the skin of a baby lamb. As was the protocol, the lamb was pure, having not yet reached sexual maturity. Beside the vellum was a quill pen he had made from the feather of a crow, a silver saucer, and three glimmering candles arranged around a solid-brass bowl. The bowl contained one inch of thick crimson liquid.

The liquid was Peter Solomon's blood.

Blood is the tincture of eternity.

Mal'akh picked up the quill pen, placed his left hand on the vellum, and dipping the quill tip in the blood, he carefully traced the outline of his open palm. When he was done, he added the five symbols of the Ancient Mysteries, one on each fingertip of the drawing.

The crown . . . to represent the king I shall become.

The star . . . to represent the heavens which have ordained my destiny.

The sun . . . to represent the illumination of my soul.

The lantern . . . to represent the feeble light of human understanding.

And the key . . . to represent the missing piece, that which tonight I shall at last possess.

Mal'akh completed his blood tracing and held up the vellum, admiring his work in the light of the three candles. He waited until the blood was dry and then folded the thick vellum three times. While chanting an ethereal ancient incantation, Mal'akh touched the vellum to the third candle, and it burst into flames. He set the flaming vellum on the silver saucer and let it burn. As it did, the carbon in the animal skin dissolved to a powdery black char. When the flame went out, Mal'akh carefully tapped the ashes into the brass bowl of blood. Then he stirred the mixture with the crow's feather.

The liquid turned a deeper crimson, nearly black.

Holding the bowl in both palms, Mal'akh raised it over his head and gave thanks, intoning the blood *eukharistos* of the ancients. Then he carefully poured the blackened mixture into a glass vial and corked it.

This would be the ink with which Mal'akh would inscribe the untattooed flesh atop his head and complete his masterpiece.

82

Washington National Cathedral is the sixth-largest cathedral in the world and soars higher than a thirty-story skyscraper. Embellished with over two hundred stained-glass windows, a fifty-three-bell carillon, and a 10,647-pipe organ, this Gothic masterpiece can accommodate more than three thousand worshippers.

Tonight, however, the great cathedral was deserted.

Reverend Colin Galloway – dean of the cathedral – looked like he had been alive forever. Stooped and withered, he wore a simple black cassock and shuffled blindly ahead without a word. Langdon and Katherine followed in silence through the darkness of the four-hundred-foot-long nave's central aisle, which was curved ever so slightly to the left to create a softening optical illusion. When they reached the Great Crossing, the dean guided them through the rood screen – the symbolic divider between the public area and the sanctuary beyond.

The scent of frankincense hung in the air of the chancel. This sacred space was dark, illuminated only by indirect reflections in the foliated vaults overhead. Flags of the fifty states hung above the quire, which was ornately appointed with several carved reredos depicting biblical events. Dean Galloway continued on, apparently knowing this walk by heart. For a moment, Langdon thought they were headed straight for the high altar, where the ten stones from Mount Sinai were embedded, but the old dean finally turned left and groped his way through a discreetly hidden door that led into an administrative annex.

They moved down a short hallway to an office door bearing a brass nameplate:

THE REVEREND DR. COLIN GALLOWAY
CATHEDRAL DEAN

Galloway opened the door and turned on the lights, apparently accustomed to remembering this courtesy for his guests. He ushered them in and closed the door.

The dean's office was small but elegant, with high bookshelves, a desk, a carved armoire, and a private bathroom. On the walls hung sixteenth-century tapestries and several religious paintings. The old dean motioned to the two leather chairs directly opposite his desk. Langdon sat with Katherine and felt grateful finally to set his heavy shoulder bag on the floor at his feet.

Sanctuary and answers, Langdon thought, settling into the comfortable chair.

The aged man shuffled around behind his desk and eased himself down into his high-backed chair. Then, with a weary sigh, he raised his head, staring blankly out at them through clouded eyes. When he spoke, his voice was unexpectedly clear and strong.

'I realize we have never met,' the old man said, 'and yet I feel I know you both.' He took out a handkerchief and dabbed his mouth. 'Professor Langdon, I am familiar with your writings, including the clever piece you did on the symbolism of this cathedral. And, Ms. Solomon, your brother, Peter, and I have been Masonic brothers for many years now.'

'Peter is in terrible trouble,' Katherine said.

'So I have been told.' The old man sighed. 'And I will do everything in my power to help you.'

Langdon saw no Masonic ring on the dean's finger, and yet he knew many Masons, especially those within the clergy, chose not to advertise their affiliation.

As they began to talk, it became clear that Dean Galloway already knew some of the night's events from Warren Bellamy's phone message. As Langdon and Katherine filled him in on the rest, the dean looked more and more troubled.

'And this man who has taken our beloved Peter,' the dean said, 'he is insisting you decipher the pyramid in exchange for Peter's life?'

'Yes,' Langdon said. 'He thinks it's a map that will lead him to the hiding place of the Ancient Mysteries.'

The dean turned his eerie, opaque eyes toward Langdon. 'My ears tell me you do not believe in such things.'

Langdon did not want to waste time going down this road. 'It doesn't matter what I believe. We need to help Peter. Unfortunately, when we deciphered the pyramid, it pointed nowhere.'

The old man sat straighter. 'You've *deciphered* the pyramid?'

Katherine interceded now, quickly explaining that despite Bellamy's warnings and her brother's request that Langdon not unwrap the package, she had done so, feeling her first priority was to help her brother however she could. She told the dean about the golden

409

capstone, Albrecht Dürer's magic square, and how it decrypted the sixteen-letter Masonic cipher into the phrase *Jeova Sanctus Unus*.

'That's all it says?' the dean asked. 'One True God?'

'Yes, sir,' Langdon replied. 'Apparently the pyramid is more of a *metaphorical* map than a geographic one.'

The dean held out his hands. 'Let me feel it.'

Langdon unzipped his bag and pulled out the pyramid, which he carefully hoisted up on the desk, setting it directly in front of the reverend.

Langdon and Katherine watched as the old man's frail hands examined every inch of the stone – the engraved side, the smooth base, and the truncated top. When he was finished, he held out his hands again. 'And the capstone?'

Langdon retrieved the small stone box, set it on the desk, and opened the lid. Then he removed the capstone and placed it into the old man's waiting hands. The dean performed a similar examination, feeling every inch, pausing on the capstone's engraving, apparently having some trouble reading the small, elegantly inscribed text.

' "The secret hides within The Order," ' Langdon offered. 'And the words *the* and *order* are capitalized.'

The old man's face was expressionless as he positioned the capstone on top of the pyramid and aligned it by sense of touch. He seemed to pause a moment, as if in prayer, and reverently ran his palms over the complete pyramid several times. Then he reached out and located the cube-shaped box, taking it in his hands, feeling it carefully, his fingers probing inside and out.

When he was done, he set down the box and leaned

back in his chair. 'So tell me,' he demanded, his voice suddenly stern. 'Why have you come to me?'

The question took Langdon off guard. 'We came, sir, because you *told* us to. And Mr. Bellamy said we should trust you.'

'And yet you did not trust *him*?'

'I'm sorry?'

The dean's white eyes stared directly through Langdon. 'The package containing the capstone was sealed. Mr. Bellamy told you *not* to open it, and yet you did. In addition, Peter Solomon himself told you *not* to open it. And yet you did.'

'Sir,' Katherine intervened, 'we were trying to help my brother. The man who has him demanded we decipher—'

'I can appreciate that,' the dean declared, 'and yet what have you achieved by *opening* the package? Nothing. Peter's captor is looking for a *location*, and he will not be satisfied with the answer of *Jeova Sanctus Unus*.'

'I agree,' Langdon said, 'but unfortunately that's all the pyramid says. As I mentioned, the map seems to be more *figurative* than—'

'You're mistaken, Professor,' the dean said. 'The Masonic Pyramid is a *real* map. It points to a *real* location. You do not understand that, because you have not yet deciphered the pyramid fully. Not even close.'

Langdon and Katherine exchanged startled looks.

The dean laid his hands back on the pyramid, almost caressing it. 'This map, like the Ancient Mysteries themselves, has many layers of meaning. Its true secret remains veiled from you.'

'Dean Galloway,' Langdon said, 'we've been over

411

every inch of the pyramid and capstone, and there's nothing else to see.'

'Not in its current state, no. But objects change.'

'Sir?'

'Professor, as you know, the promise of this pyramid is one of miraculous transformative power. Legend holds that this pyramid can change its shape . . . alter its physical form to reveal its secrets. Like the famed stone that released Excalibur into the hands of King Arthur, the Masonic Pyramid can transform itself if it so chooses . . . and reveal its secret to the worthy.'

Langdon now sensed that the old man's advanced years had perhaps robbed him of his faculties. 'I'm sorry, sir. Are you saying this pyramid can undergo a *literal* physical transformation?'

'Professor, if I were to reach out with my hand and transform this pyramid right before your eyes, would you believe what you had witnessed?'

Langdon had no idea how to respond. 'I suppose I would have no choice.'

'Very well, then. In a moment, I shall do exactly that.' He dabbed his mouth again. 'Let me remind you that there was an era when even the brightest minds perceived the earth as flat. For if the earth were round, then surely the oceans would spill off. Imagine how they would have mocked you if you proclaimed, "Not only is the world a sphere, but there is an invisible, mystical force that holds everything to its surface"!'

'There's a difference,' Langdon said, 'between the existence of gravity . . . and the ability to transform objects with a touch of your hand.'

'Is there? Is it not possible that we are still living in the Dark Ages, still mocking the suggestion of "mystical" forces that we cannot see or comprehend.

History, if it has taught us anything at all, has taught us that the strange ideas we deride today will one day be our celebrated truths. I claim I can transform this pyramid with a touch of my finger, and you question my sanity. I would expect more from an historian. History is replete with great minds who have all proclaimed the *same* thing . . . great minds who have all insisted that man possesses mystical abilities of which he is unaware.'

Langdon knew the dean was correct. The famous Hermetic aphorism – *Know ye not that ye are gods?* – was one of the pillars of the Ancient Mysteries. *As above, so below . . . Man created in God's image . . . Apotheosis.* This persistent message of man's own divinity – of his hidden potential – was *the* recurring theme in the ancient texts of countless traditions. Even the Holy Bible cried out in Psalms 82:6: *Ye are gods!*

'Professor,' the old man said, 'I realize that *you*, like many educated people, live trapped between worlds – one foot in the spiritual, one foot in the physical. Your heart yearns to believe . . . but your intellect refuses to permit it. As an academic, you would be wise to learn from the great minds of history.' He paused and cleared his throat. 'If I'm remembering correctly, one of the greatest minds ever to live proclaimed: "That which is impenetrable to us really exists. Behind the secrets of nature remains something subtle, intangible, and inexplicable. Veneration for this force beyond any-thing that we can comprehend is my religion." '

'Who said that?' Langdon said. 'Gandhi?'

'No,' Katherine interjected. 'Albert Einstein.'

Katherine Solomon had read every word Einstein had ever written and was struck by his profound respect for the mystical, as well as his predictions that the masses would one day feel the same. *The religion of the future,* Einstein had predicted, *will be a cosmic religion. It will transcend personal God and avoid dogma and theology.*

Robert Langdon appeared to be struggling with the idea. Katherine could sense his rising frustration with the old Episcopal priest, and she understood. After all, they had traveled here for answers, and they had found instead a blind man who claimed he could transform objects with a touch of his hands. Even so, the old man's overt passion for mystical forces reminded Katherine of her brother.

'Father Galloway,' Katherine said, 'Peter is in trouble. The CIA is chasing us. And Warren Bellamy sent us to you for help. I don't know what this pyramid says or where it points, but if deciphering it means that we can help Peter, we need to do that. Mr. Bellamy may have preferred to sacrifice my brother's life to hide this pyramid, but my family has experienced nothing but pain because of it. Whatever secret it may hold, it ends tonight.'

'You are correct,' the old man replied, his tone dire. 'It *will* all end tonight. You've guaranteed that.' He sighed. 'Ms. Solomon, when you broke the seal on that box, you set in motion a series of events from which there will be no return. There are forces at work tonight that you do not yet comprehend. There is no turning back.'

Katherine stared dumbfounded at the reverend. There was something apocalyptic about his tone, as if he were referring to the Seven Seals of Revelation or Pandora's box.

'Respectfully, sir,' Langdon interceded, 'I can't

imagine how a stone pyramid could set in motion *anything* at all.'

'Of course you can't, Professor.' The old man stared blindly through him. 'You do not yet have eyes to see.'

83

In the moist air of the Jungle, the Architect of the Capitol could feel the sweat now rolling down his back. His handcuffed wrists ached, but all of his attention remained riveted on the ominous titanium briefcase that Sato had just opened on the bench between them.

The contents of this case, Sato had told him, *will persuade you to see things my way. I guarantee it.*

The tiny Asian woman had unclasped the metal case *away* from Bellamy's line of sight, and he had yet to see its contents, but his imagination was running wild. Sato's hands were doing something inside the case, and Bellamy half expected her to extract a series of glistening, razor-sharp tools.

Suddenly a light source flickered inside the case, growing brighter, illuminating Sato's face from beneath. Her hands kept moving inside, and the light changed hue. After a few moments, she removed her hands, grasped the entire case, and turned it toward Bellamy so he could see inside.

Bellamy found himself squinting into the glow of what appeared to be some kind of futuristic laptop with a handheld phone receiver, two antennae, and a double keyboard. His initial surge of relief turned quickly to confusion.

The screen bore the CIA logo and the text:

SECURE LOG-IN
USER: INOUE SATO
SECURITY CLEARANCE: LEVEL 5

Beneath the laptop's log-in window, a progress icon was spinning:

ONE MOMENT PLEASE . . .
DECRYPTING FILE . . .

Bellamy's gaze shot back up to Sato, whose eyes were locked on his. 'I had not wanted to show you this,' she said. 'But you've left me no choice.'

The screen flickered again, and Bellamy glanced back down as the file opened, its contents filling the entire LCD.

For several moments, Bellamy stared at the screen, trying to make sense of what he was looking at. Gradually, as it began to dawn on him, he felt the blood draining from his face. He stared in horror, unable to look away. 'But this is . . . *impossible*!' he exclaimed. 'How . . . could this be!'

Sato's face was grim. 'You tell *me*, Mr. Bellamy. *You* tell me.'

As the Architect of the Capitol began to fully comprehend the ramifications of what he was seeing, he could feel his entire world teetering precariously on the brink of disaster.

My God . . . I've made a terrible, terrible mistake!

84

Dean Galloway felt alive.

Like all mortals, he knew the time was coming when he would shed his mortal shell, but tonight was not the night. His corporeal heart was beating strong and fast . . . and his mind felt sharp. *There is work to be done.*

As he ran his arthritic hands across the pyramid's smooth surfaces, he could scarcely believe what he was feeling. *I never imagined I would live to witness this moment.* For generations, the pieces of the symbolon map had been kept safely apart from one another. Now they were united at last. Galloway wondered if this was the foretold time.

Strangely, fate had selected two non-Masons to assemble the pyramid. Somehow, this seemed fitting. *The Mysteries are moving out of the inner circles . . . out of darkness . . . into the light.*

'Professor,' he said, turning his head in the direction of Langdon's breathing. 'Did Peter tell you *why* he wanted you to watch over the little package?'

'He said powerful people wanted to steal it from him,' Langdon replied.

The dean nodded. 'Yes, Peter told me the same thing.'

'He did?' Katherine said suddenly on his left. 'You and my brother *spoke* about this pyramid?'

'Of course,' Galloway said. 'Your brother and I have spoken on many things. I was once the Worshipful Master at the House of the Temple, and he comes to me for guidance at times. It was about a year ago that he came to me, deeply troubled. He sat exactly where you are now, and he asked me if I believed in supernatural premonitions.'

'Premonitions?' Katherine sounded concerned. 'You mean like . . . *visions*?'

'Not exactly. It was more visceral. Peter said he was feeling the growing presence of a dark force in his life. He sensed something was watching him . . . waiting . . . intending to do him great harm.'

'Obviously he was right,' Katherine said, 'considering that the same man who killed our mother and Peter's son had come to Washington and become one of Peter's own Masonic brothers.'

'True,' Langdon said, 'but it doesn't explain the involvement of the CIA.'

Galloway was not so sure. 'Men in power are always interested in greater power.'

'But . . . the CIA?' Langdon challenged. 'And mystical secrets? Something doesn't add up.'

'Sure it does,' Katherine said. 'The CIA thrives on technological advancement and has always experimented with the mystical sciences – ESP, remote viewing, sensory deprivation, pharmacologically induced highly mentalized states. It's all the same thing – tapping the unseen potential of the human mind. If there's one thing I've learned from Peter, it's this: Science and mysticism are very closely related, distinguishable only by their approaches. They have identical goals . . . but different methods.'

'Peter tells me,' Galloway said, 'that your field of study is a kind of modern mystical science?'

'Noetics,' Katherine said, nodding. 'And it's proving man has powers unlike anything we can imagine.' She motioned to a stained-glass window depicting the familiar image of the 'Luminous Jesus,' that of Christ with rays of light flowing from his head and hands. 'In fact, I just used a supercooled charge-coupled device to photograph the hands of a faith healer at work. The photos looked a lot like the image of Jesus in your stained-glass window ... streams of energy pouring through the healer's fingertips.'

The well-trained mind, Galloway thought, hiding a smile. *How do you think Jesus healed the sick?*

'I realize,' Katherine said, 'that modern medicine ridicules healers and shamans, but I saw this with my own eyes. My CCD cameras clearly photographed this man transmitting a massive energy field from his fingertips ... and literally changing the cellular makeup of his patient. If *that's* not godlike power, then I don't know what is.'

Dean Galloway let himself smile. Katherine had the same fiery passion as her brother. 'Peter once compared Noetic Scientists to the early explorers who were mocked for embracing the heretical notion of a *spherical* earth. Almost overnight, these explorers went from fools to heroes, discovering uncharted worlds and expanding the horizons of everyone on the planet. Peter thinks *you* will do this as well. He has very high hopes for your work. After all, every great philosophical shift in history began with a single bold idea.'

Galloway knew, of course, that one needn't go to a lab to witness proof of this bold new idea, this proposal of man's untapped potential. This very cathedral held healing prayer circles for the sick, and repeatedly had witnessed truly miraculous results, medically documented physical transformations. The question was not whether God had imbued man with great powers ... but rather how we *liberate* those powers.

The old dean placed his hands reverently around the sides of the Masonic Pyramid and spoke very

419

quietly. 'My friends, I do not know exactly *where* this pyramid points . . . but I do know *this*. There is a great spiritual treasure buried out there somewhere . . . a treasure that has waited patiently in darkness for generations. I believe it is a catalyst that has the power to transform this world.' He now touched the golden tip of the capstone. 'And now that this pyramid is assembled . . . the time is fast approaching. And why shouldn't it? The promise of a great transformational enlightenment has been prophesied forever.'

'Father,' Langdon said, his tone challenging, 'we're all familiar with the Revelation of Saint John and the literal meaning of the Apocalypse, but biblical prophecy hardly seems—'

'Oh, heavens, the Book of Revelation is a mess!' the dean said. 'Nobody knows how to read that. I'm talking about *clear* minds writing in clear language – the predictions of Saint Augustine, Sir Francis Bacon, Newton, Einstein, the list goes on and on, all anticipating a transformative moment of enlightenment. Even Jesus himself said, "Nothing is hidden that will not be made known, nor secret that will not come to light." '

'It's a safe prediction to make,' Langdon said. 'Knowledge grows exponentially. The more we know, the greater our ability to learn, and the *faster* we expand our knowledge base.'

'Yes,' Katherine added. 'We see this in science all the time. Each new technology we invent becomes a tool with which to invent new technologies . . . and it snowballs. That's why science has advanced more in the last five years than in the previous five *thousand*. Exponential growth. Mathematically, as time passes, the exponential curve of progress becomes almost vertical, and new development occurs incredibly fast.'

Silence fell in the dean's office, and Galloway sensed that his two guests still had no idea how this pyramid could possibly help them reveal anything further. *That is why fate brought you to me*, he thought. *I have a role to play.*

For many years, the Reverend Colin Galloway, along with his Masonic brothers, had played the role of gatekeeper. Now it was all changing.

I am no longer a gatekeeper . . . I am a guide.

'Professor Langdon?' Galloway said, reaching out across his desk. 'Take my hand if you will.'

Robert Langdon felt uncertain as he stared across at Dean Galloway's outstretched palm.

Are we going to pray?

Politely, Langdon reached out and placed his right hand in the dean's withered hand. The old man grasped it firmly but did not begin to pray. Instead, he found Langdon's index finger and guided it downward into the stone box that had once housed the golden capstone.

'Your eyes have blinded you,' the dean said. 'If you saw with your fingertips as I do, you would realize this box has something left to teach you.'

Dutifully, Langdon worked his fingertip around the inside of the box, but he felt nothing. The inside was perfectly smooth.

'Keep looking,' Galloway prompted.

Finally, Langdon's fingertip felt something – a tiny raised circle – a minuscule dot in the center of the base of the box. He removed his hand and peered inside. The little circle was virtually invisible to the naked eye. *What is that?*

'Do you recognize that symbol?' Galloway asked.

'Symbol?' Langdon replied. 'I can barely see anything at all.'

'Push down on it.'

Langdon did as he asked, pressing his fingertip down onto the spot. *What does he think will happen?*

'Hold your finger down,' the dean said. 'Apply pressure.'

Langdon glanced over at Katherine, who looked puzzled as she tucked a wisp of hair behind her ears.

A few seconds later, the old dean finally nodded. 'Okay, remove your hand. The alchemy is complete.'

Alchemy? Robert Langdon removed his hand from the stone box and sat in bewildered silence. Nothing had changed at all. The box just sat there on the desk.

'Nothing,' Langdon said.

'Look at your fingertip,' the dean replied. 'You should see a transformation.'

Langdon looked at his finger, but the only transformation he could see was that he now had an indentation on his skin made by the circular nubbin – a tiny circle with a dot in the middle.

'Now do you recognize this symbol?' the dean asked.

Although Langdon recognized the symbol, he was more impressed that the dean had been able to feel the detail of it. Seeing with one's fingertips was apparently a learned skill.

'It's alchemical,' Katherine said, sliding her chair

closer and examining Langdon's finger. 'It's the ancient symbol for *gold*.'

'Indeed it is.' The dean smiled and patted the box. 'Professor, congratulations. You have just achieved what every alchemist in history has strived for. From a worthless substance, you've created gold.'

Langdon frowned, unimpressed. The little parlor trick seemed to be no help at all. 'An interesting idea, sir, but I'm afraid this symbol – a circle with a round dot in the middle – has dozens of meanings. It's called a *circumpunct*, and it's one of the most widely used symbols in history.'

'What are you talking about?' the dean asked, sounding skeptical.

Langdon was stunned that a Mason was not more familiar with the spiritual importance of this symbol. 'Sir, the circumpunct has *countless* meanings. In ancient Egypt, it was the symbol for Ra – the sun god – and modern astronomy still uses it as the solar symbol. In Eastern philosophy, it represents the spiritual insight of the Third Eye, the divine rose, and the sign of illumination. The Kabbalists use it to symbolize the Kether – the highest Sephiroth and "the most hidden of all hidden things." Early mystics called it the Eye of God and it's the origin of the All-Seeing Eye on the Great Seal. The Pythagoreans used the circumpunct as the symbol of the Monad – the Divine Truth, the Prisca Sapientia, the at-one-ment of mind and soul, and the—'

'Enough!' Dean Galloway was chuckling now. 'Professor, thank you. You are correct, of course.'

Langdon now realized he had just been played. *He knew all that.*

'The circumpunct,' Galloway said, still smiling to

himself, 'is essentially *the* symbol of the Ancient Mysteries. For this reason, I would suggest that its presence in this box is not mere coincidence. Legend holds that the secrets of this map are hidden in the smallest of details.'

'Fine,' Katherine said, 'but even if this symbol was inscribed there intentionally, it doesn't bring us any closer to deciphering the map, does it?'

'You mentioned earlier that the wax seal you broke was embossed with Peter's ring?'

'That's correct.'

'And you said you have that ring with you?'

'I do.' Langdon reached into his pocket, found the ring, took it out of the plastic bag, and placed it on the desk in front of the dean.

Galloway picked up the ring and began feeling its surfaces. 'This unique ring was created at the same time as the Masonic Pyramid, and traditionally, it is worn by the Mason in charge of *protecting* the pyramid. Tonight, when I felt the tiny circumpunct on the bottom of the stone box, I realized that the ring is, in fact, part of the symbolon.'

'It is?'

'I'm certain of it. Peter is my closest friend, and he wore this ring for many years. I am quite familiar with it.' He handed the ring to Langdon. 'See for yourself.'

Langdon took the ring and examined it, running his fingers over the double-headed phoenix, the number 33, the words ORDO AB CHAO, and also the words *All is revealed at the thirty-third degree.* He felt nothing helpful. Then, as his fingers traced down around the outside of the band, he stopped short. Startled, he turned the ring over and eyed the very bottom of its band.

'Did you find it?' Galloway said.

'I think so, yes!' Langdon said.

Katherine slid her chair closer. 'What?'

'The degree sign on the band,' Langdon said, showing her. 'It's so small that you don't really notice it with your eyes, but if you feel it, you can tell it's actually indented – like a tiny circular incision.' The degree sign was centered on the bottom of the band . . . and admittedly looked to be the same size as the raised nubbin in the bottom of the cube.

'Is it the same size?' Katherine moved closer still, sounding excited now.

'There's one way to find out.' He took the ring and lowered it into the box, aligning the two tiny circles. As he pushed down, the raised circle on the box slid into the ring's opening, and there was a faint but decisive click.

They all jumped.

Langdon waited, but nothing happened.

'What was that?!' the priest said.

'Nothing,' Katherine replied. 'The ring locked into place . . . but nothing else happened.'

'No great transformation?' Galloway looked puzzled.

We're not done, Langdon realized, gazing down at the ring's embossed insignia – a double-headed phoenix and the number 33. *All is revealed at the thirty-third degree.* His mind filled with thoughts of Pythagoras, sacred geometry, and angles; he wondered if perhaps *degrees* had a *mathematical* meaning.

Slowly, heart beating faster now, he reached down and grasped the ring, which was affixed to the base of the cube. Then, slowly, he began turning the ring to the right. *All is revealed at the thirty-third degree.*

He turned the ring ten degrees . . . twenty degrees . . . thirty degrees –

What happened next, Langdon never saw coming.

85

Transformation.

Dean Galloway *heard* it happen, and so he didn't need to see it.

Across the desk from him, Langdon and Katherine were dead silent, no doubt staring in mute astonishment at the stone cube, which had just transformed itself loudly before their very eyes.

Galloway couldn't help but smile. He had anticipated the result, and although he still had no idea how this development would ultimately help them solve the riddle of the pyramid, he was enjoying the rare chance to teach a Harvard symbologist something about symbols.

'Professor,' the dean said, 'few people realize that the Masons venerate the shape of the cube – or *ashlar*, as we call it – because it is a three-dimensional representation of another symbol . . . a much older, two-dimensional symbol.' Galloway didn't need to ask if the professor recognized the ancient symbol now lying before them on the desk. It was one of the most famous symbols in the world.

Robert Langdon's thoughts churned as he stared at the transformed box on the desk in front of him. *I had no idea . . .*

Moments ago, he had reached into the stone box, grasped the Masonic ring, and gently turned it. As he rotated the ring through thirty-three degrees, the cube had suddenly changed before his eyes. The square panels that made up the sides of the box fell away from one another as their hidden hinges released. The box collapsed all at once, its side panels and lid falling outward, slapping loudly on the desk.

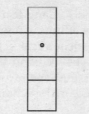

The cube becomes a cross, Langdon thought. *Symbolic alchemy.*

Katherine looked bewildered by the sight of the collapsed cube. 'The Masonic Pyramid relates to . . . Christianity?'

For a moment, Langdon had wondered the same thing. After all, the Christian crucifix was a respected symbol within the Masons, and certainly there were plenty of Christian Masons. However, Masons were also Jews, Muslims, Buddhists, Hindus, and those who had no name for their God. The presence of an exclusively Christian symbol seemed restrictive. Then the *true* meaning of this symbol had dawned on him.

'It's not a crucifix,' Langdon said, standing up now. 'The cross with the circumpunct in the middle is a binary symbol – *two* symbols fused to create *one*.'

'What are you saying?' Katherine's eyes followed him as he paced the room.

'The cross,' Langdon said, 'was not a Christian symbol until the fourth century. Long before that, it was used by the Egyptians to represent the intersection of two dimensions – the human and the celestial. As above, so below. It was a visual representation of the juncture where man and God become one.'

'Okay.'

'The circumpunct,' Langdon said, 'we already know has many meanings – one of its most esoteric being the *rose*, the alchemical symbol for perfection. But, when you place a rose on the center of a cross, you create another symbol entirely – the Rose Cross.'

Galloway reclined in his chair, smiling. 'My, my. Now you're cooking.'

Katherine stood now, too. 'What am I missing?'

'The Rose Cross,' Langdon explained, 'is a common symbol in Freemasonry. In fact, one of the degrees of the Scottish Rite is called "Knights of the Rose Cross" and honors the early Rosicrucians, who contributed to Masonic mystical philosophy. Peter may have mentioned the Rosicrucians to you. Dozens of great scientists were members – John Dee, Elias Ashmole, Robert Fludd—'

'Absolutely,' Katherine said. 'I've read all of the Rosicrucian manifestos in my research.'

Every scientist should, Langdon thought. The Order of the Rose Cross – or more formally the Ancient and Mystical Order Rosae Crucis – had an enigmatic history that had greatly influenced science and closely paralleled the legend of the Ancient Mysteries ... early sages possessing secret wisdom that was passed down through the ages and studied by only the brightest minds. Admittedly, history's list of famous Rosicrucians was a who's who of European Renaissance luminaries: Paracelsus, Bacon, Fludd, Descartes, Pascal, Spinoza, Newton, Leibniz.

According to Rosicrucian doctrine, the order was 'built on esoteric truths of the ancient past,' truths which had to be 'concealed from the average man' and which promised great insight into 'the spiritual realm.' The brotherhood's symbol had blossomed over the years into a flowering rose on an ornate cross, but it had begun as a more modest dotted circle on an unadorned cross – the simplest manifestation of the rose on the simplest manifestation of the cross.

'Peter and I often discuss Rosicrucian philosophy,' Galloway told Katherine.

As the dean began outlining the interrelationship between Masonry and Rosicrucianism, Langdon felt his attention drawn back to the same nagging thought he'd had all night. *Jeova Sanctus Unus. This phrase is linked to alchemy somehow.* He still could not remember exactly what Peter had told him about the phrase, but for some reason, the mention of Rosicrucianism seemed to have rekindled the thought. *Think, Robert!*

'The Rosicrucian founder,' Galloway was saying, 'was allegedly a German mystic who went by the name Christian Rosenkreuz – a pseudonym obviously, perhaps even for Francis Bacon, who some historians believe founded the group himself, although there is no proof of—'

'A pseudonym!' Langdon declared suddenly, startling even himself. 'That's it! *Jeova Sanctus Unus!* It's a pseudonym!'

'What are you talking about?' Katherine demanded.

Langdon's pulse had quickened now. 'All night, I've been trying to remember what Peter told me about *Jeova Sanctus Unus* and its relationship to alchemy. Finally I remembered! It's not about alchemy so much as about an *alchemist*! A very famous alchemist!'

Galloway chuckled. 'It's about time, Professor. I mentioned his name twice and also the word *pseudonym.*'

Langdon stared at the old dean. 'You *knew*?'

'Well, I had my suspicions when you told me the engraving said *Jeova Sanctus Unus* and had been decrypted using Dürer's alchemical magic square, but when you found the Rose Cross, I was certain. As you probably know, the personal papers of the scientist in question included a very heavily annotated copy of the Rosicrucian manifestos.'

'Who?' Katherine asked.

'One of the world's greatest scientists!' Langdon replied. 'He was an alchemist, a member of the Royal Society of London, a Rosicrucian, *and* he signed some of his most secretive science papers with a pseudonym – *"Jeova Sanctus Unus"*!'

'One True God?' Katherine said. 'Modest guy.'

'Brilliant guy, actually,' Galloway corrected. 'He signed his name that way because, like the ancient Adepts, he understood *himself* as divine. In addition, because the sixteen letters in *Jeova Sanctus Unus* could be rearranged to spell his name in Latin, making it a perfect pseudonym.'

Katherine now looked puzzled. '*Jeova Sanctus Unus* is an anagram of a famous alchemist's name in Latin?'

Langdon grabbed a piece of paper and pencil off the dean's desk, writing as he talked. 'Latin interchanges the letters *J* for *I* and the letter *V* for *U*, which means

Jeova Sanctus Unus can actually be perfectly rearranged to spell this man's name.'

Langdon wrote down sixteen letters: *Isaacus Neutonuus.*

He handed the slip of paper to Katherine and said, 'I think you've heard of him.'

'Isaac Newton?' Katherine demanded, looking at the paper. '*That's* what the engraving on the pyramid was trying to tell us!'

For a moment, Langdon was back in Westminster Abbey, standing at Newton's pyramidical tomb, where he had experienced a similar epiphany. *And tonight, the great scientist surfaces again.* It was no coincidence, of course . . . the pyramids, mysteries, science, hidden knowledge . . . it was all intertwined. Newton's name had always been a recurring guidepost for those seeking secret knowledge.

'Isaac Newton,' Galloway said, 'must have something to do with how to decipher the meaning of the pyramid. I can't imagine what it would be, but—'

'Genius!' Katherine exclaimed, her eyes going wide. 'That's how we transform the pyramid!'

'You understand?' Langdon said.

'Yes!' she said. 'I can't believe we didn't see it! It has been staring us right in the face. A simple alchemical process. I can transform this pyramid using basic science! Newtonian science!'

Langdon strained to understand.

'Dean Galloway,' Katherine said. 'If you read the ring, it says—'

'Stop!' The old dean suddenly raised his finger in the air and motioned for silence. Gently, he cocked his head to the side, as if he were listening to something. After a moment, he stood up abruptly. 'My friends, this pyramid obviously has secrets left to reveal. I don't know what Ms. Solomon is getting at, but if she knows your next step, then I have played my role. Pack up your things and say no more to me. Leave me in darkness for the moment. I would prefer to have no information to share should our visitors try to force me.'

'Visitors?' Katherine said, listening. 'I don't hear anyone.'

'You *will*,' Galloway said, heading for the door. 'Hurry.'

Across town, a cell tower was attempting to contact a phone that lay in pieces on Massachusetts Avenue. Finding no signal, it redirected the call to voice mail.

'Robert!' Warren Bellamy's panicked voice shouted. 'Where are you?! Call me! Something terrible is happening!'

86

In the cerulean glow of his basement lights, Mal'akh stood at the stone table and continued his preparations. As he worked, his empty stomach growled. He paid no heed. His days of servitude to the whims of his flesh were behind him.

Transformation requires sacrifice.

Like many of history's most spiritually evolved men, Mal'akh had committed to his path by making the noblest of flesh sacrifices. Castration had been less painful than he had imagined. And, he had learned, far more common. Every year, thousands of men underwent surgical gelding – orchiectomy, as the process was known – their motivations ranging from transgender issues, to curbing sexual addictions, to deep-seated spiritual beliefs. For Mal'akh, the reasons were of the highest nature. Like the mythological self-castrated Attis, Mal'akh knew that achieving immortality required a clean break with the material world of male and female.

The androgyne is one.

Nowadays, eunuchs were shunned, although the ancients understood the inherent power of this trans-mutational sacrifice. Even the early Christians had heard Jesus Himself extol its virtues in Matthew 19:12: *'There are those who have made themselves eunuchs for the sake of the kingdom of heaven. He who is able to accept this, let him accept it.'*

Peter Solomon had made a flesh sacrifice, although a single hand was a small price in the grand scheme. By night's end, however, Solomon would be sacrificing much, much more.

In order to create, I must destroy.

Such was the nature of polarity.

Peter Solomon, of course, deserved the fate that awaited him tonight. It would be a fitting end. Long ago, he had played the pivotal role in Mal'akh's mortal life path. For this reason, Peter had been chosen to play the pivotal role in Mal'akh's great transformation. This man had earned all the horror and pain he was about to endure. Peter Solomon was not the man the world believed he was.

He sacrificed his own son.

Peter Solomon had once presented his son, Zachary, with an impossible choice – wealth or wisdom. *Zachary chose poorly.* The boy's decision had begun a chain of events that eventually dragged the young man into the depths of hell. *Soganlik Prison.* Zachary Solomon had died in that Turkish prison. The whole world knew the story . . . but what they didn't know was that Peter Solomon could have saved his son.

I was there, Mal'akh thought. *I heard it all.*

Mal'akh had never forgotten that night. Solomon's brutal decision had meant the end of his son, Zach, but it had been the birth of Mal'akh.

Some must die that others may live.

As the light over Mal'akh's head began changing color again, he realized the hour was late. He completed his preparations and headed back up the ramp. It was time to attend to matters of the mortal world.

87

All is revealed at the thirty-third degree, Katherine thought as she ran. *I know how to transform the pyramid!* The answer had been right in front of them all night.

Katherine and Langdon were alone now, dashing through the cathedral's annex, following signs for 'The Garth.' Now, exactly as the dean had promised, they burst out of the cathedral into a massive, walled-in courtyard.

The cathedral garth was a cloistered, pentagonal

garden with a bronze postmodern fountain. Katherine was amazed how loudly the fountain's flowing water seemed to be reverberating in the courtyard. Then she realized it was not the fountain she was hearing.

'Helicopter!' she shouted as a beam of light pierced the night sky above them. 'Get under that portico!'

The dazzling glare of a searchlight flooded the garth just as Langdon and Katherine reached the other side, slipping beneath a Gothic arch into a tunnel that led to the outside lawn. They waited, huddled in the tunnel, as the helicopter passed overhead and began circling the cathedral in wide arcs.

'I guess Galloway was right about hearing visitors,' Katherine said, impressed. *Bad eyes make for great ears.* Her own ears now pounded rhythmically with her racing pulse.

'This way,' Langdon said, clutching his daybag and moving through the passage.

Dean Galloway had given them a single key and a clear set of directions. Unfortunately, when they reached the end of the short tunnel, they found themselves separated from their destination by a wide-open expanse of lawn, currently flooded with light from the helicopter overhead.

'We can't get across,' Katherine said.

'Hold on . . . look.' Langdon pointed to a black shadow that was materializing on the lawn to their left. The shadow began as an amorphous blob, but it was growing quickly, moving in their direction, becoming more defined, rushing at them faster and faster, stretching, and finally transforming itself into a massive black rectangle crowned by two impossibly tall spires.

'The cathedral facade is blocking the searchlight,' Langdon said.

'They're landing out in front!'

Langdon grabbed Katherine's hand. 'Run! Now!'

Inside the cathedral, Dean Galloway felt a lightness in his step that he had not felt in years. He moved through the Great Crossing, down the nave toward the narthex and the front doors.

He could hear the helicopter hovering in front of the cathedral now, and he imagined its lights coming through the rose window in front of him, throwing spectacular colors all over the sanctuary. He recalled the days when he could see color. Ironically, the lightless void that had become his world had illuminated many things for him. *I see more clearly now than ever.*

Galloway had been called to God as a young man and over his lifetime had loved the church as much as any man could. Like many of his colleagues who had given their lives in earnest to God, Galloway was weary. He had spent his life straining to be heard above the din of ignorance.

What did I expect?

From the Crusades, to the Inquisition, to American politics – the name Jesus had been hijacked as an ally in all kinds of power struggles. Since the beginning of time, the ignorant had always screamed the loudest, herding the unsuspecting masses and forcing them to do their bidding. They defended their worldly desires by citing Scripture they did not understand. They celebrated their intolerance as proof of their convictions. Now, after all these years, mankind had finally managed to utterly erode everything that had once been so beautiful about Jesus.

Tonight, encountering the symbol of the Rose Cross

had fueled him with great hope, reminding him of the prophecies written in the Rosicrucian manifestos, which Galloway had read countless times in the past and could still recall.

Chapter One: *Jehova will redeem humanity by revealing those secrets which he previously reserved only for the elect.*

Chapter Four: *The whole world shall become as one book and all the contradictions of science and theology shall be reconciled.*

Chapter Seven: *Before the end of the world, God shall create a great flood of spiritual light to alleviate the suffering of humankind.*

Chapter Eight: *Before this revelation is possible, the world must sleep away the intoxication of her poisoned chalice, which was filled with the false life of the theological vine.*

Galloway knew the church had long ago lost her way, and he had dedicated his life to righting her course. Now, he realized, the moment was fast approaching.

It is always darkest before the dawn.

CIA field agent Turner Simkins was perched on the strut of the Sikorsky helicopter as it touched down on the frosty grass. He leaped off, joined by his men, and immediately waved the chopper back up into the air to keep an eye on all the exits.

Nobody leaves this building.

As the chopper rose back into the night sky, Simkins and his team ran up the stairs to the cathedral's main entrance. Before he could decide which of the six doors to pound on, one of them swung open.

'Yes?' a calm voice said from the shadows.

Simkins could barely make out the hunched figure in priest's robes. 'Are you Dean Colin Galloway?'

'I am,' the old man replied.

'I'm looking for Robert Langdon. Have you seen him?'

The old man stepped forward now, staring past Simkins with eerie blank eyes. 'Now, wouldn't *that* be a miracle.'

88

Time is running out.

Security analyst Nola Kaye was already on edge, and the third mug of coffee she was now drinking had begun coursing through her like an electric current.

No word yet from Sato.

Finally, her phone rang, and Nola leaped on it. 'OS,' she answered. 'Nola here.'

'Nola, it's Rick Parrish in systems security.'

Nola slumped. *No Sato.* 'Hi, Rick. What can I do for you?'

'I wanted to give you a heads-up – our department may have information relevant to what you're working on tonight.'

Nola set down her coffee. *How the hell do you know what I'm working on tonight?* 'I beg your pardon?'

'Sorry, it's the new CI program we're beta-testing,' Parrish said. 'It keeps flagging your workstation number.'

Nola now realized what he was talking about. The Agency was currently running a new piece of 'collaborative integration' software designed to provide real-time alerts to disparate CIA departments when they happened to be processing related data fields. In an era of time-sensitive terrorist threats, the key to thwarting disaster was often as simple as a heads-up telling you that the guy down the hall was analyzing the very data you needed. As far as Nola was concerned, this CI software had proven more of a distraction than any real help – *constant interruption* software, she called it.

'Right, I forgot,' Nola said. 'What have you got?' She was positive that nobody else in the building *knew* about this crisis, much less could be working on it. The only computer work Nola had done tonight was historical research for Sato on esoteric Masonic topics. Nonetheless, she was obliged to play the game.

'Well, it's probably nothing,' Parrish said, 'but we stopped a hacker tonight, and the CI program keeps suggesting I share the information with you.'

A hacker? Nola sipped her coffee. 'I'm listening.'

'About an hour ago,' Parrish said, 'we snagged a guy named Zoubianis trying to access a file on one of our internal databases. This guy claims it was a job for hire and that he has no idea *why* he was being paid to access this particular file or even that it was on a CIA server.'

'Okay.'

'We finished questioning him, and he's clean. But here's the weird thing – the *same* file he was targeting had been flagged earlier tonight by an internal search engine. It looks like someone piggybacked into our system, ran a specific keyword search, and generated a redaction. The thing is, the *keywords* they used are really strange. And there's one in particular that the CI flagged as a high-priority match – one that's unique to both of our data sets.' He paused. 'Do you know the word . . . *symbolon*?'

Nola jolted upright, spilling coffee on her desk.

'The other keywords are just as unusual,' Parrish continued. '*Pyramid, portal —*'

'Get down here,' Nola commanded, mopping up her desk. 'And bring everything you've got!'

'These words actually *mean* something to you?'

'NOW!'

89

Cathedral College is an elegant, castlelike edifice located adjacent to the National Cathedral. The College of Preachers, as it was originally envisioned by the first Episcopal bishop of Washington, was founded to provide ongoing education for clergy after their ordination. Today, the college offers a wide variety of programs on theology, global justice, healing, and spirituality.

Langdon and Katherine had made the dash across the lawn and used Galloway's key to slip inside just as the helicopter rose back over the cathedral, its floodlights turning night back into day. Now, standing breathless inside the foyer, they surveyed their surroundings. The windows provided sufficient illumination, and Langdon saw no reason to turn the lights on and take a chance of broadcasting their whereabouts to the helicopter overhead. As they moved down the central hallway, they passed a series of conference halls, classrooms, and sitting areas. The interior reminded Langdon of the neo-Gothic buildings of Yale University – breathtaking on the outside, and yet surprisingly utilitarian on the inside, their period elegance having been retrofitted to endure heavy foot traffic.

'Down here,' Katherine said, motioning toward the far end of the hall.

Katherine had yet to share with Langdon her new revelation regarding the pyramid, but apparently the reference to Isaacus Neutonuus had sparked it. All she had said as they crossed the lawn was that the pyramid could be transformed using simple science. Everything she needed, she believed, could probably be found in this building. Langdon had no idea what she needed or how Katherine intended to transform a solid piece of granite or gold, but considering he had just witnessed a cube metamorphose into a Rosicrucian cross, he was willing to have faith.

They reached the end of the hall and Katherine frowned, apparently not seeing what she wanted. 'You said this building has dormitory facilities?'

'Yes, for residential conferences.'

'So they *must* have a kitchen in here somewhere, right?'

'You're hungry?'

She frowned back at him. 'No, I need a lab.'

Of course you do. Langdon spotted a descending staircase that bore a promising symbol. *America's favorite pictogram.*

The basement kitchen was industrial looking – lots of stainless steel and big bowls – clearly designed to cook for large groups. The kitchen had no windows. Katherine closed the door and flipped on the lights. The exhaust fans came on automatically.

She began rooting around in the cupboards for whatever it was she needed. 'Robert,' she directed, 'put the pyramid out on the island, if you would.'

Feeling like the novice sous chef taking orders from Daniel Boulud, Langdon did as he was told, removing the pyramid from his bag and placing the gold capstone on top of it. When he finished, Katherine was busy filling an enormous pot with hot tap water.

'Would you please lift this to the stove for me?'

Langdon heaved the sloshing pot onto the stove as Katherine turned on the gas burner and cranked up the flame.

'Are we doing lobsters?' he asked hopefully.

'Very funny. No, we're doing alchemy. And for the record, this is a *pasta* pot, not a lobster pot.' She pointed to the perforated strainer insert that she had removed from the pot and placed on the island beside the pyramid.

Silly me. 'And boiling pasta is going to help us decipher the pyramid?'

Katherine ignored the comment, her tone turning serious. 'As I'm sure you know, there is a historical and symbolic *reason* the Masons chose thirty-three as their highest degree.'

'Of course,' Langdon said. In the days of Pythagoras, six centuries before Christ, the tradition of *numerology* hailed the number 33 as the highest of all the Master Numbers. It was the most sacred figure, symbolizing Divine Truth. The tradition lived on within the

442

Masons . . . and elsewhere. It was no coincidence that Christians were taught that Jesus was crucified at age thirty-three, despite no real historical evidence to that effect. Nor was it coincidence that Joseph was said to have been thirty-three when he married the Virgin Mary, or that Jesus accomplished thirty-three miracles, or that God's name was mentioned thirty-three times in Genesis, or that, in Islam, all the dwellers of heaven were permanently thirty-three years old.

'Thirty-three,' Katherine said, 'is a sacred number in many mystical traditions.'

'Correct.' Langdon still had no idea what this had to do with a pasta pot.

'So it should come as no surprise to you that an early alchemist, Rosicrucian, and mystic like Isaac Newton *also* considered the number thirty-three special.'

'I'm sure he did,' Langdon replied. 'Newton was deep into numerology, prophecy, and astrology, but what does—'

'All is revealed at the thirty-third degree.'

Langdon pulled Peter's ring from his pocket and read the inscription. Then he glanced back at the pot of water. 'Sorry, you lost me.'

'Robert, earlier tonight, we all assumed "thirty-third degree" referred to the Masonic degree, and yet when we rotated that ring thirty-three degrees, the cube transformed and revealed a cross. At that moment, we realized the word *degree* was being used in another sense.'

'Yes. Degrees of arc.'

'Exactly. But *degree* has a *third* meaning as well.'

Langdon eyed the pot of water on the stove. 'Temperature.'

'Exactly!' she said. 'It was right in front of us all

443

night. "All is revealed at the thirty-third degree." If we bring this pyramid's temperature to thirty-three degrees . . . it may just reveal something.'

Langdon knew Katherine Solomon was exceptionally bright, and yet she seemed to be missing a rather obvious point. 'If I'm not mistaken, thirty-three degrees is almost freezing. Shouldn't we be putting the pyramid in the freezer?'

Katherine smiled. 'Not if we want to follow the recipe written by the great alchemist and Rosicrucian mystic who signed his papers *Jeova Sanctus Unus*.'

Isaacus Neutonuus wrote recipes?

'Robert, *temperature* is the fundamental alchemical catalyst, and it was not always measured in Fahrenheit and Celsius. There are far *older* temperature scales, one of them invented by Isaac—'

'The Newton Scale!' Langdon said, realizing she was right.

'Yes! Isaac Newton invented an entire system of quantifying temperature based entirely on natural phenomena. The temperature of melting ice was Newton's base point, and he called it "the zeroth degree."' She paused. 'I suppose you can guess what degree he assigned the temperature of boiling water – the king of all alchemical processes?'

'Thirty-three.'

'Yes, thirty-three! The thirty-third degree. On the Newton Scale, the temperature of boiling water is thirty-three degrees. I remember asking my brother once why Newton chose that number. I mean, it seemed so random. Boiling water is the most fundamental alchemical process, and he chose thirty-three? Why not a hundred? Why not something more elegant? Peter explained that, to a mystic like Isaac Newton, there was no number more elegant than thirty-three.'

All is revealed at the thirty-third degree. Langdon glanced at the pot of water and then over at the pyramid. 'Katherine, the pyramid is made out of solid granite and solid gold. Do you really think boiling water is hot enough to transform it?'

The smile on her face told Langdon that Katherine knew something he did not know. Confidently, she walked over to the island, lifted the gold-capped, granite pyramid, and set it in the strainer. Then she carefully lowered it into the bubbling water. 'Let's find out, shall we?'

High above the National Cathedral, the CIA pilot locked the helicopter in auto-hover mode and surveyed the perimeter of the building and the grounds. *No movement.* His thermal imaging couldn't penetrate the cathedral stone, and so he couldn't tell what the team was doing inside, but if anyone tried to slip out, the thermal would pick it up.

It was sixty seconds later that a thermal sensor pinged. Working on the same principle as home-security systems, the detector had identified a strong temperature differential. Usually this meant a human form moving through a cool space, but what appeared on the monitor was more of a thermal cloud, a patch of hot air drifting across the lawn. The pilot found the source, an active vent on the side of Cathedral College.

Probably nothing, he thought. He saw these kinds of gradients all the time. *Someone cooking or doing laundry.* As he was about to turn away, though, he realized something odd. There were no cars in the parking lot and no lights on anywhere in the building.

He studied the UH-60's imaging system for a long moment. Then he radioed down to his team leader. 'Simkins, it's probably nothing, but . . .'

'Incandescent temperature indicator!' Langdon had to admit, it was clever.

'It's simple science,' Katherine said. 'Different substances incandesce at different temperatures. We call them thermal markers. Science uses these markers all the time.'

Langdon gazed down at the submerged pyramid and capstone. Wisps of steam were beginning to curl over the bubbling water, although he was not feeling hopeful. He glanced at his watch, and his heart rate accelerated: 11:45 P.M. 'You believe something here will *luminesce* as it heats up?'

'Not luminesce, Robert. *Incandesce*. There's a big difference. Incandescence is caused by *heat*, and it occurs at a specific temperature. For example, when steel manufacturers temper beams, they spray a grid on them with a transparent coating that incandesces at a specific target temperature so they know when the beams are done. Think of a mood ring. Just put it on your finger, and it changes color from body heat.'

'Katherine, this pyramid was built in the 1800s! I can understand a craftsman making hidden release hinges in a stone box, but applying some kind of transparent thermal coating?'

'Perfectly feasible,' she said, glancing hopefully at the submerged pyramid. 'The early alchemists used organic phosphors all the time as thermal markers. The Chinese made colored fireworks, and even the

Egyptians—' Katherine stopped midsentence, staring intently into the roiling water.

'What?' Langdon followed her gaze into the turbulent water but saw nothing at all.

Katherine leaned in, staring more intently into the water. Suddenly she turned and ran across the kitchen toward the door.

'Where are you going?' Langdon shouted.

She slid to a stop at the kitchen light switch, flipped it off. The lights and exhaust fan went off, plunging the room into total darkness and silence. Langdon turned back to the pyramid and peered through the steam at the capstone beneath the water. By the time Katherine made it back to his side, his mouth had fallen open in disbelief.

Exactly as Katherine had predicted, a small section of the metal capstone was starting to glow beneath the water. Letters were starting to appear, and they were getting brighter as the water heated up.

'Text!' Katherine whispered.

Langdon nodded, dumbstruck. The glowing words were materializing just beneath the engraved inscription on the capstone. It looked like only three words, and although Langdon could not yet read what the words said, he wondered if they would unveil everything they had been looking for tonight. *The pyramid is a real map*, Galloway had told them, *and it points to a real location.*

As the letters shone brighter, Katherine turned off the gas, and the water slowly stopped churning. The capstone now came into focus beneath the water's calm surface.

Three shining words were clearly legible.

90

In the dim light of the Cathedral College kitchen, Langdon and Katherine stood over the pot of water and stared at the transformed capstone beneath the surface. On the side of the golden capstone, an incandescent message was glowing.

Langdon read the shining text, scarcely able to believe his eyes. He knew the pyramid was rumored to reveal a specific *location* ... but he had never imagined that the location would be quite *this* specific.

Eight Franklin Square

'A street address,' he whispered, stunned.

Katherine looked equally amazed. 'I don't know what's there, do you?'

Langdon shook his head. He knew Franklin Square was one of the older sections of Washington, but he wasn't familiar with the address. He looked at the tip of the capstone, and read downward, taking in the entire text.

The
secret hides
within The Order
Eight Franklin Square

Is there some kind of Order on Franklin Square?

Is there a building that hides the opening to a deep spiral staircase?

Whether or not there was actually something *buried* at that address, Langdon had no idea. The important issue at this point was that he and Katherine had deciphered the pyramid and now possessed the information required to negotiate Peter's release.

And not a moment too soon.

The glowing arms on Langdon's Mickey Mouse watch indicated that they had less than ten minutes to spare.

'Make the call,' Katherine said, motioning to a phone on the wall in the kitchen. 'Now!'

The sudden arrival of this moment startled Langdon, and he found himself hesitating.

'Are we sure about this?'

'I most certainly am.'

'I'm not telling him anything until we know Peter is safe.'

'Of course not. You remember the number, right?'

Langdon nodded and made his way over to the kitchen phone. He lifted the receiver and dialed the man's cell-phone number. Katherine came over and placed her head next to his so she could listen in. As the line began to ring, Langdon prepared himself for the eerie whisper of the man who had tricked him earlier tonight.

Finally, the call connected.

There was no greeting, though. No voice. Only the sound of breathing at the other end.

Langdon waited and then finally spoke. 'I have the information you want, but if you want it, you'll have to give us Peter.'

'Who is this?' a woman's voice replied.

Langdon jumped. 'Robert Langdon,' he said reflexively. 'Who are *you*?' For an instant he thought he must have dialed incorrectly.

'*Your name is Langdon?*' The woman sounded surprised. 'There's someone here asking for you.'

449

What? 'I'm sorry, *who* is this?'

'Officer Paige Montgomery with Preferred Security.' Her voice seemed shaky. 'Maybe you can help us with this. About an hour ago, my partner responded to a 911 call in Kalorama Heights . . . a possible hostage situation. I lost all contact with her, and so I called backup and came to check the residence. We found my partner dead in the backyard. The home owner was gone, and so we broke in. A cell phone was ringing on the hall table, and I—'

'You're inside?' Langdon demanded.

'Yes, and the 911 tip . . . was a good one,' the woman stammered. 'Sorry if I sound rattled, but my partner's dead, and we found a man being held here against his will. He's in bad shape, and we're working on him now. He's been asking for two people – one named Langdon and one named Katherine.'

'That's my brother!' Katherine blurted into the receiver, pressing her head closer to Langdon's. 'I made the 911 call! Is he okay?!'

'Actually, ma'am, he's . . .' The woman's voice cracked. 'He's in bad shape. He's missing his right hand . . .'

'Please,' Katherine urged. 'I want to talk to him!'

'They're working on him at the moment. He's in and out of consciousness. If you're anywhere in the area, you should get over here. He obviously wants to see you.'

'We're about six minutes away!' Katherine said.

'Then I suggest you hurry.' There was a muffled noise in the background, and the woman then returned to the line. 'Sorry, it looks like I'm needed. I'll speak to you when you arrive.'

The line went dead.

91

Inside Cathedral College, Langdon and Katherine bounded up the basement stairs and hurried down a darkened hallway looking for a front exit. No longer did they hear the sounds of helicopter blades overhead, and Langdon felt hopeful they could slip out unseen and find their way up to Kalorama Heights to see Peter.

They found him. He's alive.

Thirty seconds earlier, when they'd hung up with the female security guard, Katherine had hurriedly hoisted the steaming pyramid and capstone out of the water. The pyramid was still dripping when she lowered it into Langdon's leather bag. Now he could feel the heat radiating through the leather.

Excitement over Peter's discovery had temporarily trumped any further reflection on the capstone's glowing message – *Eight Franklin Square* – but there would be time for that once they got to Peter.

As they rounded the corner at the top of the stairs, Katherine stopped short and pointed into a sitting room across the hall. Through the bay window, Langdon could see a sleek black helicopter sitting silent on the lawn. A lone pilot stood beside it, facing away from them and talking on his radio. There was also a black Escalade with tinted windows parked nearby.

Staying in the shadows, Langdon and Katherine moved into the sitting room, and peered out the window to see if they could see the rest of the field team. Thankfully, the huge lawn outside the National Cathedral was empty.

'They must be inside the cathedral,' Langdon said.

'They're not,' a deep voice said behind them.

Langdon and Katherine wheeled around to see who had spoken. In the doorway of the sitting room, two black-clad figures aimed laser-sighted rifles at them. Langdon could see a glowing red dot dancing on his chest.

'Nice to see you again, Professor,' said a familiar raspy voice. The agents parted, and the tiny form of Director Sato sliced effortlessly through, crossing the sitting room and stopping directly in front of Langdon. 'You've made some exceedingly poor choices tonight.'

'The police found Peter Solomon,' Langdon declared forcefully. 'He's in bad shape, but he'll live. It's over.'

If Sato was surprised Peter had been found, she did not show it. Her eyes were unflinching as she walked to Langdon and stopped only inches away. 'Professor, I can assure you, this is nowhere *near* over. And if the police are now involved, it has only become more serious. As I told you earlier this evening, this is an extremely delicate situation. You never should have run away with that pyramid.'

'Ma'am,' Katherine blurted, 'I need to see my brother. You can *have* the pyramid, but you must let—'

'I *must*?' Sato demanded, spinning to Katherine. 'Ms. Solomon, I assume?' She stared at Katherine with fire in her eyes and then turned back to Langdon. 'Put the leather bag on the table.'

Langdon glanced down at the pair of laser sights on his chest. He set the leather bag on the coffee table. An agent approached cautiously, unzipped the bag, and pulled the two sides apart. A little puff of trapped steam billowed up out of the bag. He aimed his light

452

inside, stared for a long, puzzled moment, and then nodded to Sato.

Sato walked over and peered into the bag. The wet pyramid and capstone glistened in the beam of the flashlight. Sato crouched down, looking very closely at the golden capstone, which Langdon realized she had only seen in X-ray.

'The inscription,' Sato demanded. 'Does it mean anything to you? "The secret hides within The Order"?'

'We're not sure, ma'am.'

'Why is the pyramid steaming hot?'

'We submerged it in boiling water,' Katherine said without hesitation. 'It was part of the process of deciphering the code. We'll tell you everything, but please let us go see my brother. He's been through—'

'You *boiled* the pyramid?' Sato demanded.

'Turn off the flashlight,' Katherine said. 'Look at the capstone. You can probably still see.'

The agent flicked off his light, and Sato knelt down before the capstone. Even from where Langdon was standing, he could see that the text on the capstone was still glowing slightly.

'Eight Franklin Square?' Sato said, sounding amazed.

'Yes, ma'am. That text was written with an incandescent lacquer or something. The thirty-third degree was actually—'

'And the address?' Sato demanded. 'Is *this* what this guy wants?'

'Yes,' Langdon said. 'He believes the pyramid is a map that will tell him the location of a great treasure – the key to unlocking the Ancient Mysteries.'

Sato looked again at the capstone, her expression one of disbelief. 'Tell me,' she said, fear creeping into her voice, 'have you contacted this man yet? Have you already *given* him this address?'

'We tried.' Langdon explained what had happened when they called the man's cell phone.

Sato listened, running her tongue over her yellow teeth as he spoke. Despite looking ready to erupt with anger over the situation, she turned to one of her agents and spoke in a restrained whisper. 'Send him in. He's in the SUV.'

The agent nodded and spoke into his transceiver.

'Send who in?' Langdon said.

'The only person who has any hope of fixing the goddamn mess you made!'

'What mess?' Langdon fired back. 'Now that Peter is safe, everything is—'

'For Christ's sake!' Sato exploded. 'This is not *about* Peter! I tried to tell you that at the Capitol Building, Professor, but you chose to work *against* me rather than *with* me! Now you've made an ungodly mess! When you destroyed your cell phone, which, by the way, we *were* tracking, you cut off your communication with this man. And this address you uncovered – whatever the hell it is – this address was our *one* chance to catch this lunatic. I needed you to play his game, to *provide* him with this address so we would know where the hell to catch him!'

Before Langdon could reply, Sato directed the remainder of her wrath at Katherine.

'And *you*, Ms. Solomon! You *knew* where this maniac lived? Why didn't you tell me? You sent a rent-a-cop to this man's house? Don't you see you've ruined any chance we had of catching him there? I'm glad your brother is safe, but let me tell you this, we are facing a crisis tonight whose ramifications far outreach your family. They will be felt all around the world. The man who took your brother has enormous power, and we need to catch him immediately.'

As she finished her tirade, the tall, elegant silhouette of Warren Bellamy emerged from the shadows and stepped into the sitting room. He looked rumpled, bruised, and shaken . . . like he'd been through hell.

'Warren!' Langdon stood up. 'Are you okay?'

'No,' he replied. 'Not really.'

'Did you hear? Peter is safe!'

Bellamy nodded, looking dazed, as if nothing mattered anymore. 'Yes, I just heard your conversation. I'm glad.'

'Warren, what the hell is going on?'

Sato intervened. 'You boys can catch up in a minute. Right now, Mr. Bellamy is going to reach out to this lunatic and communicate with him. Just like he's been doing all night.'

Langdon felt lost. 'Bellamy hasn't been *communicating* with this guy tonight! This guy doesn't even know Bellamy is involved!'

Sato turned to Bellamy and raised her eyebrows.

Bellamy sighed. 'Robert, I'm afraid I haven't been entirely honest with you this evening.'

Langdon could only stare.

'I thought I was doing the right thing . . .' Bellamy said, looking frightened.

'Well,' Sato said, '*now* you will do the right thing . . . and we'd all better pray to God it works.' As if to substantiate Sato's portentous tone, the mantel clock began chiming the hour. Sato took out a Ziploc bag of items and tossed it to Bellamy. 'Here's your stuff. Does your cell phone take photos?'

'Yes, ma'am.'

'Good. Hold up the capstone.'

* * *

The message Mal'akh had just received was from his contact – Warren Bellamy – the Mason he had sent to the Capitol Building earlier tonight to assist Robert Langdon. Bellamy, like Langdon, wanted Peter Solomon back alive and had assured Mal'akh he would help Langdon acquire and decipher the pyramid. All night, Mal'akh had been receiving e-mail updates, which had been automatically forwarded to his cell phone.

This should be interesting, Mal'akh thought, opening the message.

From: Warren Bellamy

got separated from langdon
but finally have info you
demanded. proof attached.
call for missing piece. – wb

– one attachment (jpeg) –

Call for missing piece? Mal'akh wondered, opening the attachment.

The attachment was a photo.

When Mal'akh saw it, he gasped out loud, and he could feel his heart start pounding with excitement. He was looking at a close-up of a tiny golden pyramid. *The legendary capstone!* The ornate engraving on the face carried a promising message: *The secret hides within The Order.*

Beneath the inscription, Mal'akh now saw something that stunned him. The capstone seemed to be glowing. In disbelief, he stared at the faintly radiant

456

text and realized that the legend was literally true: *The Masonic Pyramid transforms itself to reveal its secret to the worthy.*

How this magical transformation had occurred, Mal'akh had no idea, and he didn't care. The glowing text was clearly pointing to a specific location in D.C., exactly as prophesied. *Franklin Square.* Unfortunately, the photo of the capstone also included Warren Bellamy's index finger, which was strategically positioned on the capstone to block out a critical piece of information.

The
secret hides
within The Order
█████ Franklin Square

Call for missing piece. Mal'akh now understood Bellamy's meaning.

The Architect of the Capitol had been cooperative all night, but now he had chosen to play a very dangerous game.

92

Beneath the watchful gaze of several armed CIA agents, Langdon, Katherine, and Bellamy waited with Sato in the Cathedral College sitting room. On the coffee table before them, Langdon's leather bag was still open, the golden capstone peeking out the top. The words *Eight Franklin Square* had now faded away, leaving no evidence that they had ever existed.

Katherine had pleaded with Sato to let her go see her brother, but Sato had simply shaken her head, eyes fixed on Bellamy's cell phone. It sat on the coffee table and had yet to ring.

Why didn't Bellamy just tell me the truth? Langdon wondered. Apparently, the Architect had been in contact with Peter's captor all night, reassuring him that Langdon was making progress deciphering the pyramid. It was a bluff, an attempt to buy time for Peter. In fact, Bellamy was doing all he could to interfere with anyone who threatened to unveil the pyramid's secret. Now, however, it seemed that Bellamy had switched sides. He and Sato were now prepared to risk the pyramid's secret in hopes of catching this man.

'Take your hands off me!' shouted an elderly voice in the hall. 'I'm *blind*, not inept! I know my way through the college!' Dean Galloway was still protesting loudly as a CIA agent manhandled him into the sitting room and forced him into one of the chairs.

'Who's here?' Galloway demanded, his blank eyes staring dead ahead. 'It sounds like a lot of you. How many do you need to detain an old man? Really now!'

'There are seven of us,' Sato declared. 'Including Robert Langdon, Katherine Solomon, and your Masonic brother Warren Bellamy.'

Galloway slumped, all his bluster gone.

'We're okay,' Langdon said. 'And we just heard that Peter is safe. He's in bad shape, but the police are with him.'

'Thank heavens,' Galloway said. 'And the—'

A loud rattling caused everyone in the room to jump. It was Bellamy's cell phone vibrating against the coffee table. Everyone fell silent.

'Okay, Mr. Bellamy,' Sato said. 'Don't blow it. You know the stakes.'

Bellamy took a deep breath and exhaled. Then he reached down and pressed the speakerphone button to connect the call.

'Bellamy here,' he said, speaking loudly toward the phone on the coffee table.

The voice that crackled back through the speaker was familiar, an airy whisper. It sounded like he was calling from a hands-free speakerphone inside a car. 'It's past midnight, Mr. Bellamy. I was about to put Peter out of his misery.'

There was an uneasy silence in the room. 'Let me talk to him.'

'Impossible,' the man replied. 'We're driving. He's tied up in the trunk.'

Langdon and Katherine exchanged looks and then began shaking their heads at everyone. *He's bluffing! He no longer has Peter!*

Sato motioned for Bellamy to keep pressing.

'I want *proof* that Peter's alive,' Bellamy said. 'I'm not giving you the rest of—'

'Your Worshipful Master needs a doctor. Don't waste time with negotiations. Tell me the street number on Franklin Square, and I'll bring Peter to you there.'

'I told you, I want—'

'Now!' the man exploded. 'Or I will pull over and Peter Solomon dies this instant!'

'You listen to me,' Bellamy said forcefully. 'If you want the rest of the address, you'll play by *my* rules. Meet me at Franklin Square. Once you deliver Peter alive, I'll tell you the number of the building.'

'How do I know you won't bring the authorities?'

'Because I can't risk double-crossing you. Peter's life is *not* the only card you hold. I know what's really at stake tonight.'

'You do realize,' the man on the phone said, 'that if I sense so much as a hint of anyone other than *you* at Franklin Square, I will keep driving, and you will never find even a trace of Peter Solomon. And of course . . . that will be the least of your worries.'

'I'll come alone,' Bellamy replied somberly. 'When you turn over Peter, I'll give you everything you need.'

'Center of the square,' the man said. 'It will take me at least twenty minutes to get there. I suggest you wait for me as long as it takes.'

The line went dead.

Instantly, the room sprang to life. Sato began shouting orders. Several field agents grabbed their radios and headed for the door. 'Move! Move!'

In the chaos, Langdon looked to Bellamy for some kind of explanation as to what was actually going on tonight, but the older man was already being hurried out the door.

'I need to see my brother!' Katherine shouted. 'You *have* to let us go!'

Sato walked over to Katherine. 'I don't *have* to do anything, Ms. Solomon. Is that clear?'

Katherine stood her ground and looked desperately into Sato's small eyes.

'Ms. Solomon, my top priority is apprehending the man at Franklin Square, and you will sit here with one of my men until I accomplish that task. Then, and only then, will we deal with your brother.'

'You're missing the point,' Katherine said. 'I know *exactly* where this man lives! It's literally five minutes up the road in Kalorama Heights, and there will be evidence there that will help you! Besides, you said you want to keep this quiet. Who knows what Peter will start telling the authorities once he's stabilized.'

Sato pursed her lips, apparently registering Katherine's point. Outside, the chopper blades began winding up. Sato frowned and then turned to one of her men. 'Hartmann, you take the Escalade. Transport Ms. Solomon and Mr. Langdon to Kalorama Heights. Peter Solomon is not to speak to *anyone*. Is that understood?'

'Yes, ma'am,' the agent said.

'Call me when you get there. Tell me what you find. And don't let these two out of your sight.'

Agent Hartmann gave a quick nod, pulled out the Escalade keys, and headed for the door.

Katherine was right behind him.

Sato turned to Langdon. 'I'll see you shortly, Professor. I know you think I'm the enemy, but I can assure you that's not the case. Get to Peter at once. This isn't over yet.'

Off to one side of Langdon, Dean Galloway was sitting quietly at the coffee table. His hands had found the stone pyramid, which was still sitting in Langdon's open leather bag on the table in front of him. The old man was running his hands over the stone's warm surface.

Langdon said, 'Father, are you coming to see Peter?'

'I'd just slow you down.' Galloway removed his hands from the bag and zipped it up around the pyramid. 'I'll stay right here and pray for Peter's recovery. We can all speak later. But when you show Peter the pyramid, would you please tell him something for me?'

'Of course.' Langdon hoisted the bag onto his shoulder.

'Tell him this.' Galloway cleared his throat. 'The Masonic Pyramid has always kept her secret ... *sincerely.*'

'I don't understand.'

The old man winked. 'Just tell Peter that. He will understand.'

With that, Dean Galloway bowed his head and began praying.

Perplexed, Langdon left him there and hurried outside. Katherine was already in the front seat of the SUV giving the agent directions. Langdon climbed in back and had barely closed the door before the giant vehicle was rocketing across the lawn, racing northward to Kalorama Heights.

93

Franklin Square is located in the northwest quadrant of downtown Washington, bordered by K and Thirteenth streets. It is home to many historic buildings, most notably the Franklin School, from which Alexander Graham Bell sent the world's first wireless message in 1880.

High above the square, a fast-moving UH-60 helicopter approached from the west, having completed its journey from the National Cathedral in a matter of minutes. *Plenty of time,* Sato thought, peering down at the square below. She knew it was critical that her men got into position undetected before their target arrived.

He said he wouldn't be here for at least twenty minutes.

On Sato's command, the pilot performed a 'touch-hover' on the roof of the tallest building around – the renowned One Franklin Square – a towering and prestigious office building with two gold spires on top. The maneuver was illegal, of course, but the chopper was there only a few seconds, and its skids barely touched the gravel rooftop. Once everyone had jumped out, the pilot immediately lifted off, banking to the east, where he would climb to 'silent altitude' and provide invisible support from above.

Sato waited as her field team collected their things and prepared Bellamy for his task. The Architect was still looking dazed from having seen the file on Sato's secure laptop. *As I said . . . an issue of national security.* Bellamy had quickly understood Sato's meaning and was now fully cooperative.

'All set, ma'am,' Agent Simkins said.

On Sato's command, the agents ushered Bellamy across the rooftop and disappeared down a stairwell, heading for ground level to take up their positions.

Sato walked to the edge of the building and gazed down. The rectangular wooded park below filled the entire block. *Plenty of cover.* Sato's team fully understood the importance of making an undetected intercept. If their target sensed a presence here and decided just to slip away . . . the director didn't even want to think about it.

The wind up here was gusty and cold. Sato wrapped her arms around herself, and planted her feet firmly to avoid getting blown over the edge. From this high vantage point, Franklin Square looked smaller than she recalled, with fewer buildings. She wondered which building was Eight Franklin Square. This was information she had requested from her analyst Nola, from whom she expected word at any moment.

Bellamy and the agents now appeared, looking like ants fanning out into the darkness of the wooded area. Simkins positioned Bellamy in a clearing near the center of the deserted park. Then Simkins and his team melted into the natural cover, disappearing from view. Within seconds, Bellamy was alone, pacing and shivering in the light of a streetlamp near the center of the park.

Sato felt no pity.

She lit a cigarette and took a long drag, savoring the warmth as it permeated her lungs. Satisfied that everything below was in order, she stepped back from the edge to await her two phone calls – one from her analyst Nola and one from Agent Hartmann, whom she had sent to Kalorama Heights.

94

Slow down! Langdon gripped the backseat of the Escalade as it flew around a corner, threatening to tip up on two tires. CIA agent Hartmann was either eager to show off his driving skills to Katherine, or he had orders to get to Peter Solomon before Solomon recuperated enough to say anything he shouldn't say to the local authorities.

The high-speed game of beat-the-red-light on Embassy Row had been worrisome enough, but now they were racing through the winding residential neighborhood of Kalorama Heights. Katherine shouted directions as they went, having been to this man's house earlier that afternoon.

With every turn, the leather bag at Langdon's feet rocked back and forth, and Langdon could hear the clank of the capstone, which had clearly been jarred from the top of the pyramid and was now bouncing around in the bottom of his bag. Fearing it might get damaged, he fished around inside until he found it. It was still warm, but the glowing text had now faded and disappeared, returning to its original engraving:

The secret hides within The Order.

As Langdon was about to place the capstone in a side pocket, he noticed its elegant surface was covered with tiny white gobs of something. Puzzled, he tried to wipe them off, but they were stuck on and hard to the touch . . . like plastic. *What in the world?* He could now see that the surface of the stone pyramid itself was also covered with the little white dots. Langdon used his fingernail and picked one off, rolling it between his fingers.

'Wax?' he blurted.

Katherine glanced over her shoulder. 'What?'

'There are bits of wax all over the pyramid and capstone. I don't understand it. Where could that possibly have *come* from?'

'Something in your bag, maybe?'

'I don't think so.'

As they rounded a corner, Katherine pointed through the windshield and turned to Agent Hartmann. 'That's it! We're here.'

Langdon glanced up and saw the spinning lights of a security vehicle parked in a driveway up ahead. The driveway gate was pulled aside and the agent gunned the SUV inside the compound.

The house was a spectacular mansion. Every light inside was ablaze, and the front door was wide open. A half-dozen vehicles were parked haphazardly in the driveway and on the lawn, apparently having arrived in a hurry. Some of the cars were still running and had their headlights shining, most on the house, but one askew, practically blinding them as they drove in.

Agent Hartmann skidded to a stop on the lawn beside a white sedan with a brightly colored decal: PREFERRED SECURITY. The spinning lights and the high beams in their face made it hard to see.

Katherine immediately jumped out and raced for the house. Langdon heaved his bag onto his shoulder without taking the time to zip it up. He followed Katherine at a jog across the lawn toward the open front door. The sounds of voices echoed within. Behind Langdon, the SUV chirped as Agent Hartmann locked the vehicle and hurried after them.

Katherine bounded up the porch stairs, through the main door, and disappeared into the entryway. Langdon crossed the threshold behind her and could see Katherine was already moving across the foyer and down the main hallway toward the sound of voices. Beyond her, visible at the end of the hall, was a dining-room table where a woman in a security uniform was sitting with her back to them.

'Officer!' Katherine shouted as she ran. 'Where is Peter Solomon?'

Langdon rushed after her, but as he did so, an unexpected movement caught his eye. To his left, through the living-room window, he could see the driveway gate was now swinging shut. *Odd*. Something else caught his eye . . . something that had been hidden from him by the glare of the spinning lights and the blinding high beams when they drove in. The half-dozen cars parked haphazardly in the driveway looked nothing like the police cars and emergency vehicles Langdon had imagined they were.

A Mercedes? . . . a Hummer? . . . a Tesla Roadster?

In that instant, Langdon also realized the voices he heard in the house were nothing but a television blaring in the direction of the dining room.

Wheeling in slow motion, Langdon shouted down the hallway. 'Katherine, wait!'

But as he turned, he could see that Katherine Solomon was no longer running.

She was airborne.

95

Katherine Solomon knew she was falling . . . but she couldn't figure out why.

She had been running down the hall toward the security guard in the dining room when suddenly her feet had become entangled in an invisible obstacle, and her entire body had lurched forward, sailing through the air.

Now she was returning to earth . . . in this case, a hardwood floor.

Katherine crashed down on her stomach, the wind driven violently from her lungs. Above her, a heavy coat tree teetered precariously and then toppled over, barely missing her on the floor. She raised her head, still gasping for breath, puzzled to see that the female security guard in the chair had not moved a muscle.

Stranger still, the toppled coat tree appeared to have a thin wire attached to the bottom, which had been stretched across the hallway.

Why in the world would someone . . . ?

'Katherine!' Langdon was shouting to her, and as Katherine rolled onto her side and looked back at him, she felt her blood turn to ice. *Robert! Behind you!* She tried to scream, but she was still gasping for breath. All she could do was watch in terrifying slow motion as Langdon rushed down the hall to help her, completely unaware that behind him, Agent Hartmann was staggering across the threshold and clutching his throat. Blood sprayed through Hartmann's hands as he groped at the handle of a long screwdriver that protruded from his neck.

As the agent pitched forward, his attacker came into full view.

My God . . . no!

Naked except for a strange undergarment that looked like a loincloth, the massive man had apparently been hiding in the foyer. His muscular body was covered from head to toe with strange tattoos. The front door was swinging closed, and he was rushing down the hall after Langdon.

Agent Hartmann hit the floor just as the front door slammed shut. Langdon looked startled and whirled around, but the tattooed man was already on him, thrusting some kind of device into his back. There was a flash of light and a sharp electrical sizzle, and Katherine saw Langdon go rigid. Eyes frozen wide, Langdon lurched forward, collapsing down in a paralyzed heap. He fell hard on top of his leather bag, the pyramid tumbling out onto the floor.

Without so much as a glance down at his victim, the

tattooed man stepped over Langdon and headed directly for Katherine. She was already crawling backward into the dining room, where she collided with a chair. The female security guard, who had been propped in that chair, now wobbled and dropped to the floor in a heap beside her. The woman's lifeless expression was one of terror. Her mouth was stuffed with a rag.

The enormous man had reached her before Katherine had time to react. He seized her by the shoulders with impossible strength. His face, no longer covered by makeup, was an utterly terrifying sight. His muscles flexed, and she felt herself being flipped over onto her stomach like a rag doll. A heavy knee ground into her back, and for a moment, she thought she would break in two. He grabbed her arms and pulled them backward.

With her head now turned to one side and her cheek pressed into the carpet, Katherine could see Langdon, his body still jerking, facing away from her. Beyond that, Agent Hartmann lay motionless in the foyer.

Cold metal pinched Katherine's wrists, and she realized she was being bound with wire. In terror, she tried to pull away, but doing so sent searing pain into her hands.

'This wire *will* cut you if you move,' the man said, finishing with her wrists and moving down to her ankles with frightening efficiency.

Katherine kicked at him, and he threw a powerful fist into the back of her right thigh, crippling her leg. Within seconds, her ankles were bound.

'Robert!' she now managed to call out.

Langdon was groaning on the floor in the hallway. He lay crumpled on his leather bag with the stone pyramid lying on its side near his head. Katherine realized the pyramid was her last hope.

'We deciphered the pyramid!' she told her attacker. 'I'll tell you everything!'

'Yes, you will.' With that, he pulled the cloth from the dead woman's mouth and firmly stuffed it into Katherine's.

It tasted like death.

Robert Langdon's body was not his own. He lay, numb and immobile, his cheek pressed against the hardwood floor. He had heard enough about stun guns to know they crippled their victims by temporarily overloading the nervous system. Their action – something called electromuscular disruption – might as well have been a bolt of lightning. The excruciating jolt of pain seemed to penetrate every molecule of his body. Now, despite his mind's focused intention, his muscles refused to obey the command he was sending them.

Get up!

Facedown, paralyzed on the floor, Langdon was gulping shallow breaths, scarcely able to inhale. He had yet to lay eyes on the man who had attacked him, but he could see Agent Hartmann lying in an expanding pool of blood. Langdon had heard Katherine struggling and arguing, but moments ago her voice had become muffled, as if the man had stuffed something in her mouth.

Get up, Robert! You've got to help her!

Langdon's legs were tingling now, a fiery and painful recovery of feeling, but still they refused to cooperate. *Move!* His arms twitched as sensation started to come back, along with feeling in his face and neck. With great effort, he managed to rotate his head, dragging his cheek roughly across the hardwood floor as he turned his head to look down into the dining room.

Langdon's sight line was impeded – by the stone pyramid, which had toppled out of his bag and was lying sideways on the floor, its base inches from his face.

For an instant, Langdon didn't understand what he was looking at. The square of stone before him was obviously the base of the pyramid, and yet it looked somehow different. Very different. It was still square, and still stone . . . but it was no longer flat and smooth. The base of the pyramid was covered with engraved markings. *How is this possible?* He stared for several seconds, wondering if he was hallucinating. *I looked at the base of this pyramid a dozen times . . . and there were no markings!*

Langdon now realized why.

His breathing reflex kick-started, and he drew a sudden gasp of air, realizing that the Masonic Pyramid had secrets yet to share. *I have witnessed another transformation.*

In a flash, Langdon understood the meaning of Galloway's last request. *Tell Peter this: The Masonic Pyramid has always kept her secret . . . sincerely.* The words had seemed strange at the time, but now Langdon understood that Dean Galloway was sending Peter a code. Ironically, this same code had been a plot twist in a mediocre thriller Langdon had read years ago.

Sin-cere.

Since the days of Michelangelo, sculptors had been hiding the flaws in their work by smearing hot wax into the cracks and then dabbing the wax with stone dust. The method was considered cheating, and therefore, any sculpture 'without wax' – literally *sine cera* – was considered a 'sincere' piece of art. The phrase stuck. To this day we still sign our letters 'sincerely' as a promise that we have written 'without wax' and that our words are true.

The engravings on the base of this pyramid had been concealed by the same method. When Katherine followed the capstone's directions and *boiled* the pyramid, the wax melted away, revealing the writing on the base. Galloway had run his hands over the pyramid in the sitting room, apparently feeling the markings exposed on the bottom.

Now, if only for an instant, Langdon had forgotten all the danger he and Katherine faced. He stared at the incredible array of symbols on the base of the pyramid. He had no idea what they meant . . . or what they would ultimately reveal, but one thing was for certain. *The Masonic Pyramid has secrets left to tell. Eight Franklin Square is not the final answer.*

Whether it was this adrenaline-filled revelation or simply the extra few seconds lying there, Langdon did not know, but he suddenly felt control returning to his body.

Painfully, he swept an arm to one side, pushing the leather bag out of the way to clear his sight line into the dining room.

To his horror, he saw that Katherine had been tied up, and a large rag had been stuffed deep into her mouth. Langdon flexed his muscles, trying to climb to his knees, but a moment later, he froze in utter disbelief. The dining-room doorway had just filled with a chilling sight – a human form unlike anything Langdon had ever seen.

472

What in the name of God . . . ?!

Langdon rolled, kicking with his legs, trying to back away, but the huge tattooed man grabbed him, flipping him onto his back and straddling his chest. He placed his knees on Langdon's biceps, pinning Langdon painfully to the floor. The man's chest bore a rippling double-headed phoenix. His neck, face, and shaved head were covered with a dazzling array of unusually intricate symbols – sigils, Langdon knew – which were used in the rituals of dark ceremonial magic.

Before Langdon could process anything more, the huge man clasped Langdon's ears between his palms, lifted his head up off the floor, and, with incredible force, smashed it back down onto the hardwood.

Everything went black.

96

Mal'akh stood in his hallway and surveyed the carnage around him. His home looked like a battle-field.

Robert Langdon lay unconscious at his feet.

Katherine Solomon was bound and gagged on the dining-room floor.

The corpse of a female security guard lay crumpled nearby, having toppled off the chair where she was propped. This female guard, eager to save her own life, had done exactly as Mal'akh commanded. With a knife to her throat, she had answered Mal'akh's cell phone and told the lie that had coaxed Langdon and

Katherine to come racing out here. *She had no partner, and Peter Solomon was certainly not okay.* As soon as the woman had given her performance, Mal'akh had quietly strangled her.

To complete the illusion that Mal'akh was not home, he had phoned Bellamy using the hands-free speaker in one of his cars. *I'm on the road,* he had told Bellamy and whoever else had been listening. *Peter is in my trunk.* In fact, Mal'akh was driving only between his garage and his front yard, where he had left several of his myriad cars parked askew with the headlights on and the engines running.

The deception had worked perfectly.

Almost.

The only wrinkle was the bloody black-clad heap in the foyer with a screwdriver protruding from his neck. Mal'akh searched the corpse and had to chuckle when he found a high-tech transceiver and cell phone with a CIA logo. *It seems even they are aware of my power.* He removed the batteries and crushed both devices with a heavy bronze doorstop.

Mal'akh knew he had to move quickly now, especially if the CIA was involved. He strode back over to Langdon. The professor was out cold and would be for a while. Mal'akh's eyes moved with trepidation now to the stone pyramid on the floor beside the professor's open bag. His breath caught, and his heart pounded.

I have waited for years . . .

His hands trembled slightly as he reached down and picked up the Masonic Pyramid. As he ran his fingers slowly across the engravings, he felt awed by their promise. Before he became too entranced, he put the pyramid back in Langdon's bag with the capstone and zipped it up.

I will assemble the pyramid soon . . . in a much safer location.

He threw Langdon's bag over his shoulder and then tried to hoist Langdon himself, but the professor's toned physique weighed much more than anticipated. Mal'akh settled on grabbing him beneath the armpits and dragging him across the floor. *He's not going to like where he ends up*, Mal'akh thought.

As he dragged Langdon off, the television in the kitchen blared. The sound of voices from the TV had been part of the deception, and Mal'akh had yet to turn it off. The station was now broadcasting a televangelist leading his congregation in the Lord's Prayer. Mal'akh wondered if any of his hypnotized viewers had any idea where this prayer really came from.

' . . . On earth as it is in heaven . . .' the group intoned.

Yes, Mal'akh thought. *As above, so below.*

' . . . And lead us not into temptation . . .'

Help us master the weakness of our flesh.

' . . . Deliver us from evil . . .' they all beseeched.

Mal'akh smiled. *That could be difficult. The darkness is growing.* Even so, he had to give them credit for trying. Humans who spoke to invisible forces and requested help were a dying breed in this modern world.

Mal'akh was dragging Langdon across the living room when the congregation declared, 'Amen!'

Amon, Mal'akh corrected. *Egypt is the cradle of your religion.* The god Amon was the prototype for Zeus . . . for Jupiter . . . and for every modern face of God. To this day, every religion on earth shouted out a variation of his name. *Amen! Amin! Aum!*

The televangelist began quoting verses from the

Bible describing hierarchies of angels, demons, and spirits that ruled in heaven and hell. 'Protect your souls from evil forces!' he warned them. 'Lift your hearts in prayer! God and his angels *will* hear you!'

He's right, Mal'akh knew. *But so will the demons.*

Mal'akh had learned long ago that through proper application of the Art, a practitioner could open a portal to the spiritual realm. The invisible forces that existed there, much like man himself, came in many forms, both good and evil. Those of Light healed, protected, and sought to bring order to the universe. Those of Dark functioned oppositely . . . bringing destruction and chaos.

If properly summoned, the invisible forces could be persuaded to do a practitioner's bidding on earth . . . thus instilling him with seemingly supernatural power. In exchange for helping the summoner, these forces required offerings – prayers and praise for those of Light . . . and the spilling of blood for those of Dark.

The greater the sacrifice, the greater the power that is transferred. Mal'akh had begun his practice with the blood of inconsequential animals. Over time, however, his choices for sacrifice had become more bold. *Tonight, I take the final step.*

'Beware!' the preacher shouted, warning of the coming Apocalypse. 'The final battle for the souls of man will soon be fought!'

Indeed, Mal'akh thought. *And I shall become its greatest warrior.*

This battle, of course, had begun long, long ago. In ancient Egypt, those who perfected the Art had become the great Adepts of history, evolving beyond the masses to become true practitioners of Light. They moved as gods on earth. They built great temples of initiation to which neophytes traveled from around the world to partake of the wisdom. There arose a race of golden men. For a brief span of time, mankind seemed poised to elevate himself and transcend his earthly bonds.

The golden age of the Ancient Mysteries.

And yet man, being of the flesh, was susceptible to the sins of hubris, hatred, impatience, and greed. Over time, there were those who corrupted the Art, perverting it and abusing its power for personal gain. They began using this perverted version to summon dark forces. A different Art evolved . . . a more potent, immediate, and intoxicating influence.

Such is my Art.

Such is my Great Work.

The illuminated Adepts and their esoteric fraternities witnessed the rising evil and saw that man was not using his newfound knowledge for the good of his species. And so they hid their wisdom to keep it from the eyes of the unworthy. Eventually, it was lost to history.

With this came the Great Fall of Man.

And a lasting darkness.

To this day, the noble descendants of the Adepts soldiered on, grasping blindly for the Light, trying to recapture the lost power of their past, trying to keep the darkness at bay. They were the priests and priestesses of the churches, temples, and shrines of all the religions on earth. Time had erased the memories . . . detached them from their past. They no longer knew the Source from which their potent wisdom had once flowed. When they were asked about the divine mysteries of their forebears, the new custodians of faith vociferously disowned them, condemning them as heresy.

Have they truly forgotten? Mal'akh wondered.

Echoes of the ancient Art still resonated in every corner of the globe, from the mystical Kabbalists of Judaism to the esoteric Sufis of Islam. Vestiges remained in the arcane rituals of Christianity, in its god-eating rites of Holy Communion, its hierarchies of saints, angels, and demons, its chanting and incantation, its holy calendar's astrological underpinnings, its consecrated robes, and in its promise of everlasting life. Even now, its priests dispelled evil spirits by swinging smoke-filled censers, ringing sacred bells, and sprinkling holy water. Christians still practiced the supernatural craft of exorcism – an early practice of their faith that required the ability not only to cast out demons but to summon them.

And yet they cannot see their past?

Nowhere was the church's mystical past more evident than at her epicenter. In Vatican City, at the heart of St. Peter's Square, stood the great Egyptian obelisk. Carved thirteen hundred years before Jesus took his first breath – this numinous monolith had no relevance there, no link to modern Christianity. And yet there it was. At the core of Christ's church. A stone beacon, screaming to be heard. A reminder to those few sages who remembered where it all began. This church, born of the womb of the Ancient Mysteries, still bore her rites and symbols.

One symbol above all.

Adorning her altars, vestments, spires, and Scripture was the singular image of Christianity – that of a precious, sacrificed human being. Christianity, more than any other faith, understood the transformative power of sacrifice. Even now, to honor the sacrifice made by Jesus, his followers proffered their own feeble gestures of personal sacrifice . . . fasting, Lenten renunciation, tithing.

All of those offerings are impotent, of course. Without blood . . . there is no true sacrifice.

The powers of darkness had long embraced blood sacrifice, and in doing so, they had grown so strong that the powers of goodness now struggled to keep them in check. Soon the Light would be entirely consumed, and the practitioners of darkness would move freely through the minds of men.

97

'Eight Franklin Square *must* exist,' Sato insisted. 'Look it up again!'

Nola Kaye sat at her desk and adjusted her headset. 'Ma'am, I've checked everywhere . . . that address doesn't exist in D.C.'

'But I'm on the roof of *One* Franklin Square,' Sato said. 'There has to be an *Eight*!'

Director Sato's on a roof? 'Hold on.' Nola began running a new search. She was considering telling the OS director about the hacker, but Sato seemed fixated on Eight Franklin Square at the moment. Besides, Nola still didn't have all the information. *Where's that damned sys-sec, anyway?*

'Okay,' Nola said, eyeing her screen, 'I see the problem. One Franklin Square is the *name* of the building . . . not the address. The address is actually 1301 K Street.'

The news seemed to confound the director. 'Nola, I don't have time to explain – the pyramid clearly points to the address Eight Franklin Square.'

Nola sat bolt upright. *The pyramid points to a specific location?*

'The inscription,' Sato continued, 'reads: "The secret hides within The Order – Eight Franklin Square." '

Nola could scarcely imagine. 'An *order* like . . . a Masonic or fraternal order?'

'I assume so,' Sato replied.

Nola thought a moment, and then began typing again. 'Ma'am, maybe the street numbers on the square changed over the years? I mean, if this pyramid is as old as legend claims, maybe the numbers on Franklin Square were different when the pyramid was built? I'm now running a search *without* the number eight . . . for . . . "the order" . . . "Franklin Square" . . . and "Washington, D.C." . . . and this way, we might get some idea if there's—' She stalled midsentence as the search results appeared.

'What have you got?' Sato demanded.

Nola stared at the first result on the list – a spectacular image of the Great Pyramid of Egypt – which served as the thematic backdrop for the home page dedicated to a building on Franklin Square. The building was unlike any other building on the square.

Or in the entire city, for that matter.

What stopped Nola cold was not the building's bizarre architecture, but rather the description of its *purpose*. According to the Web site, this unusual edifice was built as a sacred mystical shrine, designed by . . . and designed *for* . . . an ancient secret order.

98

Robert Langdon regained consciousness with a crippling headache.

Where am I?

Wherever he was, it was dark. Deep-cave dark, and deathly silent.

He was lying on his back with his arms at his side. Confused, he tried moving his fingers and toes, relieved to find they moved freely with no pain. *What happened?* With the exception of his headache and the profound darkness, everything seemed more or less normal.

Almost everything.

Langdon realized he was lying on a hard floor that felt unusually smooth, like a sheet of glass. Stranger still, he could feel that the slick surface was in direct contact with his bare flesh . . . shoulders, back, buttocks, thighs, calves. *Am I naked?* Puzzled, he ran his hands over his body.

Jesus! Where the hell are my clothes?

In the darkness, the cobwebs began to lift, and Langdon saw flashes of memory . . . frightening snapshots . . . a dead CIA agent . . . the face of a tattooed beast . . . Langdon's head smashing into the floor. The images came faster . . . and now he recalled the sickening image of Katherine Solomon bound and gagged on the dining-room floor.

My God!

Langdon sat bolt upright, and as he did, his forehead smashed into something suspended only inches above him. Pain exploded through his skull and he fell back, teetering near unconsciousness. Groggy, he reached up with his hands, groping in the darkness to find the obstacle. What he found made no sense to him. It seemed this room's ceiling was less than a foot above him. *What in the world?* As he spread his arms to his sides in an attempt to roll over, both of his hands hit sidewalls.

The truth now dawned on him. Robert Langdon was not in a room at all.

I'm in a box!

In the darkness of his small, coffinlike container, Langdon began pounding wildly with his fist. He shouted over and over for help. The terror that gripped him deepened with each passing instant until it was intolerable.

I have been buried alive.

The lid of Langdon's strange coffin refused to budge, even with the full force of his arms and legs pushing upward in wild panic. The box, from all he could tell, was made of heavy fiberglass. Airtight. Soundproof. Lightproof. Escape-proof.

I am going to suffocate alone in this box.

He thought of the deep well into which he had fallen as a young boy, and of the terrifying night he spent treading water alone in the darkness of a bottomless pit. That trauma had scarred Langdon's psyche, burdening him with an overwhelming phobia of enclosed spaces.

Tonight, buried alive, Robert Langdon was living his ultimate nightmare.

Katherine Solomon trembled in silence on the floor of Mal'akh's dining room. The sharp wire around her wrists and ankles had already cut into her, and the slightest movements seemed only to tighten her bonds.

The tattooed man had brutally knocked Langdon unconscious and dragged his limp body across the floor along with his leather bag and the stone pyramid. Where they had gone, Katherine had no idea. The agent who had accompanied them was dead. She had not heard a sound in many minutes, and she wondered if the tattooed man and Langdon were still inside the house. She had been trying to scream for help, but with each attempt, the rag in her mouth crept back dangerously closer to her windpipe.

Now she felt approaching footsteps on the floor, and she turned her head, hoping against hope that someone was coming to help. The massive silhouette of her captor materialized in the hallway. Katherine recoiled as she flashed on the image of him standing in her family home ten years earlier.

He killed my family.

Now he strode toward her. Langdon was nowhere to be seen. The man crouched down and gripped her around the waist, hoisting her roughly onto his shoulder. The wire sliced into her wrists, and the rag muffled her muted cries of pain. He carried her down the hallway toward the living room, where, earlier today, the two of them had calmly sipped tea together.

Where is he taking me?!

He carried Katherine across the living room and stopped directly in front of the large oil painting of the Three Graces that she had admired this afternoon.

'You mentioned you liked this painting,' the man whispered, his lips practically touching her ear. 'I'm glad. It may be the last thing of beauty you see.'

With that, he reached out and pressed his palm into the right side of the enormous frame. To Katherine's shock, the painting rotated into the wall, turning on a central pivot like a revolving door. *A hidden doorway.*

Katherine tried to wriggle free, but the man held her firmly, carrying her through the opening behind the canvas. As the Three Graces pivoted shut behind them, she could see heavy insulation on the back of the canvas. Whatever sounds were made back here were apparently not meant to be heard by the outside world.

The space behind the painting was cramped, more like a hallway than a room. The man carried her to the far side and opened a heavy door, carrying her through it onto a small landing. Katherine found herself looking down a narrow ramp into a deep basement. She drew a breath to scream, but the rag was choking her.

The incline was steep and narrow. The walls on either side were made of cement, awash in a bluish light that seemed to emanate from below. The air that wafted up was warm and pungent, laden with an eerie blend of smells . . . the sharp bite of chemicals, the smooth calm of incense, the earthy musk of human sweat, and, pervading it all, a distinct aura of visceral, animal fear.

'Your science impressed me,' the man whispered as they reached the bottom of the ramp. 'I hope *mine* impresses you.'

99

CIA field agent Turner Simkins crouched in the darkness of Franklin Park and kept his steady gaze on

Warren Bellamy. Nobody had taken the bait yet, but it was still early.

Simkins's transceiver beeped, and he activated it, hoping one of his men had spotted something. But it was Sato. She had new information.

Simkins listened and agreed with her concern. 'Hold on,' he said. 'I'll see if I can get a visual.' He crawled through the bushes in which he was hiding and peered back in the direction from which he had entered the square. After some maneuvering, he finally opened a sight line.

Holy shit.

He was staring at a building that looked like an Old World mosque. Nestled between two much larger buildings, the Moorish facade was made of gleaming terra-cotta tile laid in intricate multicolored designs. Above the three massive doors, two tiers of lancet windows looked as if Arabian archers might appear and open fire if anyone approached uninvited.

'I see it,' Simkins said.

'Any activity?'

'Nothing.'

'Good. I need you to reposition and watch it very carefully. It's called the Almas Shrine Temple, and it's the headquarters of a mystical order.'

Simkins had worked in the D.C. area for a long time but was not familiar with this temple or any ancient mystical order headquartered on Franklin Square.

'This building,' Sato said, 'belongs to a group called the Ancient Arabic Order of Nobles of the Mystic Shrine.'

'Never heard of them.'

'I think you *have*,' Sato said. 'They're an appendant

body of the Masons, more commonly known as the Shriners.'

Simkins shot a dubious glance at the ornate building. *The Shriners? The guys who build hospitals for kids?* He could imagine no 'order' less ominous sounding than a fraternity of philanthropists who wore little red fezzes and marched in parades.

Even so, Sato's concerns were valid. 'Ma'am, if our target realizes that this building is in fact "The Order" on Franklin Square, he won't need the address. He'll simply bypass the rendezvous and go directly to the correct location.'

'My thoughts exactly. Keep an eye on the entrance.'

'Yes, ma'am.'

'Any word from Agent Hartmann in Kalorama Heights?'

'No, ma'am. You asked him to phone you directly.'

'Well, he hasn't.'

Odd, Simkins thought, checking his watch. *He's overdue.*

100

Robert Langdon lay shivering, naked and alone in total blackness. Paralyzed by fear, he was no longer pounding or shouting. Instead, he had closed his eyes and was doing his best to control his hammering heart and his panicked breathing.

You are lying beneath a vast, nighttime sky, he tried to convince himself. *There is nothing above you but miles of wide-open space.*

This calming visualization had been the only way he had managed to survive a recent stint in an enclosed MRI machine . . . that and a triple dose of Valium. Tonight, however, the visualization was having no effect whatsoever.

The rag in Katherine Solomon's mouth had shifted backward and was all but choking her. Her captor had carried her down a narrow ramp and into a dark basement corridor. At the far end of the hall, she had glimpsed a room lit with an eerie reddish-purple light, but they'd never made it that far. The man had stopped instead at a small side room, carried her inside, and placed her on a wooden chair. He had set her down with her bound wrists behind the chair back so she could not move.

Now Katherine could feel the wire on her wrists slicing deeper into her flesh. The pain barely registered next to the rising panic she was feeling over being unable to breathe. The cloth in her mouth was slipping deeper into her throat, and she felt herself gagging reflexively. Her vision started to tunnel.

Behind her, the tattooed man closed the room's lone door and flipped on the light. Katherine's eyes were watering profusely now, and she could no longer differentiate objects in her immediate surroundings. Everything had become a blur.

A distorted vision of colorful flesh appeared before her, and Katherine felt her eyes starting to flutter as she teetered on the brink of unconsciousness. A scale-covered arm reached out and yanked the rag from her mouth.

Katherine gasped, inhaling deep breaths, coughing

and choking as her lungs flooded with precious air. Slowly, her vision began to clear, and she found herself looking into the demon's face. The visage was barely human. Blanketing his neck, face, and shaved head was an astounding pattern of bizarre tattooed symbols. With the exception of a small circle on top of his head, every inch of his body appeared to be decorated. A massive double-headed phoenix on his chest glared at her through nipple eyes like some kind of ravenous vulture, patiently waiting for her death.

'Open your mouth,' the man whispered.

Katherine stared at the monster with total revulsion. *What?*

'Open your mouth,' the man repeated. 'Or the cloth goes back in.'

Trembling, Katherine opened her mouth. The man extended his thick, tattooed index finger, inserting it between her lips. When he touched her tongue, Katherine thought she would vomit. He extracted his wet finger and raised it to the top of his shaved head. Closing his eyes, he massaged her saliva into his small circular patch of untattooed flesh.

Repulsed, Katherine looked away.

The room in which she was sitting appeared to be a boiler room of some sort – pipes on the walls, gurgling sounds, fluorescent lights. Before she could take in her surroundings, though, her gaze stopped dead on something beside her on the floor. A pile of clothing – turtleneck, tweed sport coat, loafers, Mickey Mouse watch.

'My God!' She wheeled back to the tattooed animal before her. 'What have you done with Robert?!'

'Shh,' the man whispered. 'Or he'll hear you.' He stepped to one side and motioned behind him.

Langdon was not there. All Katherine saw was a huge black fiberglass box. Its shape bore an unsettling resemblance to the heavy crates in which corpses were shipped back from war. Two massive clasps firmly locked the box shut.

'He's *inside*?!' Katherine blurted. 'But . . . he'll suffocate!'

'No, he won't,' the man said, pointing to a series of transparent pipes that ran along the wall into the bottom of the crate. 'He'll only *wish* he could.'

In total darkness, Langdon listened intently to the muffled vibrations he now heard from the outside world. *Voices?* He began pounding on the box and shouting at the top of his lungs. 'Help! Can anyone hear me?!'

Far off, a muted voice called out. 'Robert! My God, no! NO!'

He knew the voice. It was Katherine, and she sounded terrified. Even so, it was a welcome sound. Langdon drew a breath to call out to her, but he stopped short, feeling an unexpected sensation at the back of his neck. A faint breeze seemed to be emanating from the bottom of the box. *How is that possible?* He lay very still, taking stock. *Yes, definitely.* He could feel the tiny hairs on the back of his neck being tickled by air movement.

Instinctively, Langdon began feeling along the floor of the box, searching for the source of the air. It took only a moment to locate. *There's a tiny vent!* The small perforated opening felt similar to a drain plate on a sink or tub, except that a soft, steady breeze was now coming up through it.

He's pumping air in for me. He doesn't want me to suffocate.

Langdon's relief was short-lived. A terrifying sound was now emanating up through the holes in the vent. It was the unmistakable gurgle of flowing liquid . . . coming his way.

Katherine stared in disbelief at the clear shaft of liquid that was progressing down one of the pipes toward Langdon's crate. The scene looked like some kind of twisted stage magician's act.

He's pumping water into the crate?!

Katherine strained at her bonds, ignoring the deep bite of the wires around her wrists. All she could do was look on in panic. She could hear Langdon pounding in desperation, but as the water reached the underside of the container, the pounding stopped. There was a moment of terrified silence. Then the pounding started again with renewed desperation.

'Let him out!' Katherine begged. 'Please! You can't do this!'

'Drowning is a terrible death, you know.' The man spoke calmly as he paced around her in circles. 'Your assistant, Trish, could tell you that.'

Katherine heard his words, but she could barely process them.

'You may remember that I almost drowned once,' the man whispered. 'It was on your family's estate in Potomac. Your brother shot me, and I fell through the ice, out at Zach's bridge.'

Katherine glared at him, filled with loathing. *The night you killed my mother.*

'The gods protected me that night,' he said. 'And they showed me the way . . . to become one of them.'

*   *   *

The water gurgling into the box behind Langdon's head felt warm ... body temperature. The fluid was already several inches deep and had completely swallowed the back of his naked body. As it began creeping up his rib cage, Langdon felt a stark reality closing in fast.

I'm going to die.

With renewed panic, he raised his arms and began pounding wildly again.

101

'You've got to let him out!' Katherine begged, crying now. 'We'll do whatever you want!' She could hear Langdon pounding more frantically as the water flowed into his container.

The tattooed man just smiled. 'You're easier than your brother. The things I had to do to get Peter to tell me his secrets . . .'

'Where is he?!' she demanded. 'Where is Peter?! Tell me! We did exactly what you wanted! We solved the pyramid and—'

'No, you did *not* solve the pyramid. You played a game. You withheld information and brought a government agent to my home. Hardly behavior I intend to reward.'

'We didn't have a choice,' she replied, choking back the tears. 'The CIA is looking for you. They made us travel with an agent. I'll tell you everything. Just let Robert out!' Katherine could hear Langdon shouting and pounding in the crate, and she could see the water flowing through the pipe. She knew he didn't have a lot of time.

In front of her, the tattooed man spoke calmly, stroking his chin. 'I assume there are agents waiting for me at Franklin Square?'

Katherine said nothing, and the man placed his massive palms on her shoulders, slowly pulling her forward. With her arms still wire-bound behind the chair back, her shoulders strained, burning with pain, threatening to dislocate.

'Yes!' Katherine said. 'There *are* agents at Franklin Square!'

He pulled harder. 'What is the address on the capstone?'

The pain in her wrists and shoulders grew unbearable, but Katherine said nothing.

'You can tell me now, Katherine, or I'll break your arms and ask you again.'

'Eight!' she gasped in pain. 'The missing number is *eight*! The capstone says: "The secret hides within The Order – Eight Franklin Square!" I swear it. I don't know what else to tell you! It's *Eight* Franklin Square!'

The man still did not release her shoulders.

'That's all I know!' Katherine said. 'That's the address! Let go of me! Let Robert out of that tank!'

'I *would* . . .' the man said, 'but there's one problem. I can't go to Eight Franklin Square without being caught. Tell me, what's at that address?'

'I don't know!'

'And the symbols on the *base* of the pyramid? On the underside? Do you know *their* meaning?'

'*What* symbols on the base?' Katherine had no idea what he was talking about. 'The bottom has no symbols. It's smooth, blank stone!'

Apparently immune to the muffled cries for help emanating from the coffinlike crate, the tattooed man calmly padded over to Langdon's daybag and retrieved the stone pyramid. Then he returned to Katherine and held it up before her eyes so she could see the base.

When Katherine saw the engraved symbols, she gasped in bewilderment.

But . . . that's impossible!

The bottom of the pyramid was entirely covered with intricate carvings. *There was nothing there before! I'm sure of it!* She had no idea what these symbols could possibly mean. They seemed to span every mystical tradition, including many she could not even place.

Total chaos.

'I . . . have no idea what this means,' she said.

'Nor do I,' her captor said. 'Fortunately, we have a specialist at our disposal.' He glanced at the crate.

'Let's ask him, shall we?' He carried the pyramid toward the crate.

For a brief instant of hope, Katherine thought he was going to unclasp the lid. Instead, he sat calmly on top of the box, reached down, and slid a small panel to one side, revealing a Plexiglas window in the top of the tank.

Light!

Langdon covered his eyes, squinting into the ray of light that now streamed in from above. As his eyes adjusted, hope turned to confusion. He was looking up through what appeared to be a window in the top of his crate. Through the window, he saw a white ceiling and a fluorescent light.

Without warning, the tattooed face appeared above him, peering down.

'Where is Katherine?!' Langdon shouted. 'Let me out!'

The man smiled. 'Your friend Katherine is here with me,' the man said. 'I have the power to spare her life. Your life as well. But your time is short, so I suggest you listen carefully.'

Langdon could barely hear him through the glass, and the water had risen higher, creeping across his chest.

'Are you aware,' the man asked, 'that there are symbols on the *base* of the pyramid?'

'Yes!' Langdon shouted, having seen the extensive array of symbols when the pyramid had lain on the floor upstairs. 'But I have no idea what they mean! You need to go to Eight Franklin Square! The answer is there! That's what the capstone—'

'Professor, you and I both know the CIA is waiting

494

for me there. I have no intention of walking into a trap. Besides, I didn't need the street number. There is only *one* building on that square that could possibly be relevant – the Almas Shrine Temple.' He paused, staring down at Langdon. 'The Ancient Arabic Order of Nobles of the Mystic Shrine.'

Langdon was confused. He was familiar with the Almas Temple, but he had forgotten it was on Franklin Square. *The Shriners are . . . 'The Order'? Their temple sits atop a secret staircase?* It made no historical sense whatsoever, but Langdon was in no position at the moment to debate history. 'Yes!' he shouted. 'That must be it! The secret hides within The Order!'

'You're familiar with the building?'

'Absolutely!' Langdon raised his throbbing head to keep his ears above the quickly rising liquid. 'I can help you! Let me out!'

'So you believe you can tell me what this temple has to do with the symbols on the base of the pyramid?'

'Yes! Let me just look at the symbols!'

'Very well, then. Let's see what you come up with.'

Hurry! With the warm liquid rising around him, Langdon pushed up on the lid, willing the man to unclasp it. *Please! Hurry!* But the lid never opened. Instead, the base of the pyramid suddenly appeared, hovering above the Plexiglas window.

Langdon stared up in panic.

'I trust this view is close enough for you?' The man held the pyramid in his tattooed hands. 'Think fast, Professor. I'm guessing you have less than sixty seconds.'

102

Robert Langdon had often heard it said that an animal, when cornered, was capable of miraculous feats of strength. Nonetheless, when he threw his full force into the underside of his crate, nothing budged at all. Around him, the liquid continued rising steadily. With no more than six inches of breathing room left, Langdon had lifted his head into the pocket of air that remained. He was now face-to-face with the Plexiglas window, his eyes only inches away from the underside of the stone pyramid whose baffling engraving hovered above him.

I have no idea what this means.

Concealed for over a century beneath a hardened mixture of wax and stone dust, the Masonic Pyramid's final inscription was now laid bare. The engraving was a perfectly square grid of symbols from every tradition imaginable – alchemical, astrological, heraldic, angelic, magical, numeric, sigilic, Greek, Latin. As a totality, this was symbolic anarchy – a bowl of alphabet soup whose letters came from dozens of different languages, cultures, and time periods.

Total chaos.

Symbologist Robert Langdon, in his wildest academic interpretations, could not fathom how this grid of symbols could be deciphered to mean anything at all. *Order from this chaos? Impossible.*

The liquid was now creeping over his Adam's apple, and Langdon could feel his level of terror rising along with it. He continued banging on the tank. The pyramid stared back at him tauntingly.

In frantic desperation, Langdon focused every bit of his mental energy on the chessboard of symbols. *What could they possibly mean?* Unfortunately, the assortment seemed so disparate that he could not even imagine where to begin. *They're not even from the same eras in history!*

Outside the tank, her voice muffled but audible, Katherine could be heard tearfully begging for Langdon's release. Despite his failure to see a solution, the prospect of death seemed to motivate every cell in his body to find one. He felt a strange clarity of mind, unlike anything he had ever experienced. *Think!* He scanned the grid intensely, searching for some clue – a pattern, a hidden word, a special icon, anything at all – but he saw only a grid of unrelated symbols. *Chaos.*

With each passing second, Langdon had begun to feel an eerie numbness overtaking his body. It was as if his very flesh were preparing to shield his mind from the pain of death. The water was now threatening to pour into his ears, and he lifted his head as far as he could, pushing it against the top of the crate. Frightening images began flashing before his eyes. A boy in New England treading water at the bottom of a dark well. A man in Rome trapped beneath a skeleton in an overturned coffin.

Katherine's shouts were growing more frantic. From all Langdon could hear, she was trying to *reason* with a madman – insisting that Langdon could not be expected to decipher the pyramid without going to visit the Almas Temple. 'That building obviously holds the missing piece to this puzzle! How can Robert decipher the pyramid without all the information?!'

Langdon appreciated her efforts, and yet he felt certain that 'Eight Franklin Square' was *not* pointing to the Almas Temple. *The time line is all wrong!* According to legend, the Masonic Pyramid was created in the mid-1800s, decades before the Shriners even existed. In fact, Langdon realized, it was probably before the square was even called Franklin Square. The capstone could not possibly have been pointing to an unbuilt building at a nonexistent address. Whatever 'Eight Franklin Square' was pointing to . . . it *had* to exist in 1850.

Unfortunately, Langdon was drawing a total blank.

He probed his memory banks for anything that could possibly fit the time line. *Eight Franklin Square? Something that was in existence in 1850?* Langdon came up with nothing. The liquid was trickling into his ears now. Fighting his terror, he stared up at the grid of symbols on the glass. *I don't understand the connection!* In a petrified frenzy, his mind began spewing all the far-flung parallels it could generate.

Eight Franklin Square . . . squares . . . this grid of symbols is a square . . . the square and the compass are Masonic symbols . . . Masonic altars are square . . . squares have ninety-degree angles. The water kept rising, but Langdon blocked it out. *Eight Franklin . . . eight . . . this grid is eight-by-eight . . . Franklin has eight letters . . . 'The Order' has eight letters . . . 8 is the rotated symbol ∞ for infinity . . . eight is the number of destruction in numerology . . .*

Langdon had no idea.

Outside the tank, Katherine was still pleading, but Langdon's hearing was now intermittent as the water was sloshing around his head.

' . . . impossible without knowing . . . capstone's message clearly . . . the secret hides within—'

Then she was gone.

Water poured into Langdon's ears, blotting out the last of Katherine's voice. A sudden womblike silence engulfed him, and Langdon realized he truly was going to die.

The secret hides within—

Katherine's final words echoed through the hush of his tomb.

The secret hides within . . .

Strangely, Langdon realized he had heard these exact words many times before.

The secret hides . . . within.

Even now, it seemed, the Ancient Mysteries were taunting him. 'The secret hides within' was the core tenet of the mysteries, urging mankind to seek God *not* in the heavens above . . . but rather within himself. *The secret hides within.* It was the message of all the great mystical teachers.

The kingdom of God is within you, said Jesus Christ.

Know thyself, said Pythagoras.

Know ye not that ye are gods, said Hermes Trismegistus.

The list went on and on . . .

All the mystical teachings of the ages had attempted to convey this one idea. *The secret hides within.* Even so, mankind continued looking to the heavens for the face of God.

This realization, for Langdon, now became an ultimate irony. Right now, with his eyes facing the heavens like all the blind men who preceded him, Robert Langdon suddenly saw the light.

It hit him like a bolt from above.

The

secret hides

within The Order

Eight Franklin Square

In a flash he understood.

The message on the capstone was suddenly crystal clear. Its meaning had been staring him in the face all night. The text on the capstone, like the Masonic Pyramid itself, was a symbolon – a code in pieces – a message written in parts. The capstone's meaning was camouflaged in so simple a manner that Langdon could scarcely believe he and Katherine had not spotted it.

More astonishing still, Langdon now realized that the message on the capstone did *indeed* reveal exactly how to decipher the grid of symbols on the base of the pyramid. It was so very simple. Exactly as Peter Solomon had promised, the golden capstone was a potent talisman with the power to bring order from chaos.

Langdon began pounding on the lid and shouting, 'I know! I know!'

Above him, the stone pyramid lifted off and hovered away. In its place, the tattooed face reappeared, its chilling visage staring down through the small window.

'I solved it!' Langdon shouted. 'Let me out!'

When the tattooed man spoke, Langdon's submerged ears heard nothing. His eyes, however, saw the lips speak two words. *'Tell me.'*

'I will!' Langdon screamed, the water almost to his eyes. 'Let me out! I'll explain everything!' *It's so simple.*

The man's lips moved again. *'Tell me now . . . or die.'*

With the water rising through the final inch of air space, Langdon tipped his head back to keep his mouth above the waterline. As he did so, warm liquid poured into his eyes, blurring his vision. Arching his back, he pressed his mouth against the Plexiglas window.

Then, with his last few seconds of air, Robert Langdon shared the secret of how to decipher the Masonic Pyramid.

As he finished speaking, the liquid rose around his lips. Instinctively, Langdon drew a final breath and clamped his mouth shut. A moment later, the fluid covered him entirely, reaching the top of his tomb and spreading out across the Plexiglas.

He did it, Mal'akh realized. *Langdon figured out how to solve the pyramid.*

The answer was so simple. So obvious.

Beneath the window, the submerged face of Robert

Langdon stared up at him with desperate and beseeching eyes.

Mal'akh shook his head at him and slowly mouthed the words: 'Thank you, Professor. Enjoy the afterlife.'

103

As a serious swimmer, Robert Langdon had often wondered what it would feel like to drown. He now knew he was going to learn firsthand. Although he could hold his breath longer than most people, he could already feel his body reacting to the absence of air. Carbon dioxide was accumulating in his blood, bringing with it the instinctual urge to inhale. *Do not breathe!* The reflex to inhale was increasing in intensity with each passing moment. Langdon knew very soon he would reach what was called the breath-hold breakpoint – that critical moment at which a person could no longer voluntarily hold his breath.

Open the lid! Langdon's instinct was to pound and struggle, but he knew better than to waste valuable oxygen. All he could do was stare up through the blur of water above him and hope. The world outside was now only a hazy patch of light above the Plexiglas window. His core muscles had begun burning, and he knew hypoxia was setting in.

Suddenly a beautiful and ghostly face appeared, gazing down at him. It was Katherine, her soft features looking almost ethereal through the veil of liquid. Their eyes met through the Plexiglas window, and for an instant, Langdon thought he was saved. *Katherine!* Then he heard her muted cries of horror and realized she was being held there by their captor. The tattooed monster was forcing her to bear witness to what was about to happen.

Katherine, I'm sorry . . .

In this strange, dark place, trapped underwater, Langdon strained to comprehend that *these* would be his final moments of life. Soon he would cease to exist . . . everything he was . . . or had ever been . . . or would ever be . . . was ending. When his brain died, all of the memories held in his gray matter, along with all of the knowledge he had acquired, would simply evaporate in a flood of chemical reactions.

In this moment, Robert Langdon realized his true insignificance in the universe. It was as lonely and humbling a feeling as he had ever experienced. Almost thankfully, he could feel the breath-hold breakpoint arriving.

The moment was upon him.

Langdon's lungs forced out their spent contents, collapsing in eager preparation to inhale. Still he held out an instant longer. His final second. Then, like a man no longer able to hold his hand to a burning stove, he gave himself over to fate.

Reflex overruled reason.

His lips parted.

His lungs expanded.

And the liquid came pouring in.

The pain that filled his chest was greater than Langdon had ever imagined. The liquid burned as it poured into his lungs. Instantly, the pain shot upward into his skull, and he felt like his head was being crushed in a vise. There was great thundering in his ears, and through it all, Katherine Solomon was screaming.

There was a blinding flash of light.
And then blackness.
Robert Langdon was gone.

104

It's over.

Katherine Solomon had stopped screaming. The drowning she had just witnessed had left her catatonic, virtually paralyzed with shock and despair.

Beneath the Plexiglas window, Langdon's dead eyes stared past her into empty space. His frozen expression was one of pain and regret. The last tiny air bubbles trickled out of his lifeless mouth, and then, as if consenting to give up his ghost, the Harvard professor slowly began sinking to the bottom of the tank . . . where he disappeared into the shadows.

He's gone. Katherine felt numb.

The tattooed man reached down, and with pitiless finality, he slid the small viewing window closed, sealing Langdon's corpse inside.

Then he smiled at her. 'Shall we?'

Before Katherine could respond, he hoisted her grief-stricken body onto his shoulder, turned out the light, and carried her out of the room. With a few powerful strides, he transported her to the end of the hall, into a large space that seemed to be bathed in a reddish-purple light. The room smelled like incense. He carried her to a square table in the center of the room and dropped her hard on her back, knocking the wind out of her. The surface felt rough and cold. *Is this stone?*

Katherine had hardly gotten her bearings before the man had removed the wire from her wrists and ankles. Instinctively, she attempted to fight him off, but her cramped arms and legs barely responded. He now began strapping her to the table with heavy leather bands, cinching one strap across her knees and then buckling a second across her hips, pinning her arms at her sides. Then he placed a final strap across her sternum, just above her breasts.

It had all taken only moments, and Katherine was again immobilized. Her wrists and ankles throbbed now as the circulation returned to her limbs.

'Open your mouth,' the man whispered, licking his own tattooed lips.

Katherine clenched her teeth in revulsion.

The man again reached out with his index finger and ran it slowly around her lips, making her skin crawl. She clenched her teeth tighter. The tattooed man chuckled and, using his other hand, found a pressure point on her neck and squeezed. Katherine's jaw instantly dropped open. She could feel his finger entering her mouth and running along her tongue. She gagged and tried to bite it, but the finger was already gone. Still grinning, he raised his moist fingertip before her eyes. Then he closed his eyes and, once again, rubbed her saliva into the bare circle of flesh on his head.

The man sighed and slowly opened his eyes. Then, with an eerie calm, he turned and left the room.

In the sudden silence, Katherine could feel her heart pounding. Directly over her, an unusual series of lights seemed to be modulating from purple red to a deep crimson, illuminating the room's low ceiling. When she saw the ceiling, all she could do was stare. Every inch was covered with drawings. The mind-boggling collage above her appeared to depict the celestial sky. Stars, planets, and constellations mingled with astrological symbols, charts, and formulas. There were arrows predicting elliptical orbits, geometric symbols indicating angles of ascension, and zodiacal creatures peering down at her. It looked like a mad scientist had gotten loose in the Sistine Chapel.

Turning her head, Katherine looked away, but the wall to her left was no better. A series of candles on medieval floor stands shed a flickering glow on a wall that was completely hidden beneath pages of text, photos, and drawings. Some of the pages looked like papyrus or vellum torn from ancient books; others were obviously from newer texts; mixed in were photographs, drawings, maps, and schematics; all of them appeared to have been glued to the wall with meticulous care. A spiderweb of strings had been thumbtacked across them, interconnecting them in limitless chaotic possibilities.

Katherine again looked away, turning her head in the other direction.

Unfortunately, this provided the most terrifying view of all.

Adjacent to the stone slab on which she was strapped, there stood a small side counter that instantly reminded her of an instrument table from a hospital operating room. On the counter was arranged a series of objects – among them a syringe, a vial of dark liquid . . . and a large knife with a bone handle and a blade hewn of iron burnished to an unusually high shine.

My God . . . what is he planning to do to me?

105

When CIA systems security specialist Rick Parrish finally loped into Nola Kaye's office, he was carrying a single sheet of paper.

'What took you so long?!' Nola demanded. *I told you to come down immediately!*

'Sorry,' he said, pushing up his bottle-bottom glasses on his long nose. 'I was trying to gather more information for you, but—'

'Just show me what you've got.'

Parrish handed her the printout. 'It's a redaction, but you get the gist.'

Nola scanned the page in amazement.

'I'm still trying to figure out how a hacker got access,' Parrish said, 'but it looks like a delegator spider hijacked one of our search—'

'Forget that!' Nola blurted, glancing up from the page. 'What the hell is the CIA doing with a classified file about pyramids, ancient portals, and engraved symbolons?'

'That's what took me so long. I was trying to see what document was being targeted, so I traced the file path.' Parrish paused, clearing his throat. 'This document turns out to be on a partition personally assigned to . . . the CIA director himself.'

Nola wheeled, staring in disbelief. *Sato's boss has a file about the Masonic Pyramid?* She knew that the current director, along with many other top CIA executives, was a high-ranking Mason, but Nola could not imagine any of them keeping Masonic secrets on a CIA computer.

Then again, considering what she had witnessed in the last twenty-four hours, anything was possible.

* * *

Agent Simkins was lying on his stomach, ensconced in the bushes of Franklin Square. His eyes were trained on the columned entry of the Almas Temple. *Nothing.* No lights had come on inside, and no one had approached the door. He turned his head and checked on Bellamy. The man was pacing alone in the middle of the park, looking cold. Really cold. Simkins could see him shaking and shivering.

His phone vibrated. It was Sato.

'How overdue is our target?' she demanded.

Simkins checked his chronograph. 'Target said twenty minutes. It's been almost forty. Something's wrong.'

'He's not coming,' Sato said. 'It's over.'

Simkins knew she was right. 'Any word from Hartmann?'

'No, he never checked in from Kalorama Heights. I can't reach him.'

Simkins stiffened. If this was true, then something was *definitely* wrong.

'I just called field support,' Sato said, 'and they can't find him either.'

Holy shit. 'Do they have a GPS location on the Escalade?'

'Yeah. A residential address in Kalorama Heights,' Sato said. 'Gather your men. We're pulling out.'

Sato clicked off her phone and gazed out at the majestic skyline of her nation's capital. An icy wind whipped through her light jacket, and she wrapped her arms around herself to stay warm. Director Inoue Sato was not a woman who often felt cold . . . or fear. At the moment, however, she was feeling both.

106

Mal'akh wore only his silk loincloth as he dashed up the ramp, through the steel door, and out through the painting into his living room. *I need to prepare quickly.* He glanced over at the dead CIA agent in the foyer. *This home is no longer safe.*

Carrying the stone pyramid in one hand, Mal'akh strode directly to his first-floor study and sat down at his laptop computer. As he logged in, he pictured Langdon downstairs and wondered how many days or even weeks would pass before the submerged corpse was discovered in the secret basement. It made no difference. Mal'akh would be long gone by then.

Langdon has served his role . . . brilliantly.

Not only had Langdon reunited the pieces of the Masonic Pyramid, he had figured out how to solve the arcane grid of symbols on the base. At first glance, the symbols seemed indecipherable . . . and yet the answer was simple . . . staring them in the face.

Mal'akh's laptop sprang to life, the screen displaying the same e-mail he had received earlier – a photograph of a glowing capstone, partially blocked by Warren Bellamy's finger.

> *The*
> *secret hides*
> *within The Order.*
> ■■■ *Franklin Square.*

Eight . . . Franklin Square, Katherine had told Mal'akh. She had also admitted that CIA agents were staking out Franklin Square, hoping to capture

Mal'akh and also figure out what *order* was being referenced by the capstone. The Masons? The Shriners? The Rosicrucians?

None of these, Mal'akh now knew. *Langdon saw the truth.*

Ten minutes earlier, with liquid rising around his face, the Harvard professor had figured out the key to solving the pyramid. 'The Order Eight Franklin Square!' he had shouted, terror in his eyes. 'The secret hides within The Order Eight Franklin Square!'

At first, Mal'akh failed to understand his meaning.

'It's not an address!' Langdon yelled, his mouth pressed to the Plexiglas window. 'The Order Eight Franklin Square! It's a *magic* square!' Then he said something about Albrecht Dürer . . . and how the pyramid's first code was a clue to breaking this final one.

Mal'akh was familiar with magic squares – *kameas,* as the early mystics called them. The ancient text *De Occulta Philosophia* described in detail the mystical power of magic squares and the methods for designing powerful sigils based on magical grids of numbers. Now Langdon was telling him that a magic square held the key to deciphering the base of the pyramid?

'You need an eight-by-eight magic square!' the professor had been yelling, his lips the only part of his body above the liquid. 'Magic squares are categorized in *orders*! A three-by-three square is an "order three"! A four-by-four square is an "order four"! You need an "order eight"!'

The liquid had been about to engulf Langdon entirely, and the professor drew one last desperate breath and shouted out something about a famous Mason . . . an American forefather . . . a scientist, mystic, mathematician, inventor . . . as well as the creator of the mystical *kamea* that bore his name to this day.

Franklin.

In a flash, Mal'akh knew Langdon was right.

Now, breathless with anticipation, Mal'akh sat upstairs at his laptop. He ran a quick Web search, received dozens of hits, chose one, and began reading.

THE ORDER EIGHT FRANKLIN SQUARE

One of history's best-known magic squares is the order-eight square published in 1769 by American scientist Benjamin Franklin, and which became famous for its inclusion of never-before-seen 'bent diagonal summations.' Franklin's obsession with this mystical art form most likely stemmed from his personal associations with the prominent alchemists and mystics of his day, as well as his own belief in astrology, which were the underpinnings for the predictions made in his *Poor Richard's Almanack.*

Mal'akh studied Franklin's famous creation – a unique arrangement of the numbers 1 through 64 – in which every row, column, and diagonal added up to the same magical constant. *The secret hides within The Order Eight Franklin Square.*

Mal'akh smiled. Trembling with excitement, he grabbed the stone pyramid and flipped it over, examining the base.

These sixty-four symbols needed to be reorganized

52	61	4	13	20	29	36	45
14	3	62	51	46	35	30	19
53	60	5	12	21	28	37	44
11	6	59	54	43	38	27	22
55	58	7	10	23	26	39	42
9	8	57	56	41	40	25	24
50	63	2	15	18	31	34	47
16	1	64	49	48	33	32	17

and arranged in a different order, their sequence defined by the numbers in Franklin's magic square. Although Mal'akh could not imagine how this chaotic grid of symbols would suddenly make sense in a different order, he had faith in the ancient promise.

Ordo ab chao.

Heart racing, he took out a sheet of paper and quickly drew an empty eight-by-eight grid. Then he began inserting the symbols, one by one, in their newly defined positions. Almost immediately, to his astonishment, the grid began making sense.

Order from chaos!

He completed the entire decryption and stared in disbelief at the solution before him. A stark image had taken shape. The jumbled grid had been transformed . . . reorganized . . . and although Mal'akh could not grasp the meaning of the *entire* message, he understood enough . . . enough to know exactly where he was now headed.

The pyramid points the way.

The grid pointed to one of the world's great mystical locations. Incredibly, it was the same location at which Mal'akh had always fantasized he would complete his journey.

Destiny.

107

The stone table felt cold beneath Katherine Solomon's back.

Horrifying images of Robert's death continued to swirl through her mind, along with thoughts of her brother. *Is Peter dead, too?* The strange knife on the nearby table kept bringing flashes of what might lie in store for her as well.

Is this really the end?

Oddly, her thoughts turned abruptly to her research . . . to Noetic Science . . . and to her recent breakthroughs. *All of it lost . . . up in smoke.* She would never be able to share with the world everything she had learned. Her most shocking discovery had taken place only a few months ago, and the results had the potential to redefine the way humans thought about death. Strangely, thinking now of that experiment . . . was bringing her an unexpected solace.

As a young girl, Katherine Solomon had often wondered if there was life after death. *Does heaven exist? What happens when we die?* As she grew older, her studies in science quickly erased any fanciful notions of heaven, hell, or the afterlife. The concept of 'life after death,' she came to accept, was a human construct . . . a fairy tale designed to soften the horrifying truth that was our mortality.

Or so I believed . . .

A year ago, Katherine and her brother had been discussing one of philosophy's most enduring questions – the existence of the human soul – specifically the issue of whether or not humans possessed some kind of consciousness capable of survival *outside* of the body.

They both sensed that such a human soul probably *did* exist. Most ancient philosophies concurred. Buddhist and Brahminical wisdom endorsed metempsychosis – the transmigration of the soul into a new body after death; Platonists defined the body as a 'prison' from which the soul escaped; and the Stoics called the soul *apospasma tou theu* – 'a particle of God' – and believed it was recalled by God upon death.

The existence of the human soul, Katherine noted

with some frustration, was probably a concept that would never be scientifically proven. Confirming that a consciousness survived outside the human body after death was akin to exhaling a puff of smoke and hoping to find it years later.

After their discussion, Katherine had a strange notion. Her brother had mentioned the Book of Genesis and its description of the soul as *Neshemah* – a kind of spiritual 'intelligence' that was separate from the body. It occurred to Katherine that the word *intelligence* suggested the presence of *thought*. Noetic Science clearly suggested that *thoughts* had mass, and so it stood to reason, then, that the human soul might therefore also have mass.

Can I weigh a human soul?

The notion was impossible, of course . . . foolish even to ponder.

It was three days later that Katherine suddenly woke up from a dead sleep and sat bolt upright in bed. She jumped up, drove to her lab, and immediately began work designing an experiment that was both startlingly simple . . . and frighteningly bold.

She had no idea if it would work, and she decided not to tell Peter about her idea until her work was complete. It took four months, but finally Katherine brought her brother into the lab. She wheeled out a large piece of gear that she had been keeping hidden in the back storage room.

'I designed and built it myself,' she said, showing Peter her invention. 'Any guesses?'

Her brother stared at the strange machine. 'An incubator?'

Katherine laughed and shook her head, although it was a reasonable guess. The machine *did* look a bit like

515

the transparent incubators for premature babies one saw in hospitals. This machine, however, was adult size – a long, airtight, clear plastic capsule, like some kind of futuristic sleeping pod. It sat atop a large piece of electronic gear.

'See if *this* helps you guess,' Katherine said, plugging the contraption into a power source. A digital display lit up on the machine, its numbers jumping around as she carefully calibrated some dials.

When she was done, the display read:

$$0.0000000000 \text{ kg}$$

'A scale?' Peter asked, looking puzzled.

'Not just any scale.' Katherine took a tiny scrap of paper off a nearby counter and laid it gently on top of the capsule. The numbers on the display jumped around again and then settled on a new reading.

$$.0008194325 \text{ kg}$$

'High-precision microbalance,' she said. 'Resolution down to a few micrograms.'

Peter still looked puzzled. 'You built a precise scale for . . . a person?'

'Exactly.' She lifted the transparent lid on the machine. 'If I place a person inside this capsule and close the lid, the individual is in an entirely *sealed* system. Nothing gets in or out. No gas, no liquid, no dust particles. Nothing can escape – not the person's breath exhalations, evaporating sweat, body fluids, nothing.'

Peter ran a hand through his thick head of silver hair, a nervous mannerism shared by Katherine.

'Hmm . . . obviously a person would die in there pretty quickly.'

She nodded. 'Six minutes or so, depending on their breathing rate.'

He turned to her. 'I don't get it.'

She smiled. 'You *will*.'

Leaving the machine behind, Katherine led Peter into the Cube's control room and sat him down in front of the plasma wall. She began typing and accessed a series of video files stored on the holographic drives. When the plasma wall flickered to life, the image before them looked like home-video footage.

The camera panned across a modest bedroom with an unmade bed, medication bottles, a respirator, and a heart monitor. Peter looked baffled as the camera kept panning and finally revealed, near the center of the bedroom, Katherine's scale contraption.

Peter's eyes widened. 'What the . . . ?'

The capsule's transparent lid was open, and a very old man in an oxygen mask lay inside. His elderly wife and a hospice worker stood beside the pod. The man's breathing was labored, and his eyes were closed.

'The man in the capsule was a science teacher of mine at Yale,' Katherine said. 'He and I have kept in touch over the years. He's been very ill. He always said he wanted to donate his body to science, so when I explained my idea for this experiment, he immediately wanted to be a part of it.'

Peter was apparently mute with shock as he stared at the scene unfolding before them.

The hospice worker now turned to the man's wife. 'It's time. He's ready.'

The old woman dabbed her tearful eyes and nodded with a resolute calm. 'Okay.'

Very gently, the hospice worker reached into the pod and removed the man's oxygen mask. The man stirred slightly, but his eyes remained closed. Now the worker wheeled the respirator and other equipment off to the side, leaving the old man in the capsule totally isolated in the center of the room.

The dying man's wife now approached the pod, leaned down, and gently kissed her husband's forehead. The old man did not open his eyes, but his lips moved, ever so slightly, into a faint, loving smile.

Without his oxygen mask, the man's breathing was quickly becoming more labored. The end was obviously near. With an admirable strength and calm, the man's wife slowly lowered the transparent lid of the capsule and sealed it shut, exactly as Katherine had taught her.

Peter recoiled in alarm. 'Katherine, what in the name of God?!'

'It's okay,' Katherine whispered. 'There's plenty of air in the capsule.' She had seen this video dozens of times now, but it still made her pulse race. She pointed to the scale beneath the dying man's sealed pod. The digital numbers read:

51.4534644 kg

'That's his body weight,' Katherine said.

The old man's breathing became more shallow, and Peter inched forward, transfixed.

'This is what he wanted,' Katherine whispered. 'Watch what happens.'

The man's wife had stepped back and was now seated on the bed, silently looking on with the hospice worker.

Over the course of the next sixty seconds, the man's shallow breathing grew faster, until all at once, as if the man himself had chosen the moment, he simply took his last breath. Everything stopped.

It was over.

The wife and hospice worker quietly comforted each other.

Nothing else happened.

After a few seconds, Peter glanced over at Katherine in apparent confusion.

Wait for it, she thought, redirecting Peter's gaze to the capsule's digital display, which still quietly glowed, showing the dead man's weight.

Then it happened.

When Peter saw it, he jolted backward, almost falling out of his chair. 'But . . . that's . . .' He covered his mouth in shock. 'I can't . . .'

It was seldom that the great Peter Solomon was speechless. Katherine's reaction had been similar the first few times she saw what had happened.

Moments after the man's death, the numbers on the scale had decreased suddenly. The man had become *lighter* immediately after his death. The weight change was minuscule, but it was measurable . . . and the implications were utterly mind-boggling.

Katherine recalled writing in her lab notes with a trembling hand: 'There seems to exist an invisible "material" that exits the human body at the moment of death. It has quantifiable mass which is unimpeded by physical barriers. I must assume it moves in a dimension I cannot yet perceive.'

From the expression of shock on her brother's face, Katherine knew he understood the implications. 'Katherine . . .' he stammered, blinking his gray eyes as if to make sure he was not dreaming. 'I think you just weighed the human soul.'

There was a long silence between them.

Katherine sensed that her brother was attempting to process all the stark and wondrous ramifications. *It will take time.* If what they had just witnessed was indeed what it seemed to be – that is, evidence that a soul or consciousness or life force could move *outside* the realm of the body – then a startling new light had just been shed on countless mystical questions: transmigration, cosmic consciousness, near-death experiences, astral projection, remote viewing, lucid dreaming, and on and on. Medical journals were filled with stories of patients who had died on the operating table, viewed their bodies from above, and then been brought back to life.

Peter was silent, and Katherine now saw he had tears in his eyes. She understood. She had cried, too. Peter and Katherine had lost loved ones, and for anyone in that position, the faintest hint of the human spirit continuing after death brought a glimmer of hope.

He's thinking of Zachary, Katherine thought, recognizing the deep melancholy in her brother's eyes. For years Peter had carried the burden of responsibility for his son's death. He had told Katherine many times that leaving Zachary in prison had been the worst mistake of his life, and that he would never find a way to forgive himself.

A slamming door drew Katherine's attention, and suddenly she was back in the basement, lying on a cold stone table. The metal door at the top of the ramp had closed loudly, and the tattooed man was coming back down. She could hear him entering one of the rooms down the hall, doing something inside, and then continuing along the hall toward the room she was in. As he entered, she could see that he was pushing something in front of him. Something heavy . . . on wheels. As he stepped into the light, she stared in disbelief. The tattooed man was pushing a person in a wheelchair.

Intellectually, Katherine's brain recognized the man in the chair. Emotionally, her mind could barely accept what she was looking at.

Peter?

She didn't know whether to be overjoyed that her brother was alive . . . or utterly horrified. Peter's body had been shaved smooth. His mane of thick silver hair was all gone, as were his eyebrows, and his smooth skin glistened as if it had been oiled. He wore a black silk gown. Where his right hand should have been, he had only a stump, wrapped in a clean, fresh bandage. Her brother's pain-laden eyes reached out to hers, filled with regret and sorrow.

'Peter!' Her voice cracked.

Her brother tried to speak but made only muffled, guttural noises. Katherine now realized he was bound to the wheelchair and had been gagged.

The tattooed man reached down and gently stroked Peter's shaved scalp. 'I've prepared your brother for a great honor. He has a role to play tonight.'

Katherine's entire body went rigid. *No* . . .

'Peter and I will be leaving in a moment, but I thought you'd want to say good-bye.'

'Where are you taking him?' she said weakly.

He smiled. 'Peter and I must journey to the sacred mountain. That is where the treasure lies. The Masonic Pyramid has revealed the location. Your friend Robert Langdon was most helpful.'

Katherine looked into her brother's eyes. 'He killed . . . Robert.'

Her brother's expression contorted in agony, and he shook his head violently, as if unable to bear any more pain.

'Now, now, Peter,' the man said, again stroking Peter's scalp. 'Don't let this ruin the moment. Say good-bye to your little sister. This is your final family reunion.'

Katherine felt her mind welling with desperation. 'Why are you doing this?!' she shouted at him. 'What have we ever done to you?! Why do you hate my family so much?!'

The tattooed man came over and placed his mouth right next to her ear. 'I have my reasons, Katherine.' Then he walked to the side table and picked up the strange knife. He brought it over to her and ran the burnished blade across her cheek. 'This is arguably the most famous knife in history.'

Katherine knew of no famous knives, but it looked foreboding and ancient. The blade felt razor sharp.

'Don't worry,' he said. 'I have no intention of wasting its power on you. I'm saving it for a more worthy sacrifice . . . in a more sacred place.' He turned to her brother. 'Peter, you recognize this knife, don't you?'

Her brother's eyes were wide with a mixture of fear and disbelief.

'Yes, Peter, this ancient artifact still exists. I obtained it at great expense . . . and I have been saving it for you. At long last, you and I can end our painful journey together.'

With that, he wrapped the knife carefully in a cloth with all of his other items – incense, vials of liquid, white satin cloths, and other ceremonial objects. He then placed the wrapped items inside Robert Langdon's leather bag along with the Masonic Pyramid and capstone. Katherine looked on helplessly as the man zipped up Langdon's daybag and turned to her brother.

'Carry this, Peter, would you?' He set the heavy bag on Peter's lap.

Next, the man walked over to a drawer and began rooting around. She could hear small metal objects clinking. When he returned, he took her right arm, steadying it. Katherine couldn't see what he was doing, but Peter apparently could, and he again started bucking wildly.

Katherine felt a sudden, sharp pinch in the crook of her right elbow, and an eerie warmth ran down around it. Peter was making anguished, strangled sounds and trying in vain to get out of the heavy chair. Katherine felt a cold numbness spreading through her forearm and fingertips below the elbow.

When the man stepped aside, Katherine saw why her brother was so horrified. The tattooed man had inserted a medical needle into her vein, as if she were giving blood. The needle, however, was not attached to a tube. Instead, her blood was now flowing freely out of it . . . running down her elbow, forearm, and onto the stone table.

'A human hourglass,' the man said, turning to Peter. 'In a short while, when I ask you to play your role, I want you to picture Katherine . . . dying alone here in the dark.'

Peter's expression was one of total torment.

'She will stay alive,' the man said, 'for about an hour or so. If you cooperate with me quickly, I will have enough time to save her. Of course, if you resist me at all . . . your sister will die here alone in the dark.'

Peter bellowed unintelligibly through his gag.

'I know, I know,' the tattooed man said, placing a hand on Peter's shoulder, 'this is hard for you. But it shouldn't be. After all, this is not the first time you will abandon a family member.' He paused, bending over and whispering in Peter's ear. 'I'm thinking, of course, of your son, Zachary, in Soganlik prison.'

Peter pulled against his restraints and let out another muffled scream through the cloth in his mouth.

'Stop it!' Katherine shouted.

'I remember that night well,' the man taunted as he finished packing. 'I heard the whole thing. The warden offered to let your son go, but you chose to teach Zachary a lesson . . . by abandoning him. Your boy learned his lesson, all right, didn't he?' The man smiled. 'His loss . . . was my gain.'

The man now retrieved a linen cloth and stuffed it deep into Katherine's mouth. 'Death,' he whispered to her, 'should be a quiet thing.'

Peter struggled violently. Without another word, the tattooed man slowly backed Peter's wheelchair out of the room, giving Peter a long, last look at his sister.

Katherine and Peter locked eyes one final time.

Then he was gone.

Katherine could hear them going up the ramp and through the metal door. As they exited, she heard the tattooed man lock the metal door behind him and continue on through the painting of the Three Graces. A few minutes later, she heard a car start.

Then the mansion fell silent.

All alone in the dark, Katherine lay bleeding.

108

Robert Langdon's mind hovered in an endless abyss.

No light. No sound. No feeling.

Only an infinite and silent void.

Softness.

Weightlessness.

His body had released him. He was untethered.

The physical world had ceased to exist. Time had ceased to exist.

He was pure consciousness now . . . a fleshless sentience suspended in the emptiness of a vast universe.

109

The modified UH-60 skimmed in low over the expansive rooftops of Kalorama Heights, thundering toward the coordinates given to them by the support team. Agent Simkins was the first to spot the black Escalade parked haphazardly on a lawn in front of one of the mansions. The driveway gate was closed, and the house was dark and quiet.

Sato gave the signal to touch down.

The aircraft landed hard on the front lawn amid several other vehicles . . . one of them a security sedan with a bubble light on top.

Simkins and his team jumped out, drew their weapons, and dashed up onto the porch. Finding the front door locked, Simkins cupped his hands and peered through a window. The foyer was dark, but Simkins could make out the faint shadow of a body on the floor.

'Shit,' he whispered. 'It's Hartmann.'

One of his agents grabbed a chair off the porch and heaved it through the bay window. The sound of shattering glass was barely audible over the roar of the helicopter behind them. Seconds later, they were all inside. Simkins rushed to the foyer and knelt over Hartmann to check his pulse. Nothing. There was blood everywhere. Then he saw the screwdriver in Hartmann's throat.

Jesus. He stood up and motioned to his men to begin a full search.

The agents fanned out across the first floor, their laser sights probing the darkness of the luxurious house. They found nothing in the living room or study, but in the dining room, to their surprise, they discovered a strangled female security guard. Simkins was fast losing hope that Robert Langdon and Katherine Solomon were alive. This brutal killer clearly had set a trap, and if he had managed to kill a CIA agent and an armed security guard, then it seemed a professor and a scientist had no chance.

Once the first floor was secure, Simkins sent two agents to search upstairs. Meanwhile, he found a set of basement stairs off the kitchen and descended. At the bottom of the stairs, he threw on the lights. The basement was spacious and spotless, as if it were hardly ever used. Boilers, bare cement walls, a few boxes. *Nothing here at all.* Simkins headed back up to the kitchen just as his men were coming down from the second floor. Everyone shook their heads.

The house was deserted.

No one home. And no more bodies.

Simkins radioed Sato with the all-clear and the grim update.

When he got to the foyer, Sato was already climbing the stairs onto the porch. Warren Bellamy was visible behind her, sitting dazed and alone in the helicopter with Sato's titanium briefcase at his feet. The OS director's secure laptop provided her with worldwide access to CIA computer systems via encrypted satellite uplinks. Earlier tonight, she had used this computer to share with Bellamy some kind of information that had stunned the man into cooperating fully. Simkins had no idea what Bellamy had seen, but whatever it was, the Architect had been visibly shell-shocked ever since.

As Sato entered the foyer, she paused a moment, bowing her head over Hartmann's body. A moment later, she raised her eyes and fixed them on Simkins. 'No sign of Langdon or Katherine? Or Peter Solomon?'

Simkins shook his head. 'If they're still alive, he took them with him.'

'Did you see a computer in the house?'

'Yes, ma'am. In the office.'

'Show me.'

Simkins led Sato out of the foyer and into the living room. The plush carpet was covered with broken glass from the shattered bay window. They walked past a fireplace, a large painting, and several bookshelves to an office door. The office was wood paneled, with an antique desk and a large computer monitor. Sato walked around behind the desk and eyed the screen, immediately scowling.

'Damn it,' she said under her breath.

Simkins circled around and looked at the screen. It

was blank. 'What's wrong?'

Sato pointed to an empty docking station on the desk. 'He uses a laptop. He took it with him.'

Simkins didn't follow. 'Does he have information you want to see?'

'No,' Sato replied, her tone grave. 'He has information I want *nobody* to see.'

Downstairs in the hidden basement, Katherine Solomon had heard the sounds of helicopter blades followed by breaking glass and heavy boots on the floor above her. She tried to cry out for help, but the gag in her mouth made it impossible. She could barely make a sound. The harder she tried, the faster the blood began flowing from her elbow.

She was feeling short of breath and a little dizzy.

Katherine knew she needed to calm down. *Use your mind, Katherine.* With all of her intention, she coaxed herself into a meditative state.

Robert Langdon's mind floated through the emptiness of space. He peered into the infinite void, searching for any points of reference. He found nothing.

Total darkness. Total silence. Total peace.

There was not even the pull of gravity to tell him which way was up.

His body was gone.

This must be death.

Time seemed to be telescoping, stretching and compressing, as if it had no bearings in this place. He had lost all track of how much time had passed.

Ten seconds? Ten minutes? Ten days?

Suddenly, however, like distant fiery explosions in far-off galaxies, memories began to materialize, billowing toward Langdon like shock waves across a vast nothingness.

All at once, Robert Langdon began to remember. The images tore through him . . . vivid and disturbing. He was staring up at a face that was covered with tattoos. A pair of powerful hands lifted his head and smashed it into the floor.

Pain erupted . . . and then darkness.

Gray light.

Throbbing.

Wisps of memory. Langdon was being dragged, half conscious, down, down, down. His captor was chanting something.

Verbum significatium . . . Verbum omnificum . . . Verbum perdo . . .

110

Director Sato stood alone in the study, waiting while the CIA satellite-imaging division processed her request. One of the luxuries of working in the D.C. area was the satellite coverage. With luck, one of them might have been properly positioned to get photos of this home tonight . . . possibly capturing a vehicle leaving the place in the last half hour.

'Sorry, ma'am,' the satellite technician said. 'No coverage of those coordinates tonight. Do you want to make a reposition request?'

'No thanks. Too late.' She hung up.

Sato exhaled, now having no idea how they would figure out where their target had gone. She walked out to the foyer, where her men had bagged Agent Hartmann's body and were carrying it toward the chopper. Sato had ordered Agent Simkins to gather his men and prepare for the return to Langley, but Simkins was in the living room on his hands and knees. He looked like he was ill.

'You okay?'

He glanced up, an odd look on his face. 'Did you see this?' He pointed at the living-room floor.

Sato came over and looked down at the plush carpet. She shook her head, seeing nothing.

'Crouch down,' Simkins said. 'Look at the nap of the carpet.'

She did. After a moment, she saw it. The fibers of the carpet looked like they had been mashed down . . . depressed along two straight lines as if the wheels of something heavy had been rolled across the room.

'The *strange* thing,' Simkins said, 'is where the tracks go.' He pointed.

Sato's gaze followed the faint parallel lines across the living-room carpet. The tracks seemed to disappear beneath a large floor-to-ceiling painting that hung beside the fireplace. *What in the world?*

Simkins walked over to the painting and tried to lift it down from the wall. It didn't budge. 'It's fixed,' he said, now running his fingers around the edges. 'Hold on, there's something underneath . . .' His finger hit a small lever beneath the bottom edge, and something clicked.

Sato stepped forward as Simkins pushed the frame and the entire painting rotated slowly on its center, like a revolving door.

He raised his flashlight and shined it into the dark space beyond.

Sato's eyes narrowed. *Here we go.*

At the end of a short corridor stood a heavy metal door.

The memories that had billowed through the blackness of Langdon's mind had come and gone. In their wake, a trail of red-hot sparks was swirling, along with the same eerie, distant whisper.

Verbum significatium . . . Verbum omnificum . . . Verbum perdo.

The chanting continued like the drone of voices in a medieval canticle.

Verbum significatium . . . Verbum omnificum. The words now tumbled through the empty void, fresh voices echoing all around him.

Apocalypsis . . . Franklin . . . Apocalypsis . . . Verbum . . . Apocalypsis . . .

Without warning, a mournful bell began tolling somewhere in the distance. The bell rang on and on, growing louder. It tolled more urgently now, as if hoping Langdon would understand, as if urging his mind to follow.

111

The tolling bell in the clock tower rang for three full minutes, rattling the crystal chandelier that hung above Langdon's head. Decades ago, he had attended lectures in this well-loved assembly hall at Phillips Exeter Academy. Today, however, he was here to listen to a dear friend address the student body. As the lights dimmed, Langdon took a seat against the back wall, beneath a pantheon of headmaster portraits.

A hush fell across the crowd.

In total darkness, a tall, shadowy figure crossed the stage and took the podium. 'Good morning,' the faceless voice whispered into the microphone.

Everyone sat up, straining to see who was addressing them.

A slide projector flashed to life, revealing a faded sepia photograph – a dramatic castle with a red sandstone facade, high square towers, and Gothic embellishments.

The shadow spoke again. 'Who can tell me where this is?'

'England!' a girl declared in the darkness. 'This facade is a blend of early Gothic and late Romanesque, making this the quintessential *Norman* castle and placing it in England at about the twelfth century.'

'Wow,' the faceless voice replied. 'Someone knows her architecture.'

Quiet groans all around.

'Unfortunately,' the shadow added, 'you missed by three thousand miles and half a millennium.'

The room perked up.

The projector now flashed a full-color, modern photo

of the same castle from a different angle. The castle's Seneca Creek sandstone towers dominated the foreground, but in the background, startlingly close, stood the majestic, white, columned dome of the U.S. Capitol Building.

'Hold on!' the girl exclaimed. 'There's a Norman castle in D.C.?!'

'Since 1855,' the voice replied. 'Which is when this next photo was taken.'

A new slide appeared – a black-and-white interior shot, depicting a massive vaulted ballroom, furnished with animal skeletons, scientific display cases, glass jars with biological samples, archaeological artifacts, and plaster casts of prehistoric reptiles.

'This wondrous castle,' the voice said, 'was America's first real science museum. It was a gift to America from a wealthy British scientist who, like our forefathers, believed our fledgling country could become the land of enlightenment. He bequeathed to our forefathers a massive fortune and asked them to build at the core of our nation "an establishment for the increase and diffusion of knowledge."' He paused a long moment. 'Who can tell me the name of this generous scientist?'

A timid voice in front ventured, 'James *Smithson*?'

A whisper of recognition rippled through the crowd.

'Smithson indeed,' the man on stage replied. Peter Solomon now stepped into the light, his gray eyes flashing playfully. 'Good morning. My name is Peter Solomon, and I am secretary of the *Smithsonian* Institution.'

The students broke into wild applause.

In the shadows, Langdon watched with admiration

as Peter captivated the young minds with a photographic tour of the Smithsonian Institution's early history. The show began with Smithsonian Castle, its basement science labs, corridors lined with exhibits, a salon full of mollusks, scientists who called themselves 'the curators of crustaceans,' and even an old photo of the castle's two most popular residents – a pair of now-deceased owls named Diffusion and Increase. The half-hour slide show ended with an impressive satellite photo of the National Mall, now lined with enormous Smithsonian museums.

'As I said when I began,' Solomon stated in conclusion, 'James Smithson and our forefathers envisioned our great country to be a land of enlightenment. I believe today they would be proud. Their great Smithsonian Institution stands as a symbol of science and knowledge at the very core of America. It is a living, breathing, working tribute to our forefathers' dream for America – a country founded on the principles of knowledge, wisdom, and science.'

Solomon clicked off the slides to an energetic round of applause. The houselights came up, along with dozens of eager hands with questions.

Solomon called on a small red-haired boy in the middle.

'Mr. Solomon?' the boy said, sounding puzzled. 'You said our forefathers fled the religious oppression of Europe to establish a country on the principles of scientific advancement.'

'That's correct.'

'But . . . I was under the impression our forefathers were devoutly religious men who founded America as a *Christian* nation.'

Solomon smiled. 'My friends, don't get me wrong,

our forefathers were deeply religious men, but they were Deists – men who believed in God, but in a universal and open-minded way. The only *religious* ideal they put forth was religious *freedom*.' He pulled the microphone from the podium and strode out to the edge of the stage. 'America's forefathers had a vision of a spiritually enlightened utopia, in which freedom of thought, education of the masses, and scientific advancement would replace the darkness of outdated religious superstition.'

A blond girl in back raised her hand.

'Yes?'

'Sir,' the girl said, holding up her cell phone, 'I've been researching you online, and Wikipedia says you're a prominent Freemason.'

Solomon held up his Masonic ring. 'I could have saved you the data charges.'

The students laughed.

'Yes, well,' the girl continued, hesitating, 'you just mentioned "outdated religious superstition," and it seems to me that if *anyone* is responsible for propagating outdated superstitions . . . it would be the Masons.'

Solomon seemed unfazed. 'Oh? How so?'

'Well, I've read a lot about Masonry, and I know you've got a lot of strange ancient rituals and beliefs. This article online even says that Masons believe in the power of some kind of ancient magical wisdom . . . which can elevate man to the realm of the gods?'

Everyone turned and stared at the girl as if she were nuts.

'Actually,' Solomon said, 'she's right.'

The kids all spun around and faced front, eyes widening.

Solomon suppressed a smile and asked the girl,

'Does it offer any other Wiki-wisdom about this magical knowledge?'

The girl looked uneasy now, but she began to read from the Web site. ' "To ensure this powerful wisdom could not be used by the unworthy, the early adepts wrote down their knowledge in *code* . . . cloaking its potent truth in a metaphorical language of symbols, myth, and allegory. To this day, this encrypted wisdom is all around us . . . encoded in our mythology, our art, and the occult texts of the ages. Unfortunately, modern man has lost the ability to decipher this complex network of symbolism . . . and the great truth has been lost." '

Solomon waited. 'That's all?'

The girl shifted in her seat. 'Actually, there *is* a little bit more.'

'I should hope so. Please . . . tell us.'

The girl looked hesitant, but she cleared her throat and continued. ' "According to legend, the sages who encrypted the Ancient Mysteries long ago left behind a *key* of sorts . . . a *password* that could be used to unlock the encrypted secrets. This magical password – known as the *verbum significatium* – is said to hold the power to lift the darkness and unlock the Ancient Mysteries, opening them to all human understanding." '

Solomon smiled wistfully. 'Ah, yes . . . the *verbum significatium*.' He stared into space for a moment and then lowered his eyes again to the blond girl. 'And where is this wonderful *word* now?'

The girl looked apprehensive, clearly wishing she had not challenged their guest speaker. She finished reading. ' "Legend holds that the *verbum significatium* is buried deep underground, where it waits patiently for a pivotal moment in history . . . a moment when mankind can no longer survive without the truth, knowledge, and wisdom of the ages. At this dark crossroads, mankind will at last unearth the Word and herald in a wondrous new age of enlightenment." '

The girl turned off her phone and shrank down in her seat.

After a long silence, another student raised his hand. 'Mr. Solomon, you don't actually *believe* that, right?'

Solomon smiled. 'Why not? Our mythologies have a long tradition of magic words that provide insight and godlike powers. To this day, children still shout "abracadabra" in hopes of creating something out of nothing. Of course, we've all forgotten that this word is not a toy; it has roots in ancient Aramaic mysticism – *Avrah KaDabra* – meaning "I create as I speak." '

Silence.

'But, sir,' the student now pressed, 'surely you don't believe that a single *word* . . . this *verbum significatium* . . . whatever it is . . . has the power to unlock ancient wisdom . . . and bring about a worldwide enlightenment?'

Peter Solomon's face revealed nothing. 'My own beliefs should not concern you. What *should* concern you is that this prophecy of a coming enlightenment is echoed in virtually every faith and philosophical tradition on earth. Hindus call it the Krita Age, astrologers call it the Age of Aquarius, the Jews describe the coming of the Messiah, theosophists call it the New Age, cosmologists call it Harmonic Convergence and predict the actual date.'

'December 21, 2012!' someone called.

'Yes, unnervingly *soon* . . . if you're a believer in Mayan math.'

Langdon chuckled, recalling how Solomon, ten years ago, had correctly predicted the current spate of television specials predicting that the year 2012 would mark the End of the World.

'Timing aside,' Solomon said, 'I find it wondrous to note that throughout history, all of mankind's disparate philosophies have all concurred on *one* thing – that a great enlightenment is coming. In every culture, in every era, in every corner of the world, the human dream has focused on the same exact concept – the coming apotheosis of man . . . the impending transformation of our human minds into their true potentiality.' He smiled. 'What could possibly explain such a synchronicity of beliefs?'

'*Truth,*' said a quiet voice in the crowd.

Solomon wheeled. 'Who said that?'

The hand that went up belonged to a tiny Asian boy whose soft features suggested he might be Nepalese or Tibetan. 'Maybe there is a universal truth embedded in everyone's soul. Maybe we *all* have the same story hiding inside, like a shared constant in our DNA. Maybe this collective *truth* is responsible for the similarity in all of our stories.'

Solomon was beaming as he pressed his hands together and bowed reverently to the boy. 'Thank you.'

Everyone was quiet.

'Truth,' Solomon said, addressing the room. 'Truth has power. And if we all gravitate toward similar ideas, maybe we do so because those ideas are *true* . . . written deep within us. And when we hear the truth, even if we don't understand it, we feel that truth resonate within us . . . vibrating with our unconscious wisdom. Perhaps the truth is not *learned* by us, but rather, the truth is re-called . . . re-membered . . . re-cognized . . . as that which is already inside us.'

The silence in the hall was complete.

Solomon let it sit for a long moment, then quietly said, 'In closing, I should warn you that unveiling the truth is never easy. Throughout history, every period of enlightenment has been accompanied by darkness, pushing in opposition. Such are the laws of nature and balance. And if we look at the darkness growing in the world today, we have to realize that this means there is equal light growing. We are on the verge of a truly great period of illumination, and all of us – all of *you* – are profoundly blessed to be living through this pivotal moment of history. Of all the people who have ever lived, in all the eras in history . . . *we* are in that narrow window of time during which we will bear witness to our ultimate renaissance. After millennia of darkness, we will see our sciences, our minds, and even our religions unveil the truth.'

Solomon was about to get a hearty round of applause when he held up his hand for silence. 'Miss?' He pointed directly to the contentious blond girl in back with the cell phone. 'I know you and I didn't agree on much, but I want to thank you. Your passion is an important catalyst in the coming changes. Darkness feeds on apathy . . . and conviction is our most potent antidote. Keep studying your faith. Study the Bible.' He smiled. 'Especially the final pages.'

'The Apocalypse?' she said.

'Absolutely. The Book of Revelation is a vibrant example of our shared *truth*. The last book of the Bible tells the identical story as countless other traditions. They all predict the coming unveiling of great wisdom.'

Someone else said, 'But isn't the Apocalypse about the end of the world? You know, the Antichrist, Armageddon, the final battle between good and evil?'

Solomon chuckled. 'Who here studies Greek?'

Several hands went up.

'What does the word *apocalypse* literally mean?'

'It means,' one student began, and then paused as if surprised. '*Apocalypse* means "to unveil" . . . or "to reveal."'

Solomon gave the boy a nod of approval. 'Exactly. The Apocalypse is literally a *reveal-ation*. The Book of Revealation in the Bible predicts an unveiling of great truth and unimaginable wisdom. The Apocalypse is not the end of the world, but rather it is the end of the world as we *know* it. The prophecy of the Apocalypse is just one of the Bible's beautiful messages that has been distorted.' Solomon stepped to the front of the stage. 'Believe me, the Apocalypse *is* coming . . . and it will be nothing like what we were taught.'

High over his head, the bell began to toll.

The students erupted into bewildered and thunderous applause.

112

Katherine Solomon was teetering on the edge of consciousness when she was jolted by the shock wave of a deafening explosion.

Moments later, she smelled smoke.

Her ears were ringing.

There were muffled voices. Distant. Shouting.

Footsteps. Suddenly she was breathing more clearly. The cloth had been pulled from her mouth.

'You're safe,' a man's voice whispered. 'Just hold on.'

She expected the man to pull the needle out of her arm but instead he was yelling orders. 'Bring the medical kit . . . attach an IV to the needle . . . infuse lactated Ringer's solution . . . get me a blood pressure.' As the man began checking her vital signs, he said, 'Ms. Solomon, the person who did this to you . . . where did he go?'

Katherine tried to speak, but she could not.

'Ms. Solomon?' the voice repeated. 'Where did he go?'

Katherine tried to pry her eyes open, but she felt herself fading.

'We need to know *where* he went,' the man urged.

Katherine whispered three words in response, although she knew they made no sense. 'The . . . sacred . . . mountain.'

Director Sato stepped over the mangled steel door and descended a wooden ramp into the hidden basement. One of her agents met her at the bottom.

'Director, I think you'll want to see this.'

Sato followed the agent into a small room off the narrow hallway. The room was brightly lit and barren, except for a pile of clothing on the floor. She recognized Robert Langdon's tweed coat and loafers.

Her agent pointed toward the far wall at a large, casketlike container.

What in the world?

Sato moved toward the container, seeing now that it was fed by a clear plastic pipe that ran through the wall. Warily, she approached the tank. Now she could see that it had a small slider on top. She reached down and slid the covering to one side, revealing a small portal-like window.

Sato recoiled.

Beneath the Plexiglas . . . floated the submerged, vacant face of Professor Robert Langdon.

Light!

The endless void in which Langdon hovered was suddenly filled by a blinding sun. Rays of white-hot light streamed across the blackness of space, burning into his mind.

The light was everywhere.

Suddenly, within the radiant cloud before him, a beautiful silhouette appeared. It was a face . . . blurry and indistinct . . . two eyes staring at him across the void. Streams of light surrounded the face, and Langdon wondered if he was looking into the face of God.

Sato stared down into the tank, wondering if Professor Langdon had any idea what had happened. She doubted it. After all, disorientation was the entire purpose of this technology.

Sensory-deprivation tanks had been around since the fifties and were still a popular getaway for wealthy New Age experimenters. 'Floating,' as it was called, offered a transcendental back-to-the-womb experience . . . a kind of meditative aid that quieted brain activity by removing all sensory input – light, sound, touch, and even the pull of gravity. In traditional tanks, the person would float on his back in a hyperbuoyant saline solution that kept his face above the water so he could breathe.

In recent years, however, these tanks had taken a quantum leap.

Oxygenated perfluorocarbons.

This new technology – known as Total Liquid Ventilation (TLV) – was so counterintuitive that few believed it existed.

Breathable liquid.

Liquid breathing had been a reality since 1966, when Leland C. Clark successfully kept alive a mouse that had been submerged for several hours in an oxygenated perfluorocarbon. In 1989, TLV technology made a dramatic appearance in the movie *The Abyss*, although few viewers realized that they were watching real science.

Total Liquid Ventilation had been born of modern medicine's attempts to help premature babies breathe by returning them to the liquid-filled state of the womb. Human lungs, having spent nine months in utero, were no strangers to a liquid-filled state. Perfluorocarbons had once been too viscous to be fully breathable, but modern breakthroughs had made breathable liquids almost the consistency of water.

The CIA's Directorate of Science and Technology – 'the Wizards of Langley,' as they were known within the intelligence community – had worked extensively with oxygenated perfluorocarbons to develop technologies for the U.S. military. The navy's elite deep-ocean diving teams found that breathing oxygenated liquid, rather than the usual heliox or trimix, gave them the ability to dive to much greater depths without risk of pressure sickness. Similarly, NASA and the air force had learned that pilots equipped with a liquid breathing apparatus rather than a traditional oxygen tank could withstand far higher g-forces than usual because liquid spread the g-force more evenly throughout the internal organs than gas did.

Sato had heard that there were now 'extreme experience labs' where one could try these Total Liquid Ventilation tanks – 'Meditation Machines,' as they were called. This particular tank had probably been installed for its owner's private experimentation, although the addition of heavy, lockable latches left little doubt in Sato's mind that *this* tank had also been used for darker applications . . . an interrogation technique with which the CIA was familiar.

The infamous interrogation technique of water boarding was highly effective because the victim truly *believed* he was drowning. Sato knew of several classified operations in which sensory-deprivation tanks like these had been used to enhance that illusion to terrifying new levels. A victim submerged in breathable liquid could literally be 'drowned.' The panic associated with the drowning experience usually made the victim unaware that the liquid he was breathing was slightly more viscous than water. When the liquid poured into his lungs, he would often black out from fear, and then awaken in the ultimate 'solitary confinement.'

Topical numbing agents, paralysis drugs, and hallucinogens were mixed with the warm oxygenated liquid to give the prisoner the sense he was entirely separated from his body. When his mind sent commands to move his limbs, nothing happened. The state of being 'dead' was terrifying on its own, but the true disorientation came from the 'rebirthing' process, which, with the aid of bright lights, cold air, and deafening noise, could be extremely traumatic and painful. After a handful of rebirths and subsequent drownings, the prisoner became so disorientated that he had no idea if he was alive or dead . . . and he would tell the interrogator absolutely anything.

Sato wondered if she should wait for a medical team to extract Langdon, but she knew she didn't have time. *I need to know what he knows.*

'Turn out the lights,' she said. 'And find me some blankets.'

The blinding sun had vanished.

The face had also disappeared.

The blackness had returned, but Langdon could now hear distant whispers echoing across the light-years of emptiness. Muffled voices . . . unintelligible words. There were vibrations now . . . as if the world were about to shake apart.

Then it happened.

Without warning, the universe was ripped in two. An enormous chasm opened in the void . . . as if space itself had ruptured at the seams. A grayish mist poured through the opening, and Langdon saw a terrifying sight. Disembodied hands were suddenly reaching for him, grabbing his body, trying to yank him out of his world.

No! He tried to fight them off, but he had no arms . . . no fists. *Or did he?* Suddenly he felt his body materializing around his mind. His flesh had returned and it was being seized by powerful hands that were dragging him upward. *No! Please!*

But it was too late.

Pain racked his chest as the hands heaved him through the opening. His lungs felt like they were filled with sand. *I can't breathe!* He was suddenly on his back on the coldest, hardest surface he could imagine. Something was pressing on his chest, over and over, hard and painful. He was spewing out the warmth.

I want to go back.

He felt like he was a child being born from a womb.

He was convulsing, coughing up liquid. He felt pain in his chest and neck. Excruciating pain. His throat was on fire. People were talking, trying to whisper, but it was deafening. His vision was blurred, and all he could see was muted shapes. His skin felt numb, like dead leather.

His chest felt heavier now . . . pressure. *I can't breathe!*

He was coughing up more liquid. An overwhelming gag reflex seized him, and he gasped inward. Cold air poured into his lungs, and he felt like a newborn taking his first breath on earth. This world was excruciating. All Langdon wanted was to return to the womb.

Robert Langdon had no idea how much time had passed. He could feel now that he was lying on his side, wrapped in towels and blankets on a hard floor. A familiar face was gazing down at him . . . but the streams of glorious light were gone. The echoes of distant chanting still hung in his mind.

Verbum significatium . . . Verbum omnificum . . .

'Professor Langdon,' someone whispered. 'Do you know where you are?'

Langdon nodded weakly, still coughing.

More important, he had begun to realize what was going on tonight.

113

Wrapped in wool blankets, Langdon stood on wobbly legs and stared down at the open tank of liquid. His body had returned to him, although he wished it had not. His throat and lungs burned. This world felt hard and cruel.

Sato had just explained the sensory-deprivation tank . . . adding that if she had not pulled him out, he would have died of starvation, or worse. Langdon had little doubt that Peter had endured a similar experience. *Peter is in the in-between,* the tattooed man had told him earlier tonight. *He is in purgatory . . . Hamistagan.* If Peter had endured more than one of those birthing processes, Langdon would not have been surprised if Peter had told his captor anything he had wanted to know.

Sato motioned for Langdon to follow her, and he did, trudging slowly down a narrow hall, deeper into this bizarre lair that he was now seeing for the first time. They entered a square room with a stone table and eerie-colored lighting. Katherine was here, and Langdon heaved a sigh of relief. Even so, the scene was worrisome.

Katherine was lying on her back on a stone table. Blood-soaked towels lay on the floor. A CIA agent was holding an IV bag above her, the tube connected to her arm.

She was sobbing quietly.

'Katherine?' Langdon croaked, barely able to speak.

She turned her head, looking disorientated and confused. 'Robert?!' Her eyes widened with disbelief and then joy. 'But I . . . saw you drown!'

He moved toward the stone table.

Katherine pulled herself to a seated position, ignoring her IV tube and the medical objections of the agent. Langdon reached the table, and Katherine reached out, wrapping her arms around his blanket-clad body, holding him close. 'Thank God,' she whispered, kissing his cheek. Then she kissed him again, squeezing him as though she didn't believe he was real. 'I don't understand . . . how . . .'

Sato began saying something about sensory-deprivation tanks and oxygenated perfluorocarbons, but Katherine clearly wasn't listening. She just held Langdon close.

'Robert,' she said, 'Peter's alive.' Her voice wavered as she recounted her horrifying reunion with Peter. She described his physical condition – the wheelchair, the strange knife, the allusions to some kind of 'sacrifice,' and how she had been left bleeding as a human hourglass to persuade Peter to cooperate quickly.

Langdon could barely speak. 'Do you . . . have *any* idea where . . . they went?!'

'He said he was taking Peter to the sacred mountain.'

Langdon pulled away and stared at her.

Katherine had tears in her eyes. 'He said he had deciphered the grid on the bottom of the pyramid, and that the pyramid told him to go to the sacred mountain.'

'Professor,' Sato pressed, 'does that mean anything to you?'

Langdon shook his head. 'Not at all.' Still, he felt a surge of hope. 'But if he got the information off the bottom of the pyramid, we can get it, too.' *I told him how to solve it.*

Sato shook her head. 'The pyramid's gone. We've looked. He took it with him.'

Langdon remained silent a moment, closing his eyes and trying to recall what he had seen on the base of the pyramid. The grid of symbols had been one of the last images he had seen before drowning, and trauma had a way of burning memories deeper into the mind. He could recall some of the grid, definitely not all of it, but maybe enough?

He turned to Sato and said hurriedly, 'I may be able to remember enough, but I need you to look up something on the Internet.'

She pulled out her BlackBerry.

'Run a search for "The Order Eight Franklin Square."'

Sato gave him a startled look but began typing without questions.

Langdon's vision was still blurry, and he was only now starting to process his strange surroundings. He realized that the stone table on which they were leaning was covered with old bloodstains, and the wall to his right was entirely plastered with pages of text, photos, drawings, maps, and a giant web of strings interconnecting them.

My God.

Langdon moved toward the strange collage, still clutching the blankets around his body. Tacked on the wall was an utterly bizarre collection of information – pages from ancient texts ranging from black magic to Christian Scripture, drawings of symbols and sigils, pages of conspiracy-theory Web sites, and satellite photos of Washington, D.C., scrawled with notes and question marks. One of the sheets was a long list of words in many languages. He recognized some of them as sacred Masonic words, others as ancient magic words, and others from ceremonial incantations.

Is that what he's looking for?

A word?

Is it that simple?

Langdon's long-standing skepticism about the Masonic Pyramid was based largely on what it allegedly revealed – the location of the Ancient Mysteries. This discovery would have to involve an enormous vault filled with thousands upon thousands of volumes that had somehow survived the long-lost ancient libraries in which they had once been stored. It all seemed impossible. *A vault that big? Beneath D.C.?* Now, however, his recollection of Peter's lecture at Phillips Exeter, combined with these lists of magic words, had opened another startling possibility.

Langdon most definitely did *not* believe in the power of magic words . . . and yet it seemed pretty clear that the tattooed man did. His pulse quickened as he again scanned the scrawled notes, the maps, the texts, the printouts, and all the interconnected strings and sticky notes.

Sure enough, there was one recurring theme.

My God, he's looking for the verbum significatium
. . . *the Lost Word.* Langdon let the thought take shape,
recalling fragments of Peter's lecture. *The Lost Word is
what he's looking for! That's what he believes is buried here
in Washington.*

Sato arrived beside him. 'Is this what you asked
for?' She handed him her BlackBerry.

Langdon looked at the eight-by-eight grid of
numbers on the screen. 'Exactly.' He grabbed a piece of
scrap paper. 'I'll need a pen.'

Sato handed him one from her pocket. 'Please
hurry.'

Inside the basement office of the Directorate of Science
and Technology, Nola Kaye was once again studying
the redacted document brought to her by sys-sec
Rick Parrish. *What the hell is the CIA director doing
with a file about ancient pyramids and secret underground
locations?*

She grabbed the phone and dialed.

Sato answered instantly, sounding tense. 'Nola, I
was just about to call you.'

'I have new information,' Nola said. 'I'm not sure
how this fits, but I've discovered there's a redacted—'

'Forget it, whatever it is,' Sato interrupted. 'We're out
of time. We failed to apprehend the target, and I have
every reason to believe he's about to carry out his
threat.'

Nola felt a chill.

'The good news is we know exactly where he's
going.' Sato took a deep breath. 'The bad news is that
he's carrying a *laptop* with him.'

114

Less than ten miles away, Mal'akh tucked the blanket around Peter Solomon and wheeled him across a moonlit parking lot into the shadow of an enormous building. The structure had exactly thirty-three outer columns . . . each precisely thirty-three feet tall. The mountainous structure was deserted at this hour, and nobody would ever see them back here. Not that it mattered. From a distance, no one would think twice about a tall, kindly-looking man in a long black coat taking a bald invalid for an evening stroll.

When they reached the rear entrance, Mal'akh wheeled Peter up close to the security keypad. Peter stared at it defiantly, clearly having no intention of entering the code.

Mal'akh laughed. 'You think you're here to let me in? Have you forgotten so soon that I am one of your brethren?' He reached out and typed the access code that he had been given after his initiation to the thirty-third degree.

The heavy door clicked open.

Peter groaned and began struggling in the wheelchair.

'Peter, Peter,' Mal'akh cooed. 'Picture Katherine. Be cooperative, and she will live. You can save her. I give you my word.'

Mal'akh wheeled his captive inside and relocked the door behind them, his heart racing now with anticipation. He pushed Peter through some hallways to an elevator and pressed the call button. The doors opened, and Mal'akh backed in, pulling the wheelchair along with him. Then, making sure Peter could see what he was doing, he reached out and pressed the uppermost button.

A look of deepening dread crossed Peter's tortured face.

'Shh . . .' Mal'akh whispered, gently stroking Peter's shaved head as the elevator doors closed. 'As you well know . . . the secret is how to die.'

I can't remember all the symbols!

Langdon closed his eyes, doing his best to recall the precise locations of the symbols on the bottom of the stone pyramid, but even his eidetic memory did not have that degree of recall. He wrote down the few symbols he could remember, placing each one in the location indicated by Franklin's magic square.

So far, however, he saw nothing that made any sense.

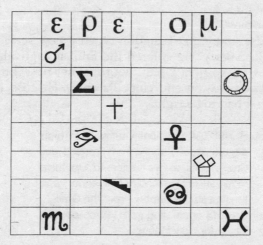

'Look!' Katherine urged. 'You must be on the right track. The first row is all Greek letters – the same kinds of symbols are being arranged together!'

Langdon had noticed this, too, but he could not think of any Greek word that fit that configuration of letters and spaces. *I need the first letter.* He glanced again at the magic square, trying to recall the letter that had been in the number one spot near the lower left corner. *Think!* He closed his eyes, trying to picture the base of the pyramid. *The bottom row . . . next to the left-hand corner . . . what letter was there?*

For an instant, Langdon was back in the tank, racked with terror, staring up through the Plexiglas at the bottom of the pyramid.

Now, suddenly, he saw it. He opened his eyes, breathing heavily. 'The first letter is *H*!'

Langdon turned back to the grid and wrote in the first letter. The word was still incomplete, but he had seen enough. Suddenly he realized what the word might be.

Ηερεδο∝!

Pulse pounding, Langdon typed a new search into the BlackBerry. He entered the English equivalent of this well-known Greek word. The first hit that appeared was an encyclopedia entry. He read it and knew it had to be right.

> HEREDOM n. a significant word in 'high
> degree' Freemasonry, from French Rose
> Croix rituals, where it refers to a mythical
> mountain in Scotland, the legendary site of
> the first such Chapter. From the Greek
> Ηερεδο∝ originating from Hieros-domos,
> Greek for Holy House.

'That's it!' Langdon exclaimed, incredulous. 'That's where they went!'

Sato had been reading over his shoulder and looked lost. 'To a mythical mountain in Scotland?!'

Langdon shook his head. 'No, to a building in Washington whose code name is Heredom.'

115

The House of the Temple – known among its brethren as Heredom – had always been the crown jewel of the Masonic Scottish Rite in America. With its steeply sloped, pyramidical roof, the building was named for an imaginary Scottish mountain. Mal'akh knew, however, there was nothing imaginary about the treasure hidden here.

This is the place, he knew. *The Masonic Pyramid has shown the way.*

As the old elevator slowly made its way to the third floor, Mal'akh took out the piece of paper on which he had reorganized the grid of symbols using the Franklin Square. All the Greek letters had now shifted to the first row . . . along with one simple symbol.

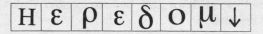

The message could not have been more clear.
Beneath the House of the Temple.
Heredom↓

The Lost Word is here . . . somewhere.

Although Mal'akh did not know precisely how to locate it, he was confident that the answer lay in the remaining symbols on the grid. Conveniently, when it came to unlocking the secrets of the Masonic Pyramid and of this building, no one was more qualified to help than Peter Solomon. *The Worshipful Master himself.*

Peter continued to struggle in the wheelchair, making muffled sounds through his gag.

'I know you're worried about Katherine,' Mal'akh said. 'But it's almost over.'

For Mal'akh, the end felt like it had arrived very suddenly. After all the years of pain and planning, waiting and searching . . . the moment had now arrived.

The elevator began to slow, and he felt a rush of excitement.

The carriage jolted to a stop.

The bronze doors slid open, and Mal'akh gazed out at the glorious chamber before them. The massive square room was adorned with symbols and bathed in moonlight, which shone down through the oculus at the pinnacle of the ceiling high above.

I have come full circle, Mal'akh thought.

The Temple Room was the same place in which Peter Solomon and his brethren had so foolishly initiated Mal'akh as one of their own. Now the Masons' most sublime secret – something that most of the brethren did not even believe existed – was about to be unearthed.

'He won't find anything,' Langdon said, still feeling groggy and disorientated as he followed Sato and the others up the wooden ramp out of the basement.

'There is no actual *Word*. It's all a metaphor – a *symbol* of the Ancient Mysteries.'

Katherine followed, with two agents assisting her weakened body up the ramp.

As the group moved gingerly through the wreckage of the steel door, through the rotating painting, and into the living room, Langdon explained to Sato that the Lost Word was one of Freemasonry's most enduring symbols – a single word, written in an arcane language that man could no longer decipher. The Word, like the Mysteries themselves, promised to unveil its hidden power only to those enlightened enough to decrypt it. 'It is said,' Langdon concluded, 'that if you can possess and *understand* the Lost Word . . . then the Ancient Mysteries will become clear to you.'

Sato glanced over. 'So you believe this man is looking for a *word*?'

Langdon had to admit it sounded absurd at face value, and yet it answered a lot of questions. 'Look, I'm no specialist in ceremonial magic,' he said, 'but from the documents on his basement walls . . . and from Katherine's description of the untattooed flesh on his head . . . I'd say he's hoping to find the Lost Word and inscribe it on his body.'

Sato moved the group toward the dining room. Outside, the helicopter was warming up, its blades thundering louder and louder.

Langdon kept talking, thinking aloud. 'If this guy truly believes he is about to unlock the power of the Ancient Mysteries, no symbol would be more potent in his mind than the Lost Word. If he could find it and inscribe it on the top of his head – a sacred location in itself – then he would no doubt consider himself

perfectly adorned and ritualistically prepared to . . .'
He paused, seeing Katherine blanch at the thought of
Peter's impending fate.

'But, Robert,' she said weakly, her voice barely
audible over the helicopter blades. 'This is good news,
right? If he wants to inscribe the Lost Word on the top
of his head before he sacrifices Peter, then we have
time. He won't kill Peter until he finds the Word. And,
if there *is* no Word . . .'

Langdon tried to look hopeful as the agents helped
Katherine into a chair. 'Unfortunately, Peter still thinks
you're bleeding to death. He thinks the only way to
save you is to cooperate with this lunatic . . . probably
to help him find the Lost Word.'

'So what?' she insisted. 'If the Word doesn't exist—'

'Katherine,' Langdon said, staring deeply into her
eyes. 'If *I* believed you were dying, and if someone
promised me I could save you by finding the Lost
Word, then I would find this man a word – *any* word –
and then I'd pray to God he kept his promise.'

'Director Sato!' an agent shouted from the next
room. 'You'd better see this!'

Sato hurried out of the dining room and saw one of
her agents coming down the stairs from the bedroom.
He was carrying a blond wig. *What the hell?*

'Man's hairpiece,' he said, handing it to her. 'Found
it in the dressing room. Have a close look.'

The blond wig was much heavier than Sato
expected. The skullcap seemed to be molded of a thick
gel. Strangely, the underside of the wig had a wire protruding from it.

'Gel-pack battery that molds to your scalp,' the
agent said. 'Powers a fiber-optic pinpoint camera
hidden in the hair.'

'What?' Sato felt around with her fingers until she found the tiny camera lens nestled invisibly within the blond bangs. 'This thing's a hidden camera?'

'*Video* camera,' the agent said. 'Stores footage on this tiny solid-state card.' He pointed to a stamp-size square of silicon embedded in the skullcap. 'Probably motion activated.'

Jesus, she thought. *So that's how he did it.*

This sleek version of the 'flower in the lapel' secret camera had played a key role in the crisis the OS director was facing tonight. She glared at it a moment longer and then handed it back to the agent.

'Keep searching the house,' she said. 'I want every bit of information you can find on this guy. We know his laptop is missing, and I want to know exactly *how* he plans to connect it to the outside world while he's on the move. Search his study for manuals, cables, anything at all that might give us a clue about his hardware.'

'Yes, ma'am.' The agent hurried off.

Time to move out. Sato could hear the whine of the helicopter blades at full pitch. She hurried back to the dining room, where Simkins had now ushered Warren Bellamy in from the helicopter and was gathering intel from him about the building to which they believed their target had gone.

House of the Temple.

'The front doors are sealed from within,' Bellamy was saying, still wrapped in a foil blanket and shivering visibly from his time outside in Franklin Square. 'The building's rear entrance is your only way in. It's got a keypad with an access PIN known only to the brothers.'

'What's the PIN?' Simkins demanded, taking notes.

Bellamy sat down, looking too feeble to stand. Through chattering teeth, he recited his access code and then added, 'The address is 1733 Sixteenth, but you'll want the access drive and parking area, behind the building. Kind of tricky to find, but—'

'I know exactly where it is,' Langdon said. 'I'll show you when we get there.'

Simkins shook his head. 'You're not coming, Professor. This is a military—'

'The hell I'm not!' Langdon fired back. 'Peter's in there! And that building's a labyrinth! Without someone to lead you in, you'll take ten minutes to find your way up to the Temple Room!'

'He's right,' Bellamy said. 'It's a maze. There *is* an elevator, but it's old and loud and opens in full view of the Temple Room. If you hope to move in quietly, you'll need to ascend on foot.'

'You'll never find your way,' Langdon warned. 'From that rear entrance, you're navigating through the Hall of Regalia, the Hall of Honor, the middle landing, the Atrium, the Grand Stair—'

'Enough,' Sato said. 'Langdon's coming.'

116

The energy was growing.

Mal'akh could feel it pulsing within him, moving up and down his body as he wheeled Peter Solomon toward the altar. *I will exit this building infinitely more powerful than when I entered.* All that remained now was to locate the final ingredient.

'*Verbum significatium,*' he whispered to himself. '*Verbum omnificum.*'

Mal'akh parked Peter's wheelchair beside the altar and then circled around and unzipped the heavy daybag that sat on Peter's lap. Reaching inside, he lifted out the stone pyramid and held it up in the moonlight, directly in front of Peter's eyes, showing him the grid of symbols engraved on the bottom. 'All these years,' he taunted, 'and you never knew how the pyramid kept her secrets.' Mal'akh set the pyramid carefully on the corner of the altar and returned to the bag. 'And this talisman,' he continued, extracting the golden capstone, 'did indeed bring order from chaos, exactly as promised.' He placed the metal capstone carefully atop the stone pyramid, and then stepped back to give Peter a clear view. 'Behold, your symbolon is complete.'

Peter's face contorted, and he tried in vain to speak.

'Good. I can see you have something you'd like to tell me.' Mal'akh roughly yanked out the gag.

Peter Solomon coughed and gasped for several seconds before he finally managed to speak. 'Katherine . . .'

'Katherine's time is short. If you want to save her, I suggest you do exactly as I say.' Mal'akh suspected she was probably already dead, or if not, very close. It made no difference. She was lucky to have lived long enough to say good-bye to her brother.

'Please,' Peter begged, his voice ragged. 'Send an ambulance for her . . .'

'I will do exactly that. But first you must tell me how to access the secret staircase.'

Peter's expression turned to one of disbelief. 'What?!'

'The staircase. Masonic legend speaks of stairs that

descend hundreds of feet to the secret location where the Lost Word is buried.'

Peter now looked panicked.

'You know the legend,' Mal'akh baited. 'A secret staircase hidden beneath a stone.' He pointed to the central altar – a huge block of granite with a gilded inscription in Hebrew: GOD SAID, 'LET THERE BE LIGHT' AND THERE WAS LIGHT. 'Obviously, this is the right place. The entrance to the staircase must be hidden on one of the floors beneath us.'

'There is no secret staircase in this building!' Peter shouted.

Mal'akh smiled patiently and motioned upward. 'This building is shaped like a pyramid.' He pointed to the four-sided vaulted ceiling that angled up to the square oculus in the center.

'Yes, the House of the Temple is a pyramid, but what does—'

'Peter, I have all night.' Mal'akh smoothed his white silk robe over his perfect body. 'Katherine, however, does *not*. If you want her to live, you will tell me how to access the staircase.'

'I already told you,' he declared, 'there *is* no secret staircase in this building!'

'No?' Mal'akh calmly produced the sheet of paper on which he had reorganized the grid of symbols from the base of the pyramid. 'This is the Masonic Pyramid's final message. Your friend Robert Langdon helped me decipher it.'

Mal'akh raised the paper and held it in front of Peter's eyes. The Worshipful Master inhaled sharply when he saw it. Not only had the sixty-four symbols been organized into clearly meaningful groups . . . but an actual *image* had materialized out of the chaos.

An image of a staircase . . . beneath a pyramid.

Peter Solomon stared in disbelief at the grid of symbols before him. The Masonic Pyramid had kept its secret for generations. Now, suddenly, it was being unveiled, and he felt a cold sense of foreboding in the pit of his stomach.

The pyramid's final code.

At a glance, the true meaning of these symbols remained a mystery to Peter, and yet he could immediately understand why the tattooed man believed what he believed.

He thinks there is a hidden staircase beneath the pyramid called Heredom.

He misunderstands these symbols.

'Where is it?' the tattooed man demanded. 'Tell me how to find the staircase, and I will save Katherine.'

I wish I could do that, Peter thought. *But the staircase is not real.* The myth of the staircase was purely symbolic . . . part of the great allegories of Masonry. The Winding Staircase, as it was known, appeared on the second-degree tracing boards. It represented man's intellectual climb toward the Divine Truth. Like Jacob's ladder, the Winding Staircase was a symbol of the pathway to heaven . . . the journey of man toward God . . . the connection between the earthly and spiritual realms. Its steps represented the many virtues of the mind.

He should know that, Peter thought. *He endured all the initiations.*

Every Masonic initiate learned of the symbolic staircase that he could ascend, enabling him 'to participate in the mysteries of human science.' Freemasonry, like Noetic Science and the Ancient Mysteries, revered the untapped potential of the human mind, and many of Masonry's symbols related to human physiology.

The mind sits like a golden capstone atop the physical body. The Philosopher's Stone. Through the staircase of the spine, energy ascends and descends, circulating, connecting the heavenly mind to the physical body.

Peter knew it was no coincidence that the spine was made up of exactly *thirty-three* vertebrae. *Thirty-three are the degrees of Masonry.* The base of the spine, or *sacrum*, literally meant 'sacred bone.' *The body is indeed a temple.* The human science that Masons revered was the ancient understanding of how to use that temple for its most potent and noble purpose.

Unfortunately, explaining the truth to this man was not going to help Katherine at all. Peter gazed down at the grid of symbols and gave a defeated sigh. 'You're right,' he lied. 'There is indeed a secret staircase beneath this building. And as soon as you send help to Katherine, I'll take you to it.'

The man with the tattoos simply stared at him.

Solomon glared back, eyes defiant. 'Either save my sister and learn the truth . . . or kill us both and remain ignorant forever!'

The man quietly lowered the paper and shook his head. 'I'm not happy with you, Peter. You failed your test. You still take me for a fool. Do you truly believe I don't understand what it is I seek? Do you think I have not yet grasped my true potential?'

With that, the man turned his back and slipped off his robe. As the white silk fluttered to the floor, Peter saw for the first time the long tattoo running up the man's spine.

Dear God . . .

Winding up from the man's white loincloth, an elegant spiral staircase ascended the middle of his muscular back. Each stair was positioned on a different vertebra. Speechless, Peter let his eyes ascend the staircase, all the way up to the base of the man's skull.

Peter could only stare.

The tattooed man now tipped his shaved head backward, revealing the circle of bare flesh on the pinnacle of his skull. The virgin skin was bordered by a single snake, looped in a circle, consuming itself.

At-one-ment.

Slowly now, the man lowered his head and turned to face Peter. The massive double-headed phoenix on his chest stared out through dead eyes.

'I am looking for the Lost Word,' the man said. 'Are you going to help me . . . or are you and your sister going to die?'

* * *

565

You know how to find it, Mal'akh thought. *You know something you're not telling me.*

Peter Solomon had revealed things under interrogation that he probably didn't even recall now. The repeated sessions in and out of the deprivation tank had left him delirious and compliant. Incredibly, when he spilled his guts, everything he told Mal'akh had been consistent with the legend of the Lost Word.

The Lost Word is not a metaphor . . . it is real. The Word is written in an ancient language . . . and has been hidden for ages. The Word is capable of bringing unfathomable power to anyone who grasps its true meaning. The Word remains hidden to this day . . . and the Masonic Pyramid has the power to unveil it.

'Peter,' Mal'akh now said, staring into his captive's eyes, 'when you looked at that grid of symbols . . . you saw something. You had a revelation. This grid *means* something to you. Tell me.'

'I will tell you nothing until you send help to Katherine!'

Mal'akh smiled at him. 'Believe me, the prospect of losing your sister is the least of your worries right now.' Without another word, he turned to Langdon's daybag and started removing the items he had packed in his basement. Then he began meticulously arranging them on the sacrificial altar.

A folded silk cloth. Pure white.

A silver censer. Egyptian myrrh.

A vial of Peter's blood. Mixed with ash.

A black crow's feather. His sacred stylus.

The sacrificial knife. Forged of iron from a meteorite in the desert of Canaan.

'You think I am afraid to die?' Peter shouted, his voice racked with anguish. 'If Katherine is gone, I have

566

nothing left! You've murdered my entire family! You've taken everything from me!'

'Not *everything*,' Mal'akh replied. 'Not yet.' He reached into the daybag and pulled out the laptop from his study. He turned it on and looked over at his captive. 'I'm afraid you have not yet grasped the true nature of your predicament.'

117

Langdon felt his stomach drop as the CIA helicopter leaped off the lawn, banked hard, and accelerated faster than he ever imagined a helicopter could move. Katherine had stayed behind to recuperate with Bellamy while one of the CIA agents searched the mansion and waited for a backup team.

Before Langdon left, she had kissed him on the cheek and whispered, 'Be safe, Robert.'

Now Langdon was holding on for dear life as the military helicopter finally leveled out and raced toward the House of the Temple.

Seated beside him, Sato was yelling up to the pilot. 'Head for Dupont Circle!' she shouted over the deafening noise. 'We'll set down there!'

Startled, Langdon turned to her. 'Dupont?! That's *blocks* from the House of the Temple! We can land in the Temple parking lot!'

Sato shook her head. 'We need to enter the building *quietly*. If our target hears us coming—'

'We don't have time!' Langdon argued. 'This lunatic is about to murder Peter! Maybe the sound of the helicopter will scare him and make him stop!'

Sato stared at him with ice-cold eyes. 'As I have told you, Peter Solomon's safety is *not* my primary objective. I believe I've made that clear.'

Langdon was in no mood for another national-security lecture. 'Look, *I'm* the only one on board who knows his way through that building—'

'Careful, Professor,' the director warned. 'You are here as a member of my team, and I *will* have your complete cooperation.' She paused a moment and then added, 'In fact, it might be wise if I now apprised you fully of the severity of our crisis tonight.'

Sato reached under her seat and pulled out a sleek titanium briefcase, which she opened to reveal an unusually complicated-looking computer. When she turned it on, a CIA logo materialized along with a log-in prompt.

As Sato logged in, she asked, 'Professor, do you remember the blond hairpiece we found in the man's home?'

'Yes.'

'Well, hidden within that wig was a tiny fiber-optic camera . . . concealed in the bangs.'

'A hidden camera? I don't understand.'

Sato looked grim. 'You will.' She launched a file on the laptop.

ONE MOMENT PLEASE . . .

DECRYPTING FILE . . .

A video window popped up, filling the entire screen. Sato lifted the briefcase and set it on Langdon's thighs, giving him a front-row seat.

An unusual image materialized on the screen.

Langdon recoiled in surprise. *What the hell?!*

Murky and dark, the video was of a blindfolded

man. He was dressed in the garb of a medieval heretic being led to the gallows – noose around his neck, left pant leg rolled up to the knee, right sleeve rolled up to the elbow, and his shirt gaping open to reveal his bare chest.

Langdon stared in disbelief. He had read enough about Masonic rituals to recognize exactly what he was looking at.

A Masonic initiate . . . preparing to enter the first degree.

The man was very muscular and tall, with a familiar blond hairpiece and deeply tanned skin. Langdon recognized his features at once. The man's tattoos had obviously been concealed beneath bronzing makeup. He was standing before a full-length mirror video-taping his reflection through the camera concealed in his wig.

But . . . why?

The screen faded to black.

New footage appeared. A small, dimly lit, rectangular chamber. A dramatic chessboard floor of black-and-white tile. A low wooden altar, flanked on three sides by pillars, atop which burned flickering candles.

Langdon felt a sudden apprehension.

Oh my God.

Filming in the erratic style of an amateur home video, the camera now panned up to the periphery of the room to reveal a small group of men observing the initiate. The men were dressed in ritual Masonic regalia. In the darkness, Langdon could not make out their faces, but he had no doubt *where* this ritual was taking place.

The traditional layout of this Lodge Room could have been anywhere in the world, but the powder-blue triangular pediment above the master's chair revealed it as the oldest Masonic lodge in D.C. – Potomac Lodge No. 5 – home of George Washington and the Masonic forefathers who laid the cornerstone for the White House and the Capitol Building.

The lodge was still active today.

Peter Solomon, in addition to overseeing the House of the Temple, was the master of his local lodge. And it was at lodges like this one that a Masonic initiate's journey always began . . . where he underwent the first three degrees of Freemasonry.

'Brethren,' Peter's familiar voice declared, 'in the name of the Great Architect of the Universe, I open this lodge for the practice of Masonry in the first degree!'

A gavel rapped loudly.

Langdon watched in utter disbelief as the video progressed through a quick series of dissolves featuring Peter Solomon performing some of the ritual's starker moments.

Pressing a shining dagger to the initiate's bare chest . . . threatening impalement should the initiate 'inappropriately reveal the Mysteries of Masonry' . . . describing the black-and-white floor as representing 'the living and the dead' . . . outlining punishments that included 'having one's throat cut across, one's tongue torn out by its roots, and one's body buried in the rough sands of the sea . . .'

Langdon stared. *Am I really witnessing this?* Masonic initiation rites had remained shrouded in secrecy for centuries. The only descriptions that had ever been leaked were written by a handful of estranged brothers. Langdon had read those accounts, of course, and yet to *see* an initiation with his own eyes . . . this was a much different story.

Especially edited this way. Langdon could already tell that the video was an unfair piece of propaganda, omitting all the noblest aspects of the initiation and highlighting only the most disconcerting. If this video were released, Langdon knew it would become an Internet sensation overnight. *The anti-Masonic conspiracy theorists would feed on this like sharks.* The Masonic organization, and especially Peter Solomon, would find themselves embroiled in a firestorm of controversy and a desperate effort at damage control . . . even though the ritual was innocuous and purely symbolic.

Eerily, the video included a biblical reference to human sacrifice . . . *'the submission of Abraham to the Supreme Being by proffering Isaac, his firstborn son.'* Langdon thought of Peter and willed the helicopter to fly faster.

The video footage shifted now.

Same room. Different night. A larger group of Masons looking on. Peter Solomon was observing from the master's chair. This was the second degree. More intense now. *Kneeling at the altar . . . vowing to 'forever conceal the enigmas existing within Freemasonry' . . . consenting to the penalty of 'having one's chest cavity ripped open and pulsing heart cast upon the surface of the earth as offal for the ravenous beasts'* . . .

Langdon's own heart was pulsing wildly now as the video shifted yet again. Another night. A much larger crowd. A coffin-shaped 'tracing board' on the floor.

The third degree.

This was the death ritual – the most rigorous of all the degrees – the moment in which the initiate was forced 'to face the final challenge of personal extinction.' This grueling interrogation was in fact the source of the common phrase *to give someone the third degree*. And although Langdon was very familiar with academic accounts of it, he was in no way prepared for what he now saw.

The murder.

In violent, rapid intercuts, the video displayed a chilling, victim's point-of-view account of the initiate's brutal murder. There were simulated blows to his head, including one with a Mason's stone maul. All the while, a deacon mournfully told the story of 'the widow's son' – Hiram Abiff – the master Architect of King Solomon's temple, who chose to die rather than reveal the secret wisdom he possessed.

The attack was mimed, of course, and yet its effect on camera was bloodcurdling. After the deathblow, the initiate – now 'dead to his former self' – was lowered into his symbolic coffin, where his eyes were shut and his arms were crossed like those of a corpse. The Masonic brothers rose and mournfully circled his dead body while a pipe organ played a march of the dead.

The macabre scene was deeply disturbing.

And it only got worse.

As the men gathered around their slain brother, the hidden camera clearly displayed their faces. Langdon now realized that Solomon was not the only famous man in the room. One of the men peering down at the initiate in his coffin was on television almost daily.

A prominent U.S. senator.

Oh God . . .

The scene changed yet again. *Outside now . . . nighttime . . . the same jumpy video footage . . . the man was walking down a city street . . . strands of blond hair blowing in front of the camera . . . turning a corner . . . the camera angle lowering to something in the man's hand . . . a dollar bill . . . a close-up focusing on the Great Seal . . . the all-seeing eye . . . the unfinished pyramid . . . and then, abruptly, pulling away to reveal a similar shape in the distance . . . a massive pyramidical building . . . with sloping sides rising to a truncated top.*

The House of the Temple.

A soul-deep dread swelled within him.

The video kept moving . . . *the man hurrying toward the building now . . . up the multitiered staircase . . . toward the giant bronze doors . . . between the two seventeen-ton sphinx guardians.*

A neophyte entering the pyramid of initiation.

Darkness now.

A powerful pipe organ played in the distance . . . and a new image materialized.

The Temple Room.

Langdon swallowed hard.

On-screen, the cavernous space was alive with electricity. Beneath the oculus, the black marble altar shone in the moonlight. Assembled around it, seated on hand-tooled pigskin chairs, awaited a somber council of distinguished thirty-third-degree Masons, present to bear witness. The video now panned across their faces with slow and deliberate intention.

Langdon stared in horror.

Although he had not seen this coming, what he was looking at made perfect sense. A gathering of the most decorated and accomplished Masons in the most powerful city on earth would logically include many influential and well-known individuals. Sure enough, seated around the altar, adorned in their long silk gloves, Masonic aprons, and glistening jewels, were some of the country's most powerful men.

Two Supreme Court justices . . .

The secretary of defense . . .

The speaker of the House . . .

Langdon felt ill as the video continued panning across the faces of those in attendance.

Three prominent senators . . . including the majority leader . . .

The secretary of homeland security . . .

And . . .

The director of the CIA . . .

Langdon wanted only to look away, but he could not. The scene was utterly mesmerizing, alarming even to him. In an instant, he had come to understand the source of Sato's anxiety and concern.

Now, on-screen, the shot dissolved into a single shocking image.

A human skull . . . filled with dark crimson liquid. The famed *caput mortuum* was being offered forth to the initiate by the slender hands of Peter Solomon, whose gold Masonic ring glinted in the candlelight. The red liquid was wine . . . and yet it shimmered like blood. The visual effect was frightful.

The Fifth Libation, Langdon realized, having read firsthand accounts of this sacrament in John Quincy Adams's *Letters on the Masonic Institution*. Even so, to *see* it happen . . . to see it calmly witnessed by America's most powerful men . . . this was as arresting an image as any Langdon had ever seen.

The initiate took the skull in his hands . . . his face reflected in the calm surface of the wine. '*May this wine I now drink become a deadly poison to me,*' he declared, '*should I ever knowingly or willfully violate my oath.*'

Obviously, this initiate had intended to violate his oath beyond all imagination.

Langdon could barely get his mind around what would happen if this video were made public. *No one would understand.* The government would be thrown into upheaval. The airwaves would be filled with the voices of anti-Masonic groups, fundamentalists, and conspiracy theorists spewing hatred and fear, launching a Puritan witch hunt all over again.

The truth will be twisted, Langdon knew. *As it always is with the Masons.*

The *truth* was that the brotherhood's focus on death was in fact a bold celebration of *life*. Masonic ritual was designed to awaken the slumbering man inside, lifting him from his dark coffin of ignorance, raising him into the light, and giving him eyes to see. Only through the *death* experience could man fully understand his *life* experience. Only through the realization that his days on earth were finite could he grasp the importance of living those days with honor, integrity, and service to his fellow man.

Masonic initiations were startling because they were meant to be transformative. Masonic vows were unforgiving because they were meant to be reminders that man's honor and his 'word' were all he could take from this world. Masonic teachings were arcane because they were meant to be *universal* . . . taught through a common language of symbols and metaphors that transcended religions, cultures, and races . . . creating a unified 'worldwide consciousness' of brotherly love.

For a brief instant, Langdon felt a glimmer of hope. He tried to assure himself that if this video were to leak out, the public would be open-minded and tolerant, realizing that *all* spiritual rituals included aspects that would seem frightening if taken out of context – crucifixion reenactments, Jewish circumcision rites, Mormon baptisms of the dead, Catholic exorcisms, Islamic *niqab*, shamanic trance healing, the Jewish Kaparot ceremony, even the eating of the figurative body and blood of Christ.

I'm dreaming, Langdon knew. *This video will create chaos.* He could imagine what would happen if the prominent leaders of Russia or the Islamic world were seen in a video, pressing knives to bare chests, swearing violent oaths, performing mock murders, lying in symbolic coffins, and drinking wine from a human skull. The global outcry would be instantaneous and overwhelming.

God help us . . .

On-screen now, the initiate was raising the skull to his lips. He tipped it backward . . . draining the blood-red wine . . . sealing his oath. Then he lowered the skull and gazed out at the assembly around him. America's most powerful and trusted men gave contented nods of acceptance.

'*Welcome, brother,*' Peter Solomon said.

As the image faded to black, Langdon realized he had stopped breathing.

Without a word, Sato reached over, closed the briefcase, and lifted it off his lap. Langdon turned to her trying to speak, but he could find no words. It didn't matter. Understanding was written all over his face. Sato was right. Tonight was a national-security crisis . . . of unimaginable proportions.

118

Dressed in his loincloth, Mal'akh padded back and forth in front of Peter Solomon's wheelchair. 'Peter,' he whispered, enjoying every moment of his captive's horror, 'you forgot you have a second family . . . your Masonic brothers. And I will destroy them, too . . . unless you help me.'

Solomon looked almost catatonic in the glow of the laptop sitting atop his thighs. 'Please,' he finally stammered, glancing up. 'If this video gets out . . .'

'If?' Mal'akh laughed. '*If* it gets out?' He motioned to the small cellular modem plugged into the side of his laptop. 'I'm connected to the world.'

'You wouldn't . . .'

I will, Mal'akh thought, enjoying Solomon's horror. 'You have the power to stop me,' he said. 'And to save your sister. But you have to tell me what I want to know. The Lost Word is hidden somewhere, Peter, and I know this grid reveals exactly where to find it.'

Peter glanced at the grid of symbols again, his eyes revealing nothing.

'Perhaps this will help to inspire you.' Mal'akh reached over Peter's shoulders and hit a few keys on the laptop. An e-mail program launched on the screen, and Peter stiffened visibly. The screen now displayed an e-mail that Mal'akh had cued earlier tonight – a video file addressed to a long list of major media networks.

Mal'akh smiled. 'I think it's time we share, don't you?'

'Don't!'

Mal'akh reached down and clicked the send button

on the program. Peter jerked against his bonds, trying unsuccessfully to knock the laptop to the floor.

'Relax, Peter,' Mal'akh whispered. 'It's a massive file. It will take a few minutes to go out.' He pointed to the progress bar:

SENDING MESSAGE: 2% COMPLETE

'If you tell me what I want to know, I'll stop the e-mail, and nobody will ever see this.'

Peter was ashen as the task bar inched forward.

SENDING MESSAGE: 4% COMPLETE

Mal'akh now lifted the computer from Peter's lap and set it on one of the nearby pigskin chairs, turning the screen so the other man could watch the progress. Then he returned to Peter's side and laid the page of symbols in his lap. 'The legends say the Masonic Pyramid will unveil the Lost Word. This is the pyramid's final code. I believe you know how to read it.'

Mal'akh glanced over at the laptop.

SENDING MESSAGE: 8% COMPLETE

Mal'akh returned his eyes to Peter. Solomon was staring at him, his gray eyes blazing now with hatred.

Hate me, Mal'akh thought. *The greater the emotion, the more potent the energy that will be released when the ritual is completed.*

At Langley, Nola Kaye pressed the phone to her ear,

barely able to hear Sato over the noise of the helicopter. 'They said it's impossible to stop the file transfer!' Nola shouted. 'To shut down local ISPs would take at least an hour, and if he's got access to a wireless provider, killing the ground-based Internet won't stop him from sending it anyway.'

Nowadays, stopping the flow of digital information had become nearly impossible. There were too many access routes to the Internet. Between hard lines, Wi-Fi hot spots, cellular modems, SAT phones, superphones, and e-mail-equipped PDAs, the only way to isolate a potential data leak was by destroying the source machine.

'I pulled the spec sheet on the UH-60 you're flying,' Nola said, 'and it looks like you're equipped with EMP.'

Electromagnetic-pulse or EMP guns were now commonplace among law enforcement agencies, which used them primarily to stop car chases from a safe distance. By firing a highly concentrated pulse of electromagnetic radiation, an EMP gun could effectively fry the electronics of any device it targeted – cars, cell phones, computers. According to Nola's spec sheet, the UH-60 had a chassis-mounted, laser-sighted, six-gigahertz magnetron with a fifty-dB-gain horn that yielded a ten-gigawatt pulse. Discharged directly at a laptop, the pulse would fry the computer's motherboard and instantly erase the hard drive.

'EMP will be useless,' Sato yelled back. 'Target is inside a stone building. No sight lines and thick EM shielding. Do you have any indication yet if the video has gone out?'

Nola glanced at a second monitor, which was running a continuous search for breaking news stories about the Masons. 'Not yet, ma'am. But if it goes public, we'll know within seconds.'

'Keep me posted.' Sato signed off.

Langdon held his breath as the helicopter dropped from the sky toward Dupont Circle. A handful of pedestrians scattered as the aircraft descended through an opening in the trees and landed hard on the lawn just south of the famous two-tiered fountain designed by the same two men who created the Lincoln Memorial.

Thirty seconds later, Langdon was riding shotgun in a commandeered Lexus SUV, tearing up New Hampshire Avenue toward the House of the Temple.

Peter Solomon was desperately trying to figure out what to do. All he could see in his mind were the images of Katherine bleeding in the basement . . . and of the video he had just witnessed. He turned his head slowly toward the laptop on the pigskin chair several yards away. The progress bar was almost a third of the way filled.

SENDING MESSAGE: 29% COMPLETE

The tattooed man was now walking slow circles around the square altar, swinging a lit censer and chanting to himself. Thick puffs of white smoke swirled up toward the skylight. The man's eyes were wide now, and he seemed to be in a demonic trance. Peter turned his gaze to the ancient knife that sat waiting on the white silk cloth spread across the altar.

Peter Solomon had no doubt that he would die in this temple tonight. The question was how to die. Would he find a way to save his sister and his brotherhood . . . or would his death be entirely in vain?

He glanced down at the grid of symbols. When he had first laid eyes on the grid, the shock of the moment had blinded him . . . preventing his vision from piercing the veil of chaos . . . to glimpse the startling truth. Now, however, the real significance of these symbols had become crystal clear to him. He had seen the grid in an entirely new light.

Peter Solomon knew exactly what he needed to do.

Taking a deep breath, he gazed up at the moon through the oculus above. Then he began to speak.

All great truths are simple.

Mal'akh had learned that long ago.

The solution that Peter Solomon was now explaining was so graceful and pure that Mal'akh was sure that it could only be true. Incredibly, the solution to the pyramid's final code was far simpler than he had ever imagined.

The Lost Word was right before my eyes.

In an instant, a bright ray of light pierced the murkiness of the history and myth surrounding the Lost Word. As promised, the Lost Word was indeed written in an ancient language and bore mystical power in every philosophy, religion, and science ever known to man. *Alchemy, astrology, Kabbalah, Christianity, Buddhism, Rosicrucianism, Freemasonry, astronomy, physics, Noetics . . .*

Standing now in this initiation chamber atop the great pyramid of Heredom, Mal'akh gazed upon the treasure he had sought all these years, and he knew he could not have prepared himself more perfectly.

Soon I am complete.

The Lost Word is found.

In Kalorama Heights, a lone CIA agent stood amid a sea of garbage that he had dumped out of the trash bins that had been found in the garage.

'Ms. Kaye?' he said, speaking to Sato's analyst on the phone. 'Good thinking to search his garbage. I think I just found something.'

Inside the house, Katherine Solomon was feeling stronger with every passing moment. The infusion of lactated Ringer's solution had successfully raised her blood pressure and quelled her throbbing headache. She was resting now, seated in the dining room, with explicit instructions to remain still. Her nerves felt frayed, and she was increasingly anxious for news about her brother.

Where is everybody? The CIA's forensics team had not yet arrived, and the agent who had stayed behind was still off searching the premises. Bellamy had been sitting with her in the dining room, still wrapped in a foil blanket, but he, too, had wandered off to look for any information that might help the CIA save Peter.

Unable to sit idly, Katherine pulled herself to her feet, teetered, and then inched slowly toward the living room. She found Bellamy in the study. The Architect was standing at an open drawer, his back to her, apparently too engrossed in its contents to hear her enter.

She walked up behind him. 'Warren?'

The old man lurched and turned, quickly shutting the drawer with his hip. His face was lined with shock and grief, his cheeks streaked with tears.

'What's wrong?!' She glanced down at the drawer. 'What is it?'

Bellamy seemed unable to speak. He had the look of a man who had just seen something he deeply wished he had not.

'What's in the drawer?' she demanded.

Bellamy's tear-filled eyes held hers for a long, sorrowful moment. Finally he spoke. 'You and I wondered *why* . . . why this man seemed to hate your family.'

Katherine's brow furrowed. 'Yes?'

'Well . . .' Bellamy's voice caught. 'I just found the answer.'

119

In the chamber at the top of the House of the Temple, the one who called himself Mal'akh stood before the great altar and gently massaged the virgin skin atop his head. *Verbum significatium*, he chanted in preparation. *Verbum omnificum*. The final ingredient had been found at last.

The most precious treasures are often the simplest.

Above the altar, wisps of fragrant smoke now swirled, billowing up from the censer. The suffumigations ascended through the shaft of moonlight, clearing a channel skyward through which a liberated soul could travel freely.

The time had come.

Mal'akh retrieved the vial of Peter's darkened blood and uncorked it. With his captive looking on, he dipped the nib of the crow's feather into the crimson tincture and raised it to the sacred circle of flesh atop his head. He paused a moment . . . thinking of how long he had waited for this night. His great transformation was finally at hand. *When the Lost Word is written on the mind of man, he is then ready to receive unimaginable power.* Such was the ancient promise of apotheosis. So far, mankind had been unable to realize that promise, and Mal'akh had done what he could to keep it that way.

With a steady hand, Mal'akh touched the nib of the feather to his skin. He needed no mirror, no assistance, only his sense of touch, and his mind's eye. Slowly, meticulously, he began inscribing the Lost Word inside the circular *ouroboros* on his scalp.

Peter Solomon looked on with an expression of horror.

When Mal'akh finished, he closed his eyes, set down the feather, and let the air out of his lungs entirely. For the first time in his life, he felt a sensation he had never known.

I am complete.

I am at one.

Mal'akh had worked for years on the artifact that was his body, and now, as he neared his moment of final transformation, he could feel every line that had ever been inscribed on his flesh. *I am a true masterpiece. Perfect and complete.*

'I gave you what you asked for.' Peter's voice intruded. 'Send help to Katherine. And stop that file.'

Mal'akh opened his eyes and smiled. 'You and I are not quite finished.' He turned to the altar and picked up the sacrificial knife, running his finger across the sleek iron blade. 'This ancient knife was commissioned by God,' he said, 'for use in a human sacrifice. You recognized it earlier, no?'

Solomon's gray eyes were like stone. 'It is unique, and I've heard the legend.'

'Legend? The account appears in Holy Scripture. You don't *believe* it's true?'

Peter just stared.

Mal'akh had spent a fortune locating and obtaining this artifact. Known as the Akedah knife, it had been crafted over three thousand years ago from an iron meteorite that had fallen to earth. *Iron from heaven, as the early mystics called it.* It was believed to be the exact knife used by Abraham at the Akedah – the near sacrifice of his son Isaac on Mount Moriah – as depicted in Genesis. The knife's astounding history included possession by popes, Nazi mystics, European alchemists, and private collectors.

They protected and admired it, Mal'akh thought, *but none dared unleash its true power by using it for its real purpose.* Tonight, the Akedah knife would fulfill its destiny.

The Akedah had always been sacred in Masonic ritual. In the very first degree, Masons celebrated '*the most august gift ever offered to God . . . the submission of Abraham to the volitions of the supreme being by proffering Isaac, his firstborn . . .*'

The weight of the blade felt exhilarating in Mal'akh's hand as he crouched down and used the freshly sharpened knife to sever the ropes binding Peter to his wheelchair. The bonds fell to the floor.

Peter Solomon winced in pain as he attempted to shift his cramped limbs. 'Why are you doing this to me? What do you think this will accomplish?'

'*You* of all people should understand,' Mal'akh replied. 'You study the ancient ways. You know that the power of the mysteries relies on *sacrifice* . . . on releasing a human soul from its body. It has been this way since the beginning.'

'You know nothing of sacrifice,' Peter said, his voice seething with pain and loathing.

Excellent, Mal'akh thought. *Feed your hatred. It will only make this easier.*

Mal'akh's empty stomach growled as he paced before his captive. 'There is enormous power in the shedding of human blood. Everyone understood that, from the early Egyptians, to the Celtic Druids, to the Chinese, to the Aztecs. There is magic in human sacrifice, but modern man has become weak, too fearful to make true offerings, too frail to give the life that is required for spiritual transformation. The ancient texts are clear, though. Only by offering what is most sacred can man access the ultimate power.'

'You consider *me* a sacred offering?'

Mal'akh now laughed out loud. 'You really don't understand yet, do you?'

Peter gave him an odd look.

'Do you know why I have a deprivation tank in my home?' Mal'akh placed his hands on his hips and flexed his elaborately decorated body, which was still covered only by a loincloth. 'I have been practicing . . . preparing . . . anticipating the moment when I am only mind . . . when I am released from this mortal shell . . . when I have offered up this beautiful body to the gods in sacrifice. *I* am the precious one! *I* am the pure white lamb!'

Peter's mouth fell open but no words came out.

'Yes, Peter, a man must offer to the gods that which he

holds most dear. His purest white dove . . . his most precious and worthy offering. *You* are not precious to me. *You* are not a worthy offering.' Mal'akh glared at him. 'Don't you see? *You* are not the sacrifice, Peter . . . *I* am. Mine is the flesh that is the offering. *I* am the gift. Look at me. I have prepared, made myself worthy for my final journey. *I am the gift!*'

Peter remained speechless.

'The secret is *how* to die,' Mal'akh now said. 'Masons understand that.' He pointed to the altar. 'You revere the ancient truths, and yet you are cowards. You understand the power of sacrifice and yet you keep a safe distance from death, performing your mock murders and bloodless death rituals. Tonight, your symbolic altar will bear witness to its true power . . . and its actual purpose.'

Mal'akh reached down and grasped Peter Solomon's left hand, pressing the handle of the Akedah knife into his palm. *The left hand serves the darkness.* This, too, had been planned. Peter would have no choice in the matter. Mal'akh could fathom no sacrifice more potent and symbolic than one performed on this altar, by this man, with this knife, plunged into the heart of an offering whose mortal flesh was wrapped like a gift in a shroud of mystical symbols.

With this offering of *self*, Mal'akh would establish his rank in the hierarchy of demons. Darkness and blood were where the true power lay. The ancients knew this, the Adepts choosing sides consistent with their individual natures. Mal'akh had chosen sides wisely. Chaos was the natural law of the universe. Indifference was the engine of entropy. Man's apathy was the fertile ground in which the dark spirits tended their seeds.

I have served them, and they will receive me as a god.

Peter did not move. He simply stared down at the ancient knife gripped in his hand.

'I will you,' Mal'akh taunted. 'I am a willing sacrifice. Your final role has been written. You will transform me. You will liberate me from my body. You will do this, or you will lose your sister and your brotherhood. You will truly be all alone.' He paused, smiling down at his captive. 'Consider this your final punishment.'

Peter's eyes rose slowly to meet Mal'akh's. 'Killing *you*? A *punishment*? Do you think I will hesitate? You murdered my son. My mother. My entire family.'

'No!' Mal'akh exploded with a force that startled even himself. 'You are wrong! I did not murder your family! *You* did! It was *you* who made the choice to leave Zachary in prison! And from there, the wheels were in motion! *You* killed your family, Peter, not me!'

Peter's knuckles turned white, his fingers clenching the knife in rage. 'You know nothing of why I left Zachary in prison.'

'I know everything!' Mal'akh fired back. 'I was there. You claimed you were trying to *help* him. Were you trying to *help* him when you offered him the choice between wealth or wisdom? Were you trying to *help* him when you gave him the ultimatum to join the Masons? What kind of father gives a child the choice between "wealth or wisdom" and expects him to know how to handle it! What kind of father leaves his own son in a prison instead of flying him home to safety!' Mal'akh now moved in front of Peter and crouched down, placing his tattooed face only inches from his face. 'But most important . . . what kind of father can look his own son in the eyes . . . even after all these years . . . and not even *recognize* him!'

Mal'akh's words echoed for several seconds in the stone chamber.

Then silence.

In the abrupt stillness, Peter Solomon seemed to have been jolted from his trance. His face clouded now with a visage of total incredulity.

Yes, Father. It's me. Mal'akh had waited years for this moment . . . to take revenge on the man who had abandoned him . . . to stare into those gray eyes and speak the truth that had been buried all these years. Now the moment was here, and he spoke slowly, longing to watch the full weight of his words gradually crush Peter Solomon's soul. 'You should be happy, Father. Your prodigal son has returned.'

Peter's face was now as pale as death.

Mal'akh savored every moment. 'My own father made the decision to leave me in prison . . . and in that instant, I vowed that he had rejected me for the last time. I was no longer his son. Zachary Solomon ceased to exist.'

Two glistening teardrops welled suddenly in his father's eyes, and Mal'akh thought they were the most beautiful thing he had ever seen.

Peter choked back tears, staring up at Mal'akh's face as if seeing him for the very first time.

'All the warden wanted was money,' Mal'akh said, 'but you refused. It never occurred to you, though, that *my* money was just as green as yours. The warden did not care who paid him, only that he was paid. When I offered to pay him handsomely, he selected a sickly inmate about my size, dressed him in my clothes, and beat him beyond all recognition. The photos you saw . . . and the sealed casket you buried . . . they were not mine. They belonged to a stranger.'

Peter's tear-streaked face contorted now with anguish and disbelief. 'Oh my God . . . Zachary.'

'Not anymore. When Zachary walked out of prison, he was transformed.'

His adolescent physique and childlike face had drastically mutated when he flooded his young body with experimental growth hormones and steroids. Even his vocal cords had been ravaged, transforming his boyish voice into a permanent whisper.

Zachary became Andros.

Andros became Mal'akh.

And tonight . . . Mal'akh will become his greatest incarnation of all.

At that moment in Kalorama Heights, Katherine Solomon stood over the open desk drawer and gazed down at what could be described only as a fetishist's collection of old newspaper articles and photographs.

'I don't understand,' she said, turning to Bellamy. 'This lunatic was obviously obsessed with my family, but—'

'Keep going . . .' urged Bellamy, taking a seat and still looking deeply shaken.

Katherine dug deeper into the newspaper articles, every one of which related to the Solomon family – Peter's many successes, Katherine's research, their mother Isabel's terrible murder, Zachary Solomon's widely publicized drug use, incarceration, and brutal murder in a Turkish prison.

The fixation this man had on the Solomon family was beyond fanatical, and yet Katherine saw nothing yet to suggest *why.*

It was then that she saw the photographs. The first showed Zachary standing knee-deep in azure water on a beach dotted with whitewashed houses. *Greece?* The photo, she assumed, could have been taken only during Zach's freewheeling drug days in Europe. Strangely, though, Zach looked healthier than he did in the paparazzi shots of an emaciated kid partying with the drug crowd. He looked more fit, stronger somehow, more mature. Katherine never recalled him looking so healthy.

Puzzled, she checked the date stamp on the photo.

But that's . . . impossible.

The date was almost a full year *after* Zachary had died in prison.

Suddenly Katherine was flipping desperately through the stack. All of the photos were of Zachary Solomon . . . gradually getting older. The collection appeared to be some kind of pictorial autobiography, chronicling a slow transformation. As the pictures progressed, Katherine saw a sudden and dramatic change. She looked on in horror as Zachary's body began mutating, his muscles bulging, and his facial features morphing from the obvious heavy use of steroids. His frame seemed to double in mass, and a haunting fierceness crept into his eyes.

I don't even recognize this man!

He looked nothing like Katherine's memories of her young nephew.

When she reached a picture of him with a shaved head, she felt her knees begin to buckle. Then she saw a photo of his bare body . . . adorned with the first traces of tattoos.

Her heart almost stopped. 'Oh my God . . .'

120

'Right turn!' Langdon shouted from the backseat of the commandeered Lexus SUV.

Simkins swerved onto S Street and gunned the vehicle through a tree-lined residential neighborhood. As they neared the corner of Sixteenth Street, the House of the Temple rose like a mountain on the right.

Simkins stared up at the massive structure. It looked like someone had built a pyramid on top of Rome's Pantheon. He prepared to turn right on Sixteenth toward the front of the building.

'Don't turn!' Langdon ordered. 'Go straight! Stay on S!'

Simkins obeyed, driving alongside the east side of the building.

'At Fifteenth,' Langdon said, 'turn right!'

Simkins followed his navigator, and moments later, Langdon had pointed out a nearly invisible, unpaved access road that bisected the gardens behind the House of the Temple. Simkins turned in to the drive and gunned the Lexus toward the rear of the building.

'Look!' Langdon said, pointing to the lone vehicle parked near the rear entrance. It was a large van. 'They're here.'

Simkins parked the SUV and killed the engine. Quietly, everyone got out and prepared to move in. Simkins stared up at the monolithic structure. 'You say the Temple Room is at the *top*?'

Langdon nodded, pointing all the way to the pinnacle of the building. 'That flat area on top of the pyramid is actually a skylight.'

Simkins spun back to Langdon. 'The Temple Room has a *skylight*?'

Langdon gave him an odd look. 'Of course. An oculus to heaven . . . directly above the altar.'

The UH-60 sat idling at Dupont Circle.

In the passenger seat, Sato gnawed at her fingernails, awaiting news from her team.

Finally, Simkins's voice crackled over the radio. 'Director?'

'Sato here,' she barked.

'We're entering the building, but I have some additional recon for you.'

'Go ahead.'

'Mr. Langdon just informed me that the room in which the target is most likely located has a very large skylight.'

Sato considered the information for several seconds. 'Understood. Thank you.'

Simkins signed off.

Sato spit out a fingernail and turned to the pilot. 'Take her up.'

121

Like any parent who had lost a child, Peter Solomon had often imagined how old his boy would be now . . . what he would look like . . . and what he would have become.

Peter Solomon now had his answers.

The massive tattooed creature before him had begun life as a tiny, precious infant . . . baby Zach curled up in a wicker bassinette . . . taking his first fumbling steps across Peter's study . . . learning to speak his first words. The fact that evil could spring from an innocent child in a loving family remained one of the paradoxes of the human soul. Peter had been forced to accept early on that although his own blood flowed in his son's veins, the heart pumping that blood was his son's own. Unique and singular . . . as if randomly chosen from the universe.

My son . . . he killed my mother, my friend Robert Langdon, and possibly my sister.

An icy numbness flooded Peter's heart as he searched his son's eyes for any connection . . . anything familiar. The man's eyes, however, although gray like Peter's, were those of a total stranger, filled with a hatred and a vengefulness that were almost otherworldly.

'Are you strong enough?' his son taunted, glancing at the Akedah knife gripped in Peter's hand. 'Can you finish what you started all those years ago?'

'Son . . .' Solomon barely recognized his own voice. 'I . . . I loved . . . you.'

'Twice you tried to kill me. You abandoned me in prison. You shot me on Zach's bridge. Now *finish* it!'

For an instant, Solomon felt like he was floating outside his own body. He no longer recognized himself. He was missing a hand, was totally bald, dressed in a black robe, sitting in a wheelchair, and clutching an ancient knife.

'Finish it!' the man shouted again, the tattoos on his naked chest rippling. 'Killing me is the only way you

594

can save Katherine . . . the only way to save your brotherhood!'

Solomon felt his gaze move to the laptop and cellular modem on the pigskin chair.

SENDING MESSAGE: 92% COMPLETE

His mind could not shake the images of Katherine bleeding to death . . . or of his Masonic brothers.

'There is still time,' the man whispered. 'You know it's the only choice. Release me from my mortal shell.'

'Please,' Solomon said. 'Don't do this . . .'

'*You* did this!' the man hissed. 'You forced your child to make an impossible choice! Do you remember that night? Wealth or wisdom? That was the night you pushed me away forever. But I've returned, Father . . . and tonight it is *your* turn to choose. Zachary or Katherine? Which will it be? Will you kill your son to save your sister? Will you kill your son to save your brotherhood? Your country? Or will you wait until it's too late? Until Katherine is dead . . . until the video is public . . . until you must live the rest of your life knowing you could have stopped these tragedies. Time is running out. You know what must be done.'

Peter's heart ached. *You are not Zachary,* he told himself. *Zachary died long, long ago. Whatever you are . . . and wherever you came from . . . you are not of me.* And although Peter Solomon did not believe his own words, he knew he had to make a choice.

He was out of time.

* * *

Find the Grand Staircase!

Robert Langdon dashed through darkened hallways, winding his way toward the center of the building. Turner Simkins remained close on his heels. As Langdon had hoped, he burst out into the building's main atrium.

Dominated by eight Doric columns of green granite, the atrium looked like a hybrid sepulcher – Greco-Roman-Egyptian – with black marble statues, chandelier fire bowls, Teutonic crosses, double-headed phoenix medallions, and sconces bearing the head of Hermes.

Langdon turned and ran toward the sweeping marble staircase at the far end of the atrium. 'This leads directly to the Temple Room,' he whispered as the two men ascended as quickly and quietly as possible.

On the first landing, Langdon came face-to-face with a bronze bust of Masonic luminary Albert Pike, along with the engraving of his most famous quote: WHAT WE HAVE DONE FOR OURSELVES ALONE DIES WITH US; WHAT WE HAVE DONE FOR OTHERS AND THE WORLD REMAINS AND IS IMMORTAL.

Mal'akh had sensed a palpable shift in the atmosphere of the Temple Room, as if all the frustration and pain Peter Solomon had ever felt was now boiling to the surface . . . focusing itself like a laser on Mal'akh.

Yes . . . it is time.

Peter Solomon had risen from his wheelchair and was standing now, facing the altar, gripping the knife.

'Save Katherine,' Mal'akh coaxed, luring him toward the altar, backing up, and finally laying his own body down on the white shroud he had prepared. 'Do what you need to do.'

As if moving through a nightmare, Peter inched forward.

Mal'akh reclined fully now onto his back, gazing up through the oculus at the wintry moon. *The secret is how to die.* This moment could not be any more perfect. *Adorned with the Lost Word of the ages, I offer myself by the left hand of my father.*

Mal'akh drew a deep breath.

Receive me, demons, for this is my body, which is offered for you.

Standing over Mal'akh, Peter Solomon was trembling. His tear-soaked eyes shone with desperation, indecision, anguish. He looked one last time toward the modem and laptop across the room.

'Make the choice,' Mal'akh whispered. 'Release me from my flesh. God wants this. *You* want this.' He laid his arms at his side and arched his chest forward, offering up his magnificent double-headed phoenix. *Help me shed the body that clothes my soul.*

Peter's tearful eyes seemed to be staring through Mal'akh now, not even seeing him.

'I killed your mother!' Mal'akh whispered. 'I killed Robert Langdon! I'm murdering your sister! I'm destroying your brotherhood! Do what you have to do!'

Peter Solomon's visage now contorted into a mask of absolute grief and regret. He threw his head back and screamed in anguish as he raised the knife.

Robert Langdon and Agent Simkins arrived breathless outside the Temple Room doors as a bloodcurdling scream erupted from within. It was Peter's voice. Langdon was certain.

Peter's cry was one of absolute agony.

I'm too late!

Ignoring Simkins, Langdon seized the handles and yanked open the doors. The horrific scene before him confirmed his worst fears. There, in the center of the dimly lit chamber, the silhouette of a man with a shaved head stood at the great altar. He wore a black robe, and his hand was clutching a large blade.

Before Langdon could move, the man was driving the knife down toward the body that lay outstretched on the altar.

Mal'akh had closed his eyes.

So beautiful. So perfect.

The ancient blade of the Akedah knife had glinted in the moonlight as it arched over him. Scented wisps of smoke had spiraled upward above him, preparing a pathway for his soon-to-be-liberated soul. His killer's lone scream of torment and desperation still rang through the sacred space as the knife came down.

I am besmeared with the blood of human sacrifice and parents' tears.

Mal'akh braced for the glorious impact.

His moment of transformation had arrived.

Incredibly, he felt no pain.

A thunderous vibration filled his body, deafening and deep. The room began shaking, and a brilliant white light blinded him from above. The heavens roared.

And Mal'akh knew it had happened.

Exactly as he had planned.

*   *   *

Langdon did not remember sprinting toward the altar as the helicopter appeared overhead. Nor did he remember leaping with his arms outstretched . . . soaring toward the man in the black robe . . . trying desperately to tackle him before he could plunge the knife down a second time.

Their bodies collided, and Langdon saw a bright light sweep down through the oculus and illuminate the altar. He expected to see the bloody body of Peter Solomon on the altar, but the naked chest that shone in the light had no blood on it at all . . . only a tapestry of tattoos. The knife lay broken beside him, apparently having been driven into the stone altar rather than into flesh.

As he and the man in the black robe crashed together onto the hard stone floor, Langdon saw the bandaged nub on the end of the man's right arm, and he realized to his bewilderment that he had just tackled Peter Solomon.

As they slid together across the stone floor, the helicopter's searchlights blazed down from above. The chopper thundered in low, its skids practically touching the expansive wall of glass.

On the front of the helicopter, a strange-looking gun rotated, aiming downward through the glass. The red beam of its laser scope sliced through the skylight and danced across the floor, directly toward Langdon and Solomon.

No!

But there was no gunfire from above . . . only the sound of the helicopter blades.

Langdon felt nothing but an eerie ripple of energy that shimmered through his cells. Behind his head, on the pigskin chair, the laptop hissed strangely. He spun in time to see its screen suddenly flash to black. Unfortunately, the last visible message had been clear.

SENDING MESSAGE: 100% COMPLETE

Pull up! Damn it! Up!

The UH-60 pilot threw his rotors into overdrive, trying to keep his skids from touching any part of the large glass skylight. He knew the six thousand pounds of lift force that surged downward from his rotors was already straining the glass to its breaking point. Unfortunately, the incline of the pyramid beneath the helicopter was efficiently shedding the thrust sideways, robbing him of lift.

Up! Now!

He tipped the nose, trying to skim away, but the left strut hit the center of the glass. It was only for an instant, but that was all it took.

The Temple Room's massive oculus exploded in a swirl of glass and wind . . . sending a torrent of jagged shards plummeting into the room below.

Stars falling from heaven.

Mal'akh stared up into the beautiful white light and saw a veil of shimmering jewels fluttering toward him . . . accelerating . . . as if racing to shroud him in their splendor.

Suddenly there was pain.

Everywhere.

Stabbing. Searing. Slashing. Razor-sharp knives piercing soft flesh. Chest, neck, thighs, face. His body tightened all at once, recoiling. His blood-filled mouth cried out as the pain ripped him from his trance. The white light above transformed itself, and suddenly, as if by magic, a dark helicopter was suspended above him, its thundering blades driving an icy wind down into the Temple Room, chilling Mal'akh to the core and dispersing the wisps of incense to the distant corners of the room.

Mal'akh turned his head and saw the Akedah knife lying broken by his side, smashed upon the granite altar, which was covered in a blanket of shattered glass. *Even after everything I did to him . . . Peter Solomon averted the knife. He refused to spill my blood.*

With welling horror, Mal'akh raised his head and peered down along the length of his own body. This living artifact was to have been his great offering. But it lay in tatters. His body was drenched in blood . . . huge shards of glass protruding from his flesh in all directions.

Weakly, Mal'akh lowered his head back to the granite altar and stared up through the open space in the roof. The helicopter was gone now, in its place a silent, wintry moon.

Wide-eyed, Mal'akh lay gasping for breath . . . all alone on the great altar.

122

The secret is how to die.

Mal'akh knew it had all gone wrong. There was no brilliant light. No wondrous reception. Only darkness and excruciating pain. Even in his eyes. He could see nothing, and yet he sensed movement all around him. There were voices . . . human voices . . . one of them, strangely, belonging to Robert Langdon. *How can this be?*

'She's okay,' Langdon kept repeating. 'Katherine is *fine*, Peter. Your sister is *okay*.'

No, Mal'akh thought. *Katherine is dead. She must be.*

Mal'akh could no longer see, could not tell if his eyes were even open, but he heard the helicopter banking away. An abrupt calm settled through the Temple Room. Mal'akh could feel the smooth rhythms of the earth becoming uneven . . . as if the ocean's natural tides were being disrupted by a gathering storm.

Chao ab ordo.

Unfamiliar voices were shouting now, talking urgently with Langdon about the laptop and video file. *It's too late*, Mal'akh knew. *The damage is done.* By now the video was spreading like wildfire into every corner of a shocked world, destroying the future of the brotherhood. *Those most capable of spreading the wisdom must be destroyed.* The ignorance of mankind is what helped the chaos grow. The absence of Light on earth is what nourished the Darkness that awaited Mal'akh.

I have done great deeds, and soon I will be received as a king.

Mal'akh sensed that a lone individual had quietly approached. He knew who it was. He could smell the sacred oils he had rubbed into his father's shaved body.

'I don't know if you can hear me,' Peter Solomon whispered in his ear. 'But I want you to know something.' He touched a finger to the sacred spot atop Mal'akh's skull. 'What you wrote here . . .' He paused. 'This is *not* the Lost Word.'

Of course it is, Mal'akh thought. *You convinced me of that beyond a doubt.*

According to legend, the Lost Word was written in a language so ancient and arcane that mankind had all but forgotten how to read it. This mysterious language, Peter had revealed, was in fact the oldest language on earth.

The language of symbols.

In the idiom of symbology, there was *one* symbol that reigned supreme above all others. The oldest and most universal, this symbol fused all the ancient traditions in a single solitary image that represented the illumination of the Egyptian sun god, the triumph of alchemical gold, the wisdom of the Philosopher's Stone, the purity of the Rosicrucian Rose, the moment of Creation, the All, the dominance of the astrological sun, and even the omniscient all-seeing eye that hovered atop the unfinished pyramid.

The circumpunct. The symbol of the Source. The origin of all things.

This is what Peter had told him moments ago. Mal'akh had been skeptical at first, but then he had looked again at the grid, realizing that the image of the pyramid was pointing *directly* at the lone symbol of the circumpunct – a circle with a dot in its center. *The Masonic Pyramid is a map,* he thought, recalling the legend, *which points to the Lost Word.* It seemed his father was telling the truth after all.

All great truths are simple.

The Lost Word is not a word . . . it is a symbol.

Eagerly, Mal'akh had inscribed the great symbol of the circumpunct on his scalp. As he did so, he felt an upwelling of power and satisfaction. *My masterpiece and offering are complete.* The forces of darkness were waiting for him now. He would be rewarded for his work. This was to be his moment of glory . . .

And yet, at the last instant, everything had gone horribly wrong.

Peter was still behind him now, speaking words that Mal'akh could barely fathom. 'I lied to you,' he was saying. 'You left me no choice. If I had revealed to you the true Lost Word, you would not have believed me, nor would you have understood.'

The Lost Word is . . . not the circumpunct?

'The truth is,' said Peter, 'the Lost Word is known to *all* . . . but recognized by very few.'

The words echoed in Mal'akh's mind.

'You remain incomplete,' Peter said, gently placing his palm on top of Mal'akh's head. 'Your work is not yet done. But wherever you are going, please know this . . . you were loved.'

For some reason, the gentle touch of his father's hand felt like it was burning through him like a potent catalyst that was initiating a chemical reaction inside Mal'akh's body. Without warning, he felt a rush of blistering energy surging through his physical shell, as if every cell in his body were now dissolving.

In an instant, all of his worldly pain evaporated.

Transformation. It's happening.

I am gazing down upon myself, a wreck of bloody flesh on the sacred slab of granite. My father is kneeling behind me, holding my lifeless head with his one remaining hand.

I feel an upwelling of rage . . . and confusion.

This is not a moment for compassion . . . it is for

revenge, for transformation . . . and yet still my father refuses to submit, refuses to fulfill his role, refuses to channel his pain and anger through the knife blade and into my heart.

I am trapped here, hovering . . . tethered to my earthly shell.

My father gently runs a soft palm across my face to close my fading eyes.

I feel the tether release.

A billowing veil materializes around me, thickening and dimming the light, hiding the world from view. Suddenly time accelerates, and I am plunging into an abyss far darker than any I have ever imagined. Here, in the barren void, I hear a whispering . . . I sense a gathering force. It strengthens, mounting at a startling rate, surrounding me. Ominous and powerful. Dark and commanding.

I am not alone here.

This is my triumph, my grand reception. And yet, for some reason, I am filled not with joy, but rather with boundless fear.

It is nothing like I expect.

The force is churning now, swirling around me with commanding strength, threatening to tear me apart. Suddenly, without warning, the blackness gathers itself like a great prehistoric beast and rears up before me.

I am facing all the dark souls who have gone before.

I am screaming in infinite terror . . . as the darkness swallows me whole.

Inside the National Cathedral, Dean Galloway sensed a strange change in the air. He was not sure why, but he felt as if a ghostly shadow had evaporated . . . as if a weight had been lifted . . . far away and yet right here.

Alone at his desk, he was deep in thought. He was not sure how many minutes had passed when his phone rang. It was Warren Bellamy.

'Peter's alive,' his Masonic brother said. 'I just heard the news. I knew you'd want to know immediately. He's going to be okay.'

'Thank God.' Galloway exhaled. 'Where is he?'

Galloway listened as Bellamy recounted the extraordinary tale of what had transpired after they had left Cathedral College.

'But all of you are okay?'

'Recuperating, yes,' Bellamy said. 'There is one thing, though.' He paused.

'Yes?'

'The Masonic Pyramid . . . I think Langdon may have solved it.'

Galloway had to smile. Somehow he was not surprised. 'And tell me, did Langdon discover whether or not the pyramid kept its promise? Whether or not it revealed what legend always claimed it would reveal?'

'I don't know yet.'

It will, Galloway thought. 'You need to rest.'

'As do you.'

No, I need to pray.

When the elevator door opened, the lights in the Temple Room were all ablaze.

Katherine Solomon's legs still felt rubbery as she hurried in to find her brother. The air in this enormous chamber was cold and smelled of incense. The scene that greeted her stopped her in her tracks.

In the center of this magnificent room, on a low stone altar, lay a bloody, tattooed corpse, a body perforated by spears of broken glass. High above, a gaping hole in the ceiling opened to the heavens.

My God. Katherine immediately looked away, her eyes scanning for Peter. She found her brother sitting on the other side of the room, being tended to by a medic while talking with Langdon and Director Sato.

'Peter!' Katherine called, running over. 'Peter!'

Her brother glanced up, his expression filling with relief. He was on his feet at once, moving toward her. He was wearing a simple white shirt and dark slacks, which someone had probably gotten for him from his office downstairs. His right arm was in a sling, and their gentle embrace was awkward, but Katherine barely noticed. A familiar comfort surrounded her like a cocoon, as it always had, even in childhood, when her protective older brother embraced her.

They held each other in silence.

Finally Katherine whispered, 'Are you okay? I mean . . . really?' She released him, looking down at the sling and bandage where his right hand used to be. Tears welled again in her eyes. 'I'm so . . . so sorry.'

Peter shrugged as if it were nothing of consequence.

'Mortal flesh. Bodies don't last forever. The important thing is that you're okay.'

Peter's lighthearted response tore at her emotions, reminding her of all the reasons she loved him. She stroked his head, feeling the unbreakable bonds of family . . . the shared blood that flowed in their veins.

Tragically, she knew there was a *third* Solomon in the room tonight. The corpse on the altar drew her gaze, and Katherine shuddered deeply, trying to block out the photos she had seen.

She looked away, her eyes now finding Robert Langdon's. There was compassion there, deep and perceptive, as if Langdon somehow knew exactly what she was thinking. *Peter knows*. Raw emotion gripped Katherine – relief, sympathy, despair. She felt her brother's body begin trembling like a child's. It was something she had never witnessed in her entire life.

'Just let it go,' she whispered. 'It's okay. Just let it go.'

Peter's trembling grew deeper.

She held him again, stroking the back of his head. 'Peter, you've *always* been the strong one . . . you've *always* been there for me. But I'm here for *you* now. It's okay. I'm right here.'

Katherine eased his head gently onto her shoulder . . . and the great Peter Solomon collapsed sobbing in her arms.

Director Sato stepped away to take an incoming call.

It was Nola Kaye. Her news, for a change, was good.

'Still no signs of distribution, ma'am.' She sounded

hopeful. 'I'm confident we would have seen something by now. It looks like you contained it.'

Thanks to you, Nola, Sato thought, glancing down at the laptop, which Langdon had seen complete its transmission. *A very close call.*

At Nola's suggestion, the agent searching the mansion had checked the garbage cans, discovering packaging for a newly purchased cellular modem. With the exact model number, Nola had been able to cross-reference compatible carriers, bandwidths, and service grids, isolating the laptop's most likely access node – a small transmitter on the corner of Sixteenth and Corcoran – three blocks from the Temple.

Nola quickly relayed the information to Sato in the helicopter. On approach toward the House of the Temple, the pilot had performed a low-altitude flyover and pulsed the relay node with a blast of electro-magnetic radiation, knocking it off-line only seconds before the laptop completed its transfer.

'Great work tonight,' Sato said. 'Now get some sleep. You've earned it.'

'Thank you, ma'am.' Nola hesitated.

'Was there something else?'

Nola was silent a long moment, apparently considering whether or not to speak. 'Nothing that can't wait till morning, ma'am. Have a good night.'

125

In the silence of an elegant bathroom on the ground floor of the House of the Temple, Robert Langdon ran warm water into a tile sink and eyed himself in the mirror. Even in the muted light, he looked like he felt . . . utterly spent.

His daybag was on his shoulder again, much lighter now . . . empty except for his personal items and some crumpled lecture notes. He had to chuckle. His visit to D.C. tonight to give a lecture had turned out a bit more grueling than he'd anticipated.

Even so, Langdon had a lot to be grateful for.

Peter is alive.

And the video was contained.

As Langdon scooped handfuls of warm water onto his face, he gradually felt himself coming back to life. Everything was still a blur, but the adrenaline in his body was finally dissipating . . . and he was feeling like himself again. After drying his hands, he checked his Mickey Mouse watch.

My God, it's late.

Langdon exited the bathroom and wound his way along the curved wall of the Hall of Honor – a gracefully arched passageway, lined with portraits of accomplished Masons . . . U.S. presidents, philanthropists, luminaries, and other influential Americans. He paused at an oil painting of Harry S. Truman and tried to imagine the man undergoing the rites, rituals, and studies required to become a Mason.

There is a hidden world behind the one we all see. For all of us.

'You slipped away,' a voice said down the hall.

Langdon turned.

It was Katherine. She'd been through hell tonight, and yet she looked suddenly radiant . . . rejuvenated somehow.

Langdon gave a tired smile. 'How's he doing?'

Katherine walked up and embraced him warmly. 'How can I ever thank you?'

He laughed. 'You know I didn't *do* anything, right?'

Katherine held him for a long time. 'Peter's going to be fine . . .' She let go and looked deep into Langdon's eyes. 'And he just told me something incredible . . . something *wonderful*.' Her voice trembled with anticipation. 'I need to go see it for myself. I'll be back in a bit.'

'What? Where are you going?'

'I won't be long. Right now, Peter wants to speak with you . . . *alone*. He's waiting in the library.'

'Did he say why?'

Katherine chuckled and shook her head. 'You know Peter and his secrets.'

'But—'

'I'll see you in a bit.'

Then she was gone.

Langdon sighed heavily. He felt like he'd had enough secrets for one night. There were unanswered questions, of course – the Masonic Pyramid and the Lost Word among them – but he sensed that the answers, if they even existed, were not for him. *Not as a non-Mason.*

Mustering the last of his energy, Langdon made his way to the Masonic library. When he arrived, Peter was sitting all alone at a table with the stone pyramid before him.

'Robert?' Peter smiled and waved him in. 'I'd like a word.'

Langdon managed a grin. 'Yes, I hear you *lost* one.'

126

The library in the House of the Temple was D.C.'s oldest public reading room. Its elegant stacks burgeoned with over a quarter of a million volumes, including a rare copy of the *Ahiman Rezon, The Secrets of a Prepared Brother*. In addition, the library displayed precious Masonic jewels, ritual artifacts, and even a rare volume that had been hand-printed by Benjamin Franklin.

Langdon's favorite library treasure, however, was one few ever noticed.

The illusion.

Solomon had shown him long ago that from the proper vantage point, the library's reading desk and golden table lamp created an unmistakable optical illusion . . . that of a pyramid and shining golden capstone. Solomon said he always considered the illusion a silent reminder that the mysteries of Freemasonry were perfectly visible to anyone and everyone if they were seen from the proper perspective.

Tonight, however, the mysteries of Freemasonry had materialized front and center. Langdon now sat opposite the Worshipful Master Peter Solomon and the Masonic Pyramid.

Peter was smiling. 'The "word" you refer to, Robert, is not a legend. It is a *reality*.'

Langdon stared across the table and finally spoke. 'But . . . I don't understand. How is that possible?'

'What is so difficult to accept?'

All of it! Langdon wanted to say, searching his old friend's eyes for any hint of common sense. 'You're saying you believe the Lost Word is *real* . . . and that it has actual *power*?'

'Enormous power,' Peter said. 'It has the power to transform humankind by unlocking the Ancient Mysteries.'

'A *word*?' Langdon challenged. 'Peter, I can't possibly believe a word—'

'You *will* believe,' Peter stated calmly.

Langdon stared in silence.

'As you know,' Solomon continued, standing now and pacing around the table, 'it has long been prophesied that there will come a day when the Lost Word will be rediscovered . . . a day when it will be unearthed . . . and mankind will once again have access to its forgotten power.'

Langdon flashed on Peter's lecture about the Apocalypse. Although many people erroneously interpreted *apocalypse* as a cataclysmic end of the world, the word literally signified an 'unveiling,' predicted by the ancients to be that of great wisdom. *The coming age of enlightenment.* Even so, Langdon could not imagine such a vast change being ushered in by . . . a word.

Peter motioned to the stone pyramid, which sat on the table beside its golden capstone. 'The Masonic Pyramid,' he said. 'The legendary symbolon. Tonight it stands unified . . . and complete.' Reverently, he lifted the golden capstone and set it atop the pyramid. The heavy gold piece clicked softly into place.

'Tonight, my friend, you have done what has never been done before. You have assembled the Masonic Pyramid, deciphered all of its codes, and in the end, unveiled . . . *this*.'

Solomon produced a sheet of paper and laid it on the table. Langdon recognized the grid of symbols that had been reorganized using the Order Eight Franklin

Square. He had studied it briefly in the Temple Room.

Peter said, 'I am curious to know if you can *read* this array of symbols. After all, you are the specialist.'

Langdon eyed the grid.

Heredom, circumpunct, pyramid, staircase . . .

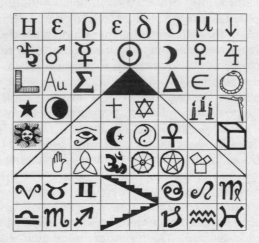

Langdon sighed. 'Well, Peter, as you can probably see, this is an allegorical pictogram. Clearly its language is metaphorical and symbolic rather than literal.'

Solomon chuckled. 'Ask a symbologist a simple question . . . Okay, tell me what you see.'

Peter really wants to hear this? Langdon pulled the page toward him. 'Well, I looked at it earlier, and, in simple terms, I see that this grid is a *picture* . . . depicting heaven and earth.'

Peter arched his eyebrows, looking surprised. 'Oh?'

'Sure. At the top of the image, we have the word *Heredom* – the "Holy House" – which I interpret as the House of God . . . or *heaven*.'

'Okay.'

'The downward-facing *arrow* after *Heredom* signifies that the *rest* of the pictogram clearly lies in the realm *beneath* heaven . . . that being . . . *earth*.' Langdon's eyes glided now to the bottom of the grid. 'The lowest two rows, those *beneath* the pyramid, represent the earth itself – terra firma – the lowest of all the realms. Fittingly, these lower realms contain the twelve ancient *astrological* signs, which represent the primordial religion of those first human souls who looked to the heavens and saw the hand of God in the movement of the stars and planets.'

Solomon slid his chair closer and studied the grid. 'Okay, what else?'

'On a foundation of astrology,' Langdon continued, 'the great pyramid rises from the earth . . . stretching toward heaven . . . the enduring symbol of lost wisdom. It is filled with history's great philosophies and religions . . . Egyptian, Pythagorean, Buddhist, Hindu, Islamic, Judeo-Christian, and on and on . . . all flowing upward, merging together, funneling themselves up through the transformative gateway of the pyramid . . . where they finally fuse into a single, unified human philosophy.' He paused. 'A single universal consciousness . . . a shared global vision of God . . . represented by the ancient symbol that hovers over the capstone.'

'The circumpunct,' Peter said. 'A universal symbol for God.'

'Right. Throughout history, the circumpunct has

been *all* things to *all* people – it is the sun god Ra, alchemical gold, the all-seeing eye, the singularity point before the Big Bang, the—'

'The Great Architect of the Universe.'

Langdon nodded, sensing this was probably the same argument Peter had used in the Temple Room to sell the idea of the circumpunct as the Lost Word.

'And finally?' Peter asked. 'What about the staircase?'

Langdon glanced down at the image of the stairs beneath the pyramid. 'Peter, I'm sure you know as well as anyone, this symbolizes the Winding Staircase of Freemasonry . . . leading upward out of the earthly darkness into the light . . . like Jacob's ladder climbing to heaven . . . or the tiered human spine that connects man's mortal body to his eternal mind.' He paused. 'As for the *rest* of the symbols, they appear to be a blend of celestial, Masonic, and scientific, all lending support to the Ancient Mysteries.'

Solomon stroked his chin. 'An elegant interpretation, Professor. I agree, of course, that this grid can be read as allegory, and yet . . .' His eyes flashed with deepening mystery. 'This collection of symbols tells another story as well. A story that is far more revealing.'

'Oh?'

Solomon began pacing again, circling the table. 'Earlier tonight, inside the Temple Room, when I believed I was going to die, I looked at this grid, and somehow I saw *past* the metaphor, *past* the allegory, into the very heart of what these symbols are telling us.' He paused, turning abruptly to Langdon. 'This grid reveals the *exact* location where the Lost Word is buried.'

'Come again?' Langdon shifted uneasily in his chair, suddenly fearing that the trauma of the evening had left Peter disorientated and confused.

'Robert, legend has *always* described the Masonic Pyramid as a map – a very *specific* map – a map that could guide the worthy to the secret location of the Lost Word.' Solomon tapped the grid of symbols in front of Langdon. 'I guarantee you, these symbols are exactly what legend says they are . . . a *map*. A specific diagram that reveals exactly where we will find the staircase that leads down to the Lost Word.'

Langdon gave an uneasy laugh, treading carefully now. 'Even if I believed the Legend of the Masonic Pyramid, this grid of symbols can't possibly be a map. Look at it. It looks *nothing* like a map.'

Solomon smiled. 'Sometimes all it takes is a tiny shift of perspective to see something familiar in a totally new light.'

Langdon looked again but saw nothing new.

'Let me ask you a question,' Peter said. 'When Masons lay cornerstones, do you know why we lay them in the northeast corner of a building?'

'Sure, because the northeast corner receives the first rays of morning light. It is symbolic of the power of architecture to climb out of the earth into the light.'

'Right,' Peter said. 'So perhaps you should look *there* for the first rays of light.' He motioned to the grid. 'In the northeast corner.'

Langdon returned his eyes to the page, moving his gaze to the upper right or northeast corner. The symbol in that corner was ↓.

'A downward-pointing arrow,' Langdon said, trying to grasp Solomon's point. 'Which means . . . *beneath* Heredom.'

'No, Robert, not *beneath*,' Solomon replied. 'Think. This grid is not a metaphorical maze. It's a *map*. And on a map, a directional arrow that points *down* means—'

'South,' Langdon exclaimed, startled.

'Exactly!' Solomon replied, grinning now with excitement. 'Due south! On a map, *down* is south. Moreover, on a map, the word *Heredom* would not be a metaphor for heaven, it would be the name of a geographic location.'

'The House of the Temple? You're saying this map is pointing . . . due south of this building?'

'Praise God!' Solomon said, laughing. 'Light dawns at last.'

Langdon studied the grid. 'But, Peter . . . even if you're right, due south of this building could be *anywhere* on a longitude that's over twenty-four thousand miles long.'

'No, Robert. You are ignoring the legend, which claims the Lost Word is buried in D.C. That shortens the line substantially. In addition, legend *also* claims that a large stone sits atop the opening of the staircase . . . and that this stone is engraved with a message in an ancient language . . . as a kind of *marker* so the worthy can find it.'

Langdon was having trouble taking any of this seriously, and while he didn't know D.C. well enough to picture what was due south of their current location, he was pretty certain there was no huge engraved stone atop a buried staircase.

'The message inscribed on the stone,' Peter said, 'is right here before our eyes.' He tapped the third row of the grid before Langdon. '*This* is the inscription, Robert! You've solved the puzzle!'

Dumbfounded, Langdon studied the seven symbols.

Solved? Langdon had no idea whatsoever what these seven disparate symbols could possibly mean, and he was damned sure they were *not* engraved anywhere in the nation's capital . . . particularly on a giant stone over a staircase.

'Peter,' he said, 'I don't see how this sheds any light at all. I know of no stone in D.C. engraved with this . . . message.'

Solomon patted him on the shoulder. 'You have walked past it and never seen it. We *all* have. It is sitting in plain view, like the mysteries themselves. And tonight, when I saw these seven symbols, I realized in an instant that the legend was true. The Lost Word *is* buried in D.C. . . . and it *does* rest at the bottom of a long staircase beneath an enormous engraved stone.'

Mystified, Langdon remained silent.

'Robert, tonight I believe you have earned the right to know the truth.'

Langdon stared at Peter, trying to process what he had just heard. 'You're going to *tell* me where the Lost Word is buried?'

'No,' Solomon said, standing up with a smile. 'I'm going to *show* you.'

Five minutes later, Langdon was buckling himself into the backseat of the Escalade beside Peter Solomon.

Simkins climbed in behind the wheel as Sato approached across the parking lot.

'Mr. Solomon?' the director said, lighting a cigarette as she arrived. 'I've just made the call you requested.'

'And?' Peter asked through his open window.

'I ordered them to give you access. Briefly.'

'Thank you.'

Sato studied him, looking curious. 'I must say, it's a most unusual request.'

Solomon gave an enigmatic shrug.

Sato let it go, circling around to Langdon's window and rapping with her knuckles.

Langdon lowered the window.

'Professor,' she said, with no hint of warmth. 'Your assistance tonight, while reluctant, was critical to our success . . . and for that, I thank you.' She took a long drag on her cigarette and blew it sideways. '*However*, one final bit of advice. The next time a senior administrator of the CIA tells you she has a national-security crisis . . .' Her eyes flashed black. 'Leave the bullshit in Cambridge.'

Langdon opened his mouth to speak, but Director Inoue Sato had already turned and was headed off across the parking lot toward a waiting helicopter.

Simkins glanced over his shoulder, stone-faced. 'Are you gentlemen ready?'

'Actually,' Solomon said, 'just one moment.' He produced a small, folded piece of dark fabric and handed it to Langdon. 'Robert, I'd like you to put this on before we go anywhere.'

Puzzled, Langdon examined the cloth. It was black velvet. As he unfolded it, he realized he was holding a Masonic hoodwink – the traditional blindfold of a first-degree initiate. *What the hell?*

Peter said, 'I'd prefer you not see where we're going.'

Langdon turned to Peter. 'You want to *blindfold* me for the journey?'

Solomon grinned. 'My secret. My rules.'

127

The breeze felt cold outside CIA headquarters in Langley. Nola Kaye was shivering as she followed syssec Rick Parrish across the agency's moonlit central courtyard.

Where is Rick taking me?

The crisis of the Masonic video had been averted, thank God, but Nola still felt uneasy. The redacted file on the CIA director's partition remained a mystery, and it was nagging at her. She and Sato would debrief in the morning, and Nola wanted all the facts. Finally, she had called Rick Parrish and demanded his help.

Now, as she followed Rick to some unknown location outside, Nola could not push the bizarre phrases from her memory:

Secret location underground *where the . . . somewhere in* Washington, D.C., *the coordinates . . . uncovered an* ancient portal *that led . . . warning the* pyramid *holds dangerous . . . decipher this* engraved symbolon *to unveil . . .*

'You and I agree,' Parrish said as they walked, 'that the hacker who spidered those keywords was definitely searching for information about the Masonic Pyramid.'

Obviously, Nola thought.

'It turns out, though, the hacker stumbled onto a facet of the Masonic mystery I don't think he expected.'

'What do you mean?'

'Nola, you know how the CIA director sponsors an internal discussion forum for Agency employees to share their ideas about all kinds of things?'

'Of course.' The forums provided Agency personnel a safe place to chat online about various topics and gave the director a kind of virtual gateway to his staff.

'The director's forums are hosted on his private partition, and yet in order to provide access to employees of all clearance levels, they're located *outside* the director's classified firewall.'

'What are you getting at?' she demanded as they rounded a corner near the Agency cafeteria.

'In a word . . .' Parrish pointed into the darkness. *'That.'*

Nola glanced up. Across the plaza in front of them was a massive metal sculpture glimmering in the moonlight.

In an agency that boasted over five hundred pieces of original art, this sculpture – titled *Kryptos* – was by far the most famous. Greek for 'hidden,' *Kryptos* was the work of American artist James Sanborn and had become something of a legend here at the CIA.

The work consisted of a massive S-shaped panel of copper, set on its edge like a curling metal wall. Engraved into the expansive surface of the wall were nearly two thousand letters . . . organized into a baffling code. As if this were not enigmatic enough, positioned carefully in the area around the encrypted S-wall were numerous other sculptural elements –

granite slabs at odd angles, a compass rose, a magnetic lodestone, and even a message in Morse code that referenced 'lucid memory' and 'shadow forces.' Most fans believed that these pieces were clues that would reveal how to decipher the sculpture.

Kryptos was art . . . but it was also an enigma.

Attempting to decipher its encoded secret had become an obsession for cryptologists both inside and outside the CIA. Finally, a few years back, a portion of the code had been broken, and it became national news. Although much of *Kryptos*'s code remained unsolved to this day, the sections that *had* been deciphered were so bizarre that they made the sculpture only more mysterious. It referenced secret underground locations, portals that led into ancient tombs, longitudes and latitudes . . .

Nola could still recall bits and pieces of the deciphered sections: *The information was gathered and transmitted underground to an unknown location . . . It was totally invisible . . . hows that possible . . . they used the earths magnetic field . . .*

Nola had never paid much attention to the sculpture or cared if it was ever fully deciphered. At the moment, however, she wanted answers. 'Why are you showing me *Kryptos*?'

Parrish gave her a conspiratorial smile and dramatically extracted a folded sheet of paper from his pocket. 'Voilà, the mysterious redacted document you were so concerned about. I accessed the complete text.'

Nola jumped. 'You snooped the director's classified partition?'

'No. That's what I was getting at earlier. Have a look.' He handed her the file.

Nola seized the page and unfolded it. When she saw

the standard Agency headers at the top of the page, she cocked her head in surprise.

This document was *not* classified. Not even close.

EMPLOYEE DISCUSSION BOARD: KRYPTOS
COMPRESSED STORAGE: THREAD #2456282.5

Nola found herself looking at a series of postings that had been compressed into a single page for more efficient storage.

'Your keyword document,' Rick said, 'is some cipher-punks rambling about *Kryptos*.'

Nola scanned down the document until she spotted a sentence containing a familiar set of keywords.

> Jim, the sculpture says it was transmitted to a
> *secret location UNDERGROUND where the*
> *info was hidden.*

'This text is from the director's online Kryptos forum,' Rick explained. 'The forum's been going for years. There are literally thousands of postings. I'm not surprised one of them happened to contain all the keywords.'

Nola kept scanning down until she spotted another posting containing keywords.

> Even though Mark said the code's lat/long
> headings point somewhere in WASHINGTON,
> D.C., the coordinates he used were off by one
> degree--Kryptos basically points back to itself.

Parrish walked over to the statue and ran his palm across the cryptic sea of letters. 'A lot of this code has yet to be deciphered, and there are plenty of people who think the message might actually relate to ancient Masonic secrets.'

Nola now recalled murmurs of a Masonic/*Kryptos* link, but she tended to ignore the lunatic fringe. Then again, looking around at the various pieces of the sculpture arranged around the plaza, she realized that it was a code in pieces – a symbolon – just like the Masonic Pyramid.

Odd.

For a moment, Nola could almost see *Kryptos* as a modern Masonic Pyramid – a code in many pieces, made of different materials, each playing a role. 'Do you think there's any way *Kryptos* and the Masonic Pyramid might be hiding the same secret?'

'Who knows?' Parrish shot *Kryptos* a frustrated look. 'I doubt we'll *ever* know the whole message. That is, unless someone can convince the director to unlock his safe and sneak a peek at the solution.'

Nola nodded. It was all coming back to her now. When *Kryptos* was installed, it arrived with a sealed envelope containing a complete decryption of the sculpture's codes. The sealed solution was entrusted to then-CIA director William Webster, who locked it in his office safe. The document was allegedly still there, having been transferred from director to director over the years.

Strangely, Nola's thoughts of William Webster sparked her memory, bringing back yet another portion of *Kryptos*'s deciphered text:

> IT'S BURIED OUT THERE SOMEWHERE.
> WHO KNOWS THE EXACT LOCATION?
> ONLY WW.

Although nobody knew exactly *what* was buried out there, most people believed the *WW* was a reference to William Webster. Nola had heard whispers once that it referred in fact to a man named William Whiston – a Royal Society theologian – although she had never bothered to give it much thought.

Rick was talking again. 'I've got to admit, I'm not really into artists, but I think this guy Sanborn's a serious genius. I was just looking online at his *Cyrillic Projector* project? It shines giant Russian letters from a KGB document on mind control. Freaky.'

Nola was no longer listening. She was examining the paper, where she had found the third key phrase in another posting.

> Right, that whole section is verbatim from
> some famous archaeologist's diary, telling
> about the moment he dug down and
> <u>uncovered an ANCIENT PORTAL that led</u> to
> the tomb of Tutankhamen.

The archaeologist who was quoted on *Kryptos*, Nola knew, was in fact famed Egyptologist Howard Carter. The next posting referenced him by name.

> I just skimmed the rest of Carter's field notes
> online, and it sounds like he found a clay
> tablet <u>warning the PYRAMID holds</u>
> <u>dangerous</u> consequences for anyone who
> disturbs the peace of the pharaoh. A curse!
> Should we be worried? ☺

Nola scowled. 'Rick, for God's sake, this idiot's pyramid reference isn't even right. Tutankhamen wasn't buried in a *pyramid*. He was buried in the Valley of the Kings. Don't cryptologists watch the Discovery Channel?'

Parrish shrugged. 'Techies.'

Nola now saw the final key phrase.

> Guys, you know I'm not a conspiracy theorist, but Jim and Dave had better <u>decipher this ENGRAVED SYMBOLON to unveil</u> its final secret before the world ends in 2012 . . . Ciao.

'Anyhow,' Parrish said, 'I figured you'd want to know about the Kryptos forum before you accused the CIA director of harboring classified documentation about an ancient Masonic legend. Somehow, I doubt a man as powerful as the CIA director has time for that sort of thing.'

Nola pictured the Masonic video and its images of all the influential men participating in an ancient rite. *If Rick had any idea . . .*

In the end, she knew, whatever *Kryptos* ultimately revealed, the message definitely had mystical undertones. She gazed up at the gleaming piece of art – a three-dimensional code standing silently at the heart of one of the nation's premier intelligence agencies – and she wondered if it would ever give up its final secret.

As she and Rick headed back inside, Nola had to smile.

It's buried out there somewhere.

128

This is crazy.

Blindfolded, Robert Langdon could see nothing as the Escalade sped southward along the deserted streets. On the seat beside him, Peter Solomon remained silent.

Where is he taking me?

Langdon's curiosity was a mix of intrigue and apprehension, his imagination in overdrive as it tried desperately to put the pieces together. Peter had not wavered from his claim. *The Lost Word? Buried at the bottom of a staircase that's covered by a massive, engraved stone?* It all seemed impossible.

The stone's alleged engraving was still lodged in Langdon's memory . . . and yet the seven symbols, as far as he could tell, made no sense together at all.

The Stonemason's Square: the symbol of honesty and being 'true.'

The letters Au: *the scientific abbreviation for the element gold.*

The Sigma: the Greek letter S, the mathematical symbol for the sum of all parts.

The Pyramid: the Egyptian symbol of man reaching heavenward.

The Delta: the Greek letter D, the mathematical symbol for change.

Mercury: as depicted by its most ancient alchemical symbol.

The Ouroboros: the symbol of wholeness and at-one-ment.

Solomon still insisted these seven symbols were a 'message.' But if this was true, then it was a message Langdon had no idea how to read.

The Escalade slowed suddenly and turned sharply right, onto a different surface, as if into a driveway or access road. Langdon perked up, listening intently for clues as to their whereabouts. They'd been driving for less than ten minutes, and although Langdon had tried to follow in his mind, he had lost his bearings quickly. For all he knew, they were now pulling back into the House of the Temple.

The Escalade came to a stop, and Langdon heard the window roll down.

'Agent Simkins, CIA,' their driver announced. 'I believe you're expecting us.'

'Yes, sir,' a sharp military voice replied. 'Director Sato phoned ahead. One moment while I move the security barricade.'

Langdon listened with rising confusion, now sensing they were entering a military base. As the car began moving again, along an unusually smooth stretch of pavement, he turned his head blindly toward Solomon. 'Where are we, Peter?' he demanded.

'Do *not* remove your blindfold.' Peter's voice was stern.

The vehicle continued a short distance and again slowed to a stop. Simkins killed the engine. More voices. Military. Someone asked for Simkins's identification. The agent got out and spoke to the men in hushed tones.

Langdon's door was suddenly being opened, and powerful hands assisted him out of the car. The air felt cold. It was windy.

Solomon was beside him. 'Robert, just let Agent Simkins lead you inside.'

Langdon heard metal keys in a lock . . . and then the creak of a heavy iron door swinging open. It sounded like an ancient bulkhead. *Where the hell are they taking me?!*

Simkins's hands guided Langdon in the direction of the metal door. They stepped over a threshold. 'Straight ahead, Professor.'

It was suddenly quiet. Dead. Deserted. The air inside smelled sterile and processed.

Simkins and Solomon flanked Langdon now, guiding him blindly down a reverberating corridor. The floor felt like stone beneath his loafers.

Behind them, the metal door slammed loudly, and Langdon jumped. The locks turned. He was sweating now beneath his blindfold. He wanted only to tear it off.

They stopped walking now.

Simkins let go of Langdon's arm, and there was a series of electronic beeps followed by an unexpected rumble in front of them, which Langdon imagined had to be a security door sliding open automatically.

'Mr. Solomon, you and Mr. Langdon continue on alone. I'll wait for you here,' Simkins said. 'Take my flashlight.'

'Thank you,' Solomon said. 'We won't be long.'

Flashlight?! Langdon's heart was pounding wildly now.

Peter took Langdon's arm in his own and inched forward. 'Walk with me, Robert.'

They moved slowly together across another threshold, and the security door rumbled shut behind them.

Peter stopped short. 'Is something wrong?'

Langdon was suddenly feeling queasy and off balance. 'I think I just need to take off this blindfold.'

'Not yet, we're almost there.'

'Almost *where*?' Langdon felt a growing heaviness in the pit of his stomach.

'I told you – I'm taking you to see the staircase that descends to the Lost Word.'

'Peter, this isn't funny!'

'It's not *meant* to be. It's meant to open your mind, Robert. It's meant to remind you that there are mysteries in this world that even *you* have yet to lay eyes upon. And before I take one more step with you, I want you to do something for me. I want you to *believe* . . . just for an instant . . . *believe* in the legend. Believe that you are about to peer down a winding staircase that plunges hundreds of feet to one of humankind's greatest lost treasures.'

Langdon felt dizzy. As much as he wanted to believe his dear friend, he could not. 'Is it much farther?' His velvet hoodwink was drenched in sweat.

'No. Only a few more steps, actually. Through one last door. I'll open it now.'

Solomon let go of him for a moment, and as he did so, Langdon swayed, feeling light-headed. Unsteady, he reached out for stability, and Peter was quickly back at his side. The sound of a heavy automatic door rumbled in front of them. Peter took Langdon's arm and they moved forward again.

'This way.'

They inched across another threshold, and the door slid closed behind them.

Silence. Cold.

Langdon immediately sensed that this place,

whatever it was, had nothing to do with the world on the other side of the security doors. The air was dank and chilly, like a tomb. The acoustics felt dull and cramped. He felt an irrational bout of claustrophobia settling in.

'A few more steps.' Solomon guided him blindly around a corner and positioned him precisely. Finally, he said, 'Take off your blindfold.'

Langdon seized the velvet hoodwink and tore it from his face. He looked all around to find out where he was, but he was still blind. He rubbed his eyes. Nothing. 'Peter, it's pitch-black!'

'Yes, I know. Reach in front of you. There's a railing. Grasp it.'

Langdon groped in the darkness and found an iron railing.

'Now watch.' He could hear Peter fumbling with something, and suddenly a blazing flashlight beam pierced the darkness. It was pointed at the floor, and before Langdon could take in his surroundings, Solomon directed the flashlight out over the railing and pointed the beam straight down.

Langdon was suddenly staring into a bottomless shaft . . . an endless winding staircase that plunged deep into the earth. *My God!* His knees nearly buckled, and he gripped the railing for support. The staircase was a traditional square spiral, and he could see at least thirty landings descending into the earth before the flashlight faded to nothing. *I can't even see the bottom!*

'Peter . . .' he stammered. 'What *is* this place!'

'I'll take you to the bottom of the staircase in a moment, but before I do, you need to see something else.'

Too overwhelmed to protest, Langdon let Peter

guide him away from the stairwell and across the strange little chamber. Peter kept the flashlight trained on the worn stone floor beneath their feet, and Langdon could get no real sense of the space around them . . . except that it was small.

A tiny stone chamber.

They arrived quickly at the room's opposite wall, in which was embedded a rectangle of glass. Langdon thought it might be a window into a room beyond, and yet from where he stood, he saw only darkness on the other side.

'Go ahead,' Peter said. 'Have a look.'

'What's in there?' Langdon flashed for an instant on the Chamber of Reflection beneath the Capitol Building, and how he had believed, for a moment, that it might contain a portal to some giant underground cavern.

'Just look, Robert.' Solomon inched him forward. 'And brace yourself, because the sight *will* shock you.'

Having no idea what to expect, Langdon moved toward the glass. As he neared the portal, Peter turned out the flashlight, plunging the tiny chamber into total darkness.

As his eyes adjusted, Langdon groped in front of him, his hands finding the wall, finding the glass, his face moving closer to the transparent portal.

Still only darkness beyond.

He leaned closer . . . pressing his face to the glass.

Then he saw it.

The wave of shock and disorientation that tore through Langdon's body reached down inside and spun his internal compass upside down. He nearly fell backward as his mind strained to accept the utterly unanticipated sight that was before him. In his wildest dreams, Robert Langdon would never have guessed what lay on the other side of this glass.

The vision was a glorious sight.

There in the darkness, a brilliant white light shone like a gleaming jewel.

Langdon now understood it all – the barricade on the access road . . . the guards at the main entrance . . . the heavy metal door outside . . . the automatic doors that rumbled open and closed . . . the heaviness in his stomach . . . the lightness in his head . . . and now this tiny stone chamber.

'Robert,' Peter whispered behind him, 'sometimes a change of perspective is all it takes to see the light.'

Speechless, Langdon stared out through the window. His gaze traveled into the darkness of the night, traversing more than a mile of empty space, dropping lower . . . lower . . . through the darkness . . . until it came to rest atop the brilliantly illuminated, stark white dome of the U.S. Capitol Building.

Langdon had never seen the Capitol from this perspective – hovering 555 feet in the air atop America's great Egyptian obelisk. Tonight, for the first time in his life, he had ridden the elevator up to the tiny viewing chamber . . . at the pinnacle of the Washington Monument.

129

Robert Langdon stood mesmerized at the glass portal, absorbing the power of the landscape below him.

Having ascended unknowingly hundreds of feet into the air, he was now admiring one of the most spectacular vistas he had ever seen.

The shining dome of the U.S. Capitol rose like a mountain at the east end of the National Mall. On either side of the building, two parallel lines of light stretched toward him . . . the illuminated facades of the Smithsonian museums . . . beacons of art, history, science, culture.

Langdon now realized to his astonishment that much of what Peter had declared to be true . . . was in fact true. *There is indeed a winding staircase . . . descending hundreds of feet beneath a massive stone.* The huge capstone of this obelisk sat directly over his head, and Langdon now recalled a forgotten bit of trivia that seemed to have eerie relevance: the capstone of the Washington Monument weighed precisely thirty-three hundred pounds.

Again, the number 33.

More startling, however, was the knowledge that this capstone's ultimate peak, the zenith of this obelisk, was crowned by a tiny, polished tip of aluminum – a metal as precious as gold in its day. The shining apex of the Washington Monument was only about a foot tall, the same size as the Masonic Pyramid. Incredibly, this small metal pyramid bore a famous engraving – *Laus Deo* – and Langdon suddenly understood. *This is the true message of the base of the stone pyramid.*

The seven symbols are a transliteration!

The simplest of ciphers.
The symbols are letters.

> *The stonemason's square – L*
> *The element gold – AU*
> *The Greek Sigma – S*
> *The Greek Delta – D*
> *Alchemical mercury – E*
> *The Ouroboros – O*

'Laus Deo,' Langdon whispered. The well-known Latin phrase – meaning 'praise God' – was inscribed on the tip of the Washington Monument in script letters only one inch tall. *On full display . . . and yet invisible to all.*

Laus Deo.

'Praise God,' Peter said behind him, flipping on the soft lighting in the chamber. 'The Masonic Pyramid's final code.'

Langdon turned. His friend was grinning broadly, and Langdon recalled that Peter had actually *spoken* the words 'praise God' earlier inside the Masonic library. *And I still missed it.*

Langdon felt a chill to realize how apt it was that the legendary Masonic Pyramid had guided him *here* . . . to America's great obelisk – the symbol of ancient mystical wisdom – rising toward the heavens at the heart of a nation.

In a state of wonder, Langdon began moving counterclockwise around the perimeter of the tiny square room, arriving now at another viewing window.

North.

Through this northward-facing window, Langdon gazed down at the familiar silhouette of the White

House directly in front of him. He raised his eyes to the horizon, where the straight line of Sixteenth Street ran due north toward the House of the Temple.

I am due south of Heredom.

He continued around the perimeter to the next window. Looking west, Langdon's eyes traced the long rectangle of the reflecting pool to the Lincoln Memorial, its classical Greek architecture inspired by the Parthenon in Athens, Temple to Athena – goddess of heroic undertakings.

Annuit coeptis, Langdon thought. *God favors our undertaking.*

Continuing to the final window, Langdon gazed southward across the dark waters of the Tidal Basin, where the Jefferson Memorial shone brightly in the night. The gently sloping cupola, Langdon knew, was modeled after the Pantheon, the original home to the great Roman gods of mythology.

Having looked in all four directions, Langdon now thought about the aerial photos he had seen of the National Mall – her four arms outstretched from the Washington Monument toward the cardinal points of the compass. *I am standing at the crossroads of America.*

Langdon continued back around to where Peter was standing. His mentor was beaming. 'Well, Robert, this is it. The Lost Word. *This* is where it's buried. The Masonic Pyramid led us *here.*'

Langdon did a double take. He had all but forgotten about the Lost Word.

'Robert, I know of nobody more trustworthy than you. And after a night like tonight, I believe you deserve to know what this is all about. As promised in legend, the Lost Word is indeed buried at the bottom of a winding staircase.' He motioned to the mouth of the monument's long stairwell.

Langdon had finally started to get his feet back under him, but now he was puzzled.

Peter quickly reached into his pocket and pulled out a small object. 'Do you remember this?'

Langdon took the cube-shaped box that Peter had entrusted to him long ago. 'Yes . . . but I'm afraid I didn't do a very good job of protecting it.'

Solomon chuckled. 'Perhaps the time had come for it to see the light of day.'

Langdon eyed the stone cube, wondering why Peter had just handed it to him.

'What does this look like to you?' Peter asked.

Langdon eyed the 1514🝕 and recalled his first impression when Katherine had unwrapped the package. 'A cornerstone.'

'Exactly,' Peter replied. 'Now, there are a few things you might not know about cornerstones. First, the *concept* of laying a cornerstone comes from the Old Testament.'

Langdon nodded. 'The Book of Psalms.'

'Correct. And a true cornerstone is always *buried* beneath the ground – symbolizing the building's initial step upward out of the earth toward the heavenly light.'

Langdon glanced out at the Capitol, recalling that its cornerstone was buried so deep in the foundation that, to this day, excavations had been unable to find it.

'And finally,' Solomon said, 'like the stone box in your hand, many cornerstones are little vaults . . . and have hollow cavities so that they can hold buried treasures . . . talismans, if you will – symbols of hope for the future of the building about to be erected.'

Langdon was well aware of this tradition, too. Even today, Masons laid cornerstones in which they sealed

meaningful objects – time capsules, photos, pro-
clamations, even the ashes of important people.

'My purpose in telling you this,' Solomon said,
glancing over at the stairwell, 'should be clear.'

'You think the Lost Word is buried in the *cornerstone*
of the Washington Monument?'

'I don't *think*, Robert. I *know*. The Lost Word was
buried in the cornerstone of this monument on July 4,
1848, in a full Masonic ritual.'

Langdon stared at him. 'Our Masonic forefathers
buried a *word*?!'

Peter nodded. 'They did indeed. They understood
the true power of what they were burying.'

All night, Langdon had been trying to wrap his
mind around sprawling, ethereal concepts . . . the
Ancient Mysteries, the Lost Word, the Secrets of the
Ages. He wanted something solid, and despite Peter's
claims that the key to it all was buried in a cornerstone
555 feet beneath him, Langdon was having a hard time
accepting it. *People study the mysteries for entire lifetimes
and are still unable to access the power allegedly hidden
there.* Langdon flashed on Dürer's *Melencolia I* – the
image of the dejected Adept, surrounded by the tools
of his failed efforts to unveil the mystical secrets of
alchemy. *If the secrets can actually be unlocked, they will
not be found in one place!*

Any answer, Langdon had always believed, was
spread across the world in thousands of volumes
. . . encoded into writings of Pythagoras, Hermes,
Heraclitus, Paracelsus, and hundreds of others. The
answer was found in dusty, forgotten tomes on alchemy,
mysticism, magic, and philosophy. The answer was
hidden in the ancient library of Alexandria, the clay
tablets of Sumer, and the hieroglyphs of Egypt.

'Peter, I'm sorry,' Langdon said quietly, shaking his head. 'To understand the Ancient Mysteries is a life-long process. I can't imagine how the key could possibly rest within a single word.'

Peter placed a hand on Langdon's shoulder. 'Robert, the Lost Word is not a "word." ' He gave a sage smile. 'We only call it the "Word" because that's what the ancients called it . . . in the beginning.'

130

In the beginning was the Word.

Dean Galloway knelt at the Great Crossing of the National Cathedral and prayed for America. He prayed that his beloved country would soon come to grasp the true power of the Word – the recorded collection of the written wisdom of all the ancient masters – the spiritual truths taught by the great sages.

History had blessed mankind with the wisest of teachers, profoundly enlightened souls whose understanding of the spiritual and mental mysteries exceeded all understanding. The precious words of these Adepts – Buddha, Jesus, Muhammad, Zoroaster, and countless others – had been transmitted through history in the oldest and most precious of vessels.

Books.

Every culture on earth had its own sacred book – its own Word – each one different and yet each one the same. For Christians, the Word was the Bible, for

Muslims the Koran, for Jews the Torah, for Hindus the Vedas, and on and on it went.

The Word shall light the way.

For America's Masonic forefathers, the Word had been the Bible. *And yet few people in history have understood its true message.*

Tonight, as Galloway knelt alone within the great cathedral, he placed his hands upon the Word – a well-worn copy of his own Masonic Bible. This treasured book, like all Masonic Bibles, contained the Old Testament, the New Testament, and a treasure trove of Masonic philosophical writings.

Although Galloway's eyes could no longer read the text, he knew the preface by heart. Its glorious message had been read by millions of his brethren in countless languages around the world.

The text read:

TIME IS A RIVER . . . AND BOOKS ARE BOATS. MANY VOLUMES START DOWN THAT STREAM, ONLY TO BE WRECKED AND LOST BEYOND RECALL IN ITS SANDS. ONLY A FEW, A VERY FEW, ENDURE THE TESTINGS OF TIME AND LIVE TO BLESS THE AGES FOLLOWING.

There is a reason these volumes survived, while others vanished. As a scholar of faith, Dean Galloway had always found it astonishing that the ancient spiritual texts – the most studied books on earth – were, in fact, the least understood.

Concealed within those pages, there hides a wondrous secret.

One day soon the light would dawn, and mankind would finally begin to grasp the simple, transformative truth of the ancient teachings . . . and take a quantum leap forward in understanding his own magnificent nature.

131

The winding staircase that descends the spine of the Washington Monument consists of 896 stone steps that spiral around an open elevator shaft. Langdon and Solomon were making their way down, Langdon still grappling with the startling fact that Peter had shared with him only moments ago: *Robert, buried within the hollow cornerstone of this monument, our forefathers placed a single copy of the Word – the Bible – which waits in darkness at the foot of this staircase.*

As they descended, Peter suddenly stopped on a landing and swung his flashlight beam to illuminate a large stone medallion embedded in the wall.

What in the world?! Langdon jumped when he saw the carving.

The medallion depicted a frightening cloaked figure holding a scythe and kneeling beside an hourglass. The figure's arm was raised, and his index finger was extended, pointing directly at a large open Bible, as if to say: 'The answer is in there!'

Langdon stared at the carving and then turned to Peter.

His mentor's eyes shone with mystery. 'I'd like you to consider something, Robert.' His voice echoed down the empty stairwell. '*Why* do you think the Bible has survived thousands of years of tumultuous history? Why is it still here? Is it because its stories are such compelling reading? Of course not . . . but there *is* a reason. There is a *reason* Christian monks spend lifetimes attempting to decipher the Bible. There is a *reason* that Jewish mystics and Kabbalists pore over the Old Testament. And that *reason*, Robert, is that there exist powerful secrets hidden in the pages of this ancient book . . . a vast collection of untapped wisdom waiting to be unveiled.'

Langdon was no stranger to the theory that the Scriptures contained a hidden layer of meaning, a concealed message that was veiled in allegory, symbolism, and parable.

'The prophets warn us,' Peter continued, 'that the language used to share their secret mysteries is a cryptic one. The Gospel of Mark tells us, "Unto you is given to know the mystery . . . but it will be told in parable." Proverbs cautions that the sayings of the wise are "riddles," while Corinthians talks of "hidden wisdom." The Gospel of John forewarns: "I will speak to you in parable . . . and use dark sayings."'

Dark sayings, Langdon mused, knowing this strange phrase made numerous odd appearances in Proverbs as well as in Psalm 78. *I will open my mouth in a parable and utter dark sayings of old.* The concept of a 'dark saying,' Langdon had learned, did not mean that the saying was 'evil' but rather that its true meaning was shadowed or obscured from the light.

'And if you have any doubts,' Peter added, 'Corinthians overtly tells us that the parables have two layers of meaning: "milk for babes and meat for men" – where the *milk* is a watered-down reading for infantile minds, and the *meat* is the true message, accessible only to mature minds.'

Peter raised the flashlight, again illuminating the carving of the cloaked figure pointing intently at the Bible. 'I know you are a skeptic, Robert, but consider this. If the Bible does *not* contain hidden meaning, then why have so many of history's finest minds – including brilliant scientists at the Royal Society – become so obsessed with studying it? Sir Isaac Newton wrote more than a *million* words attempting to decipher the true meaning of the Scripture, including a 1704 manuscript that claimed he had extracted hidden *scientific* information from the Bible!'

Langdon knew this was true.

'And Sir Francis Bacon,' Peter continued, 'the luminary hired by King James to literally *create* the authorized King James Bible, became so utterly convinced that the Bible contained cryptic meaning that he wrote in his *own* codes, which are still studied today! Of course, as you know, Bacon was a Rosicrucian and penned *The Wisdom of the Ancients*.' Peter smiled. 'Even the iconoclastic poet William Blake hinted that we should read between the lines.'

Langdon was familiar with the verse:

BOTH READ THE BIBLE DAY AND NIGHT,
BUT THOU READ BLACK WHERE I READ WHITE.

'And it wasn't just the European luminaries,' Peter continued, descending faster now. 'It was here, Robert, at the very core of this young American nation, that our brightest forefathers – John Adams, Ben Franklin, Thomas Paine – all warned of the profound dangers of interpreting the Bible *literally*. In fact, Thomas Jefferson was so convinced the Bible's true message was hidden that he literally cut up the pages and reedited the book, attempting, in his words, "to do away with the artificial scaffolding and restore the genuine doctrines." '

Langdon was well aware of this strange fact. The Jeffersonian Bible was still in print today and included many of his controversial revisions, among them the removal of the virgin birth and the resurrection. Incredibly, the Jeffersonian Bible had been presented to every incoming member of Congress during the first half of the nineteenth century.

'Peter, you know I find this topic fascinating, and I can understand that it might be *tempting* for bright minds to imagine the Scriptures contain hidden meaning, but it makes no logical sense to me. Any skilled professor will tell you that *teaching* is never done in code.'

'I'm sorry?'

'Teachers *teach*, Peter. We speak *openly*. Why would the prophets – the greatest teachers in history – *obscure* their language? If they hoped to change the world, why would they speak in code? Why not speak plainly so the world could understand?'

Peter glanced back over his shoulder as he descended, looking surprised by the question. 'Robert, the Bible does not talk *openly* for the same reason the Ancient Mystery Schools were kept hidden . . . for the same reason the neophytes had to be initiated before learning the secret teachings of the ages . . . for the same reason the scientists in the Invisible College refused to share their knowledge with others. This information is *powerful*, Robert. The Ancient Mysteries cannot be shouted from the rooftops. The mysteries are a flaming torch, which, in the hands of a master, can light the way, but which, in the hands of a madman, can scorch the earth.'

Langdon stopped short. *What is he saying?* 'Peter, I'm talking about the *Bible*. Why are you talking about the *Ancient Mysteries*?'

Peter turned. 'Robert, don't you see? The Ancient Mysteries and the Bible are the same thing.'

Langdon stared in bewilderment.

Peter was silent for several seconds, waiting for the concept to soak in. 'The Bible is one of the books through which the mysteries have been passed down through history. Its pages are desperately trying to tell us the secret. Don't you understand? The "dark sayings" in the Bible are the whispers of the ancients, quietly sharing with us all of their secret wisdom.'

Langdon said nothing. The Ancient Mysteries, as he understood them, were a kind of instruction manual for harnessing the latent power of the human mind . . . a recipe for personal apotheosis. He had never been able to accept the power of the mysteries, and certainly the notion that the Bible was somehow hiding a key to these mysteries was an impossible stretch.

'Peter, the Bible and the Ancient Mysteries are total *opposites*. The mysteries are all about the god *within* you . . . man as god. The Bible is all about the God *above* you . . . and man as a powerless sinner.'

'Yes! Exactly! You've put your finger on the precise problem! The moment mankind *separated* himself from God, the true meaning of the Word was lost. The voices of the ancient masters have now been drowned out, lost in the chaotic din of self-proclaimed practitioners shouting that they alone understand the

Word . . . that the Word is written in *their* language and none other.'

Peter continued down the stairs.

'Robert, you and I both know that the ancients would be horrified if they saw how their teachings have been perverted . . . how religion has established itself as a tollbooth to heaven . . . how warriors march into battle believing God favors their cause. We've lost the Word, and yet its true meaning is still within reach, right before our eyes. It exists in all the enduring texts, from the Bible to the *Bhagavad Gita* to the Koran and beyond. *All* of these texts are revered upon the altars of Freemasonry because Masons understand what the world seems to have forgotten . . . that each of these texts, in its own way, is quietly whispering the exact *same* message.' Peter's voice welled with emotion. ' "Know ye not that ye are gods?" '

Langdon was struck by the way this famous ancient saying kept surfacing tonight. He had reflected on it while talking to Galloway and also at the Capitol Building while trying to explain *The Apotheosis of Washington*.

Peter lowered his voice to a whisper. 'The Buddha said, "You are God yourself." Jesus taught that "the kingdom of God is within you" and even promised us, "The works I do, *you* can do . . . and greater." Even the first antipope – Hippolytus of Rome – quoted the same message, first uttered by the gnostic teacher Monoimus: "Abandon the *search* for God . . . instead, take yourself as the starting place." '

Langdon flashed on the House of the Temple, where the Masonic Tyler's chair bore two words of guidance carved across its back: KNOW THYSELF.

'A wise man once told me,' Peter said, his voice faint

now, 'the only difference between you and God is that *you* have forgotten you are divine.'

'Peter, I hear you – I *do*. And I'd love to believe we are gods, but I see no gods walking our earth. I see no super-humans. You can point to the alleged miracles of the Bible, or any other religious text, but they are nothing but old stories fabricated by man and then exaggerated over time.'

'Perhaps,' Peter said. 'Or perhaps we simply need our science to catch up with the wisdom of the ancients.' He paused. 'Funny thing is ... I believe Katherine's research may be poised to do just that.'

Langdon suddenly remembered that Katherine had dashed off from the House of the Temple earlier. 'Hey, where did she go, anyway?'

'She'll be here shortly,' Peter said, grinning. 'She went to confirm a wonderful bit of good fortune.'

Outside, at the base of the monument, Peter Solomon felt invigorated as he inhaled the cold night air. He watched in amusement as Langdon stared intently at the ground, scratching his head and looking around at the foot of the obelisk.

'Professor,' Peter joked, 'the cornerstone that con-tains the Bible is underground. You can't actually access the book, but I assure you it's there.'

'I believe you,' Langdon said, appearing lost in thought. 'It's just ... I noticed something.'

Langdon stepped back now and surveyed the giant plaza on which the Washington Monument stood. The circular concourse was made entirely of white stone ... except for two decorative courses of dark stone, which formed two concentric circles around the monument.

'A circle within a circle,' Langdon said. 'I never realized the Washington Monument stands at the center of a circle within a circle.'

Peter had to laugh. *He misses nothing.* 'Yes, the great circumpunct . . . the universal symbol for God . . . at the crossroads of America.' He gave a coy shrug. 'I'm sure it's just a coincidence.'

Langdon seemed far off, gazing skyward now, his eyes ascending the illuminated spire, which shone stark white against the black winter sky.

Peter sensed Langdon was beginning to see this creation for what it truly was . . . a silent reminder of ancient wisdom . . . an icon of enlightened man at the heart of a great nation. Even though Peter could not *see* the tiny aluminum tip at the top, he knew it was there, man's enlightened mind straining toward heaven.

Laus Deo.

'Peter?' Langdon approached, looking like a man who'd endured some kind of mystical initiation. 'I almost forgot,' he said, reaching into his pocket and producing Peter's gold Masonic ring. 'I've been wanting to return this to you all night.'

'Thank you, Robert.' Peter held out his left hand and took the ring, admiring it. 'You know, all the secrecy and mystery surrounding this ring and the Masonic Pyramid . . . it had an enormous effect on my life. When I was a young man, the pyramid was given to me with the promise that it hid mystical secrets. Its mere existence made me *believe* there were great mysteries in the world. It piqued my curiosity, fueled my sense of wonder, and inspired me to open my mind to the Ancient Mysteries.' He smiled quietly and slipped the ring into his pocket. 'I now realize that the Masonic Pyramid's true purpose was not to reveal the answers, but rather to inspire a fascination with them.'

The two men stood in silence for a long while at the foot of the monument.

When Langdon finally spoke, his tone was serious. 'I need to ask you a favor, Peter . . . as a friend.'

'Of course. Anything.'

Langdon made his request . . . firmly.

Solomon nodded, knowing he was right. 'I will.'

'Right away,' Langdon added, motioning to the waiting Escalade.

'Okay . . . but one caveat.'

Langdon rolled his eyes, chuckling. 'Somehow you always get the last word.'

'Yes, and there *is* one final thing I want you and Katherine to see.'

'At this hour?' Langdon checked his watch.

Solomon smiled warmly at his old friend. 'It is Washington's most spectacular treasure . . . and something very, *very* few people have ever seen.'

132

Katherine Solomon's heart felt light as she hurried up the hill toward the base of the Washington Monument. She had endured great shock and tragedy tonight, and yet her thoughts were refocused now, if only temporarily, on the wonderful news Peter had shared with her earlier . . . news she had just confirmed with her very own eyes.

My research is safe. All of it.

Her lab's holographic data drives had been destroyed tonight, but earlier, at the House of the Temple, Peter had informed her that he had been secretly keeping backups of all her Noetic research in the SMSC executive offices. *You know I'm utterly fascinated with your work,* he had explained, *and I wanted to follow your progress without disturbing you.*

'Katherine?' a deep voice called out.

She looked up.

A lone figure stood in silhouette at the base of the illuminated monument.

'Robert!' She hurried over and hugged him.

'I heard the good news,' Langdon whispered. 'You must be relieved.'

Her voice cracked with emotion. 'Incredibly.' The research Peter had saved was a scientific tour de force – a massive collection of experiments that proved human thought was a real and measurable force in the world. Katherine's experiments demonstrated the *effect* of human thought on everything from ice crystals to random-event generators to the movement of sub-atomic particles. The results were conclusive and irrefutable, with the potential to transform skeptics into believers and affect global consciousness on a massive scale. 'Everything is going to change, Robert. *Everything.*'

'Peter certainly thinks so.'

Katherine glanced around for her brother.

'Hospital,' Langdon said. 'I insisted he go as a favor to me.'

Katherine exhaled, relieved. 'Thank you.'

'He told me to wait for you here.'

Katherine nodded, her gaze climbing the glowing

651

white obelisk. 'He said he was bringing you here. Something about "*Laus Deo*"? He didn't elaborate.'

Langdon gave a tired chuckle. 'I'm not sure I entirely understand it myself.' He glanced up at the top of the monument. 'Your brother said quite a few things tonight that I couldn't get my mind around.'

'Let me guess,' Katherine said. 'Ancient Mysteries, science, and the Holy Scriptures?'

'Bingo.'

'Welcome to *my* world.' She winked. 'Peter initiated me into this long ago. It fueled a lot of my research.'

'Intuitively, some of what he said made sense.' Langdon shook his head. 'But intellectually . . .'

Katherine smiled and put her arm around him. 'You know, Robert, I may be able to help you with that.'

Deep inside the Capitol Building, Architect Warren Bellamy was walking down a deserted hallway.

Only one thing left to do tonight, he thought.

When he arrived at his office, he retrieved a very old key from his desk drawer. The key was black iron, long and slender, with faded markings. He slid it into his pocket and then prepared himself to welcome his guests.

Robert Langdon and Katherine Solomon were on their way to the Capitol. At Peter's request, Bellamy was to provide them with a very rare opportunity – the chance to lay eyes upon this building's most magnificent secret . . . something that could be revealed only by the Architect.

133

High above the floor of the Capitol Rotunda, Robert Langdon inched nervously around the circular catwalk that extended just beneath the ceiling of the dome. He peered tentatively over the railing, dizzied by the height, still unable to believe it had been less than ten hours since Peter's hand had appeared in the middle of the floor below.

On that same floor, the Architect of the Capitol was now a tiny speck some hundred and eighty feet below, moving steadily across the Rotunda and then disappearing. Bellamy had escorted Langdon and Katherine up to this balcony, leaving them here with very specific instructions.

Peter's instructions.

Langdon eyed the old iron key that Bellamy had handed to him. Then he glanced over at a cramped stairwell that ascended from this level ... climbing higher still. *God help me.* These narrow stairs, according to the Architect, led up to a small metal door that could be unlocked with the iron key in Langdon's hand.

Beyond the door lay something that Peter insisted Langdon and Katherine see. Peter had not elaborated, but rather had left strict instructions regarding the precise *hour* at which the door was to be opened. *We have to wait to open the door? Why?*

Langdon checked his watch again and groaned.

Slipping the key into his pocket, he gazed across the gaping void before him at the far side of the balcony. Katherine had walked fearlessly ahead, apparently unfazed by the height. She was now halfway around the circumference, admiring every inch of Brumidi's *The Apotheosis of Washington*, which loomed directly over their heads. From this rare vantage point, the fifteen-foot-tall figures that adorned the nearly five thousand square feet of the Capitol Dome were visible in astonishing detail.

Langdon turned his back to Katherine, faced the outer wall, and whispered very quietly, 'Katherine, this is your conscience speaking. Why did you abandon Robert?'

Katherine was apparently familiar with the dome's startling acoustical properties . . . because the wall whispered back. 'Because Robert is being a chicken. He should come over here with me. We have plenty of time before we're allowed to open that door.'

Langdon knew she was right and reluctantly made his way around the balcony, hugging the wall as he went.

'This ceiling is absolutely amazing,' Katherine marveled, her neck craned to take in the enormous splendor of the *Apotheosis* overhead. 'Mythical gods all mixed in with scientific inventors and their creations? And to think *this* is the image at the center of our Capitol.'

Langdon turned his eyes upward to the sprawling forms of Franklin, Fulton, and Morse with their technological inventions. A shining rainbow arched away from these figures, guiding his eye to George Washington ascending to heaven on a cloud. *The great promise of man becoming God.*

Katherine said, 'It's as if the entire essence of the Ancient Mysteries is hovering over the Rotunda.'

Langdon had to admit, not many frescoes in the world fused scientific inventions with mythical gods and human apotheosis. This ceiling's spectacular collection of images was *indeed* a message of the Ancient Mysteries, and it was here for a reason. The founding fathers had envisioned America as a blank canvas, a fertile field on which the seeds of the mysteries could be sown. Today, this soaring icon – the father of our country ascending to heaven – hung silently above our lawmakers, leaders, and presidents . . . a bold reminder, a map to the future, a promise of a time when man would evolve to complete spiritual maturity.

'Robert,' Katherine whispered, her gaze still fixated on the massive figures of America's great inventors accompanied by Minerva. 'It's prophetic, really. Today, man's most advanced inventions are being used to study man's most ancient ideas. The science of Noetics may be new, but it's actually the *oldest* science on earth – the study of human thought.' She turned to him now, her eyes filled with wonder. 'And we're learning that the ancients actually understood *thought* more profoundly than we do today.'

'Makes sense,' Langdon replied. 'The human mind was the only technology the ancients had at their disposal. The early philosophers studied it relentlessly.'

'Yes! The ancient texts are obsessed with the power of the human mind. The Vedas describe the flow of mind energy. The *Pistis Sophia* describes universal consciousness. The *Zohar* explores the nature of mind spirit. The Shamanic texts predict Einstein's "remote influence" in terms of healing at a distance. It's all there! And don't even get me started about the Bible.'

'You, too?' Langdon said, chuckling. 'Your brother tried to convince me that the Bible is encoded with scientific information.'

'It certainly *is*,' she said. 'And if you don't believe Peter, read some of Newton's esoteric texts on the Bible. When you start to understand the cryptic parables in the Bible, Robert, you realize it's a study of the human mind.'

Langdon shrugged. 'I guess I'd better go back and read it again.'

'Let me ask you something,' she said, clearly not appreciating his skepticism. 'When the Bible tells us to "go build our temple" ... a temple that we must "build with no tools and making no noise," what *temple* do you think it's talking about?'

'Well, the text does say your body is a temple.'

'Yes, Corinthians 3:16. *You* are the temple of God.' She smiled at him. 'And the Gospel of John says the exact same thing. Robert, the Scriptures are well aware of the power latent within us, and they are urging us to harness that power ... urging us to build the temples of our *minds*.'

'Unfortunately, I think much of the religious world is waiting for a *real* temple to be rebuilt. It's part of the Messianic Prophecy.'

'Yes, but that overlooks an important point. The Second Coming is the coming of *man* – the moment when mankind finally builds the temple of his mind.'

'I don't know,' Langdon said, rubbing his chin. 'I'm no Bible scholar, but I'm pretty sure the Scriptures describe in detail a *physical* temple that needs to be built. The structure is described as being in two parts – an outer temple called the Holy Place and an inner sanctuary called the Holy of Holies. The two parts are separated from each other by a thin veil.'

Katherine grinned. 'Pretty good recall for a Bible skeptic. By the way, have you ever seen an actual human brain? It's built in two parts – an outer part called the dura mater and an inner part called the pia mater. These two parts are separated by the arachnoid – a *veil* of weblike tissue.'

Langdon cocked his head in surprise.

Gently, she reached up and touched Langdon's temple. 'There's a reason they call this your *temple*, Robert.'

As Langdon tried to process what Katherine had said, he flashed unexpectedly on the gnostic Gospel of Mary: *Where the mind is, there is the treasure.*

'Perhaps you've heard,' Katherine said, softly now, 'about the brain scans taken of yogis while they meditate? The human brain, in advanced states of focus, will *physically* create a waxlike substance from the pineal gland. This brain secretion is unlike anything else in the body. It has an incredible healing effect, can literally regenerate cells, and may be one of the reasons yogis live so long. This is real *science*, Robert. This substance has inconceivable properties and can be created *only* by a mind that is highly tuned to a deeply focused state.'

'I remember reading about that a few years back.'

'Yes, and on that topic, you're familiar with the Bible's account of "manna from heaven"?'

Langdon saw no connection. 'You mean the magical substance that fell from heaven to nourish the hungry?'

'Exactly. The substance was said to heal the sick, provide everlasting life, and, strangely, cause no waste in those who consumed it.' Katherine paused, as if waiting for him to understand. 'Robert?' she prodded. 'A kind of nourishment that fell from *heaven*?' She tapped her temple. 'Magically heals the body? Creates no waste? Don't you see? These are *code words*, Robert! *Temple* is code for "body." *Heaven* is code for "mind." *Jacob's ladder* is your spine. And *manna* is this rare brain secretion. When you see these code words in Scripture, pay attention. They are often *markers* for a more profound meaning concealed beneath the surface.'

Katherine's words were coming out in rapid-fire succession now, explaining how this same magical substance appeared *throughout* the Ancient Mysteries: Nectar of the Gods, Elixir of Life, Fountain of Youth, Philosopher's Stone, ambrosia, dew, *ojas*, soma. Then she launched into an explanation about the brain's pineal gland representing the all-seeing eye of God. 'According to Matthew 6:22,' she said excitedly, ' "when your eye is *single*, your body fills with light." This concept is also represented by the Ajna chakra and the dot on a Hindu's forehead, which—'

Katherine stopped short, looking sheepish. 'Sorry . . . I know I'm rambling. I just find this all so exhilarating. For years I've studied the ancients' claims of man's awesome mental power, and now *science* is showing us that *accessing* that power is an actual physical process. Our brains, if used correctly, can call forth powers that are quite literally superhuman. The Bible, like many ancient texts, is a detailed exposition of the most sophisticated machine ever created . . . *the human mind*.' She sighed. 'Incredibly, science has yet to scratch the surface of the mind's full promise.'

'It sounds like your work in Noetics will be a quantum leap forward.'

'Or *backward*,' she said. 'The ancients already knew many of the scientific truths we're now rediscovering. Within a matter of years, modern man will be forced to accept what is now unthinkable: our minds can generate energy capable of *transforming* physical matter.' She paused. 'Particles *react* to our thoughts . . . which means our *thoughts* have the power to change the world.'

Langdon smiled softly.

'What my research has brought me to believe is *this*,' Katherine said. 'God is very real – a mental energy that pervades everything. And we, as human beings, have been created in *that* image—'

'I'm sorry?' Langdon interrupted. 'Created in the image of . . . mental energy?'

'Exactly. Our physical bodies have evolved over the ages, but it was our *minds* that were created in the image of God. We've been reading the Bible too literally. We learn that God created us in his image, but it's not our *physical* bodies that resemble God, it's our *minds*.'

Langdon was silent now, fully engrossed.

'This is the great gift, Robert, and God is waiting for us to understand it. All around the world, we are gazing skyward, waiting for *God* . . . never realizing that God is waiting for *us*.' Katherine paused, letting her words soak in. 'We are *creators*, and yet we naively play the role of "*the created*." We see ourselves as helpless sheep buffeted around by the God who made us. We kneel like frightened children, begging for help, for forgiveness, for good luck. But once we realize that we are truly created in the Creator's image, we will start to understand that we, *too*, must be Creators. When we understand this fact, the doors will burst wide open for human potential.'

Langdon recalled a passage that had always stuck with him from the work of the philosopher Manly P.

Hall: *If the infinite had not desired man to be wise, he would not have bestowed upon him the faculty of knowing.* Langdon gazed up again at the image of *The Apotheosis of Washington* – the symbolic ascent of man to deity. *The created . . . becoming the Creator.*

'The most amazing part,' Katherine said, 'is that as soon as we humans begin to harness our true power, we will have enormous control over our world. We will be able to *design* reality rather than merely react to it.'

Langdon lowered his gaze. 'That sounds . . . dangerous.'

Katherine looked startled . . . and impressed. 'Yes, exactly! If *thoughts* affect the world, then we must be very careful *how* we think. Destructive thoughts have influence, too, and we all know it's far easier to destroy than it is to create.'

Langdon thought of all the lore about needing to protect the ancient wisdom from the unworthy and share it only with the enlightened. He thought of the Invisible College, and the great scientist Isaac Newton's request to Robert Boyle to keep 'high silence' about their secret research. *It cannot be communicated,* Newton wrote in 1676, *without immense damage to the world.*

'There's an interesting twist here,' Katherine said. 'The great irony is that all the religions of the world, for centuries, have been urging their followers to embrace the concepts of *faith* and *belief.* Now science, which for centuries has derided religion as superstition, must admit that its next big frontier is quite literally the science of *faith* and *belief* . . . the power of focused conviction and intention. The same science that eroded our faith in the miraculous is now building a bridge back across the chasm it created.'

Langdon considered her words for a long time. Slowly he raised his eyes again to the *Apotheosis.* 'I have a question,' he said, looking back at Katherine. 'Even if I could accept, just for an instant, that I have the power to change physical matter with my mind, and literally manifest all that I desire . . . I'm afraid I see nothing in my life to make me believe I have such power.'

She shrugged. 'Then you're not looking hard enough.'

'Come on, I want a real answer. That's the answer of a *priest.* I want the answer of a *scientist.*'

'You want a real answer? Here it is. If I hand you a violin and say you have the capability to use it to make incredible music, I am not lying. You *do* have the capability, but you'll need enormous amounts of practice to manifest it. This is no different from learning to use your mind, Robert. Well-directed thought is a learned skill. To manifest an intention requires laser-like focus, full sensory visualization, and a profound belief. We have proven this in a lab. And just like playing a violin, there are people who exhibit greater natural ability than others. Look to history. Look to the stories of those enlightened minds who performed miraculous feats.'

'Katherine, please don't tell me you actually *believe* in the miracles. I mean, seriously . . . turning water into wine, healing the sick with the touch of a hand?'

Katherine took a long breath and blew it out slowly. 'I have witnessed people transform cancer cells into healthy cells simply by *thinking* about them. I have witnessed human minds affecting the physical world in myriad ways. And once you see that happen, Robert, once this becomes part of your reality, then some of the miracles you read about become simply a matter of degree.'

Langdon was pensive. 'It's an inspiring way to see the world, Katherine, but for me, it just feels like an impossible leap of faith. And as you know, faith has never come easily for me.'

'Then don't think of it as *faith*. Think of it simply as changing your perspective, accepting that the world is not precisely as you imagine. Historically, every major scientific breakthrough began with a simple idea that threatened to overturn all of our beliefs. The simple statement "the earth is round" was mocked as utterly impossible because most people believed the oceans would flow off the planet. Heliocentricity was called heresy. Small minds have always lashed out at what they don't understand. There are those who create . . . and those who tear down. That dynamic has existed for all time. But eventually the creators find believers, and the number of believers reaches a critical mass, and suddenly the world becomes round, or the solar system becomes heliocentric. Perception is transformed, and a new reality is born.'

Langdon nodded, his thoughts drifting now.

'You have a funny look on your face,' she said.

'Oh, I don't know. For some reason I was just remembering how I used to canoe out into the middle of the lake late at night, lie down under the stars, and think about stuff like this.'

She nodded knowingly. 'I think we all have a similar memory. Something about lying on our backs staring up at the heavens . . . opens the mind.' She glanced up at the ceiling and then said, 'Give me your jacket.'

'What?' He took it off and gave it to her.

She folded it twice and laid it down on the catwalk like a long pillow. 'Lie down.'

Langdon lay on his back, and Katherine positioned his head on half of the folded jacket. Then she lay down beside him – two kids, shoulder to shoulder on the narrow catwalk, staring up at Brumidi's enormous fresco.

'Okay,' she whispered. 'Put yourself in that same mind-set . . . a kid lying out in a canoe . . . looking up at the stars . . . his mind open and full of wonder.'

Langdon tried to obey, although at the moment, prone and comfortable, he was feeling a sudden wave of exhaustion. As his vision blurred, he perceived a muted shape overhead that immediately woke him. *Is that possible?* He could not believe he hadn't noticed it before, but the figures in *The Apotheosis of Washington* were clearly arranged in two concentric rings – a circle within a circle. *The* Apotheosis *is also a circumpunct?* Langdon wondered what else he had missed tonight.

'There's something important I want to tell you, Robert. There's another piece to all this . . . a piece that I believe is the single most astonishing aspect of my research.'

There's more?

Katherine propped herself on her elbow. 'And I promise . . . if we as humans can honestly grasp this *one* simple truth . . . the world will change overnight.'

She now had his full attention.

'I should preface this,' she said, 'by reminding you of the Masonic mantras to "gather what is scattered" . . . to bring "order from chaos" . . . to find "at-one-ment."'

'Go on.' Langdon was intrigued.

Katherine smiled down at him. 'We have scientifically proven that the power of human thought grows *exponentially* with the number of minds that share that thought.'

Langdon remained silent, wondering where she was going with this idea.

'What I'm saying is this ... two heads are better than one ... and yet two heads are not *twice* better, they are many, *many* times better. Multiple minds working in unison magnify a thought's effect ... *exponentially*. This is the inherent power of prayer groups, healing circles, singing in unison, and worshipping en masse. The idea of *universal consciousness* is no ethereal New Age concept. It's a hard-core scientific reality ... and harnessing it has the potential to transform our world. This is the underlying discovery of Noetic Science. What's more, it's happening right now. You can feel it all around you. Technology is linking us in ways we never imagined possible: Twitter, Google, Wikipedia, and others – all blend to create a web of interconnected minds.' She laughed. 'And I guarantee you, as soon as I publish my work, the Twitterati will all be sending tweets that say, *"learning about Noetics,"* and interest in this science will explode exponentially.'

Langdon's eyelids felt impossibly heavy. 'You know, I still haven't learned how to send a twitter.'

'A *tweet*,' she corrected, laughing.

'I'm sorry?'

'Never mind. Close your eyes. I'll wake you when it's time.'

Langdon realized he had all but forgotten the old key the Architect had given them ... and why they had come up here. As a new wave of exhaustion engulfed him, Langdon shut his eyes. In the darkness of his mind, he found himself thinking about *universal consciousness* . . . about Plato's writings on 'the mind of the world' and 'gathering God' . . . Jung's 'collective unconscious.' The notion was as simple as it was startling.

God is found in the collection of Many . . . rather than in the One.

'Elohim,' Langdon said suddenly, his eyes flying open again as he made an unexpected connection.

'I'm sorry?' Katherine was still gazing down at him.

'Elohim,' he repeated. 'The Hebrew word for God in the Old Testament! I've always wondered about it.'

Katherine gave a knowing smile. 'Yes. The word is *plural*.'

Exactly! Langdon had never understood why the very first passages of the Bible referred to God as a *plural* being. *Elohim*. The Almighty God in Genesis was described not as One . . . but as Many.

'God is plural,' Katherine whispered, 'because the minds of man are plural.'

Langdon's thoughts were spiraling now . . . dreams, memories, hopes, fears, revelations . . . all swirling above him in the Rotunda dome. As his eyes began to close again, he found himself staring at three words in Latin, painted within the *Apotheosis*.

E PLURIBUS UNUM.

'*Out of many, one*,' he thought, slipping off into sleep.

665

Robert Langdon awoke slowly.

Faces gazed down at him. *Where am I?*

A moment later, he recalled where he was. He sat up slowly beneath the *Apotheosis*. His back felt stiff from lying on the hard catwalk.

Where's Katherine?

Langdon checked his Mickey Mouse watch. *It's almost time.* He pulled himself to his feet, peering cautiously over the banister into the gaping space below.

'Katherine?' he called out.

The word echoed back in the silence of the deserted Rotunda.

Retrieving his tweed jacket from the floor, he brushed it off and put it back on. He checked his pockets. The iron key the Architect had given him was gone.

Making his way back around the walkway, Langdon headed for the opening the Architect had shown them . . . steep metal stairs ascending into cramped darkness. He began to climb. Higher and higher he ascended. Gradually the stairway became more narrow and more inclined. Still Langdon pushed on.

Just a little farther.

The steps had become almost ladderlike now, the passage frighteningly constricted. Finally, the stairs ended, and Langdon stepped up onto a small landing. Before him was a heavy metal door. The iron key was in the lock, and the door hung slightly ajar. He pushed, and the door creaked open. The air beyond felt cold. As Langdon stepped across the threshold into murky darkness, he realized he was now outside.

'I was just coming to get you,' Katherine said, smiling at him. 'It's almost time.'

When Langdon recognized his surroundings, he drew a startled breath. He was standing on a tiny sky-walk that encircled the pinnacle of the U.S. Capitol Dome. Directly above him, the bronze Statue of Freedom gazed out over the sleeping capital city. She faced the east, where the first crimson splashes of dawn had begun to paint the horizon.

Katherine guided Langdon around the balcony until they were facing west, perfectly aligned with the National Mall. In the distance, the silhouette of the Washington Monument stood in the early-morning light. From this vantage point, the towering obelisk looked even more impressive than it had before.

'When it was built,' Katherine whispered, 'it was the tallest structure on the entire planet.'

Langdon pictured the old sepia photographs of stonemasons on scaffolding, more than five hundred feet in the air, laying each block by hand, one by one.

We are builders, he thought. *We are creators.*

Since the beginning of time, man had sensed there was something special about himself . . . something more. He had longed for powers he did not possess. He had dreamed of flying, of healing, and of trans-forming his world in every way imaginable.

And he had done just that.

Today, the shrines to man's accomplishments adorned the National Mall. The Smithsonian museums burgeoned with our inventions, our art, our science, and the ideas of our great thinkers. They told the history of man as creator – from the stone tools in the Native American History Museum to the jets and rockets in the National Air and Space Museum.

If our ancestors could see us today, surely they would think us gods.

As Langdon peered through the predawn mist at the sprawling geometry of museums and monuments before him, his eyes returned to the Washington Monument. He pictured the lone Bible in the buried cornerstone and thought of how the Word of God was really the word of *man*.

He thought about the great circumpunct, and how it had been embedded in the circular plaza beneath the monument at the crossroads of America. Langdon thought suddenly of the little stone box Peter had entrusted to him. The cube, he now realized, had unhinged and opened to form the same exact geometrical form – a cross with a circumpunct at its center. Langdon had to laugh. *Even that little box was hinting at this crossroads.*

'Robert, look!' Katherine pointed to the top of the monument.

Langdon lifted his gaze but saw nothing.

Then, staring more intently, he glimpsed it.

Across the Mall, a tiny speck of golden sunlight was glinting off the highest tip of the towering obelisk. The shining pinpoint grew quickly brighter, more radiant, gleaming on the capstone's aluminum peak. Langdon watched in wonder as the light transformed into a beacon that hovered above the shadowed city. He pictured the tiny engraving on the east-facing side of the aluminum tip and realized to his amazement that the first ray of sunlight to hit the nation's capital, every single day, did so by illuminating two words:

Laus Deo.

'Robert,' Katherine whispered. 'Nobody ever gets to come up here at sunrise. This is what Peter wanted us to witness.'

Langdon could feel his pulse quickening as the glow atop the monument intensified.

'He said he believes this is why the forefathers built the monument so tall. I don't know if that's true, but I do know *this* – there's a very old law decreeing that nothing taller can be built in our capital city. *Ever.*'

The light inched farther down the capstone as the sun crept over the horizon behind them. As Langdon watched, he could almost sense, all around him, the celestial spheres tracing their eternal orbits through the void of space. He thought of the Great Architect of the Universe and how Peter had said specifically that the treasure he wanted to show Langdon could be unveiled *only* by the Architect. Langdon had assumed this meant Warren Bellamy. *Wrong Architect.*

As the rays of sunlight strengthened, the golden glow engulfed the entirety of the thirty-three-hundred-pound capstone. *The mind of man . . . receiving enlightenment.* The light then began inching down the monument, commencing the same descent it performed every morning. *Heaven moving toward earth . . . God connecting to man.* This process, Langdon realized, would reverse come evening. The sun would dip in the west, and the light would climb again from earth back to heaven . . . preparing for a new day.

Beside him, Katherine shivered and inched closer. Langdon put his arm around her. As the two of them stood side by side in silence, Langdon thought about all he had learned tonight. He thought of Katherine's belief that everything was about to change. He thought of Peter's faith that an age of enlightenment was imminent. And he thought of the words of a great prophet who had boldly declared: *Nothing is hidden that will not be made known; nothing is secret that will not come to light.*

As the sun rose over Washington, Langdon looked to the heavens, where the last of the nighttime stars were fading out. He thought about science, about faith, about man. He thought about how every culture, in every country, in every time, had always shared one thing. We all had the Creator. We used different names, different faces, and different prayers, but God was the universal constant for man. God was the symbol we all shared . . . the symbol of all the mysteries of life that we could not understand. The ancients had praised God as a symbol of our limitless human potential, but that ancient symbol had been lost over time. Until now.

In that moment, standing atop the Capitol, with the warmth of the sun streaming down all around him, Robert Langdon felt a powerful upwelling deep within himself. It was an emotion he had never felt this profoundly in his entire life.

Hope.

Angels &
DEMONS

An ancient secret brotherhood
A devastating new weapon
An unthinkable target

CERN Institute, Switzerland:
a world-renowned scientist is found
brutally murdered with a mysterious
symbol seared onto his chest.

The Vatican, Rome: the College of
Cardinals assembles to elect a new
pope. Somewhere beneath them, an
unstoppable bomb of terrifying power
relentlessly counts down to oblivion.

In a breathtaking race against time,
Harvard professor Robert Langdon
must decipher a labyrinthine trail of ancient
symbols if he is to defeat those responsible – the Illuminati –
a secret brotherhood presumed extinct for nearly four hundred years,
reborn to continue their deadly vendetta against their most hated enemy,
the Catholic church.

'A breathless, real-time adventure' *SAN FRANCISCO CHRONICLE*

'A no-holds-barred, pull-out-all-the-stops, breathless tangle of a thriller…
A heck of a good read' *AMAZON.COM*